Corrupt
GODS

A DARK MAFIA ROMANCE COLLECTION

CORRUPT GODS DUET

USA Today BESTSELLING AUTHOR
CORA KENBORN
INTERNATIONAL BESTSELLING AUTHOR
CATHERINE WILTCHER

Corrupt Gods
A Dark Mafia Romance Collection
Copyright © 2021
by Cora Kenborn and Catherine Wiltcher
Cover design by Maria at Steamy Designs
Editing by N. Isabelle Blanco & Gillian Leonard
Proofreading by Saints and Sinners Proofreading
Formatting by Midnight Designs

All rights reserved, including the right to reproduce this book or portions thereof in any form whatsoever.

The story in the following publication contains mature themes, strong language, and sexual situations. It is intended for adult readers.

No part of this publication may be reproduced in any form or by any electronic or mechanical means, including photocopying, recording, or by any information storage and retrieval systems, without written permission from the author in writing. No part of this book may be uploaded without permission from the author, nor be otherwise circulated in any form of binding or cover other than which it is originally published.

This book is a work of fiction. Names, characters, places, and incidents are either products of the author's imagination or are used fictitiously. Any resemblance to actual persons, living or dead, business establishments, events or locales is entirely coincidental.

The author acknowledges the trademarked status and trademark owners of various products referenced in the work of fiction, which have been used without permission. The publication/use of these trademarks is not authorized, associated with, or sponsored by the trademark owner.

CORRUPT GODS DUET

AUTHOR NOTE

Dear Reader,

Corrupt Gods is a thrilling arranged marriage mafia romance collection where every choice has a consequence. This collection features both books in the duet, the prequel novella, **PLUS exclusive bonus material**.

Bad Blood and Tainted Blood are Books 1 and 2 of the duet and includes five extra chapters **ONLY** available in the collection.

Born Sinner is a standalone prequel, featuring Lola Carrera and Sam Sanders, who are prominent characters in the duet. *It can be read before or after the duet.*

We welcome you to our next generation of ruthless kingpins and their fiery queens.

"These violent delights have violent ends…"
—William Shakespeare

xoxo,

Cora and Catherine

BOOK
CORRUPT GODS DUET

BAD BLOOD

A Santiago is a lesson in ruin.
A Carrera bleeds for revenge.

Thalia Santiago is the daughter of my enemy.
A beautiful rebel with a single cause.
Impulsive.
Fearless.
And ripe for her father's undoing.

I recognized her the moment she stepped into my casino.
I watched her start the fires that burned her pretty fingers, then poured gasoline on the flames.
Now she's in my debt, and her dues are a shiny gold ring and a vow of deception.

I'll bend her.
I'll break her.
I'll turn our mockery of a marriage into a battlefield.
And that river of bad blood that flows between our two families?
I'll make it an ocean of hate.

"The sins of the father are to be laid upon the children."
—*William Shakespeare*

PLAYLIST
In no particular order…

Gasoline - Halsey
Kill or Be Killed - New Years Day
Beast Within - In This Moment
The Archer - Taylor Swift
Fine Line - Mabel, Not3s
Only Love - Ben Howard
Bartering Lines - Ryan Adams
Gypsy - Fleetwood Mac
Goddess - Xana
Only Happy When It Rains - New Years Day (feat. Lzzy Hale)
Crazy On You - DIAMANTE
Hit Me Like a Man - The Pretty Reckless
I Really Want You To Hate Me - Meg Myers
Sick Like Me - In This Moment
Turn You On - Stitched Up Heart

Bad BLOOD

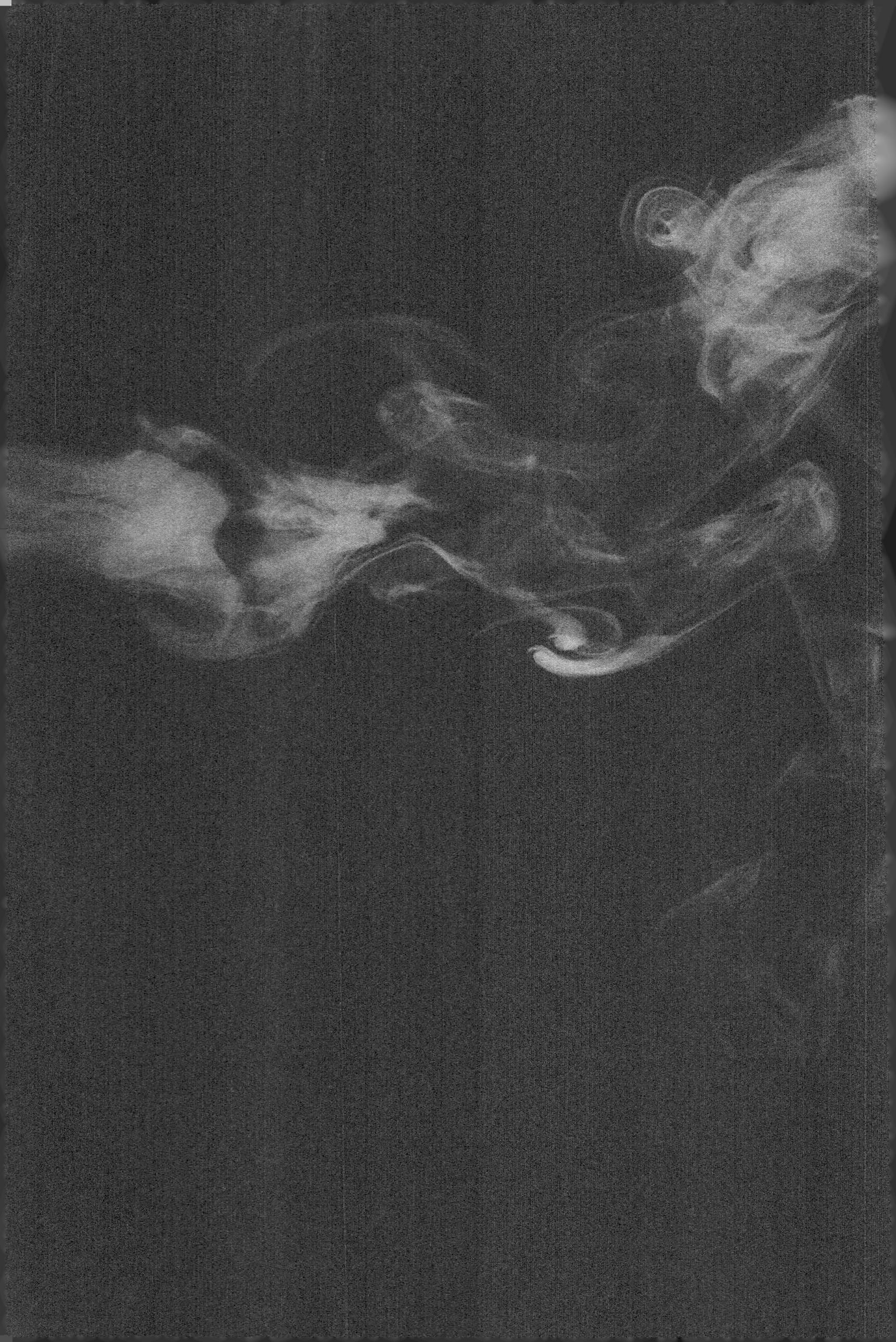

PROLOGUE

Mexican folklore calls it *La Boda Roja*, the Red Wedding—a day meant for celebration, but one that ended in death and betrayal.

Once the toasts were made, the bullets started flying, though who fired the first shot remains shrouded in mystery. Valentin Carrera loyalists claim that the ill-fated truce between the two most powerful cartels in the world was severed by a Colombian trigger finger, while Dante Santiago's men maintain that war was declared by Mexican treachery.

Others say that there are two sides to every story, and somewhere in the middle lies the truth.

To the next generation, their hate became a new hate. Their pain became a new pain. *La Boda Roja* became as real to them as if they'd stood on the battleground themselves that day.

Eventually, they took their bad blood across the border.

New York fell to the new Santiago Cartel order. New Jersey fell to the Carrera regime.

Twenty years ago, two kings declared war…

And only one dark prince can end it.

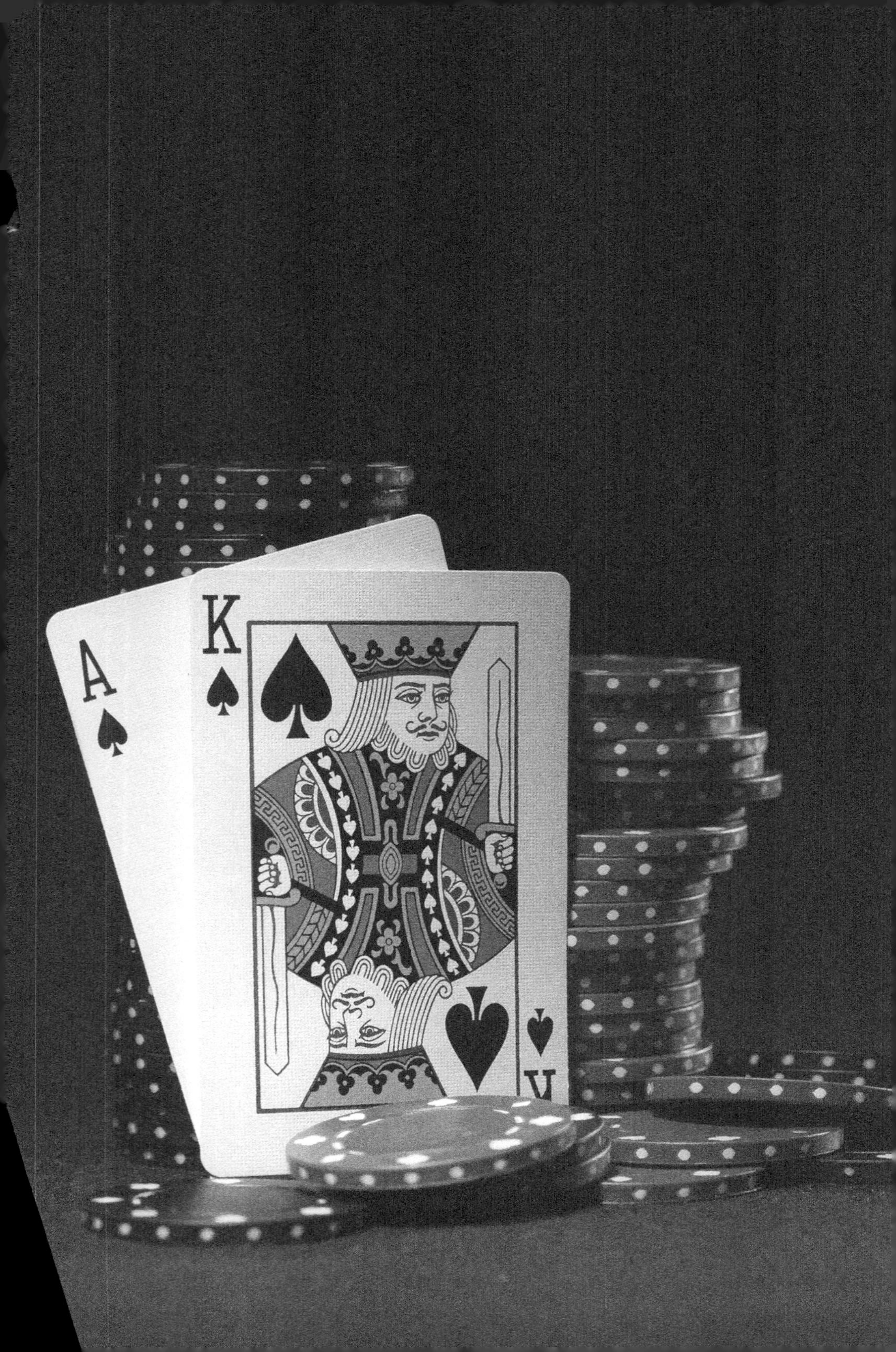

CHAPTER
One

THALIA
Ten Years Ago

It started snowing an hour ago. Thick, swirling mists of white fell upon our stolen car like hungry animals with soft teeth. Edier switched the wipers on, then turned them off again when the curtains in the old house opposite started twitching.

Fast forward, and the storm is a never-ending eddy as we sit and wait—though what we're waiting for hasn't been explained to me, yet. The flakes on the glass are as big as my fist. Drifts are forming against the line of big black cars parked outside the abandoned church, a little way up the street. Our windows keep getting fogged up, but nothing much else seems to be happening out there anyway.

"Do you think they're praying?" I ask doubtfully.

"Not unless they're praying for their lives," Sam jokes from the back seat.

"Zip it, shithead," Edier mutters, folding a new piece of Juicy Fruit gum into his mouth. "Thalia's nine, not nineteen. Don't go giving her nightmares, or else."

"Or else what?"

"Or else you can find your own way back to New York."

"They've been in there for *ages*," I say, screwing up my face. "We watched them go in an hour ago."

Edier shoots me a sideways glance. "You worried, bug?"

I shake my head. "I never worry about *papá*. He's indestructible." *I-n-d-e-s-t-r-u-c-t-i-b-l-e*. I spell the word out a couple of times under my breath. I heard a man say it about him once, and it stuck in my head like a piece of Edier's gum.

"Me either," he mutters.

It's not just my *papá* in there; it's his and Sam's, too.

I'm tempted to tell him that I don't really care what's happening, and that I'm only here because sleep is boring. I saw them sneaking out of the apartment earlier and I made them take me. Otherwise, I told them I'd squeal.

I never would. These boys are my brothers by a different kind of blood.

Cartel blood.

C-a-r-t-e-l.

I didn't understand what that meant until I saw our *papás* beat a man to death last year—until I saw the same shade of crimson smearing their knuckles.

Ours are clean, but it's only a matter of time.

I know that in the same way I know my sister, Ella, is really sick, and she might not be getting better.

Glancing out of the car window again, I watch the gargoyles on the outside walls of the church turn from stone-gray to white. They're starting to look like angry angels. I guess *papá* was right. Some monsters *can* be beautiful at night.

"Why the hell is it so cold in New Jersey?"

Edier yanks his gray beanie down lower over his face until it's hugging his eyelashes. He's nine years older than me, but he never treats me like a little kid. He once told me he did most of his growing up when he was my age. I know bad things happened to him before he was adopted by one of *papá's* friends, but I don't know what. Sometimes you only need to look into a boy's eyes to see their truth, and his are swimming in it.

He's slouched in the driver's seat, chewing his gum. There's a notebook balancing on his knee, and he's pencil-sketching the church. His drawings are unreal. My bedroom walls back home are covered in them. In another life, he might have been an artist, but he's stuck in this one now, and there's only one job description.

"Anywhere is cold outside of Colombia, numbnuts." Sam appears in the gap between the two front seats again, scraping his scruffy brown hair out of his eyes. "This weather is so chilly…*it's 'snow' joke*," he says, grinning goofily at me.

"Ugh, Sam, you're so lame."

"Lame-o, same-o." He laughs. He's only happy when he's breaking rules, and we've broken *a lot* of them tonight. Sneaking out of *papá's* apartment after a family party... Stealing Edier's bodyguard's car... Driving across state lines to a place that's forbidden...

Edier wouldn't let it go. After our fathers left during dessert, he'd wanted to follow, and nothing was stopping him.

"Cut it out," I say crossly, as Sam tries to ruffle my hair.

"Where do sheep go to get a haircut? *The baa baa shop.*" He collapses with laughter again, so I smack his shoulder a couple of times with my glove. "Ouch! Stop! Thalia, that hurts!"

I hate it when he takes our age gap and stuffs it full of bad jokes. He thinks he's funny, but he's nowhere near as funny as his stepdad is.

"What's that?" he says suddenly, his face turning serious.

"What's what?"

He jabs a finger between us. "That."

Edier leans forward in the driver's seat to swipe his sleeve across the fogged-up glass. One of the black car doors has opened up. As we watch, a dark shape climbs out and walks slowly in our direction. His head is braced against the storm, his arms wrapped tight around his body. Meanwhile, the black car has zoomed off down the street and disappeared into the night.

He stops under a streetlight that's more mellow yellow than amber, a couple of feet away from us. He looks both ways, and then he's raising a cell phone to his ear.

It's the shortest conversation ever. Before I can blink, he's pocketing it again.

"Do you think he's part of the meeting, Sam?" I whisper.

"He'd be inside the church if he was."

"Can he see us?"

"I doubt it." Even so, Edier leans across and shoves his notebook in the glove box—just in case we need to make a quick getaway.

"What if he's cold?" I muse out loud. "He looks cold. It's so cold out there."

"You can't tell from this distance if a person's cold or not, dummy," Sam mutters.

"But his ride went and left him!"

Just then, a violent gust of wind divides the driving snow like curtains. At the same time, the hunched figure turns in our direction, and our eyes meet in the darkness.

"He's a boy," I gasp in surprise. "He's the same age as you, Sam."

"I am *not* a boy," he huffs out, sounding offended.

"Twelve is *not* a man," I retort, tossing him a look.

"Thirteen last month, actually."

"Quiet," Edier hisses. "I'm the oldest here, I'm driving, so it's my rules."

I watch the boy in the snow jerk his head left and right again. It's almost like he's waiting for something.

Well, he can't wait out there. It's freezing.

Before Edier can stop me, I'm opening the passenger door. The bad weather muffles the sound, but the movement catches the boy's attention.

"Bug, come back," Edier hisses again, swiping for the back of my jacket, but all I give him is sliding fingertips.

I kick my boots through the fallen snow. It's nearly up to my knees.

"Are you waiting for someone?" I call out. "Do you want to come sit with us?"

The boy doesn't move. He's watching me with deep, dark eyes like distant planets.

"Did you hear what I—?"

"Go," he snarls, leaping toward me suddenly. "Get out of here. It's not safe!"

His English is hesitant, his accent oozy like soup.

"Go!" he says again, pushing me backward.

The force makes me stumble. His words are confusing me.

"Leave her alone!" I hear Edier shout as the squealing of tires cuts through the storm. Seconds later, the sound of gunfire inside the church explodes into the night like the flames from a bonfire.

The next few minutes happen loud and fast.

I see Sam yanking Edier back into the driver seat as another two black cars scream past us out of nowhere.

I feel something vicious whiz past my woolly red toboggan.

I taste ice in my mouth as the boy grabs me by the waist and drives me down into the ground—the heat of his body pushing me deeper into the snow as he curls around me, protecting me like a brave knight would.

More gunfire from the church.

More shouts.

Edier's yelling out my nickname again. He's spun the stolen car away from the curb, swung it around, and skidded to a stop by the sidewalk I'm now sprawled across.

"Bug—"

His next words are cut short as a bullet hits the trunk.

"Shit!"

Sam kicks open the back door. I feel his hand dragging me toward the car, with the boy still attached to me, but he rolls away at the last second, leaving me free to be yanked to warmth and safety.

"Go," I hear him croak in his strange accent from the white ground. "You don't belong here, *muñequita*... Go!"

"Shut the door! We need to get out of here!" Sam sounds scared as he reaches around me for the handle.

"We can't leave him!"

"He's a Carrera." He spits out the word as if it were poison. "He's their look-out. He gave the signal. Don't you see? This whole meeting was a trap. He deserves to die like a dog for that."

The boy in the snow unleashes a rush of angry Spanish at him.

He doesn't look scared. Not like us. *Maybe he's a knight, after all.*

Another bullet bounces off the trunk. A hundred feet away, men are still fighting and killing.

Men including *papá*.

But he's invincible, right?

Are the Carreras invincible, too?

Carrera.

I spell out the word under my breath: *C-a-r-r-e-r-a*.

Sam's wrong. He doesn't deserve to die. He tried to warn me. He tried to save me.

"Come with us!" I reach out my hand to him as Edier revs the engine in warning.

The boy shakes his head, his dark eyes blinking something unreadable into mine. "I can't. I won't... This isn't our war yet. But it will be soon."

I open my mouth to ask for more, but he swings his foot out and kicks my door shut. Sam pulls me back just in time. Edier hits the gas with the sound of police cars rising above the gunfire flames.

No one speaks until we reach the bridge.

We plot our alibis before Manhattan.

All the while, I'm thinking about a knight in the snow and a war that's coming for me.

CHAPTER
Two

THALIA
Present Day

Living up to your parents' expectations is a losing game.

The dice are loaded. The odds are stacked. But when you're the daughter of a Colombian cartel king and an American angel...? That's like surviving a snake pit with a fading flashlight and a water pistol.

Maybe that's why, at nineteen, I find myself stranded on the island of Manhattan, somewhere between breaking all the rules and doing the right thing.

Stranded between doubt and determination.

Fear and fury.

"He wants to speak with you, Thalia," comes a gruff voice as I'm attempting to slip into the apartment I share with my older sister, Ella, undetected. "And just so you know, he's called three times this morning already."

—Stranded between my father's oppression and the keys to my freedom.

Spinning around on last night's heels, I find the tall figure of Reece Costello bruising up my shadow. He's our head of security in New York—a tough Irishman in his fifties, who lost any trace of an accent around the same time he lost his hair.

He's holding out a cell to me, but it may as well be a loaded gun.

"Call him," he urges.

"At least let me have a double espresso first."

"Not this time."

"Please, Reece." I clasp my hands together. "It's too early in the morning to be dealing with parental disapproval."

"You spit in the devil's face when you keep a man like him waiting."

But he pockets the cell with a grimace. I can tell it's physically hurting him to do it, though.

"Thank you," I whisper in relief, wishing for the hundredth time that my father was more like him. There's a layer of sympathy behind those cool, gray eyes—the likes of which never blessed Dante Santiago's DNA. "Besides," I add, with a hopeful grin, "ten extra minutes isn't going to hurt."

"Wanna bet?"

I watch his eyebrows knit together as he takes in my extra short, overly expensive, silver designer cocktail dress, with the deep 'v' lace decolletage that kisses my belly button. Reece has been working for my family for longer than I've been screwing shit up on this planet, so I know what he's thinking. This outfit is anathema to all the ripped skinnies and leopard print Chucks I usually wear. The thing is, I'm on the edge of a life precipice and it's throwing all my norms into chaos. If that means resorting to every cheap trick in the book, so be it.

"You need to be smarter than this," he warns, leaning over to shove the apartment door open for me. "He knows you slipped your bodyguards again last night. Even before I made the call."

"Of course, he does," I say flatly. "He knows everything." *Except why I'm acting out so much.* "Listen, I'll deal with him later. I swear."

His grunt of disbelief speaks more truth than I ever will. I haven't spoken to my father in over a month. Our last words were poisoned with blame and anger, and I can't bring myself to taste the antidote of forgiveness, yet.

I shift my weight from foot to foot to offset my blister pain. "Did he give you a hard time about it?"

He chuckles darkly. "Santiago's threats lose their jagged edge when they're delivered from a thousand miles away." His grin fades. The rifts in his face deepen. "I can't keep you safe if you keep flying south on me, sweetheart. If you're in some kind of trouble—"

"I'm not," I say quickly.

"Where did you go last night?"

"Some bar."

Another lie.

"You know the dangers—"

"I didn't cross the Brooklyn Bridge, Reece. I didn't go anywhere near New Jersey, if that's what you're implying."

"Then where—"

"I went hunting... Oh God, not for *that*," I groan, seeing dark things flash across his face. "Nothing occurred that was A—love related, or B—sex related."

"Now you're talking stupid."

No, solutions, Reece.

Bad solutions to bad problems.

Like the forty-thousand dollars that's burning a hole in the bottom of my Gucci silk purse.

"Have you been drinking?" he says suspiciously.

"Nope. Gotta go. Have a phone call to make."

I slam the door and rest my forehead against cool wood, my panic rising up inside me like a flock of birds. I have a secret: a dark and dangerous thing that's slowly ripping me apart. But I have a plan to make it go away, too. It's cradled tight to my chest, and I can feel it fluttering wildly as I wait for the birds to disperse.

I find my sister sitting hunched over and cross-legged on the living room couch, her fingers weaving last minute college assignments out of a flurry of furious laptop clicks, a frown of concentration crumpling up her beautiful face.

She hasn't heard me enter, so I'm gifted a rare moment to watch her unnoticed. She's a carbon copy of our mom—with the same shiny dark waterfall of hair grazing her shoulders, the same thoughtful gaze, the same quietly ambitious nature... The minute we found out mom used to be an award-winning reporter, there was never any other future for Ella. Getting accepted into NYU and then majoring in Journalism were the two best days of her life. Not even the heavy crown that comes with being cartel royalty was going to crush them for her.

Not even a bad secret is going to derail them.

My sister chooses her family battles carefully.

I fight with all of my tiger heart, too, but I always come up short, even when I'm winning. I begged for years to attend a US college like Ella, and then

I dropped out after one semester.

One whole semester.

Sam calls it the Freshman Fuck-up Special. He lasted a whole two years before he was tossing his frat house keys in the trash. There was only one way he was going, and that was straight into the family business…

The Santiago Cartel business.

As for me, I'm like one of those insects that dances above treetops on a summer's evening, with too much energy and no place to go.

"Good night, last night?" Ella finally glances up from the screen as I stumble into the room, leaving a trail of bleeding Louboutin's behind me.

"It was okay." I reach for the volume control on the portable speaker, hitting the mute button with a frown. "You know you're the only person under forty-five who thinks Fleetwood Mac are cool, right?"

"Don't diss the Mac," she whispers in mock horror, raking red-rimmed eyes over my non-existent cocktail dress. "And what the heck are you wearing? You'll give Reece a heart attack."

"Heck" is the closest Ella ever comes to cursing.

"Reece was already flat-lining in the hallway about something else." I go to pick up her iPhone from the coffee table.

Now it's Ella's turn to cluck with disapproval. "Don't tell me you ditched your security again? You know it's not safe on the East Coast. Edier warned us about standing too close to Mexican fire." She waves her hand. "Or something like that."

Ignoring her, I flick through her Spotify playlist for something that wasn't born and bred in the era of bad fashion sense. "Does Edier know you're a flower-powered soul trapped inside the body of a twenty-one-year-old goddess?"

Ella blushes. "Why would Edier give a damn what I am, or what I wear, for that matter?"

"Damn" is her second closest word to cursing. Somehow, she ended up with all the good girl genes.

She's making me feel guilty again. The heat on her face is like a love declaration with a megaphone. Ella's had a secret, long-term crush on another of our childhood friends, Edier Grayson, for longer than she's dreamed of being a reporter.

Unfortunately, Edier doesn't know she exists beyond the parameters of their friendship. Or if he does, he's smart enough not to cross those lines. He's another man who's fully entrenched in my father's cartel. He runs the New York Santiago territory with Sam as his second, and despite their yin and yang personalities there's not a whole lot of mercy going on between them. Sam's the hot-headed arrogant one, with smooth dealings and fatalistic charm. Edier's like deadly nightshade in comparison—deceptively handsome, but lethal as hell. Sometime over the last decade, my childhood friends turned into killers and sinners, and I guess I'm still mourning the loss of their innocence.

"What's your assignment about?" I ask her.

My sister is so out of place in this dangerous world of ours, and I worry about her constantly. The slightest knock sends her spiraling. I once heard Sam describe her as a fragile flower trying to flourish on a mountain of shit.

She has health issues, too. Ten years ago, I found her crying on the bathroom floor, curled up in a ball of agony. Every muscle in her body was on fire. Next, her knees and fingers swelled up, and then came the rash, ulcers, and the fever. After seven doctors, we finally had a diagnosis, and our father had a new enemy—Lupus.

Her future is unpredictable, a lengthy remission damn near impossible… I toss the iPhone back down on the coffee table with far more force than necessary. I can't think about that right now. I can't think about an existence without her. She's the person I adore most. The one person I would do anything for.

My thoughts stray to last night's blackjack table.

I'm winning.

I'm losing.

"Fascism during the second world war," she answers with a frown. *Did I mention she's a history major, too?* "By the way, *papá* called."

"Fascism, huh?" Oh, the irony. "Speaking of which…"

"You're going to have to speak to him sometime, Thalia." She candy-coats her censure with a smile, but all I see is her sadness. She hates it when we fight, but it's the one thing I refuse to compromise on. "That's unless you want him turning up here in New York…"

A shiver of fear hits my spine. He's too perceptive. He'll know something's wrong the moment his boots cross the threshold of our apartment.

"I'm going to go take a shower," I say, backing out of the room.

"You know what your problem is?" Her soft words trail me into the hallway.

"You and he are *way* too similar."

I stop dead, clutching at the door frame as a deep-seated pain takes hold of my stomach and twists...*hard*.

"*Mamá's* not going to let this go, either. If we can see the good in him, so can you."

"You know what he is, right?" I swing back around, fighting to keep my cool. "Those scars on his chest aren't just tattoos, Ella. When he does wrong, he doesn't just shrug his shoulders and learn his lesson. He *is* the lesson... I suggest you make your assignment all about blood-thirsty Colombian dictators. You have a ton of research already. Twenty-one years, to be exact."

Her face pales. "Drop it, Thals."

"Never going to happen."

CHAPTER
Three

THALIA

I cross the hallway to my bedroom under a cloud of black thoughts. Most days, I feel like I'm punching underwater, though what or whom I'm punching is usually up for debate.

Today, I have a face and a name.

Marco Bardi.

He's a small-time mafiosi from Canal Street with an even smaller dick—better known as my latest battle, and the man on the cusp of my older sister's ruin. He's also blowing up my cell as I slam my bedroom door shut, his slimeball aura seeping into my life again.

"How much?" he demands as soon as the call connects.

"Forty-thousand." I scoop out the wads of crumpled dollars from my purse and toss them onto the bed. The notes scatter, tainting the crisp, white sheets with a dirty green.

"Not enough," he states bluntly.

My teeth slash bloody lines into my lower lip. When all of this is over, I'm giving his name, address, and social security number to Edier. After that, Marco Bardi will never see another sunset again.

"I need more time. Too many of the casinos in Pennsylvania are Santiago-associated. I'm running out of—"

"Not possible. Try another state."

Damn the assholes who revoked New York's gambling laws five years ago.

"My father's security is all over me! I can't travel to Massachusetts—"

"There's an obvious answer, bitch." He chuckles, but it's an unclean, hostile shock of a sound, like finding unwanted grit in my favorite clam chowder. "Are you going to say it, or should I?"

Shit.

"How are you going to get your fifty-thousand if I get my throat slit?" I say desperately.

"Don't get cute with me, Thalia Santiago. All I need to do is to press that button and Pornhub gets super juicy."

Panic fills my mouth. "Okay, wait!" *Don't say it. Don't say it.* "Fine. Atlantic City, it is then. As long as I'm there and back in one evening, Bardi."

There's a long pause. Even Marco the super creep knows I'm playing fast and loose with my life by venturing into a rival cartel territory controlled by Valentin Carrera and his son.

Is he having second thoughts?

"Do you want your money, or not?" I say, now forcing this decision down his throat as much as I'm forcing it down mine. "I'm all out of options. Atlantic City is the gambling mecca of the East Coast."

One chance to win all the money I need.

One night to save my sister's reputation.

Everyone falls, and Bardi was the high cliff edge that Ella never saw coming.

It's my fault. I *made* her join me in that bar last June where he bought her drinks all evening. I wouldn't let up at her. I'd practically dragged her there in her nightgown.

He was my sister's one moment of tasting reckless, a stupid drunken mistake, and now there's footage of it—grainy images tainting something sweet and precious.

Ella doesn't know about the tape, yet. Bardi came straight to me. If I can somehow raise the half million dollars he's demanding, her big mistake never has to see the light of day. But, like he said, I'm fifty grand short and my deadline is one day away.

Sam and Edier would help me in a flash, but I'm too scared to ask them. One slip up… one loose word… That's all it'll take to smear the colors of a rainbow.

I know my sister. This kind of humiliation will disfigure her with cuts that will never, ever fade.

If I told *papá*, he'd shoot first and dissect the consequences later, and by then it would be too late—the footage would have bled its filth all over the internet, soiling the pages of her history forever. As for me, I don't have that kind of money. Ella and I were never destined to be playthings maneuvered around a cartel power board, but our father snapped invisible collars around us just the same. We have a cool apartment, cars, drivers, but we'll never have enough cash in the bank to lead us into trouble.

Or out of it…

When Bardi started blackmailing me, I had no choice but to lie, to distance myself from my family, to tumble headfirst into a world that I'm not even legal enough for in the eyes of the law.

Gambling.

Ella must have told Bardi I have the kind of memory that retains things at a single glance—book pages, images, the patterns and sequences of playing cards… Last summer in Monte Carlo, my father let me sit in on one of the private tables at Black Skies Casino. Within half an hour, I could predict what cards the dealer was going to turn.

Still, there's a 101 for counting cards and not getting caught. I never get greedy, I start small, and I only play a six-deck game. I move from casino to casino and keep in the shadows of the big players, wearing shorter and shorter dresses as a camouflage and the bright white smile of youth and inexperience.

In four days, I've won four-hundred and fifty-thousand dollars.

"New Jersey it is, then," Bardi agrees.

I sit down hard on the bed, crunching loose dollars, feeling like a cornered animal.

I must be insane to even consider this.

"Does Carrera's influence extend to the casinos?"

"Not by choice, but I believe his son has designs."

Shit.

"Do you know which ones?"

"No idea. Why don't you pay the gambling commission a visit on your way in? If you drop to your knees and kiss their dicks, you might get your answer."

Bastard. "Like I said, do you want your money, or not?"

"You're fifty grand short, sugar. And you've one more day to get it for me."

The next thing I hear are the moans and groans of a woman in the throes of the hardest fuck of her life.

It might be regular porn.

It might be Ella.

Irrespective, it's a shotgun incentive.

"Meet me outside The Haven at eight p.m.," I tell him, as soon as the sex gets muted. "If I'm doing this, you're driving."

"I'll be there."

"The second I hit fifty-thousand, I want that footage, Bardi."

Instead of answering, the line goes dead, stranding me all alone in the wicked wasteland of no guarantees.

With a curse, I chuck my cell across the room, and it hits the carpet with a muffled thud. Down the hallway, I can hear Ella chatting with one of her friends. Her laughter floats into my room, via the crack under the door.

I have to protect that sound.

I can't let it fade away.

Tonight, it's play or pay.

CHAPTER
Four

SANTI

"Good men follow the rules. Smart men follow their instincts." Locking eyes with Legado's casino manager, I raise my glass, letting the words hang in the air.

The man's face blanches, and with good reason. While mildly entertaining, the pathetic song and dance routine he just performed broke two of my three cardinal rules.

Never lie to me.

Never waste my time.

I can't decide if it's because he's scared, stupid, or shrewd. All three can be dangerous to a man like me, which is why I don't care to delve into what drove him to commit his first sin.

Never steal from a Carrera.

"Santi…" He swallows hard, his Adam's apple bobbing in his throat. "You don't understand…"

"See, that's where you're wrong," I offer calmly. "I understand you perfectly, Ashford. You've reeked of desperation for weeks."

A bead of sweat rolls down his temple. "Santi..."

"Your priorities shifted from the bottom line to a white line." A tinge of anger seeps through my cool façade.

He lifts his chin. "A little hypocritical from a man who imports and distributes it."

Well, look who decided to grow a pair of balls.

"I sell it, *cabrón,* not snort it. That shit rots the brain, and like I said, smart men follow their instincts. If you'd followed yours, you would've come to me for a loan. Instead, you helped yourself."

I've known for months that the man was up to his ass in debt and addiction. *Not my problem.* As long as he came to work, did his job, and kept his mouth shut, he could snort fucking bath salts for all I cared.

But he stuck his hand in my pocket and made it my problem.

"Yeah," he huffs, more sweat glistening his forehead. "At forty percent interest."

"This is Atlantic City, *pendejo.* You play, you pay." Finishing my drink, I set the glass on the table before adding, "One way or another."

I don't elaborate. My reputation speaks for me. At twenty-two, I've accomplished more than men twice my age. New Jersey's playground bows to me. For two years, I've owned its cocaine distribution, and now I've seized control of another of its vices.

Gambling.

It's a side venture that feeds my hunger for power and vengeance. The only thing I love more than the smell of money is the scent of blood.

Neither masks the scent of a traitor.

Does forty-thousand-dollars make a difference in my bottom line? Not in the least. I've made twice that during the span of our conversation.

Could I forgive it? *Probably.*

Will I? *No.*

"I swear, Mr. Carrera," he pleads, his knees bouncing with the frantic cadence of his words. "Nothing like this will ever happen again."

More empty promises fall from his lips, faster than a golden-tongued auctioneer. Pointless, of course. They're nothing but wasted energy and white noise.

That's when I hear a familiar, throaty laugh behind me. One that knows better than to show up three hours early.

Good men follow the rules. Smart men follow their instincts.

My own words chisel into my skull as I rise from my chair, ignoring the frantic bargaining still going on. Ashford is throwing himself on the mercy of the devil's court, and at any other time, I'd enjoy delivering his sentence.

But not today.

He gets a reprieve.

She doesn't.

Pulling out my phone, I make my way over to her, unsurprised when RJ answers before it even rings—a hallmark of his upbringing. "Platinum Bar Lounge," I say before disconnecting the call and tucking the device back inside my jacket. In five wide steps, I make my way to the counter, my hands fisted by my side. "Still can't follow directions, I see."

Two slender shoulders stiffen under a curtain of long, dark hair. "Why start now?"

"You weren't supposed to be here until five o'clock. Explain yourself."

"Boss." Like a phantom, RJ, my second in command, appears by my side.

Announcing his presence wasn't necessary. I knew he'd arrived by the sudden wave of whispers rippling across the bar. The man is a genetically engineered tank stuffed inside a designer suit. It's what makes him so dangerous. People focus on the muscles shaping his body, ignoring the most lethal one of all.

His brain.

A diabolical machine with the IQ of a genius.

Despite his appearance, RJ Harcourt can blend in better than any of us. Having been born in Mexico City and raised in Houston, he's a cultural chameleon—able to look the part of a hardened narco and speak with the eloquence and civility of a silver-spoon fed CEO.

I nod at my ill-fated casino floor manager, still sitting motionless where I left him. "Please escort Mr. Ashford downstairs."

Where he'll pay until his skin drips red.

RJ crosses the room and engulfs Ashford's arm in his grip. Impressively, the doomed man doesn't say a word, simply stumbling along the trajectory of his fate, his face the color of spoiled milk.

Once they're both out of sight, I shift my attention to my left and the college asshole at the bar with his eyes attached to my sister's chest. "Leave."

Cocking a blond eyebrow, he offers a disinterested scan down my handmade Italian suit. "Man, fuck off. I'm buying the lady a drink."

I don't argue; I act.

One glance at the bartender is all it takes. With a subtle nod, he discreetly hands me a credit card.

I glance down. "Channing Yeager." *Stupid name for a stupid fucker.*

"Santi..." a soft voice groans next to me.

"Quiet," I snap. "I'll deal with you in a minute. Now, Mr. Yeager..." I say, redirecting my focus. "You have thirty seconds to leave the premises of your own free will"—leaning in, I lower my voice—"and in one piece."

That cocky smirk melts off his face like a crayon in the sun. "Y-you're Santi Carrera..." I have to admit, my blood sings at the terror my name etches into his face. With a shaking hand, he retrieves his card. Glancing briefly at the fuming woman beside him, he sprints toward the exit. "You're on your own."

Silence dances an out of step beat between us as I slide into the newly vacated barstool. Both of us wait for the other to speak first, neither wanting to concede.

Without asking, a glass of *Añejo* tequila appears in front of me. Biding my time, I lift my glass, savoring the familiar burn to the familiar tune of spinning slot machines in the background.

"That was a little over the top, don't you think?" she says finally.

Setting my glass down, I fight a smirk. "No."

"What are you going to do?" She peers up at me from underneath those dark lashes. "Run every guy who looks at me out of town?"

I'm rarely questioned, even less so in such a petulant tone. Biting back a knee jerk response, I filter my words through clenched teeth. "If I have to."

There's a long pause before my little sister tilts her face up at me, the stubborn set of her jaw frustratingly familiar. "It has been a year and a half. How long are you going to punish me?"

Until every trace of Sam Sanders is gone and forgotten.

Until I raze New York to the ground, leaving nothing but a bad memory.

I gaze at her, refusing to give my pain a voice. Emotion equals weakness, and all a man's enemy needs is one crack. "I'm not punishing you, Lola," I offer solemnly. "I'm protecting you."

She stares at me, those bright blue eyes wide with something dangerously close to pity. "Do you know the difference?"

"What's that supposed to mean?" With a growl, I slam the glass down so hard, a piece chips off the bottom and skids across the bar.

She sighs. "Santi, you're my big brother. I love you. But I'm family, not one of your men." Lowering her gaze, she spins a silver bracelet on her wrist. "I wear the Carrera name, too," she adds quietly.

"And the Santiago brand."

Lola stiffens, her palm dropping from her wrist to cover her right hip. "That's not fair."

She's right. She didn't ask to get stalked and kidnapped by one of our family's enemies. She didn't carve a rival cartel's initial into her own skin.

None of that was her fault.

My sister may have grown up as a cartel princess, but she's hopelessly idealistic. She still sees the good in people.

"Life isn't fair, *chaparrita*. The sooner you realize that the better off you'll be."

I brace for another argument. To my surprise, she inhales a breath and exhales resignation. "*Ugh*. I outgrew that nickname years ago, Santi."

She didn't, but "*shorty*" likes to think of herself as a cartel badass in stiletto heels.

"Too bad your height didn't follow suit."

Groaning at the jab, she leans in and bumps my shoulder. "I've missed you, you big asshole."

My lips twitch, a rare smile threatening to break across my face. "I may have noticed your absence, once or twice."

"Careful," she says, lazily spinning a cocktail napkin with the tip of her fingernail. "That almost sounded like actual emotion."

Anyone else would be picking up their teeth after such audacity, but my little sister is given liberties no one else is allowed.

In America, I am an island, a solitary extension of Mexico's underground. *An empire of one.* The men in my inner circle are invaluable but not irreplaceable. But Lola is different.

Family is priceless. Other than power and vengeance, it's the only thing I live for, and the one thing I'd die for. And, for as much danger as my sister's presence brings, it also brings comfort.

Reaching across the bar counter, I tip her chin toward me. "No more surprises, okay? When I give you an order, it's for a reason." *Her protection and my sanity.*

She nods reluctantly, so I let it go.

Lifting my glass, I motion around the bar. "So, how long have you been here?"

Her gaze travels toward the empty chair of my soon-to-be ex-floor manager. "Long enough."

Growing up as the child of one of the most feared men in the world doesn't allow for the luxury of ignorance. She knows his fate.

That off-beat silence dances between us again, and this time it's laced with tension.

As if desperate to change the subject, Lola surveys the bar. "Swanky place, Santi. It's different."

And by different, she means flashy.

Un-Carrera-like.

Legado Casino is a purchase my father and I didn't agree on. The kingpin of Mexico's Carrera Cartel is old-school. He prefers to fly under the radar. Keep a low profile. Remain an international ghost and blend in.

Fuck that.

I've run our East Coast operation his way for two years. All it's gotten me is a one port cocaine distribution and ridicule on the other side of the river. Now, it's time to do things my way. I'm making noise and lighting cannons. When I'm done, everyone will know the name Santi Carrera.

"Different." I repeat. "So is that dress." I narrow my eyes at the skimpy black material suctioned to her body like Saran Wrap. "Where's the rest of it?"

Those pale blue eyes darken. *Trophy eyes*, my father calls them. Ones that left a string of shattered hearts and broken bones back in Mexico. "Don't start."

I don't plan to.

For now.

"Come on..." Placing my empty glass on the bar, I stand and offer her my hand. "I'll give you a tour."

Lola slides out of her chair with a grin. "Does it include a free stop at the blackjack table?"

"No," I murmur, dragging her behind me.

It's going to be a long fucking summer.

A half hour later, I've paraded Lola through Legado's main casino floor, four more bars, a world-renowned restaurant, two spas, and finally the executive offices on the third floor.

The minute I open the door, a short, perky blonde pushes away from her desk and catapults herself out of her chair. "Good afternoon, Mr. Carrera. Mr. Spader confirmed your appointment for tonight."

It's about time.

The Atlantic City Gaming Commissioner has kept me waiting for forty-eight hours. That's not how I do business. People wait on me, not the other way around.

"Thank you, Audrey." Pressing my palm against Lola's back, I maneuver her toward my office, adding over my shoulder, "By the way, you're fired."

"I d-don't..." she stutters, her eyes glazing over. "What did I—?"

Do? Nothing. She's simply not needed, and I always trim excess.

My focus returns to Lola as she takes a leisurely stroll around the executive office lobby.

"Cheerful setup you have here." She folds her arms across her chest while taking in the dominant dual color scheme. One that carries through to every single office—especially mine.

Black and red.

Two colors that not only match my mood, but also hide more incriminating colors.

Yet I don't owe her an explanation, so I don't offer one.

"So, you've kept me in suspense long enough." Circling around me, she perches on the corner of the desk. "What am I going to be doing here all summer? Director of Marketing? VP of Operations?"

"Secretary."

One word, and my sister's smile drops. "Santi! I'm your sister, not your damn secretary."

Dios mío. Did I not just order her to stop questioning me?

She needs an internship for college credit, so I'm giving her one.

I'm on her in less than two strides, my hands gripping her slim shoulders. "That's right. You *are* my sister, and that's why I can't have you flaunting your ass all over my casino. You're a liability, Lola. I need you in a position that keeps you out of the public eye but always in my sight."

A muffled sniffle causes me to glance over my shoulder where I find Audrey watching us with glassy eyes and quivering lips.

"Why are you still here?"

Blinking, she backs up, nearly tripping over her own feet.

"You okay?" Lola asks. When Audrey nods, she swings her heated gaze back to me. "I don't want to spend three months locked in an office, Santi."

"It's the safest place for both of us," I say, pinching the bridge of my nose. "You have to admit, you're a goddamn magnet for trouble."

That's putting it mildly. Carrera women are the sirens of the underworld.

"Santi, you—"

A crash interrupts her, and we both turn to find Audrey on her hands and knees, frantically shoving the strewn contents of her purse back inside it as if her life depends on it. We watch in silence as she stumbles to her feet, clutching her bag to her chest and trembling as she closes the door behind her.

Lola sighs. "You're a bastard."

"Don't…" I warn, shoving a finger in her face before turning toward my office with her right on my heels. "She'll be well compensated for her troubles."

"If you keep treating people like that, you're going to die alone."

The words snake around my neck, sinking their truth into my jugular. "Didn't you learn anything growing up?" I say, my tone razor-thin. "Carreras can't outrun destiny."

CHAPTER
Five

THALIA

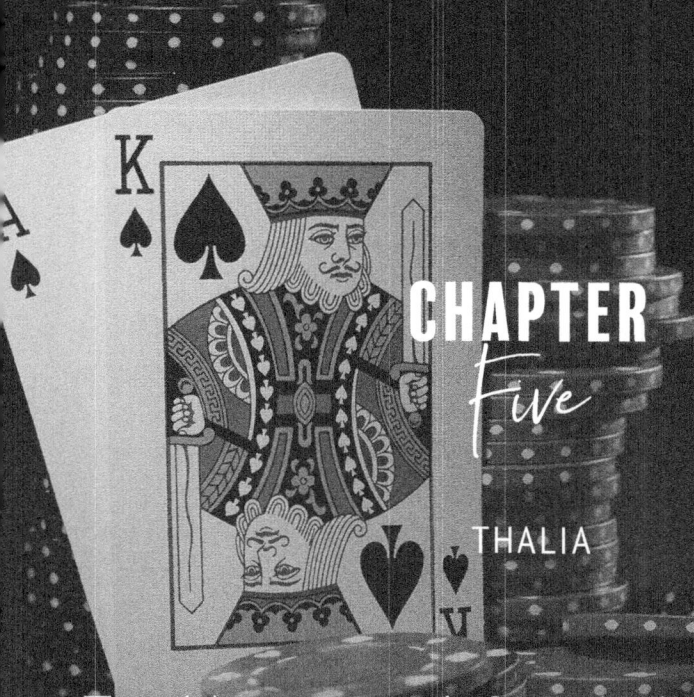

Legado is more extravagant than I expected. And taller... Like a glimmering, rose-gold castle of sin, rising up from the depths of hell to high five the skyline.

The *porte-cochère* is dripping with thick green ivy and big enough to fit at least a dozen cars. Bardi pulls up behind a Porsche Cayenne and we sit in silence, watching parades of money exit their rich-people vehicles and sashay up the black marble front steps and into the glass-fronted lobby. There's not a hint of Vegas cliché about any of it. All the prowling bride-to-be packs have been herded up and penned into some other, less exclusive casino down the road.

The muscles-in-tuxes on the front door have a mean gangster look about them that's ricocheting unease around my stomach. I know security like that. I've been around them all my life. In fact, I'm straight-up ignoring mine...

My cell has eighteen missed calls from Reece already. I won't be able to joke my way out of this one. The new guys he'd put in charge of my security were doing a great job, until I used the bathroom window escape route from a bar on 16th Avenue. As arranged, Bardi was out front waiting for me.

Thirty minutes later...

"Why here?" I ask, tugging the hemline down on tonight's designer dress—a claret-red showstopper with embellished maroon detail that rises and falls with the curves of my body like the waves of an ocean. I hate it, but not as much as

I hate the asshole sitting in the seat next to me. Bardi's been staring at my legs all journey long, and the unwanted attention has left me with two clenched fists.

It doesn't help that I'm running on empty. Adrenaline hasn't allowed me much sleep this week, but it's a small price to pay. I just want out of this mess, and to go back to playing family politics and looking after my sister again.

Fifty thousand. That's all I need."

"Legado is the best in America's Playground." Bardi gives me one of his irritating laughs. "I thought you could start with pure gold and end up with the shitty bronzes where old folk mainline slot machines like junkies."

I glance at the casino entrance again. In a place like this—if I play super smart—I'll be coasting home on a tank of relief by midnight.

"Nice dress." He shifts in his seat, and I catch the foul odor of a fresh wave of sleaze. "Maybe we can come to some arrangement if you come up short... I suppose you'd be worth a couple of grand."

I grind my teeth together before one of my fists makes another dent in his eye socket. He's twenty-five, and not nearly as hot as he thinks he is.

He's smart, though... Like back-up plan smart. Like don't fuck with me, bitch, because I'll press that button regardless smart. He knows there's no way out for me tonight, other than up those damn marble steps.

"Are you sure it's not Carrera affiliated?" For some reason, this place is making me nervous.

"Life's a fucking gamble, right, babe?" He appraises me with half-lidded eyes that dare to stray southward again. "On second thought, you'll never look as hot as your sister. Now, when *she* wrapped her lips around my cock—"

"Go fuck yourself, Bardi!" Angrily, I swipe at the door handle. How dare he disrespect Ella like that. *How dare I lead her astray and get her into this mess in the first place.*

Swinging out of the passenger seat, I grind my five-inch heels into the gray stone driveway. "Little tip for you," I say, leaning back inside the vehicle. "Keep your eyes off my legs, or I'll be showing you this real neat knife trick my father taught me."

I regret my words instantly.

Little tip for myself? Don't piss off the guy with my sister's reputation in his hands.

"Go count your cards, Thalia Santiago," he calls out from the driver seat.

"Go make Daddy proud."

With his words stinging my ears, I slam the door and make my way into the casino, tensing my stomach muscles as I pass through security. Fortunately, my fake ID checks out. They don't even glance at my face as they sweep my purse for hidden bombs.

Whoever owns this place has their market by the throat. The main gaming floor is a silky-smooth set-up, with a black and gold decor, mirrored walls, and crystal chandeliers hanging from high domed ceilings. The acoustics are amplifying the sound of the play, making me feel like I'm entering a Gladiatorial arena where success hangs on the mercy of the cards and the lions of failure are constantly prowling the perimeter.

I take my time, buying up a couple of grand's worth of chips, drifting between tables—my free cocktail in hand—catching hot glances and returning them with an icy-cold detachment that freezes their hopeful balls off. Eventually, I settle at a table, sliding into the Third Base seat of seven, and stifling my grin. It's a great position. The one I've been waiting for. I can see all the other player's cards dealt before mine and I'm always the last to hit, split or surrender.

"How many decks?" I ask the dealer, signaling to one of the circling waitresses for another drink.

"Eight," she says curtly, loading up the shoe. "We only use eight at Legado."

My grin slips as I watch her insert a red plastic card into the decks. I'm used to counting six. The house edge here just made my job a hell of a lot harder.

The chairs are soon filling up.

I lose a thousand on the first five games—partly intentional, partly out of nerves. There's some beefy Texan and his trophy wife next to me who are determined to be the big stakes at the table, betting higher and higher to match their egos, like new money often does.

Settling into a groove, I keep my bets under five hundred as I start to see the rhythm in the cards. Before long, I'm ten thousand up, and three drinks down.

Half an hour later, I've gained another ten after a tactical, diversionary loss of four.

"Paint it, paint it!" the Texan yells, clawing at the table behind his cards like he's cat-scratching the felt. The requested card sends him crashing over with a bust hand of twenty-two and a volley of Dallas profanity.

I glance at the dealer's "upcard" and the one she just revealed. It's a shiny red ace of hearts and a nine of clubs.

Total of twenty.

I glance at my cards again.

Another blackjack hand.

Twenty-one.

I wave at her and slide the cards under my bet, calculating that I've just netted myself another three thousand, when there's a flash of black and blue to my left.

Two men are moving through the gaming floor on a fast trajectory that'll bring them within spitting distance of my table. One is short and nondescript, wearing a cheap navy suit and glasses that make him look like a Pro Bono from the ass-end of Queens, but the other... My breath catches... *The other is sinful royalty himself.*

He's taller than most, making him even harder to ignore. Tousled dark hair, hard penetrating brown eyes that are taking a sledgehammer to my senses, a devilishly-well cut black suit to match... His skin is a rich golden color that only adds to that mysterious aura of money and power, and the high cut of his cheekbones is casting serious shade over a fierce expression.

His movements are sleek and precise. One hand hangs loose from his suit pant pocket, but I can tell it's more from habit than some masculine, dick-swinging statement. It's pulling his white dress shirt taut against his lower torso, outlining the wall of muscle underneath which barely shifts as he walks.

Stalks.

Fear ignites in my veins again, and this time it's the kind that no amount of free drinks can extinguish.

"Ma'am," snaps the dealer, losing patience with me.

I play my cards while I'm still staring at the man, oblivious to the excited gasps all around me as I claim another win.

He's close now. I can see the satisfied twist to his cruelly sensual mouth. He's younger than I'd first figured—maybe mid-twenties—but he's the sort to view his age as a disadvantage. Maybe that's why he's overpromoting his dangerous vibe.

At the last second, I drop my eyes to the table. I feel the heat of his gaze passing over my lowered head like a blast from a furnace, and then he's offering up his broad back to me as some kind of "fuck you, I'm not interested."

He skims past the poker tables, and then he and the other guy disappear into a door marked "private", adjacent to the long bar.

His shadow continues to linger over the floor.

I glance at my fellow players to see if anyone else is affected by the Tornado of Danger that just blew through the casino, but all eyes are fixed on the dealer.

Without thinking, I chuck a couple of thousand in chips into the betting circle, and then scramble to remember the last cards that were played. *Come on, Thalia... keep it together.* But it's like my concentration just disappeared through a door marked "private", too. The urge to run is so strong, my fingers start gripping the edge of the table. My father always swore that instinct was his greatest weapon.

Whoever that man is, I need to stay away from him at all costs.

That's when I do something I've never done at a blackjack table before—I make a stupid, rash decision that sets my destiny on a collision course with the Prince of Darkness himself.

I add every single chip I've won tonight to my pile on the betting circle before a single card is dealt.

I need to get the hell out of here, and I need to do it fast.

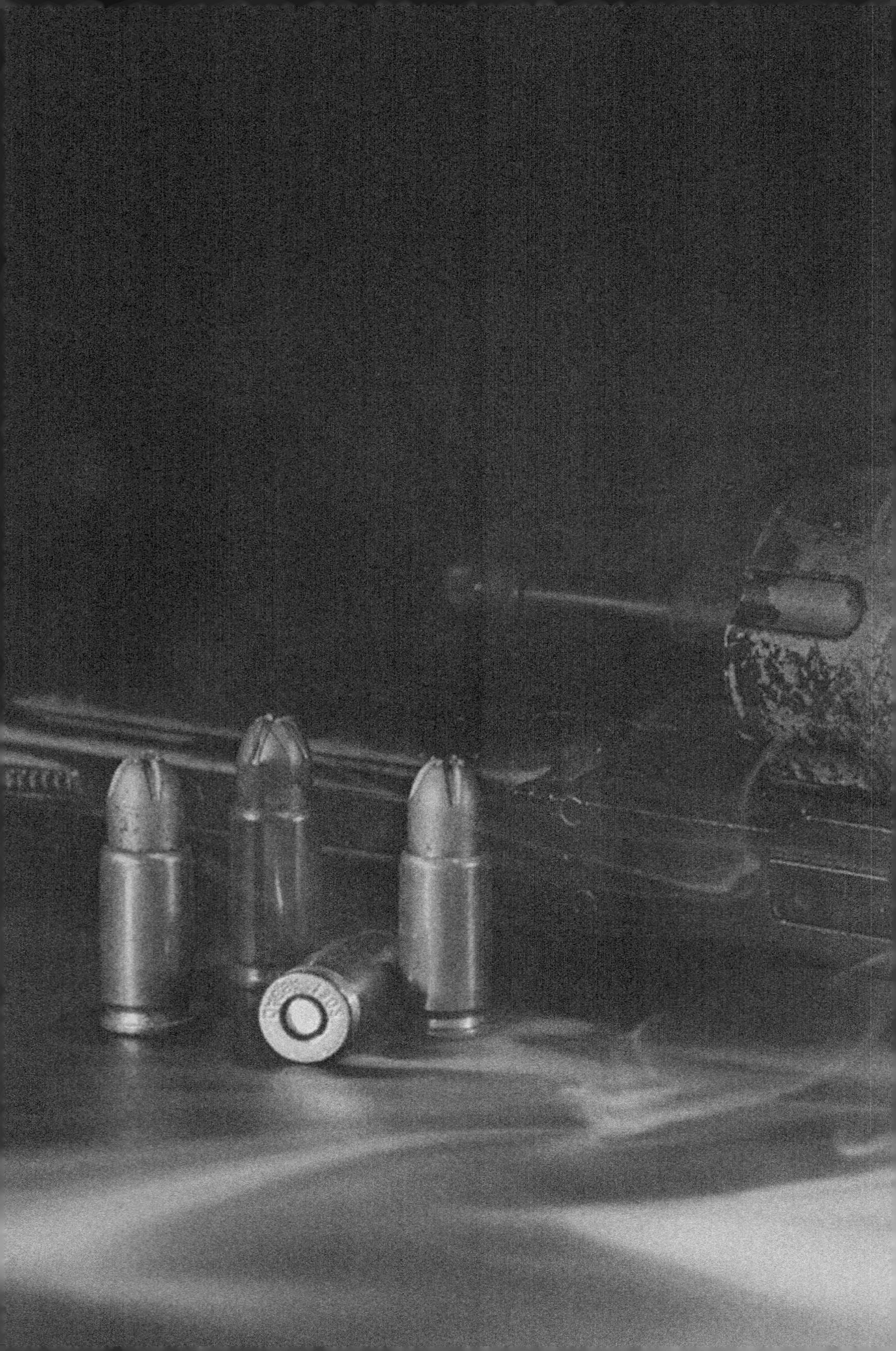

CHAPTER
Six

SANTI

I dreamed of her again last night.

The young girl in the red toboggan with the brown eyes.

Like always, I see her spilling out of the black sedan, the snow crunching beneath her boots as a nickname trails behind her. She pays no attention to it. We're too locked in our own world—her bright curiosity tainted by my dark purpose.

"Are you waiting for someone?" she asks.

Yes, you…

"Do you want to come sit with us?"

I want her to move so that I can fire two bullets into the car behind her, but I stand frozen, just like the barrier of snow between us.

She shouldn't be here… It isn't safe. I'm a falcon—eyes, ears, and wall of protection for the men inside that church. And right now, the only one I want to protect is her.

Last night was different.

Instead of rushing forward and shielding her from the gunfire, the dream I've had for nearly ten years extended into something new. Something so hauntingly disturbing, I can't get it out of my head.

The young girl in the red toboggan was a woman in a white dress. Her head was bowed, her face hidden behind a thick curtain of onyx hair. A flickering light swung above the corner of the damp, dark room where she knelt with her hands bound behind her back. Even in her vulnerable position, she never cried. Her shoulders never shook with fear.

"*I trusted you,*" she whispered. "*You failed us.*"

Us.

She whispers the word each time I see her, only she's always alone—this unknown woman I shouldn't waste a spare moment thinking about. Yet, her accusation pierces like a dagger to my heart.

The image has haunted me all day, following me about like a phantom. It occupies unwanted space in my mind, bleeding its chaos into my business.

I'm silent as the elevator doors slide open, my gaze settling on the steel door a few feet in front of me. This is where everything makes sense. Four floors below the most exclusive casino in Atlantic City lies the gate to hell.

Down here, nothing matters but what's behind that door. My focus should be the slow build of adrenaline pumping through my veins, but it's not. It's still locked on that damn woman, and it's pissing me off.

She pisses me off.

A manifestation of my own guilt.

My mind devours the word as I press my thumb against the access pad and a faint click grants me entry. Shoving the door open, I step inside my sanctuary of sin.

Fuck it.

Drowning in a sea of guilt is a waste of time and mistakes are nothing but stagnant water: they'll never flow differently. Revenge, on the other hand, is a rushing rapid that, without warning, plummets off the side of a cliff.

It's revenge that fuels my appetite for power and my thirst for blood.

It's in the air tonight. I can smell its coppery scent.

It's time a certain traitor choked on it.

There's a trace of a smile on my lips as I close the door behind me. "Rough day, Ashford?"

An understatement. Getting hit by an eighteen-wheeler would've been *rough.* Ten hours of being tied to a chair and slowly mutilated is a fate worse than death.

Unfortunately for him, that was just the prelude.

My former casino floor manager lifts his chin, and I take a moment to appreciate RJ's artwork. The man has skill. Angry, purple bruises paint the canvas of Ashford's alabaster skin like a damn Picasso.

"Santi, please..." he begs, blood streaming from both corners of his mouth. "I'll get you your money. I swear."

I don't dignify that with an answer.

Removing my jacket, I drape it over a nearby table and roll up my sleeves as he grovels for his life.

Then I drive my fist into what's left of his nose.

Ashford's head snaps back with a satisfying crack, a fresh river of blood coating his face. "Cleaver," I order, opening my stained hand.

The command needs few words. One is enough for RJ to place a meat cleaver in my waiting palm. As my second, it's his job to anticipate and act. Of course, the fact that he's also my cousin adds a layer of depth rarely found in our line of work.

Depth, not trust.

I depend on a few. I *trust* no one.

Glancing down, I loosen my grip around the cleaver's worn handle and give it a light spin. Simple, but effective. I usually prefer more sophisticated toys, but I'm late for a meeting. Tried and true will have to suffice.

I hold it up just to watch Ashford's swollen eyes well up with tears, and a wet stain appears at his crotch as he pisses himself. "You're making a fucking mess in my casino, Ashford."

"P-please..." he gurgles.

"My father always believed in the punishment fitting the crime." Folding my arms across my chest, I tap the flat end of the cleaver against my chin. "You stole from me, so maybe I should make sure that never happens again." Without taking my eyes off him, I nod my head. Before I can blink, RJ has a folding table placed between Ashford and me.

"N-no. No, please!"

RJ disappears behind him with a switchblade, slicing through the zip tie binding Ashford's hands within seconds. Wrapping his fingers around the man's wrist, he slams his palm onto the table and firmly holds it in place.

Ashford is so fucking dazed he doesn't bother using his free arm to fight back. The *cabrón* just leaves it hanging by his side like an overcooked noodle.

Who am I to refuse an open invitation?

Without hesitation or remorse, I slam the cleaver down, unbothered as his pinkie and ring finger scatter across the tarp. I stare down at the severed digits, kicking the one imprisoned by a gold band out of my sight.

There. I did us both a favor.

Ashford's screams are a calming melody, and I hum the familiar tune. This is where my demons dance. Uncaged, they chant their oaths to the devil while reveling in their own sin.

Four floors up, I am a shark in a designer suit.

Below their feet, I am *El Muerte.*

My shirt is no longer white. Streaks of red soak the front, sealing it to my chest like a second skin.

RJ grabs a handful of Ashford's dark blond hair, snapping the man's head back like a rubber band. Barely conscious, he stares up at me through glassy eyes. He's no longer sniveling. There's a calmness blanketing him that I don't like. It's as if he's straddling two worlds, and the gateway is an opaque window.

"Your guilt will force you to choose one day," he wheezes, death rattling in his chest.

Leaning down, I flash a rare smile. "I always choose revenge."

Drawing my arm back, I swing the cleaver, lodging it deep into his carotid artery.

Lola's head snaps up as I open the glass doors to the executive offices. Shoving her chair back, she glides around her desk, her high heels clicking in a staccato rhythm. "Where have you been?"

"Out."

Frowning, she slams the heel of her palm against my chest, halting my movement. "It's ten o'clock at night. Normal secretaries don't keep these kinds of hours, *Santi.*"

"Normal secretaries don't have three-fourths of her family plastered across the Ten Most Wanted list, *Lola.*"

That shuts her up, which would give me a modicum of satisfaction if this entire day hadn't gone completely left of center.

Leaving her to roll that around in that stubborn head of hers, I take a step forward only to find her blocking my path again. "I've called you six times. That Spader guy has been waiting in your office for over forty minutes." Huffing out a breath, she glances over her shoulder at my closed office door. "He's a real barrel of laughs, huh?"

I know that tone. Subtlety isn't one of my sister's finer qualities. Instead of tiptoeing around a subject, she prefers to hit it head on, run it over, and drag it a couple miles.

On edge from a lack of sleep and waning adrenaline, I scrub my hand down my face—two days of stubble scraping my palm. "Tell me you didn't mouth off to Atlantic City's chief gaming commissioner."

"Okay, I won't tell you."

"Lola," I warn.

"¡Ay, Dios mío! I'm kidding." She pats my chest. "Lighten up or you're going to have a stroke before you're thirty." When I don't laugh, she sighs. "Look, you may have saddled me with a shitty, and frankly demeaning job, but I'm not going to make my own brother look bad."

I stiffen at her affection but force myself not to react. No one is allowed to touch me. It's an unfortunate by-product of having a mother who didn't fully know who I was until I was nearly eight years old. That kind of shit damages a kid. Although it wasn't her fault, the scars run deep.

Not her fault.

A common theme in my family with one twisted Colombian root.

The smile on Lola's face slips along with her hand. "I told him your meeting was running late, and you'd be here in ten minutes—of course that was four ten minutes' ago..." Her voice trails off as she tilts her head, her focus dropping from my face. "What's that?"

"What's what?"

"You have something on your neck." Before I can stop her, she licks her thumb and scrubs at a patch of skin below my ear. Drawing her arm back, she rubs the pads of her thumb and index finger together, the leftover evidence of my sins coating her skin. As her pursed lips slowly part, I brace myself for what I know is coming next. "It's—"

"Nothing you need to concern yourself with." Taking hold of her wrist, I wipe the red stain onto my black suit jacket. "I cut myself shaving."

She doesn't answer, and with good reason. We both know I'm full of shit.

My sister grew up on a compound in Mexico City surrounded by guards armed with military grade artillery where a day's body count was nothing more than dinner conversation.

I've never hidden who I am or what I do from her. However, I prefer to keep her on the outskirts of it, if at all possible.

Releasing her wrist, I slide my gaze toward my office. Smoothing the frayed ends of my patience, I push my family out of my mind and center myself on the business at hand.

"Clear my schedule," I instruct, following the stench of corruption and cheap aftershave into my office.

Opening the door, I find Monroe Spader bent over the side of my desk, the back of his greasy brown hair bobbing as he tries every drawer like his life depends on it.

"They're all locked," I note, closing the door behind me. Monroe's spine stiffens as he slowly rises to his full height. *All five foot eight inches of it.* "Nice try, though."

"Carrera," he stammers, flashing a smile as sincere as a used car salesman. "I was just—"

"Save it." Motioning for him to get the fuck out of my way, I collapse into my desk chair. "I'd be more offended if you *didn't* try to break into my files. Any business partner worth my time would never take a man's word at face value."

None that are still alive at least.

"So are we...?" He hesitates, fisting the lapels of his suit jacket. *Nerves. They always manifest whether you want them to or not.* At my silence, he clarifies, "Business partners I mean."

"You tell me."

The answer had better be a confident "yes" with a lot of ass kissing. Our proposed partnership stands to not only line our pockets, but to carve deep inroads into enemy territory as well.

A deal that infiltrates the one place they aren't protecting, and all arranged by the stupid grinning puppet staring down at me.

I've known for a while that Atlantic City's chief gaming commissioner is a pious prick with his hand out. Like most politicians, Monroe's morality is a two-faced whore: one face spews political promises while the other sits on a back-alley auction block.

One who can be collared and screwed for the right price.

Then again, the video footage I sent of him fucking his mistress sped things along.

"I don't like the imbalance of risk, Santi," he says, tugging at his collar.

I cock an eyebrow. "Meaning?"

"I'm the one shouldering all of it. If this deal goes south, I lose everything—my job, my reputation—hell, if enough violations add up, maybe even my freedom. What the hell do you have at stake?"

The fact that he has to ask irritates the shit out of me.

"Fuck your stakes. Your white-washed political risk means nothing. Jobs can be replaced. Reputations can be rebuilt. Even freedom can eventually be reclaimed." Gritting my teeth, I jab my finger onto my desk. "But if this fucks up, I don't get a reprimand, *pendejo*. I get tossed in the Hudson with a bullet in the back of my skull. You wanted to play in the big leagues, well here it is." I spread my arms wide. "Welcome to the upper echelon. You either win big or lose your life. Those are the stakes. You still want to play?"

Sweat beads across his forehead, but to his credit, he doesn't fold. Instead, he releases his death grip on his lapels. "Yeah, I still want in."

Dance, puppet, dance.

"Good." Turning, I motion across the black lacquer desk at the two empty chairs. "Have a seat and update me on the status of the New York situation."

The New York situation has been a thorn in my side for months. After successfully turning Legado into a gold-plated laundromat, it only made sense to replicate a winning formula and spread it across enemy territory. Unfortunately, a bunch of sanctimonious pearl clutchers managed to get New York's gambling ordinance revoked five years ago.

But I don't accept defeat. I always find a way around it.

"I don't know how he did it," he says, shaking his head while lowering himself into the chair directly across from me. "But Senator Rick Sanders managed to get another 'State gaming commission proposal' passed through the General Assembly. After burying it deep within an eight-hundred-and-ninety-page Senate bill, all that's left is to get it approved by the State."

"Any chance they'll kill it?"

"Not likely. Sanders has solidified a damn-near unanimous vote."

Unsurprising. New York's flashiest senator is used to swaying the opposition in his favor. Twenty years ago, he ran New York's cocaine distribution for Dante Santiago. These days, he hides behind that American seal pinned to his lapel while his adopted son plays bitch boy to Santiago's newest protege.

Edier Grayson: the other side of this fucked up East Coast coin. A piece of currency he's going to wish he never stamped his face on.

A smirk tugs at the corners of my mouth. It seems Slick Rick has lost his edge. For all his street smarts, the Brooklyn asshole-turned-political prick didn't think twice in sliding a few hundred thousand Monroe's way in exchange for his expertise in crafting a new gaming bill.

And in screwing me over.

Well, surprise, fucker. That piece of shit's name has been on my payroll for two years.

"And he has no idea what's about to happen?" I ask, steepling my fingers.

Monroe's eyebrows shoot up to his hairline. "Senator Sanders? No, none. And as far as Sanders's son and Edier Grayson are concerned, this is a New York power play." Mimicking my gesture, he steeples his fingers under his chin. "Once the bill passes, they're free and clear to turn their bars and clubs into high-end casinos so they can—"

"Get a piece of Legado's action," I finish for him.

Of course. Why wouldn't they? With the current ban against any legalized gambling that doesn't involve a scratch off, New Jersey is siphoning money straight out of Santiago's deep pockets. Pissed off New Yorkers have no problem crossing state lines to blow their paychecks at the toss of the dice.

And Legado is more than happy to oblige.

Folding my hands, I tap the pad of my thumb against my bottom lip. "So we're firmly on the offense?"

"Acquisition of Bar None is a solid lock," he answers confidently. "I have a contact at the health department who owes me a favor. After Sanders was served a laundry list of code violations…" He smirks, flashing teeth straight out of an orthodontist's wet dream. "Well, let's just say, the 'good' senator isn't one to bother with renovations and upgrades."

Or with details.

"So he's set an asking price?"

He nods. "And he's highly motivated to sell. We should be able to add his club to our assets by the month's end. Your first behind enemy lines."

The first of many.

"*Our* assets?" I flash him a heated stare.

A nervous laugh escapes his crooked smile. "My apologies, Santi. It was a slip of the tongue. I meant *your* assets, of course."

"See that it doesn't happen again, Spader," I warn darkly. "Or the next 'slip' may be onto the floor."

Wincing, he pushes his falling glasses back up his nose. "There could be one slight hiccup."

"How *slight?*"

Pulling a handkerchief from the inside pocket of his cheap blue suit, he dabs his forehead. "Another buyer has thrown his hat in the ring, and he's offering twice what we are."

I don't like the hesitation in his voice. "Who?"

He winces again. "His son."

I slam my palm onto the desk. "*¡Hijo de su puta madre!*"

Sam Sanders is like the gift that keeps on giving. A goddamn poison repeatedly infecting my family. Two years ago, Valentin Carrera sent his only daughter to the United States, and I allowed her to fall into *his* hands.

One blink and the Santiago Cartel left their stain on one of my own.

My little sister.

A kid who mistook affection for annihilation.

Lola was my responsibility, and I failed her.

And here this *pinche cabrón* is again, sticking his dick where it doesn't belong.

This war between the Carreras and the Santiagos may have started a generation ago, but its legacy has been fed by the river of bad blood dividing New Jersey and New York. Between Carrera-ruled territory and Santiago-owned grounds. Between a new generation hell-bent on stoking the fires of a twenty-year feud. Between the son of Valentin Carrera and the spawn of Dante Santiago's inner circle.

The original debt has yet to be paid.

The sin against my sister has yet to be atoned.

And now with the Santiagos attempting to backdoor my backdoor, the East Coast just became a powder keg of anarchy.

"If Sanders wants to join the game, let him," I say, meeting Spader's surprised gaze with a hardened stare.

"What?"

"Have your New York contact double Sanders's offer." *Compliments of an offshore shell corporation.* "While he's there, have him drop by Sanders's father's office and give him this." Pressing my thumb against another access pad, I wait for it to click before opening my desk drawer and pulling out a brown office-sized envelope. Monroe doesn't say a word as I toss it across the desk. "That should deflate his balls for a while."

He reaches forward, then stalls. He doesn't want to look inside, but he will. The envelope is a forbidden apple, as tempting as it is poisonous.

It takes less than three seconds for him to give in. Dragging it off my desk and into his lap, he unpins the top, bows his head and peers inside, all the color draining from his ruddy cheeks. "Jesus, Carrera. Remind me never to get on your bad side."

"You're already on it, Spader. It's the only side I have."

"Santi?" Monroe and I both turn as Lola appears in the doorway.

I toss her a hardened glare, her casual tone grating on me like nails on a chalkboard.

She rolls her eyes. "I mean, *Mr. Carrera.*"

Still petulant, but a concession.

"I'm busy, Lola."

"I know, but—"

"That means no calls, and no interruptions," I say, in a clipped tone. "If I need something, I'll let you know."

The temperature in the room plummets as her fingers tighten around the doorframe. I smile to myself as I catch a flicker of the infamous Carrera temper dancing in those icy blue eyes.

"Understood, *sir.* However, I thought you'd like to know that I just got a call from surveillance. One of your guests has been caught on closed-caption counting cards."

"Then have security deal with it."

"It's your casino." She shrugs, slowly closing the door. "So, if you don't care about getting cheated out of fifty-thousand dollars..."

I'm rising from my chair before she can finish her sentence. Gripping the edge of the door, I swing it open, fire blazing through my veins. "Some bastard just gamed me out of fifty grand?"

"Oh, trust me." Lola laughs, trailing behind me as I push past her. "The only *bastard* around here is you."

Monroe and his sweaty forehead are forgotten as I exit the executive lobby with murder on my mind. I've already killed one man for stealing from me.

Spilling blood twice in the same day is only going to worsen my mood.

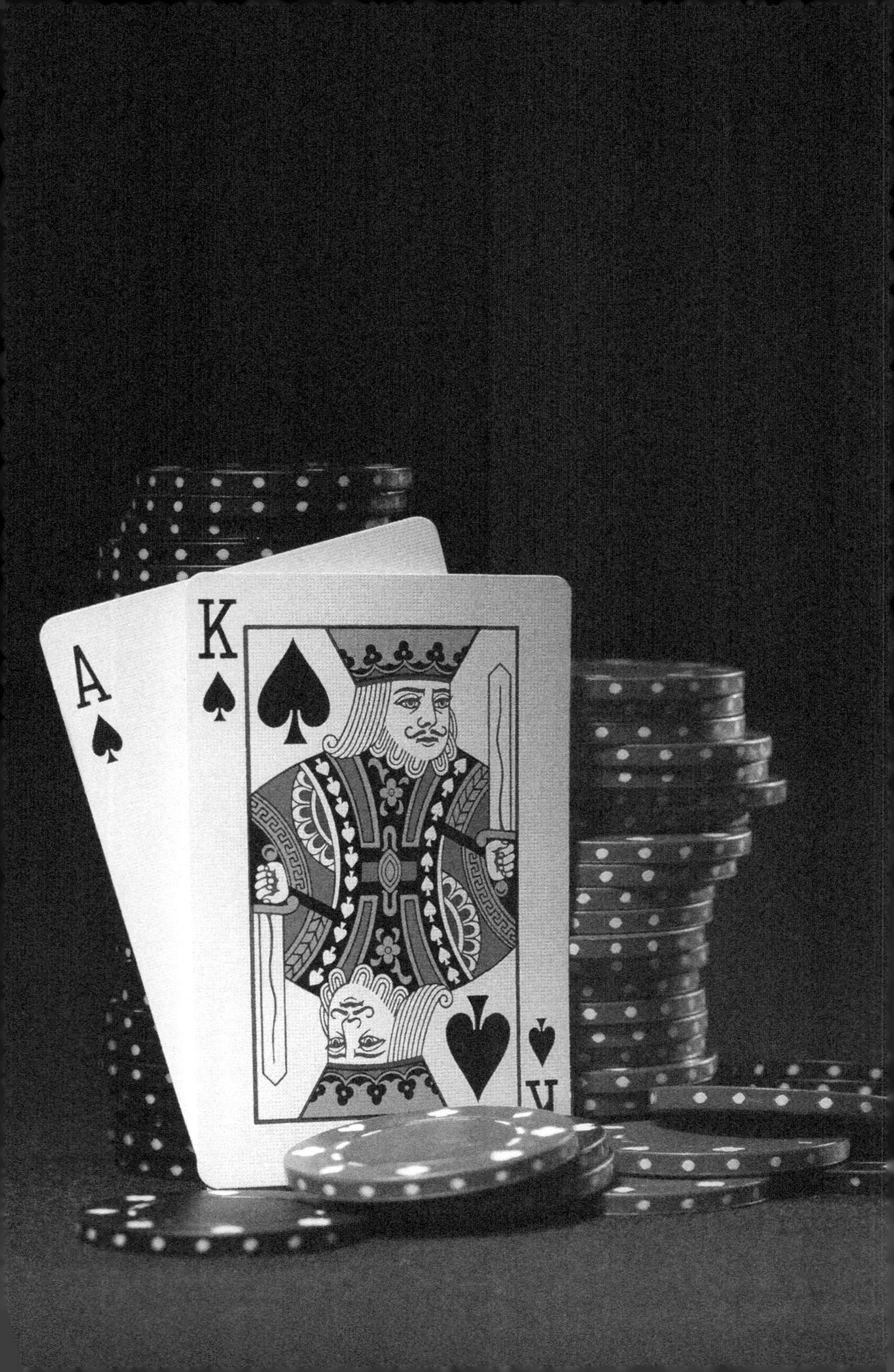

CHAPTER Seven

THALIA

There's a word for that moment when victory is snatched from you, when you're stretching for the finishing line and someone overtakes you with less than a foot to go.

Disbelief.

It fuses with another when there's fifty thousand dollars-worth of casino chips stashed in your purse, and the heavy hand of authority just smacked down on your left shoulder.

"You need to come with us, ma'am."

No, thank you.

His accent is scaring me more than his tone. It's all flat vowels and thick syrup...

Mexican.

"W-why?" Heart thudding, I rise from my seat to find a wall of those muscles-in-tuxes behind me. I glance at each of them in turn, but their blank expressions are like a second uniform. "Is something wrong?"

The hand on my shoulder tightens. A second later, my exit from the table is an embarrassment and a stumble as I'm yanked out onto the gaming floor and flanked, two-deep, while I'm forced to undertake the gambler's walk of shame.

So much for my gladiatorial contest. The emperor just condemned me, and now the lions are loose.

"Is this how you treat all your patrons?" I shove the hand away, recovering some of my bite, but it fizzles out again when we skirt the main entrance and head straight for the door marked *"private"*. "Look, if you're going to throw me out, just throw me out, okay?"

"Can't do that." A hand finds my shoulder again.

"This is bullshit! I won that money fair and square!"

But it's like talking to concrete. Golden-skinned concrete, with flat, black eyes that are unnervingly similar to those of the man I saw walking through the casino half an hour ago.

"We can't throw you out for counting cards," the tallest admits. "Too bad the state laws aren't the only laws in this place."

Too bad for me, you mean.

I'm man-handled into an elevator carriage that's wall-to-wall mirrors. I keep my eyes fixed to the floor as they pile in too, filling up the small space with their unspoken threats. I don't want to see my fear reflected back at me. *I don't want to see my failure.*

"At least let me have my purse."

"Can't do that."

If he says that to me one more time, I'm shredding his boot with my stiletto heel.

I then watch, incensed, as he opens it up, removes my phone and pockets it.

"You make any calls on that thing, you're paying the bill!"

"Whatever you say, *ma'am*."

The elevator carriage stops at the third floor. I'm led out and marched down a long, hallway toward a pair of double doors. There's a receptionist's desk to my left, but the chair is empty.

One of the tuxes raps his knuckles and a deep voice answers.

"Bring her in."

"Your funeral, *puta*," hisses one of the tuxes, opening up and giving me a hard shove inside. "Don't forget to smile for the camera when *Santa Muerte* blows you a kiss."

"Who the hell is—?"

My question is drowned out by their laughter, and then the doors slam shut behind me.

Silence.

"Welcome."

It's a black greeting, but all I see is crimson. It's all around me, boxing me in—a deep, punishing color that makes the walls look like they're bleeding out.

The whole effect is so distracting it takes me a minute to focus on the tall, dark man leaning against the front of his desk, with his fingers curled around the lip of the polished glass and his long legs stretched out and crossed at the ankles.

The Prince of Darkness himself.

At first glance, it's a pretty *laissez-faire* stance considering the reason why he's dragged me all the way up here. After all, he just caught me scamming fifty-grand out of—*what I assume*—is his casino.

The thing is, I've never relied much on first glances. Look harder, and you find the tiny details that paint the real truth—stuff like the unpleasant tilt of his lips, the rigidity in his broad shoulders, the still manner, and the faint bloodstains on the collar of his white dress shirt. He's not the first man I've met who's swapped lipstick for carnage.

I straighten my dress and stand as tall as my five-foot-six frame in five-inch heels will allow.

"Why am I here?"

It's a question we both know the answer to, but when there's a sticky moment, I tend to run my mouth off, and it's usually a sprint toward trouble.

"Why do *you* think you're here?" he says slowly.

His voice is like the darkest richest chocolate cake I've ever tasted, only to find it stuffed with Carolina Reaper chilis after the first chew. He has an accent too, and it's one I'm trying very hard not to place in case it lets the fear back in.

"Because you're impressed with my blackjack skills?"

He doesn't answer at first. Instead, he tilts his head to cover every inch of my body with those terrifying dark eyes.

If hate had a name, he owns the copyright. I've never seen so much antipathy in a man's expression.

In turn, I can feel my own force shield of hostility coming into play. Yes, I screwed up, but he doesn't have to do the whole Miami Vice interrogation thing on me. I'd rather take my chances with the cops.

"Correct me if I'm wrong, *sir*," I say, taking a couple of steps toward him. "But isn't it customary to sit *behind* your desk in an office environment, instead of against it?"

His lips don't even twitch. "It all depends on the type of business. Paperwork necessitates chairs. Reprimanding a thief requires something a little more *inventive*."

My stomach drops. I know a threat when I hear it.

"What's your name?"

"Mickey Mouse," I blurt out. "But only on the weekends. What's yours?"

"Don't play stupid games with me. How old are you?"

"Twenty-one."

He scoffs. "*Maldita mentirosa.* Show me some ID."

"I am *not* a fucking liar" *As far as he knows.* "And that might be tricky," I say, glaring at him. "Considering your security just walked off with my purse."

"Stealing is a contagious disease, *muñeca.*"

"But easily explainable if you're innocent in the first place," I lie, bristling at his contempt. *Doll?* I'm not his damn doll. I'm half Colombian, which means I'm fluent in Spanish and bullshit names from men who refuse to tell me theirs.

"We'll see about that." He pushes off from his desk and walks toward the door, blasting me as he passes with a scent-rush of spice, cedarwood, and sinister, and an overriding sense that there's a subtext here I'm still not grasping. "RJ," I hear him bellow into the hallway. "Get me her purse."

There's a flash of silver as it's handed over to him, and then the door slams shut again.

Seconds tick as he makes his way back to me, dangling my purse between his fingers like it's something repellent.

Firing his scornful gaze into mine, he upends the entire contents onto the floor. The sound of plastic clattering across the black marble tiles is the noise of my last hope crashing and burning.

"You bastard!"

"*¡Silencio!*"

Once done, he tosses the empty purse away, and circles back to stand behind me. I flinch as a couple of casino chips hit my toes and go rolling off into death spirals.

"Eyes to the front," he snaps when I try turning to face him.

"Are you some kind of weird—?"

"Don't test me, *muñeca*!"

"Fine," I mutter, doing as he says, but only because his close proximity is malfunctioning my defenses. My body braces as his cologne seeps into my skin. In my mind, he's already tilting his head again and glazing my back with more of his hate.

"I don't see any ID down there, Mickey," I hear him murmur. "I don't even see a credit card."

"I must have left them downstairs," I say stiffly. "Maybe your men took them when they took my phone."

"Admit it, *muñeca*. You haven't spoken a word of truth since you entered my office."

I can't bring myself to answer that when my sister's happiness is lying in ruins at my feet.

"I'm going to require compensation for the inconvenience you've given me and my men tonight."

"I don't have any money," I grit out, shivering with fear and loathing when I feel his hot breath lacing the nape of my neck.

He laughs—thick, throaty, and disbelieving.

More of that hot breath.

More fear and loathing.

"Do you see that picture behind my desk?"

Somehow, I drag my eyes from the mess on the ground to a gilt-framed, six by four, oil painting hanging on the wall, depicting a smiling skull of a woman with red feathers braided through her long, dark hair. She's terrible in her beauty. Haunting, intimidating... She's also half in profile—enveloped in a cloud of thick, gray smoke—and something tells me I never want her turning her empty gaze in my direction.

"What is she?" I whisper.

"*Who* is she," he corrects, moving in so close I can feel the outline of his snarl against my hair. "*Nuestra señora de la Santa Muerte.* Mexico's venerable Lady of the Dead."

If he hears my sharp intake of breath at this, he doesn't comment.

"*Santa Muerte* serves as protection from my enemies...*Thalia Santiago.*"

Shit.

Before I can run, a steel-like vise is wrapped around my wrist, and I'm being spun around to face him.

"You're Santi... Valentin Carrera's son," I gasp out in horror.

"And you're trespassing into *very* dangerous territory. Why the fuck are you here, *señorita*?"

"I-I didn't know this was your casino, I swear."

"You cross that state line, you may as well have Carrera stamped all over your fucking passport. Did your father send you to spy? To steal from me?"

"No!" I try to yank my wrist away, but his grip is too firm. "He doesn't even know I'm here!"

"*¡Maldita mentirosa!*" he curses again.

"I'm not a fucking liar! And neither am I a *muñeca*!"

"All dolls break if you apply the right kind of pressure. Did the poor little cartel princess decide to have her fun at my expense, or is this Edier Grayson's doing?"

Oh Jesus, he's terrifying. I'm never getting out of here alive.

"I needed the money!"

He drops my wrist as if it's burning him—as if he can't bear my touch for a single second longer. "You expect me to believe the daughter of one of the richest sinners in the world is coming up short on pocket change?"

"It's the truth!"

"In a thousand-dollar dress?" He studies my face for a beat, and then takes a step back. "Prove it."

"I don't think I—"

"Drop to your knees, Colombian *princesa*," he clarifies scornfully. "Go ahead, gather up your winnings if you need them so badly." He kicks a couple of loose chips in my direction with the toe of his dress shoe. "I've always wanted to see how low a Santiago can go."

He can't be serious?

That's when I know his hate for me will never match my hate for him.

"Well?" He slides his hands into his pockets and waits, daring me to expose myself as an even greater fraud than he thinks I am already.

It's just a power thing, I tell myself as I sink to the floor. *Think of Ella. Think of the bonfire I'm going to make with that footage.*

Still, it doesn't stop the tears of shame from burning my eyes as I gather up pieces of black and gold plastic at the feet of one of my father's greatest enemies.

"Why did you ask me for my name if you knew it already?" I mutter.

There's movement in my periphery as he squats down on his haunches, bringing his face level with mine. "Because big cats like to play with their mice before the kill…*Mickey*." There's a pause. "*Dios mío*, look at you," he mutters in disgust. "On your hands and knees like a whore. Why do you need it so badly, anyway? Daddy cut your allowance?"

"Like I said," I rasp out, my voice trembling. "He doesn't know."

I find myself staring down the barrel of his gun.

"Wait!"

"I'm not known for my patience, *señorita*," he says, slowly flexing his fingers around the grip. "If I were you, I'd start talking. Because on my side of the river, the punishment fits the crime, and I've already ruined one thief's day. Would you like me to make it two?"

Hell no. But I can't afford to back down now.

"You're not known for your compassion either, Santi Carrera," I grit out. "Why the hell would I bother telling you anything if you're just going to kill me anyway?"

"You have three seconds."

"Go ahead. Pull that trigger. Start the war to end all wars. See how far my father will go to avenge the death of his youngest daughter." Now it's my turn to shake my head in disgust. "I know all about you Carreras and your dirty tricks and deceit. You call me a *maldita mentirosa,* but tell me, have you taken a good look in the mirror lately?"

I'm rewarded for my words with cool steel pressed against my forehead. Whatever strings of patience this man had just snapped at my insults.

Me and my big mouth...

I close my eyes and wait for the bullet.

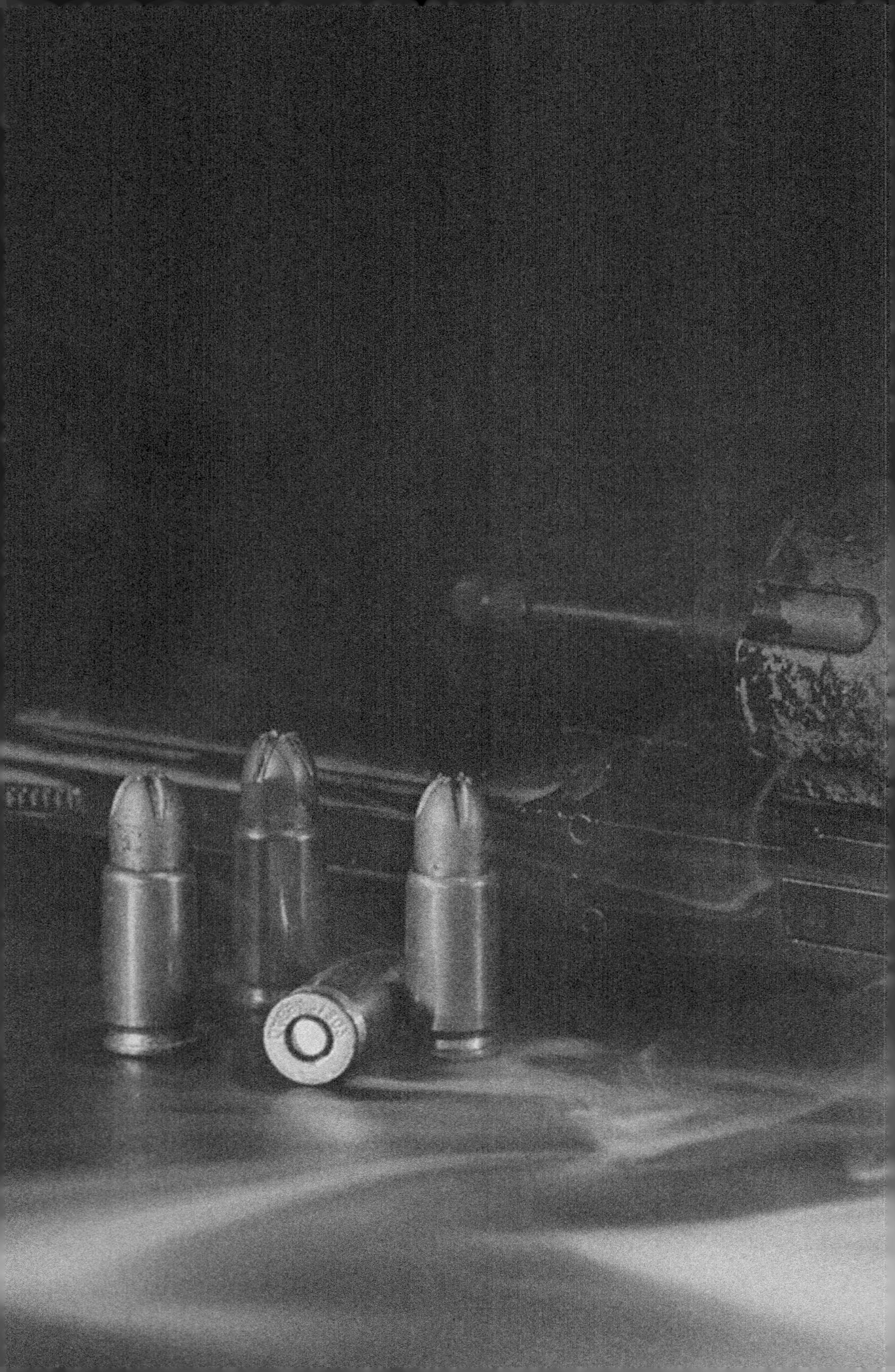

CHAPTER
Eight

SANTI

I t's her unapologetic insolence that shreds what little restraint I have left.

What the fuck happened to the pathetic *princesa* who was just crawling around on her hands and her knees in front of me, scraping up casino chips like they were her last meal ticket?

Now there's this…*fearlessness,* but that emotion sits too close to stupidity. Thalia Santiago seems to have confused the two. There's no other explanation for her to fling insults at me with a loaded Glock pressed against her forehead.

After I'd stopped pacing long enough to watch the video footage, I'd recognized her immediately. Cartel warfare isn't contained by border walls. It spills out like poison, turning foreign soil into a game of land chess. The difference between a good boss and a dead one is knowing all the players. And just like in regular chess, I know when to watch and when to attack. Once I saw that heart-shaped face and long dark hair—a vision that struck a hauntingly familiar chord inside me—playing strategically was no longer an option.

A Santiago is a threat—*whatever form it takes.*

"Either answer the question or pull the trigger." Her breathy voice fans across my face. "Indecisiveness is a poor quality in a leader, *Señor* Carrera."

A valiant effort, but I see right through her. It's like my father always said, *an enemy in a designer dress is still an enemy, and seduction wrapped in forced bravado is still fear.*

She's scared, but her pride has her walking a very thin line with no safety net. It shouldn't surprise me. After all, it's the first of the seven deadly sins—closely followed by greed—the one that landed her here in the first place. So why have I absorbed the razor-sharp barbs spilling from those luscious lips and not pulled the trigger?

I have no idea.

Thalia Santiago should have drawn her last breath already. Instead, my finger is curled around the trigger, the bullet still lodged inside the magazine.

"You're a brave little thief, *señorita*."

"I'm not a thief," she says, her nostrils flaring.

"Right. And I'm not a killer." I reach out to trail a finger down the long, graceful line of her neck. The move catches her off guard. She flinches, her body betraying her. Smiling to myself, I brush my thumb against the erratic beat of her pulse point. "Nobody likes labels, but reality doesn't give a fuck about your feelings. Besides, considering your bloodline, you should be used to hearing much worse."

Those midnight eyes shift to the side, avoiding my stare. Her mouth may spew venom, but her eyes speak the truth.

I was right. This girl is hiding something.

And this standoff just took an interesting detour.

"I'm not a thief," she repeats, her voice brittle with emotion. "I earned that money."

"By cheating me out of mine. Are we adding 'liar' to your list of offenses, as well?"

Thalia snaps that fiery gaze back to me, her small show of weakness now firmly tucked away behind that beautiful exterior.

An exterior I find much too intriguing.

I can't allow desire to distort reality. Not here. Not with *her*. Business is my lover, power my mistress. Women are simply an enjoyable pastime, not a necessity. Watching my father's humanity erode away after my mother's "accident" taught me to detach emotions from physical needs.

La Boda Roja. The Red Wedding.

The day my father held my mother in his arms as the light slowly drained from her eyes. Luckily, she survived—but miracles come at a cost. The woman who held his black heart awoke to find that a brain hemorrhage had stolen three years of her life—including memories of her husband and children.

Truth became inconsequential. In my father's eyes, Dante Santiago had cursed him with a fate far worse than my mother's death. He erased her love.

Twenty years have passed, and while the wounds have healed, scars never fade…

"Screw you, Carrera," she hisses, her outburst drawing my attention back to her. "Counting cards isn't illegal in New Jersey. Your men just said as much. You'd think as a casino owner, you'd be more familiar with local law. In fact, I could have *you* arrested."

"For what?" I ask, mildly amused.

"Harassment. Assault." She glances down at the strewn contents of her purse. "Robbery. Take your pick. All three would hold up in a court of law."

Her offended tone makes me laugh. Santiagos only care about laws when they're trying to circumvent them. Not that a Carrera has ever been accused of planting a bloodstained flag on moral high ground. However, I'm not the one standing here spouting judicial jargon like Lady *fucking* Liberty.

Hauling her to her feet, the sweet scent of jasmine disorients me as I trap her against the wall. Irritated by my body's response to it, I revel in her sharp inhale as my forearm settles deep within the plunging neckline of her dress. "The only law that matters here, *muñeca*, is mine."

"I told you, I'm not your doll!"

"And I told you…" The rest of my threat dies in my throat as the sound of gunfire erupts outside my office door. It's not just a shot or two, either.

My mind is already three steps ahead of my feet. Grabbing Thalia's wrist, I tug her away from the wall to go and investigate when a dead weight drags me back again.

I swear to God, this woman…

I glance down to find her crouched low, her heels digging into the floor. "Get the fuck up," I command through clenched teeth. "You're leaving scuff marks all over my Lux Touch marble."

"Where are you taking me?"

"On a date," I growl, weighing the consequences of putting a bullet between those pretty eyes right here. "Where do you think?" I wave my gun toward the closed door. "Out there to see what the fuck is going on."

"But those were gunshots."

And the wide-eyed innocent act continues.

Pressing the grip of the Glock to my forehead, I fight to rein in my temper as another round of gunfire lights up the lower level of my casino. "Yes, and those are, too." A flicker of emotion flares across her face at my sardonic tone. "If we wait another thirty seconds, they'll explode the back of our heads against that wall. Now, get up!"

Whether motivated by intimidation or by the thought of dying alongside a Carrera, Thalia climbs to her feet. Dragging her behind me, I storm across the lobby and barrel through the double glass doors. Glancing to my left, I make a snap decision.

There's no time for the elevator.

Thalia stumbles in my wake as I sprint down the hallway and into a small alcove. Opening a camouflaged square within the wall, I press my thumb against a hidden access pad. Within seconds, a sealed door opens, granting us entry to the fastest and most discreet access to the main casino floor—a private stairwell.

Taking a calculated risk, I release my hold on Thalia to shove my hand in my pocket and pull out my phone. With one press of a familiar button, I lift it to my ear. After the first ring, I glance over my shoulder to find Thalia still matching me step for step. On the second ring, RJ answers, the sound of war waging in the background.

"What the fuck?" I roar, my pulse matching the cadence of my steps.

"Invasion," he answers, his even-keeled tone out of place among the turmoil. "Ten—at least twelve men came out of nowhere and started firing. There were a few AR-15s but, Santi…"

"What?" I snap.

"Most are packing M27s." He says nothing else. We both know what he's implying. M27s are infantry automatic rifles—military grade. A fan favorite of the Marine Corps.

My grip tightens around my phone as the scent of jasmine floats over my shoulder. *And guess whose daddy is an ex-marine?*

"Casualties?" I ask, my voice tight. *I'll deal with her later.*

"Negative."

Gracias a Dios. Not that I'd mourn faceless people, but spilled civilian blood is bad for business. "Contact Rocco. Have him meet me at the west executive door." I don't wait for an answer. Disconnecting the call, I slide my phone back in my pocket.

Thalia remains silent, her high heels clicking a frantic tempo as we make our way down the third and final flight of stairs, through a second door, and straight into the jaws of anarchy.

Screams bounce off the chrome and crystal as well-dressed patrons scatter like prey. They're trapped in a chaotic web spun from the heart of the casino floor: an epicenter of destruction where at least a dozen pairs of black combat boots are crushing the expensive green felt of my gaming tables.

I assess the situation. With steel-plated eyes, I scan the black military fatigues of the ski masked intruders opening fire, the *rat-tat-tat* of their automatic rifles nearly drowning out the cries. Rage does nothing but dilute critical thinking and incite costly mistakes, so I lock it away and aim my gun.

"Don't shoot them!" Thalia screams, grabbing hold of my arm.

Un-*fucking*-believable.

"Would you prefer to be on the receiving end?" I say, pushing her away. "It would be my pleasure to arrange it." Taking aim again, I fire, not bothering to hide the smile that curves my lips as my bright green blackjack table stains a deep shade of red.

"Oh my God."

As my target falls to the floor, Thalia looks shocked. We catch each other's gazes and find we can't look away. For the first time since she stepped into my office, there's no façade, pretense, or bravado between us. We see each other for who and what we are—two products of a dark and twisted history.

"Boss…"

A rough voice on my left breaks the stand-off, and I turn to find Rocco Altieri, my best lieutenant and head of security appearing out of nowhere, fists clenched, and gun drawn. He looks like hell, which is exactly where he's headed.

Thalia is forgotten as I lunge and shove my gun under his chin. "How the hell did they get through security?"

"They didn't," he says, looking me dead in the eye. *No fear.* Having a gun pulled on him is simply part of the job. "I've been stationed at the front entrance all night. They didn't come through my detectors." He slides a hardened gaze over my shoulder. "*Someone* let them in through the back."

I've heard enough.

Retracting my gun, I spin around to take Thalia's arm. Looking dazed, she doesn't protest as I slingshot her into Rocco's chest. "Here. Take her back to my office. And don't let her out of your sight." He gives a curt nod, and I watch with clenched teeth as her delicate wrist is swallowed by his huge hand.

"No, wait!" As he drags her toward the stairwell, Thalia tosses a panicked look over her shoulder. "You can't just leave me with him!"

I don't offer her an answer as I turn my back and fight my way through the rush of patrons still pushing and trampling each other toward the exit.

First, I'll deal with the destruction and carnage she caused.

Then I'll return and create my own.

As more of my men flood the casino floor, the ambush settles to a dull roar. I fire a couple more shots, sending two more motherfuckers six feet under.

With the main floor less congested, I survey the damage.

My casino is a mess, but the only bodies littering the floor are swathed in black and cloaked in ski masks. It makes no sense. Why barge in guns blazing, only to miss every goddamn target?

It's almost as if this wasn't intended to be a mass murder as much as…

I stop cold.

A suicide mission.

The gun sits like concrete in my hand as I stalk forward, past a row of silent slot machines. As I turn the corner into one of the private poker rooms, every muscle in my body coils in hatred. Every drop of blood boils for revenge. And every instinct I had from the moment I laid eyes on that surveillance footage roars with vindication.

Because that's when I see it… A declaration of war—perfectly drawn graffiti on the back wall by a hailstorm of bullets, its tail curled up like an exclamation point.

The Santiago Scorpion.

Thalia.

Icy numbness overtakes me as I turn slowly, her name a rhythmic chant in my head.

Thalia. Thalia. Thalia.

My mind is a spinning funnel of revenge as I make my way back through the now quiet casino. It isn't until a hand grabs my shoulder that the funnel touches down, leveling everything in its path.

"Boss."

The deep, accented voice is familiar, but I'm too far gone to discern an ally from an enemy.

"Santi," he tries again, stepping in front of me.

The black haze clears, and I blink him back into focus.

RJ.

"Call a clean-up crew," I instruct, shoving him out of my way. "Get those dead Colombians out of my casino."

"Santi."

"And call Chief Rinaldi at the Atlantic City PD. If that *cabrón* knows what's good for him, he'll make sure there's no trace of a report."

"Santi!" he shouts.

"What?" I snap, finally turning back to face him.

"It's Lola…"

For the second time in less than ten minutes, I stop cold. Suddenly, it's no longer Thalia's name drumming a furious beat inside my head.

Lola.

I've been so consumed by the daughter and the attack, I pushed everything else to the side—including the whereabouts and safety of my own family.

After I'd recognized Thalia on the surveillance footage, I'd sent Lola to the lobby and Monroe back to the hole he crawled out of. I needed to be alone when she was brought to me. I couldn't protect and punish at the same time, but while I bore my fangs upstairs, the wolves had already sunk theirs into a main artery.

"Where is she?" I demand.

His answer is to walk back toward the destruction, knowing damn well I'll follow.

My own casino becomes a maze of lights and blind turns. All I can hear is the punishing thud of my heart slamming against my ribcage.

My movements are mechanical as we reach the lobby. Lola is on the floor, her back against the wall, her bare legs sprawled out in front of her like a rag doll. Her eyes are closed, and her sun-kissed skin is the color of chalk. The tight, black dress I've spent all day bitching about is ripped from her mid-thigh all the way up to her hip.

And coated in thick, sticky blood.

I drop to my knees. "*chaparrita…*"

Lola opens her eyes and forces a weak smile. "I'm fine."

I can't think straight. The black haze is back, and this time, it's suffocating me. "They'll pay," I swear, brushing a piece of drenched hair away from her face as I press a kiss to her forehead. "They'll all pay."

"Santi, it's just a nick."

"Flesh wound," RJ notes behind me. "Barely grazed the skin. A few stitches and she'll be as good as new."

Dragging my finger through the puddle of blood staining the floor, I rise to my feet and shove it in his face. "Do you see that? *That* is Carrera blood. *Family blood.* What does that mean to you, RJ?"

"Vengeance," he says solemnly.

"Take her to the car," I instruct as *El Muerte* awakens. "I'll be there in a minute."

"What?" Lola's eyes widen as I round the front desk and head back toward the main casino. "RJ! Put me down! Where's he going? Santi!"

I keep walking, forbidding myself to look back. If I do, I'll insist on taking her to the hospital myself—and I can't.

Not when I have a dark promise upstairs still waiting to be kept.

CHAPTER
Nine

SANTI

I kick my office door open to find Thalia pacing like a caged animal. The moment she sees me, she freezes, the breath whooshing from her chest. "Where have—?"

The remainder of her words are cut off. In four wide steps, I'm across the room with my hand around her throat. Those dark eyes flare in panic seconds before I'm pinning her against the wall. "*You*," I say with a growl.

She claws at my hand, her toes barely dusting the floor. "You're hurting me!"

Grabbing her chin with my other hand, I turn her head to the side and press my lips against her ear. "Bruises are a blessing, Thalia Santiago," I murmur, my tone deceptively calm. "They should be bullets for what you've done."

"I don't know what you're—"

"Don't lie to me!" I roar. "A dozen men just shot up my casino. My fucking sister got caught in the crossfire."

Thalia stills. "Is she…?"

"Dead? No, unfortunately, you failed."

"Me?" Startled, she blinks at me as if I've slapped her. "You can't think that I planned this?"

Not at nineteen…

I know how old she is, and it sure as hell isn't twenty-one like she claims. No, this turn of events has Edier Grayson written all over it.

"I think you were the decoy—a shiny distraction who opened the gates and diverted my attention. Someone should have warned you, *muñeca*. I always win in the end."

"You're wrong!"

Tightening my grip, I push her harder into the wall, the space between us all but evaporating. "Those scorpions now decorating my walls contradict you. If Grayson wanted you to walk out of here alive, he should have calmed the theatrics."

I'm pretending not to notice the softness of her breasts pressed up against my chest. But my body notices. In fact, that traitorous fuck is having a hard time focusing on anything else.

Damn this woman.

"Theatrics aren't Edier's style."

"Maybe not. But they're definitely your father's."

That strikes a nerve—a raw one.

Stiffening, Thalia glances away. *Interesting.* There seems to be dissension on Santiago Island. A loose thread just begging to be pulled... One that could unravel an entire dynasty.

The corners of my mouth twitch as a plan takes shape in my head. One where I don't end Thalia Santiago right here for the sins she has committed tonight, but one where I use her to my advantage.

One where I avenge an attack with one of my own.

An eye for an eye.

"Take her upstairs to my penthouse and lock her in the east wing," I instruct the man who has been silently watching our confrontation with interest.

Thalia glances over my shoulder as Rocco rises from one of the two chairs in front of my desk. As his heavy footsteps draw closer, she tries, and fails, to push me away.

"What? No! I'm not going anywhere with him!"

"Oh, *muñeca*," I chuckle, releasing my hold on her throat. "You don't have a choice." Giving her a wink, I nod at Rocco. "Go."

"This is kidnapping!" she screams as the behemoth of a man picks her up and tosses her over his shoulder like she weighs nothing at all. I watch in amusement as she drives her fist into his back, but it's like beating a brick wall with a pillow.

"Didn't your father teach you that actions have consequences?" I call out, laughing at my own question. "Then again, I guess a man like that wouldn't."

As Rocco crosses the threshold between my office and the lobby, Thalia lurches forward and grabs the door frame with both hands. "I swear, I didn't do this. I just came here to win enough money for…" She curses as her fingers are pried off one by one. "I came to win money, not to hurt anyone."

If she were anyone else, I might believe her.

But she's not. So, I don't.

"I don't care," I say, my smirk fading as Rocco readjusts his hold and carries her through the executive office lobby. "You drew Carrera blood, *muñeca*. So, you'd better hope to God or the devil or whoever your family prays to, that my sister lives. Because if she doesn't? You don't either."

I revel in the shock playing out across her face as Rocco carries her through the lobby and disappears through the glass doors.

Will I follow through?

Maybe.

But I'd sooner destroy the priceless *Santa Muerte* painting above my head than a work of art like Thalia Santiago. However, wants and needs come second to honor and oath. Sometimes beauty has to be destroyed to feed a greater good.

And a life-long vendetta.

Running a hand through my disheveled hair, the events of tonight land on my shoulders like a cinder block. The tension between New York and New Jersey has finally come to a head. The new blood in the Santiago Cartel has fired first. A retaliation is warranted and expected—and the one I'll deliver will be a bouncing red ball that distracts Edier Grayson from the waiting bomb.

I'm my father's son. I don't play by rules, and I don't follow expectations. I'll make my move, but it will be one they aren't expecting. Besides, the only advantage a man has over his enemies is the element of surprise.

With another revered glance at my prized *Santa Muerte* painting, I button my suit jacket and make my way into the executive lobby. I only make it a few steps before I find RJ standing at the entrance, a pinched look on his face.

My heart stops. "Lola?"

"Is fine," he answers calmly. "She's on the way to the hospital along with three of our best *sicarios*. I'll have Rocco meet them there to supervise."

A hundred wouldn't be enough. "I told *you* to take her."

"I couldn't drive her *and* handle retaliation, Santi."

"Family comes first."

"Even Lola insisted I stay," he says, his dark eyes flashing with restrained fury. "An attack like this can't go unanswered."

He's right. I dislike being disobeyed, but I dislike being caught off guard even more. I need RJ on offense rather than defense.

"You know what to do," I say, moving to push past him. *If Grayson wants to soil my baby with bullets, I'll set fire to one of his.*

"Santi…"

"Move." As volatile as I feel, it's the only word I can muster and remain in control.

Instead of following a direct order, RJ stands his ground, his body rigid, rage swimming in his dark eyes. "We need to talk."

"It can wait." I go to push past him, when he takes two steps back to block my path. "RJ, you'd better have a damn good reason for doing that. This is not the time to test boundaries."

He doesn't flinch at my threat. "During the attack, we secured the grounds. Our men didn't come back empty handed."

There's no need to elaborate. I can smell his thirst for blood, and it drives my own.

"Alive?"

It's the only word I speak. The only question I want answered. When he nods, we both exit the lobby and walk silently toward the elevators.

Four floors below ground level, the carriage doors slide open, and my pulse jumps.

Someone was left behind…. And now, that someone will pay.

RJ is first through the steel door, holding it open for me as I step through to find a calming sense of *déjà vu*. A metal chair sits on top of the tarp in the middle of the room, and in that chair sits a man. One in a bad suit, a broken nose, and two swollen eyes. Pleas to Catholic deities fall from his split lips.

Words are his only weapon since kneeling and lifting his hands in prayer are out of the question. Both are a little tied up at the moment.

"Name's Marco Bardi," RJ divulges, nodding toward the sniveling piece of shit. "Security caught him outside with this…" Reaching into his pocket, he produces a cell phone. "Same number dialed twelve times in twenty minutes. Two guesses who he was calling."

I don't have to *guess*. It's written in drywall like a chicken shit calling card. Too bad he didn't have the common sense to realize when a plan had taken a major detour.

In the wrong direction.

Taking the phone, I scroll through it, recognizing the number my men pulled from Thalia's phone. "Any texts or voicemails?"

He shakes his head. "No. At least the asshole was smart enough to delete those. But I put a call out to Gianni Marchesi and discovered Bardi and Thalia's sister had a one-night thing last year."

Gianni Marchesi. Boss of New Jersey's extension of the East Coast Italian mafia and firmly planted on the Carrera side of the cartel war.

"Which one?"

"Ella. Two years older. They live together."

Well, this just got messy.

Did she realize what a piece of shit he was and raise her standards, or did he simply grow tired and make a lateral move to the more gullible sister?

Either way, their taste leaves a lot to be desired. He's not only out of the Santiago sisters' league…he's a couple miles past the ballpark selling handjobs for a dimebag.

Concrete proof would have expedited the hell out of this, but, then again, I didn't get to where I am today by waiting for opportunity to fall in my lap.

"Has he broken?"

"Not yet." RJ glares in disgust as Bardi hiccups through another snivel. "Our *sicarios* didn't hold back, but the *pendejo* still refuses to talk."

Oh, he'll talk.

"Bardi," I call out, leisurely making my way toward him. "It seems you've found yourself in quite the predicament."

"I don't know anything, Carrera."

"Well, that puts you at a disadvantage, doesn't it?"

His head flops around like a fish. "What's that supposed to mean?"

"Well, if you don't know anything, then I have no use for you," I say, my arrogance taking center stage as I hold up his phone. "Because these phone calls to Thalia Santiago are all I need to condemn you. Right here. Right now."

"Maybe I'm screwing her too."

And maybe you don't need a tongue. "Don't insult my intelligence," I warn, my hand clenching around the back of his chair. "This is a business deal gone wrong. See, Bardi, I think you were outside my casino because you were waiting for Thalia Santiago to return." Leaning down, I offer a cold smile. "With her stolen earnings, of course."

It's an educated guess. I have no idea if they were working together to split the money or if there were a few more moving parts. What I do know is that Marco Bardi is a simple-minded criminal. One lacking finesse and style.

He'll crumble like a stale donut if given the *wrong* incentive.

"Fuck you, Carrera!"

Strong insult. Weak delivery.

They're the words of a cornered man. He has no rebuttal, so I sharpen my knives and go for the kill. "She's in my penthouse, right now. Whatever you offered must not have satisfied her needs, Marco," I lie. "Because when I bartered protection for truth, she threw you under the bus faster than you can say 'traitor.'"

"Bullshit."

"Think so? Then tell me why, just half an hour ago, she fell to her knees begging for her life while selling you out? She told me everything you're doing to her."

More lies. I have no fucking clue what he's doing to her. This is a power play with a fifty/fifty odds payout.

"You're lying."

"Maybe," I say, tucking his phone into my inside suit jacket pocket. "Maybe not. Are you willing to take that risk?" Pushing off his chair, I hold up a finger. "Before you answer, let me give you a tip—there's already a deal on the table. There can be two, and you can prove your worth to me, or you can keep protecting the woman who sold you out and watch as RJ here carves your heart out of your chest." I motion behind me where RJ spins a vintage dagger in his palm.

My fist aches to drive into his face, but I fight the urge, leaving the threat to detonate by itself.

I don't have to wait long.

Bardi's frantic gaze bounces between RJ and me. "It wasn't me!" he sputters, spittle forming at the corners of his mouth. "It was that bitch's idea to come here and steal from you."

"That's not what she said." Sighing, I glance over my shoulder. "This is going nowhere. You know what to do."

RJ advances with a nod, the dagger in one hand, a pistol in the other.

That's all it takes for Marco Bardi to tattle like a little bitch. His body jerks, causing the chair to skid a couple of inches. "No! No!" He swallows hard, sweat staining the front of his shirt. "So you know about the video..."

No, but I do now.

"What do *you* think?"

His face blanches. "Fine, so I may have used the skin flick of *sweet little Ella* as incentive for extra cash. It's half a million, for Christ's sake. She's a fucking Santiago. It's not like they can't afford it."

I control a knee-jerk reaction to put a bullet between his eyes. *Jesus Christ.* This son of a bitch was blackmailing Thalia with a sex tape of her sister? Is that why she was so desperate for money?

"Incentive..." I say, walking around him like a tiger assessing his prey. "Is that what we're calling extortion these days?"

Bardi's bound hands tug on their restraints. "Why do you care?"

I don't give him an answer because, frankly, I don't fucking have one. "Was shooting up my casino part of your *incentive*, Marco?"

"I told you...I had nothing to do with that. I'm opportunistic, not suicidal."

Condemned men will say anything to save their own asses. Marco Bardi is a waste of space who exploits women at their weakest—a wanna-be gangster with the intelligence of a dishrag and the balls of a toddler.

However, he didn't mastermind the attack on my casino tonight. This dumb fuck was just in the wrong place at the wrong time.

So, what to do...

I could kill him just for being an idiot. That'd be the easiest and most satisfying end to the night. But it's obvious how easily he's manipulated.

Moldable.

Usable.

Thalia stole from me and refused to tell me why. Now that I know, it's information easily leveraged to my advantage.

RJ steps forward, the knife tucked tightly in his fist. "Can I slit his throat now? This *pinche cabrón* is giving me a headache."

I hold up a hand. "Where's the tape, Bardi?"

"Why?"

"Because unlike you, I have plans for it that don't involve jerking off into a Kleenex."

Bardi's swollen face puckers. "If I give it to you, what's in it for me?"

"You live to see tomorrow," I say, bracing both hands on the arms of his chair. "And maybe even a few after that..."

A defeated glaze coats his bloodshot eyes. "It's in a safety deposit box in Queens." At my raised eyebrow, he sighs, adding, "The bank account is under Donatella Bardi—my grandmother."

He sold out his own grandmother?

I hated this motherfucker before, but now I not only want to cut off his fingers, but the traitorous lips of a treacherous grandson.

Family disloyalty is the deadliest sin in the eyes of a Carrera.

"Does *Nonna* Donatella know her piece of shit grandson has involved her in a goddamn cartel war?"

"No," he admits, shaking his head weakly. "She didn't ask questions."

"Of course she didn't." I grit my teeth. Why would she? She's just another innocent life tainted by his greed. "Take a trip to Queens," I instruct RJ, my eyes still locked on Bardi. "Escort Donatella Bardi to the bank to retrieve our stolen property."

"It's not stolen—"

"Shut up!" I growl, forcing myself not to ram my fist into his face. Fucking him up won't do me any favors with Thalia. "Don't scare the woman. Tell her whatever lie she needs to hear in order to comply. Return with the tape, not blood. *¿Comprendes?*"

Bardi's eyes shift between us. "I've given you everything you've asked for, Carrera. Now let me go."

He's right. Which proves he's telling the truth about one thing—he's not working with the Santiagos. Any cartel associate knows the only thing ever standing between life and death is information.

It's time to turn up the heat and watch this piece of shit burn.

I glance over my shoulder where RJ still fists both weapons. "Go for the carotid and make it messy…"

"No, wait!" Bardi's tied limbs thrash in the chair. "That's not everything! If you kill me, you'll never know what he has planned!"

"He?"

"Edier Grayson," he says hesitantly. "That's who shot up your casino, right? There's more coming your way than just a few stray bullets hitting the wall, Carrera. And this shot will be heard round the world."

I stiffen, grabbing him by the throat. "I thought you were here just for a handout, Bardi. What the fuck do you know? And don't lie to me this time."

Bardi's Adam's apple bobs against my palm. "If I tell you, you won't turn me over to Grayson?"

"Now why would I do that when you can be much more useful with your hands still attached." My slow smile punctuates the thinly-veiled threat as I release my grip.

If Thalia's extended family found out Bardi not only filmed Ella in a compromising position, but then proceeded to blackmail her with it, his death would become Colombian folklore. Nothing I could do to him would be half as sadistic. Revenge takes a much sharper blade when family is involved.

"No, Bardi. I won't turn you over to Grayson."

I prefer to end problems myself.

"Then I'll tell you," he says, flipping his newfound bargaining tool in the air like a fifty-thousand-dollar poker chip. "*After* I walk out of here and collect my money."

"You're a greedy little fuck, you know that?" Irritated, I stroke my chin, the thickening stubble raking across the pads of my finger and thumb. He could be lying, but instinct tells me otherwise.

He's balls deep in Santiago shit. Until I have that tape in hand, I'll need to keep him alive so his tongue can spill its secrets.

And then I'll cut it out.

"You have a temporary reprieve, Bardi," I tell him. "I have more pressing business to attend to at the moment. However, when I return, you and I are going to have another chat." I give his bruised cheek a firm tap. "And you're going to tell me everything you know, or not only is the deal off, but I'll also toss you into the river missing a few limbs. Are we clear?"

He nods so hard I'm surprised his neck doesn't snap. "Y-yes. Whatever you say, Carrera."

Pushing away from the chair, I give him a slow, brittle smile, which he devours like it's his last meal. I'm not fooled by his fervor. A man dying of thirst will drink his own piss if he's desperate enough.

I didn't lie to him. I just didn't tell the whole truth.

CHAPTER
Ten

SANTI

"Where is she?" I say, storming down the hallway of AtlantiCare Medical Hospital with the devil coursing through my veins.

Startled nurses back away as I charge forward, my hand on my gun. I'm intercepted by a looming shadow and a hand on my shoulder.

"That way." Rocco tips his bald head toward a room tucked away in a corner at the far end of the hallway.

I don't wait for an escort. Knocking his hand away, I close the distance in five long strides and barrel through the door. "Lola, are you—?"

"Nice of you to join us," my sister chirps, flashing me a condescending smile.

Exhaling a relieved breath, I glance over my shoulder at Rocco. "What did the doctor say?"

"Hey!" I turn back to find Lola snapping her fingers at me. "Why are you asking him?"

"He's the one who brought you here,"

"And I'm the one who took the bullet, remember?" she says, throwing back her blanket.

Rocco was right. Her injury is barely a flesh wound. Only seven small stitches mar her skin. It's a sight that should calm me…

But it doesn't.

I'm too wound up over Marco Bardi and my Colombian houseguest.

Exhausted, I scrub my hand across my face, and then a scuffling movement draws my attention toward the bed. "What the hell are you doing?" I say, as she swings both legs off the side of the bed.

"What does it look like I'm doing?" She gives me her best deadpan stare. "I'm leaving."

"Like hell you are!"

"Santi, I've been discharged," she says with a groan." Clean bill of health, and prescriptions already filled." She motions to the side table where two pill bottles sit next to a water pitcher. "We could've left an hour ago, but *somebody* kept blocking the door." She wrinkles her nose at Rocco, who answers with a hand gesture.

"You're not going anywhere."

"But Santi—"

"Don't push me on this, Lola. I'm not in the fucking mood."

Having her discharged poses a major problem. She's living with me at Legado where I have Thalia on lockdown. I need time to figure out what the hell I'm going to do with her before adding yet another irate female into the mix.

One call to the Chief of Medicine. That's all it will take. Every key player in this town owes me a favor, and he's no exception.

Giving her a quick kiss on the forehead, I turn to Rocco. "Don't let her out of your sight until RJ gets here."

"Got it, boss."

"You can't do this!" Lola says angrily as I step into the hall.

I pause in the doorway. "I can do anything I want, *chaparrita*," I tell her calmly. "I own this motherfucking city."

"You can't keep people locked away against their will, Santi!"

"Watch me." Giving her a deliberate smile, I close the door behind me.

Traffic is nearly at a standstill on the Atlantic City-Expressway Connector, but I'm weaving in and out of both lanes like I'm threading a needle, Lola's protests ringing in my ear.

"You can't keep people locked away against their will, Santi!"

That's where she's wrong.

I can, and I have. *More than one, in fact.*

I hit the gas harder as my mind drifts to the Colombian princess locked away in my penthouse on the top floor of Legado.

Which is precisely the moment my phone rings.

I don't have to look at it to know who it is. I've been expecting this call. Any man remotely connected to him couldn't take a shit in Siberia without word crossing the border. Hell, he probably knew what was happening by the time the first bullet hit the wall.

Exhaling a hard breath, I hit the answer button. "Good news travels fast."

"How were Santiago's men able to infiltrate Legado?" a thick accent growls over a staticky connection.

My father is asking *me*? He's Valentin Carrera, Mexican kingpin and a god amongst thieves. If anything, I assumed I'd get my ass handed to me for allowing his sworn enemy's daughter to walk through the door of my...

He doesn't know about Thalia.

Interesting...

I should tell him what she did, where she is, and my plans for her. I've never lied to my father. The Carreras operate better as a machine, not loose parts. But the anger in his voice drives a sharp knife straight into everything I hold sacred.

"What are you going to do?" he bellows, breaking my internal tug-of-war. The one between upholding my oath and fulfilling a need.

"What do you think I'm going to do?"

There's only one way to cut off the head of a snake and that's to become the snake. I'm going to leverage my two assets and infiltrate from the inside.

But I don't say any of that. Instead, I clench my jaw as a dangerous chuckle rumbles in my ear.

"This is the second time your sister has been hurt under your watch, Santi. *Si esta vez no te vengas en nombre de tu hermana, estarás acabado.*"

"What the hell do you mean, if I 'don't get revenge, I'm finished'?"

"Exactly what I said, son," he says, matter-of-factly—as if he didn't just drop a bomb on me from twenty-five hundred miles away. "Carreras protect their own. It's the first lesson I taught you, remember?"

Do I remember?

He never lets me forget. It's my first memory as a child. Most kids got bedtime stories like *Goodnight Moon.* I sat in my father's lap listening to tales of revenge, blood, devils, and destiny.

"I remember," I answer coolly.

"Then if I can't trust you to uphold our family's most basic rule, how am I supposed to trust you to run an entire cartel?"

And there's the dangled carrot. The promise of an empire outside of American borders. One that spans the globe, built off the backs of three generations of Carrera men.

"The Santiagos will suffer for what they've done," I swear through clenched teeth. It's a vow I'll honor with my dying breath, which if what Bardi claims is true, may come sooner than later.

"See that they do. Because, Santi, if they don't...? I'll have to assume I made a grave error in judgment." He offers no other words and no goodbye before there's a subtle click and the line goes dead.

My grip tightens on the steering wheel.

He means New Jersey—a grave error in handing me control of the East Coast.

My father may be head of this cartel, but I'm not some wide-eyed teenager who worships the ground he walks on anymore. I respect him, but I'm a man now, and New Jersey is mine. The only way I'll be returning to Mexico is in a body bag.

No one is going to take what I've spent the last two years building.

Even Valentin Carrera

An eye for an eye.

To prove myself, I'll take more than a life to make the Santiagos pay. I'll find another way to rip at the heart of their seams. Something more personal. Something that will brand the Carrera name into *their* legacy for generations to come.

"Carrera." As my own name rolls off my tongue, my pulse roars with the shape of a new plan. A plan so dangerous, it will either make me a god or destroy everything.

Pulling into my private parking spot behind Legado, I kill the ignition and stare up at the brightly lit penthouse—the one licking the sky four hundred and thirty-one feet in the air. Thalia needs money. I want revenge. The debt she owes is so personal, she'll do almost anything for it...

I smile to myself.

Even commit the ultimate sin.

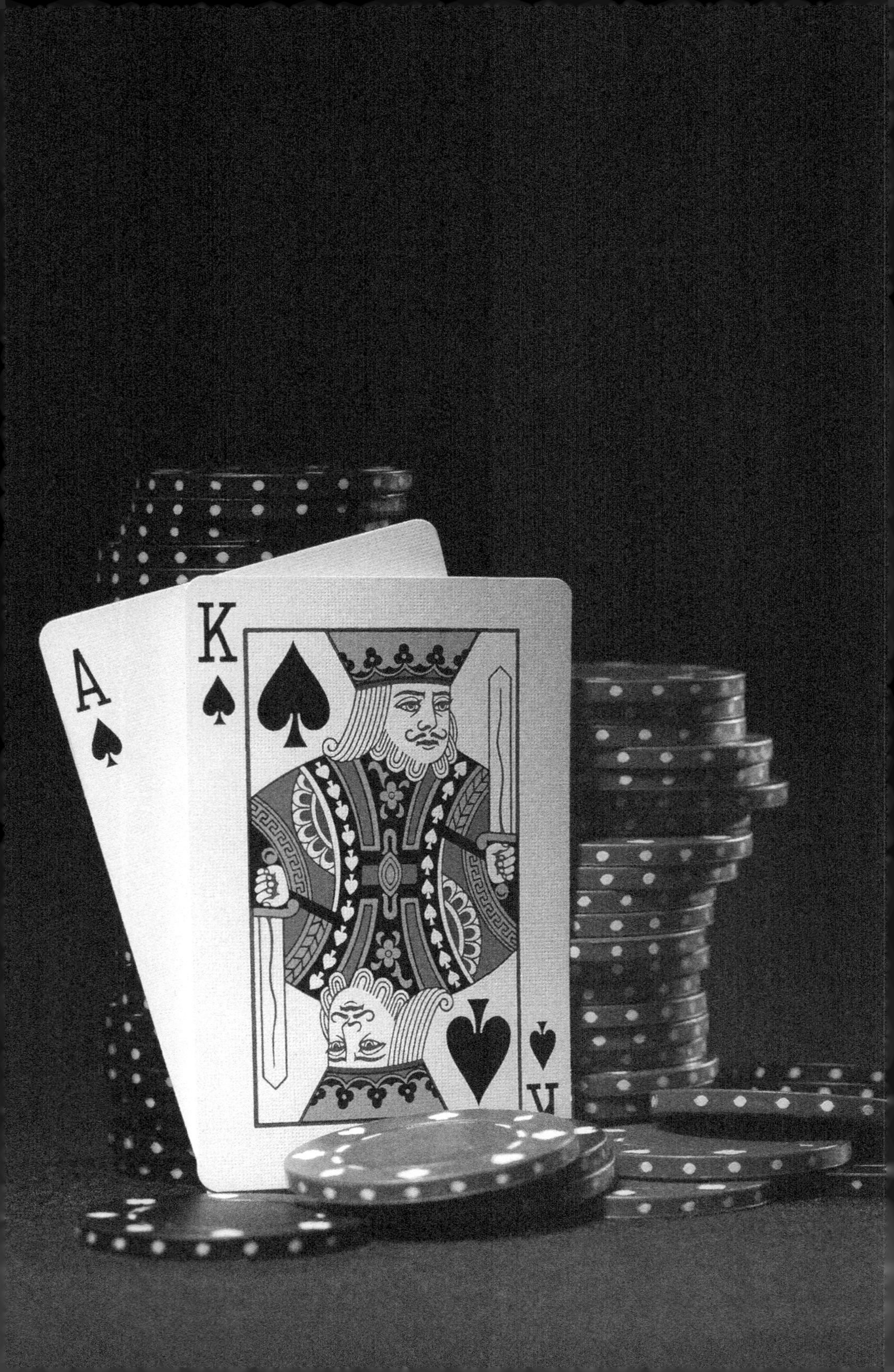

CHAPTER
Eleven

THALIA

History repeats itself, and then you die—preferably not in some cartel boss's penthouse apartment in the middle of Atlantic City. The End.

I tuck my knees to my chest and pull the black comforter tighter around my shoulders. Everything in this room is that color—from the expensive side table and nightstands, to the chaise lounge in front of the huge, floor-to-ceiling windows, to the high thread count Egyptian cotton sheets I'm lying on. The violent beast who locked me in here was born without an imagination it seems—along with decency, acceptable social skills, and a pleasant attitude to be around.

My fingers drift to the marks on my neck where he held me up against the wall of his office. No one has ever laid their hands on me like that before. No one has dared… And then to accuse me of having his precious casino targeted? *Of hurting his sister in the crossfire?*

From the Prince of Darkness to the King of *Loco*. He's a dual nationality of crazy.

The more I think about it, the more nothing about tonight makes sense. It's not Edier's style to shoot up a casino like that. As for me, I tolerate violence because it runs through my veins. It scorches the edges of my life like a match to paper, but I never seek it out, except when they deserve it.

Like Santi Carrera, for holding me against my will like this.

Like Marco Bardi, for terrorizing my sister

My heart jolts unpleasantly when I think about the sleazy Italian. Is he still waiting for me outside the casino? Did he get hurt in the chaos? The way this night is unraveling, I wouldn't be that lucky…

I toss and turn a couple more times. I can't get comfy in any position. There's so much uncertainty, it's like trying to rest on a bed of nails. *There's so much history in danger of repeating itself.*

Perhaps it's a form of destiny. You can fight it all you want, but it still happens anyway, leaving you with even more scars to contend with. Not so long ago, my father stole my mother and locked her up in a bedroom like this. She doesn't know I know, of course. Her housekeeper, Sofia, told me after she'd drunk too much *Aguardiente* last Christmas. It sort of slipped out, like the worst kind of punchline: "Oh, by the way, your father is this brutal man who chops up people for fun, but don't worry he only held your mother against her will and made her marry him, too."

What does that make me? The forced spawn of the devil? Did she even want me and Ella in the first place, or did he take away that decision from her as well?

Rolling onto my back, I stare up at the ceiling, blinking back hot, angry tears. I always do this to myself. I'm a world champion self-masochist. I'm thinking horrible things to punish myself for letting Ella down so badly.

I won her future, and then I blew it.

I counted cards, but I never counted on *him* ruining my plan.

Santi Carrera.

I shiver at the memory of those first moments together in his office. Who knew hate could spark electricity between people? Who knew dead eyes could glint with flecks of gold, like hidden secrets in a pool of darkness?

Outside, the first colors of dawn are painting carnage onto the horizon, and worse is to come. Reece won't have kept quiet about my latest escapade. My father is most likely plotting World War Three with Edier already, and Ella…? I scrunch my eyes up as tightly as I can.

I'm so sorry, Ella.

There's the sound of footsteps in the hallway outside. The lock on my door clicks open and the soft reds and pinks illuminating the far wall are snuffed out by a tall dark shadow.

A shadow who smells far better than he ought to.

"Get up."

His voice isn't chocolate and chili cake anymore. It's Mississippi Mud Pie with a twist of arsenic.

Throwing off the black comforter, I scramble to my feet as the shadow reveals the man who is currently sharing the top spot on my Worst Man Alive List.

"Sleep well?"

"Like a baby," I lie, tugging my dress down, but I lose the attitude as soon as I spot more bloodstains on his white dress shirt.

There's a pause. "How's your sister?"

He freezes in the doorway, my concern catching him off guard.

He recovers quickly.

"The fact that you're still alive and breathing should give you an indication." He kicks the door shut behind him, and there's something in that casual, I fucking-loathe-you movement that jolts a pulse between my legs.

"Listen, I know you don't believe a word I say, but I swear I hadn't nothing to do with this. Sam—"

"¡*Silencio*!" At the mention of Sam's name, his handsome face twists into something savage. "I swear to *you*, *muñeca*, if you mention him again in my presence, I'll be sending you back to your father in pieces."

He takes a step toward me, and I shift one back so fast I hit the side of the mattress. I've never met a man with so much rage and intensity spilling out of him. He's like a volcano in permanent eruption.

"Here."

I flinch as he tosses something onto the bed next to me. There's a soft flutter against my leg, and then another sea of dirty green is messing up another counterpane.

"You're giving me money?" I say stupidly.

"Fifty thousand in one-hundred-dollar bills. That's what you 'won', right?"

I don't like the implied quotation marks around the word "won." I like the Machiavellian look on his face even less.

"What's the catch?"

"First, tell me why you need it."

I glance away, aiming for anywhere other than him or at the money, which pretty much just leaves the floor. "Is it a deal breaker, if I *don't* tell you?"

"I'll get it out of you eventually, but a swift confession is preferred."

Arrogant bastard. "Has anyone added you to the donor list for a personality transplant yet?" I say bitterly. "If not, I'd be more than happy to oblige."

His resulting smile resembles that of a cold, dead fish. "I'm not the one who dropped to the floor over a couple of casino chips... Sell your soul often?"

"At least I still have one to sell."

His next step toward me is a threat in an expensive suit with blood stains.

"You have an unfortunate mouth on you, Thalia Santiago. One of these days it will carve your name into the side of a bullet."

"Really, *señor*?" I say, losing my temper again. "All threats and no decorum make the Mexican cartel boss an even bigger piece of shit."

He stills a couple of feet away from me—as still as a statue and as brittle as a pyre.

"Come on then, explain my *investment* in this deal," I say, nodding at the money. *Investment. Solution. Same thing, different colors.* "I'm sure nothing comes for free around here. What glorious indignity will I have to suffer for it this time? Pick the bills up with my bare teeth? Strip naked on top of them with rainbows shooting out of my ass?"

There's the briefest tug at his mouth and then it's gone again. The rarest of things. *Now, I'm intrigued...* Is there another man dancing beneath his surfaces? One who doesn't act like a character from the *Godfather* Hall of Fame?

"Before you ask, I'm not giving up information about my family," I warn, pouncing on the obvious trade-off before he has a chance to speak it.

"Who says you'd have to do anything that dramatic?" He saunters closer, but this time I stand my ground. He's at least a foot taller than me without my heels on. Most of that is hate. "You need the money, and I need revenge, *señorita*. Some might say that's a match made in hell."

"I don't need it that badly," I lie, feeling a rush of impending doom.

"Oh yes, you do. You can't count your cards out of this one, *muñeca*. I can smell desperation a mile off. In my office, you fucking reeked of it."

"I have a question for you," I say shakily. "Do you hate me more for my name, or for what you 'think' I did last night?"

"*Muñeca*, you will never know how much I hate you. *All* of you... There's not an abyss in this world that is deep enough to contain it." I recoil at the bite behind his words. *The sureness.* "Now, I have a question for *you*... Are you planning to wear white to your forthcoming wedding?"

"*Wedding?*" I bow forward slightly, certain I've misheard. "What wedding?"

He offers me another of his arctic smiles. "In sickness and in health, señorita." He gives me a wink that's more a threat. "Let's make your *papá* really mad, shall we?"

Oh.

My.

God.

The air lodges at the back of my throat and it doesn't shift. "You really *are* insane," I whisper, scanning his face for mockery, but seeing only blank certainty. "One minute you're siding me with Hitler and the next you want to…"

I can't even say the words, let alone breathe in oxygen.

Then I remember why I took this trip to Atlantic City in the first place, and suddenly the future is paved with black and gold and mutual animosity of the murderous kind.

"There must be another way," I stammer.

"You either take the money and accept, or I can end it all now." He opens the left side of his suit jacket to reveal his gun and holster.

More blackmail?

What a week.

"This isn't a choice. This is basement extortion. Congratulations, Carrera, you just created a new bullying low point." I start to sway. I think I'm going to faint.

"Get used to that name, *muñeca*. In twenty-four hours, you'll be wearing it too."

Thalia *Carrera?*

My heart lurches in protest.

"Look at me." Lunging forward, he holds my face prisoner, inches from his own. I feel the bite of his touch, but it's nothing compared to the sting of his indecent proposal. "You're right. You don't have a choice, so I won't waste words trying to spin this into something it's not."

"I'm nineteen," I gasp out. "Girls my age think about marrying Henry Cavill, not the devil."

"You can set a fucking precedence then, can't you?" He lets go of me, and this time I lose my balance in my haste to get away—sprawling backward across the mattress, and covering hundred-dollar bills in shock, shame, and a crushing inevitability. "You want that money?" He stares down at me with that same look of distaste on his face that he wore last night. "Then this is my price."

"I hate you too," I croak, as a crimson jewelry box is tossed carelessly down next to my head.

Prince of Darkness.

King of Loco

Soul Crusher Extraordinaire.

"I take it that's a 'yes'? I hope the ring fits, *fiancée*."

"I hope you rot in hell," I hiss, scrambling to sit up and regain what little dignity he's left me with.

"I'll defer that honor to your father and his *sicarios* in New York."

Oh fuck, my father. Santi Carrera has no idea what he's about to unleash.

"White dress it is," I hear him say. "Though if you're a virgin, I'm *Santa Muerte* herself. Santiago gave you too much freedom. I won't be making the same mistake. Maybe we'll start with a wardrobe that doesn't pussy-flash every man in the room."

"How dare you," I seethe, lobbing the first thing I can lay my hands on which happens to be a Legado branded notepad on the nightstand.

With no weight behind it, it fizzles to a pathetic nosedive between us—which, to be honest, is a pretty good representation of how much control I have over my life right now.

He lifts a withering eyebrow at me. "Either way, we'll find out soon enough."

Don't tell me I'll have to share a bed with this monster, as well?

Turning on his heel, he starts walking toward the door. "We'll marry tomorrow. You'll live here with me. I'll release that money to you in exactly one week. And don't bother running. There's a hundred armed guards between you and your freedom."

"A *week*?" Panic blooms in my stomach. Bardi's deadline has already passed.

"In that time, you will be respectful and dutiful to me and everyone who works for me. You'll convince your family how fucking irresistible you find me, and that free will is a twenty-four-hour party in this penthouse. Understood?"

"I need it now, Carrera," I say, rising to my feet. "He won't—" I stop myself just in time. "Please, I'm begging you."

"One week. No less… To sweeten the deal, here's an early wedding gift." He tosses a burner cell on the table as he passes. "You can use it to tell Daddy all about the good news, or maybe not. When's the last time you spoke to him again?"

Without waiting for an answer, the door slams shut behind him.

A beat later, I'm grabbing the cell and dialing out Bardi's number. I feel like crying when it clicks straight to voicemail.

"Bardi, it's me. I have your money, but I need a couple more days. Meet me at that bar you picked me up outside yesterday at nine p.m., next Friday. Look, I'll even take a photo of it, so you know I'm not bullshitting you." I glance at the dirty dollars on the bed. "I know it's a lot to ask, but I'm begging you not to do anything stupid with that tape until you speak to me. Please… Damn. Call me." I ring off as my voice starts to crack.

I slide down the wall in a crumpled heap of anger and confusion. Not only have I been kidnapped at gunpoint, but I'm also being forced to marry against my will, just like my mother did.

History really does *repeat itself.*

But this is where it ends.

I'll play his stupid games. I'll wear his stupid ring, but as soon as Bardi is paid off and I get that footage, I'll be serving Santi Carrera with an annulment so fast he'll be bleeding out from all the paper cuts.

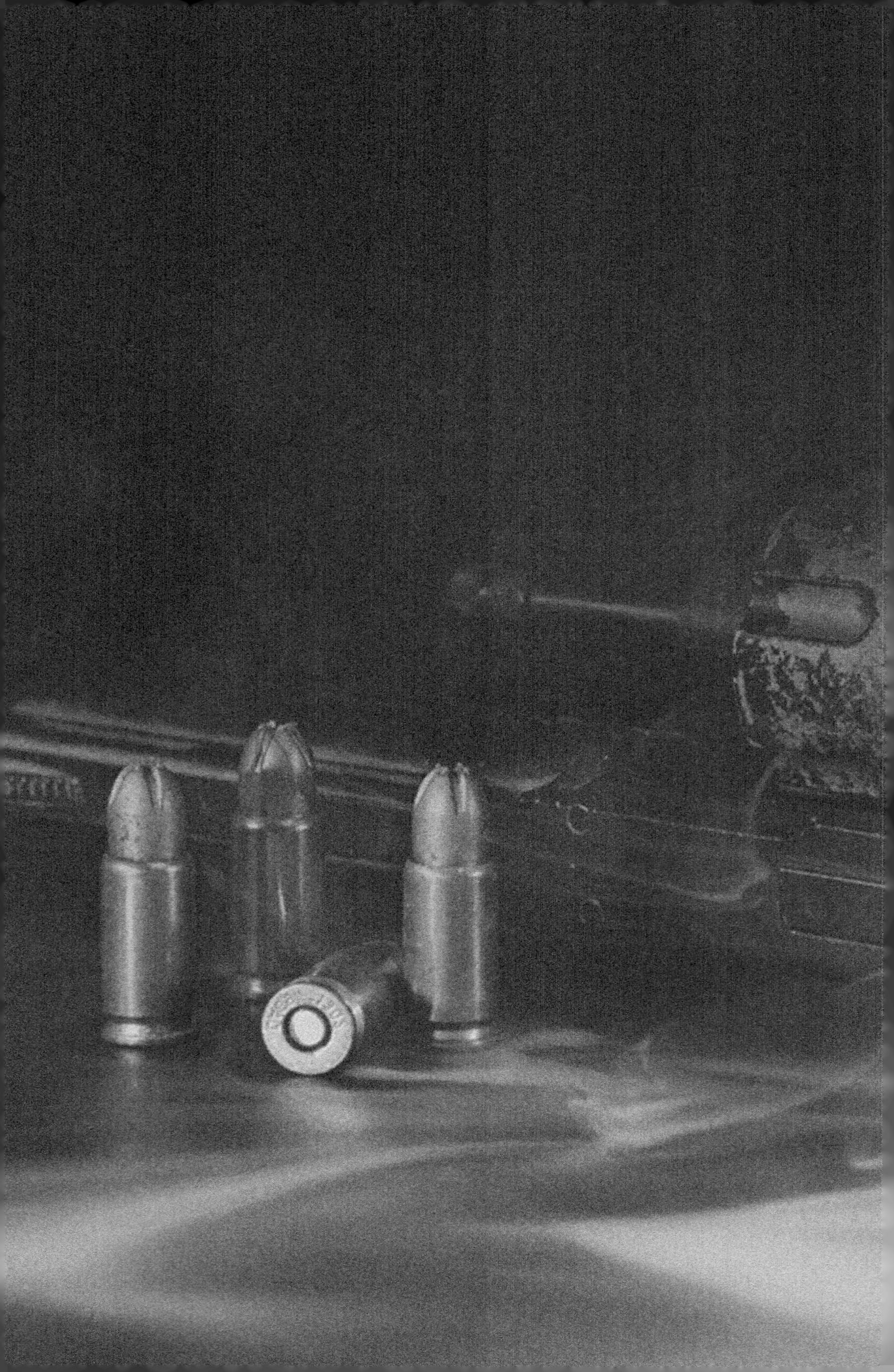

CHAPTER
Twelve

SANTI

Driving is becoming a reckless endeavor.

"Bardi, it's me. I have your money, but I need a couple more days. Meet me at that bar you picked me up outside yesterday at nine p.m., next Friday."

That's the third time I've listened to her begging that Italian piece of shit to call her back. I have to tighten my grip on the steering wheel just so I don't drive my fist through the windshield. She sounds desperate. Panicked. *So fucking broken.*

She was telling the truth last night. She didn't toss Bardi whatever information he's clinging to like a lifeline. Even so, an innocent Santiago is the living definition of an oxymoron.

Still, I think of how she'd stood up to me in my office last night, with her attitude and confidence. How she'd absorbed my threats—choosing to face her fate head on with dignity instead of tears. I think of the woman who'd sashayed into my casino in a crimson dress, laying her life on the line to salvage her sister's.

I listen to it again.

Hearing the pain in her voice makes me crave to hear *him* beg. To break him like he broke her. I have no idea how to reconcile the urge to protect a Santiago with the hate I'm supposed to feel for her.

I knew she'd call him. I'd counted on it. My plan can't proceed without a scheduled rendezvous between my bride-to-be and the man who betrayed her. Thalia has no idea I'm pulling all the strings in this puppet show. Now that there's a confirmed date, all that's left to do is open the curtain and make my marionettes dance.

"You know the definition of insanity, Santi?" Lola asks, nodding to where Bardi's phone is still plastered to the side of my head.

"Picking you up, instead of calling Uber?"

Cocking her head, she wrinkles her nose. "Cute, but no. It's doing the same thing over and over and expecting a different result. Like listening to the same message four times, thinking maybe the fifth won't cause that vein in the middle of your forehead to pop and give you an aneurysm."

Scowling, I drop Bardi's phone in the console.

Lola mutters a string of curses and scrambles for the overhead handle as I take the car in a sharp hairpin turn toward Legado. "*Dios mío*, slow down!" she yells, wincing as her shoulder slams against her window. "I didn't survive getting shot only to die by vehicular manslaughter."

"You were grazed by a bullet. Don't be dramatic."

"*I'm* being dramatic? You kept me locked in a hospital room for *observation*." She punctuates the word with air quotes. "A few stitches and you acted like I needed to be given last rites."

I'm not having this argument with her again. She's pissed and rightly so. I've given her a string of vague answers and half-truths concerning the events from last night and my reason for, *and I quote*, "acting like a total shitbag and treating her like a criminal."

I want to tell her that what I'm doing is for *her*. For my mother. For the Carrera name. For two decades of sins against all three.

I pull the car into the circular valet station in front of the casino's main entrance. As the car slows to a stop, I steal a look at her out of the corner of my eye. "After what happened at Rutgers, can you blame me for being overprotective?"

My words hit their mark. Lola flinches, her shoulders curving at the direct hit. Regardless of what she claims, she didn't spill the *entire* truth about what happened between her and Sam Sanders last year. The "kidnapping" story she spun to our father had more holes than a slice of Swiss cheese.

However, the truth will come out eventually.

It always does.

Just like it will with Thalia.

Thalia...

Her name spreads an unfamiliar warmth throughout my chest. She's a welcome departure from the parade of vapid whores constantly vying for my attention. The youngest Santiago may be intimidated by me, but that acid tongue of hers is so easily provoked.

Most women I encounter open their mouths for one thing, and it tends to impede further conversation. But Thalia... That iron will and sharp wit hardens my dick more than any blow job ever could. I shift uncomfortably in my seat. *Something I'll have to take care of myself, sooner rather than later.*

More memories of her efforts to stand her ground last night bring a ghost of a smile to my lips. My little thief is holding her cards close, but she forgets that this is my casino. My playground. My rules. Last night, she agreed to the highest stakes game of her life—and I never sit at the table without an ace up my sleeve.

I think of the horror on her face when I tossed that diamond ring at her. Perk of owning a casino? There are always drunken assholes willing to tie the knot over the spin of a roulette wheel. Legado caters to their every need, as long as their credit is good.

A chapel. A justice of the peace. A florist. A boutique.

And a jeweler.

Thalia looked as sick at hearing the words as I felt saying them. *Marriage?* I'd never intended on marrying anyone, much less a Santiago—the fucking root of all evil. However, a couple of vows and a piece of paper isn't what's important.

It's what it all symbolizes.

Possession.

My father demanded revenge, but staining my hands would simply be a warning flare—a short-term solution to a much bigger problem. The Colombians would retaliate, resulting in a never-ending see-saw of death and loss, and a lack of retribution.

Blood and bullets are temporary, but betrayal... Well, that's forever. And there's no greater betrayal to a father than his daughter taking the name of his enemy.

Marco Bardi gave me the perfect bargaining chip, and if the events of the last twenty-four hours have revealed anything, it's that Thalia will sacrifice everything to protect her sister—including herself.

I'll keep my word. I'll pay her debt. I'll salvage her sister's reputation. But my generosity comes with a price—a plant in the heart of New York.

Dante Santiago will suffer in a way he never imagined.

And his daughter will orchestrate it all.

Lola glares down at the offered crutches in my hand like they just insulted our mother.

"Are those really necessary?"

Is this whole goddamn conversation really necessary?

"Unless you want to walk with a limp for the rest of your life, yes. Now stop arguing."

Snatching the crutches out of my hand, she scowls while muttering to herself in Spanish. Still, she flops onto the crutches without protest and hobbles toward the front entrance of Legado.

The moment we enter the grand foyer, her breath catches. "*Whoa.*"

A sentiment lacking in eloquence, but accurate, nonetheless.

Construction crews are crammed into every available corner in a state of perpetual motion. My Legado, the most luxurious and high-end casino in Atlantic City, has gone from the epicenter of opulence to a hub of demolition.

While Lola gapes, I settle my gaze a few feet away where RJ stands talking to a stocky man I assume to be the crew foreman. "I'll be right back," I say to her over my shoulder, not waiting for a response.

As if sensing my presence, RJ stiffens, giving the worker a curt nod and then sending him away.

Frowning, I tap the sole of my Santoni dress shoe over a missing chunk of marble. "I'd ask how it's going, but I'm not sure I want to know."

"Repairs should take no more than seventy-two hours."

I raise an eyebrow. Expedited work usually comes with a hefty price tag. I'll have to do a rinse and spin on a few offshore accounts to cover the cost, but if the bullet holes are gone, and there's not a drop of Santiago blood staining my marble anymore, it's worth it.

"And the *nonna* situation...?"

"Will be handled by tomorrow. Procuring things *delicately* isn't a usual practice, Santi."

Delicate isn't a familiar word to any *sicario*. We want, we take—by any means necessary. Pasting on an ingenuous smile and sweet-talking little old ladies isn't a tactic in our wheelhouse.

I don't tolerate delays, but this is one concession I'm willing to give. Besides, there are more pressing matters to discuss. "Did you do what I asked?"

He crosses his arms, a smirk playing on his lips. "Sanders's club got lit up like the Fourth of July. You should have come along. We could have roasted marshmallows and watched it burn."

I'll give it to him; the man is efficient as hell. Not only that, he also takes pride in molding even the simplest acts of violence into a work of art.

"Maybe some other time." *Because if Bardi is telling the truth, there will be many more opportunities.* "What about the other thing?"

RJ offers a hesitant nod, his fists clenching. *Jesus.* The man has zero poker face. He wears his disapproval like a cheap suit. If body language had a voice, RJ's would be a string of obscenities hurled right in my face.

He thinks I'm making a mistake. If anyone should be ready and willing to charge into battle, it should be him. After all, Dante Santiago murdered his birth father in cold blood—a brutal act that left him orphaned at three years old.

RJ Harcourt would probably be dead right now if my *Tiá* Adriana and *Tío* Brody hadn't taken him in, eventually "adopting" him. I don't care that he grew up in Houston. His loyalty is tied to a falsified document buried deep within the borders of Mexico.

"Wipe the judgment off your face," I warn. "Your job is to be my second, not my conscience."

He scoffs. "You don't have one."

"Something you should keep in mind, *primo*." The stressed *"cousin"* isn't a familial term of endearment. It's a subtle reminder. When he doesn't respond, I take that as a silent acquiescence. "Good, then I'll expect everything to go as planned later. I want double the security." At his raised eyebrow, I palm the back of my neck in frustration. "In case two cold feet try to do something stupid."

He knows how to read between the lines. There will be no runaway bride today.

Leaving him to handle the details, I turn back toward the front desk, only to collide with a five-foot three tornado, holding a steel crutch like a Samurai Warrior.

Shoving a hand through my hair, I exhale a sigh. "We need to work on your inability to follow instructions, *chaparrita*."

"What the hell was that all about?" Lola demands, jabbing the rubber-tipped end of her crutch into my chest.

I know she overheard pieces of our conversation. The question is, how many, and were they enough to cause a problem. I have no doubts where my sister's loyalty lies. However, I don't trust women. I especially don't trust women with commonalities.

Two cartel princesses.

Two daughters of sin.

Two women whose lives are controlled by the very power that created them.

I've already determined it's best if Lola is introduced to her new sister-in-law *after* the ink dries on our marriage certificate.

"Business," I answer curtly. By the way her lip curls, I might as well have told her we were trading DIY tips. I'm both irritated and impressed. She's acting like a Carrera. Which is exactly the problem. *She's acting like a Carrera—*suspicious, ruthless, and relentless in getting what she wants.

"Don't give me that bullshit 'cartel king' rhetoric. I was shot in the leg, not the head."

I look away to keep from laughing.

"It's not funny!" The crutch jabs deeper into my sternum. "I'm serious, damn it."

I am, too. Keeping my impending nuptials from my sister is a strategic move, not a punitive one. Eventually, I'll have to inform my parents of my actions and then weather the repercussions. It's safer for Lola if she's as blindsided as the rest of my family.

My father will condemn my methods. A lethal storm will make its way across the border, and the less of an accessory Lola is to my crime, the less of a chance *papá's little girl* will get swept into its path. Besides, she'd only try to talk me out of it—which we both know would be a waste of time. Once I make a decision, I don't waver. The first domino has been tipped, and the chain reaction is already in play.

There's no stopping an avalanche once it crests the top of a mountain.

Gripping the steel rod of Lola's crutch, I calmly push it away from my chest, lowering it between us until balance forces her to drop it onto the floor. "I'm serious too, *chaparrita*. You're my secretary, not my business partner. If information is needed to do your job, I'll tell you."

It comes out harsher than I intended, but *my* job is to ensure her safety, not to stroke her ego.

"Does this have something to do with Thalia Santiago?" Lola's matter-of-fact delivery catches me off guard.

"What makes you think that?"

"Oh, I don't know, maybe common sense? I was there in the control room, remember? I stood right behind you when you saw her face on that surveillance screen. You whispered her name under your breath, for Christ's sake."

"*Dios mío*, Lola!" Pressing my hand to her lower back, I gently but firmly maneuver her toward the elevators.

Once the doors slide shut, I lift a slot below the row of buttons and press my thumb against a hidden access pad. Right away, it illuminates, and we start to rise. I watch as the floors tick away, my anger slowly fading with each one. By the time we pass the twenty-second floor, I'm calm enough to face her again.

"That was reckless. Anyone could have overheard you."

"Maybe if you'd stop treating me like a child, I wouldn't have to resort to drastic measures." She slams her crutch onto the floor. "I recognize a blitz attack when I see one. It doesn't take a genius to see two plus two always adds up to four." Sighing, she leans her head back against the elevator wall. "I know you, Santi. If Dante's daughter is responsible for turning Legado into a goddamn turkey shoot, you're not going to sit back and take it."

Folding my arms across my chest, I stare at her—straight through her clipped words to the tremble on her lips. Her nerves are showing, along with her humanity. *There's so much of our mother in her.*

"Why do you care so much?"

"I-I don't," she stammers, my question catching her off-guard. "I just don't like being forced on the outside of my own inner circle, that's all."

Before I can answer, the elevator dings, and the doors slide open revealing the entrance to my sister's "summer home"—an extravagant apartment, one floor below mine.

"It's late," I say, guiding her across the threshold and into the lavish accommodations. "You need your rest, and I need a drink. We'll talk about this tomorrow."

Surprisingly, she doesn't argue. After getting her settled in her bedroom, I slip away toward the kitchen—a room with enough bells and whistles to employ an entire fleet of Michelin star chefs. It's bright, too. The kind of bright that makes you wonder if you're about to sit down to a meal or meet your maker.

That's by design.

I renovated the entire place when Lola announced her plans to spend the summer in New Jersey. I wanted her surroundings to be bright, white, and pure.

Unlike the penthouse sitting directly above it.

It's that need to preserve her innocence that ultimately drives me to destroy her trust.

CHAPTER
Thirteen

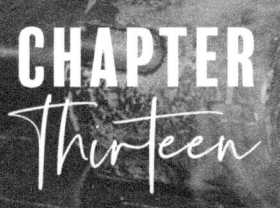

SANTI

Filling a crystal glass with juice, I set it on the counter and retrieve two prescription bottles from the inside pocket of my suit jacket. Placing one beside the glass, I pop the cap on the other and shake two capsules into my palm.

I don't stop to think about what I'm doing. If I do, I'll change my mind. Breaking each capsule open, I dump ten milligrams of OxyContin into the orange liquid. Giving it a stir, I grab the glass in one hand and the second prescription bottle in the other before crossing the open-floor plan back to the bedroom.

Lola is tucked under the covers, stress and fatigue already claiming her.

"Here," I say, offering her the glass and the pill bottle. "Take your antibiotics so you don't get gangrene."

"Funny." She pops two pills in her mouth, and I hold my breath as she washes them down with half the glass.

"Finish it. You need the Vitamin C." *And I need assurance my wedding won't be disturbed.*

She rolls her eyes but doesn't argue.

Fifteen minutes later, a wrecking ball could barrel through the floor to ceiling windows and Lola would be none the wiser. That's because she'll be spending the next ten to twelve hours in a narcotic wonderland.

Was it a dirty play? Of course.

The brother in me hates myself for drugging my own flesh and blood.

However, the cartel boss accepts it for what it is—a necessary evil. This is a war, and sometimes the ends justify the means.

As I stare down at my sister, her face clean of makeup and her dark hair strewn across her cheeks, I'm struck with how young she looks. *Barely twenty.* Older than Thalia, but still younger than Ella. My chest flares with rage at the thought of anyone trying to hurt her. I'd turn the heavens black and the seas red in order to protect her.

Just like Thalia did for her sister.

At that moment, my hate for Marco Bardi becomes a living, breathing thing. Ella Santiago could have easily been Lola Carrera—and then a sister's jaded desperation would have become a brother's unholy crusade.

I can't excuse her methods, and I won't ignore her role in what I still believe to be a planned attack on my casino... But as a devoted brother, I respect the lengths Thalia was *and still is,* willing to go to in the name of family.

Turning out the light, I kiss Lola's forehead. "I'm sorry," I whisper. "*Te amo, chaparrita.*"

Stepping back onto the elevator, all traces of regret fade away as it ascends one final floor. As the doors part, I button my suit jacket and take a step into my onyx lair—five thousand square feet of banished sunlight and weighted tension—only to come face to face with a set of wringing hands and a pinched face.

I can feel my eyebrows arching. My housekeeper isn't easily rattled. It's one of the reasons I keep her around. Not only is she efficient, but she also knows how to keep her mouth shut.

"Svetlana."

"Sir, your *guest*..."

For some reason, I bristle at her tone. "She has a name."

She flinches, but I offer no apology or explanation. I don't need my housekeeper and my betrothed to be best friends, but I'd prefer to keep the bloodshed to a minimum.

"Of course," she says, dialing back the attitude. "Miss Santiago refuses to eat. Francois has prepared her three meals, and she... Well, sir, she vehemently rejected them."

"How *vehemently?*"

"She threw them across the room, sir," she answers, indignation flaring in her eyes.

Not a crisis in my opinion, but Svetlana takes offense to waste. And justifiably so. She's a Russian mail order bride, left behind by Legado's previous owner as if she were a broken slot machine. Svetlana has known hunger few will ever suffer.

To refuse food is to sin.

"Has my package been delivered?"

She nods, motioning behind her where a long, rectangular box rests on a black lacquer and glass coffee table.

RJ may not agree with my tactics, but he has one hell of a follow through.

"Key," I say, extending my palm. Svetlana digs a small keyring out of her apron and places it in my hand without question.

"*Spasibo*," I thank her in Russian while crossing the foyer into the main living room. A dark laugh rumbles in my chest as I tuck the box under my arm, spinning the keyring around my index finger as I head toward the spiral staircase that sits in the dead center of the room.

Two floors, two hallways, and one quick detour later, I unlock the door and let myself into the room where I find Thalia sitting on the floor with her back against the opposite wall, hugging her knees to her chest.

She drops her legs as soon as she sees me.

"*Feliz noche de bodas, muñeca.*"

She scowls, but the dark circles under her eyes betray her. "You're in a good mood. Did you kick a few puppies on your way up here?"

"I'll chalk the rudeness up to pre-wedding jitters." Stepping further into the room, I clench my teeth as the heel of my shoe sinks into something soft and sticky. Glancing down, I exhale in annoyance. "Crème Brûlée is a French classic, not a congealed weapon."

"I believe the word you're looking for is *concealed*," she grits out.

"Not when it's defiling my shoe."

That brief spark of fire flickers and dies when she sees the box I'm carrying. "I don't want anything from you."

She turns her head away sharply, her long, dark hair tangling around her shoulders. Her body language is hellfire and brimstone, but her profile is a raw canvas of water-colored worry. The corners of her mouth curve down, making her seem less like the tool of the devil as much as his pawn.

This Thalia is the one I heard on Bardi's voicemail.

This Thalia is fragile—a broken doll hidden beneath a layer of thinning steel.

This Thalia ignites that foreign warmth in my chest again. The one I don't understand and don't care to dissect.

This Thalia strikes a chord deep within a shadowy corner of my mind. One with a solitary hanging light.

Get a grip, Santi. This is what she wants. One chink is all she needs...

"This hunger strike of yours isn't hurting anyone but yourself," I say, regrouping while shaking custard off the sole of my shoe. "We both know that you're not going to starve yourself. Self-destruction isn't in your DNA. So, you can eat what's on your plate now or eat it off the floor later and risk salmonella. Your choice."

Her response is a middle finger.

Bad girl.

I glance across the room where the burner phone I gave her sits silently on the nightstand. "Does Daddy know his little girl is about to shit all over his legacy?" When she doesn't answer, I chuckle again to myself and give the package tucked under my arm a light tap. "Aren't you going to ask what's in the box?"

"Nope."

That fucking mouth of hers. "That's foolish. What if it's a plane ticket? Or a check for fifty-thousand, free and clear?"

She shoots me a withering look. "You aren't that stupid and I'm not that gullible. Try again."

"Well, look at that. We *can* agree on something."

Her disgusted snort draws a smirk to my lips.

Winking, I toss the box at her feet. "Smart and beautiful. My bride is quite the catch."

Beautiful.

Thalia freezes at the word, and I kick myself internally, drawing blood.

Giving the box a quick scan, she looks away again, disinterested "Go to hell."

"Oh, *mi amada.*" My tone is thick with condescension as I lower to my haunches in front of her. "That wish was granted a long time ago. Let's strive for a little originality, shall we?"

A moment of uncertainty glazes her brown eyes, and then it's gone—quickly replaced by a deadly cocktail of fatigue and loathing. "What do you want, Santi? I've already agreed to marry you. Do you want it signed in blood?"

Yes. Just not yours. "Maybe later. For now, opening the box will suffice."

"Fine." She hisses the submission between clenched teeth. "If it will make you go away."

Crossing her legs, she leans forward, tearing the gold ribbon off the box as if the keys to her freedom are buried in there somewhere. The top is ripped off just as *delicately*, derision coiling her lips as paper is tossed over her shoulder like garbage…

And then she freezes.

"What the hell is this?"

"I believe in America it's called a wedding dress."

"Is this your idea of a joke?" she says, holding up the swathe of white satin.

My smirk fades. "I rarely joke, Thalia, and never about business."

"Business," she repeats, spitting out the word as if its taste of torture. "Well, take it back. I'm not selling my soul in some cheap knock-off gown."

"Try a twenty-thousand-dollar gown."

If I hadn't been watching her so closely, I would've missed the way her shoulders jolted, as if the price tag itself delivered a hard punch to her chest.

"It's not my size."

"Check the tag. You're a four, if I'm not mistaken."

Her jaw drops. "How…?"

"I pay attention to detail. It's a skill you should learn if you plan to survive a week in my world."

Technically, it's not a lie. I paid an exorbitant amount of attention to the shape of her body when I had her pressed up against the wall in my office. Every curve. Every valley. Every single fucking inch of her. "Look underneath," I instruct, nodding toward the gown. "There's more."

She doesn't want to, but she can't help herself. After all, curiosity and impulsiveness are the two endearing traits that landed her ass here in the first place. I don't have to look to know the exact moment she sees it.

That gasp is music to my ears… *And my aching dick.*

Thalia lifts the black lace bustier and matching thong in the air as if they were just peeled off a dead hooker. "Oh, fuck you, Carrera!" she breathes. "There's no way in hell I'm wearing this."

"Maybe I was unclear," I say patiently. "It wasn't a request."

Despite what she wants to believe, I'm not a soulless monster. *At least not completely.* This may not be the wedding day she dreamed for herself, but she deserves to have beautiful things to wear, regardless. The gown isn't a designer slap in the face. It's an attempt to counteract the cheapness Bardi made her feel.

However, the lingerie? That's to show her that even though we're standing on opposite sides of the battle line, I'm still a man who can appreciate a confident woman.

However, the color isn't for her.

It's for me.

It's a symbol of dark consuming light. A reminder that while heart and innocence may radiate on the outside, underneath all that satin and crystal, sin and lace wrap around her in blasphemy.

Blinking away her shock, she climbs to her feet. "This isn't a dream wedding, Santi. This is…" Her words trail off as her eyes settle on the lace dangling from her outstretched hands. "This is matrimonial terrorism." She exhales dramatically, and then she blushes as the sexy lingerie flutters under the force of her breath.

The truth stains her cheeks like a scarlet letter. Basic animal instinct can't be controlled. It knows no boundaries and doesn't give a fuck about crossing enemy lines. *Right now, Thalia is imagining me ripping this off her tight little body.*

I don't even try to stifle my laugh.

"You think this is funny?" she says, the blush on cheeks darkening with anger.

No, Thalia Santiago. Nothing I want to do to you is funny.

"I told you, I never joke, *mi amada*."

"I'm not your beloved. I'm your prisoner, and this"—balling her fists, she hurls the scraps of lace at my chest—"is revolting. If you think a couple of meaningless vows entitles you to anything other than a cold shower, you're very much mistaken. You lay a finger on me, and I'll break it."

Dislodging the thong hooked around one of my shirt buttons, I step forward, erasing all but an inch of space between us. "Big words for such a small woman."

I expected her to crumble under my wicked torture, but I should've known better. This girl is no wilted daisy. She's a wild rose with thorns the size of her petals.

"Haven't you ever heard that dangerous things come in small packages?"

"No, I'm used to handling...*large things*." I lower my eyes toward my tailored pants. As if pulled by an invisible tether, hers follow. The innuendo isn't veiled. It's framed by a flashing neon sign. Her lips round in shock and I let out another laugh. "It's a gift, Thalia. A simple gesture."

Composing herself, she kicks the lingerie and the box across the room. "You want to be generous? Bring me a long black dress and a veil."

"It's a wedding, not a funeral."

"Semantics."

Okay, that's it. I've indulged her tantrum long enough.

A low growl rumbles in my throat as I stalk toward her. A startled gasp escapes those tempting lips as Thalia takes a step backward—right into the wall. Placing a palm on either side of her head, I cage her in with nowhere to go...

Nowhere to run.

"You want to talk funerals, *muñeca*? Last night, you came within an angel's breath of being the guest of honor at your own. The only reason you still have breath in here"—I don't ask for permission before dragging a hand from the wall and placing it between her breasts—"is because I allow it."

"But you—"

"*You* chose life, Thalia. *You* chose our unholy union. *You* chose debt over loyalty. So don't act like you're doing me any favors by following through."

She's quiet for a moment, her heart thumping wildly beneath my palm. "You still don't believe I had nothing to do with the attack last night."

It's not a question.

"The word of a Santiago means nothing to me."

"And the promise of a Carrera means nothing to *me*." Raw hate flares in her eyes, turning the warmth in my chest into a goddamn inferno. "You're a bastard."

"And you're soon to be fifty thousand dollars richer. So, what does that make *you, señorita*?"

I may as well have struck her. As my words sink in, Thalia visibly deflates— any lingering boldness dissipating in a cloud of truth and deceit. Nobody likes having a mirror shoved in front of their face—especially when the reflection isn't pretty.

"I need to get out of this room, Santi," she whispers. "At least let me go home and offer up an explanation to my—"

"Do I look like a fucking moron to you?"

"They'll be looking for me. They'll trace me here, and when they do—"

"Let them come." My challenging tone is as dark as a starless Mexican sky. "You won't be the only thing I take from them. It's only a matter of time before New York is mine as well."

The moment Thalia says, "I do," I'm lighting a fire under Monroe Spader's ass. If Grayson thinks he can keep me out of New York, he has a surprise coming.

Regardless of what he might have planned.

For the second time since she stumbled through the doors of my office, my bride-to-be drops the queen bitch act. That scorched gaze dims, only to be filled by unshed tears. "Please..." she chokes out, pressing her hand against my chest. "I know you—"

One touch. One simple touch sparks a deadly live wire. My skin sizzles under my shirt, the pressure of her hand burning a permanent tattoo on my chest.

Everything distorts.

Wrapping my fingers tightly around her wrist, I pull her hand away and slam it against the wall above her head. "Don't. Touch. Me," I growl, my voice razor-thin. "Don't *ever* touch me without my permission."

"I'm s-sorry," she stutters. "I didn't know."

How could she? I'm the heir to a cartel empire. I don't explain myself to anyone.

I need to get out of here.

Twisting around, I drive both hands into my hair as I stalk toward the door.

"Santi..."

I pause with my back to her. I don't acknowledge her, but I can't seem to walk away either. *Stuck in fucking limbo—as usual.*

"What's in this for you?" she asks softly.

"What's in this for *you*?" I counter, flinging her own words back at her. "What does my fifty-grand buy?"

Neither of us answers.

"Be ready in an hour." I turn to leave. "I'll have Svetlana bring makeup and a brush and whatever the hell else it is girls need to look presentable."

"And if I'm not?"

"Then you'll need that black veil after all," I warn, locking the door behind me.

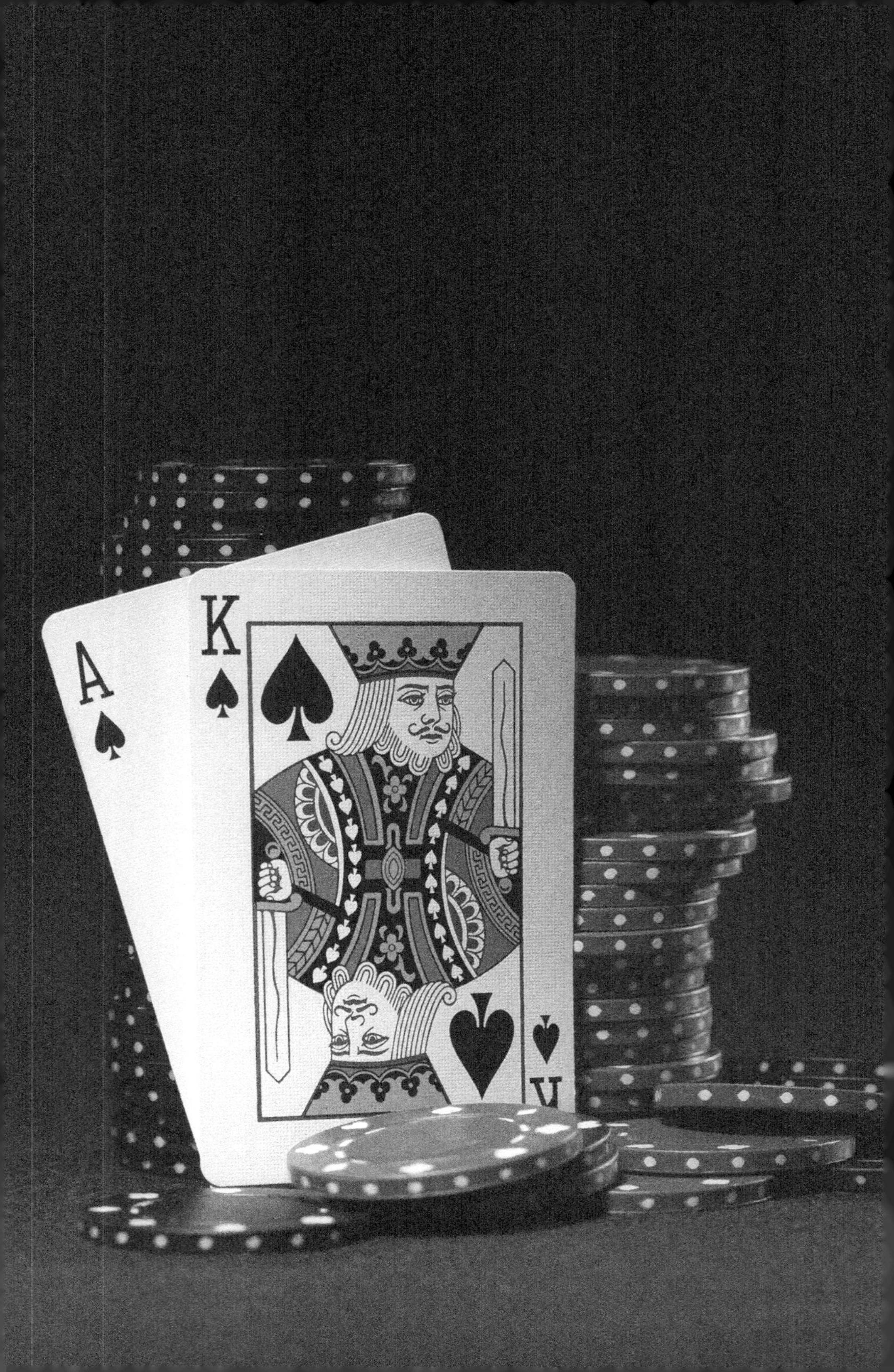

CHAPTER
Fourteen

THALIA

I've never considered myself to be a rebel.
It's hard to break the rules when you spend the first eighteen years of your life on an armed island compound in the middle of the Pacific Ocean, surrounded by more guns than fun. Even my words don't carry that much of a shock value anymore. My mouth has always been a box with a broken lid.

That's until Santi Carrera left me all alone with an expensive wedding dress and a pair of nail scissors I just found in the bottom drawer of the ensuite's vanity unit. Now, dissidence is my New Jersey state of mind.

Kneeling down on the cool tiles, I pick the scissors up and examine them again, sliding my fingers into the eyes and feeling how snug the metal fits against my skin. They're too blunt to cause any real damage, but they're sharp enough to make a scene. And that's the aim of the game now—to slide myself like a piece of glass underneath Carrera's surfaces until I bleed his patience dry.

Beyond my father's protection, I'm learning that rules can be bent by the subtlest of mutinies. I won't push Carrera so far that my money comes into jeopardy—but by the end of this week, he'll be begging me to leave.

Walking back into the bedroom, I stare down at the silky white material spilling out of the box on the floor. *And this cost him twenty thousand dollars?* I grind my teeth together in frustration. That's nearly half the money I need to pay Bardi off.

The wedding dress itself screams money and status—from the intricate Swarovski crystals sewn into the neckline, to the detailed stitching on the bodice. Even if I felt a modicum of emotion for him, *which I don't,* I wouldn't be caught dead in something so flashy. This man wouldn't know refinement if it smacked him over the head with a loaded Glock.

It takes me over an hour, and by the time I'm done, my forefinger and thumb are throbbing with pain. For the final touches, I rip the velveteen petals off the red rose bouquet that his blonde housekeeper delivered with her bags of makeup, and then I arrange them into two words on the bed's counterpane that speak for me and every member of the Santiago Cartel.

Fuck.

You.

Catching my reflection in the mirror, I smile at the carnage.

And then I wait.

CHAPTER
Fifteen

SANTI

I've never imagined my wedding day.

Not because I haven't found the right woman, or because I'm too busy sampling all the wrong ones. It's not even because I likened the institute of marriage to a six by eight prison cell complete with a warden and fifty-year march toward Death Row.

It's because of who I am. What I've done. The soil I've stained.

It's because a man like me spends a lifetime acquiring just as many debts as he collects. They come in the form of a scorned business partner. A grieving widow. A jealous friend.

A dangerous rival.

Over the years, each debt darkens to a sworn vow, and unatoned sins tip the scale of judgment against his favor. From the day I was born, I've been living on borrowed time. And those debts? Those vows? Those sins? They all have an expiration date.

Like me.

I was too young to remember the day my father's world stopped turning, but he made damn sure the images painted in my head as I grew up did it justice.

Skyfall, he called it.

La Boda Roja. The Red Wedding. The day the heavens opened, and angels wept. The day our family's tragedy set the course of destiny hurling my way.

The day a bullet meant for him almost took my mother from this world. And the day two years later, when my father dropped three bullets in the chamber of a revolver, gave it a spin, and stared down the barrel of his own gun.

That's when I knew I'd never allow myself to be so consumed by a woman that I'd rather die by my own hand than live in a world without her.

That's why I never imagined my wedding day, because marriage is nothing but a game of Russian Roulette, too. The sins of the father may be laid upon his children, but his mistakes are his to keep. When *Santa Muerte* comes for me, I plan to leave this world the same way I came into it.

Alone.

But that all went to hell last night, when, in a snap decision, I bartered my soul and Thalia's as well. I broke my own rules. Now, with two shiny gold rings, not only will I have a partner in life, but thanks to the *shiny gold* bullet inevitably coming our way for this, I'll have one in death too.

I tug at the collar of my white shirt. The dark gray suit I chose to wear feels more like a silk coffin than formal wear—something I'd prefer not to have amplified in a thirty-six by forty-six-inch mirrored funhouse, *thank you very much*. Whoever decided to plate the inside of this goddamn elevator with angled mirrors should be executed inside of it.

I don't want to see *one* image of myself dressed like this, much less a couple dozen. Not because the suit costs more than most people's houses. Excess is my calling card. It's because the image staring back at me looks less like me...

And exactly like *him*.

From my slicked back dark hair to the five o'clock shadow that never lasts a minute past six, Valentin Carrera's image is etched across every line and crevice of my face like cursed stone.

It's a realization that sours my mood even more.

"Fuck destiny," I mutter as the elevator doors slide open, revealing my devil's paradise.

"Thalia?" I call out, hearing nothing but my own echo bouncing off the black walls. "Thalia Santiago," I repeat, every vowel in her last name like a mouthful of broken glass. "Get out here now. It's bad luck to arrive late to your own wedding."

As far as I'm concerned, all weddings are bad luck...*period.*

"I'm marrying *you*," a voice calls out. "Obviously, Lady Luck already slammed the door in my face."

I scan a restless gaze across the room, only to have my eyes assaulted by what can only be described as a visual blitzkrieg.

"What. The. Fuck?"

Thalia is standing on the bottom step of the spiral staircase, her body draped across the coiled banister like a serpent. Cradled in her hands is a bouquet of long green stems, every single one plucked clean of their petals.

And that's only the beginning…

While I spent the day ensuring every detail of my plan was executed to my specification, this crazy woman has gone fucking *Edward Scissorhands* on a twenty-thousand-dollar wedding gown.

What used to be a full skirt with a long, ornate train, now looks like a demented cocktail dress. Miles of smooth, golden legs pave a deadly pathway from her ivory Louboutins to the jagged material that's now barely covering her ass.

At least she's wearing the black bustier I gave her—as a fucking tube top.

However, it's her face that causes my jaw to drop. Not only does her makeup look like she fell into a box of sixty-four count crayons, but she's also fashioned her hair into pigtails.

Goddamn pigtails.

I stepped out of the elevator expecting to find Grace Kelly and got bitch slapped by Harley Quinn, instead.

"Do you like it?" she says, peeling herself off the railing and sauntering toward me with a dramatic spin. "I wanted all the joy I felt inside at becoming your wife to be reflected on the outside." A wicked smile dances across her bright purple painted lips. "Now, I'm not one to brag, but I think I nailed it."

If I wasn't so pissed, I'd be impressed at the steel *cojones* on this woman.

"You *nailed* it, all right," I say dryly. "Straight through the part of your brain that controls your common sense." I grab at her arm to stop her incessant twirling. "Is this your idea of a joke?"

"Oh, Santi… *I rarely jok*e," she says, pleased as hell with herself as she repeats my own words from earlier.

"You look like a psychopath."

"Oh no!" Gasping dramatically, Thalia presses a hand over her heart. "My betrothed is displeased. But I worked *so* hard to look the part of a *Carrera*."

"Watch it," I warn, swallowing the string of Spanish obscenities resting on my tongue. Her little insults are becoming a big problem—one I plan to address *after* the ceremony.

I inherited my father's temper, but I also know when to pick my battles. Thalia's act of defiance was a commendable effort, but a complete waste of energy. This woman thinks that by shredding her gown and then covering it with the bustier like a confused whore in a brothel, I'll assume she's *loca en la cabeza* and send her on her merry way?

Hell no.

Thalia *wants* me to lose my temper so she can hate me even more. She *wants* my anger. She *wants* my hate and her fear all twisted up and displayed in all its fucked-up glory.

And she almost had it.

My initial instinct was to drag her back into the ensuite bathroom and force her to change after scrubbing all that shit off her face. *But why?* This isn't a real wedding, at least not in any traditional sense. It's nothing more than a binding agreement—a gold shackle that ensures her a front row seat to her family's destruction.

If Thalia wants to walk down the aisle dressed like a circus freak, so be it. Her act of rebellion is nothing more than an eyesore.

The Colombian *princesa* is about to get a lesson in playing with fire.

"It's short," I note, my eyes tracing the uneven cut barely grazing the tops of her thighs. "I thought I told you to stop pussy-flashing my men, *muñeca?*"

"What's wrong, Carrera?" she purrs, batting those long eyelashes. "Don't you like what you see?"

Like it? I could devour it. Even a package wrapped in a shitty attitude still shines. If the blood of my enemy didn't flow through her veins, I'd happily wreck that pretty little cunt she keeps parading in front of my face. However, I'd chop off my own dick before I'd fuck a Santiago, despite my unspoken thoughts to the contrary.

"It definitely makes a statement."

She pauses, clearly taken off guard. "Wait, you're not mad?"

"Should I be?"

That proud jaw tightens as I step closer. "You're toying with me, aren't you?"

I catch the faint scent of jasmine as I lower my mouth to her ear. "Not yet," I whisper, that charged electricity crackling between us again as I call her bluff. "I'm saving that for our wedding night." Reveling in her breathy gasp, I bend my elbow, offering her my arm with a salacious grin. "Shall we, *mi amada*?"

"I'm not your *beloved*—or your wife," she mutters, looping her arm around mine before sinking her bright yellow nails deep into my skin. "A least not for the next few minutes."

I choose to ignore her final act of defiance. It's not the first time a woman has tried to leave scars, and it won't be the last.

She draws blood under my suit jacket as I walk us to the elevator. "Enjoy *those few minutes*, Thalia," I warn. "Because after you say, 'I do', all of the minutes after belong to me."

Fueling hope is like feeding a wishing well.

You can walk by the same one every day for years, blindly tossing in penny after penny, believing that eventually, one magical coin will make all your dreams come true.

Here's the cold, hard truth—it won't. Because a penny is just a dirty piece of copper, and a pool of water doesn't give a fuck about your wishes.

Wishes can't deliver dreams.

And hope doesn't change fate.

Two hard lessons Thalia Santiago is learning today.

She hasn't opened her mouth since we left the penthouse. Not that I expected much more than the blank stare currently painted across her face as we make our way down a narrow hallway toward Legado's "chapel."

Part me wonders if, despite her sharp tongue and acid words, there was a small part of her that believed fate wouldn't be so cruel as to deliver back-to-back blows. That surely, she wouldn't be forced to sell her soul to two evil men twice in one week. That if she stayed strong and just *believed*, at the last minute, the family she holds in such high regard would ride in on their black horses and save the day.

But there are no horses here.

No saviors.

And only one Santiago.

Her.

A half a dozen guards in dark sunglasses stand motionless in front of the closed double doors. As Thalia and I round the corner, they nod in quiet respect, parting like the Red Sea.

As the chapel doors open, Thalia inhales sharply. It's her first emotive concession since taking my arm.

"I'd ask if you're having second thoughts," I say, scanning the curious faces of the few trusted men I've allowed to be in attendance, "but I assume that's rather rhetorical at this point."

Thalia's answer is to dig her nails even deeper into my arm.

I'm not offended. In fact, the less my intended speaks, the less chance there is of anything veering off course. I've afforded her tantrums. I've put up with her disrespect and destruction of my generosity. I've even tolerated her recent attempt at physical violence. However, this ceremony is one thing I won't allow anyone to impede—especially the bride.

There's a side of me Thalia has never seen.

And I promise her, she doesn't want to.

Sliding my gaze to my left, I stare at Rocco's shaded eyes and arch an eyebrow. He dips his chin in a silent affirmation to my unspoken question.

Excelente.

Words aren't needed for me to know what has transpired. After settling Lola earlier, I provided Rocco with a specific task—*track the scorpion*. His findings were just as I anticipated. Edier Grayson already knows about our impending union, and Daddy Dante's private jet has already landed in New York.

Everything is unfolding perfectly.

With one final nod toward Rocco, I smile inwardly as he reaches into his suit pants and pulls out his phone.

"Smile, *muñeca.*"

Thalia snaps her face toward me, but before she can utter a single protest, there's a click and a bright flash of light.

"Did he just take our picture?" she says, sounding shocked.

"Yes," I answer. Lifting my chin, I offer an unapologetic stare.

"I don't want any mementos of this day."

"They're not for you, *mi esposa.*" Thalia flinches as I punctuate the words "*my wife*" with a slow smirk. "They're for my new father-in-law."

For once, she's rendered speechless.

As the reality of my words sink in, that rainbow of color splashed across her face vanishes underneath a thick veil of chalky-white fear.

They say a picture is worth a thousand words.

This one is worth fifty-thousand of them, but Dante Santiago's reaction when he sees it...?

Priceless.

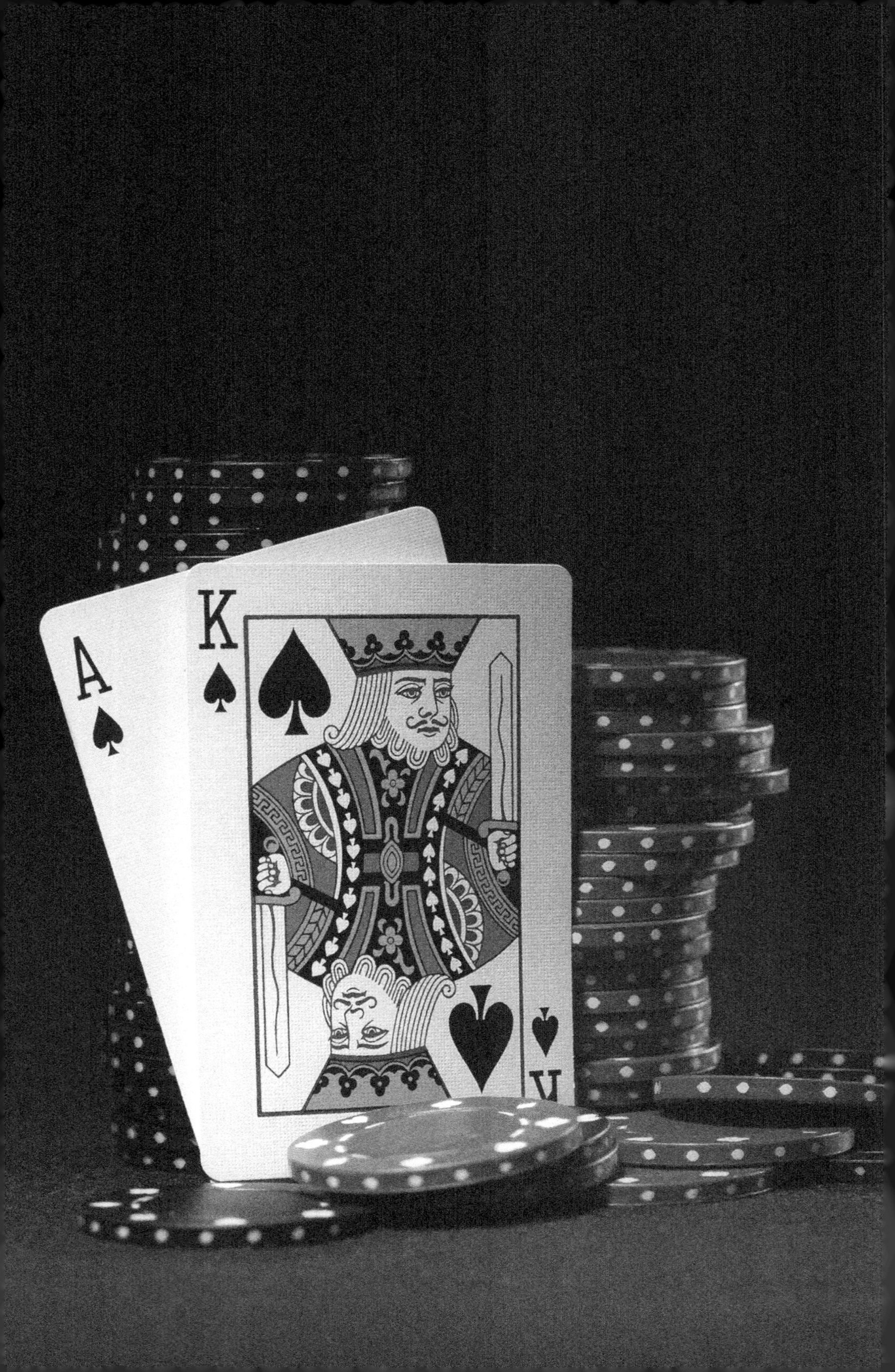

CHAPTER Sixteen

THALIA

There's more danger in silence than with a spoken threat.

My father taught me that.

When I was twelve, we visited Edier's family in Colombia for a whole summer. One evening, after dinner, a man was brought to the main house in chains. I remember watching from an upstairs window as he and Edier's father stepped onto the front porch below to receive him. I'd cranked the glass open in the hopes that I'd overhear what this man's offense was, but all I'd heard were his begs and pleas for forgiveness.

There wasn't a word from anyone else—not even from the guards.

After ten minutes of this, I saw the flash of silver in my father's hand. The man was dead before he hit the ground, his mournful eyes staring up at a night he'd never get to fill with begging and pleading again.

It wasn't the murder that shocked me. It was the brutal way in which his justice was delivered.

Silently.

I sometimes wonder if that's the reason why I talk too much. Why I spill my thoughts and emotions into a room to keep some kind of a messed-up equilibrium, because when the world goes quiet, things get serious.

Like the long, painful pause last month before I told my father that I never wanted to see him again. That I spent every day wishing I'd be born to another man.

Like when Bardi showed me his tape...

Like now.

There's no finesse to how I'm being marched up the chapel's aisle. It's the only room in his casino that isn't black and gold. The walls are white, and daylight is streaming in through another of those dome glass ceilings, making me feel like I'm under some kind of divine interrogation.

Sorry, God, but there's nothing holy about this marriage.

I stumble in my heels as we pass by the rows of empty pews, but his tight grip on my arm doesn't give me a chance to fall. I hate that he's won the first battle in this marriage. My outfit missed the mark, and now I feel like an idiot.

As we reach the altar, he spins me around to face him. "Well?" he says irritably.

"Well, what?"

"I'm bracing myself for your last stab of hostility as an unmarried woman."

"*Stab?*" I yank my arm free, refusing to acknowledge how the cut of his dark gray wedding suit is doing strange butterfly-like things to my stomach. "That's an interesting word to use with your partner-in-hate... And it will be my pleasure to disappoint you, *señor*. I'm all out of words."

"Except for the ones that count in a place like this."

"I'm a liar, remember?" I say through gritted teeth. "This should come easy to me."

He lifts a slanted eyebrow, but he doesn't comment.

There's a scuffling noise behind us as a couple of his muscles-in-tuxes enter the chapel and take their seats in the furthest pew. Trailing behind them is a short man in a blue suit, with a pinched face and thinning brown hair. I recognize him as the man I saw walking through the casino a couple of nights ago with Santi.

"Ah, the witnesses," he says, nodding at the justice of the peace who's been staring in open-faced horror at my face and outfit. "You can begin."

"Wait!"

All heads turn toward me. A flash of annoyance dances across Santi's face but he kills it, stone dead. "I figured as much. Come on then, spit it out."

"No, it's not that..." I trail off, struggling to put into words the deep sadness I'm suddenly feeling.

Is this how my mother felt on her wedding day?

My fingers fumble for the pendant around my neck, the one she gave to me when I turned eighteen. The one I'd always admired as a child, and the one I wear every day. The same one my father gifted to her over two decades ago.

It's a silver chain with three diamond-encrusted numbers that seem so fitting for today.

666

"Well?"

If this pendant protected her from the worst of her devil, maybe it can do the same for me.

"Thalia?" he snaps. "I'm waiting."

"I was just giving you the opportunity to back out of the deal," I say, smiling at him sweetly—my sadness turning to acid. "My father always said it was a specialty of the Carreras."

Angry murmurs rise up behind us.

Santi's smile is the stuff of torture porn.

"Begin," he snaps at the officiant again. "And this time don't stop until this Santiago *puta* has a new last name."

It turns out it doesn't take long to dishonor your entire family. Five minutes, to be exact... In the end, it's all a countdown of numbers to the ultimate anti-prize:

Three witnesses with their fingers on the trigger, should I decide to run.

Two vows of gut-churning deception.

One marriage, borne out of blood and thorns.

As a wedding ring is rammed onto my finger, I allow a single tear to escape from its strict confinement, turning my head away so my new husband doesn't see. This is a temporary deal for me, but for Edier and Sam...for Ella... They won't understand. Not until the truth comes to light.

Until then, I'm stuck with Carrera, for better or for worse.

As if it could be any worse.

There's no reception afterward. No celebratory drink to mark the occasion. Instead, he leaves me hanging in the lobby while he conducts a brief exchange of words with the man in the blue suit. Afterward, I'm led down a flight of stairs to a private underground garage where a black Aston Martin DBS is parked.

Trust him to drive a car as beautifully brutal as he is.

"Get in, *mi esposa*." Swinging my door open, he all but hustles me into the passenger seat.

I wish he'd stop calling me his wife. It's revolting.

I watch him slide in next to me. "Where are we going?"

"Time for another wedding gift." With that, he accelerates down the driveway and sets a course for the Garden State Parkway.

More silence.

More lost words.

My heart is sinking like the sun overhead as we cross into Manhattan.

"If this is a concession from you, it's a really shitty one," I tell him. "Thanks to that wedding photo, I'm now as unwelcome in this city as you are."

"Pariahs in matrimony," he murmurs.

"Who was that man at the wedding?" I blurt out as we're driving up 9th Avenue.

"One of my security guards."

"No, the short guy. The limp lettuce in between the meathead sandwich. Looked like a rat in a suit."

"Rodents *are* the most loyal and dedicated animals."

He's mocking me now. I can tell.

"Oh, forget it," I say, as he pulls up to the curb a hundred feet from my apartment block. "What are you doing now?"

"*I'm* not doing anything. You, however, are going to get your things." He cuts the engine and yanks at his silver necktie so as to loosen his top button. At the same time, he reaches for his gun and rests it on his lap. "You have thirty minutes, and then you won't be returning."

That's what he thinks. One week. Seven days. One-hundred and sixty-eight hours, and I definitely will be.

I go to grab the door handle and feel his heavy hand on my thigh.

"Remember the rules, Thalia. One week of happy, fake-smile honeymooning, or my half of the arrangement is off. You know damn well your sister isn't going to be the only member of the Santiago Cartel in your apartment right now. Fake it, or fuck it up. ¿*Comprendes*?"

Without answering, I push his hand away and exit the car, catching sight of myself in the window. *God, I look ridiculous.*

Ripping off the black bustier, I chuck it back on the seat, and lose the pigtails. I go to slam the door and catch him staring at me.

"Cartel pervert," I hiss, flicking him my middle finger.

"*Your* cartel pervert," he corrects coldly. "Signed, sealed, delivered."

"Not in this lifetime," I mutter under my breath as I cross the street, aware of his dark gaze on me constantly.

Entering the building, I head straight for the elevator. I'm so nervous I could die. *Is Ella ever going to speak to me again? Is Edier going to line me up against a wall and shoot me?* My knees keep doing a weird shaking thing, so I kick my high heels off to give me a shot at some semblance of balance. I'm still frantically scrubbing off the last of the crazy makeup as the elevator doors slide open.

Scooping up my heels, I go to exit, and then freeze. Two of the most lethal men in New York are leaning against the far wall, waiting for me. From their stiff stances and sour expressions, I'm guessing this isn't a friendly fly-by. Sam looks like I just took his Bugatti for a test-drive and hit every street light post from here to Central Park, while Edier's face is as impenetrable as his father's these days, but his brown eyes are dancing with rage.

That's when I know the next thirty minutes are going to be the longest of my life.

"What the *fuck* have you done, Thalia?" Sam roars, leaping away from the wall to slam his hand across the closing doors. "You just took this war to the next level."

Edier pulls him back again as I shrink against the carriage wall. "Leave it," he murmurs, authoritative as always. "She'll explain herself when she's ready."

"Damn right, she will." Taking a step back, Sam flings open my apartment door for me. "Get inside and take that stupid dress off. You look like a clown."

"A clown, huh?" For a second, I'm so angry, I can't speak. "Try walking a mile in these, Sam Sanders." I surge forward to shake my Louboutins in his handsome face. "Believe me when I say you'd break your fucking ankles before you hit the sidewalk."

"Do you have any idea how much trouble you've caused?"

"Why don't I take an extra-long shower, and then you can tell me all about it?"

His gaze dips to what's left of my wedding dress again. "You can wash all you want, but you'll still stink of Carrera."

"Tell that to your dick after you screwed his sister last year."

"Cut it out," Edier snarls at the both of us. "Don't let that Carrera bastard divide us any more than he has already."

That's when it hits me. The weight of this bad blood was always going to drown us, but standing here in this hallway with two boys I used to steal cars with, for the first time I can feel our heads slipping under.

We're all connected now, whether we want to be or not—Santi, me, Edier, Ella, Sam, Lola... It's a generational fuck-up, like a computer glitch in our matrix. We're programmed to hate each other for as long as our fathers tell us to, no matter the pain, the anguish, the violence...

I glance down at my wedding ring, and catch Sam doing the same.

Cursing under his breath, he stalks off down the hallway, and for a fleeting moment I wonder if he knows that Lola was shot the other day. I don't know the details of what went down between them, but it was enough to turn the most popular boy on Rutgers campus into a killing machine.

"Are you going to take aim at me, too?" I ask Edier warily.

He regards me for a moment, all six-foot-two inches of cool self-assurance. No one else would dare provoke him like this and expect to get away with it.

Ella and I have special decompensation, though. Or Ella does... I think my status got revoked a couple of hours ago.

"Jesus, Thalia, why did you do it?" he says, shaking his head at me. "You have a problem in this city, you come to me?"

The disappointment in his voice kills me more than his words.

Shame turns to accusation.

"Did you guys shoot up Legado last night?"

"What the fuck are you talking about?"

Even Sam stops and turns at this.

"He told me, Edier."

"And you believed him?"

"Just tell me it isn't true..."

"You heard what he wanted you to hear." He catches Sam's eye over my shoulder and mouths a name at him, but he says it so fast I don't have a chance to lip read.

"So, you're saying you *didn't* order it?"

"I'm saying that Santi Carrera has an agenda, and it doesn't include giving a damn about you, whatever you might think." Edier jerks his head toward the open door. "Time to face the music. He's been waiting up most of the night for you."

I bet he has.

Assuming he means Reece, I'm dragging my guilt behind me as I enter the apartment. He's been good to me over the years, and I've gone and thrown it in his face. My father won't be happy either, so that'll necessitate a dreaded phone call to deflect *that* bullet. I'm going to need to do some serious groveling to make this right.

My bare feet sound like sighs on the mahogany floorboards. I'm right outside the living room when a familiar rich scent wraps itself around my throat, making me stop dead—my heart exploding in my chest.

It can't be...

And then I watch in horror as his presence fills the doorway—a man far taller and broader than Reece Costello, with a firestorm raging in his brooding black eyes, and his expression as dark as the shadows stretching out behind him.

Age hasn't softened him. If anything, it's made him sharper, harder... Deadlier.

The only man in the world who scares me more than Santi Carrera.

The shoes in my hand clatter to the floor.

"Hello, *papá*," I whisper.

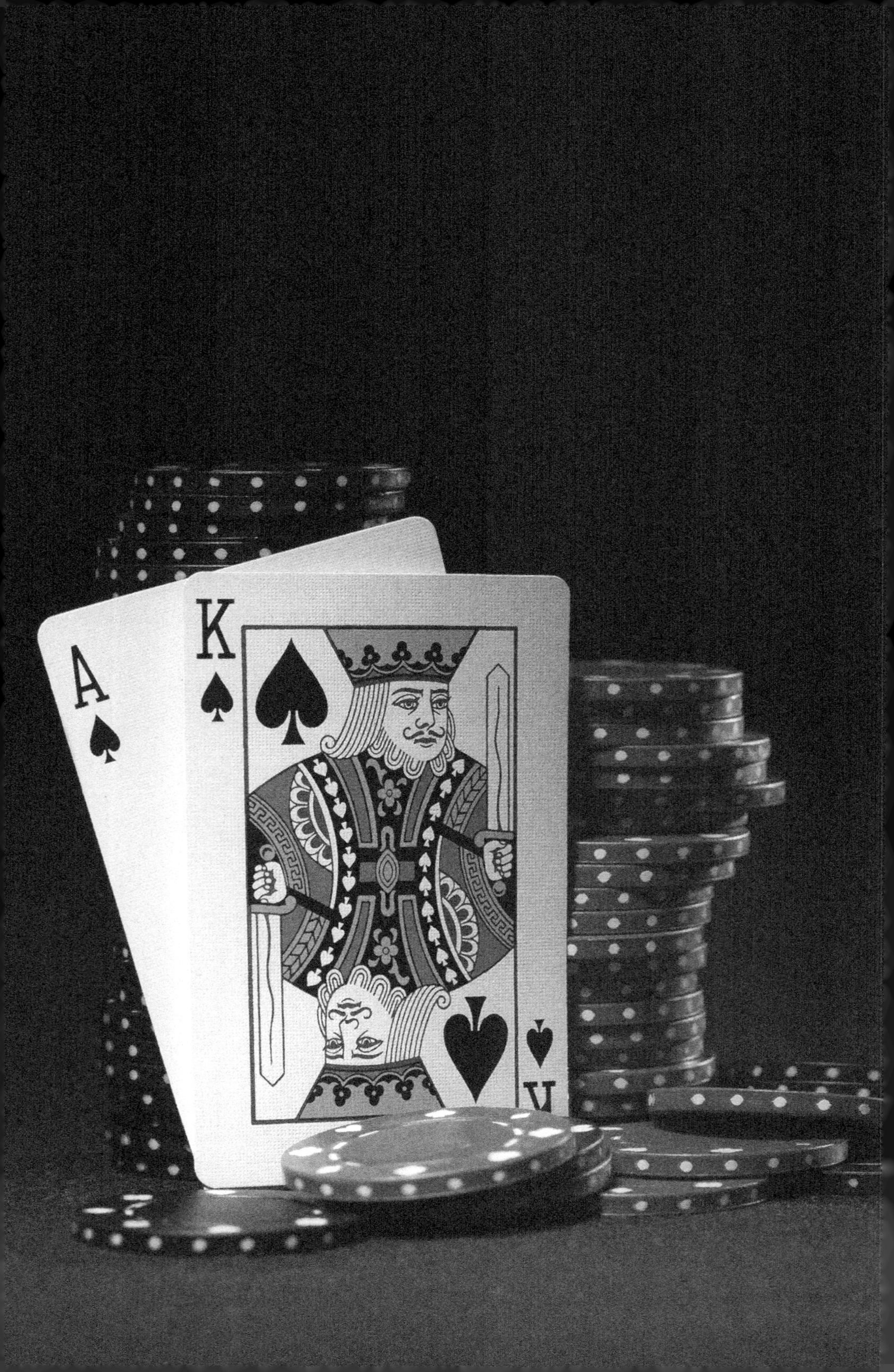

CHAPTER
Seventeen

THALIA

There's that silence again… That long, painful precursor to hell.

It takes me back to a snowy night ten years ago, sitting in a stolen car outside an abandoned church, waiting for something to happen and knowing I wouldn't like it when it did. That was the night I first heard the name "Carrera"—the night I first learned anything about this war.

Who double-crossed who first doesn't matter anymore. All I know is a tentative truce became a bloodbath, and it hasn't stopped splashing over the sides ever since.

Through the years, there have been more bullets fired, deals undercut, lives lost… Like my knight in the snow predicted, it passed down to the next generation, and now I've been forced to marry into it and face the consequences.

My father doesn't comment on my appearance at first, but the downturn of his mouth does all the talking for him.

"Thalia," he greets, in that drawling, mocking intonation of his that delivers kill orders in the same way he used to tell me bedtime stories. "Nice of you to join us."

"I can explain…"

"I can't wait to hear it."

"About the dress…"

"No need to start there, *mija*," he says, lifting his eyebrows at me. "Clearly,

Santi Carrera isn't picky about what the fuck his vengeance looks like."

And so it begins...

"Don't. Just don't." Brushing past him, I flop down on the nearest couch and pull a cushion to my stomach for protection.

"Don't, what?"

"Don't... *this*." I gesture at his casually deceptive stance. He's leaning against the doorframe with his arms folded, but I'm not fooled for a second. He's so unapologetic about everything. It's his way, or he's blowing up the highway. There's a good reason why I never went to him about Bardi's footage in the first instance. The situation needed tact, and he only knows how to stomp.

"You mean I'm not allowed to congratulate my youngest daughter on her wedding?"

His tone could flay skin... Which is something he'd know all about.

"Next, you'll be telling me you're in love with him."

"I *am* in love with him," I lie. "It's been a perfect day."

"I see."

"Shame *mamá* couldn't say the same about her own wedding day."

My cheap shot chills the atmosphere in the room to minus figures. Even in his fifties, *papá* carries a gravitas that reduces grown men and wayward daughters to trembling, self-doubting heaps.

"Don't try and understand it, *mija*," he warns. "Just know that it brought light into a dark place."

"You kidnapped her and forced her to marry you!"

"And she's so *fucking* unhappy about it."

There's a tic working hard in his jaw.

That's another thing about my father. He doesn't like to be questioned about anything. He parked his conscience a long time ago and lost the valet ticket on purpose.

"I don't think much of your husband's deference to his new family." Taking a step toward me, he tosses his phone onto my lap. "Is this meant to be some kind of reverse dowry with spikes?"

Glancing sideways, I suddenly see why Sam was so angry.

"What happened?" I whisper, knowing how much he loved that place. The Barfly was Sam's favorite property in Manhattan—the bar his father gave to him on his twenty-first birthday.

136

It's nothing but burning embers and ash now.

"Unsubstantiated kitchen fire." He takes back the cell with a vicious swipe. "I'll give you one guess whose lieutenant was caught standing by the oven with a box of matches in his hand."

"Maybe you shouldn't have provoked him by graffitiing your scorpion all over his casino."

"Maybe you should have stayed the right side of the fucking river," he snarls, losing his temper. "This madness ends today, Thalia. You've had your fun. You've caught my attention—"

"Your *attention*?" I jump to my feet, the sharp claws of indignation slashing at my self-control. "I've been ignoring your calls for the past month because I didn't *want* your damn attention! I needed to fly—without getting my wings pulled off for once."

"Straight into Carrera's net?" He shakes his head in disgust. "I gave you too much freedom, *mija*. I never should have let you come to New York."

"I never expected you to like this. I know how you feel about—"

"I've never much cared for the word 'like'," he muses darkly. "It doesn't describe 'premeditated murder' in the way it should."

"You're unbelievable!" I cry. "Stomp, stomp, stomp, all over everything. I'm done talking about this. You can see yourself out."

I'm halfway to the door when he starts speaking again.

"There's a bag packed and ready on your bed, *mija*... I suggest you choose wisely."

"Choose what?" I say, turning back slowly, knowing that any option he gives me is going to be a one-way ticket to heartache.

"You can either leave with me today and return to the island, or the sniper I have trained on the black Aston Martin halfway down the street outside gets the call he's been waiting for." He holds up his cell to show me he's not messing around. *Not that I'd ever accuse him of that.* "Santi Carrera is a vindictive shit... Yesterday, he sent an envelope of fake documents to Rick Sanders's office which showed him rigging ballet boxes. It took ten million dollars to make it go away."

"How do you know they were fake?" I mutter defiantly. "Uncle Rick doesn't strike me as the kind of man who always plays by the rules."

"That's beside the point," he snaps. "Carrera will be reaping the repercussions of that little stunt very soon. Rick's son is seeing to it personally."

I don't like the sound of that. I know what Sam's like. Revenge is his favorite pastime.

I feel tired suddenly. So very tired.

"How's *mamá*?" I ask, missing her quiet diplomacy, now more than ever. She's the only person who can calm *papá* when he's a raging inferno of malevolence like this.

"Pissed... Hurt." His eyes narrow, and my stomach drops. When Ella and I were young we were always in the worst kinds of trouble with him when we did something to upset her. "Same as your sister, in fact."

Ella.

I've been trying to reach her for a whole day now, and she's still not picking up. I glance around for her stuff, but there's no laptop, no speaker system, none of her clothes are draped over the back of the couches...

"Where is she?" I say, feeling panicky.

"It's not safe for her in New York... Not now that her sister has lit a bomb under a box of fireworks."

"But she has her finals next month! She won't graduate!"

Oh God, it's like Bardi just demanded another half a million from me.

"And who's fault is that?"

"Don't do this." I reach out to touch his arm—to halve some of the distance between us for Ella's sake. "Let her come back. I'll speak to Santi. Call a truce with Valentin Carrera before it wrecks all our lives."

"Have you lost your fucking mind?" he roars. "The sooner you come to your senses and hire a fucking divorce lawyer, the sooner she can return and graduate."

Is there anyone not trying to blackmail these days?

"Where's Reece?"

"Re-deployed," he says viciously.

"Did you hurt him?"

He smiles, but there's no warmth to it. "I might have shown him and his team my displeasure for letting you fall amongst the sharks of Atlantic City. Your security won't be so lax in the future."

The bars of my prison cell start looming again.

"What does the son have over you, Thalia?"

I swallow quickly. "I have no idea what you're talking about."

"I want the truth, *mija*, so I can ram it into his chest before I rip his heart out."

Shit. Shit. Shit. I knew he'd see through this wedding in a hot minute, but I refuse to ruin my sister's life any more than I already have.

"Don't bullshit me, *mija*..."

"The marriage is real," I croak. "My life is in New Jersey now. With him."

"Shame." His word sounds like a bullet hitting bone. In a daze, I watch him lift the phone to his ear. "Just know that I never wanted this life for you, Thalia. You sought this out yourself."

"You're wrong," I say, shaking my head. "You had this life and all its petty vengeances wrapped around me like a straitjacket from the day I was born. I couldn't escape it, even if I tried, so I had to adapt. I learned to live with it... To survive. And now you want to punish me for it."

"Jackson," he snaps into the mouthpiece. "One minute."

"One minute to what?" I demand.

He gives me that cold smile again. "One minute before the Aston Martin receives a new paint job."

"Please don't shoot him," I whisper. "For me."

If Carrera dies. I won't get the money I need. Bardi wins.

That tic starts jumping in his jaw again.

Without waiting for his response, I turn and run.

With my overnight bag in my hand, I can feel his dark shadow moving up behind me as I reach the front door.

"You walk out like this, Thalia Santiago, and you'll be a fucking widow by nightfall," he warns.

I close my eyes as something jagged rips strips inside of me.

"I'm walking out of here as Thalia Carrera," I tell him softly—*regretfully*. "And she makes her own decisions now."

Who knew heartbreak could be such a physical thing? There's pain in every part of my body as I hit the elevator call button.

Spilling out into the lobby, I make it all the way to Santi's car before the first bullet is ricocheting off the sidewalk behind me.

I freeze, too shocked to move.

Is my father shooting *at me?*

"Thalia!" Santi erupts from the Aston Martin with his gun in his hand as another bullet strays too close to my head. "Get in the car!"

I watch in a daze as he fires five rounds in the direction of my apartment block, the squeals and gasps of passers-by resonating all around. As they crouch for cover in shop doorways, another stray bullet hits the sidewalk, and I'm throwing myself into the Aston Martin. A beat later, a string of returning fire is shattering the back windshield.

"Keep your head down," Santi orders, swinging in beside me. He's cool as ice, but his grip on his gun is a white-knuckled ride. "I take it our happy news didn't go over so well?"

Not waiting for my reply, he spins the car into a savage one-eighty in the middle of the street. With steam still rising up from the tires, he fires three more shots as a final goodbye before his foot hits the gas and I'm being flung backward into my seat.

He's running red lights like he's on a suicide mission, weaving in and out of yellow cabs to put as much distance between us and 9th Avenue as possible.

As for me, I'm too numb to cry. For all the angry words exchanged, for all the resentment and frustration I've felt toward him and this life he brought me into, deep down I've always loved my father.

I thought we were unbreakable.

But the way he looked at me back there... The fury in his voice. The betrayal he heard in my words... I know there's no coming back from that.

I didn't count the cards right.

There were too many shots fired.

I've gambled and lost everything to a man who flat-out despises me.

CHAPTER Eighteen

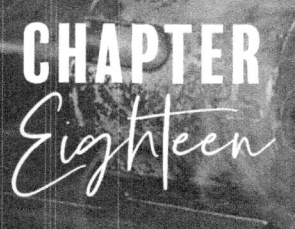

SANTI

I keep the pedal to the floor until we're on the Atlantic City Expressway. It's hard to let up when there's more octane than blood pumping through my veins.

The back windshield is completely blown out. The only thing circulating in my Aston Martin is air. No conversation. No explanation. We haven't spoken since 9th Avenue, but she doesn't like the silence. It's there in the way she's hugging her arms across her body and gazing out of the window, the breeze from the blown-out window wrapping her long hair around her neck like a black silk noose.

She looks trapped.

She is trapped.

But what to do with my prey now?

As a wedding gift, her father just pulled the pin on an invisible grenade and tossed it into the backseat. It's as if she's shielding herself, waiting for me to explode.

Not today, mi amada.

Controlled composure elicits a stronger reaction than rage. If I push her hard enough, maybe she'll start opening up to me. Maybe we'll finally have a fucking conversation in this marriage, instead of trading insults with one another.

As I pull the car into Legado's underground parking garage, the overhead lighting slices through the shattered windshield, casting a serrated prism across

Thalia's face.

How appropriate: shadow and light, twisted together in a forbidden union.

Killing the ignition, I sit there for a moment, absorbing the tension—growing stronger from it... Harder.

Thalia opens her mouth to say something and then quickly snaps it shut again.

If it's an apology, she can save it. I'm pissed—and it's not just because Santiago opened fire and destroyed my car. I would have been more suspicious if he *hadn't* tried to take a shot at me.

It's because he took a shot at *her*.

I keep seeing her face when the first bullet hit the sidewalk. It shattered something inside Thalia, more than when she was standing at an altar promising to honor and obey with her fingers crossed behind her back. She doesn't approve of her father's business practices any more than she approves of mine, but she still loves him. What happened back there was a violent turning point in a father-daughter relationship.

I should be fucking ecstatic about it. I should be swimming in *Dom Pérignon*. Wasn't this my plan all along? To break that family apart, piece by piece? The deepest and most permanent cuts are always through the heart.

But I'm not.

Why the fuck am I not?

I glance across at her again. She's chewing on her fingernail, head bowed. I can't shake the feeling that we're veering off course toward an unknown destination.

The tension finally snaps. She tries to open the passenger's side door, her small hands fighting with a handle that won't relent. Giving up, she lets out a frustrated sigh.

"Unlock it... *Please.*"

"I will when you tell me what happened back there."

I follow the glide in her throat as she swallows, wondering what her skin would taste like if I followed that same route with my tongue.

"Someone fired a bullet that came within a couple inches of ruining my dress." She glances at me, her lips tipping into a reluctant smile as she motions at the already-wrecked garment. "Oh wait... Too late."

"I'm serious, Thalia."

"What would you like me to say? That my father was there waiting for me? That when his tough love tactics didn't work, he resorted to more drastic measures?" I can hear the vulnerability seeping through her cracks of confusion. "God, you must be loving this!"

Far from it.

"That's not what—"

"Those bullets were meant for *you*." Her tone is sharp, but the false certainty woven through it is all too familiar. Children of criminals are so fucking proficient at lying, especially to themselves.

Shooting me a dirty look, she starts beating her fist against the passenger's side window. "Unlock this door, Santi. You got what you wanted. At least let me go inside so I can lie down, close my eyes, and pretend it's all a bad dream."

Offering comfort isn't a part of my skill set. I'm usually the one inflicting pain, not soothing it, but something compels me to reach over and tilt her face toward me as gently as possible.

"Let's just say the celebration is on hold."

"Why, because you feel *guilty*?" She jerks her head away, letting out a scornful laugh. "Can a Carrera even spell that word?"

She's lashing out with good reason, but I'm not a reasonable man. She can insult me all she wants, but never my family.

That's what I get for giving a shit.

Unlocking the doors, I climb out of the Aston Martin, slamming mine behind me. I make it all the way to the elevator before I feel her fingers close around my bicep. Just that small impact is enough to cause a short circuit in my brain.

Fire.

Her skin feels like fire burning mine.

Before I can react, she curses and quickly releases her hold. "Shit, I forgot… No touching."

Silently, I reach for the call button, her shallow breaths falling into rhythm with the chaotic beat of my heart.

What the fuck is happening to me today?

"Look, I'm sorry. That was disrespectful. All the stuff I said about guilt and the Carreras? Well, it's not like I have the moral ground to be throwing stones…" Her voice trails off again, and she lets out a sigh. "Can we call a temporary truce and go back to hating each other tomorrow?"

I give her a curt nod in response.

"I'm sorry about your Aston Martin, too." She steps into the carriage beside me, looking even more like a doll without her shoes on. "Though my *mamá* always told me that big, expensive cars were an overcompensation for something."

I catch a small smile twitching at the corners of her mouth.

"I hear your father has quite the collection."

That same smile disappears, and I'm suddenly angry at myself for mentioning him.

"Still," she says, her tone stilted once again. "It's a good thing he hit the side of the car rather than the side of your head."

I arch an eyebrow. "I'm surprised to hear you say that, *mi amada*. You've already stated your preference for a black veil over white lace. I assumed being given the opportunity to wear it would've been the perfect ending to your day."

She drops her eyes to the floor. "Not if I'm fifty thousand dollars short."

Because it's all about the money, right?

And revenge... Let's not forget that beautiful, toxic cherry.

My phone beeps. Glancing down, I find more missed calls from my father than I can count and a short message from Monroe.

The bill passed.

I type out a quick reply.

Excellent. Meeting at Legado 10 a.m. tomorrow.

It seems Rick Sanders can check off another box on his corrupt political scorecard—a prepaid victory. Not only has he already bought his constituents' votes, but he's now purchased the rights to his fellow senators' opinions. A couple more insignificant steps and the bright lights of Vegas will shine on the Big Apple once more.

New York is reopened for business.

And mine for the taking.

When we reach the top floor, I hang back to allow Thalia to exit first. She turns in mild surprise when I don't follow her out.

"Business," I murmur, sliding my hands into my pockets and reaching for the button again.

As they close, I swear I see a flicker of frustration on her face.

Dropping one floor to Lola's apartment, I'm relieved to find my sister fast asleep.

Even under sedation, she's a creature of habit. Ever since she was a little girl, she's slept in the fetal position. *Autodefensa mental*, my father calls it. Defense mechanism. He claims it's due to the residual trauma still floating around in her subconscious from almost dying in utero, thanks to another of Santiago's bullets.

He got real philosophical after my mother's accident. There was a lot of talk about fate and scars and destiny. He started to believe that all sins committed were reenacted over and over on a continual loop, in a realm between dreams and reality. Like reincarnation, only no one ever learns. No one repents. All that's waiting there is a never-ending punishment.

The sins of the father are to be laid upon the children.

Like a war that stains a new generation, and the next, and the next...

For the second time, I brush the hair away from my sister's face.

"Autodefensa mental..." he would say. *"Even in sleep, the soul remembers."*

Hopefully, she won't remember being drugged by her own brother. I'm guessing I have another four or five hours left before the narcotics wear off and she comes looking for answers.

Hopefully, by then, I'll have some.

A shrill ring fills the quiet room, causing Lola to stir.

"Shit," I mutter, reaching for my phone again. Silencing the ringer, I catch a glimpse of the coded number flashing on the screen.

It's another hand-held warning flare. His twentieth today...

I should answer it.

Instead, I slide it back into my pocket. There will be repercussions for ignoring Valentin Carrera, but I'm in no mood to deal with my father right now. He's another who'll want answers I can't give.

Leaving Lola to sleep, I make my way downstairs to the Platinum Bar where RJ is waiting for me. There's a glass of whiskey in hand and judgment scrawled across his face.

"Don't start," I warn, unbuttoning my jacket before collapsing into one of the oversized chairs across from him.

"Wasn't planning on it." Raising his palm in peace, he nods toward another drink placed on the table between us.

I can't pick it up fast enough. *Añejo* tequila. Straight and strong. I'll need more than one after today.

"What has our Italian guest down below been up to?" I ask.

"Shitting his pants, mostly."

I laugh for the first time in what seems like forever. *What a dickless fuck.* Not that I expected much more out of a man like Marco Bardi. "So, am I to assume he's sung like the piece of shit canary he is?"

"Not exactly," he grumbles. "He keeps yapping about irrelevant stuff nobody gives a fuck about." The rest of his sentence is drowned in fifteen-year-old Glenfiddich Special Reserve.

Damn it. I assumed that *idiota* would have broken by now.

"Do we have the tape?"

He nods. "Original, plus seven copies and a plate of lasagna." At my raised eyebrow, he adds, "*Nonna* Bardi was more than cooperative to help her little '*patatino*'... And insisted on thanking us with frozen casseroles."

I chuckle at the nickname. Her *little potato* has become a huge liability.

"*Muy bien...*" I say, lifting my glass in honor of a job well done.

RJ frowns, hesitation playing across his face as he pulls his cell from his pocket. A long pause extends between us as he stares down at it.

"Spit it out, RJ. I'm too tired for mind games."

"I watched it," he says slowly.

"So?"

"I think you should, too."

I shake my head. "Hard pass. Not into homemade porn, thanks."

"I'm serious." He lowers his gaze to his phone, his heavy tone dragging mine along for the ride. "You need to see this."

My gut churns as I lean forward and take it. The video is already queued up. I know it's the sister on that tape, not Thalia, but something inside me is warning me not to look.

Autodefensa mental.

Ignoring it, I press play, and quickly see what RJ's so twisted up about.

There's a naked girl passed out on a bed. Not just any girl—one with the same heart-shaped face as Thalia's and the same luscious black hair spilling all around her face like a dark promise.

The same way I've imagined the wife I claim to hate would look lying underneath me.

We watch in silence as the camera pans this way and that, covering every inch of her tan skin, before Bardi is roughly pushing her onto her front and continuing. When he turns her back and starts spreading her legs, I hit the pause button and toss the phone across the table.

"I've seen enough. What the fuck is he doing to her? Measuring her for a new dress?"

"It's an audition."

"A *what*?"

"For a sex trafficking auction, I believe."

The air comes shooting out of my lungs. For all of my family's sins, flesh trade is a barter we don't tolerate. A few thousand kilos of cocaine couldn't care less how it's cut or defiled, but a human being—a woman whose only crime was to exist—never recovers. Sex slave trade scars are permanent.

Provided she survives the bite of its blade.

"*¡Hijo de su puta madre!*" I bite out between clenched teeth. "He never had any intention of handing this over to Thalia."

RJ shakes his head. "Can we kill him now?" There's murder in his voice. The kind that would give even the hardest of criminals pause.

"Not until he's served his purpose."

He grunts his displeasure. "What's the plan, then?"

"To win."

"Santi…"

"This isn't up for debate, Harcourt." In truth, I need time to formulate a new one after everything that's come to light tonight. "Look into the group behind this auction. See what you can find out."

"There's one other thing," RJ notes, draining his glass. "Bardi is still claiming to have no knowledge of what happened here the other night."

"I think it's pretty obvious he's not working for Santiago if he's using a skin flick of one daughter in an attempt to blackmail the other." Raking a frustrated hand through my hair, I dislodge the last remaining remnants of its slicked back style. None of the pieces of this puzzle are fitting together. They're all different sizes and shapes with entirely separate pictures on the front.

"Should we put the bar buyout on hold for a while?"

"No." If anything, I want control of New York even more. "I have another meeting with Monroe scheduled for tomorrow morning."

"In the interim, this should cheer you up." RJ flicks through his phone again and holds out a photo of the burning wreckage that used to be Sam Sanders's flagship bar—The Barfly.

"Tell Rocco he did well," I say with a grim smile. "Send him an extra grand as a bonus."

Is this what finally made Santiago snap and fire a "Daddy gunfire special" at his youngest daughter?

The thought makes my lips flatten in a tight line.

"Thalia has requested to meet with Bardi on Friday night. Speaking of which…" Reaching into the inside pocket of my suit jacket, I pull out the Italian's phone. It's time my new bride receives the answer she's been waiting for.

Happy fucking wedding day, Thalia Carrera.

Draining the last of my tequila, I type out a short text, mentally punching that asshole's face as I hit send.

It's about time. Friday at nine. Don't be late, bitch.

I'm about to pocket the phone when I change my mind and type one final line.

Nice pic of MY money... Next time, send me one with your legs open.

Disgusted, I hit send, and toss the phone back onto the glass table, quickly ordering another drink to dilute my guilt.

RJ lowers his gaze, chuckling as he scans the text. "Are you asking for Marco or for yourself?"

"Fuck off." Swiping the phone off the table, I flip him my middle finger as I rise to my feet to head back upstairs. "I don't touch Colombian pussy... I marry it, and then I ignore it."

CHAPTER Nineteen

SANTI

There's a rock sitting in the pit of my stomach as I prowl the black hallways of my penthouse apartment.

Craving a glass of *Gran Patrón Burdeos Añejo* tequila, I'm irritated as hell when I discover my office bar empty. Striding into the kitchen, thinking dark thoughts about my housekeeper, I'm greeted by the sight of a perfectly rounded ass in a pair of denim cutoffs, with the seams stretching in all the right places.

¡A la verga! I'm going to need something stronger than tequila.

"Can I help you?"

Thalia's head quickly re-emerges from the refrigerator. She straightens and turns with a jerk, her cheeks flushing. "What are you doing here? I thought you were out for the evening." She glances at the door. "Do you want me to stay in my room? It wasn't locked, so I figured—"

"We're married. Do whatever the fuck you want. You know the rules." Leaning over the kitchen island, I crush my elbows onto the cool surface, pretending to ignore the hurt look on her face. This woman is a goddamn guilt machine. It's all I seem to be feeling today.

I'm not telling her I have the tape, though. Bardi is my one bargaining chip—I control him, I control her—and I can do a lot of damage to the Santiago Cartel in a week with Thalia in my corner.

Hell, I already have.

"Does this mean the hunger strike is officially over?" I watch her stirring a saucepan, the fragrant aroma of garlic and tomatoes sweetening the tension between us. "Or will I be sliding into bed later, courtesy of another crème brûlée floor wax?"

The stirring stops. "I thought you said we had separate bedrooms?"

"Relax. It's a joke," I say, watching her shoulders deflate in relief. "What the hell are you eating anyway? I'm sure there's something more refined that my Paris-trained chef has made in the—"

"I like spaghetti and tomato sauce," she says flatly, spinning around to switch the gas off.

"Suit yourself." I flick through the messages on my phone, overlooking another two from my father, all the while stealing more glances at her. She's wearing a loose white T-shirt tucked into the front of her dick-tease shorts. It's molding her small breasts into something far more appetizing than dinner.

She's also looking every minute of nineteen and vulnerable as hell.

"Do you have anything in particular against French cuisine?" I ask her.

"I'm in need of comfort food tonight."

"Autodefensa mental," I mutter.

She cocks her head, her eyebrows drawn tight. "Huh?"

"Defense mechanism," I repeat in English. Holding up the empty box of processed pasta, I give it a shake. "This isn't comfort food, *mi esposa*; it's a heart attack in a bowl." Leaning into the refrigerator myself, I remove a plate of foie gras pâté.

"At least it's not pureed animal livers," she says, frowning at me.

"This is a French luxury. Here, try it." Digging out a fork, I attempt to lift a portion up to her lips, but she backs away with a disgusted look on her face.

"Ugh. No thanks, I'm a vegetarian. And do you know how cruel that stuff is? They force feed the ducks and geese until their liver explodes. Not to mention they keep them in tiny cages."

"Cruel food for a cruel man," I say dryly, adding it to a piece of brioche and popping the entire thing in my mouth.

Shooting me a withering look, she turns back to the stove, rewarding me with another view of those shorts as my dessert. *Comfort food, indeed...*

"The best meals don't always have to come from animals, you know."

"Okay, Miss PETA. Educate me."

"Speak to my sister. She's the vegetarian cook."

I try not to think about the images on the tape. The indignity of those ten minutes has ensured that Bardi will be missing a few fingers before dawn.

As for the rest of him…

I watch her drain the water from the pot and mix in the jar of sauce. "Tell me your sister is a better cook than this."

"She's great. And a brilliant writer too." There's a sudden warmth in her voice. "It's amazing really, after everything she's been…" She stops abruptly, as if her words have strayed somewhere they shouldn't.

"What's amazing?" I push the foie gras to the side. Now I'm craving spaghetti, and I never eat that shit. It's official. My taste buds have ADHD.

Thalia tosses a fork into the pot, her dark eyebrows bunching together again as she stirs. "She's sick… Lupus. She was diagnosed ten years ago. The symptoms come and go, but when she's in a flare, it's…" The stirring stops. "It's really bad."

Bardi just lost a fucking hand now.

"What can they do for her?"

The stirring resumes, this time in a swift and punishing rhythm. "Nothing," she clips, the word swaddled in anger. "There's no cure. Her body will keep attacking itself until one day…"

"I get it," I say stiffly, eyeing my missing bottle of *Gran Patrón Burdeos Añejo* sitting on the counter behind her.

Dios mío, I need a fucking drink…

"Yeah, sure you do," she mutters under her breath.

I don't share kills, and I sure as hell don't share my family's personal shit with my enemy's daughter, but my mouth is playing mutineer tonight.

"My *Tía* Adriana, my father's sister, was born with Type 1 Juvenile Diabetes. When I was a baby, she went into kidney failure."

"Oh God, I'm so sorry." She spins around, her delicate features creased in sympathy. It's such a genuine reaction that it has me reaching around her for the bottle of *Añejo* and pouring myself a large double. "Did she—?"

"Die along with her kidneys?" I finish, causing Thalia to flinch. Shaking my head, I place the bottle back down on the counter. "No. She got herself a brand new one."

"Let me guess… The King of Mexico made his *sicarios* draw straws, and the poor bastard who pulled the short one '*volunteered*' a vital organ."

"No, *he* did."

Fuck off, mouth. Just. Fuck. Off.

"Are you serious?" She looks shocked.

"Blood is blood. Even criminals wear capes once in a while… Speaking of which, when did you learn to count cards?" I take a swig of my drink, not only savoring the burn, but that blush staining her face. *Maybe even more so…*

There's a pause. "Did you have your cameras on me the whole time?"

My lips turn up in a reluctant smirk. "Only when you passed twenty-thousand on the same table. House policy."

"Damn. I knew I should have moved on. It's part of my 101."

"My wife, the master criminal," I mock. "How much have you won from other casinos?"

"Four hundred and forty-five thousand dollars," she says quietly. "In four days."

"*Four days?*" I slam my glass back down on the counter. Shit. I need her on my payroll. Even my best dealers can't move enough shipments of cocaine fast enough for that kind of payout.

"I hate doing it, though. It doesn't feel right."

"Don't tell me I married the only Santiago with a conscience?"

"No, that's my sister. I've done plenty bad." She points to the bottle of *Gran Patrón Burdeos Añejo*. "Can I have one?"

"Be my guest." I unscrew the cap and pour out another double. "Unlike you, I don't mind breaking the law. Serving alcohol to a minor is at the bottom of a long list of offenses in my lifetime." Extending my arm, I offer the glass. She takes it, and then retreats back to her half of the kitchen.

"Did you ever want to do anything different with your life?" she asks as I slip off my jacket and holster, placing my gun on the island between us.

"No," I answer tersely, shooting her look over the rim of my glass. "The penthouse apartment and the millions in the bank are a real kick in the balls at the ripe old age of twenty-two."

I'm the first-born son of Mexico's bloody version of Camelot. *This* is what was expected of me. I never cared to explore other options because to me, there were none. Carrera men honor their families by protecting them and raining hell on anyone who tries to hurt them. My father's name is sacred. Our way of life isn't always honorable, but it's never disloyal.

A man doesn't choose his destiny. It chooses him.

"*Twenty-two?*" she looks surprised. "I figured you were older."

"Looks can be deceiving, *mi amada*... What about you? College? Job?"

"Tried college. Lasted one semester. Wanted a job. Wasn't allowed." She scans my gun again and then frowns. "Violence is like an earthquake, don't you think? There are so many aftershocks and consequences, even if you can't see them. The man you killed might have had a family who now miss him. A trafficked woman might have been lucky enough to escape, but she'll always have severe PTSD."

"I'm more of a survive-the-moment kind of crime lord," I say, leaning back against the counter, intrigued by her strange outburst of metaphorical wisdom—wanting more, even though it's painting me in every shade of asshole.

One thing's for sure. Thalia Santiago is much smarter than I ever perceived her to be. Atlantic City is full of eager women willing to bend to my every command. However, I'm a man who fulfills his needs and then moves on. I have no interest in anything more than a hard fuck. Plus, there's usually nothing between their ears except for air and a wicked tongue. A week ago, that's all it took to satisfy me.

Things change.

My new bride doesn't follow rules, and she sure as hell doesn't fit in any premade box. She's perceptive and brave and cunning—a woman who understands this savage life fate has chosen for us.

Thalia Santiago Carrera stimulates more than my dick. She challenges my mind.

And *that* turns me on more than I could've ever imagined.

Her defiance and intellect, the two attributes that landed her in my clutches, are the same damn things making me want to keep her there.

That's some psychological bullshit I don't care to analyze.

"My friend's mom runs a women's sanctuary in Colombia," she continues, spooning the spaghetti into two bowls, taking it upon herself to assume I want one. "She supports abuse victims and victims of trafficking... I helped out one summer, and I really enjoyed it."

Tactfully done, Thalia. Her so-called "friend" is my number one rival, Edier Grayson. I know all about him and his family's *telenovela*-worthy drama.

I bite my tongue at my own words. *You're one to talk, Carrera.*

Still, it strikes me that our two families have something in common: a shared aversion to human trafficking. Neither of our cartels supports it. In fact, we both actively condemn it.

Thalia clears her throat. "Listen, I'm not saying I'm a saint or anything—"

"Cheating casinos out of half a million this week certainly puts you in a gray area." I yank at my tie and loosen the top button of my white dress shirt.

"Oh, forget it," she scowls, pushing one of the bowls toward me. "Here you go, *dear*."

I'm starting to enjoy her acid tongue. *Maybe a little too much.*

Leaning over the island, she takes a bite from her bowl, and the obscene noise she makes hits me straight in the dick.

"Are you going to tell me what you need the money for?" I ask, mimicking her stance. We're barely a couple of feet away from each other now, but I can smell that sweet jasmine perfume as strongly as if we were skin to skin.

"You have your deal clauses," she says, shaking her head. "This is mine."

Those dark eyes catch me staring.

"Are you 'cartel-perving' on me again?"

"Can't 'perve' on someone you hate."

Her fork clatters back to her bowl. "This is officially the worst week of my life," she mutters, "and there are still six more days to go."

As far as she knows... "You'll live."

"I need to breathe, Santi," she pleads. "Can't you at least try giving me an inch?"

I flash a salacious smile. "I'd give you all ten, but I doubt you could handle them."

"God, you're such an arrogant..." The next thing I know, I'm wearing a fistful of spaghetti—the tomato sauce spreading like blood stains all over my Tom Ford dress shirt.

Neither of us speaks until the spaghetti finally loses its traction on the eight-hundred-dollar material and hits the tiles by my feet with a *splat.*

"You really shouldn't have done that," I say slowly.

Thalia's dark eyes sparkle with triumph. "Why? What are you going to do about it? Force me to marry you? Too late, you already—"

She shuts up pretty fucking quick when a fistful of my own spaghetti hits the front of her white T-shirt.

"You're a bastard," she hisses.

"And you're a spoiled Colombian *princesa*," I snarl.

"At least when I marry for real, I won't have to blackmail my fiancé up the aisle!"

"You're not going anywhere, *mi amata*," I growl, an unfamiliar emotion rising up inside me as I circle the island to reach her like I'm an animal stalking my next meal. "When this week is over, you'll be begging me for a key to the Carrera castle."

"Stop calling me that! I'm not your *beloved* anything. In fact, when this week is over, you'll be begging me to leave!" She seals the promise with a flick of her middle finger before swiping the lingering strands of spaghetti off her chest—a move that leaves a wet smear across her breasts, turning her T-shirt transparent. I can see the hard outline of her nipples beneath, but it's nowhere nearly as hard as my dick is right now. "I'll never forgive you for what you made me do today!"

"I don't remember asking for your fucking forgiveness!"

"You're a cruel, heartless, murdering—"

"You're running out of words there, *wife*." I crowd her up against the counter, and she shoves both palms into the mess on my chest, freezing as I emit another low growl.

She opens her mouth, and I'm not sure if it's to scream, apologize, or hurl another fucking insult, but my self-control has heard enough. Her warmth, her scent, her spirit... *It's all too damn much.*

Fisting the ends of her long hair, I yank her head back and crash my mouth onto hers before I can talk myself out of it.

I feel her softness turn to stone, and then her fingers become twisting vines in my hair. But when I drive my tongue past her lips...? That's when shit gets really messy.

"Fuck... *Me vuelves loco.*" Hooking my arms underneath her thighs, I hoist her onto the counter and roughly part her legs.

"Say it in English," she gasps out.

"You make me crazy, Thalia. So fucking crazy."

I slide a trail of heat to her breast, feeling her pounding heart beneath my fingertips as she grinds against my dick. "Did you do this on purpose, *pequeña seductora*? Parade around my penthouse in those shorts just to tempt me?"

"No... I.... Oh God..."

"There's no God, here, *mi amada*. He left my life the day your family entered it."

I feel her reaching out to touch me again, so I pin her hands to the counter, resisting the urge to sink my teeth into her pouty lower lip just to taste the flavor of Santiago blood.

"You like to break rules, don't you?" Smirking down at her, I feel her flinch. With just one kiss, she's mine for the taking. "Lift your hips. I want to know if your pussy feels as good as the rest of you."

I catch the beat of her hesitation before she complies, and then I'm ripping denim down her long legs. Dragging her to the edge of the counter, I tug the crotch of her panties to one side and rest my middle finger against the entrance to her soaking-wet pussy.

Wet for me, and only me.

This is wrong.

She's a fucking Santiago.

Less than an hour ago, I was telling RJ, I'd never touch her.

My hate is all twisted up. I feel it more for myself than I do for her right now.

"Beg me to finger fuck you, Thalia Carrera," I demand, looming over her like the devil I am.

"W-what?" Her eyelids flicker open in surprise.

"Beg me, *mi pequeña seductora*."

"Okay then, fuck me," she whispers.

I offer her a smile with the warmth of a sheet of black ice, and then I drive my finger deep inside her, right up to the knuckle.

She opens up wider, letting out a helpless moan as I swipe her needy clit with my thumb.

"Now, beg me to make you come."

As I say it, I start pumping in and out, waiting for her words to become a triumphant melody to my ears.

"No."

I pause, feeling her soft muscles pulling me in deeper. "*No?*"

She's so fucking close already. But if she refuses to submit to me, I'll make us both suffer.

Fisting her hair again, I hold her head prisoner as I slide my finger out of her tight heat and smear her desire for me across her lips.

"W-why did you stop?" she rasps in confusion.

"Because, despite what's written on a piece of paper, you're still a Santiago, Thalia," I murmur, leaning in extra close to deliver my truth. "And if you won't beg for it from a Carrera, then I'm not fucking interested."

Running my tongue across the seam of her mouth, I taste her addictive sweetness before I'm pushing her away.

"Pleasant dreams," I say, turning on my heel and swinging a goddamn hammer into her guilt machine.

For one brief moment, I touched her light. I imagined another version of Camelot.

Then I saw it for what it really was—a beautiful bullet in a spinning chamber.

I lost sight of what's important.

I lost sight of the end game.

I will never lose control like that with her again.

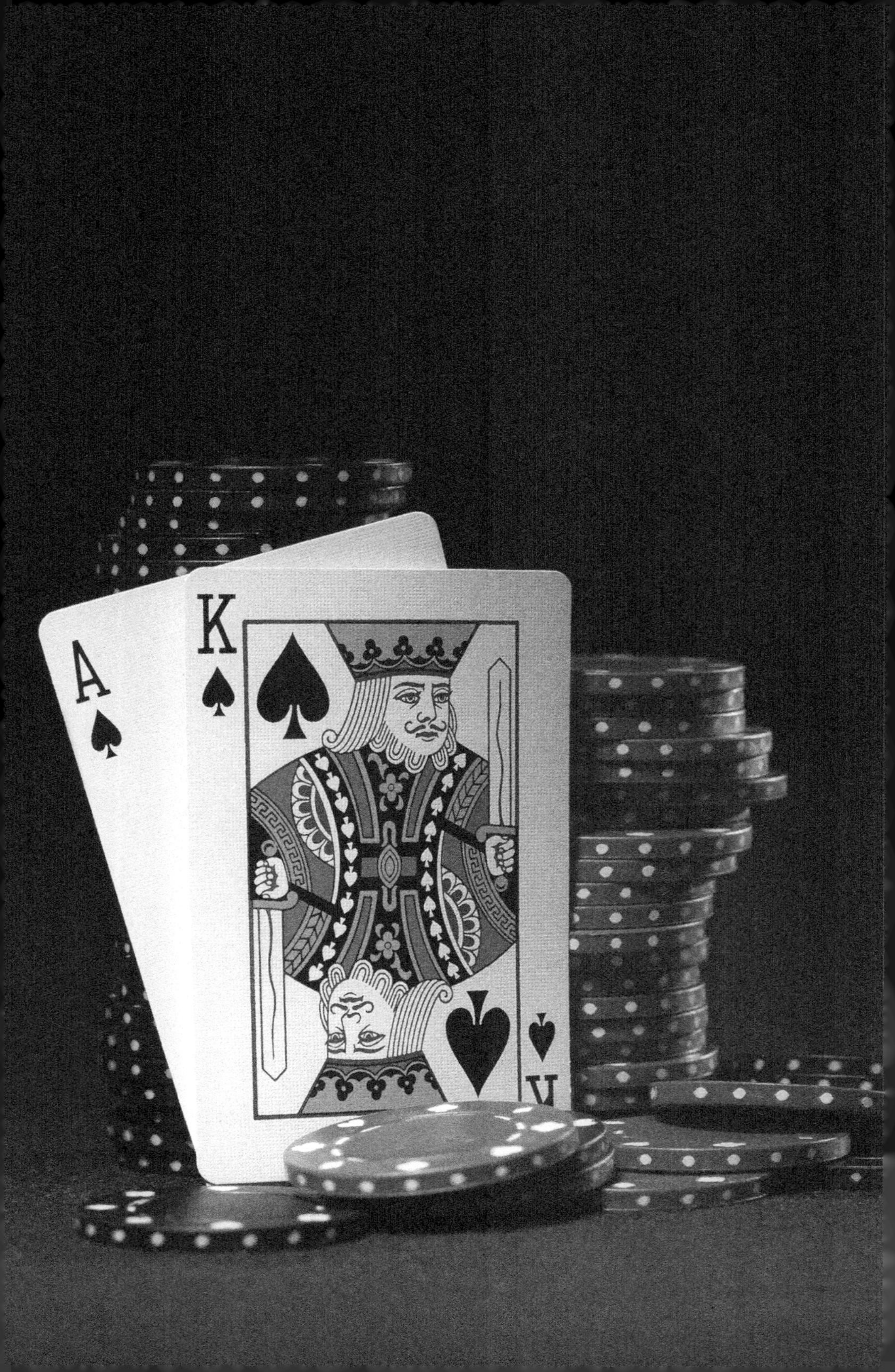

THALIA

Shame is a cloth held tight across your face as you're splashed with cold cruelty. Pride is the air you try desperately to suck back into your lungs, even when it's an elusive prize.

An hour later, I still haven't moved from the kitchen counter. I know what and who I am now. I'm one of Santi Carrera's torture victims, but instead of missing fingers, my scars are on the inside, like survival lines scratched into a prison wall.

The seconds tick.

I think I've forgotten how to move.

From feeling everything with him to feeling nothing at all... I offered up a piece of myself, and what did he do? He crushed it with his fist.

Lesson learned.

Move, Thalia. Move.

Ella uses a meditation app to help her stress levels. I can hear the soothing voice in my head, as my feet hit the tiles, my stiff muscles aching in protest.

Breathe in.

Hold.

Breathe out.

I do this for a couple of minutes, feeling the cloth slowly slipping from my face and my lungs expanding again.

Breathe in. *Bardi finally messaged me back. The meet is confirmed.*

Hold. *In six days, I'll be gone from this place and that man forever.*

Breathe out. *I'll make all of this right somehow. I know I will.*

Placing the discarded bowls in the sink, I set about cleaning the remains of dinner away and tidying up the kitchen. It takes me ages to scrub dried sauce from the countertops and the floor, but once I'm done the place is gleaming, and it's after midnight.

I'm reaching into a cabinet to put the saucepans away, when Santi's housekeeper, Svetlana, comes barreling into the kitchen. She stops dead when she sees me, her gaze dipping to the state of my clothes, and then she's backtracking fast and closing the door as quietly as she can.

"I've cleaned up as best I—"

"Shhh," she whispers fiercely, bringing her finger to her mouth. Grabbing my hand, she pulls me sideways into a pantry. "Are you alright, *zvezda moya*?" Her hands are all over me, patting me down as if searching for bullet holes.

"I'm fine," I say, cringing away. It's weird behavior for someone who's barely even talked to me. Plus, I've had more than enough of being manhandled for one evening. "It's just sauce. I had an accident."

One I won't be repeating anytime soon.

"I meant from earlier," she urges. "The gunshots outside your apartment?"

My mouth drops. "How did you—?"

She pulls me even deeper into the pantry. "I have been asked by a business associate of your father's to deliver a message."

The air comes whooshing out of my lungs again. I should have known his spies would be everywhere.

"What message?"

"He did not fire those bullets at you, *zvezda moya*. He would never, ever harm you."

Tears of relief prick my eyelashes. "But my father had a sniper—"

"He was killed during the shooting. *Señor* Santiago found his body a couple of hours ago."

Even in the dim light of the pantry, I can see the dark circles under her eyes. The lines on her face look like crevasses. She's risking *everything* to tell me this.

"But if it wasn't my father...?"

"He does not know who is behind it yet. All he has is a discarded M27 rifle.

His men are tracing it now." She glances over her shoulder at the closed door. "I must go, *zvezda moya*." *Señor* Carrera would kill me if he knew I was talking to you. He is much more dangerous than you think he is."

"Wait," I hiss again, as she's reaching for the door handle. "Can you deliver a message back to my father for me?"

She nods, her movements jerky and jittery like a frightened mouse.

"Can you ask him to trust me?"

Another nod. She turns to leave again.

"One more thing..." She waits impatiently. "Tell him I'm sorry."

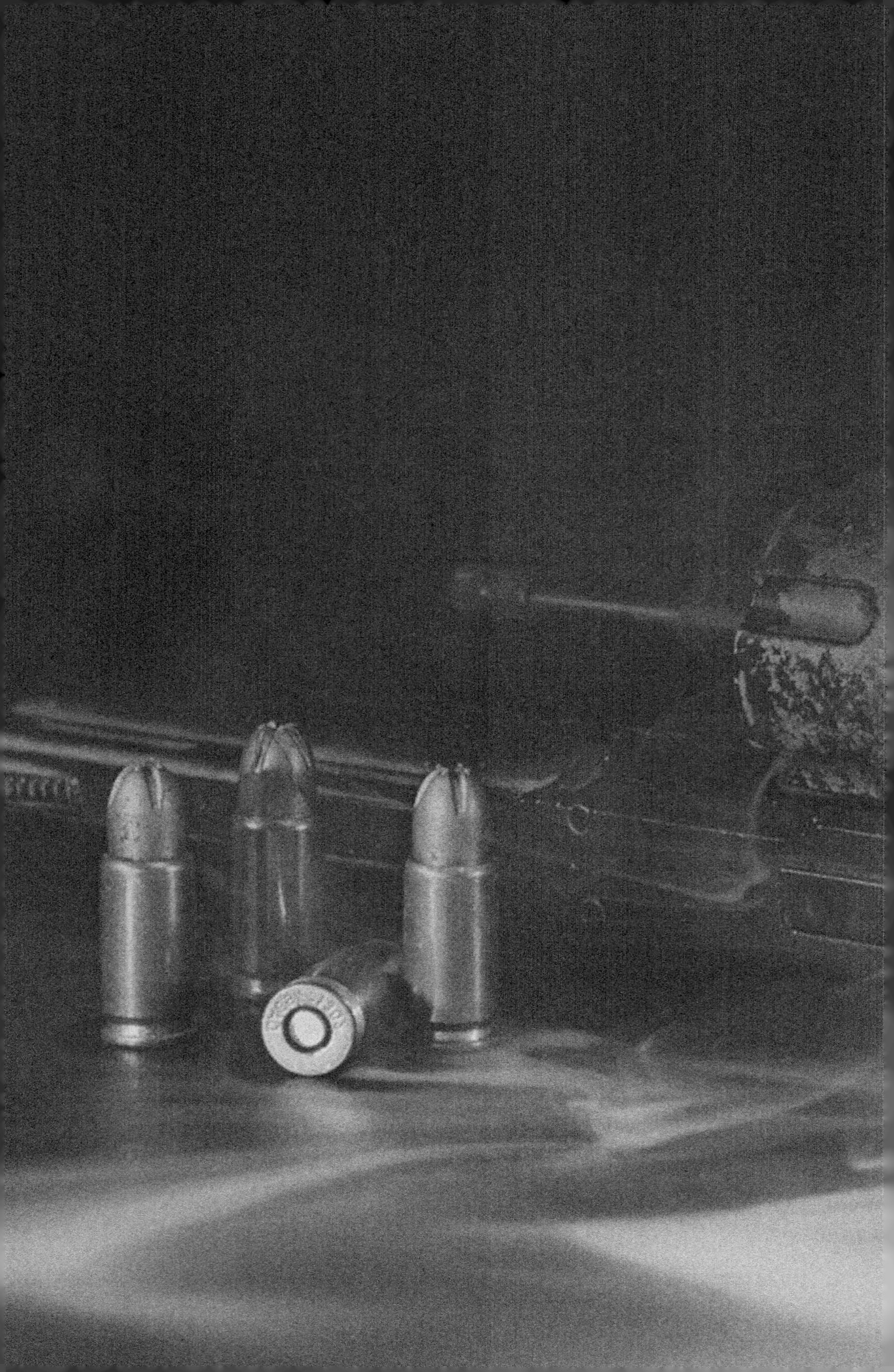

CHAPTER
Twenty-One

SANTI

Thalia Santiago's pussy is going to send me to an early grave.

I slam my bedroom door, unsure if I'm about to put a bullet in the wall or in my own head. I wanted her to beg for me. No, I *needed* her to beg for me.

For my touch… My kiss… My cock.

Please.

One word and I would have devoured her. I would've made her come with my fingers and then sank my tongue into that greedy pussy until she screamed for mercy.

Screamed my fucking name.

I can't decide if I'm more furious with myself for letting it get so far or with her for denying me the pleasure of breaking her. One simple word from those lips, and I would've taken more than her name.

The scent of her arousal still coats my fingers as I rip off my tie. It's an infuriating cocktail of jasmine and pussy juice, causing me to tear at my shirt until the buttons pop off. Shrugging it off my shoulders, I break the zipper on my pants in a desperate attempt to free my swollen cock.

The moment it curls against my stomach, I turn and drive my fist into the wall.

It only hardens my dick even more.

Taking a vicious hold at the root, I pump my hand, my cock enduring a savage punishment meant for her.

The faster I stroke, the harder my fist pounds into the wall.

Pound. Pump. Pound. Pump.

"*Dios mío*, fuck... Thalia..." She's all around me—her face in my head, her scent in the air, her taste on my tongue. As my hips thrust into my hand, I imagine it's her cunt I'm driving into. Her cunt I'm fucking. Her Santiago cunt I'm going to stain with Carrera cum.

It's that image that pushes me over the edge.

My balls tighten as my rhythmic strokes and punches become frenzied and frantic.

Pound. Pump. Pound. Pump. Pound. Pump.

I close my eyes and see her face—cheeks flushed, and eyes glazed with desire. My breath comes hard and ragged. In my fantasy, I'm grabbing the back of her neck and pulling her upright off the counter.

"Look," I rasp, thrusting harder. "Watch the moment I own you, Thalia Carrera."

Then my mind goes blank, and I roar out my release, like I'm spilling every drop of cum inside her.

When the fog clears, I draw air back into my lungs and slowly open my eyes.

My clenched fist is encircled by countless dents in a wall, where a few inches below, a trail of cum slowly drips down the dark paint.

Pushing away, I step back and stare at it—and decide not to clean it up.

Let it stain.

Let it be a reminder to us both.

She's a little girl playing with a box of matches and a can of gasoline.

I forced myself to walk away tonight, but next time...

Next time, I won't have the control.

Next time, I'll fan the flame and toss us both into the fire.

I wake to the sound of incessant ringing.

Rolling over, I land a heavy hand onto my nightstand, searching for the source while managing to knock over a half empty glass of *Añejo*.

"Son of a bitch…" I mutter, swiping my phone into my hand seconds before it swims in tequila. Rolling back over, I glance at the flashing screen and groan.

RJ…

And how the hell is it nine o'clock already? I just closed my eyes.

"This had better be important," I say with a growl into the mouthpiece.

"What are you doing?"

"Having a goddamn tea party." I drop my forearm over my eyes. *Fucking sunlight.* "What do you think? I'm sleeping—or at least I was."

"Get dressed. You need to come to Elizabeth right now."

Elizabeth Marine Terminal—the Carrera owned Newark shipping port used for cocaine import and distribution. Two years ago, when my father handed me New Jersey on a silver platter, I flipped it over and launched an attack on Red Hook Terminal in Brooklyn—Santiago territory.

The Carreras lost eight loyal men, and I lost something it has taken me two years to regain—Valentin Carrera's trust.

It was a hard lesson in reckless ambition.

However, it's this same lesson that allows me to catch the subtle shift in my cousin's tone. He sounds rattled. In twenty years, I've never known RJ Harcourt to be anything but apathetic to the unforgiving reality of cartel life.

I sit up, fully alert. "What's happened?"

"Santiago diverted a hundred kilos of an incoming shipment from Guadalajara. Three dock workers were found nearby with their throats slit."

"Are we sure it was a Santiago hit?" There's a hesitation I don't like. "RJ…?"

"An 'S' was carved into all three chests," he says quietly.

The scorpion calling card.

Memories I've tucked away for eighteen months rise to the surface. Ones of me sitting across from Lola at a pizzeria in New Brunswick, New Jersey, my heart impaled on the jagged image in my hand. A picture she begrudgingly took of the "S" for slut some frat boy cut into her hip after spiking her drink.

Only it wasn't any frat boy. It was Sam Sanders.

And the "S" wasn't for slut. It was for Santiago.

That bastard branded my sister with the same mark I'd found carved into a dead dockhand not twenty-four hours earlier.

Unstable feet carry me toward the shower as my lungs fight for air. "I'm on my way."

Before I can end the call, I hear my name. "Santi?"

I freeze, my hand on the shower door. There's that tone again. That unfamiliar rattled lilt giving conscience to a killer. "What now?"

"The stolen shipment and dead workers were the opening act to their shitshow. There's more."

"How much more?"

There's a tense pause and then, "The main event."

The main event consists of seventeen dead girls—stripped of their clothing and dignity and dumped like garbage in a forty-foot shipping container.

Some as young as ten, some as old as twenty litter a dark, damp mausoleum. Some healthy, others starved to nothing but a layer of skin and bones. Some with painted faces and nails while others wear the gaunt mask of poverty.

Death doesn't discriminate. It just takes.

"Did they arrive this way?" I ask, unable to look away from their faces.

Frozen in fear for eternity.

Nodding, RJ palms the back of his neck. "Rocco got here first. He's the one who discovered the missing shipment and this…" He jerks his head toward the stench, as if unable to stomach another look. "When he opened the container, the bodies had already started to…"

He doesn't finish. We both know what he means.

Decompose.

"That didn't come from Guadalajara," I say.

No one in Mexico would dare to traffick women behind my father's back. His fight to end it resulted in the origins of *La Boda Roja.*

The Red Wedding.

The start of everything.

"No," RJ agrees, sliding his hand up to rub the back of his closely cropped dark hair. "But someone sure as hell wanted it to look that way."

My mind flashes back to a conversation four floors below Legado's marble surface.

"No, wait!" Bardi's tied limbs thrash in the chair. "That's not everything!

If you kill me, you'll never know what he has planned!"

"He?"

"Edier Grayson," he says hesitantly. "That's who shot up your casino, right?"

Son of a bitch...

"Not someone," I grit out as another piece of the puzzle clicks into place. "Grayson."

RJ's thick dark eyebrows shoot up to his hairline. "Not Santiago?"

"Even Santiago wouldn't stain his hands in trafficked blood. The man has left a trail of body parts from here to Romania for over thirty years in revenge for shit like this." At RJ's sideways glance, I tighten my jaw. "Personal reasons."

"You think Grayson has the *cojones* to go against him?"

"*Cojones*? No. Reckless ignorance? Yes." *Even the smallest taste of power can do damage.* "We're the second generation of this war, RJ. You included. Sometimes as it evolves, so do values."

Neither of us speaks again. Partly out of anger, but mostly out of respect. Seventeen innocent girls just became a casualty of a war they knew nothing about. They were someone's daughter... Someone's sister...

And my final straw.

The reverence is shattered by a shrill ring coming from my pocket. I don't bother to pull out my phone and see who's calling.

I know who's on the other line.

"Get a clean-up crew down here immediately, and then see to it that they get a proper burial." With a final glance toward the shipping container, I allow the image to imprint its evil into my mind before turning to walk away.

"Where are you going?" he calls after me.

"To tie up loose ends."

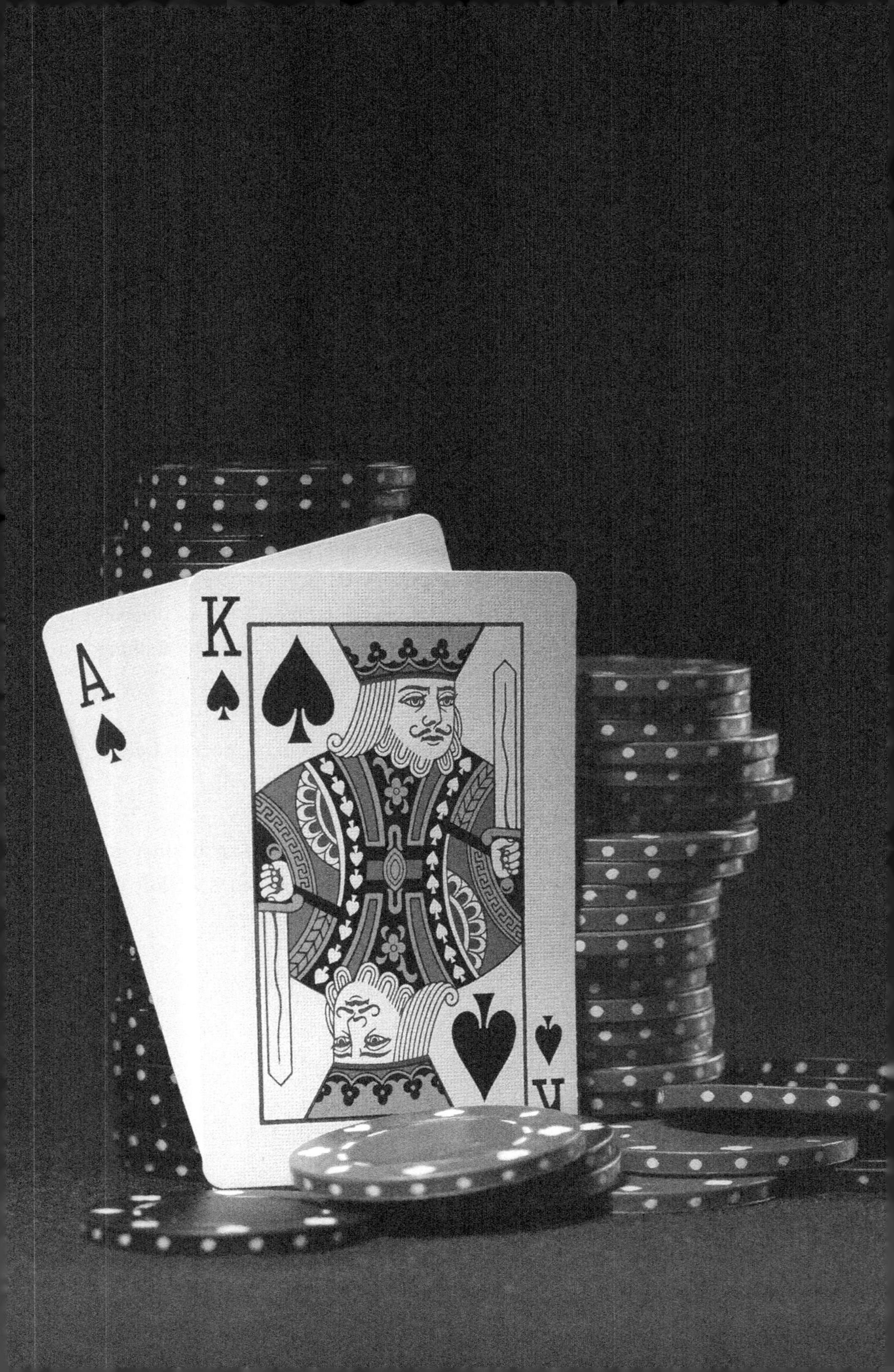

CHAPTER
Twenty-Two

THALIA

I sleep fitfully, tossing and turning in a strange bed with sheets that are cold, stiff, and unwelcoming. The darkness is weakening my defenses, and bad thoughts keep pouring into my head—like how stupid I was to believe that swapping secrets could bridge two worlds.

How I fell for his touch so easily.

I wake up feeling even more angry and confused, with sunlight streaming onto my pillow. Dressing in black skinny jeans, a clean white T-shirt, and my favorite leopard print Chucks, I check the burner phone to see if Ella's called—I've left her this number repeatedly—and groan in frustration when I'm greeted with another blank screen.

I hope she's okay.

I hope she's not too mad at me.

I hope she's looking after herself.

Next, I fire off another message to Bardi. For someone who wants his money so badly, he's being unusually cool about the delay. *More worry. More blind faith.*

I'm tempted to storm into my new husband's office and demand he gives me my own phone back, but when I finally pluck up the courage to do so, the room is empty.

It still smells of him, though: rich, woody, masculine… *Irredeemably cruel.*

Shutting the door behind me, I take in the expensive furniture, the shelves, the bar in the corner with his beloved *Gran Patrón Burdeos Añejo* tequila. He tasted of it last night—mixed with a persuasive invitation and a heavy dash of sin.

Walking over to the bar, I unscrew the lid and take a sip. It's not the most reckless thing I've ever done before breakfast, but it's pretty close.

I take another, the flames of the liquor burning away the memory of Santi Carrera's tongue. I take a third to make sure my mouth is cleaned of him forever, and then I'm emptying the rest of a six-hundred-dollar bottle down the sink and filling it up with water.

That should serve him right for being such a cold-hearted bastard.

You don't get to play with Santiago hearts and expect to celebrate with a drink afterward.

There's still no sign of Santi when I leave his office. The hallways are empty. The kitchen, barren. After the *Añejo* incident, I'm feeling audacious, so I head for the front door, expecting to feel a disapproving hand on my arm at any moment.

It never comes.

Even the blank-eyed security guards blocking the route from his penthouse to the elevator part to let me through.

Exiting on the ground floor, I find myself stepping into a hive of activity. Legado's casino restoration is near completion. A quick peek through the double glass doors reveals a new carpet, new black and gold décor, new pristine-green gaming tables… Santi's gambling gladiatorial arena is close to being back in business, and as I pass by a couple construction workers, I overhear them mentioning how the place is on schedule to reopen on Thursday night.

A wicked thought steals into my head as I return to the lobby. I could slip Santi a couple of Oxy and sneak down here to win the rest of my money while he's passed out and dribbling. But as tempting as it sounds, my plan would necessitate being within ten feet of him, and right now I'd rather stick pins in my eyeballs.

I follow signs for the Platinum Bar. It's another swanky room with high domed ceilings and mirrored walls. Fleetwood Mac is playing softly on the stereo. Ella's favorite. It's a musical dart to the heart.

Five days to go, and then we're all free.

There's a bartender polishing an already-gleaming counter. He glances up and notices me standing in the doorway.

"Can I get you something to drink, Mrs. Carrera?"

That wipes the smile off my face.

"Juice, please," I say sliding onto one of the stools at the bar. *I may as well throw in a mixer with all the Añejo tequila lining my stomach.*

He places a clean coaster and a glass in front of me and then glances up again.

"Mr. Spader," he says, not sounding nearly as enthusiastic with *that* greeting.

"Andrew," comes a thin, reedy voice. "The usual, if you will."

The stool next to me gets pulled out and "unwanted company" parks his slight frame with a grunt.

"Mrs. Carrera," he says, bowing his thinning head.

"That's the second time I've been called that in the last sixty seconds," I muse, taking in his blue suit, thick, black-rimmed glasses, and drawn appearance.

The rat in the suit.

"New names can take a little time to get used to," he says, patting my hand.

His touch is cold and clammy, like a lizard deprived of sunlight.

"New names can also be reversed." I withdraw my hand, resisting the temptation to wipe it on my jeans.

"You're looking very well." His beady gaze lasers in on my chest. "Married life must be agreeing with you."

Who the hell is this guy? He's giving me serious Marco Bardi sleaze vibes.

"I take it Santi hasn't mentioned me?" He frowns as I fold my arms on purpose to nix his view. "How remiss of him when I was invited to your wedding."

"Santi and I have a language barrier," I state bluntly. "He speaks in threats, and I ignore him."

The sarcasm is strong in me today. *I'm blaming the Añejo.*

The man laughs. At least I think it's a laugh. It sounds more like a hyena on speed.

"How amusing... I'm Monroe Spader," he says, as the bartender places a Bloody Mary in front of him. "I'm the gambling commission in this state."

"Ah, so you're one of Santi Carrera's minions?"

"I prefer the term 'business associate'."

"I get the impression you do more than just issue gambling licenses to my husband, Mr. Spader."

He pushes his glasses back up his nose. "I'm afraid I don't know what you mean."

I follow his eyes to my crotch, and then back to my face. It's creepy and evasive, but it's also oddly methodical, like he's committing my vital statistics to memory.

"I'm guessing you've heard the news."

"What news?"

"Senator Sanders passed his bill through the State Senate yesterday. Next stop is the Assembly, and then it lands on the good Governor's desk." He leans in close. "She won't be a problem. Soon, gambling will be legal in New York again. It's going to open up the gates to all sorts of exciting new business ventures."

"Ventures like Carrera-owned casinos, you mean," I say, catching on fast.

The King of Loco strikes again.

It's madness for Santi to even consider this. Edier would raze any establishment of his to the ground before the doors opened.

"Perceptive little thing, aren't you?"

Condescending piece of shit, aren't you?

Taking a cautious sip of his Bloody Mary, he rises to his feet. "I'm afraid I must leave it there. I have a meeting with your husband in five minutes." After this declaration, he's draining the rest of the drink in one gulp, like he's the Jekyll and Hyde of cocktail consumption. "Delicious," he says, smacking his lips together. "Enjoy the rest of your honeymoon."

"You mean the one spent in a cage," I say sweetly.

"One woman's bars are another woman's freedom, Mrs. Carrera. No doubt we'll see each other again soon."

I can't wait.

I'm still contemplating his words when there's an exasperated sigh behind me.

"Andrew, hit me up with something strong and fast. My brother is in a bad mood again, and if he tells me I make a shit cup of coffee one more time, I'm going to throw it at his damn head."

A pair of gray crutches and two slim elbows hit the counter next to me, followed by a mass of dark silky hair that's not unlike mine.

"Hi there, sorry about the drama…" Her words die a death on her lips as she turns to look at me. A beat later, she's staggering back from the counter as if it's burning hot.

"*Hijo de su puta madre…*"

"You must be Lola," I say calmly.

"And you're a Santiago scorpion in Chucks," she gasps back. "You do know who owns this place, right? When my brother finds out—"

"Oh, he knows." I hold up my hand to show her my ring finger and her brilliant blue eyes widen to saucers.

"Andrew?" she breathes, sitting down hard on Mr. Spader's recently vacated stool. "You better make it a double, and fast."

"How's your leg?" I ask, nodding at her crutches.

"How's your mental state after agreeing to marry a Carrera?"

"Questionable."

She points to her thigh. "Hurts."

"Stitches?"

"Seven, not the thirty-seven my brother seemed to think I needed. Your *papá's* bullet missed the mark," she adds, aiming a vicious smile at me.

It's no less than what I deserve, sitting here in the center of the Carrera lair with all fingers pointing squarely at me.

"Edier didn't destroy Legado, Lola."

She scoffs. "You expect me to believe that? After the hell your father has put my family through?"

"I think you'll find there are two hells to every story."

"You know my *mamá* and I nearly died that night of the wedding…"

"So did mine."

"Your father fired first."

"Not according to him."

Her sneer glides effortlessly into a frown. "We're just going to have to agree to disagree then, aren't we? Without the guns, though," she adds dryly. "Crimson doesn't match my outfit."

"Mine either," I say, my mouth twitching.

I'm beginning to understand how Sam fell so hard for her a year and half ago. He could have any woman he wanted. God knows, he's sampled most of them over the years. It was always going to take someone truly spectacular to knock my playboy friend on his ass.

A long pause follows, filled with a thousand possibilities, as Andrew places another juice down on the counter with an apologetic wince.

"I'm sorry, Miss Carrera. You know that Mr. Carrera won't let you have alcohol at this time of the morning."

"Controlling fuck," I hear her mutter as she tosses it back and offers out the empty glass for a refill. "If you don't mind?"

Andrew smiles, looking relieved. "My pleasure."

I catch her glancing at my ring finger again. "Now I know why he slipped me those OxyContin last night."

"He *what*?"

Don't act so shocked, Thalia. You were just considering doing the same to him.

"He knew I'd try and talk him out of the wedding, the fucking hypocrite." Her expression hardens. "So tell me, oh, voodoo temptress. How did you go from counting cards in his casino to marrying my brother in two days? I was there when he saw the surveillance footage," she confides, seeing my confusion. "He went *loco*. I thought he was going to punch RJ in the face."

"We, uh, came to an...arrangement."

"That's more beneficial for him, I can imagine. I know my brother well, *señorita*."

She can hide it all she wants, but I see the love behind her brutal mockery of him too.

"My name's Thalia."

"Thalia." She repeats it slowly. "So, what's in it for you?"

"Money," I say honestly, staring down at my untouched juice.

"That's something I didn't expect to hear from a Santiago."

"It's complicated."

"The best stories always are." She catches my eye again. "How's Sam?"

"Pining."

I can tell she's weighing her next words carefully.

"Did he ever tell you what happened?"

I shake my head. "Not much. It changed him, though."

"It changed us both." She glances at her phone. "Shit. I need to get back up there before Santi detonates another nuclear bomb on me for not answering his phone."

"He has you working as his secretary?" I ask in surprise.

"The worst kind of penance for daring to love the wrong man," she says, rolling her eyes at me. "He won't let me out of his sight after what happened with Sam. He blames himself. It's also to fill a college internship requirement. Lucky me, right? Come. I'll show you around if you like..." She picks up her crutches. "Let me be your hobbling tour guide for today."

By the time we reach his office, I'm wound up to the point of detonation myself. As much as the thought of seeing him after what happened last night makes me want to puke, there's another emotion drawing me here.

Curiosity.

I knew I was a self-masochist.

"Coffee?" Lola asks, as I collapse into the chair in front of her desk.

"Does it come with a toxic sweetener?"

"I imagine sharing a bed with my brother is toxic enough," she answers with a slow grin.

I blush to the roots of my dark hair. "We don't... We haven't—"

"Of course not," she clips, sensing my discomfort. "I've only known you for five minutes, and I already know you're not stupid."

"Just a viper," I say slyly. *And desperate.*

"Well, we can't all be perfect." She gives me the ghost of a wink.

"I'm so far from perfect it's unreal," I say with a sigh, thinking of Ella.

She pauses and starts nibbling on her lower lip. "He doesn't *hurt you*, does he?"

Not physically.

"Actually, don't answer that."

"Tell me about him," I ask, curious again. "All my experiences so far haven't exactly been—"

"Complimentary?" She laughs. "What did you expect? When it comes to the Santiago Cartel, our father taught him to hate first, love never." She wanders backs over to me and leans against the side of the desk. "Unfortunately, the main thing that drives Santi is family. Considering who your father is, I don't think it bodes well for the success of your marriage."

"I don't want our marriage to be golden," I tell her. "I just want to survive it."

CHAPTER
Twenty-Three

SANTI

Leaning back in my chair, I pinch the bridge of my nose in a futile attempt at warding off the headache that's been brewing for the last hour.

Instead of taking it as a cue to shut the fuck up, Monroe drapes himself across the opposite end of my desk and lets out a huff. "I have to admit, Carrera, I thought you'd be happier about the Senate vote."

Glancing up, I stare at him through parted fingers. Type in *sleazy politician* on any search engine, and Monroe Spader's plastic smile and pock-marked face would pop up like an STD.

I have no clue how this *idiota* got appointed to the Atlantic City Gaming Commission. With his cheap suits, parted and slicked back brown hair, and black rimmed glasses that refuse to stay on his face, he looks like he should be hanging out next to a white van passing out candy rather than issuing gaming citations.

Then again, good things happen to bad people. Especially when their brother is banging the Governor.

"What do you want, Spader? A parade? You didn't fuck up simple instructions. Dropping my hand, I give him a slow clap. "Congratu-*fucking*-lations."

"Someone's in a bad mood." Settling back into his chair, he reaches inside his suit jacket and pulls a half-eaten bag of peanuts. Shaking a handful into his palm, he tosses one into the air, missing his mouth by a good six inches.

"In case you've forgotten, my casino was shot up the other night. You were there, I believe…until you weren't."

"I don't stick around for fireworks, Carrera." Tossing another peanut in the air, he curses as it bounces off one of the lenses in his glasses. "Speaking of fireworks, how's that new wife of yours treating you?"

I'm suddenly regretting my choice to have him attend my wedding—even if it was strategic. "She's an unhappily married woman, as expected."

"Gotta admit, that was one hell of an outfit she—"

"Is there a reason you're still here?" I ask, cutting him off. I'm not discussing Thalia with him. I don't even want him speaking her name. A second glance at his lecherous smirk almost has me reaching for my gun.

I don't want him thinking of her at all.

She's mine.

Wait, where the fuck did that come from?

The only claim I have on Thalia is a legal one. Just because she let me touch her pussy last night, that doesn't mean we'll be getting his and hers monogrammed towels.

"The new Mrs. Carrera is the least of my concerns since a shipment of dead women was dropped on my doorstep."

A third peanut flies in the air, this time hitting its target. Monroe's eyes widen, and he lets out a hacking cough.

I'm not sure if he's choking on the peanut or my revelation.

"I heard." He clears his throat, tucking what's left of the bag of peanuts back inside his jacket. "One of the port terminal operators is an old friend. We…talk."

John Wentworth. Another *pendejo* on my payroll with his hand out. Meaning that the two associates whose asses I own because of the morality I bought, have been trading war stories.

"You know what they say about loose lips, don't you, Monroe?"

"Santi—"

"They sink ships…and careers. So, I suggest you shut yours."

His face pales. "I want out."

"What did you just say?"

"Look, I know who your family is, Santi. I know what they do…" He pushes his glasses back onto his nose, swallowing hard as I grip the edge of my desk. "I took your deal because it's none of my business if somebody wants to take a line up the nose. But I didn't sign on for dead hookers."

"They're not hookers," I say, my tone low and deadly. "They were trafficked women."

He waves his hand. "Either way, they're dead. Something I don't want to be. I agreed to pull some political strings, but no amount of money is worth this, Carrera. Not at the risk of getting caught in the middle of a cartel war."

"The risk?" I bark out a dark laugh. "Monroe, there's no risk anymore. You sank balls deep in this shit the minute you walked through my door. There's only one way out of our arrangement, and it leads six feet under."

"But I've done my part. The Barfly is nothing but soot and ash."

A cold smile slowly parts my lips. "You wanted to be business partners, remember? I warned you then if you chose to play in my league, you'd either win big or lose your life. You reached for the brass ring, Monroe. Whether it stays in your hand or gets wrapped around your neck is up to you." I wait a beat or two and let that sink in before nodding toward the door. "Now, get out. I have work to do."

Within seconds, his chair flies backward, and Monroe Spader becomes nothing more than a department store-suited blur.

Once my office door closes behind him, I spin away from my desk and collapse back into my chair. *Dios mío, what the fuck else is going to go wrong?*

My eyes travel up to the oil painting above my head where my silent challenge is met by the smiling skull-faced reverence of *Santa Muerte* herself. "Don't answer that..." I tell her, and after another glance at her haunting stare, I quickly add, "*Por favor.*"

Even with the weight of the Terminal attack weighing heavy on me, my thoughts drift back to Thalia. She let her guard down last night. Not only did she offer me a glimpse behind that iron wall she's always hiding behind, but she also offered me herself.

I took what I wanted.

And then I broke what was left.

Loosening my tie, I unbutton the first button on my shirt. Something inside aches. It burns. I press my palm against my chest. It's starting to spread.

Fuck, maybe Lola was right. I *am* going have a stroke before I'm thirty.

As if summoned, my gaze drifts back to *Santa Muerte* who is staring down at me in judgment. "Fine," I grumble, digging my phone from my pocket. "I get it."

Svetlana picks up on the first ring. "Sir?"

"Have Francois make spaghetti for dinner." Before she can ask any questions, I add, "And none of that boxed shit. I want fresh pasta and gourmet sauce."

"Of course, Mr. Carrera." I can hear the smirk in her voice so loudly she might as well have ended it with, *you overbearing fuck.*

"And throw out that Day-glo bullshit she smeared on her face for the wedding. Buy her some classy makeup and a new dress. What else do women need to feel secure?"

"Freedom," she says flatly.

"So just the spaghetti then."

A low chuckle rumbles on the other end of the line just before I end the call.

Fucking women.

Speaking of women…

Spader was already in my office waiting for me by the time I made it back from Newark. I didn't get the chance to speak to her, but judging by the pinched look on Lola's face as I rushed past her desk, I didn't need to.

The fire burning in her blue eyes said it all.

Spaghetti won't cut it with my sister. If I hope to have any sense of peace in a life that's already imploding, I'm going to have to swallow my pride and apologize.

Apologize.

Cursing under my breath, I stride across my office and open the door to find that my two worlds have collided, spewing twisted wreckage and brunette-infused gasoline across every inch of the executive lobby.

Thalia sits perched on the edge of a chair, while my sister rests against the side of her desk like the queen of the damned. They're deep in conversation, and although I can't make out their words, I have a pretty good idea who's the topic of their conversation.

The pinche cabrón who let time get away from him, only to have it bite him in the ass.

Women talking is never a good thing. But two *Carrera* women in deep discussion? That's a Molotov cocktail.

I clear my throat, and a set of bright blue eyes swing my way.

"Santi..." Lola flashes me a lethal smile. "We were just talking about you."

"I'll bet." *Probably about which common household cleaner can be used to induce a cardiac arrest.* "Thalia... My office. Now."

She doesn't budge.

"I said, *now*."

Flashing me daggers, she slowly rises to her feet. Before she can take a single step, Lola clamps a hand around her wrist. "Your wife is not a Cocker Spaniel, Santi. Try again."

I grit my teeth. "Please."

I'm going to demote her to toilet attendant after this.

"Now that wasn't so hard, was it?" Grinning, she releases Thalia's wrist and flops down into her own chair. "You two kids have fun."

Turning on my heel, I stalk back into my office before I throw something at that grin and knock out a tooth. By the time the door closes behind me, I'm already pacing. I'm pissed, and it's not just because Lola challenged me in front of Thalia.

It's because I wouldn't put it past my new wife to try and draw my sister into her corner.

What just happened out there was Lola being...well, *Lola*. I'd planned to tell her about my marriage.

Me. Her brother.

It wasn't Thalia's place to cross that line.

Thalia...with her long dark hair piled on top of her head in a messy bun that's somehow classy in its chaos.

Thalia...her face fresh and beautiful with only a hint of color on her lips and lashes.

Thalia...in tight black jeans showcasing her long legs and another dick-tease white T-shirt.

"You don't need to worry," I hear her say. "I played my role, but your sister isn't stupid. I had to be honest about us—"

"*Us?*" Pausing mid-pace, I cock an eyebrow at her.

In response, she gives me the look of a woman who has spent the last twelve hours plotting my painful demise. "Don't worry, *husband*. Lola already knows her brother is a *pinche sangrón*."

My head snaps up. "Did you just call me a fucking jerk?"

"I'm half-Colombian. You don't think I know Spanish, too? Now if that's all…"

Fuck, she's beautiful when she's angry.

I grab her arm before she can take a single step. "About last night—"

"It was a mistake—on both our parts. I have my agenda, and you have yours. As long as we remember that, there will be no more of *this*." She motions between us with a disgusted look on her face.

"And what is *this*?" I demand, mimicking her gesture.

She smiles sweetly, venom dripping from her lips. "Emotional extortion. Something I've become depressingly familiar with over the past week." Thalia turns back to the door and once again, I find myself stopping her with a firm grip on her arm. Her body tenses beneath my fingertips. "I've said all I have to say, Santi."

"Good, then maybe you'll listen for once."

"Fuck you," she snarls, pushing me away. There's fire in her eyes, but it's not a solitary emotion. Somewhere, in that river of molten rage, there are ribbons of pain too. "I may be your wife, but I won't let you treat me like a whore."

"You're no one's whore, *mi amada*."

A bruised laugh rumbles in her throat. "After the way you acted last night? I let my guard down. I confided in you about my sister's illness, and you twisted it into something ugly."

"You don't think I let mine down, too?" I'm advancing closer and closer to her as I speak. At this rate, we'll both be crashing into that wall.

"For a second maybe," she admits reluctantly. "Then it shot up pretty goddamn fast again."

"And with good reason."

Damn it. I didn't want to have this conversation, but she's forcing my hand. She doesn't want amends, she wants blood.

Fine.

I'll slice a vein for her, but what spills out isn't going to be what she expects.

"I am *not* a monster." Reaching out, I trail the back of my hand across her rigid jaw. "Not all the time, anyway. I'm a man of extremes. If there's a middle ground, I've never found it. The line between hate and lust blurs too easily for me. Once it's crossed, I crave…*something more*."

She swallows hard, her throat constricting against my skin. "Did you want to hurt me?"

"Yes."

"That's why you wanted me to beg for it last night," she whispers. "Because you knew I wouldn't."

The stark truth in her words is something she'll never understand. It's a truth buried deep within the dents peppering my bedroom wall. Her refusing me was the only salvation I could offer her.

My cruelty wasn't simple malice. It was a lifeline.

I cradle her face in my hands—a tender gesture wrapped in a sharp warning. "I'm not a gentle man…in or out of bed. And you, *mi esposa*, are a virgin." She opens her mouth to refute my words, but I press my thumbs over her lips. "You have no idea what I'd do to you, Thalia Carrera. Vile things no virgin should ever know."

Silence tucks itself into every corner of the room. Waiting… Listening…

"I just want to go home," she says, her lips trembling beneath my touch.

Those deep brown wells are brimming with unshed tears. One finally breaks free and trails down her cheek. When it hits my thumb, instead of wiping it away, I smear it into her skin. "You and I were born into a nightmare, and we'll die in one too. This is the hand we've been dealt. But even in nightmares, we can control our own destiny. We can claim what's ours and live by our own rules… our own desires."

Her breath catches.

"What do you desire, *Señora* Carrera?"

Holding my gaze, Thalia opens her mouth and wraps her lips around my thumb. There's a skipped heartbeat where we stare at each other—one of us testing boundaries, the other daring them to be crossed.

Then she hollows her cheeks…and sucks.

And once again, my prized control snaps like a dry twig.

I drag my thumb from her mouth, only to slam her up against the wall and replace it with my tongue. Diving my fingers in her messy bun, I pull at the strands while grinding against her.

Her moans are feeding the monster I warned her about.

I fucking warned her…

She kisses me back just as hard, taking everything I have to give, but the harder we kiss, the more I know her lips won't be enough to calm this storm.

I want more.

I want her.

I reach for the zipper on her jeans, and she stiffens. "Santi…stop. *Stop!*"

But it's too late. My monster has already consumed me. All I can do is brace my palms against the wall and lock my arms to keep from doing something I can't take back.

After a couple of wide-eyed blinks, Thalia ducks under my arm. Pressing her fingertips against her swollen lips, she backs away, her eyes never leaving me. "I can't… Not after…"

"Thalia."

"I'll stay out of your way." She reaches behind her for the door handle. "I…I have to go."

I close my eyes, trying to breathe through the thick haze of unsatisfied lust. *She did it again. She fucking made me lose control again.* This hot and cold seesaw has to stop. I can't destroy someone and hunger for them at the same time.

I have to get my shit together.

When my head finally clears, I open the door and barrel straight into a five-foot three tornado ready to level me to the ground.

"Was it worth it?"

"If you're referring to my new bride, you're going to have to be more specific." I go to step around my sister when she hobbles in front of me, blocking my path.

"While I have no doubt backing her into a corner was the highlight of your year, I'm referring to me."

Okay, so we're doing this right now. "What egregious sin have I committed this time?" I say, crossing my arms over my chest with a sigh.

"How about drugging me so I couldn't attend my own brother's wedding?"

I stiffen. The bite in her delivery tells me it's not just an accusation. When Lola is mad, she reacts like a Carrera—methodical and calculating with very little emotion. But when she's hurt, she's vicious.

"I'm not stupid, Santi," she scowls, shoving a surprisingly powerful jab into my chest. "I was roofied, remember? I know what being drugged feels like." The tightness in her face fades, only to be replaced by a devastated frown. "But until now, I didn't know what it felt like to be drugged by my own brother."

Fuck, she went straight for the kill shot.

"I did it for your protection."

"Bullshit," she hisses, her eyes narrowing in accusation. "You did it for your own protection."

"From whom?" I shout, the pain in my gut turning into something much darker. "You? I'm king of this empire."

Those light blue eyes narrow again as she studies me. "Well, your highness, bullets aren't as sharp as arrows."

"You should probably take the rest of the day off. It appears the drugs aren't fully out of your system." I push past her again. This time she doesn't try to stop me.

"I saw the way you looked at her," she calls after me. "This isn't just about revenge, Santi. She's getting to you."

Fuck.

I don't know why I stop. I should just keep walking—only I don't.

"You don't know what you're talking about."

"Don't I? You can't choose who you fall for, Santi. The heart doesn't care about battle lines."

"Are you speaking from experience, *chaparrita?*" *She's not the only one who can throw stones.* I glance over my shoulder to find her glaring at me. "Because that worked out so well for you."

As usual, any mention of Sam Sanders and Lola's big mouth turns into a sealed vault. Bowing her head, she exhales a defeated breath. "I'm not fighting with you, Santi. I'm on your side."

"Could have fooled me. From the way things looked when I walked in here, you've already jumped onto Thalia's she-ship and set sail."

She groans, shaking her head. "Just because I feel for the girl, it doesn't mean I don't know how dangerous she can be." I hear her crutches drag across the marble and then still.

I tell myself to walk. *Just fucking walk away.* But, once again, I stand there, stock still, as my sister rests her hand on my shoulder before quickly drawing it back.

"We're Carreras. I understand we have to break rules. Just promise me you won't break *her.*"

"You really think I'm a bastard, don't you?"

"No. I think you'd do anything to prove your loyalty to *papá*...and to yourself."

Just the mention of his name and my chin slingshots back over my shoulder. "What's that supposed to mean?"

She stares into my eyes, her gaze softening. "Loyalty isn't always a straight path, Santi. Sometimes it forks when we least expect it."

CHAPTER
Twenty-Four

THALIA

I don't want to go back upstairs. I don't want to dissect the state of my one-day marriage inside an empty room again. It's a dangerous activity when you're forty-two floors up and the sky is within touching distance. If Santi were to wander in unannounced for another round of unresolved sexual-hate tension, I might end up pushing him off the balcony.

Instead, I find myself back in the Platinum Bar, ordering another orange juice from Andrew that I know I'm not going to drink.

"Here you go," he says with a wry smile. He knows I'm not going to drink it either, but he's too polite to say anything.

I watch him polish the counter for the umpteenth time, until I can see my misery reflected back to me in perfect definition.

"How long have you worked here?"

"Two years."

"Do you like it?"

He laughs. "Is that a loaded question? I know who you're married to, Mrs. Carrera, and I value my…*employment*."

"Fair enough," I say, grinning back at him.

I watch him place a box of Johnnie Walker Blue on the counter and start unpacking the bottles. He's handsome in an All-American quarterback kind of way, but I know that if I were to ever find myself alone with him, his touches wouldn't sear my skin, and his kisses wouldn't burn like fire.

Not like another's... When *he* touches me, I know I'm already in hell.

Damn you, Santi. Why did you have to go and make everything so confusing?

"Are you a New Jersey native?"

"Born and bred," he says proudly.

"Tell me a joke," I say suddenly, and then I blush, realizing how forward that sounded.

"Are you okay?" he says, frowning down at me.

"It's not a come-on, I swear," I stammer. "When I was a kid, my friend used to try and make me laugh with bad jokes all the time." I shrug helplessly. "I guess I could use that right now."

He side-eyes me with a slow grin. "A joke, huh?" Leaning across the counter, he nods and accepts my challenge. "Okay then, two guys walk into a bar... The third guy ducks."

It's way too stupid to be funny, but I find myself laughing anyway.

Or I do until a fist comes flying past my face and slams into Andrew's jaw before he has a chance to duck himself.

"Get the fuck out of my casino!" Santi roars, taking the polished counter like he's Bo Duke from *Dukes of Hazzard* sliding across the hood of a car, just as Andrew reels backward into a shelf of vodkas.

"Santi, stop!" I scream, climbing up onto the bar myself to try and haul him away, but it's like trying to calm an angry wasp. The harder I try, the more stings keep raining down on the bartender.

"Did he touch you?" He whirls around suddenly and catches my chin in a vise-like grip. His face is blazing. His touch, savage.

"Oh my God, *are you jealous*?" I gasp out.

"You're mine, Thalia Carrera," he growls. "That fucking ring on your finger proves it."

"A piece of metal proves nothing! I'm filing for an annulment unless you hire Andrew back right away."

"First name basis with the staff, already? You *do* move fast, Thalia."

"In five days, I'll be fucking sprinting out of this place. See how fast I move then!"

Mouthing an apology to Andrew who's holding the left side of his jaw and looking dazed, I push backward to free myself, vowing to speak to Lola as soon as I can about her brother's unreasonable behavior. If Andrew isn't rehired within twenty-four hours, I'll do more than fill his bottles of *Gran Patrón Burdeos Añejo* up with water.

"Thalia Carrera, come back here," I hear him thunder as I reach the entrance to the bar.

Ignoring him, I flick my middle finger up as an *au revoir* and then wait for the thunder of angry footsteps to follow me.

He catches up as I'm stepping into the elevator.

"Leave me alone," I grit out, as he barges into the carriage after me, crowding me into a corner as the doors *ding* shut.

"Did he touch you?" he repeats as the carriage starts to rise—along with the temperature inside it.

"I asked him to tell me a joke," I respond, bitterly. "I didn't expect my husband to be the *punchline*."

It's a great pun, but neither of us are in a laughing mood right now.

"You're lying!"

"And you're the King of *Loco*!" I say, jabbing my finger into his chest.

"The, *what*?"

"It's the name I've been calling you in my head since the day we met. You make these crazy, mad decisions all the time, and only you can see the logic. Is it true you're going to open casinos in New York now that Uncle Rick's bill passed through the Senate?"

"Oh, *hija de tu puta madre*!" he spits out. "Don't say it like you care about my safety."

"You're right; I don't!"

Our chests are heaving in time with each other's now. We're standing so close, we're creating our own friction from the movement.

I can feel his hard erection pressing up against my stomach. My nipples are like bullets.

"You're lying to me again," he accuses harshly.

"Fuck you!"

"Good idea."

Just then, the elevator gives a lurch. It may as well have snapped its wires for all the self-control left inside the carriage.

It's hard to tell who moves first. *Who started this war first?* But suddenly,

I'm full of him again. Possessive, strained kisses that drive his tongue so deep into my mouth, there's no amount of *Añejo* that's going to burn this memory away.

In turn, I take my anger out on his body—twisting my fingers into his thick black hair and yanking hard. He groans, spilling Spanish curses and filthy words into our kiss as the heat between my legs ignites into a pulsing inferno.

Sliding his hands to my ass, he lifts me up, forcing my legs around his waist, and pins me against the carriage wall.

"If you ever…"

Kiss

"Laugh like that with another man again…"

Kiss

"I will fucking murder him…"

Kiss.

"And then I will fucking murder you."

Kiss.

"That's if you can catch me," I rasp, tipping my head back to offer him my throat for the killer finale.

Somewhere in the distance, the doors *ding* open again.

He carries me wrapped around him like this into his apartment, shouting at his security guards to avert their eyes as we pass.

Kicking the door shut, he lays me down on the table in the middle of the hallway, rips at my jeans and panties, and then sinks to his knees between my legs.

"I thought I was the one who had to beg," I pant, lifting my head.

Our gazes meet.

Our worlds collide.

"Oh, you'll beg, *mi amada*," he says with an evil smile, spreading my legs even wider for him. "I won't stop devouring this pussy until you do, and then I'm turning you over and tongue-fucking your ass until you forget you ever had a name before Carrera."

All of my thoughts fragment, except one.

"What about…?"

"I can wait," he says, guessing at my question. "Because when you're ready to take my cock… When you come to me willingly... I know your innocence will be worth every second spent desiring it."

I'd never stopped to consider how it would feel to have a man kissing me *down there*, but when his tongue paints a hard line up through my folds, I don't recall much of anything anymore. When he wraps his lips around my clit and draws hard, the universe ceases to exist.

When he wrings his first orgasm out of me so violently my back arches up from the table and his name becomes permanently tattooed on my lips, I think I've reached oblivion.

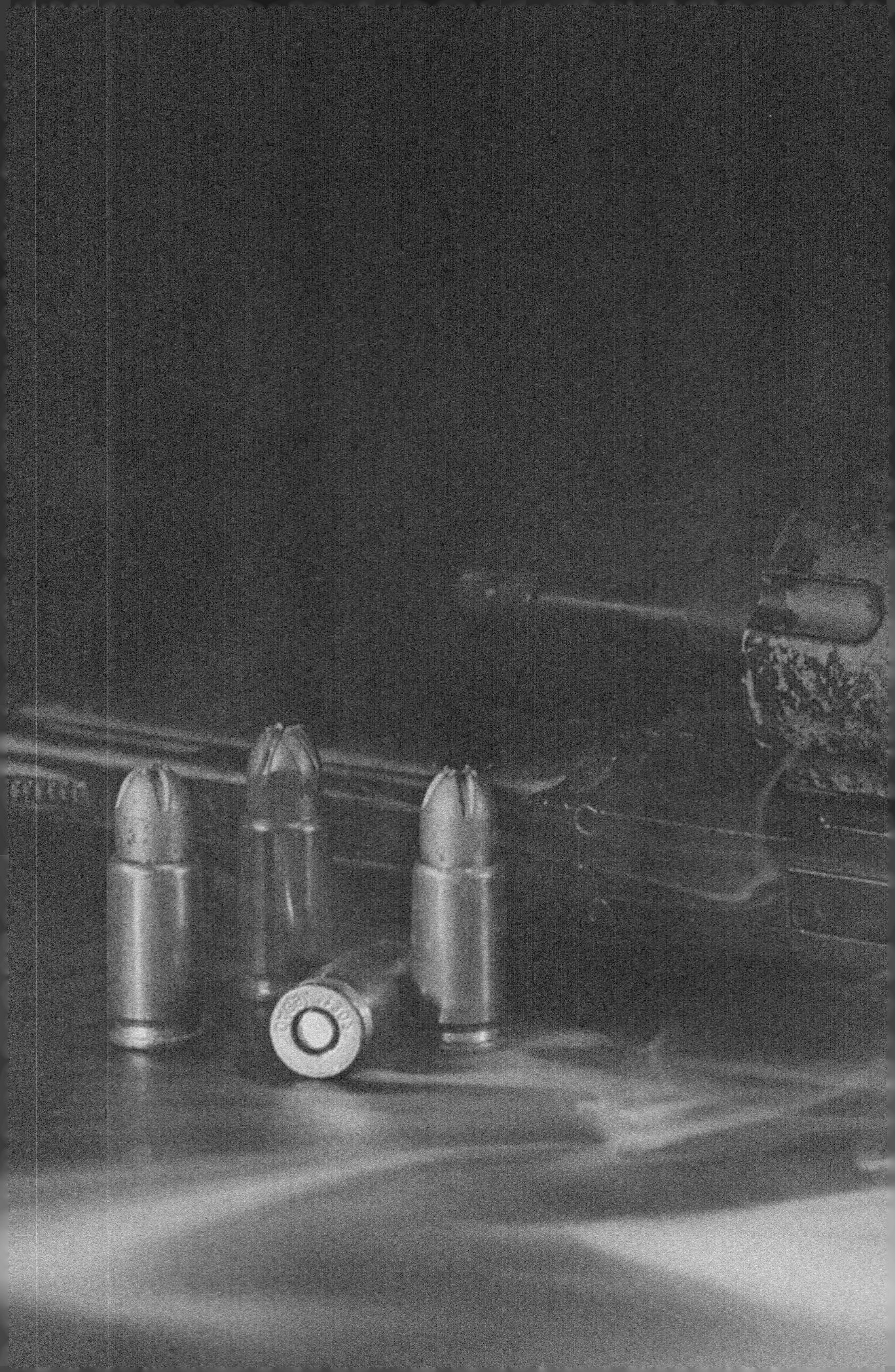

CHAPTER
Twenty-Five

SANTI

My phone is ringing again by the time I make my way back down to the Platinum Bar an hour later. RJ already has a full glass of *Añejo* tequila waiting for me. For the first time, I stare at my poison of choice with mixed emotion.

I need a drink. This day is starting to warrant many of them. However, I've just sampled a much more powerful vice, and now the familiar, soothing burn has competition.

I roll my neck, my tight muscles stiffening in protest. While taking that first sip may ease the knots created by Grayson's counterattack and Monroe's pathetic bullshit, it will also erase the taste of her. And right now, the sweet essence of my wife's lust is the only thing keeping Marco Bardi's skull in one piece.

I reach into my pocket to silence its incessant ringing before unbuttoning my jacket and sliding onto the barstool. With one sideways glance, the bartenders scatter, busying themselves with mopping up invisible spills at the other end of the counter.

Luckily, that *pendejo*, Andrew, is nowhere to be found. Thalia's warning filters through my head... *Hire him back, my ass*... He's lucky he still has hands to lift his dick to take a piss, much less pour drinks in my casino.

After what just happened upstairs, the stakes are even higher. Thalia isn't just a pawn anymore. My hunger for her is tipping the scales in the wrong direction.

I wanted to own the world.

Now, she's flipping it upside down.

I've never walked away from pussy so many times without fucking it. Yet here we are again—the virgin and the villain—charging the same lust-laden battlefield. Advance and retreat. Attack and surrender. We're crossing two territories filled with hidden landmines, and eventually, one of them is going to explode.

I'm going to need that drink, after all...

"*Gracias*," I mutter, downing half of the glass before taking a breath.

RJ places his half-empty whiskey on the counter next to it. "Rough day with the missus?"

Rough and brutally delicious. An image of Thalia lying on her back, legs spread, and neck arched in ecstasy invades my thoughts, and my cock swells again with the need to possess her.

All of her.

Her inexperience drew me in, but it's her vulnerability that keeps me interested.

I pause, the tequila halfway to my mouth, and flick him a hard stare. "Keep that shit up, and I'll be sending your nuts back to Houston in a Ziploc."

He laughs, the sound grating on my last nerve.

"What did our friend Bardi have to say about the *gift* Grayson left on our dock?"

"Haven't asked him yet. I figured you'd want to do the honors."

My cousin knows me too well. After having my port turned into a crime scene and watching my sister stage a mutiny, there's nothing I want more than to beat a confession out of that Italian motherfucker.

"Well, at least we know he wasn't responsible," I offer, settling back onto the barstool with exaggerated casualness. "He's a little tied up at the moment."

The joke goes over about as well as the bartender's did earlier.

"Speaking of which," RJ says. "If you're done using his phone to catfish your wife, hand it over. I'll have one of our hackers see if they can pull anything off it."

"Already done. Nothing but bootleg porn and dick pics."

He's reaching for more whiskey when his phone starts ringing. It's quickly followed by mine—*again.*

There's a hard set to his jaw as he slides his phone from his pocket and notices I'm not doing the same. "Aren't you going to answer that?"

"Nope."

"Harcourt," he answers.

A tap of my empty glass on the bar sends the bartenders scattering once again. Within seconds, a new drink is placed in front of me, all wrapped up with an invisible bow.

"What do you mean?" A sharp note in RJ's voice catches my attention. I glance over to find him gripping his phone so hard, I'm surprised it hasn't turned to dust. "Well, fucking find him, you stupid *pinche cabrón*!"

"Tell me." It's all I can do to force out the command through clenched teeth.

"Bardi is gone."

Three words.

Three fucking words, and all my best laid plans crumble like a house of cards.

"What do you mean, 'he's gone'?" I grit out. "Where the fuck could he go? The son of a bitch was tied to a chair in a locked room!"

RJ stands, raking his fingers through his short hair. "I need to find out. Rocco just went down there, and the door was open along with two dead *sicarios*. No chair. No Bardi."

My fingers tighten around my glass moments before I'm hurling it across the bar, watching as it shatters the mirrored walls. "So what? Did he sprout wings and levitate his way to freedom? Fucking find him! Now!"

"Santi, I—"

He's cut off by yet another shrill ring, and then I fucking snap.

Reaching for my own phone, I silence it before slamming it onto the bar. "Don't you know how to leave a fucking message?"

"Yes, but I prefer to deliver them in person."

Every muscle in my body tenses as the deep, familiar accent amplifies in surround sound, controlled and deceptively smooth in its delivery. Slowly, I turn to find the cold, unforgiving eyes of my father staring back at me.

Phone held to his face.

Murder darkening his eyes.

Valentin Carrera doesn't sit. He stands like Zeus himself, presiding over my office like it's Mount Olympus.

He hasn't spoken a word since I closed the door, but to be fair, neither have I. Our chilly reunion drew more than a few stares in the bar, so my only reaction was to suggest we move it elsewhere.

Somewhere more private—with fewer witnesses who could be called to testify in the event of a murder.

I lean back in my chair, widening my fingers and pressing my fingertips together. Choosing to sit rather than stand was a strategic move. My desk chair is a seat of power—a self-built throne under the watchful eye of *Santa Muerte*.

This isn't Mexico.

This is New Jersey.

And here, I'm king, not him.

My phone chimes, alerting me to a recently left voicemail. I'm in no mood to deal with anything else right now, so I toss it onto the desk between us like a grenade.

Lowering his eyes, my father gives it a half-interested glance. "So, your phone isn't broken after all."

I'm also not in the mood for explanations, so I reach for the crystal decanter sitting beside me and pour myself a drink. "Help yourself," I murmur.

His dark gaze lowers to the decanter and then settles back on me. "I don't like to be ignored, Santi."

With my glass in hand, I sit back in my chair and mimic his calm, lethal tone. "And I don't like to be questioned. You demanded I handle Grayson's attack on Legado, so I did. I wasn't aware my decisions needed a prior authorization." Holding his stare, I take a long drink, letting the challenge hang in the air. I've never been anything but reverent toward my father, so we're both treading in uncharted waters here.

"Depends on the decision," he says, scanning my office with the same stormy eyes I see in the mirror every day. Dark brown with flickering glints of gold, which means he's barely containing his rage. "This is quite a place you have here, son."

It's not a compliment.

And a flicker is nothing more than an impending fire.

Although my father's hands are tucked loosely in the pockets of his black suit pants, it's a dubious stance. Judging by the hard set of his jaw and unwavering stare, I wouldn't be surprised if he drew out a thunderbolt and hurled it at my face.

"Repairs went well, I see."

I nod. "The Carrera name has a way of expediting things."

"You're welcome."

My blood pumps a furious rhythm at the insinuation. "For what?" I ask, struggling to keep my temper under control. "You think *you* did this? You think it's *your* name they fear in this town?"

He lets out a dark chuckle. "They fear *El Muerte*."

Those two words are like a gunshot. *The Reaper.* A name he's referred to in hushed whispers all across Mexico.

"On this side of the border, I am *El Muerte*," I say, baring my teeth and slamming my glass onto the desk.

My father's lips curl into a tepid smile. *Son of a bitch.* He provoked me on purpose. He wanted me to break first.

My empty stomach churns on nothing but acid and tequila.

"You didn't come all this way to talk about building structure," I say idly. "I know you have falcons planted up and down the East Coast reporting back to you. You know I have a caged songbird in my penthouse."

He doesn't confirm nor deny, but he doesn't have to. We both know I'm right.

"Legado..." he notes, ignoring me, the heavily accented word rolling off his tongue. "It's ironic, don't you think?"

"What is?"

"That you'd name your casino after your *legacy*..." His smirk vanishes, the black calm of a cartel kingpin sweeping across his face as his palms smack onto my desk. "Only to put a ring on a Santiago, and shit all over it."

"Watch it," I warn in a low tone, but I don't know what I'm defending more—my casino, or my wife.

"Have you let her pussy poison your brain, Santi?" he seethes, his palms curling into tight fists. "That woman is *not* your ally. Have a few days between her legs made you forget everything I've taught you? Everything her father did to your mother? The pain he caused our family? The time he stole from *you*?"

That last one was a well-flung dart to the weakest part of me. A dark corner inside my head filled with nothing but scorched hope and unanswered prayers.

"No, I haven't forgotten," I counter, recapturing my deadly tone, only this time, it's sliced paper-thin. "How could I? You've never let me."

"What the hell is that supposed to mean?"

I don't answer him. It's not a conversation I care to have, now or ever. Arguing about the past is like spinning circles inside a hamster wheel and expecting to travel in a straight line.

"Seventeen dead women washed up in a shipping container in my port this morning," I say flatly, changing the subject.

He grinds his teeth. "*Si*, I know."

Of course, he does. This war has escalated to a new level, and now it's resting in my hands.

On my fucking shoulders.

"My casino got shot up." I rake my hand through my hair and tug at the roots. "Lola got hurt. Sanders's bar is a pile of ash and stale memories. Santiago used his own daughter as target practice for Christ's sake."

He's quiet for a moment and then cocks his chin, the gold flecks in his eyes turning from a flicker to a spark. "You knew this was always your destiny. My battle is your battle."

"No!" I accuse, jabbing my finger across the desk. "It was always your battle. You made it my burden."

"You are a Carrera. A sin against one is a sin against all. We don't rest until vengeance has been claimed and blood has been spilled."

"That's *your* truth."

The spark becomes a flame, his knuckles flattening into my desk. "And you made it *your* truth when you took the oath and accepted a seat at *Senado*," he hits back, his accent thickening as his anger escalates. "I may have groomed you to be a king, Santi, but you coveted the crown all on your own."

He's right. And I want to hate him for it—only I can't. Valentin Carrera molded me to be his successor. To bloody my hands and absorb his hate as mine. But in the end, I chose this life. As young as eight years old, I'd sneak out of the house and follow my father and uncles to the one-room building at the far end of the estate.

Senado. The Carrera Senate.

The only law that exists within those four walls is the law of the cartel.

The men inside that room earned their seat. They took an oath. I coveted what they had. My soul burned to belong. To claim what was rightfully mine.

I earned *my* seat the night I stood with New Jersey snow under my feet and gunfire erupting all around me. The night I took my first life…

And faced my first weakness.

As I stare at my father, I suddenly realize how much I've become him. Not only physically, it's also there in our mannerisms and words. My office is bathed in darkness, just like his. My Italian suits are made of only the finest silk, black and dark grays, just like his. While his hair is now salt and pepper, and mine is still jet-black, they both act as mood barometers—slicked back when we're in control and chaotic when we're not.

Truth's reflection is a bitter pill. Even now, we're both leaned forward on opposite sides of my desk, fists clenched, jaws tight, unrelenting, and stubborn as fuck.

Mirror images.

Mirror sins.

The sins of the father…

I can feel a cold smile spreading across my face. "It seems I am my father's son, in more ways than one."

He cocks a dark eyebrow. "Meaning?"

"Thalia Santiago came here trying to win money to protect her sister from an Italian piece of shit who was blackmailing her. Instead of letting her keep her earnings, I've held her against her will and used her to my advantage in the middle of a cartel war." I hold his stare, my sadistic smile widening. "Sound familiar?"

For the first time, I see my father flinch. He was just a few years older than me when my grandfather sent him to Houston to run stateside operations for the Southeastern leg of the cartel. My mother was a bartender at a Carrera-owned cantina, and somehow, her whole family got trapped in the middle of a Mexican cartel rivalry.

Which ended with my father kidnapping her.

He claims it was to protect her, but Valentin Carrera does nothing that doesn't benefit him.

I never asked the details. I didn't want to know. Now, I'm thinking maybe I should have…

Stretched silence paints the room in even more volatile darkness. Only a single breath separates action and consequence.

Until the door flies open.

"Santi, I'm sorry to barge in, but you aren't answering your…" Lola's voice trails off as her gaze settles on the opposing force standing across from me. "*Papá?*" she whispers.

My father shifts his attention toward the open door, his scowl softening. "*Hola, cielito.*"

His little sky. His greatest weakness, second only to my mother.

"What are you doing here?" she asks incredulously. "I didn't…" When his gaze locks onto the crutches tucked under her arms, she shoots me a panicked look.

All I can do is shrug. Trying to contain his vengeance now would be like trying to capture a breeze. *Futile as fuck.* Whether she has a flesh wound or a paper cut, it won't matter to Valentin Carrera.

Someone drew blood from his little *cielito.*

So someone will die.

Lola clears her throat nervously. "Is *mamá* here?"

He nods. "*Sí,* she's resting in a room upstairs."

The words are aimed at her, but they punch me straight in the chest. "You're staying here? At Legado?"

"*Sí,*" he answers again, and I don't like the look in his eyes. "In fact, she is very much looking forward to tonight."

Lola gasps. "Tonight?"

My father strides across the office, gently cupping her cheek. "Didn't Santi tell you? The five of us are having our first family dinner together."

Santi didn't know shit about it.

Wait…

"Five?" I ask, realizing I'm about to steer myself right into another shithole.

I grip the edge of my desk, bracing for the response that is every bit as toxic as I anticipate.

"Yes, you, me, your *mamá,* your sister…and our new daughter-in-law."

CHAPTER
Twenty-Six

SANTI

My father glares down at his plate in disgust. "What the fuck is this?"

The waiter becomes a wax statue, his face frozen in terror as he glances across the table at me for guidance. Unfortunately, I can't pull him from this fire.

I'm the one who lit the match.

Legado's Cellar Bistro is a world-renowned five-star restaurant occupying a large portion of the eighth floor. The food is high-end and eclectic, which, besides being completely empty due to renovations, is one of the main reasons I chose it for tonight's festivities. My father is a product of his environment and a creature of habit.

Valentin Carrera will charge into enemy territory with nothing more than a vendetta and a steak knife, but when it comes to his food, he rarely strays outside his comfort zone. If his plate doesn't have Mexican roots or come with a hefty side of Texan nostalgia, he isn't interested.

So, I may have enjoyed it a little too much when the waiter set a plate of sautéed baby octopus in front of him.

Bon appetit, Zeus.

My mother, however, isn't so amused. *Or at all.* In fact, if looks could kill, I'd have eight baby octopus legs tied in knots around my neck.

"It's *Jjukkumi Gui*, s-sir. I-it's a K-korean delicacy."

The man can't form a sentence without stuttering, and instead of reveling in it, I find myself feeling sorry for the *idiota*. This newfound guilt Thalia has shoved down my throat is putting a damper on my fun.

Flashing the waiter a gracious smile, *mamá* leans in close to my father. "That looks delicious. Val, do you mind?" Without missing a beat, she switches plates, placing her roasted duck in front of him while taking the octopus for herself.

Delicious, my ass. She's full of shit, but no one dares argue with her.

Crisis averted. *For now.*

Mamá glares across the table at me, her red lips pursing in that familiar, disapproving way—the one that always hits in the same raw places. The same scars. But it's her eyes that wipe all traces of smugness from my face—narrow slits of blue, identical to Lola's but much less innocent. Eyes that have always held an endless well of devotion and the deepest source of pain.

For both of us.

She hasn't changed much in two years. Even in her late forties, Eden Lachey Carrera is still striking. The long, cherry red hair I used to grasp as a young boy, now dusts her shoulders, but it's still just as vibrant.

I wish happy memories were the only ones I had of her. The ones where I tugged on that hair and she laughed and squeezed me so hard I thought I'd pop.

But they're not, and I have Dante Santiago to thank for that.

Thankfully, the view to my right helps. I had to put the brakes on the spaghetti extravaganza, but Svetlana delivered on the dress.

This time, Thalia didn't turn it into a Halloween costume—a concession that didn't even require heated debate.

She looks like an angel, with those sexy loose curls flowing down her back. But it's her dress that's the star of the show. It's white—elegant and sophisticated, while still showing enough skin to make me contemplate the ramifications of escorting her to the restroom for round two.

That Russian needs a raise.

Refusing to give the roasted duck a second glance, my father raises a stem glass of *Gran Patrón Burdeos Añejo* to his mouth and takes a slow sip, his dark gaze settling to my right as well. "I would toast to the happy couple, but it seems I wasn't invited to the festivities."

"Val..." my mother warns. I can tell they've already had words—none of them pleasant.

"*Cereza...*" he counters, his tone thickening with reverence as he speaks his private name for her.

"It's fine, *mamá,*" I murmur, because *fuck that.* I'm a grown man. I don't need anyone fighting my battles. "There wasn't time to invite anyone." I glance at Thalia, reaching for her hand under the table, more for solidarity than anything else.

As soon as my skin touches her, she jerks it away.

Orgasms are not concessions in her book.

Noted.

"...From either side," I finish, glaring straight at my father.

"You'll have to excuse my son, Thalia," he says smoothly. "He seems to have forgotten his manners. Please...tell us about yourself." He pins her with a lethal stare. "You are, after all, *family* now."

The insult is unspoken, but it's loud and clear. Thalia will never be a part of our family, in this life or the next.

I slam my wine glass down, but my retort dies on my tongue when I catch Thalia shaking her head at me. "Santi, it's fine. Your father has every right to be curious about me. And every right to have his question answered."

I know she's putting on a show to hold up her end of our agreement, and I can tell she's nervous from the slight edge to her voice. Thalia isn't afraid to stand up for herself, but her bravery has limits, and those limits have a distinct tell:

The sharper her words, the greater her fear.

All her life, she's been taught to hate the very people she's being forced to make polite conversation with tonight. I expected tantrums. What I'm receiving is fucking Oscar-worthy.

Is it for her, or for me?

We made a deal, but somewhere along the line the terms started blurring.

"I'm nineteen," she says, glancing around the table, meeting everyone's curious eyes in turn, even the ones flashing unwelcome signs at her. "I moved to Manhattan to be with my older sister, Ella, a year ago"

"Do you attend college, or does your father not allow it?"

"College isn't my thing," she admits, ignoring the jab. "I lasted one semester."

The contradiction of that acerbic tongue and innocent appearance holds me captive. I couldn't look away, even if I wanted to.

"And what is your *'thing,' Señorita* Santiago?"

"*Señora Carrera*," she corrects softly.

What the fuck?

My father leans forward as if he's misheard, but his brief glance my way has all the charm of a razor blade. "What was that?"

"You called me *Señorita* Santiago," says Thalia, meeting his gaze. "As you pointed out, I'm part of the family now, and that includes my name."

Lola's mouth drops open.

My mother laughs softly.

My dick turns to stone.

But my father's jaw ticks as he says, "*Lo siento, Señora* Carrera. My apologies."

"And my 'thing' as you put it…" she adds sweetly. "Well, I guess I'm still figuring that out. All I know is that there's a lot of ruin in this world, *Señor Carrera*. Perhaps, some things need to be put right."

I'm not sure if I want to hold my hand over her mouth or drive my tongue into it and kiss her senseless. Other than my mother and my aunt, I've never seen any woman dare to stand up to my father like this.

She's fucking fearless.

I wait for the explosion, but instead, my father indulges in a long, slow drink, studying every facet of her face as he does.

"I'm surprised to hear that, *señora*. You sound more philanthropic than ambitious. I thought charity was one of the Santiagos' deadly sins."

Boom.

There it is.

Thalia's polite smile slips as she returns my father's weighted stare, neither of them blinking. "I want to help the world, not make it spin for me—something that you and my father seem to take great pleasure in."

No one breathes.

No one dares.

What's happening here is so casual in its destruction, there will be nothing left of Legado to repair.

"Painting pretty colors over bloodstains won't make them go away, *Señora*

Carrera," he counters finally, the cords in his neck straining. "Eventually, the paint chips away, and the blood reveals itself."

"That's enough," I warn between clenched teeth.

The sins of the father are to be laid upon the children.

That's what his whole paint and blood metaphor bullshit means.

It doesn't matter what I do or what Thalia does. Hell, for that matter even Lola or RJ or those fuckers Grayson and Sanders. We could cure cancer or fly to the moon, but it's all just colored paint covering our fathers' sins.

Their blood will always be our stain.

And this isn't a family dinner. It's a slaughter. And I led Thalia here like a sacrificial lamb.

"So, am I supposed to dissect this thing first or just hack a leg and go for it?" my mother asks loudly, attempting to force a distraction by jabbing her fork into a tentacle.

"What's out of line is this whole act you two are putting on," my father snaps, ignoring her. "I don't care what you convinced that bastard father of yours, but I know my son." Thalia flinches, and he takes that opportunity to turn his vitriol on me. "I know you, Santi," he repeats viciously. "This whole family knows you. And we all know *why* you put a ring on this woman's finger. There's nothing real about a bartered marriage. What I really want to know is what made her agree," he adds, flashing Thalia a look of derision. "What would make a Santiago open her legs for a Carrera?"

I rise to my feet so fast, my own legs collide with the table, tipping over wine glasses. "I said that's enough!" I roar, not giving a fuck who hears me. "You're my father. I respect you, and I love you, but this isn't Mexico. This is my territory and my casino. The minute you stepped foot inside it, your authority ended. As such, you will *not* disrespect my wife."

Lola places a hand on my arm. "Santi—"

"No..." My father stretches out the word with full confidence. "Let him speak. I'd like to hear this."

Apparently, so would the rest of Cellar Bistro's wait staff because every eye in the whole damn place is on us, waiting for the conclusion.

Drawing in a deep breath, I try to remember whose side I'm on. Whose name I bear. Whose blood runs through my veins. But all I can see is white. All I can smell is jasmine.

"Why Thalia married me isn't important, and frankly it isn't any of your business," I tell him, lowering my voice. "The only thing that matters is that she did." I reach again for Thalia's hand, unable to stop the torrent of rage as I flash her ring across the table, a part of me registering that she isn't jerking it away this time. "You can either accept it, or you can leave."

There's a tense moment where nobody knows what to say or do. I've just thrown down the gauntlet, and part of me is starting to question my own sanity. This is Valentin Carrera. Anything could happen. He could storm out and disown me or put a bullet between my eyes and enjoy a Chianti.

He does neither.

What he does shocks everyone.

A slow, arrogant smile lifts the corner of his mouth. "Sit down, son. I'm not going anywhere until I finish my drink. Leaving good *Añejo* on the table is as much of a sin as pouring it down the drain." He turns toward Thalia, his smile widening. "Wouldn't you agree, *Señora* Carrera?"

At that, Thalia pales.

"So, I'm failing chemistry, in case anyone cares..." Lola pipes up, trying to ease the tension.

Nobody cares.

As I lower back down into my chair, my father holds his glass at his lips. "I do have one question for you..."

I grit my teeth.

"How philanthropic will your wife be when another shipment of dead trafficked women is dumped on your dock?"

You bastard.

"Trafficked women?" Thalia recites the words as a whisper—as if refusing to give them a voice will make it untrue.

Shit. Shit. Shit.

Only then does my father pick up his knife and fork and begin vigorously sawing at the now cold duck on his plate. "*Dios mío*, did he not tell you?" Pausing, he points his knife across the table. "Communication is the key to a lasting marriage, Santi... Deception after only a few days isn't a good sign."

I clench my fists. "Don't..."

"Danger..." my mother cautions, trying to diffuse him with a soft but stern whisper of the name only she calls him.

He ignores both of us. "Then allow me, *señora*. This morning, your childhood friend, Edier Grayson, intercepted a Carrera shipment arriving from Guadalajara. Recreational goods, of course. However, in exchange, he left us a present. A forty-foot shipping container filled with seventeen dead naked women. Trafficked women."

"No..." She shakes her head vehemently, her hands white-knuckling the table. "You're wrong. Edier would never do that." Her breathing is erratic, her pupils dilated and wild as she turns to me. "His mother is the one who runs the women's shelter in Colombia. His mother *was* a victim herself. He's grown up with his father's hatred for the business all his life. My own father abhors it. He would never sanction this. Tell him, Santi!" she says desperately, turning to me. Though what the fuck she wants me to do about it is anyone's guess. "Tell him Edier wouldn't do that!"

The strange clamp around my chest is back...squeezing harder and harder. But I can't tell her what she wants to hear just to spare her feelings.

Before was personal, this is business.

"There's no other explanation," I state bluntly. "He's right. Revenge changes people, Thalia. It's changed us all." *Me and you, included.* "It makes them do things they never thought themselves capable of doing."

Glancing at my father's callous stare, I deliver the final blow. "You of all people should know that."

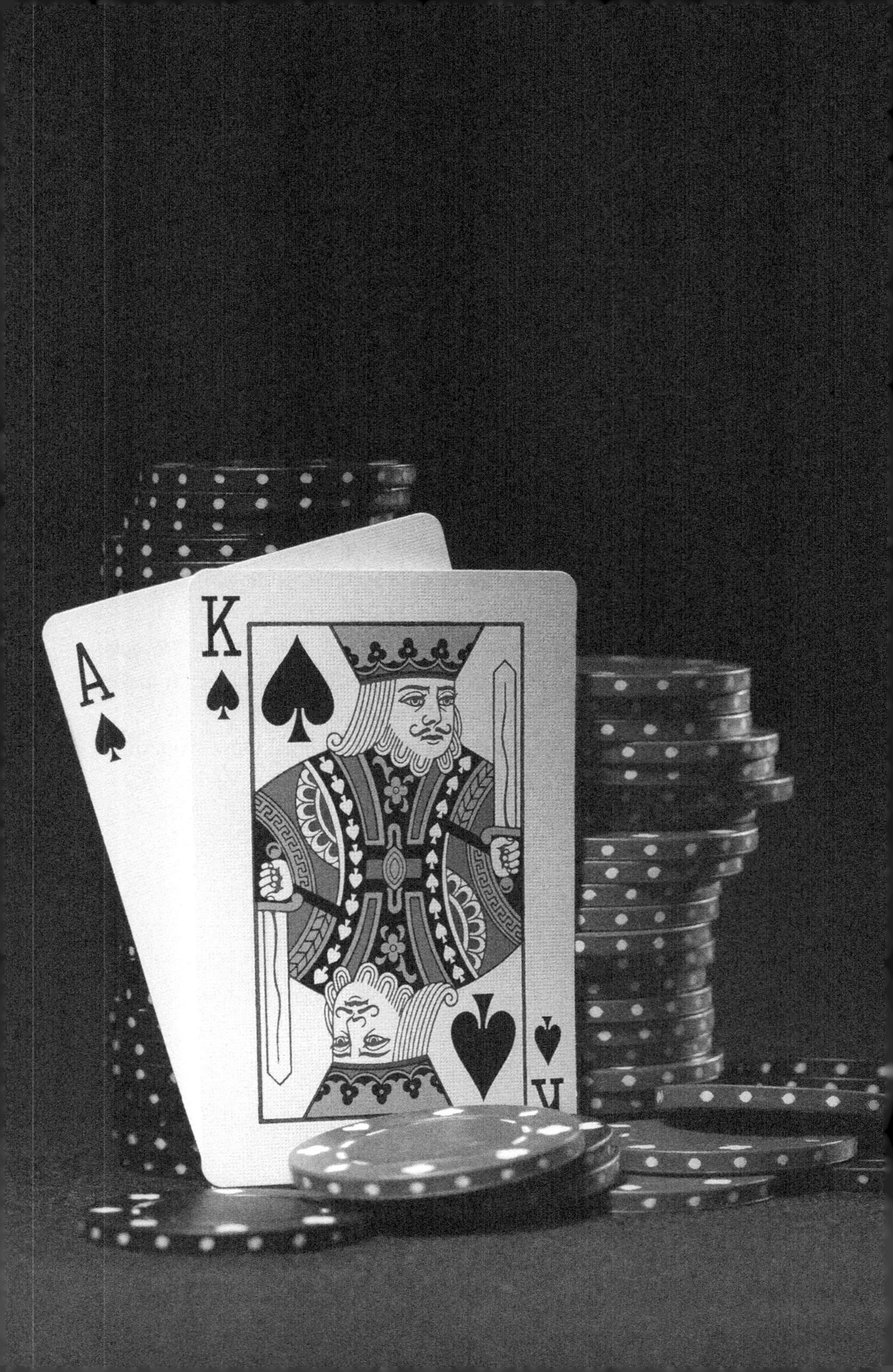

CHAPTER
Twenty-Seven

THALIA

It wasn't easy for me to walk away from that fight, and I can't deny that it hurt my heart to do so.

My damn Santiago heart.

Ella was right. I *am* similar to my father in some respects, no matter how much I argue to the contrary. Our shared stubbornness is what drove me to Santi's casino in the first place. I made the problem, so there was only one person who was going to fix it.

It's this same stubbornness that keeps me playing along with Santi Carrera's mind games.

Swinging my legs out of bed, I check my phone on the nightstand.

Still no call from Ella.

Still no message from Bardi.

Still no closer to morning.

Three a.m. is a dead time—*the worst time*—shipwrecked between night and dawn. Still, I need a drink of water and a pee, so another day in captivity is going to have to start extra early for me today.

Pulling a hoodie over my old gray sleeping T-shirt, I follow a long black hallway all the way to the kitchen. Part of me hopes that I'll run into Svetlana again, just in case she has another message from my father, but when I hit the lights, the place is sterile and empty.

I pour myself a chilled glass from the bottle in the fridge and lean against the island to survey the scene of our food fight explosion the other night. Turns out, it was just the beginning because we haven't stopped exploding since. Every day, every minute, every hour brings with it a new bomb—the latest being the table of doom last night.

I came straight back to the penthouse after the meal. I didn't expect him to come and find me because he'd made his feelings clear. When all is said and done, Santi will never trust me. I will always be the enemy. My words and opinions mean less than nothing to him.

I shouldn't care, but I do.

Finishing up my glass of water, I place the empty back in the sink and head for the door. I see us for what we are now—we're a war within a war—fighting for ascendency on a slippery slope. I find myself conceding a little more with each hour I spend in his black tower. With each time he infuriates me, confuses me...*touches me.*

A few days ago, I wouldn't have been caught dead in a white dress without a Santiago special makeover.

A few days ago, I hated him with every breath in my body.

A few days ago, I hadn't felt my whole axis shift when his tongue carved the promise of his own concession into my pussy.

And it's all because of a brutal, demanding, passionate man who presides over a kingdom of bones.

I'm heading back to my bedroom when I hear a scuffling noise coming from his office.

Back-tracking fast, I open the door to find him sitting in his black leather chair, with his feet up on the desk, his head facing the ceiling, and a half-drunk tumbler of something brown and alcoholic in front of him.

For a man who prides himself on his appearance, he didn't get the memo today. His gray tie is a coiling snake across his chest, the top two buttons of his crumpled white dress shirt are wide open, and both sleeves have been rolled up to the elbows.

He's a silent statue until the door clicks shut behind me. The sound echoes like gunfire. He drops his head and pins me with his hard brown eyes, looking stupidly angry, and stupidly handsome, and very, very drunk.

"You're up early."

"Never went to bed." Blowing out a sigh, he slides his tumbler across the table in my direction. "Care to join me? It's your father's favorite."

He's clumsy with his movements and the whole thing starts to topple. I hold my breath before it miraculously rights itself.

"I don't like bourbon," I confess, curling up in the chair opposite. "It reminds me of family parties invariably cut short when he went off to murder someone."

He grunts and doesn't comment. His hair is a disheveled, furious mess like the rest of him, and I'm aching to run my fingers through it.

"I was looking forward to my bottle of *Añejo*, until some fucking liver liberator sneaked in here and swapped it out for water."

I blush beet red. "Guess she was a, uh, liver-tarian?" I say, wincing slightly.

"Never knew you cared." He gestures toward the bourbon. "Thought I'd try drinking alongside the enemy for a change instead of trying to bury him."

"How did your father know it was me who poured out your bottle?" I ask, curious all of a sudden.

His palms flex into fists as he slides them behind his head. "My father knows everything."

"Sounds familiar," I say, hugging my knees to my chest.

"It's not fun, is it, *mi amada*?" He drops his fists again. "Getting born into chaos and spending your whole life trying to make sense of it."

"I think you've done okay," I say, glancing around his office. "You built your own empire of sin."

"You say it like it's a *very* bad thing."

"Just because I don't appreciate the process, doesn't mean I can't appreciate the results. It couldn't have been easy to step out of Valentin Carrera's shadow."

I'm still learning to step out of my own father's.

"Cut the bullshit," he says, narrowing his eyes at me. "You'll only be happy when my head is on a spike."

"Likewise," I say, trying not to smile.

"I'd rather see it in my bed, attached to the rest of you."

He's only saying it because he's drunk.

With a shaking hand, I pick up the bourbon and take a sip. He chuckles when I make a face and put it straight back down again.

"God, that's disgusting."

"There's a Coke in the refrigerator, if you'd prefer."

"All the better to drown you with, you patronizing asshole," I say, my temper flaring.

"It's called gratitude, Colombian *princesa*."

We glare at each other as our war within a war spills out into early morning.

"Fucking fearless," he muses eventually.

"Prince of Darkness," I retort.

He barks out a laugh. "That's a new one." He considers me for a moment. "You have a fire inside you, Thalia Carrera, and it's too goddamn distracting. Was this your plan all along? To infiltrate my kingdom and implode it? My father wants to murder me, my mother is a close second, and my sister… Fuck!"

"Edier *didn't* plant those bodies, Santi," I say softly. "The same way my father didn't storm this casino, and he didn't fire those bullets—"

"Don't be so naïve." He yanks his tie off and chucks it across the room.

"Don't be so short-sighted! I know you want this battle, but what if we're not the only sides playing?"

"Did Grayson put you up to this?"

"No."

"Do you really want to change the world or just make it more palatable?" he asks, changing the subject.

"Is that a serious question?"

"I liked it when you came on my face earlier." He drops his feet and leans forward over his desk. "My benevolent, little virgin."

I grab the bourbon again. It's a reflex action. This time my sip is enough to make my eyes water.

"My virginity seems to be a bigger deal to you than it is to me."

The atmosphere in the room recharges with something other than liquor fumes.

"That's because I'm going to be the one to break you. My wife. My pussy."

I blush again. "You can't claim ownership of everything, Santi."

"Says the woman who hasn't fucked me yet."

I roll my eyes in mock disgust. "How does your ego even fit in the *door*?"

"Turns out I have a big penthouse." I watch him pull out a sheet of white paper from his drawer and a pen. "New deal terms," he announces, and I watch him write a sentence in a jagged, inelegant scrawl. "Let's expedite this shit. One night with me, and you get your fucking money in the morning."

"That's not fair," I whisper, the blood draining from my face. "You'd be an even crueler man than I thought if you made me make that choice."

A beat later, he's balling up the paper and throwing it in the trash.

"You're right. Stupid idea."

He looks like he wants to say something else, but he stops himself in time.

"You could just give me the money now," I say hopefully.

"And have a chorus of slammed doors ten seconds later as you hightail it back to New York?"

Something in his voice makes me pause.

"Is that why you're dragging your feet, Santi?" I say slowly. "Do you not want me to make that decision? To leave as soon as my locks turn? You could have given me that money from the start, but you made me wait a week, even though the maximum damage you could inflict on my family was made the moment I said, 'I do.' The rest was just cartel posturing. A blown-up bar here, a political hit there—"

"A crate full of dead women down on my fucking dockside." He leans back in his chair again to study me. "Are you saying you *wouldn't* leave if I gave you the fifty-thousand?"

"You and I could never work, Santi," I say with a sigh. "Even if we wanted it, there's too much bloodshed under the bridge. What we have is hate lust. Hate fascination. It's toxic and it's beautiful, but it only ends one way."

I remove the rings from my finger and place them on the desk between us.

"I'm not going to sleep with you because I want your money, or because I'm your wife and it's my duty. I'm going to sleep with you, simply because I want to. Because it's something that's mine to give, without threats or coercion. You say that you're this big, terrible man, so come on… Show me your worst. Destroy your enemy's daughter's innocence. Deliver that killer blow to my father or deliver that killer blow to me if you refuse."

Rising to my feet, my heart pounding, I slip my hoodie from my shoulders and pull my gray tee over my head.

His eyes darken, but he doesn't move a muscle as I climb across his desk in my black panties. I'm halfway there when his willpower snaps, and he's pulling me the rest of the way into his arms.

"You have no idea what you're offering me," he warns, settling me astride him. "But my dick can't handle the way you just pussy crawled across my desk like that."

"Good thing *I* can handle it," I whisper, digging my fingers into his hair like I've been wanting to do since I first entered his office.

"So young...so fucking delusional."

"Kiss me... Make me forget."

He tastes of bourbon and temptation—*the devil's favorite cocktail.*

I can't get enough of it.

I can't get enough of him.

"Fucking fearless," he repeats, placing a hand over my heart, and then he's pushing me off him and rising from his chair. There's a primal look on his face that's both scaring and thrilling me.

Spinning me around, he bends me over his desk, thrusting against my ass so violently that I'm forced to lock my fingertips around the edges for purchase.

"Shit!"

"Firebird." He covers me with his body crushing my breasts against the cool glass surface. "My beautiful, fearless firebird... I'm not capable of being gentle on a good day, but when I'm half a bottle of bourbon down, I'm goddamn vicious."

Taking a step back, he flips me over again and drags my panties down my thighs.

"Open up," he orders, ripping at the buttons of his shirt. "I know you're going to feel as good as you taste."

His body is to die for—broad, tan, bullet-scarred, tattooed, perfect—with a wall of muscle behind a trail of black hair.

"Pretend I'm not a Santiago," I say, groaning as he trails a hand down the center of my naked body, while the other rips at his belt and zipper. "Pretend—"

"No pretending." He pinches my nipple between his fingers, sending another bolt of desire shooting through my pelvis. "Not tonight."

His clenched fist comes crashing down next to my head as he leans over me to trail that same wicked finger up through my soaking wet folds.

"This pussy," he groans, shaking his head at me. "This *fucking* pussy..."

He doesn't ease me in with a finger. The smooth head of his cock is already pressing against my entrance. Like everything else with us, we're pushing boundaries, breaking rules—

"Look at me."

My eyes snap open.

"You're right. I am going to destroy this cunt," he says savagely. "I'm going to fucking mold it to me."

"Is this the part where I have to beg for it?" I whisper, feeling the heat and fullness of him and wanting more. *So much more.*

"No, *mi amada*," he says, his fingers tracing my 666 pendant. "This is where *I* do some of the begging for once. Because if you don't let me inside you, if you don't let me fill you up, I won't be held responsible for the carnage I'll be causing to this office."

"Beg for it then, Carrera," I whisper, pushing back on him, feeling him slide in slowly until he hits resistance. "Beg for pleasure from your Santiago wife."

He slides in a little deeper and the first bite of pain makes me groan with pleasure.

"Fuck, you're tight."

"Santi…"

His fingers find the hollow of my neck. I can feel the warmth of his palm wrapping around my skin—pressing, squeezing... "On second thought, I'll ask for your permission instead."

Good enough.

"It's yours."

His hand tightens around my neck. *Another inch.* "Like you had any fucking choice in the matter."

His next thrust buries his cock so deep inside me, his name on my lips is a scream and a prayer.

He curses.

"Santi!"

There's nothing tender about the way he fucks. He means to shatter me. Pain turns to pleasure as he forces every inch inside me with every thrust. His hands are on my breasts, my ass, my mouth. There's nowhere that doesn't bear his delicious scars.

His control is insane. It's as ruthless as he is. When he picks up his pace, each stroke—each vicious grunt—is a masterclass in expelling air from my lungs and more screams from my lips, as the glass desk below me turns as wet and slippery as my inner thighs.

I start to free-fall, and he forces his fingers into my mouth, turning my final scream into a twisted mess of skin and desire. As my back arches and my body shudders, he pulls out of me, his hand pumping viciously until thick ropes of cum cover my aching slit.

"Mine," he grits out, giving me one of those blazing hard stares that turn our lies into truth.

"Ours," I whisper, pulling him into my arms.

CHAPTER
Twenty-Eight

SANTI

The road to hell is paved with good intentions.

The road to this bed was paved with bad.

Thalia sighs in her sleep and rolls onto her side, tucking her hands beneath her chin and bringing her knees up to her chest, as if she's keeping all her dreams hostage. The twisted white sheet that was wrapped around her naked body falls away, and I'm drunk off the sight it leaves behind.

No matter what happens, I'll always own a piece of her. I'll always be the first man to sample that helpless, rasping melody she makes when she comes… Tearing my gaze away, I lean back against the headboard and close my eyes.

The first to ruin her…

The empty glass in my hands demands a refill because that's what happens when the woman you're supposed to hate flips the fucking script on you. You start your drinking day before dawn.

I was supposed to use her and then toss her back to her family broken and shamed. Now, she's lying in a bed I've never allowed another woman to sleep in before and stealing more than just my sheets.

Her debt chains her to me, and the key is buried in a vow of lies. But Bardi is gone, along with all my fucking leverage, so there's no reason to keep her here.

So why can't I let her go?

Placing the glass on the nightstand, I lean over and brush a lock of her dark hair away from her face. *So beautiful. So dangerous.*

She calls me the Prince of Darkness, but after last night—after she broke in my arms—I'm now the Prince of Deception.

CHAPTER Twenty-Nine

SANTI

Three days later, and the truth is still hanging around my neck like a noose. Each time we touch, I can feel it tightening more and more.

And there's still no fucking sign of Bardi.

"Are you sure this isn't some kind of trick?"

I scan down the length of Thalia's outfit. *Jeans and a T-shirt again.* Her style leaves a lot to be desired, but it's growing on me.

"Are you going to elaborate, or do I have to read between the lines of your skepticism?" I say, straightening my tie.

"You're allowing me to leave Legado to go shopping." Her eyes narrow to sharp slits as she adds, "*Alone.*"

"You'll have an escort."

She rises to her feet. "Your sister? *That's* your security guard?"

"Yes," I lie. *As if I'd leave Thalia and Lola unprotected for a moment.*

"Are we talking about the same person? Five-three, a hundred pounds, likes to push your buttons and make that vein"—she waves her finger at my forehead—"swell as big as your…" She trails off, her cheeks staining red again.

Once upon a time, that mouth drove me to hold a loaded gun to her head. Now, it makes me want to defile her even more.

"My what, *mi amada*?" I say, my voice dangerously low. Closing the distance between us, my fingers stray a little too close to her heart. "Say it…"

"Your cock," she rasps.

I claim that dirty, fucking mouth with a kiss.

"You'll come back today, *mi amada*."

"Give me one reason why I should?"

"I'll give you fifty thousand of them."

At that, a shadow crosses her face. It passes a mirror image across my chest.

"Did I interrupt something?" an amused voice comes from the doorway.

Perfect timing as ever, Lola.

"Nope," says Thalia, ducking out of my embrace. "Santi was just giving me his credit card."

I arch an eyebrow at her. Opening my wallet, I hand her my AmEx Black. "With a pre-set ten-grand limit," I add, icily.

Her smile falters as she finally sees this domestic illusion for what it is.

I still don't trust her.

I don't even trust myself.

As the door closes behind them, my phone rings.

I answer, ready to lay into RJ for giving me radio silence all day when he cuts me off before I can say a word. "Come to the control room. There's something you need to see."

I stare at the black and white screen, every instinct of mine straining to put a bullet through it.

"You told me the security footage was hacked and erased."

"It was." RJ pauses the video. "But Legado's previous owner installed backup servers. It took us a day to hack, and we weren't able to recover all of it, but I think this is enough to determine we have a problem."

"Play it again."

He starts the surveillance footage from the beginning. We watch as a large man, dressed in similar black fatigues to the bastards who destroyed my casino, enters the basement. A beat later, he's firing two bullets at my *sicarios* that they never saw coming. Stepping over one body, he grabs the corpse's wrist and wrenches it upward, pressing the dead man's thumb against the access pad.

This wasn't an accident.

This was intel.

I remain silent as the man approaches Bardi, who's sitting slumped and bound to the chair. He keeps his back to the camera, but the look on Bardi's face when he sees him tells me all I need to know.

Recognition.

I watch the relief washing over that bastard's face. "Is there sound on this?"

RJ shakes his head. "Just images."

From there, it's the same flurry of motion as during the last two times I've watched it. The man pulls a knife from his pocket, slices through Bardi's restraints, and then the two of them exit the camera's line of vision.

"Here, take a look at this." RJ backs the tape up to the moment right before the man pulls out a switchblade to free Bardi. "There," he says, pointing at the screen. "Look familiar?"

I lean closer. The image is grainy, but those harsh black outlines cut through the static. The tattoo on the side of his neck is blazing—black and ugly—like a beacon.

"Is that an ax?"

We exchange glances.

RJ grits his teeth. "The New York Italian mafia insignia."

"Ricci." The name burns as it passes my lips. "That's an unwelcome blast from the past."

Twenty years ago, Don Ricci ran New York's cocaine distribution—a billion-dollar baton handed over by Rick Sanders when he stepped into the political arena.

Don Ricci. The same man who turned state's witness against his own Syndicate, inciting an underworld civil war and leaving New York ripe for the taking—a territory both my father and Dante Santiago were determined to control.

What the hell is a dead man doing back in the fucking picture?

Thalia was right. This isn't just an East Coast rivalry anymore. There are more seats at this table than we thought.

"Find out who that man is, and how he got into my casino."

RJ scrubs a hand across his unshaven face and nods.

"Until you have an ID on whoever has picked up Ricci's reins, and find intel on how Bardi's involved, we keep this between us. ¿*Comprendes*?"

"Yeah, I got it."

Fucking Ricci. Even from the grave, he's still waging war against us.

I'm pulling out my phone as I exit the control room. "Rocco, it's me. Are you still tailing them?"

"Yep."

"Step it up and be vigilant. Call for backup."

He doesn't ask questions. The tone of my voice is warning enough.

Until I know how deeply the remains of Ricci's fractured Syndicate are involved in this, *all* Carreras are in danger.

And as my wife, that includes Thalia.

Four hours...

That's how long it's been since I met with RJ, and everything went sideways.

I once read that the art of war was to know your enemy better than you know yourself, but it's not that fucking simple when one of them is a ghost from the past who's started haunting our cartel again.

Why him?

Why now?

Fixing the collar of my tuxedo, I fire off another message to my second in command. If someone so much as breathes the wrong way tonight, we'll know about it. There are more armed men surrounding this casino than guests, but there's a storm coming from an undisclosed direction, and we need to be prepared.

"Thalia!" I call out, checking my watch again as I'm hit with a jarring sense of *déjà vu.* "Get down here. We're going to be late."

These were my exact words six days ago—right before she appeared looking like a carnival sideshow act.

"Okay, I'm coming."

Expecting black jeans—hell, maybe a clean T-shirt if I'm lucky—the vision standing at the bottom of the spiral staircase drop-kicks my preconceived notions right out of the penthouse door.

She does a long, slow twirl that has all of my attention. The floor-length, crimson halter dress exposes curves in all the right places. Her dark hair is styled in a low bun at her nape, exposing a stretch of flawless tan skin that's begging for my mouth.

"Red," I muse, the corners of my mouth tipping.

Giving me a coy shrug, she runs a hand down the delicate beaded fabric. "What can I say? I was feeling nostalgic."

"Nostalgic or vindictive?"

Her seductive smile hits a straight line to my cock. "To quote my husband, 'the line between nostalgia and vindictiveness blurs too easily."

"I believe that referred to hate and lust."

"You have your interpretation. I have mine."

"You're playing a dangerous game, *mi amada*," I warn, stalking up to her. "That sultry insolence is severing what little control I have left. Are you trying to provoke me?"

She lifts her chin and holds my gaze. "What if I am?"

Don't ask questions you don't want the answers to.

Trailing my hand down her spine, I feel her shiver as I lean in to whisper a dark promise in her ear. "Oh, I'm sure I'll think of something for your retribution."

"Do your worst," she whispers back, her brown eyes sparkling. "You only have twelve more hours to corrupt me."

Spoken like a true Carrera.

Legado shines like a diamond tonight.

The jewel in my empire of sin.

As we make our way through the crowds toward the Platinum Lounge, I lean in and graze Thalia's ear with a heated promise. "I've decided to take another of your firsts later."

She stops and turns, a question forming in her eyes.

Sliding my hand from her waist to her face, I press my thumb against her lips. "I dream of these, you know that? Hurling insults… Wrapped around my cock…" Hooking my fingers under her chin, I force her to look at me—savoring her embarrassment like it was my finest bottle of *Añejo*. "When this night is over, I want you on your knees in that dress, *mi amada*. You're going to open this beautiful mouth and take me. *All of me.* And you'll be looking up at me the whole time as I fuck my pleasure into you until the tears stream down your face."

"Would you like me to beg for it?" she asks softly.

"I wouldn't have it any other way." Over her shoulder, I catch my father staring at us from across the lounge. "Have a drink. Have three." I say, my mood souring. "You're going to need them."

His stare is unwavering. Seconds pass like minutes until finally, he lifts his glass of tequila and nods.

A silent message... *We'll talk later.*

Turning back, I find Thalia already at the counter. I watch without taking a breath as Monroe Spader slides onto the spare barstool next to her. That fucking man is beginning to outlive his usefulness.

The bill has passed.

Sanders's bar is a pile of dust.

Our business has concluded.

I stare as she offers him a polite smile. *A fuck off smile.* Only he can't take a hint, pushing those black-rimmed glasses back up his nose as he leans in closer.

If he touches her, I'll rip his arms off.

"Green is an interesting color on you, Santi." I turn to find my mother has materialized beside me with a glass of my finest Malbec wine in her hand.

She thinks I'm jealous.

She's right.

"She's a Santiago," I say grimly, taking her inference and turning it into something unpleasant. "She serves a purpose, *mamá*. Nothing more."

Her thoughtful gaze travels back to the bar. "If you push people away enough, eventually they don't come back."

And so she fucking shouldn't.

I make my decision, then and there. It's time to let my firebird fly and see if she leaves me for heaven or sits by my side in hell. After tonight—*after one more taste of her*—that footage is hers.

"Santi."

We turn to find RJ standing behind us. I've never seen him so tense.

He gives my mother a respectful nod. "Aunt Eden..."

She smiles warmly. "It's good to see you, Rafael."

He flinches at hearing his given name. Understandable. It's a permanent reminder of the man slaughtered by my wife's father.

Quickly recovering, he turns to me with a grave expression. "There's a man outside requesting to talk to you."

Something in his voice makes me pause. There's anger there. Pain... *History.*

"Go," my mother says, stepping back, her eyes shifting to my father. "I'll handle him."

"Tell me," I say, falling into step with RJ as we exit the bar.

"Ten minutes ago, he walked up to the security at the front entrance," he clips out. "Unarmed and uninvited. He's waiting for you by the front steps outside. We have thirty guns trained on him and his men as a precaution. Just give us the order when you're ready."

"That's quite a welcome," I say, shooting him a look. "Who's the VIP, and why the fuck is he so deserving?"

"It's Edier Grayson," RJ says grimly. "He says he wants to talk."

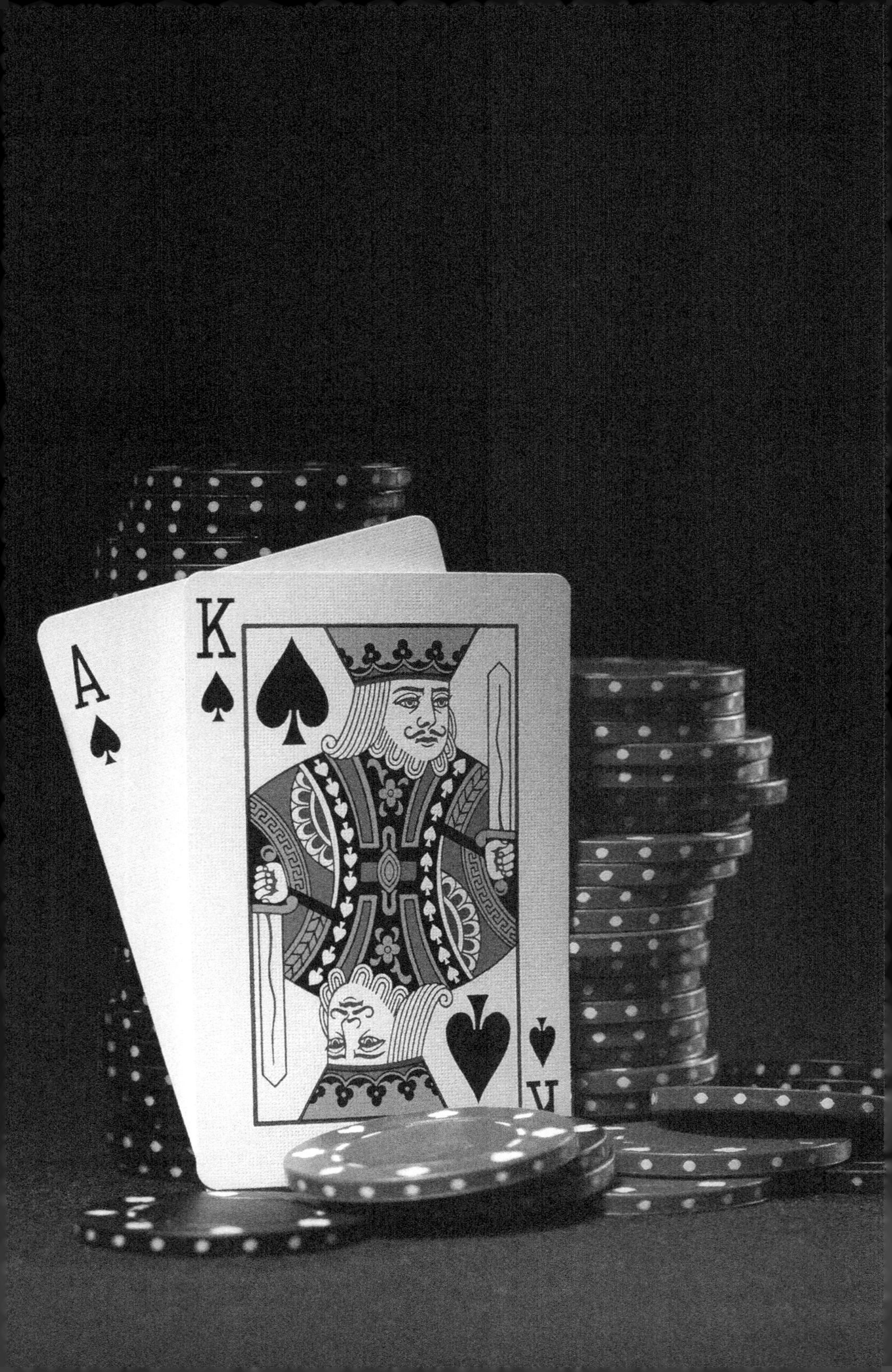

CHAPTER
Thirty

THALIA

"If I ask Santi to buy you diamonds, will you teach me how to count cards?" Lola swivels on her barstool to study the empty blackjack table behind her. We both needed a break from all the Carrera tension threatening to break bottles in the Platinum Bar, so we're swapping Rapple cocktails and relief in one of the empty private gambling rooms off the main floor.

It has free drinks and no drama, so we're both in heaven.

"I would if I could." Leaning over the bar counter for more ice, I *plink* a couple more cubes into my highball. "Some people assign values to each card in a deck, but it's more of a visual thing for me. It's like my brain is hardwired to be a criminal, even when the rest of my body is resisting."

"I'm envious," she whistles. "I could totally clean up in here, and Santi wouldn't be able to do shit about it."

"Knowing your brother, he'd find a way," I say with a laugh.

"At least it wouldn't be a ring on my finger." She swivels back to the bar to drain the rest of her drink.

Not for much longer I reflect, glancing down at mine.

Kicking off my red heels, I flex out my aching toes and take another sip of my Rapple. Tomorrow has all the ingredients of an emotional cocktail. There'll be relief at finally being able to pay Bardi off and secure the tape; fear about coming clean to *papá* and being ordered back to his island with his next breath…

And then there's something else—an unwanted flavor that's sitting uneasy in the pit of my stomach.

I don't want to go back to being like one of those directionless insects above trees in summertime. *I don't want to miss the way he fucks his anger into me, like I'm to blame for blurring these lines, only for him to kiss me like I'm the only clarity in his life.*

"I need to pee," Lola announces, rising to her feet.

I drain the rest of my drink and eye the rows of tequila behind the bar. "When you're back, I'll mix us up a couple of margaritas."

"My national drink," she says with a grin. "Don't fuck it up. I'll make sure the private sign is up so no one barges in."

"Thanks."

I hear the door click shut behind me. Silence pervades, and then there's another click, followed by a turning lock.

"That was fa—"

My words become a muffled scream as a large hand clamps across my mouth.

"Thalia, it's me," comes a familiar drawl. "Don't fucking bite, or I'll torture you to death with bad jokes until the end of time."

"Sam?" I gasp out. As rough skin turns to air again, I whip around to confront him. He's dressed in a black tux, like some kind of criminal mastermind version of James Bond, but with a much smoother smirk. "What the *hell* are you doing here?"

He slaps a finger to his lips as my voice rises to an undignified screech.

A Santiago on Carrera territory is never a good thing, but tonight it's suicide.

"I've come for you... Orders from above." He points to the heavens, but we both know that finger should be pointing in the other direction. "Edier wanted discretion. There's some bigger shit at play."

"I can't, Sam—"

"We know."

Two words. Numerous possibilities. *An ocean of heartbreak.*

"We know everything, you crazy, beautiful, brave, total fuck-up of a woman," he continues, sounding exasperated. "What the *hell* were you thinking trying to deal with this shit on your own? I nearly put a bullet in your brain for your alleged betrayal six days ago. Edier wanted to throw you in the Hudson."

"How much do you know?" I whisper, realizing my lungs haven't actually expanded since those two words entered the room.

His expression darkens. "You mean the tape?"

"Oh God." I sit back down on my stool with a *whoosh*, frantic tears filling up my eyes. "Shit, Sam, you can't tell him, you can't tell him! Please, you can't tell. You can't—"

"*He* knows as well," he says heavily, cutting across my hysteria. "Marco Bardi is a dead man walking."

I let out a sob. This is my worst-case scenario—the one thing I've ripped myself in two to avoid these past few weeks.

"If you kill him, he's going to release another copy! You don't know him like I do. He'll find a way. Ella—"

"Is fine," he says soothingly, wiping the tears away from my cheeks. "She's safe. She doesn't know about any of this and she never fucking will. Edier is bartering for the last remaining copies now. He'll kill everyone in America before he walks away empty-handed. He can protest it until his blue balls fall off, but we all know how he feels about her."

My hand flies to my mouth, pressing hard to stem a thousand different emotions for spilling out. I start to sway on my barstool.

"Jesus." Sam grabs my arm to steady me before sliding it around my shoulder and pulling me in for a hug that smells of sandalwood and cast-iron guarantees. "You're free, Thalia," he murmurs into my hair. "Chuck your rings over the side of the Bridge when we cross it doing one-ninety later. The divorce lawyers are on stand-by. You're walking out of Atlantic City tonight, sweetheart, and you're never coming back. You hear?"

I think of that one ingredient again.

The one thing I can't bring myself to consider.

"How did you even find out about Bardi?" I stammer.

"We caught him trying to blow up one of our shipment warehouses down at Red Hook Terminal yesterday. Edier followed a trail of fuckery which led us to a very sweet old lady in Queens who was more than happy to give up her grandson. Last night, your father cut the truth from his tongue." I watch Sam's smirk slip into something more unpleasant, *more befitting* of the man he's become. "Bardi is currently sitting in a car outside your soon-to-be-ex-husband's casino with an 'S' carved into his chest. Or what's left of him."

"Wait." I grab his arm in confusion. "You're telling me you've given Bardi to *Santi*? After everything he's done? When did Edier and *papá* learn such restraint?"

"He's a peace offering," he says, leaning over the bar to help himself to a vodka bottle. Pouring himself a double, he knocks it back before continuing. "He's the foundations of a temporary truce. Bardi is Carrera's, as long as he agrees to talk with Edier and not blow the back of his head off."

I watch him pour out another in a daze. "Has the world stopped turning since I've been locked up in a penthouse tower? My father actually *agreed* to this?"

"After what we uncovered yesterday, it's in all our best interests to shut the fuck up and listen to each other for once, instead of trying to turn the East Coast into World War Three." He takes my hand and yanks me off the barstool. "Time to go," he announces. "My car's outside."

"But why would Santi want Bardi?" I say, scrambling to slip my heels back on as he marches me toward the door. "How is he a bargaining chip?"

"The fact that he spent most of this week as an inmate of his fucking basement is pretty indicative." He lets go of my arm to unlock the door. "Carrera chopped off half the fingers on his left hand before he escaped. Edier took great pleasure in evening it up on the right."

I screech to a halt, my heart following suit. "Are you saying Santi *knew* about the tape?"

Sam frowns and nods. "From the first night you met."

The pain explosion in my chest steals my breath away.

Santi knew how badly I needed that money. Instead, he chose to use that knowledge to turn every kiss, every touch, every fuck into a lie.

"Bardi was the one blackmailing me," I gasp out. "I needed fifty-grand, but I never told Santi what it was for."

All he ever cared about was winning jabs in a war he never even started in the first place.

"Take me home, Sam," I whisper. "I'm done with Atlantic City."

CHAPTER
Thirty-One

SANTI

In the end, the storm came from the Northeast, bringing with it a dangerous man from New York, wearing cold curiosity and black.

With ten men arranged in a semi-circle behind him.

They're not pointing their guns. They're still concealed. But their threat lingers over the *porte-cochère* like a bad secret waiting to be shared.

Loosening my bow tie, I leave the silk strands hanging as I slow to a stop right outside Legado's tinted front doors. I slide my hands into my pockets, keeping my cool on the outside, even when I'm raging behind my mask.

It's my first tactical move of this meeting. Five marble front steps separate us, and guess who has the height advantage…

Edier Grayson stands like a statue in front of me, his hands clasped in front of him, wearing the same uniform as his men. On them, they look like soldiers. With Grayson, he looks like a motherfucking assassin.

He's a suave bastard—as tall as me, with a Colombian heritage that shows in his features, and an adopted upbringing that has sharpened them into the ultimate weapon.

His stillness is unnerving.

His dark gaze, unswerving.

I sense RJ falling in beside me, his hand hovering over his gun, but this is the last place I need bullets to fly. We're already giving my guests a free show.

Steeling my jaw, I glance over at Rocco, who's hovering a few steps behind. "Secure the entrance. I don't want anyone walking through those doors. Got it?"

He offers a curt nod before retreating inside.

"You brought our war back to my casino, Grayson" I say idly, turning to my uninvited guest and breaking our standoff with a casual accusation. "Are you here to piss on my walls this time instead of shoot them?"

His face darkens. *Finally, a reaction.* "You know that wasn't us, Carrera. If that was the play, I would've aimed a scorpion bullet at your head, not the wall."

He's right. Grayson would consider it a waste of time and good artillery. If he aims, he aims to kill. Which is why his presence is like a downed power line—calm exterior but filled with enough voltage to light up a man with a single word.

"I'm surprised you have the balls to cross that Bridge. You're gate-crashing my big night."

He doesn't react. Not one damn smirk cracks that facade. "I'm sure I would have enjoyed myself immensely, but my invitation got lost in the mail."

"Yet here you are...and you brought friends." Spreading my arms wide, I gesture to his ninja-clad entourage. "Obsession isn't a good look for you, Grayson."

Taking one slow step at a time, playing fast and loose with the swagger, I hold his icy stare until we're face to face. Two feet apart. Boss to boss.

Prince to prince.

I don't need to look behind me to know that RJ is right there, or to know that the thirty sniper guns we have trained on the situation need only one good reason to fire.

"You have sixty seconds to tell me why you're here. After that, you and that piece of shit car you hauled over state lines are getting a remodel." I direct his gaze to where a long, dark sedan is parked, blocking my valet stand.

Arrogant fuck couldn't even park like a normal person.

"You dare to ask me that, Carrera, after all the trouble you've caused?"

"That *I've* caused?"

"You forced Thalia to marry you. You made her look her *father* in the face and lie. That's the kind of shit, Santiago remembers." His own mask is slipping, and I want nothing more than to rip it off and shove it down his throat. "We both have blood on our hands. That truth is as real as our hate, but you went too far when you stained hers."

My smirk disappears. "No more than Sam Sanders did with my sister last year."

He considers this for a moment, and who am I to interrupt?

Let him tie his own knot and hang with it.

"This isn't over," he says, stepping forward to meet me halfway. "That shot *will* be returned at some point. But right now, there are more important things to discuss."

"Enough dick swinging," I snap. "Tell me what you want or get the fuck out of New Jersey."

He straightens up, rolling his shoulders back like he's gearing up for the fight of his life. "You have something of mine, and I want it back."

Over my dead body.

"Thalia is a Carrera now." I cut the distance between us to a single foot, escorted by the sound of ten Santiago rifles preparing to spill their deadly secret. "She's my wife—in *every* sense of the word."

Let that sink in for a minute, you Colombian asshole.

His eyes narrow as he holds up his hand for his men to stand down.

My amusement doesn't last. As usual, his allergy to emotion is a buzzkill.

"Classless innuendoes," he tuts. "How very *Carrera* of you. You're becoming annoyingly predictable, Santi. Which is why I've come prepared to offer an incentive."

"Fuck off," I reply, succinct as always.

"I'm not here for Thalia."

I pause. "Why the incentive then?"

He gives me a chilly smile. "Hear me out before your snipers"—he gestures to the windows of the casino behind me—"decide to ruin my evening."

"Spit it out, Grayson. I bore easily."

His jaw flexes. I'm pushing him closer and closer to the edge. "You give me what I want, and I'll give you something you've been looking for." He nods to one of his men, who turns and opens the rear passenger's side door of the sedan.

I'm not sure what I'm seeing at first, and then it hits me.

Bardi.

He's slumped over in the backseat with what's left of his hands bound in front of him. I thought he looked like shit the last time I saw him, but *shit* is a step up from what's staring back at me. His face is a goddamn color parade—at least the parts I recognize. Most of it is a canvas of bloody gashes and open flesh. He's still struggling though, but it's a waste of everyone's time and energy. Unless he plans to log roll his way down the Atlantic City Expressway, he's fucked.

I don't care why he's here.

I care about *how*.

"How the fuck do you know Bardi?" I demand, forcing down a visceral reaction to put a bullet in both of them. "You have no idea what he's done to Thalia. *Dios mío*, to Ella!"

Her name is a cracked whip, and suddenly all the monsters here are dancing.

"Of course, we know what he did," Grayson snarls. "Why the hell do you think I'm here? Cocktails are for pussies, and poker is a cunt's game. We caught Bardi at Red Hook Terminal with a bag of napalm and a smile, attempting to blow up a shipment of ours all the way back to *Barranquilla*." He tosses a disgusted look at him. "Goddamn idiot nearly blew his nuts off."

What has this Italian idiota gotten himself involved in?

"You're telling me he was trying to sabotage a Santiago import?"

A curt nod is his only affirmation I get. "Our *sicarios* brought him back to the warehouse, and we had ourselves a messy conversation. I'd planned to remove a finger for every ten minutes he kept his mouth shut." Something like a smirk threatens to tilt his lips. "Then I saw you and I like to have the same fun." He motions to Bardi's three remaining fingers. "Turns out, he only needed two to sell you out."

"Shit," RJ mutters beside me.

"He was playing both sides." Grayson's lips tilt even more. He's enjoying digging the knife in and giving it a good, hard twist. "But with a little motivation, we made him sing."

"You drove all the way out to New Jersey to tell me this? Don't you have technology back in the Big Apple?"

"I know about the tape, Carrera. And I know you have it." His smirk disappears. "Give it to me now, and then we can all be home in time for milk and cookies."

Now?

Bad move, Grayson. I don't bow down to demanding fucks.

"Are you expecting me to be impressed by your intimidation act?" I say with an exaggerated sigh.

"I know exactly what's on that footage," he says, losing his cool. "If you think I'm going to leave an audition tape of Ella Santiago that was made for some mafia princess trafficking ring with *you*, you're wrong. I'll fucking shoot it out of your hands, if I have to."

My blood runs cold.

We suspected there was a ring, but we didn't know all the fucked-up details.

"It was requested by a specialized ring," he continues. "One that comes with the highest price tag on the market. Crime boss's daughters. Cartels, bratvas, mafia... Those Romanian bastards don't discriminate, as long as the bloodline is certified." He glances back at the sedan again. "It was another confession from our mutual friend, Bardi. I didn't believe him until our docks turned into a graveyard."

Fuck.

"Let me guess... A shipping container with a bad surprise."

He nods, the muscles in his neck pulling as taut as a bowstring. "Eleven dead girls... That was personal to us, Carrera. That was personal to *me*."

I remember what Thalia said during the dinner from hell. How his own mother was a victim of trafficking.

"I was about to burn this place down to the ground thinking you were responsible until Sanders reminded me of something." We're nose to nose now. *This could go one of two ways, and neither of them ends well.* "Despite all the betrayal, despite the death and destruction, despite the years of bad blood, the Santiagos and Carreras will always have one thing in common... We don't trade flesh. That's one sin neither of us is willing to lay claim to."

It's true. This swings back to *La Boda Roja*.

Son of a bitch.

La Boda Roja...

Old scars are reopening, hemorrhaging their truth for a new battle.

One neither of us saw coming.

"It's not the Romanians," I tell him coldly. "It's Ricci."

"Ricci? As in Don Ricci?" He lets out a clipped laugh. "The traitor wearing a pair of concrete shoes at the bottom of the Hudson?"

"No, a restructuring of his Syndicate." Saying the words out loud is enough to stir the monster inside me. "And if I'm right, history is about to repeat itself."

He stills. "Explain."

I turn and catch RJ's eye. Nodding, he steps forward.

"We have surveillance footage of the man who helped Bardi escape," he says. "There's an ax tattoo on his neck."

Grayson's fury swings back to me, and he jabs a finger into my chest. "If I find out you're lying about this, Carrera…"

He's riding that edge again.

"He fucked with my business," I snarl, shoving his finger away. "He was wearing the same fatigues as the men who destroyed my casino six days ago. Now why do you suppose they'd shoot scorpions into my wall?"

He doesn't hesitate. "To make it look like a Santiago attack and ensure a retaliation."

"War is starting again with the Italians just like it did twenty years ago. Only this time, *we've* brought it to American soil, and they have the home advantage. They're behind this mafia princess ring…not the Romanians." Side-stepping Grayson, I glare at Bardi. "He lied to hold on to the one card he had left."

A fact proven by the frantic screams now coming from the black sedan.

I half expect my enemy to level the barrel of his gun to the back of my head. Instead, he moves to stand beside me, and I know we both feel something shift.

Standing toe to toe.

Talking instead of killing.

"If Bardi is working with the Italians, why hold the tape over Thalia's head? Why blackmail her with it?"

"He didn't," I grit out. "Bardi was never planning to make the tape public. He counted on Thalia's love for her sister outweighing everything. He played on her worst fears and used it to pad his own pocket. The blackmail was a side venture to go along with the main event."

There's a flicker of respect in his eyes. "How can you be so sure?"

"Thalia told me about her sister's illness." I catch a muttered curse under his breath. "To the men Bardi works for, she's damaged goods. She won't fetch the same price." I stiffen as the final piece clicks into place. "Not like Thalia will… He didn't bring her here that night to collect a debt. He brought her here to deliver one. It was pre-arranged. Swap out one sister for the other. Even better when they look like twins."

RJ exhales a weighted breath.

"If I hadn't caught her counting cards, she'd be theirs already."

"Motherfucker!" Grayson roars, causing all ten guards to aim their guns at my head again. "Thalia—"

"Is safe," I grit out.

"And your sister?"

A beat later, the barrel of my Glock is being introduced to his forehead. "Are you questioning my abilities to keep them safe, Grayson?"

In his defense, he doesn't even blink. "If history *is* repeating itself, it's up to us to change the outcome."

"I'm listening." *With my gun still cocked and loaded.*

"Twenty years ago, Dante and your father agreed to a temporary truce in order to bring down a common enemy. Let's make this come full circle. We blow up this ring, we stop trying to kill each other, and we end these bastards, once and for all."

"Because that went so well last time," I drawl.

He lets out a dark chuckle. "Don't get me wrong; this changes nothing. My emphasis is on the 'temporary' here. When all of this is over, I'm still putting a bullet in the back of your skull and smiling while doing it."

"Not if I have that pleasure first. Considering I'm holding a gun to your head right now, I'm fucking calling it."

"Lower it, Carrera. I came here with a show of good faith. Give me the tape, and you get Bardi's severed head as a new wall mount, and we both stop dead girls from turning up on our docks."

Common sense tells me this is a bad idea. *Never trust a Santiago.* The past doesn't lend itself to a happy outcome.

But the alternative...

Fuck.

I can't even think about that.

"There's one copy of the footage on RJ's phone. You can watch him delete it." Lowering my gun, I turn toward my stunned looking second. "Call Rocco. Have him bring the other copies out."

"It's official... Hell is freezing over." Grayson holds my gaze for a beat before nodding at his men. Two of them lower their guns to drag Bardi from the car, forcing his frantically twisting body to his knees in front of us. "He's all yours."

Usually, I like to fuck with my prey before I kill them, but not today.

Lifting my gun, I aim right between his eyes. "For Thalia," I murmur, refusing to consider the alternatives.

If that red dress hadn't strutted into my office and fired her own calling card at me...

If my fearless firebird had fallen into the hands of monsters who are even worse than I am...

For my wife.

When I fire, the bullet is dried ink on a truce we just made in blood.

Temporarily, of course.

Tucking my gun back in its holster, I glance at Grayson. "Take him back to New York. I don't want that kind of shit stain on my doorstep."

There's a flurry of motion behind me as Rocco appears with the footage and hands it over to Grayson.

"Watch your back, Carrera," he murmurs, as I turn to leave. "We both have traitors in our midst for this carnage to have been orchestrated this smoothly."

My thoughts exactly.

"One last thing..."

Pausing halfway up the steps, I watch the Colombian lean against the side of the car and cross his arms, while his men throw the piece of dead meat into the sedan's trunk.

Something in his casual stance makes my trigger finger itchy again.

"I have a confession to make."

From the look on his face, he's not sorry about it either.

"Considering my state's newly reinstated gaming laws, I was intrigued by the competition... Tonight, Sanders has been inside your casino, taking notes and catching up with old friends. He should be long gone by now, though."

As soon as I hear that *pendejo's* name again, I freeze.

Lola.

Goddamn it, Lola was in there.

"He had strict instructions to avoid your sister," he reassures me. "This time, anyway. Truth is, we missed Thalia. We wanted to bring her up to speed with the fact you've had Bardi's tape all along. We thought it might help with her *lucidity* toward the true state of her marriage."

I watch in mounting fury as he opens the passenger door and slides into the seat, calm as fuck—as if he didn't just pull the trigger on me after all.

"She's coming home with us, Carrera," he says, reaching for the handle, and then rolling down the window to continue his backhanding clusterfuck. "Santiagos don't belong on this side of the East Coast. You know that as well as I do."

But firebirds do.

They can fly anywhere.

"I thought we weren't fucking each other over," I snarl.

The bomb I'd planned for another of Sanders's bars is about to get predated.

"Starting now," he calls out in mock apology, rapping his knuckles on the roof of the car. "You know, all this could have been avoided if I'd just shot you that night outside the church. You're lucky I'd never aim a bullet near her."

I stand there long after the taillights disappear into the night, in the ruins of a ten-year-old grenade he just tossed at my feet.

The girl outside the church.

The one I risked everything to protect.

The one who haunts my dreams.

Thalia.

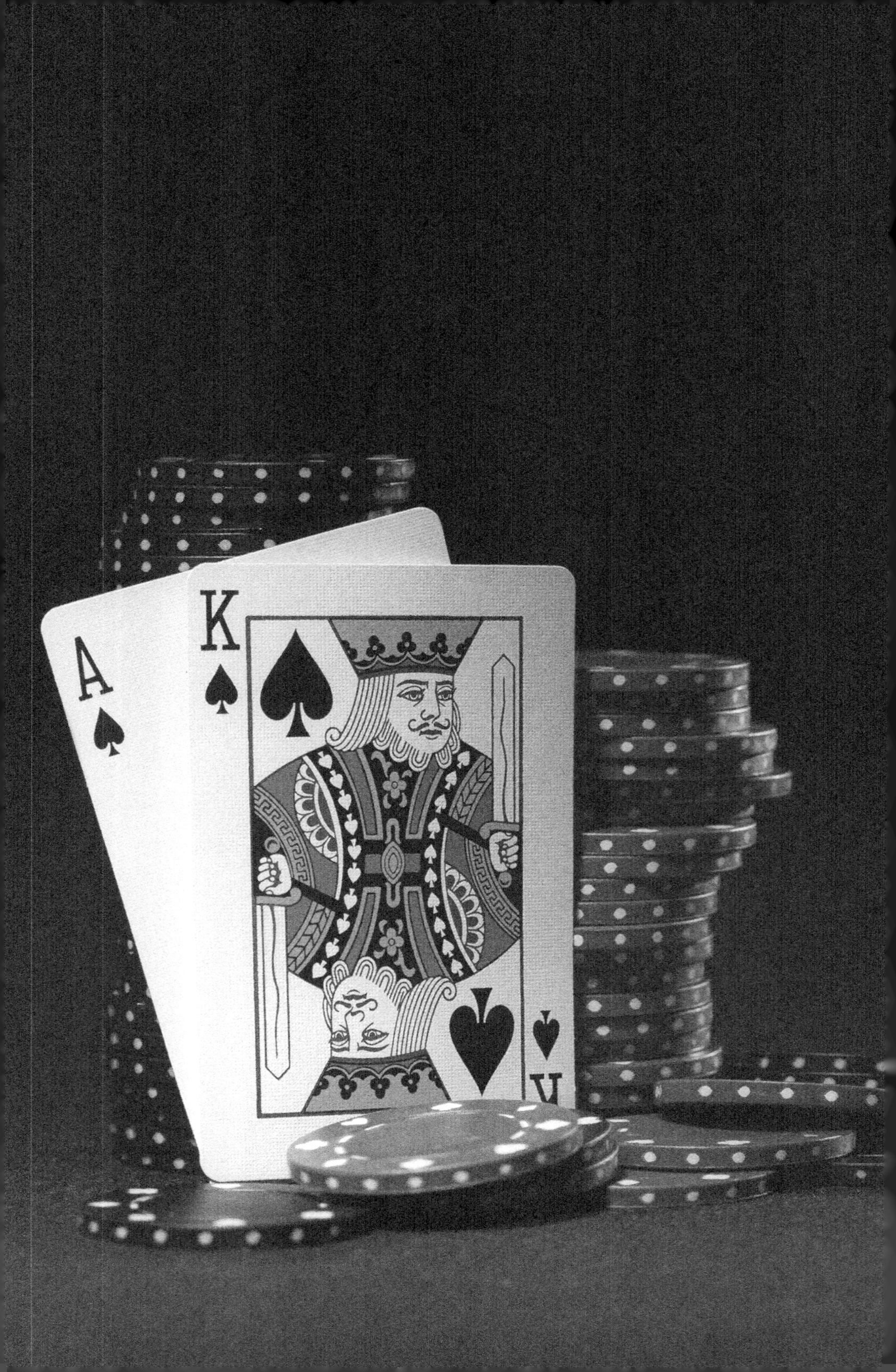

CHAPTER
Thirty-Two

THALIA

H urt is a hammer designed to break you apart.
Pain is what happens on impact.

I'm feeling the brutal effects of both as Sam leads me through Legado's back entrance and out into the deserted parking lot. At any other time, this would be at full capacity, but tonight was "by invitation only" for a select few.

A night of celebration.

A night of last memories.

A night of betrayal.

Don't look back, I tell myself as my heels spark misery off the asphalt. Our future isn't written in the stars. It's scrawled on a note passed back and forth between enemy lines.

And then he was caught.

And now I hate him more than I ever did. *So why the hell are there tears in my eyes?*

"Am I going to have to deprogram you?" Sam asks as we reach his Bugatti. "What the fuck are you so upset about? The man duped you into marrying him. He forced you to betray your family. He lied to your face about—"

"Okay, enough."

I'd forgotten his sympathy chip was ripped out and stamped on the day he made his first kill.

Freeing myself from his grip, I take a step back as he opens the door for me. "We were a war within a war, Sam," I say quietly, casting one final look at Legado—shimmering high against a skyline, as black on the inside as her emperor's heart. "You and Edier didn't get to fight this one."

"No, we just fucking liberated you from it." He gestures for me to get in the car.

When I refuse, he shakes his head at me slowly. "Thalia Santiago... Always wanting to save the world. Never realizing that it's better to push certain people off it first... *Especially a Carrera.*"

"That's a little hypocritical, don't you think?"

His face loses all traces of amusement. "Get in the car, Thalia."

"Wait."

Sighing, he braces his hand against the door frame.

"How did you do it?"

"Do what?"

I hesitate. "How did you stop feeling for Lola, if it's so wrong to care about a Carrera?"

I wait for him to blow up at me, but he gives me a gray smile that's neither a lie nor an admission.

"You just do."

"That doesn't answer my question."

"Jesus, Thalia..." He runs a frustrated hand through his dark hair. "You're a fucking Santiago. This family comes first. Follow that rule, and you'll figure out the rest."

Deeply profound and evasive as hell.

"And you *still* haven't gotten in the car."

I steal one more look at the place I called my reluctant home for six days.

"Okay, Sam, I'm—"

Boom

The gunshot shatters the night, blasting chaos into the space between us. My heart slams against my chest, and I fall back against the Bugatti door frame. Then I look to my left and find an ugly bloom of red spreading across Sam's white dress shirt.

Oh God! Oh God, no!

"Sam!" Terror buckles my knees as I shove away from the car, watching as he skids down the side panel with a hissing curse and a final order.

"Run, Thalia... Get the fuck out of here!"

I have to get to him. I have to help him. He's going to die.

I'm on my knees and reaching for him, when rough hands grab me from behind, squeezing so hard around my middle, I can only wheeze out a shocked scream.

As I'm lifted into the air, a bag is pulled over my head while another gunshot rings out.

Sam!

I can't breathe.

I can't breathe.

I fight as hard as my father taught me to.

I kick.

I twist.

I buck.

Then something sharp pierces the side of my neck, and my whole world slides into darkness.

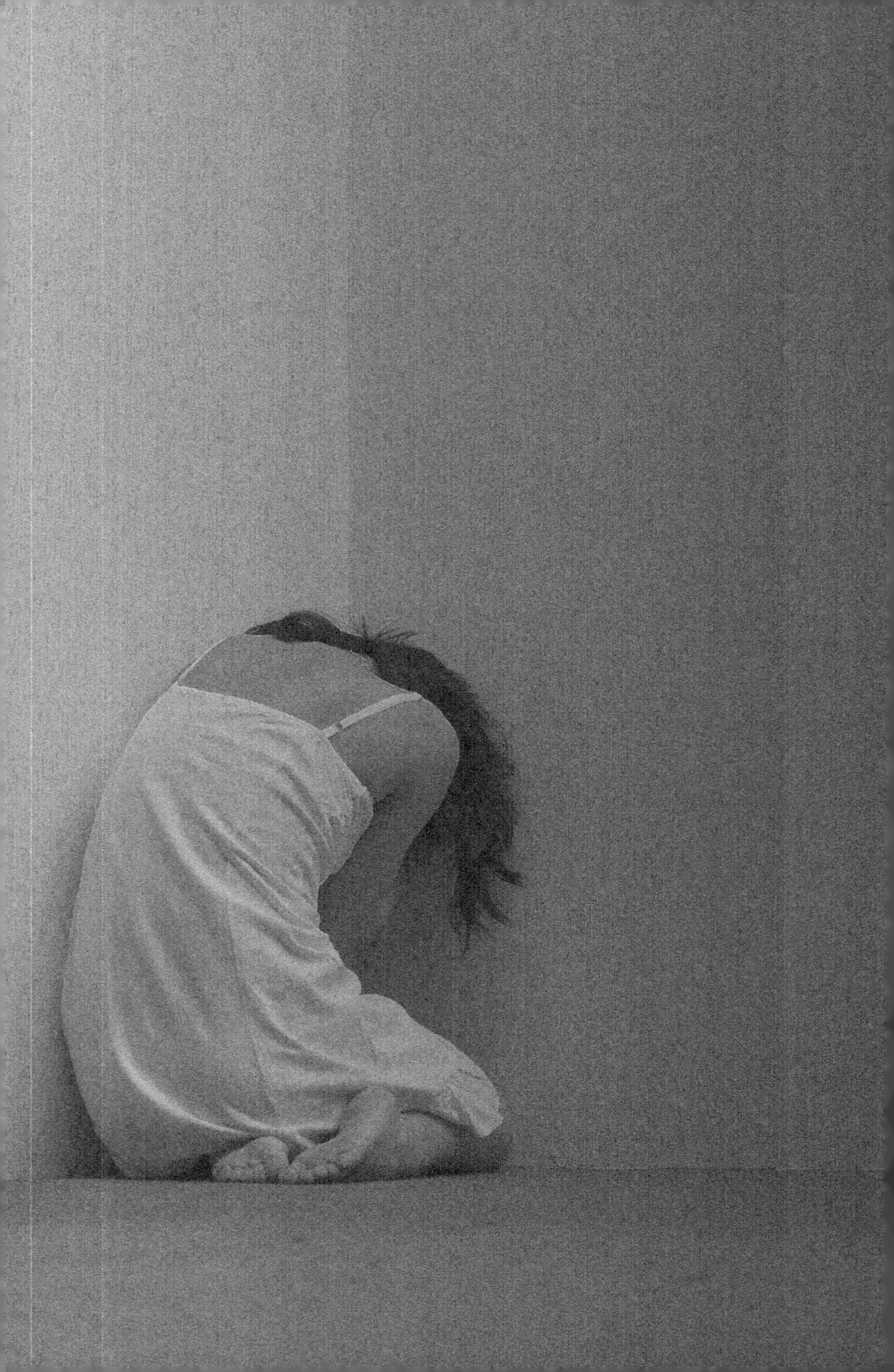

EPILOGUE

THALIA

It's pitch black.

My eyelids feel like concrete.

I keep them shut tight until I can muster enough strength to open them. When I do, a hot and sticky world comes rushing in—blanketed by a cloudy haze.

It smells of metal and salt. I can hear something, too. There's a buzzing noise above my head. I try to look up, but my head feels even heavier than my eyelids.

There's a flickering LED tube light running along the ceiling.

Flick. Buzz. Flick. Buzz. Flick. Buzz.

Watching it makes me feel sick, so I close my eyes again and concentrate on forcing back the waves of nausea. It finally subsides, only to be replaced by a drilling ache inside my head.

Dizzy.

Why am I so dizzy?

It feels like my brain is sloshing back and forth.

Am I hungover?

I go to rub my temple, but I can't.

I try again.

I still can't.

Opening my eyes wider, I force myself to focus on the light. That's when I notice it's not my brain that's sloshing back and forth. It's the floor.

My pulse thumps a wild beat in my ears as I try to move my arms again.

"What's happening?" I beg the haze, my voice hoarse and unrecognizable to me.

Only silence answers.

I hate silence.

Squeezing my eyes shut again, I force myself to remember snapshots from *before*...

I was with Santi at Legado's reopening night... And then...

There's a sharp pain in my chest when I remember what Sam told me.

There's another when I remember the sound of two gunshots.

"Sam," I rasp, tears spilling down my cheeks.

After that, everything comes back in a rush of choking fear—the hands, the bag, the pain. I'm too scared to look down. *I'm too scared not to.* My hands and feet are bound together with black duct tape, and I'm wearing a white satin slip dress that's ridden up past my knees.

Last night, I was wearing red.

Look around, Thalia... Assess your surroundings... Fighters survive...

I blink back my tears and force myself to concentrate. I'm in a box—a damp, dark, gray, steel box—that's gently rocking back and forth. There are no markings on the corrugated walls, and no signs to tell me where I am, or who has taken me.

That's when I hear soft crying.

Frantic, I scan the darkness again, and then I see her. There's another woman in here, wearing the same white dress as me. She's slumped in the corner, her head pitched into her knees, her long dark hair a messy contrast to her tan and bruised skin.

I'm about to call out for help when the crying stops.

"Perdona nuestras ofensas, como también nosotros perdonamos a los que nos ofenden."

Forgive our offenses, as we also forgive those who offend us.

"No nos dejes caer en tentación y líbranos del mal."

Do not allow us to fall into temptation and deliver us from evil.

I know those words. They're the ending verse of the Lord's Prayer... whispered in Spanish.

I know that voice, too.

"Lola?" I hiss.

She lifts her forehead from her knees, tears matting her hair to her cheeks.

No. No, no, no, no.

As we stare at each other, Valentin Carrera's words come rushing back, soaking me in their dark candor.

Shipping container.

Dead women.

Trafficked women.

We weren't just kidnapped.

We're being sold.

They say that when you're desperate, your mind swings a pendulum back and forth between survival and comfort...

In this moment, I only see him.

Brutal, demanding, passionate him.

"Find me, Santi," I whisper to our new hell. "Find us both."

Tainted BLOOD

BOOK 2
CORRUPT GODS DUET

TAINTED BLOOD

A Carrera is a master of deception.
A Santiago never forgets.

Santi Carrera is the war I never saw coming.
A beautiful liar.
Ruthless.
Captivating.
The architect of my own undoing.

He twisted my loyalty into an ultimatum.
He chained me to his side with a vow of deceit.
I should despise him for all he's done to me...
But behind those dark eyes, I see his pain.
I recognize his conflict because it's ours to share.

Now, I'm a pawn in a new war.
Stolen by a stranger, I've been taken to a foreign land.
My fate rests in the fragile truce between our families.
They will tear this world apart to find me.
But he's the only man who can save me.

"Goonies never say die…"

PLAYLIST
In no particular order…

If We Never Met - John K., Kelsea Ballerini
Black Sea - Natasha Blume
Dirty Mind - Boy Epic
Umbrella (Epic Trailer Version) - J2, JVZEL
Fight For My Survival - The Phantoms
Dead Man Walking - WAR*HALL
Like That - Bea Miller
Black Widow - Iggy Azalea, Rita Ora
Sucker For Pain - Lil Wayne, Wiz Khali
Heathens - Twenty-One Pilots
Gangsta - Kehlani
Devil Eyes - Hippie Sabotage
You Should See Me In a Crown - Billie Eilish
Prisoner - Raphael Lake, Aaron Levy
Give Em Hell - Everyone Loves An Outlaw
Finish Line - SATV Music
The Hunted - The Rigs
Do It For Me - Rosenfeld
Drink Me - Michele Morrone
Feeling Good - Michael Bublé

PROLOGUE

SANTI
Ten Years Ago

The snow is falling harder now.

It's settling on the windshield. Fading the whole world to white.

I check my phone again, my pulse kicking into overdrive when I see RJ's text.

Got it. Call you in five.

I knew it.

I'm already stepping out of the SUV by the time Tito, my cartel-appointed babysitter, shakes his fist at me across the console. "*¡Maldito niño estúpido!* Get back in the fucking car, kid!"

"I'll only be a minute."

"Where the hell are you going?"

I shift my gaze toward the old church. "To prove a point."

Slamming the door, I make my way across the street, a thick blanket of snow climbing up to my calves and soaking my jeans.

I can hear my father's voice with every step.

Choices have consequences, Santi.

Even as a reckless thirteen-year-old, I understand the meaning of the phrase, and the warning that comes with it. He's drilled it into me so many times it's become like second nature.

Today, I've made three choices, but the consequences are still a mystery.

The first was crossing the Mexican border into America. The second was my decision to join this war. And the third? That happened ten seconds ago, when I chose to ignore a direct order.

The snow is up to my knees. I decide I'm not a fan as I trudge a path through it, adrenaline rushing through my veins.

I can't screw this up.

I won't screw this up.

I glance down at my phone.

Three minutes to go.

I slow my stride as I reach my destination, the muted yellow street lights above me casting a wide glow. With its menacing stone gargoyles, Sacred Heart Church looks out of place on the quiet street in Hasbrouck Heights, New Jersey. It's a little town right outside Hackensack, coated in Americana and family values. Mom and Pop shops line one side of the narrow streets, while parks and little league fields dominate the other.

Simple.

But that's another thing I've learned. The simplest solutions are often the smartest, like hiding in plain sight, for instance.

While I wait for RJ's call, my gaze strays toward the jagged New York City skyline. Something stirs inside me. Something I can't explain. Those bright lights might as well be spelling out my name. One day, I'll rule the entire East Coast. Not just New Jersey. I'll take New York too, and the Carreras will rule it all.

My breath comes hot and heavy at the thought, billowing out in front of me like a cloud of smoke. The gun shoved in the waistband of my jeans feels even heavier, pressed against the small of my back. I want it in my hand. I want to feel the grip. To curl my finger around the trigger… *To know the power of deciding someone's fate.*

Just as I reach for it, my phone rings.

"Well?"

"Definitely stolen," he confirms.

I rake an icy hand through my hair. "Damn it."

As soon as I saw that dark sedan park down the street, my suspicion shot off like a bottle rocket. Once I had the license plate, I texted RJ.

My cousin lives for this shit. If you want a database hacked or record unsealed, RJ's your guy. At fourteen, the kid is already a menace to society. In a few more years, he'll be a national threat.

Cops are the last thing we need. "Has it been reported?"

"About twenty minutes ago. Which gives you about forty before your quiet little suburban neighborhood turns into a SWAT team party."

"I'll get back to you." Ending the call, I type out a quick text to my father.

Surprise blue light show in forty.

Hitting send, I shove my phone in my back pocket.

Packed snow crunches under my feet as I brace against the bitter wind, all the while keeping a steady gaze on the dark sedan.

Fucking stolen.

Stolen means things are about to get really messy.

Cupping my hands around my mouth, I exhale a few hard breaths, trying to coax the feeling back in my fingers. *Can't pull the trigger if my hand is numb.*

Whoever is inside that car isn't here to pray for their sins. They're here to dance with two devils. But until they make the first move, all I can do is watch and wait, which is the story of my life.

You're not ready, Santi…

Watch and learn, Santi…

Wait until you're eighteen, Santi…

Well, screw that. I'm not a little kid anymore, and I'm tired of waiting.

I kick at the piles of snow in frustration. Now that I've been given the chance to prove myself, I've been regulated to "falcon"—*a fucking watchdog…*

Dios mio, I'm Santi Carrera—the kingpin's son. I shouldn't be hiding out, reduced to surveillance like a low-ranking soldier. I belong inside where the action is. Seated next to my father, Valentin Carrera. Staring into the black eyes of our enemy, Dante Santiago.

The snow keeps falling. It's like Mother Nature is trying to counteract all the darkness seeping from the church. It could bury us neck deep, and it still wouldn't matter. Light never triumphs over dark.

Inside, a muffled string of heated Spanish fights for dominance.

I check my watch.

Eleven minutes.

I'm surprised they lasted that long. My father and Santiago haven't been in the same room together—hell, in the same country—in eleven years.

Not since *La Boda Roja*.

Leave it to Gianni Marchesi, head of the New Jersey Syndicate to mediate a sit-down between the Devil and the Reaper. When your family deals on the wrong side of the law, even a thirteen-year-old knows egos and grudges take a backseat when it comes to the DEA. Handcuffs and prison bars don't discriminate, and Feds don't come for one—they come for all.

Which is why they're all inside, and I'm out here freezing my nuts off.

Santiago and my father would rather spend the rest of their lives behind bars than align again, but both men will do anything to protect their families. Even if it means being inside the same room.

From what I gather, an agent flipped a couple of dockhands on both sides of the river, putting not only Santiago's and my father's asses on the line, but Gianni's too. The Italian mob boss is the one who carved the path for the Carrera Cartel into New Jersey eleven years ago. It's never a smart move to owe a favor to a man like my father—the trade-off is never equitable.

Out of nowhere, a brutal gust of wind hurls a sheet of wet snow at my face. Blinking the flakes from my eyes, I turn toward the dark sedan again in time to see the rear passenger's side door swing open.

"Fuck." I fumble for my gun.

"Bug!" I hear a deep voice hiss from the driver's side. "Come back!"

A red, wooly toboggan breaks through the wall of white. It's a girl. *A young girl.* She's kicking up waves of snow as she runs toward me.

Shit!

"Shoot her," a voice in my head says. *"Shoot her now."*

"But she's just a kid," I whisper.

"Enemies come in all forms," it growls back. *"The sweetest faces are often the most deceiving."*

My throat tightens.

"Are you waiting for someone?" she calls out. "Do you want to come sit with us?"

"Do it," the silent voice commands. *"Prove yourself."*

She can't be more than nine or ten years old. *Innocent.* What the hell is she doing in the backseat of a stolen car?

Reluctantly, I release the trigger. *No, I can't. My first kill won't be her.*

I want to tell her to get back in the car, but I can't find my voice. I'm too wrapped up in those rosy, wind-bitten cheeks. She looks like an angel lost inside the walls of a white jungle. I want to look away. Instead, I watch, mesmerized as she draws closer, snowflakes dotting her long dark hair like a domino.

The shouts from the church are escalating. This time, it's more than a clash of egos. Something doesn't feel right. *Blood instinct,* my father calls it.

Still holding my gun, I grab my phone from my back pocket. Something bad is about to happen. I can feel it in my bones. And despite what my father thinks, I'm ready to take charge. I'm going to lead a *sicario* ambush inside that church. I have to get my father out of there.

I glance back at the girl.

I have to get her out of here, too.

She tilts her chin. "Did you hear what I—?"

"Go," I snarl, eating up the distance between us in a couple of strides and shoving her backward. "Get out of here. It's not safe!"

She stumbles, those soft brown eyes widening in shock. She doesn't understand.

"Leave her alone!" the older boy shouts.

That's when all hell breaks loose.

Out of nowhere, engines rev—plowing at full speed through the dense white curtain, just as gunfire erupts inside the church. My heart slams against my chest. Loyalty tells me to run inside.

But this girl…

Unfamiliar men pour from the cars as more shots ring out. Before I know it, I'm barreling straight toward her. Gripping her waist, I shove her to the ground, her small frame sinking deep into the snow as I shelter her with my body.

Choices have consequences.

I'll face mine.

If I live that long.

More squealing tires. More bullets fly but I refuse to move. I won't let this little girl die.

Not tonight.

Not ever.

"Bug!" I look up to find the older boy swinging the sedan alongside the sidewalk we're lying on. A spray of bullets hits the trunk. "Shit!"

The back door opens, and another boy about my age leaps out, frantically digging in the snow until he finds the girl's hand. Glaring at me, he tugs her toward the car.

I'm wrapped around her so tightly he's dragging me with her. Then logic kicks in, and I roll to the side, releasing her.

She came here with them.

They're taking her out of here.

To safety.

Away from me.

I'm not prepared for the knot those three words twist inside my chest. My head knows she's better off with them, but there's something ingrained which hates them for it. It hates them for being her heroes instead of me.

The second boy pauses before he lifts her inside. She locks eyes with me again, an unspoken question on her face.

"Go," I repeat. "You don't belong here, *muñequita*... Go!"

The boy yells something at her, but their argument is muffled by another vicious blast of wind. As it clears, I watch him turn toward me.

"He's a Carrera," I hear him say. "He's their look-out. He gave the signal. Don't you see? This whole meeting was a trap. He deserves to die like a dog for that."

The hatred in his words gives him away. Many fear my family. A few loathe us. But only one lives to see us suffer.

Santiago.

"*¡Hijo de tu puta madre!*" I curse at him. He's a lying son of a bitch. Whoever they are in Santiago's organization, they live in a bubble. That *pendejo* knows nothing of my world. Nothing of what I just sacrificed. Tonight, I chose a stranger over my own family.

Surprisingly, the boy's lies don't seem to affect her. Instead, she reaches out her hand to me. "Come with us!"

Innocent and *brave*.

In that moment, I know I've made the right choice. I may be a boy, but I'm also a Carrera. There will never be a place in Heaven for me, so when an angel falls at my feet, I have two choices: clip her wings, or help her fly.

In another time, in another place, maybe I'll be selfish, but not tonight.

Shaking my head, I offer her a parting gift—*the truth*. "I can't. I won't... This isn't our war yet. But it will be soon."

She doesn't get the chance to answer. The door slams shut, the sedan speeds away, and I watch as it's swallowed up by the storm.

Everything feels colder suddenly. Heavier. Darker... For the first time since landing in New Jersey earlier, I shiver.

Gathering every thought of her together, I lock them in a box at the back of my mind.

It's time to be a Carrera. It's time to prove I *am* my father's son.

Coolly and methodically, I rise from the sidewalk and walk, stone-faced, straight into the line of fire.

"You did well tonight, Santi," my father says, lifting his glass.

He looks so blasé and unaffected sitting there, sipping tequila at forty-one thousand feet, as if nothing has happened.

As if he doesn't have eleven new stitches holding his right side together.

As if we didn't lose four of our best *sicarios* tonight.

As if a bullet didn't graze my shoulder.

As if his thirteen-year-old son didn't just take his first life tonight—he took five.

In the end, the lit match was dropped from Irish fingers. Sean Mahoney, boss of the New Haven Irish Mob, was tipped off about the meeting and wasn't too thrilled with his lack of an invitation. He crashed the party and, as a result, not one damn Mahoney made it back to Connecticut.

"Thanks," I say, tonelessly, anticlimax choking out the last of my adrenaline.

"I never meant to bring you into the cartel this soon. You're thirteen, Santi. That's too young to understand the consequences of this life."

I think of the locked box tucked safely away in the back of my mind. *That's what he thinks.*

"Then why did you bring me with you?" *Why did you give me this choice?*

It's a question that's been eating at me since we left Mexico.

"I've made no secret of my intentions. I expect you to take over one day."

"And I've made no secret of mine. That's what I want."

His hand tightens around his glass. "Eventually, everything *will* be yours—the cartel, the Carrera name, our legacy, and the responsibility that accompanies all three."

I arch an eyebrow. "Responsibility?"

"*La Boda Roja.*" The three words roll off his tongue in a twisted mix of reverence and disgust.

He doesn't have to explain. *La Boda Roja* has been drilled into my head since I was a toddler.

"*Nuestra lucha no tiene fin.* Our fight has no end, Santi. It's a vicious circle that will be handed down for generations to come. So to answer your question, I brought you to New Jersey to show you what lies ahead. To bring you face to face with Santiago, so that circle will burn just as brightly for you as it does for me.

"I hate him."

Hate isn't a strong enough word for what I feel for the Colombian. We locked eyes the moment I stormed through the doors of that church, and he looked right through me. Bullets flew past his head like torpedoes as he dismissed me like I was nothing more than a kid in the wrong place at the wrong time.

Like I wasn't even a Carrera.

My father pins me with a lethal stare. "Remember that hate, Santi. Feed it. Build upon it. Use it to your advantage. But whatever you do, never underestimate the same hate that burns for *you.*"

"So, who will be joining me in this ring of fire?"

His lips twitch. "It remains to be seen. The universe has seen fit to deny Santiago an heir." The twitch becomes a smirk. "Still, a rebel can't escape his destiny."

I have no idea what he means. *Pápa* has never been one for directness. He enjoys pulling people's strings and making them dance for his own entertainment—until he's bored enough to cut them and get to the point.

I usually don't take the bait... But this has my attention.

"Who would anyone try to run from power?"

"You'd be surprised. Not everyone is like you, Santi." The pride in his voice makes my chest swell. "But there are some who refuse to see the value in our way of life."

Then those people are as blind as they are short-sighted. Respect is everything in this world. When I grow up, I'll have everyone's, one way or another.

"Who are these *idiotas*?" I scoff.

"The sons of Santiago's second-in-command and a close business associate. They'll form the next generation of the Santiago Cartel, despite their present distaste for it."

"Does this 'dream team' have names?" My sarcasm is pushing boundaries, but he doesn't look pissed about it. Instead, he seems amused by my newly-inflated balls.

"Edier Grayson and Sam Sanders."

I test them out in my head, deciding I don't care much for either one.

He glances at me out of the corner of his eye, his stare turning deadly. "Grayson is the older of the two."

That must be who was driving the sedan. Which, by default, makes the jackass with the big mouth Sanders. I grit my teeth, his words cemented in my head.

"He's a Carrera. He's their look-out. He gave the signal. Don't you see? This whole meeting was a trap. He deserves to die like a dog for that."

No, *he* deserves to die for being a lying shit. It's just like *pápa* has always told me—*a Santiago doesn't deal in truth; he plays whatever narrative fits his needs.*

I could've died right there in the goddamn snow, protecting the girl, and it wouldn't have mattered. To them, I'll never be more than that dog who should've stained it red.

I hope *pápa* is right. I hope someday those two boys accept their destiny. Then, when I'm in charge, I'll show them exactly who deserves to die.

But that still leaves one unanswered question... *Who is the girl in the red toboggan?*

"*Muñequita*," I murmur.

"What was that?"

I shake my head quickly. "Nothing."

I've already told my father about the stolen sedan parked outside the church, but I've said nothing about who was inside it. And I sure as hell don't tell him about *her*.

Choices have consequences.

There's a stretch of silence as *pápa* drains what's left in his glass, then clears his throat. "How's your shoulder?"

"Hurts. How's your side?"

"Filleted."

I laugh at the absurdity of the conversation. Sometimes I wonder what it would've been like to have been born into a normal family. One that watches *America's Most Wanted* instead of starring in it.

"Get some sleep, son," he says, rising slowly from his seat. "We have about four hours until we land in Mexico City." He motions toward my swollen eye. "We'll both need our strength to deal with your mother once she sees your face." With that, he disappears into the small bedroom at the back of the jet.

Left alone with a million questions, I recline my chair, allowing a single word to stain my lips once more.

Someday, I'll return.

To rule.

To reign.

To blur the sky with bullets.

Someday, I'll see my *muñequita* again. And when I do, I'll tell her about the night I chose her innocence over my loyalty.

CHAPTER
One

SANTI
Present Day

I'm standing on the marble steps outside Legado Casino. Unable to move. Unable to breathe. Unable to right everything that's just been wronged. Watching as Grayson's taillights disappear into the darkness, like a thief in the night.

A thief who just stole my wife.

The Colombian's revelation spins in my head until every word hums a sinister melody. *"You know, all this could have been avoided if I'd just shot you that night outside the church. You're lucky I'd never aim a bullet near her."*

Her.

The angel I chose to let fly, rather than clip her wings.

The signs had been there all along, dancing in the shadows. They'd watched and taunted, waiting for me to look past my own blind revenge and see the truth.

The girl in the red toboggan. The innocence I chose above honor.

Muñequita.

Thalia.

Everything has always been red.

Red Wedding.

Red toboggan.

Red dresses.

"Santi?"

I glance over my shoulder to find a gathered crowd of *sicarios* waiting for a command, anticipating a volatile reaction to the grenades Grayson just tossed out the window of his piece of shit car.

This wasn't so much a truce as a diversion. That Colombian bastard lured me outside so he could drive his way in. He dangled a Bardi-shaped carrot in front of my face, distracting me with warnings of princess rings and trafficking auctions, allowing Sanders enough time to turn my wife against me.

With the truth.

I grit my teeth. "I want this place surrounded," I say, forcing a calm I don't feel. "No one leaves the vicinity."

They all look at each other. One finally clears his throat. "What about the invited guests, boss? What if they're already leaving?"

"Then fire bullets into their tires until they're not." I don't wait for any more questions. Turning, I take two steps at a time, with RJ and Rocco falling in behind me as I barrel through the doors of my casino.

Curious eyes turn our way, but no one speaks.

"Have two guards stationed at every exit and the rest searching every inch of this place for Thalia like their lives depend on it." Pausing, I hold Rocco's stare. "Because they do."

My threat doesn't fall on deaf ears. As it shouldn't. I'm dead serious. Nodding, he slips out from behind us, his phone already to his ear, barking out orders.

RJ doesn't question where I'm going as I continue my path. He silently shadows my heavy footsteps as I weave through the layers of smiling patrons and make my way toward the Platinum Bar Lounge.

I don't hold out much hope, but it's the last place I saw her.

I scan the sea of faces, finding nothing but old money and ambitious socialites laughing as they turn a blind eye to Legado's bloody foundations. Six days ago, I looked at them and saw dollar signs. Now I just see my own fallibility.

But no red...

She's not here.

Fucking Grayson.

All I needed was a few more hours. I was going to tell her everything tonight—about Bardi, about finding the tape, about there being no debt to pay off...

About my decision to let my *muñequita* fly away. Again.

"What happened?"

I'm straddling the line between control and chaos as my father steps in front of me, a glass of *Añejo* tequila in his hand. It's not a question. It's a demand, delivered with the casual bite of a snake. Calm and controlled. *Almost fucking pleasant.* Valentin Carrera doesn't shout. Men like him wield much more power in a steady tone than a deafening roar. The danger lies in the delivery.

Despite all that, I don't bother to answer. The explanation of tonight's events would take too long, and frankly, I'm not in the mood to watch my father's head explode when he finds out I've ignored everything he ever taught me. Instead, I focus on more pressing issues.

"Have you seen Thalia?" I grit my teeth, adding, "Or Sam Sanders?"

At the mention of Sanders's name, he stiffens—his fingers clenching so tightly around the glass I'm surprised it doesn't shatter. "Why would a Santiago *pinche cabrón* be in this casino, Santi?"

That's a no, then.

Sanders is a reckless son of a bitch, but he's not stupid. You don't violate a man's daughter and then dance at his party. If Grayson sent him in here for Thalia, he'd stay out of sight until she stepped into view.

The irritating sound of spinning slot machines chisel down into my brain as I stand locked in a battle of wills with *El Muerte* himself.

I have to get out of this damn place.

Just as I turn to leave, my father's firm grip clamps down on my shoulder. "I repeat… Why would that *pinche cabrón* dare step foot in New Jersey, much less on Carrera ground?"

"I'll explain later."

"You'll explain now."

"I'll explain when I have something to say," I appease with a low growl, shrugging him off. I'm not doing this with him. *Not here. Especially not now.* "In the meantime if you happen to see my wife, please escort her to my office."

They say when you find yourself standing at the end, return to the beginning.

So that's where I am—at the beginning. More specifically, the desk I was leaning against as she walked through my door that night.

I glance at the floor where she stood, head held high, lying to my face as her knees shook with fear, then at the wall I shoved her against seconds before putting a gun to her head... My office is a battlefield of scattered landmines, all of them filled with reminders of *her*.

I can't think straight when she's invading my head like this.

Knocking the top off the crystal decanter sitting on my desk, I lift it, and take a long hard drink, not bothering with a glass. Strangling the neck of the bottle with one hand, I shove the other in my hair, tugging at the roots as I pace the length of my office.

RJ remains uncharacteristically quiet, as I come undone.

"She can't just leave like that," I say, swiping the back of my hand across my chin. "We're fucking married. I don't care what shit Grayson convinces her to pull, I won't give her a divorce. She's a Carrera for as long as I say she is, goddamn it!" The decanter shatters against the wall as I hurl it across the room. Staring at the jagged pieces of glass strewn across the floor, my tone lowers. "The only way Santiago is going to cut that tie is by cutting my throat."

I'm spiraling. Half an hour ago, I had every intention of telling Thalia the truth and letting her go. But now... Now, I'm irritated, concerned, and pissed the fuck off—a dangerous cocktail with a hairpin trigger.

As I pass my desk for the fourth time, I stop to check my phone.

Nothing.

"Have you heard from Rocco?"

When all I get in return is an incoherent mumble, I glance up from my screen, narrowing a suspicious glare at my second-in-command. He's perched on the edge of the couch, an elbow braced on each knee, his phone tucked protectively in his hands. Now that I think about it, he hasn't taken his eyes off it since we caught the finale of Grayson's orchestrated shit show.

"I asked you a question, RJ."

His thick eyebrows knot. "In a minute."

No. That's not how this works. Especially tonight. "Put the damn phone away, or I'll shove it somewhere you won't like."

Holding my stare, he presses another button, flipping his middle finger as he lifts it to his ear. "Go to hell, Santi."

Too late. I'm already there.

In two strides, I have his phone in my hand. In response, RJ catapults off the couch, his fists clenching by his side. He wants to take a swing at me. I can see it in his eyes. But we both know he won't.

"Give me my fucking phone," he bites out between clenched teeth.

This kind of volatile reaction isn't like him. He's the still waters to my raging tempest. But those lines darting across his forehead are new. This distraction he's had since Grayson's visit is out of character.

I don't like it. And if he's not going to give me an answer as to why, then I'll find it myself.

Illuminating the screen, I stare down at the contact name, and the nine unanswered calls. "Rachel Marlow?" I spit the name out, my anger cranking up about ten notches. "What the hell, RJ? My whole operation just went up in flames, and you're worried about getting your dick sucked?"

"It's not like that."

"No? Then explain it to me?"

"Why don't you worry about finding your wife?" he bites back, snatching the phone out of my hand.

It's the wrong thing to say.

Red mist clouds my eyes and uncertainty clouds my judgement as I shove him up against the wall. The dam breaks, and RJ pushes back, causing the lid to blow off what little restraint I have left. Drawing my fist back, I aim for his nose.

"I'd go for the throat myself."

I freeze mid-swing, releasing my grip on RJ's neck. Turning, I find my father leaning casually against the doorframe to my office, his arms crossed, wearing a look of amused boredom.

"Collapses the larynx," he adds. "Then you get the pleasure of watching them suffocate."

"What the hell are you doing here?" I demand.

"You said you'd explain later." He shrugs. "It's later."

Forgetting about RJ, I shove another hand through my hair. I'm irritated yet unsurprised. "You know that's not what I meant."

"And *you* know I'm not accustomed to waiting."

And *I'm* not accustomed to answering to anyone. *Dios mío*, I need time to plan. To find Thalia and somehow get her back under my roof.

"You left *máma* alone at a party?" I accuse, dealing my father a low blow.

When he cocks a dark eyebrow, I add, "Do I have to remind you what happened last time you did that?"

A chilling smile spreads across his face. "No, that won't be necessary... I never make the same mistake twice."

He pushes away from the doorframe to reveal my mother standing right behind him. She's staring at me just as intently, maybe even more so. But what I notice most is the determined lift of her chin, as if she's stepping into old, but familiar skin.

"*Mijo*," she says, baiting me with a name she hasn't called me since I left Mexico. "Let us help you."

I glare at my father. The bastard knew exactly what he was doing in bringing her here.

I shake my head. "Not this time—"

The crack from a single gunshot swallows the rest of my protest. It's a stab of adrenaline straight to the chest. When the second blast sounds, we all have our guns out.

"Grayson." RJ hurls his large frame off the wall, our fight already forgotten, but there's another name in my head as I lead the charge.

Thalia.

My father falls into line as we cross into the lobby. When I turn to stop him from coming any further, it's not a power play, it's a plea. "Don't tempt fate." I draw his volatile stare to my mother. "Lightning *can* strike twice."

His scowl hardens, but he steps back. The man may be a killer, but the mind is an unforgiving sadist. All my father's demons are carved into three jagged words:

La Boda Roja.

I can't run fast enough. *I'll burn this city to the ground if she's hurt.* Throwing the stairwell door open, I run straight into the heavily armed chest of Rocco. Before I can demand answers, he's jerking his chin over his shoulder.

"Shots came from the rear parking lot."

With my gun drawn and finger wrapped tight around the trigger, I storm ahead, giving zero fucks about protocol or protection.

The rhythmic click of boots scatter across the asphalt as swarms of *sicarios* pour in from every direction. The ones I commanded to secure the perimeter have already arrived, forming a half-circle around a black sports car.

They're silent.

Unmoving.

Guns lowered.

No.

Time slows, each second stretching long into the next. My throat tightens. My heart stutters.

"Move," I order. My men glance up, their unreadable stares feeding the monster inside me. "I said 'move!'"

As soon as they part, I take a step forward. Then another. I don't stop until the soles of my Santoni dress shoes are submerged in the spreading pool of blood. I take in the crumpled body lying motionless on the asphalt—the two gunshot wounds turning his white shirt an angry red.

Thank God.

The pile of bricks crushing my chest lifts as RJ lets out a staggered breath.

"What the fuck? Is that *Sam Sanders*?"

"What's left of him," I say, not bothering to hide the elation in my voice. "Point blank range. Nice work, men."

Grayson's invasion never made it past the parking lot, although my men's aim leaves a lot to be desired. One bullet tore through his abdomen, but the other barely hit his shoulder. I've trained them better than that. There's no second-guessing a bullet aimed at the head. *Always go for the kill shot.*

"Boss, we didn't do this."

My head snaps up. "What do you mean?"

I don't like the look in my *sicario's* eyes. It's one of caution. Like he's tiptoeing around a hungry lion.

"Most of us were on the east side when the first shot rang out. By the time we got here, he was already down."

"Did you do a sweep?"

He nods. "Every inch within a hundred-foot radius. The snipers at the front moved position to try and get a visual but found nothing."

"My wife?"

"Negative. Sanders was alone when he was hit."

The relief flooding through me could drown out an ocean. But this is war, so a brief moment of solace is all I allow myself.

"Santiago wouldn't take out one of his own, Santi."

Bending down on his haunches, I watch RJ press two fingers against Sanders's neck. "Well?"

"He's only got two, maybe three minutes before *Santa Muerte* comes for him." He rises to his feet. "Someone's already fired the first two shots. It's your call. What do you want to do?"

I glance down as the American starts gurgling incoherent nonsense, blood streaming from the corners of his mouth, and leaving red track marks down the sides of his face. Those smug dark eyes are barely open, but we still lock gazes. Even in his final moments, after all he's done to my family, he doesn't look away.

As for me?

I don't have a damn thing to prove.

Lifting my arm, I aim my gun at his head. "Fire the last," I say coolly.

As I prepare to pull the trigger and send the East Coast up in flames, Rocco crashes into me from behind, knocking my aim sideways—his hurried movements sending a spray of crimson down the front of my tux.

"Wait!" he hisses.

"For what?" I roar.

"He's talking!"

"He always talks. Bastard never shuts up." I aim again, only this time he steps into the line of fire.

"Santi, listen! *Listen!* He's saying her name."

Glancing down, I watch as Sanders's pale lips mouth a name that, in six days, has branded itself across my heart. Right away, I'm dropping to my knees, my face so close to him I can smell the death on his breath. "Where is she?" I snarl. "Where's my wife?"

His voice is faint, strangled by blood and weakened by the bullets of an unknown enemy. "Run," he rasps. "Run, Thalia. Fucking run..."

"Where is she, you son of a bitch?" I yell, grabbing handfuls of his crimson-stained shirt. "What happened to her?"

"Santi..."

I turn to find RJ on his knee beside me, holding out a diamond engagement ring and a gold band.

Both abandoned.

Both stained with blood.

"They were under the car," he says, with a grim expression.

Mi amada.

Steeling my jaw, I tear my gaze away from my broken wedding vows and back to the dying man in front of me. I'd love to send the asshole who branded his name on my sister to his grave, but as long as his heart still beats, then so does mine.

Rising to my feet, I shove my gun back in its holster. "Take him downstairs."

Without another word, I head back inside. Thalia is out there somewhere, and I'll stop at nothing to find her.

And when I do…?

God help the motherfucker who took her from me.

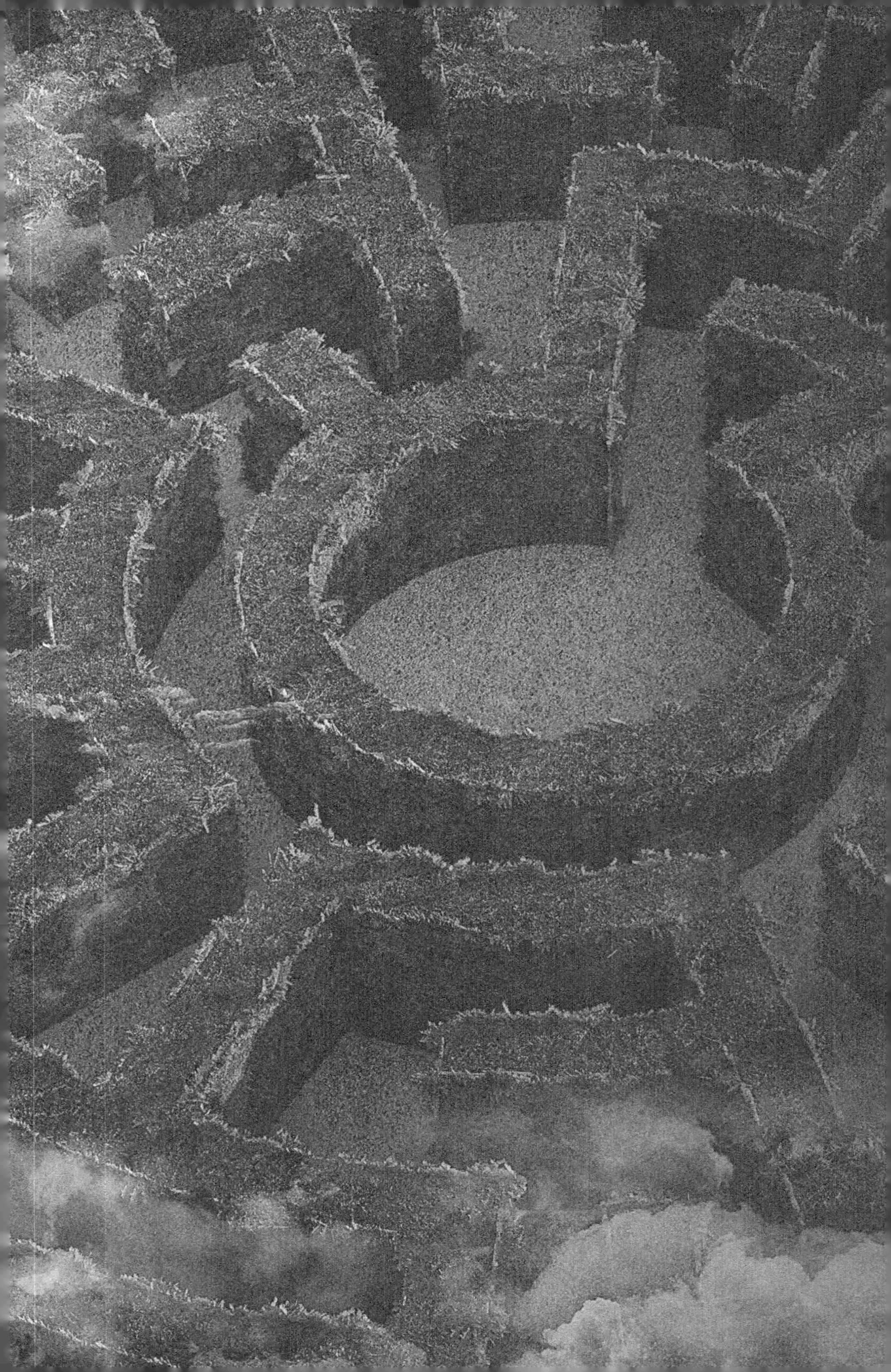

CHAPTER Two

THALIA

The lark is back again.

It must be nearly dusk.

I watch as the little brown bird hops his usual path along the alabaster stone ledge outside our prison cell. With no clocks in this room, he's all we have to stop time sliding into a black hole.

He's here at daybreak.

He's here at the end of the day when it's our hope that is breaking.

The lark pauses suddenly, cocking his head to listen to the blood-curdling screams rising up from the castle's grounds below us. It's an ugly sound that not even his sweet lullaby can remedy—a sound that has haunted me, ever since we arrived at this hellhole yesterday.

For a while, the bird remains a twitching silhouette against the bars at our window. I hate those bars, not so much for what they represent as for the perfect vista they crisscross with black metal. Closed shutters and total darkness would have been less cruel. I don't want to see paradise. I don't want to see the wildflowers and the sweeping lines of poplar and cypress trees that border the sun-soaked hills—a view that, no doubt, graces a billion holiday postcards from Florence to Rome.

We're in Italy: a beautiful country with a hidden dark corner that's reserved just for us.

We've yet to face the evil that orchestrated our capture, but I sense him all the time. He hangs like a thick fog over everything—even thicker than the white mist that smothers those hilltops every morning before the hot Tuscan sun burns it away.

Eventually, the lark starts hopping again, taunting us with his frantic movements. Only one of us has their freedom, and it isn't me.

Or Lola.

She's lying on the bed next to me, curled up in a ball to protect herself. She tells me she's always slept that way. Her father calls it *autodefensa mental*. I call it preemptive, and it frightens me more than anything. It's like her subconscious knows what's lurking around the corner for us.

She coughs in her sleep—her slim body rattling with the violence of it. I hold my breath as I wait for hers to even out again. She's been throwing up all day. She finally passed out from exhaustion around an hour ago.

My gaze switches to the locked door, and I utter a silent prayer for it to stay shut. So far, the men with empty eyes have left us alone, but their absence is nothing more than a stay of execution. The screams below us are never at the same pitch.

Different girls.

Different hours.

Soon, those screams will be ours.

I dared myself to look outside earlier. That's when I saw the lines and lines of neat, green, yaupon holly hedges for the first time—as sinisterly uniformed as they were terrifying. The garden maze was a myriad of brutal twists that turned my stomach into knots, and every instinct I had, *every instinct my father's world has forced me to nurture*, told me that this was a place I needed to fear.

The screams were coming from the center of it. The pleading went on and on…

Lola coughs again. She needs to be stronger before they attempt to destroy us with whatever sick perversion they have planned. *I need to figure a way to get us out of here before they do.*

Since we were taken, it's been one inescapable cage after another—from the dirty shipping container to the private plane, to the black van that wound around the spiraling narrow roads up to this creepy-as-fuck hilltop town, with the thick stone perimeter wall. Presently, we're in a shitty room with bars on the window and bolts on the door.

I dread to think how many women must have been held captive here before us. Our mattress was threadbare with desperation when we arrived. The pillowcases were still damp with another's tears...

"Larks can only sing when they're in flight," comes a weak voice as Lola rolls over to face me, her eyelids fluttering open. "Did you know that?"

Firebirds can only sing when their wings haven't been pulled off.

Tonight, in the fading light, she looks so much like Santi it stings my eyes.

I try not to think about him here, despite the constant reminder. It makes me weaker and more vulnerable. When he finally manages to hijack my thoughts, I tell myself I hate everything about him to toughen up what's left of my heart.

I hate the power he wields over me, his viciousness, his filthy mouth... I hate how his kisses are like the sweetest lie and his fucking, as hard as the truth. He knew how worried I was about Ella. He knew how sick she was. He could have set my fears to rest at any time by telling me he had the tape.

But I also know why he didn't. Because it's the same reason why I can't bring myself to hate him as much as I desperately want to.

It's a reason I refuse to acknowledge, and one I refuse to accept.

"I'm amazed anything can sing around here," I say, pulling her arm around my waist, welcoming the extra heat, even though the humidity in the air is crushing my lungs.

I remember reading about a derelict Second World War concentration camp in Poland once. There was never any birdsong in the trees surrounding it. Some wickedness was built to endure.

We lie like statues until the little lark flies off into a world that we don't belong to anymore. Lola's silence is agony. The pieces of her broken heart are even more jagged than mine. When I told her about Sam getting shot in Legado's parking lot, something about the way her face crumpled tore their year and a half deception to pieces.

The truth fell like dominoes after that.

The man she loves is dead.

The man she loves will never hold their child.

She hasn't confirmed her pregnancy to me yet, but it's obvious from the way her hand hovers over her stomach, and from her never-ending bouts of sickness. There's no bump, but it's only a matter of time.

It makes me so full of fear for her.

We hardly know each other, but I feel a fierce, almost violent protectiveness toward her and her baby. I'm stepping up to fulfill Santi's role. We're sisters now. We're family. I'm quickly learning that a Santiago and a Carrera are so much stronger together than when they're ripping each other apart.

Maybe if Santi and I hadn't been fighting like cats and dogs all the time, we might have seen this hell coming.

"Shit, what's that?"

Lola sits up in a rush, and I scramble to follow. There are loud male voices in the hallway outside, speaking a language that neither of us understand. The bolts groan in protest. The lock in the heavy wooden door turns. A beat later, a young woman with matted dark curls is being pushed into our room.

With a muffled cry, she lands on the cold flagstones as the door slams shut again.

At first, she doesn't move. She's dressed in a dirty white slip dress like us, but every inch of her bare skin is covered in cuts and bruises. She's shaking like a leaf, the strands of black hair slithering free across her shoulders to reveal six jagged welts. They're all around ten inches in length, interlacing a crimson pattern into her tan skin.

My blood turns cold.

Whip lashes.

"Who did this to you?" I whisper in horror, sliding from the bed.

She raises her face to us, and I stop dead. One cheek is swollen purple, and her lower lip is split and bleeding. There's still a flame of defiance in her dark eyes, though... A burning hate for the men who did this to her. They may have crushed her body, but her soul is still fighting.

"Them." It's a single accusation spoken in perfect English, her accent cutting its teeth on New Jersey glass. Her gaze darts from me to Lola, who is sitting rooted to the mattress in shock. I watch her eyes widen slightly. "When did they bring you here?"

"Yesterday."

She waves away my attempts to help her up. "Then tomorrow is your first auction."

"Auction?" Lola pounces on the word as the woman slowly rises to her feet.

"It's Sunday," she states, wincing as she straightens up, as if that's all the explanation we need. "It's time for them to bid on the new girls to enter *Il Labirinto.*"

My stomach lurches. "What the hell is *Il Labirinto?*"

But I already know the answer. It's the place I can see from our window where your mind gets twisted up and your screams are made.

"One of you will be chosen," she says regretfully. "It's inevitable."

"Why?"

"Because *you* are a Santiago, and *you* are a Carrera." She swings her bruised gaze between us again. "That means you're the ultimate game, and the ultimate prize... Tomorrow night, you will run in *Il Labirinto,* and if you're lucky, like me, then maybe you'll survive it."

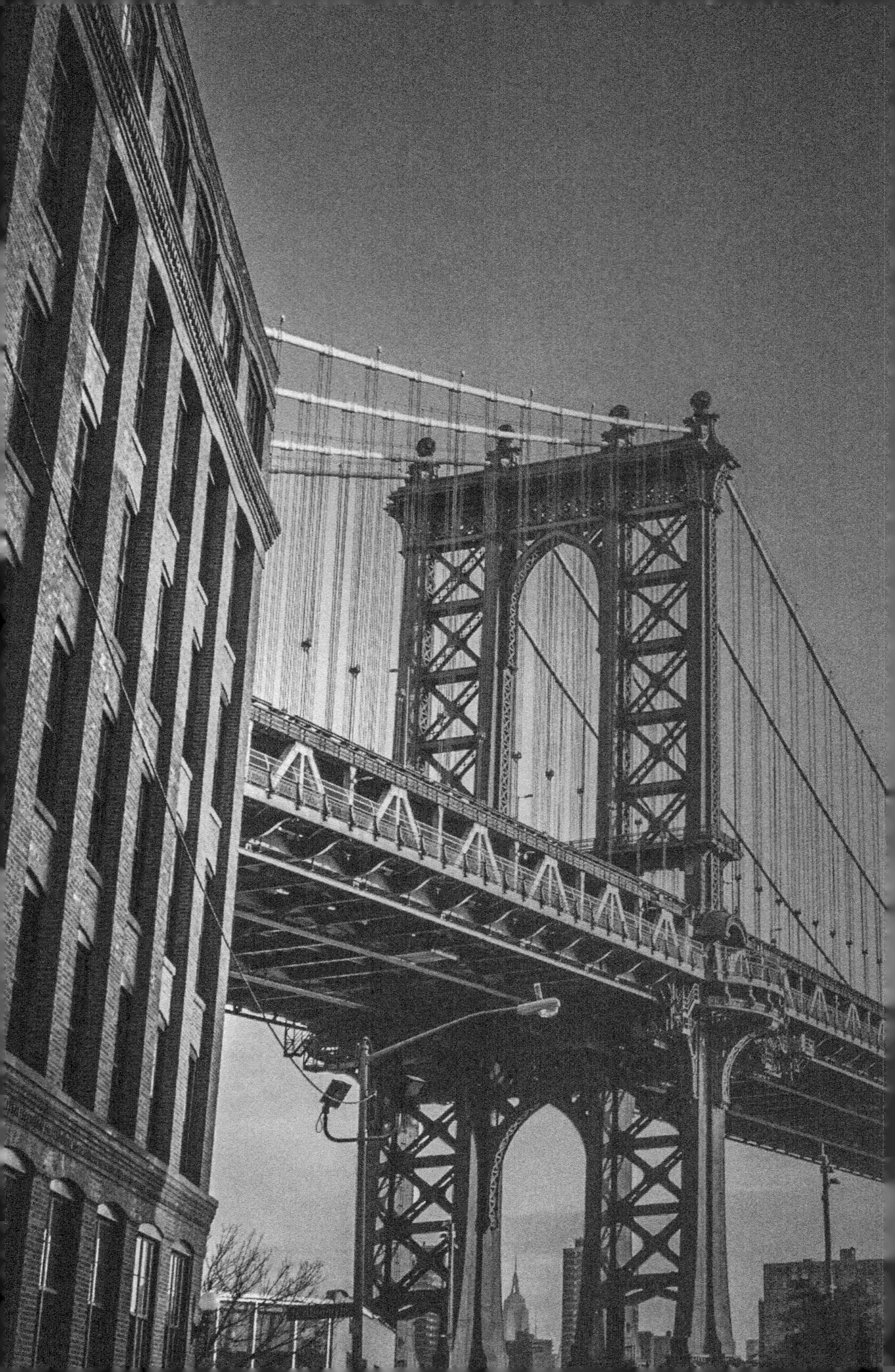

CHAPTER
Three

SANTI

D eath is as unique as a fingerprint. No two people exit this world the same way. Some are shoved into the next life courtesy of a bullet between the eyes, while others are cursed with a slower, more painful crawl. I've watched hundreds of men die, some intentionally, some by circumstance. The end comes with a set of snapping jaws, and an iron grip. It's a sight that you either pray to forget or crave to watch again and again.

I shift my weight, another rough patch of the concrete wall digging into my spine. It might as well be a razor blade, because tonight that craving is absent. Instead, it's being overpowered by fear.

Fear of death claiming a man I hate.

Fear for *her*.

It's an unfamiliar feeling that has every muscle in my shoulders twisted up in knots.

Tilting my head from side to side, I tap the barrel of my gun against my bicep while keeping a steady gaze on the other side of the room. *The basement.* Legado's dark underbelly. A place where debts are silenced by four blood stained walls. A place where, tonight, I've gone against every instinct to rise and ruin.

After bringing Sanders downstairs as ordered, Rocco managed to control the bleeding, using gravity, tape, and a piece of plastic. Thanks to six months of paramedic training, my head of security has kept my enemy on this side of death's door.

That was an hour ago. An hour since I called in a favor to save my enemy. An hour since Atlantic City's most heralded chief of medicine quietly pulled a "borrowed" EMS truck around to the back, only to have swarms of Carrera *sicarios* strip it clean of supplies. An hour since RJ escorted him down four floors, and I pointed a gun in his face and warned him that his fate depended on Sanders's.

An hour since Santiago-affiliated blood started staining the floor of my sanctuary.

I'm done waiting.

As I push off the wall, RJ grabs my arm, jerking his head across the room to where Elias Baxter is ripping off his bloody gloves and tossing them onto the stained table beside him. His shoulders round in fatigue as the pretty blonde nurse standing beside him casts her eyes to the floor.

"Well?" I demand. "Is he dead?"

Fucker better not be dead. If he's dead, I'll kill him.

The surgeon turns to me, sweat beading along his upper lip. *Good. Fear is the best motivator.* "No, Mr. Carrera, he's not dead," he says solemnly. "He came close a couple times, though." He motions to where Sanders is lying on an eight-foot banquet table, then to a smaller one scattered with supplies from the EMS truck, along with an array of switchblades, kitchen knives, and a half empty bottle of vodka. "This isn't exactly a sterile working environment..."

"*Lo siento, señor.* My apologies," I say sharply. "How inconsiderate of me to be so ill-prepared for the emergency surgery I had no idea would be performed in my casino tonight."

He swallows hard, but wisely chooses to keep his mouth shut. My tone may be calm, but inside I'm an avalanche of emotions. *Rolling faster. Growing deadlier. Minutes away from taking out everything in its path.*

Avoiding my stare, he runs his palm along the ring of thinning white hair at the back of his head. "The young man was lucky."

"You call that lucky?" I ask, waving my gun in Sanders's direction.

"Yes, I do. Your friend should be dead. The first bullet passed clean through his shoulder, miraculously missing the brachial plexus *and* subclavian artery..."

I don't have time for this shit.

His breath hitches as I center my Glock on his bloodstained lab coat. "*Muy bien.* Now try it again—in English."

At the nurse's gasp, he turns toward her, giving her a small shake of his head in warning. *Naive girl. Smart man.* Focusing his attention back on me, he tries to regain whatever authority that title embroidered on his lab coat gives him, but it's too late for that. His breathing is as rattled as Sanders's is.

"I-I just meant that no main artery was hit. I've stitched the wound, and—barring infection—I don't foresee any blood vessel damage, loss of motor skills, or worse, risk of amputation."

Shame. Maybe in losing a limb, he'd gain some humility.

"And the second bullet?"

Baxter glances back at Sanders, the corners of his mouth turning down. "That one is more serious, I'm afraid. Whoever shot him, shot to kill. I can only assume they were aiming for his heart. From the angle of the bullet entry, he moved at the last moment, catching it in the upper abdomen."

"Any organ damage? Liver? Kidneys? Spleen?" RJ asks, his tone almost as clinical as Baxter's.

If the situation wasn't so fucked up, I'd laugh. Blood and bullets are an occupational hazard in our line of work. Getting shot is just part of the job, a rite of passage every *sicario* wears as a badge of honor. We've both watched many men fall. We know what's survivable and what's fatal.

"I managed to repair the bowel and place a tube in to drain any excess fluid. That tends to happen when there's inflammation and traumatic injury, but…" He stares down at the front of his own stained shirt. "It was a mess. There was a lot of blood… A lot of blood."

No shit. Legado's tarp lined floors are flooded with it.

"He's stable for now," he continues, gathering up the salvageable supplies. "But I urge you to let me take him to the hospital, and fast. I may have stopped the bleeding, but I can't fight sepsis."

"No hospitals."

Ignoring me, RJ clears his throat. "When will he regain consciousness?"

"If he even does?" Baxter mutters, and it's all I can do not to put a few bullet holes in *him.* "Could be hours, could be days. When he does, he's going to be groggy and weak. Best not to get him worked up if you want him to recover."

"Fuck that," I say with a growl. "I didn't have you save him so he could *recover*. I want answers, and then what happens, happens."

The wave of horror washing across Elias Baxter's face never gets old. He's both disgusted and terrified at my lack of regard for human life, but I bankroll his gambling habit, so the good doctor knows to keep his opinions to himself.

Without another word, he motions toward the nurse. Both of them slip past me, a soft breath exiting his chest when I don't stop him. *Why would I?* He's of no use to me anymore. He'll go home, crawl in bed, and cry himself to sleep over the loss of his precious morality.

Fuck morality.

Then again...

"Baxter?" I call out over my shoulder.

He stiffens, his fingers curled around the door handle.

"Get some rest and be back here in a few hours with whatever you need to turn this basement into a state-of-the-art hospital room."

"But...but, I have a job, Carrera," he stutters. "Responsibilities..."

"Correct. And that job is doing exactly what I say, and your only 'responsibility' is to keep that son of a bitch alive." I swing my gun toward Sanders.

He whips his head around, his eyes wide. "You can't do that."

"That fifty-thousand-dollar tab pinned to my blackjack table says I can do whatever the fuck I want, Dr. Baxter."

This time, his shoulders slump. He drops his head, a harsh breath spilling from his mouth. "Fine. Come, Gina." The doe-eyed nurse follows him out, her face tipped in shock.

"Gina..." I say her name slowly, causing her to stumble into Baxter's back. Once I catch her glazed stare, I give her a chilling smile. "Gina Pruitt from Ridgefield. I believe your parents still live there, am I right?"

All the color drains from her face, her slight frame trembling with fear.

"Tell me, Gina, do you know what separates smart women from dead ones?"

At that, the tears filling her eyes spill down her cheeks as she shakes her head.

"The ability to keep their mouths shut. Do I make myself clear?"

"Y-yes, sir," she whispers, crowding against Baxter again. As a guard opens the door, she hastily pushes her way out of the room.

RJ gives me a side-eyed glare. "Was that necessary?"

"Is that a rhetorical question?"

Tucking his gun back into its holster, he moves toward Sanders, rubbing his chin. There's something on his mind—something besides the half-dead Santiago bleeding all over the floor.

"What's up with you?" I ask.

"We should take him to the hospital."

I groan. "*Dios mío*, not you, too."

"You heard the man... That hit to the stomach isn't just a nick a few stitches can solve. You're only going to get answers from Sanders if he's alive to tell them. I know you hate him, Santi, but if he dies, so do our chances of finding Thalia."

"*Our* chances?"

"She's your wife. I'm your cousin. That makes us all one big fucked-up family."

Scowling, I tuck my own gun away, flipping him my middle finger as I cross the room. *Family*... The word doesn't even make sense anymore. Six days ago, "family" was a word reserved for those with Carrera blood flowing through their veins. Then Thalia showed up, smearing her color all across my dark world. I'd planned to use her. Degrade her. Destroy her. Then throw her away. Now, all I want to do is find her and take it all back.

Swiping what's left of the vodka bottle off the table, I tip it up, inhaling the burn...welcoming it. *If it can cleanse Sanders's wounds, maybe it can cleanse mine.*

"You can't let go, can you?" he says, gesturing at my clenched hand.

"Find your own damn bottle."

"Not the vodka. I mean what's in your other hand. You've held onto those things ever since leaving the parking lot."

I glance down, surprised to find my fingers wrapped in a death grip around Thalia's wedding rings.

As the seconds tick away, my eye twitches under the weight of RJ's stare. I should throw them on the floor, just like she did. *But I can't.* Because they're hers—and right now, they're all I have left.

I flip the focus back on him. "No more than you've held onto that thing," I say, nodding to where his hand is coiled around his cell phone. "Care to tell me about Rachel Marlow?"

That wipes the confident smirk off his face. "Some woman. Not important."

I don't believe him, but who he fucks is his own business, as long as he does it on his own time. And until we find Thalia? All his time is my time.

The moment stagnates, filling the damp room with tension and something I can't put a name to. But it's heavy and filled with a darkness ten times more potent than the one lurking inside these four walls. The same darkness hit me when I watched that Italian motherfucker free Marco Bardi on the security feed.

My head snaps up.

The security feed.

"Check the cameras. We run surveillance in the rear lot."

RJ shakes his head. "Already made the call. Nothing."

"What about the backup? You said something before about Legado's previous owner installing backup surveillance."

"That's just wired for the inside."

Then Sanders really is my only hope in finding Thalia.

Damn it.

I own a casino. I know bad odds when I see them. I had no intention of betting Thalia's life on the slim-to-none chance that Sanders would live long enough to make it to the basement, much less talk. So, once again, I went against every instinct and had every patron questioned and interrogated.

No one left the premises without clearance.

Was it financial suicide? *Probably.*

Like it matters.

Tonight was the second shooting at Legado in six days. There's no way it can withstand this kind of bad publicity. Keeping it out of the press and off police records once was a feat in itself. This time, I'll be lucky to avoid jail, much less keep his casino operational.

"Think he's gonna make it?"

Following RJ's gaze, I stare down at Sanders' face. The fucker looks gone. If it wasn't for the shallow rise of his chest, I'd call the time of death, and pull the sheet over his head.

"If he doesn't, the news is going to travel fast." I catch his eye. "After that, a scorpion shitstorm is going to blow hard across state lines and land right on our doorstep."

CHAPTER
Four

SANTI

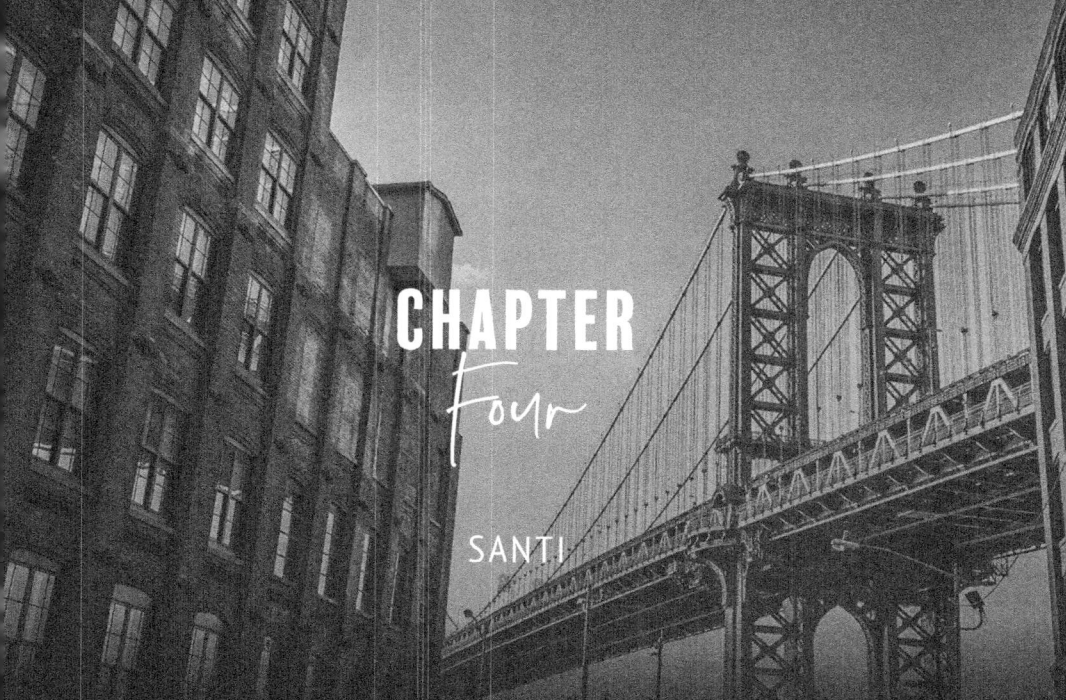

The last of the vodka is long gone. Now I'm passing the time by counting Sanders's shallow breaths.

Twelve hundred in twenty minutes equals ten breaths per minute.

Not great odds.

I'm about to send out one of the guards for another bottle when I hear muffled arguing outside the door. RJ and I lock gazes, both of us drawing our guns, moments before the basement door swings open and stone-faced *sicarios* spill into the room with clenched fists and darting eyes.

"Sorry, boss," one says, his chin snapping toward the intimidating man a few steps in front of him. "We told him we had Carrera orders, but…" He grits his teeth. "He pulled rank."

A slow smile tips the corners of my mouth. "Is that right?"

Glancing over his shoulder, my father pins him with a stare that could melt steel. "I'm *the* Carrera, you *pendejo*." Straightening his suit jacket, he offers a passing glance at Sanders's bloodstained body, then centers his attention back on me. "What the hell is going on?"

I look behind him, not bothering to stand. "Where's *máma*?"

He scowls. "Surrounded by *sicarios*. Now, answer my question."

RJ catches my eye again. I can read his expression. He wants me to tell my father the truth so he can step in and take control. So he can unfuck the mess

I've made, proving he was right—that I acted irrationally in marrying Thalia. That I let lust and ambition cloud my judgment. That I became short-sighted and impatient instead of continuing to play a strategic chess game.

"It's an East Coast problem," I say calmly.

"It's a Carrera problem," he explodes, crossing the rest of the room in three wide strides, his icy stare snapping to Sanders's motionless body again. "What happened to him?"

"He tripped on his way out," I say dryly. "What do you think happened? You heard the shots."

"Why is he here?" he demands, ignoring my jab.

I motion at the IV stand and bloodied surgical instruments. "Again, I'm going to defer to the obvious."

A chill sweeps through the room. "You seem to have misplaced your respect. Do you need a reminder of who still runs this cartel, *chico*?"

My spine stiffens at the condescending nickname. I meet his furious gaze, mirrored eyes battling for power. "No. But it seems you need a reminder of which side of the border you're on."

He steps forward, only inches separating us. "I own New Jersey."

"No, *I* own New Jersey," I correct. "You gave it to me, remember? If I'm to take over this cartel one day, you have to back off, and let me do things my way."

As we glare at each other, I can't help wondering how it's come to this. How I've found myself fighting for my rival while waging war with my own father.

"I wasn't aware that *your way* included marrying the enemy."

The fire in my veins turns to ice. "Go back to Mexico, *pápa*," I say, enunciating each word, my tone deceptively calm.

"I don't take orders from anyone, Santi. Especially not from my own son."

"My wife is missing. Did you know that?" Curling my lip, I deliver a lethal smile. "Of course you do—you're Valentin Carrera. So, why do you want to stay? Because you want to help me find her and bring her home, or because you want to make sure she never makes it back?"

Behind me, I hear RJ suck in a sharp breath through his teeth.

"Choose your next words very carefully," my father warns, staring at me with the look he reserves for those who stand against him. "A Carrera doesn't betray his own blood."

"No? So my *Abuelo* Alejandro welcomed *máma* with open arms, then?"

He flinches. It's the second low blow I've dealt him in less than twelve hours, but he keeps forcing my hand.

"That's not the same."

"Isn't it? You've told me the story enough times."

I hear RJ murmuring my name in warning, but I'm too worked up to stop.

"Your father hated *máma*," I press. "He considered her American blood to be poison to his cartel. He didn't give a shit about what you wanted, or had to say. To him, *she* was the enemy."

"That was different."

"Right." Shaking my head, I turn away, only to have his fingers clamp around my bicep in a vise-like grip. *Fuck, the man could crush steel.* Gritting my teeth, I force myself not to react as I slowly turn to meet his unrelenting stare.

"I am *nothing* like him," he grits out. "My father was a sadistic son of a bitch who didn't give a shit about my mother or his children. He wanted an heir, not a son."

Sins of the father.

I lift an eyebrow.

"You've never been just an heir to me, Santi," he says, his nostrils flaring as his anger escalates. "You're my flesh and blood." Releasing his hold on me, he slams his fist against his chest. *"Mi maldito corazón!"*

My fucking heart.

"Then prove it." I gesture toward Sanders. "Either help me save two Santiagos, or go back to Mexico, and I'll do it on my own."

We stare at each other in a rare moment of silence, the only sound between us being the steady *drip drip drip* of the IV machine.

Seconds feel like minutes, before he finally heaves out a rough breath and rakes a bronzed hand down his stubbled face. *"Dios mío.* You love this girl."

It's a hit I don't see coming.

Shoving my hands in the pockets of my crumpled tuxedo pants, I glance toward Sanders with a condescending laugh. "I'd prefer her alive rather than dead. That hardly constitutes love. Besides, it's only been six goddamn days."

"That's true," he states. "Two days longer than it took for me to fall for your mother."

Jesus. He's angry, then he's calm. One minute he's telling me I've disgraced his name, the next he's telling me that I love her... Is this what Thalia had to deal with? A volatile pendulum swinging from one unpredictable extreme to the next?

No wonder she hates me.

"Thalia and I are nothing like you and *máma*," I insist. The vehemence in my tone falters as I add, "Especially after tonight."

As my father and I stand there observing our fallen enemy, something shifts between us. The power struggle we've been fighting since he landed on American soil fades away as he, too, tucks his hands into his pockets, the tension easing from his shoulders.

"Tell me everything, Santi."

My pride is a crumbling wall. For twenty-two years, I've been taught a man is nothing without power and strength. *Control fear and you'll control the world.* I've lived by those words. I've justified every decision and choice by them.

The world was all I ever wanted, until Thalia became the center of it. Now my world is gone, and the man who raised me—the one who taught me how to hate, while warning me to keep love trapped inside our tightly guarded circle—is the only one who can help me get her back.

 I start from when Thalia stumbled into my office, and I end with how I blackmailed the chief of medicine into performing surgery in the basement of my casino. He doesn't interrupt. He listens quietly, taking it all in, until the very last word.

"She won't forgive me, and why the fuck should she?" My chest is hollow from expelling six days of truth. "If she's even still alive..."

Fuck, I can't go there. I won't.

He rubs his chin. "I was indirectly responsible for your uncle Nash's death... I didn't think your mother could ever forgive me for that, but she did."

I turn to face him, my guard down, my bloody, black heart in my hands. "How'd you get her to listen?"

"I let her go."

His solution pisses me off. It's not the answer I want. Besides, I've already let her go—twice—and look where it's gotten us.

I hear him chuckle. "Santi, we're Carrera men... Patience isn't one of our strongest traits. However, a wounded bird can't fly with clipped wings. You have to give them time to heal for it to fly back to you."

Clipped wings.

I'm immediately transported back to a snowy street in Hasbrouck Heights.

To a little girl in a red toboggan who was worried I was cold.

Ten years ago, I almost made her my first kill. Instead, I let her fly. Now, someone else holds that choice in the palm of his hands.

"I need to find her before they clip her wings."

"You're right. You're in charge here, not me." When I glance up, I find a determined look on his face. "I'll back off, but I won't return to Mexico. This family sticks together. We're powerful men, but we're not invincible." Giving RJ a conciliatory nod, he turns and walks out.

RJ stares after him, his eyebrows drawn together in confusion. "What the hell was that?"

For the first time since Thalia left my side, I smile.

"Respect."

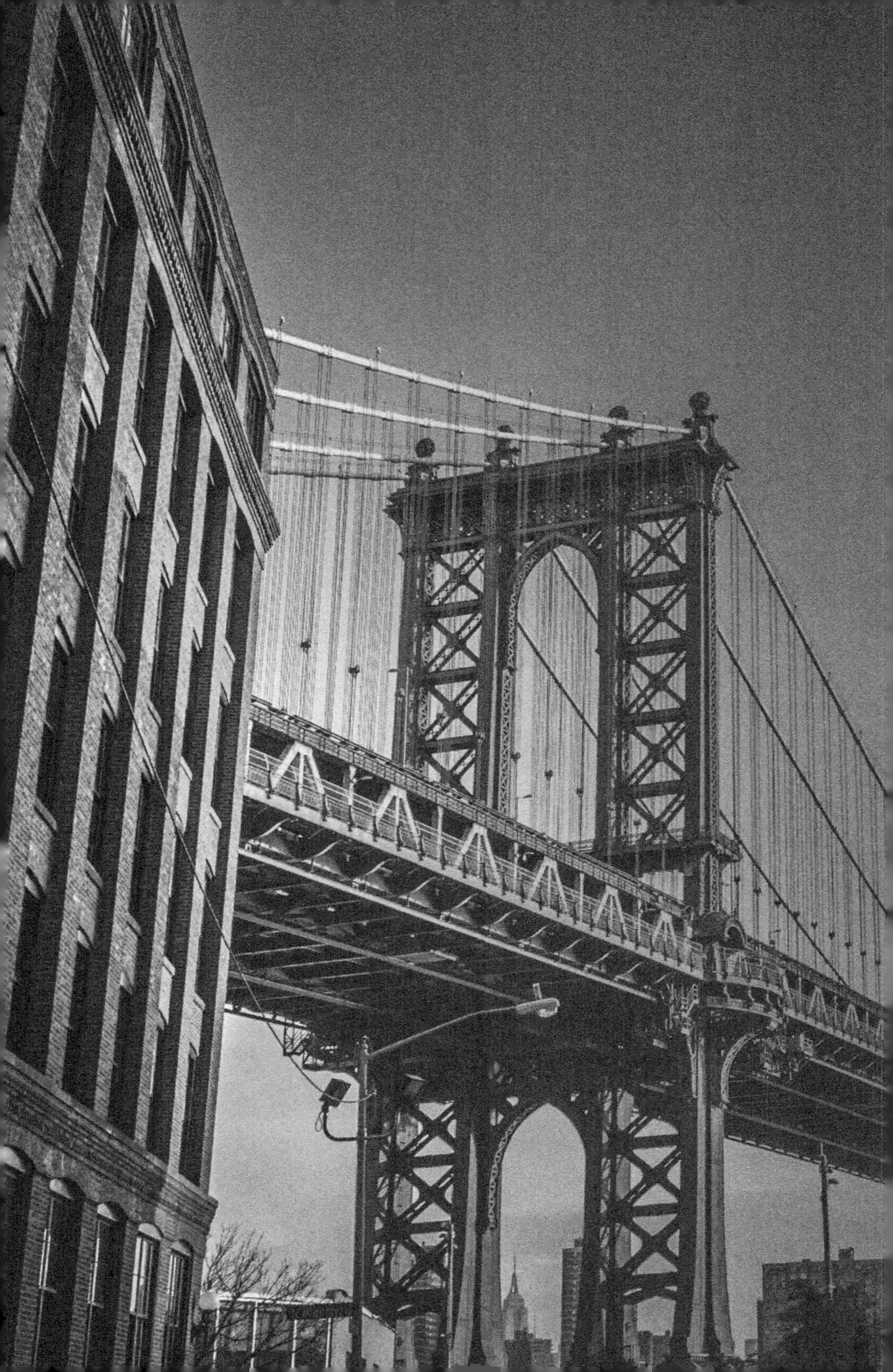

CHAPTER
Five

SANTI

Give a man enough incentive, and he'll exceed your expectations.
 I told Baxter to return in a few hours with more supplies. Instead, he showed up fifty minutes later, bleary-eyed, with damn near a whole operating room in tow.
 He said nothing as he and his protégé, Gina, worked like an over-caffeinated machine, replacing the earlier eighty-proof antiseptic with a sterile version, along with medical grade instruments, multiple IV drips and drainage tubes, and one highly-contested epidural to deliver a steady stream of pain-killing narcotics into the main wound site.
 I conceded to saving Sanders's life. I never said anything about not wanting him to suffer. Now, my dark basement is an obscenely bright hospital room, and there are enough wires and tubes protruding from him to power all of Atlantic City.
 RJ and I stand, side by side, our arms folded across our chests, neither of us saying a word as we stare at a still-unconscious Sanders. It's a familiar scene, one that keeps circling around to repeat itself.
 Bleed.
 Watch.
 Wait.
 Eventually, RJ breaks the silence. "They need to know, Santi."

Jesus, he's starting to sound like a broken record. "Don't start that shit again. I've already told you this is—"

"This *isn't* a Carrera problem," he argues in a tone I don't particularly care for. "In case you haven't noticed, none of our men took a bullet. They wanted Sanders dead and Thalia taken."

He doesn't have to remind me. It's all I can think about.

"Santiagos were targeted," he adds, loosening his bowtie. "They need to know what happened to their own. No one will bathe the world in blood to find Thalia like Santiago will."

"Wrong."

"She's his daughter, Santi."

"And she's my wife." I can hear the defiant passion in my tone. My father's accusation is still lingering in the room. Strangling me… Haunting me…

"Dios mio. You love this girl."

"I have an obligation," I add, gritting my teeth.

He huffs out a dry laugh. "Right."

"What's that supposed to mean?"

He stares at me for a moment, thumbs tucked in his pockets and lips pressed together as if weighing his options. I'm not sure which I'm hoping to provoke—his honesty or his silence. Both come with risks.

Honesty takes the win. RJ lifts his chin, his stance unapologetic. "You think I'm blind? I see it—hell, everyone sees it—except you. Or maybe you do, and you just refuse to admit how much she slipped through your defenses while you were busy plotting world domination."

Son of a bitch.

He watches me clench my fists, then his earlier hesitation vanishes, a smug smile tugging at his mouth. "Despite all your efforts, the great Santi Carrera has been brought to his knees by a Santiago."

His words burrow deep, then detonate. I let an unnerving silence hang in the air before turning to face him. "I kneel for no one," I say darkly, each word edged with sharp intent. "You got that?"

"Santi, I—"

The pained groan from a few feet away claims our attention. Both of us turn, not daring to breathe as, five hours after undergoing a risky and illegal operation, Sanders's lips part, and he lets out a rattled hiss.

"No... *Hmmphh*... Run..."

Shit, he's in bad shape. Baxter warned us that his chances of survival were still slim. Hell, I almost feel sorry for the bastard as we listen to him wheezing and coughing his way around to consciousness. His face is the color of chalk mixed with dirty dishwater. It reminds me of the grimy snow coating a dark street, ten years ago. The night I first met the cocky American.

The moment I see his eyelids flicker, I stride forward, only to have RJ slam his arm across my chest. "Give him a minute. You can't force answers from a dead man."

A minute turns into twelve.

I rub my thumb across the back of my wedding ring, spinning it like a Roulette wheel just to keep my mind occupied. To keep from peeling that bastard's eyelids back myself and shaking him until some fucking answers fall out.

Luckily for us both, they finally open on their own. Squinting against the harsh lights, it takes him a few minutes to focus, and then he's darting his eyes around the room, absorbing every detail as the cartel underboss in him takes over.

I say nothing, continuing to spin my ring.

Until his gaze lands on me.

I anticipate the moment his confusion morphs into rage. I wait for it... Salivate for it. Instead, his lips flatten into a grimace.

"Great party, Carrera," he croaks, his gaze lowering to all the tubes protruding from his chest. "Your hospitality skills could use a little work, though."

I pause my relentless spinning. "Is that supposed to be a joke?"

"No. That was sarcasm." He coughs again, his brittle voice getting lost in his fight to breathe. "Then again, I wouldn't expect a Carrera to know the difference."

I lunge toward him. "You motherfucking—"

"Do you know where you are, Sanders?" RJ asks, blocking me from strangling him with another swing of his arm across my chest.

He's overstepping, and it's about to cause me to redirect my rage.

"I assume"—Sanders clenches his teeth as his chest rattles again—"Carrera took a cheap shot at me."

¡Hijo de su puta madre!

Granted, I had him carved up in the basement of a casino, but you'd think the asshole could show a little gratitude for not leaving him to bleed to death.

"It wasn't me, you *idiota*. You'd remember my fucking smile if I pulled that trigger."

"Then why go to all this trouble?" He narrows his eyes at me in suspicion. "I don't play games, Carrera. Especially ones that end with my guts on display."

"You seem to be under the impression you have a choice."

RJ steps in front of me to diffuse the tension. "We heard shots, then found you in the back parking lot with two rounds in you."

"And I'm supposed to believe a bunch of Carreras have been standing vigil over my bedside?" he hisses. "Give me a fucking break."

I've had enough of this. Pushing RJ aside, I lean over him, slamming both my hands on either side of the gurney. "I don't give a shit what you believe, Sanders. I didn't fix you so you could live a long, happy life, *pendejo*. You got that? You walked, uninvited, into my party and then walked Thalia into a goddamn trap!" I roar out the final two words, the gurney shaking as I smack my palms against the edge.

I'd prefer to be smacking eight inches north, but I need him conscious.

I watch the wheels spinning in his head as the clouds thin. I sense the conflict as his loyalty fights a winless battle against the reality that's slowly taking hold of him. Then, I feel the moment truth grabs him by the throat.

Sam's icy facade is swallowed by blunt fear. "Thalia. Is she…?"

"If I knew the answer to that, do you think you'd still have air in your lungs?" Pushing away from the gurney, I cross the room in a couple of strides, shoving my hand into my pocket and clenching it around Thalia's rings. "This is all that's left of her," I roar, shoving them in his face. "Now, where is she?"

"Where did you find those?" His voice is starting to slur. "I told her…told her to wait and toss them in the Hudson."

A bloom of warmth spreads inside my chest. *She didn't take them off herself.* Then the gravity of his words take root in my chest, turning a bloom of warmth into molten lava.

She didn't take them off.

That means someone else did.

"Santi, he's going back under," RJ notes.

The fuck he is.

I give his cheek a firm smack, causing his eyes to flutter back open. "Focus, Sanders. When we found you, you said, '*Run. Run, Thalia. Fucking run.*' You saw someone. You saw them coming. Who was it?"

"I don't know," he repeats.

I smack his other cheek. "Don't lie to me!"

This time, his eyes don't just flutter—they snap wide open, the fire from before reigniting to a full blaze. "Hit me again, and I'll cut your fucking hand off. If I knew where she was, don't you think"—he heaves out a ragged breath—"don't you think I'd tell you?"

Typical Santiago. Talking bullshit, even when on death's door.

"Then do it," I say with a growl. "Because if she shows up in a shipping container next week, her blood is on your hands."

"Care to rephrase that? You know damn well her blood will be staining the both of us."

"What the fuck did you say?"

He exhales with a cough and a grimace. "She should never have been in that parking lot in the first place. She should never have been in New Jersey."

I bite down on my tongue so hard I taste metal. My head knows what he says is true, but my Thalia-torn heart, that traitorous piece of shit, has a mind and a mouth of its own.

For once, I don't combat RJ's look of warning. I heed it. Locking my fingers around the back of my neck, I walk away, pacing the back of the room as Sanders floats in and out of consciousness. It takes every ounce of restraint I have to maintain distance between us, when all I want to do is reach inside his head and drag his memories out myself.

Finally, after fifteen more minutes of babbling, he lets out three clear words. "They took her."

His revelation is like a shot to my heart. Still, I remain silent, waiting for him to continue. *Waiting to know Thalia's fate.*

Sanders holds RJ's stare, and then slowly slides his gaze to me. The moment we lock eyes again, my stomach churns.

"I found her in one of your private gambling rooms." He tosses me a look of derision. "Your security is shit, by the way."

"Fuck you."

He shifts his weight, and pain blankets his face. "Grayson wanted her to know everything. Said she'd come home easier once she knew you'd lied to her. That Ella was fine. That she'd betrayed her family for nothing."

The hatred in his voice is palpable.

RJ mumbles out a hushed, "Don't," under his breath, but it's unnecessary. While I don't appreciate his tone, I can't argue with the truth.

"It worked. She wanted to be back in New York that night," he rasps, twisting the knife in even deeper. "We were walking back to my car. I remember opening the door for her, and that's when they hit me with the first shot. That's when I told her to run—"

"And did she?" I demand.

He levels me with a stare. "What do you think?"

Of course she didn't. *She's a fearless firebird, remember?*

"Then they hit me with the second."

I run my fingers across my mouth and into my thickening stubble. "Do you remember seeing Thalia after that?"

Sam wheezes through a scowl. "No, I was too busy bleeding all over your goddamn parking lot." I'm about to tell him where he can shove his attitude when his eyes darken. "Wait... She was swimming."

I pause, certain I've misheard. "I'm sorry, *swimming?*"

"Like treading water, but in the air." His scowl returns. "Fuck, I don't know. I was halfway to hell by then."

"Treading water." RJ shoots me a look. "As in kicking... That's when they grabbed her."

I fight the image in my head—of Thalia fighting for her life. Begging for help. Pleading for mercy.

Dios mío, did she scream my name?

The thought calls to all my demons.

"Did you see who shot you?"

"They had masks. Black fatigues..." Determination creases his face. "Carrera, you need to call Grayson."

I flash him a cold smile. "You don't get to call the shots with two holes in you."

"Don't do it for me. Do it for Thalia," he gasps out, his brief burst of energy fading. "This is bigger than all the shit between our cartels. She's family."

"She's *my* wife."

"We need that truce, Carrera. At least until we figure out who's behind this."

When I don't answer, he clenches his fist by his side, "What if it were Lola?"

Pulling my gun from its holster, I shove the muzzle under his chin before RJ can stop me. "Don't you dare say her name, you piece of shit. Not only did you steal her innocence, but she ended up taking a bullet because of your *affiliations*."

To his credit, he doesn't flinch. "Those are some big fucking stones you're throwing. Your glass house is about to shatter, too."

"Are we reduced to talking in riddles now?"

"Thalia," he says, slurring her name. "You used her. You tried to turn her against Santiago, and for what? Some stupid revenge that isn't even ours?"

"This is different."

"How?"

I hesitate, the words resting on my tongue. Admitting it weakens me, but denying it weakens *her*.

Stepping back, I lower my gun. "Because I give a damn about her."

"And I give a damn about—"

"Where is she?" The door flies open, and for the second time tonight my father storms in, trailed by an army of *sicarios*. "Where is she, you *pinche cabrón*?" he roars again, shoving his gun right between Sanders's eyes.

Both RJ and I try to pull him back, only to get an elbow to the throat for our efforts.

Sanders gazes up at him with mild disinterest, as if it's normal to have a gun shoved in his face every five minutes. "You must be Daddy Carrera."

"Where's my daughter, *maricón*? Where's Lola?"

His facade slips, his foundations shaking. There's an unfiltered look in his eyes, as if every truth he's ever held sacred just turned to dust. That rawness... It's a strong current that drags a man under. I know, because I'm drowning in it, too.

"She's upstairs," I say, answering for him. "Where she should be."

My father explodes at this. "She's not. She's nowhere. While you've been fixated on keeping this *idiota* alive, our men have torn this entire place to hell. All they found was this..." He hurls a silver bracelet onto the bed.

It's Lola's. I remember sitting next to her in the Platinum Bar the day she showed up unannounced, watching her spin it around her wrist. She never took the damn thing off.

"What makes you think he'd know?" I motion to Sanders's hacked-up body. "He's been a little incapacitated this evening."

But as I say it, there's a gnawing in the pit of my stomach. Something that doesn't feel right. *Something I'm missing.*

Picking up the bracelet, my father reads the words engraved on the inside as if he's spitting out a mouthful of nails. "My only love sprung from my only hate–SS."

"Romeo and Juliet," I drawl, recognizing the quote. "How fatalistic of you, Sanders."

But he isn't looking at either of us anymore. His eyes are glued to the bracelet. "It was a gift," he says flatly.

My father either doesn't hear him, or he doesn't care. The pressure of the gun on his forehead increases. "I warned you to leave my daughter alone, but you fucking Santiagos... You have to destroy everything good and pure in this world, don't you?"

That particular bullet strays a little too close to home.

The gnawing sensation in my chest chews its way up my chest, sinking its teeth into the dark place I keep it caged. I let it feed on the realization, slowly bleeding its way into clarity.

Two stray bullets. Two criminals who can't see beyond their own hate. Two innocent targets.

That's when I know.

"She's with Thalia. They were taken together."

My father swings around to face me. "What makes you think that?"

"This mafia princess trafficking ring... Whoever took Thalia wouldn't just settle for her. They'd make the effort worth their while."

His eyes close. "*Dios ayude a mi cielito.*"

"God can't help them. But we can." My heart pounds a disjointed rhythm of fury and hope against my ribcage as I focus on the dying American. "We can't find them without him. We need him alive."

Glancing at my father, I see the fury straining his neck muscles.

Seconds tick, and then he's sliding his Glock back in its holster. "Make it fast."

I turn to Sanders. "We need more. Think hard."

Nodding, he closes his eyes, and I count every second of silence.

One. Two. Three.

Dark images slither into my head.

Four. Five. Six.

Thalia and Lola, trapped in some hellhole with no escape.

Seven. Eight. Nine.

Thalia and Lola, covered in blood.

At ten, I'm at breaking point, and reaching for my own gun when his eyes suddenly pop open.

"*I vecchi....*" He shakes his head, his fingers taking hold of the sheet. "*I vecchi pecca...* Shit, what did I hear them say...?"

"*I vecchi peccati hanno le ombre lunghe.*"

Every eye swings to where my father stands, one hand gripping his gun, the other clenching Lola's bracelet.

Sanders glares at him, daring him to explain. "I heard a voice saying those words. Like he was mocking me."

"Italian," I spit in frustration. "We need a fucking translator in here."

"Old sins have long shadows" my father murmurs, surprising us all. "I haven't heard that phrase in over twenty years. I thought it was dead and buried."

"What the hell does it mean?"

"It's the creed of *La Societá Villefort*," he says heavily. "An elite underground criminal organization with roots all over the world." He takes my arm in a vise-like grip again. "Call Edier Grayson," he orders, turning back to the gurney. "Set up a meeting right away."

"What the *fuck*?" I roar, shoving a hand through my hair. This night is exposing more than a few skeletons.

There's a distant look in my father's eyes, accompanied by a faint film of resignation. "There's one man who knows more about this organization than anyone... The same man who brought it crashing down two decades ago, and he happens to be a close business associate of Santiago's."

Sanders murmurs something in agreement, then lifts his arm. "Hand me a phone. I'll make the call."

I shoot him a blistering look. "I thought I'd made it clear who gives the orders around here. If anyone's going to make that call, it's me."

My father's grip on my arm tightens. "Then do it. My daughter's life is on the line. *Your sister's life.* It's time for the Carreras to put our pride aside and make a concession. Tell Grayson we'll cross the river and come to him this time." Grinding his teeth, he slides Lola's bracelet back into his pocket. "I refuse to let *La Boda Roja* become my daughter's *Funeral Rojo*. If there's the slightest chance this associate knows where Lola and Thalia are, the walls between New Jersey and New York need to come crashing down... Starting tonight."

CHAPTER
Six

THALIA

I was born with a price on my head.

Not the FBI one, but another that's whispered about in dark corners of the underworld. It promises revenge over dollars… Innocence for blood.

My father has many enemies.

Enemies have a habit of laying low.

Enemies bite when you least expect it, and it's usually those closest who end up hurting the most.

Today, those enemies are here to collect, and I'm his collateral… Or rather, I'm his and Santi's. I bear two cartel names now, which means I'm twice as valuable to those who seek to profit from whatever this horror show is.

They come for us in the afternoon, just like Rosalia—the girl who was shoved into our room yesterday—said they would.

With their guns pointing in our faces, we're made to shower and put on clean, white slip dresses, without being allowed to dry ourselves first.

The flimsy material is still clinging to our bodies as we're forced down the winding stone steps to the ground floor. I do as they demand, but I'm counting everything… The guard with his eyes glued to my breasts? He has two missing fingers on his right hand. The crimson key insignia pin badge that they wear on their lapels? It matches the insignia on the twenty-three doors we pass. There are five security cameras in total above the lines of faded frescos, and exactly forty-five steps from the bottom of the staircase to the steel front door.

If there's a chink in the armor of this place, I'm going to find it.

We're pushed through a double doorway, down another flight of stone steps, and out into a small courtyard. The sight that greets me makes my steps falter. More young women—all dressed in the same stupid white dresses and invisible chains.

No one speaks as we're herded together like sheep, ring-fenced by a pack of snarling guards.

There are sixty-three of them in total.

There are only thirty-one of us.

"Don't make eye contact," Rosalia whispers, her soft plea melting into all the whimpers going on around us. "Whatever you do, don't catch their attention."

I jerk out a nod as I'm sucked deeper into the group, allowing dread and uncertainty to seep further into my bones. There's a shadow forming inside me, a bullet wrapped up in barbed wire that's dragging along the walls of my soul— ripping and tearing—freeing emotions I've never dared allowed myself to entertain.

Hate.

Hurt.

Anger.

These feelings terrify me. I've fought them all my life. Reviled them. Shoved them in a lost and found box for my father to claim, not me. Despised him because of it. Despised my husband for embracing them, too.

I see a fancy dining table.

I hear my own words echoing in my head.

"I want to help the world, not make it spin for me..."

My naivety makes me want to puke. Right now, that same woman wants nothing more than to make the whole world burn for her.

Lola slips her hand into mine, as if she can sense the shock and chaos going on beneath my frozen expression.

My tainted blood has been there all along, flowing through my veins. Lying dormant. Waiting for a dark awakening to finally set it free...

Breathe, Thalia. Breathe.

I need a sliver of Ella's happiness to bring me back. A chink of my mother's light... Desperately, I cling to a Pinterest collage of sepia tone memories in my head. I see the cerulean borders of my father's island. I see Ella waving to me from the shoreline, wearing a wide-brimmed straw hat two sizes too big for her. I hear my husband's laugh... The rarest of rough diamonds, yet somehow the most precious.

"Stay strong. We'll get through this, Thalia," I hear her whisper.

I wonder if she knows that her tainted blood is slowly poisoning her too.

They make us stand in the courtyard for an hour, spotlighted by the blazing sunshine—sweating and shivering, and bracing ourselves for the next blow.

Finally, there's movement in the doorway. An uneasy hush descends over the courtyard as a tall man emerges from the castle. He pauses on the top step, casting a long shadow that divides us like a blade. His expensive black suit flatters a cruel expression. His eyes are the dead calm of a bitter-blue ocean.

I wince as Lola's grip starts crushing my bones. We've been around bad men all our lives, but pure evil has a face, and this man is wearing it.

"*Le mie puttane vestite di bianco,*" he declares, his thick accent ripe with disdain. "My whores in white... Today is another glorious day to cry and kneel and submit." He laughs, and then gestures at his men. "Begin."

I feel a rough shove between my shoulder blades.

"Move, *puttana.*"

Rosalia grabs my other hand and tugs us toward a stone archway. "Stay close to me. They make us walk all the way to the town square. This is where the auction is."

Auction.

The word swirls around my head like hot sauce, burning every thought it touches. Rosalia didn't say much about it last night, other than to expect hell today. We begged and pleaded, but she only gave us crumbs. It's like she wanted us to have one last night of ignorance.

That night is over, and ignorance is about to be damned to the same place we're all headed.

"Who are these girls?" I hear Lola whisper.

"They're like us... Camorra. Bratva. Cartel. Born into leading underworld families—"

"Wait. I swear I know you from somewhere." I can see the dots connecting in her head, but they're not moving fast enough. Not here. Not now. Not with the devil breathing down our necks. "I thought you looked familiar last night—"

"My father is Gianni Marchesi. The New Jersey don." Rosalia's eyes dart to the side before she adds, "Italian mafia."

"*Silenzio!*" the guards snarl, and Rosalia draws us tighter into the group again.

"Whatever happens, don't react," she warns. "They want to see your fear. They get fucking loaded off of it. This place is like a bad virus, and everyone is infected."

"What do you mean...?" I trail off as we enter a narrow cobblestone street. That's when I see them all waiting for us. Lines and lines—two, sometimes three-locals deep.

Our degradation is to be a public spectacle here in Creepsville, Italy.

The next few minutes are the worst of my life. I count off every torturous meter as old men jeer at us from the doorways and women shout vile foreign words and slap and pinch our skin as we stumble past them. Their hate for us is tangible, but there's not much of 'us' to warrant such animosity. Stripped of our underwear, our shoes, our families' protection, we're about as threatening as the lark from our window ledge.

"Why the fuck are they doing this?" Lola gasps, her face white with fear.

"We're our father's atonement," Rosalia mutters. "Our families disgust them. We're the reason why their harvests fail, or why their kids never make it into the right college... That's what *he* tells them, anyway, and they revere him like a fucking god. He turns us into mafia scapegoats to justify what really goes on around here."

"Are you talking about the guy in the courtyard?"

Before she can answer, she's ducking to avoid a thrown bottle. It smashes next to us, and another girl cries out in pain as the broken pieces cut her feet to ribbons.

"They call him *Il Re Nero, The Black King.* But others call him by his birth name—Lorenzo Zaccaria. He sells our bodies to the highest bidder to fund his secret criminal organization. The men who pay the most get to take us into *Il Labirinto* and do whatever the hell they want with us."

Holy shit.

"You mean—?"

"*Silenzio,*" growls a nearby guard again, giving me another rough shove that pitches me forward into the girl in front.

This time when I glance at my fellow captives, I do so with fresh eyes. Rosalia isn't the only one here sporting whip marks and bruises, smashed up souls and burned-out courage. *This is so much worse than being sold to one cruel bastard.* We're about to be trapped in a cycle of hell. We're going to be used and abused until death is a mercy.

Find us Santi. Hurry.

Kill them all, pápa. Violently.

The grim procession continues into the next street.

Something wet and warm hits my bare shoulder. *Did someone just spit at me?* I stagger sideways in shock and, once again, Lola is there to steady me.

We didn't need Rosalia's warning. We're smart enough not to react to the abuse. We swallow down our humiliation like it's a bad meal, knowing we can puke it up later, but others in our group aren't so restrained. One girl tries to break formation and she's dragged back by her hair and beaten right in front of us, her screams and pleas prompting a round of applause.

What is *this place?*

Something unlocks inside me again as I watch the cobblestones run red with her blood.

With each new punch and kick, I feel that same shadow unfurling in the pit of my stomach. By the time we reach *la piazza cittadina, the town square,* I'm shaking from my efforts to contain it.

There's a new crowd waiting for us here, one that reeks of a refined brutality that promises to crush us even more. No women. Just men, dressed like *Il Re Nero*—their black suits accessorized with black masquerade masks to conceal their own evil. There are more crimson key symbols on their lapels. Every house we passed had that same motif carved in stone above the doorways.

We're led like cattle onto a wooden platform in the center of the square. Right away, I move to stand in front of Lola.

"What the hell are you doing?" she hisses, trying to pull me back.

"If anyone's being chosen today, it's me."

"Bullshit!"

"Think of the baby, Lola," I mutter, and her breath hitches sharply.

Before she can respond, *Il Re Nero* steps into the square. He's not alone. There's a man walking next to him, so short in comparison he's barely a footnote, wearing a crumpled blue suit, black-rimmed glasses, and the same punchable, rat-like face that, once upon a time, I joked to my husband about.

No. It can't be…

Lola's seen him too, judging by all the angry Spanish going on behind me.

Monroe Spader.

Santi's ex-business partner.

But when…? How…?

Our eyes meet, and his smirk widens.

As I watch in muted shock, he turns to say something to *Il Re Nero* whose dark gaze seeks out my face as well. His chilly smile turns my insides to ice, before he nods at Spader. The exchange is a dirty agreement. It's a reward for a job well done.

That's when I know this "auction" is nothing more than a shitshow.

I've already been bought and sold by the ultimate deception.

CHAPTER
Seven

SANTI

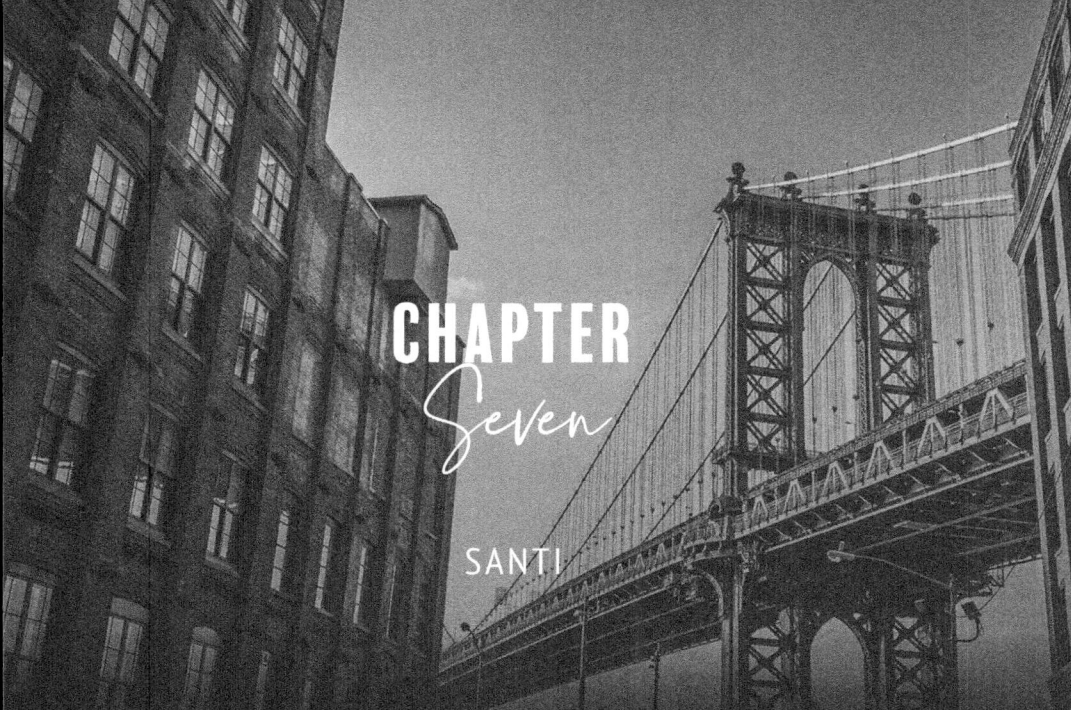

The storm that blew in from the Northeast twelve hours ago is nothing compared to the one breezing in from the south, late morning, in two Black SUVs and an Aston Martin with a shattered windshield.

In the end, I made the call. Sanders had passed out shortly before, mumbling my sister's name like it was a goddamn prayer, proving he still gives a fuck about her.

It pissed me off enough to demand that his painkillers be halved for the next few hours. This meeting may be a concession, but bad blood doesn't dilute like oil. There's never a clean separation, and he'd do well to remember that.

I kept the conversation with Grayson as brief as possible. We needed to talk, and we needed to do it before every McDonald's up and down the East Coast started serving a new "lunchtime special."

Thalia's whereabouts wasn't something to be casually dropped over a phone-line. The gravity of what we'd learned deserved a face-to-face delivery.

In turn, I decided the truth about Sanders would be held over their heads like an insurance policy. If Grayson and Santiago played nice for the next few hours and agreed to cooperate, Rick Sanders would get his stepson back in one piece, minus eight inches of damaged colon.

Edier Grayson was his usual monosyllabic self, but knowing what was at stake, he agreed right away. Sixty seconds later, a text message arrived containing one location and two assurances.

No bullets allowed, and The Devil himself would be in attendance.

It's eleven a.m. by the time we arrive at an address in downtown Brooklyn. It's a red brick building, with broken windows, located on a quiet street with a dozen other empty warehouses on either side. Four stories high of *nothing-going-on-here-officer.* The kind of place I'd choose myself.

As we pull up to the curb, I see a beast of a man lurking just inside the doorway. The minute I step out of the Aston Martin, he emerges from the building.

"*Señor* Carrera," he says, directing his greeting at me, not my father, which amuses only one of us. "Our lookout notified us of your arrival. Santiago and Grayson have already been informed. Keep your guns out of sight and follow me."

He leads us into a large open space with a network of rusted metal beams latticing the high ceiling, but I'm not here to admire the architecture. There's a line of thirty-five armed *sicarios* blocking our access.

"Wait here."

The beast moves toward a side door as I give the order for our men to fan out either side of us, their air of "no fucks given" turning their ten into the threat of twenty. It's still not enough. I left Rocco in charge of Sanders, and I'm starting to miss the moody bastard already.

RJ scans a calculated eye down the line of heavily armed *sicarios*. "Have we been led to a meeting or a slaughter?"

I slide my hands into the pockets of my clean black slacks, grateful to be rid of Sanders's blood. Now I can focus without smelling the stench of his and my sister's lies.

Hypocrite, a voice in my head whispers.

That voice can fuck off.

"It's a strategic move." I meet his side-eyed stare with a shrug. "Basic checks and balances. Numbers keep the odds in Grayson's favor. It's a truce, not a tea party."

My father straightens his tie, his focus never straying from Santiago's ninja army. "Remember to keep it in check, Santi."

At first, I'm more intrigued by the fact that he's finally speaking, rather than what he's saying. The whole trip from Atlantic City to Brooklyn has been a lesson in silence. Not that RJ and I had a whole lot to say, but in growing up under my father's command we learned a valuable truth early in life:

A man is most dangerous when he's calm.

And Valentin Carrera has had two and a half hours of raw tranquility.

"Keep what in check?" I ask.

He stands like a statue, giving nothing away. "Your temper. Your reactions. Your expressions. All of the above. Santiago has built an empire on his ability to mindfuck the soulless. Don't let him feed you a spark and let it draw you into an inferno."

Dios mío, not him, too. I'm so sick of hearing about "Stone Cold Dante" and his blindsides. He didn't seem so covert when he was pulling a Lee Harvey Oswald out the window of Thalia's high-rise last week.

"He's not God, for fuck's sake. He's just a man. Cut him, and he still bleeds like everyone else."

He nods. "True. Contrary to popular belief, even Dante Santiago isn't immortal. But arrogance is a thin shield, son. This will be the first time he lays eyes on the man who blackmailed his daughter into marriage. Don't expect anything but six days-worth of resentment."

"This also isn't Colombia, or some off-the-grid Pacific island," I argue. "This is New York. Isn't Grayson the boss around here? Or is he just an extension of Santiago's overinflated ego?"

The words are barely out of my mouth before he's spinning around and jabbing a finger in my face. "That's exactly what I'm talking about. You're projecting your anger, and that's what's going to end this meeting before it begins."

It pisses me off how well he reads me sometimes. All I can think about is my sister and my wife and what could be happening to them. *Who could be hurting them.* What cuts the deepest is I'm powerless to stop it. I have a reach that stretches across all seven continents, but it's still not enough.

I have to find a way to bottle that hatred—*self-directed or otherwise*. This paper-thin truce is the only thing preventing the bullets from flying.

"Whose side are you on?" I grit out eventually.

Without warning, my father's mask drops back into place, and just like that, his break in character is over. *Curtain call. Take a bow.*

"I'm not going to dignify that with an answer. However, if the situation were reversed and Sanders had forced your sister into marriage against her will"—his nostrils flare, the thought filling him with fury—"let's just say I'm not sure there wouldn't be a bullet waiting for him in the next room."

He doesn't elaborate further, and neither do I. The image hangs in the air—a blunt reminder of why we're here in the first place.

The beast returns, and motions for us to enter the side room. Our men follow in our wake, the sound of marching footsteps filling the tense beats of silence.

This warehouse is smaller than the last, with that same latticework of rusted brown beams. Once again, I couldn't give a fuck about the architecture, not when I see the long, low mahogany table set in the center, and the two men sitting behind it.

Of all the things to focus on, I can't take my eyes off a half-drunk bottle of bourbon on the table. It makes me think of Thalia crawling across my desk and into my heart.

As Grayson's men move to stand behind their boss, my own men position themselves behind us. Everyone is watching and waiting for history to repeat itself as I force my gaze from the bourbon to a couple of dangerously still expressions. *Not that I can blame them...* After all, the definition of insanity is doing the same thing, over and over, and expecting a different result.

Good thing we're all a little mad here.

Grayson is the first to acknowledge our presence. Rising to his feet, he slowly makes his way around the table to where we're standing. He's wearing the same all-black attire again—as is every other member of his unwelcome party. It tells me Santiagos are creatures of habit. Either that, or they have a severely stunted imagination.

"Carrera." My name rolls off Grayson's tongue like a sharpened dart as his gaze slides to where my father stands stoically to my right. "Carrera..." Shifting down the line to RJ, he arches an eyebrow in disinterest. "*Not* Carrera..."

"Your powers of observation astound me," I say dryly.

My sarcasm is lost on him. Instead, he offers a curt nod. "My second-in-command is bleeding all over your casino. We'd like him back. I assume the only reason you're here is to arrange his safe return."

"Fuck his return. I'm more concerned with who shot him twice at close range, and why."

His cool facade slips a notch. I may be holding the details of Thalia's kidnapping close to my chest, but during our call, I had no problem giving this bastard a detailed, play-by-play of his right-hand-man's near demise in the parking lot of my casino—swiftly followed by hours of agonizingly primitive surgery.

RJ called it reckless.

My father called it *infantil*.

I call it payback.

Grayson quickly tempers his expression. "How is he?"

"Alive..." At his almost imperceptible exhale, I add, "For now. How long that continues is up to you."

Tired of dancing around the volatile elephant in the room, I turn to Santiago. He's leaning forward, forearms on the table—his posture deceptively calm.

A man is most dangerous when he's calm, remember?

"Dante Santiago, I presume." Lifting my chin, I meet his glacial glare with one of my own, my bottled-up anger spilling all over the floor like Anthrax. "Or would you prefer it if I called you, *pápa*?"

Well, that didn't take long.

To his credit, my father doesn't react, even though I just pissed all over his warning.

There's no mistaking RJ's exhaled, "*Fuck*," though. He's already reaching for his gun. In response, five others are aimed at the back of our heads.

Santiago's gaze never wavers as he lifts his hand. A beat later, his men's bullets are back aiming at the floor.

"*I'd prefer* it if you didn't address me at all, Carrera." The temperature in the room drops sharply as he rises to his feet, his voice a deep, mocking drawl. "Most of all, I'd *prefer* it if you left my daughter alone."

"I could say the same to you, *amigo*." Three deadly syllables roll into six as my father turns camaraderie into a thrown gauntlet.

I guess his own advice to "not let Santiago draw you into an inferno" becomes null and void when Lola's the one trapped in the middle of it.

At this, his rival slams his palms to the table. "Then I suggest you check your fucking sources. Grayson and I control where our men aim their guns, not their dicks. Whatever Sanders did with your precious *cielito* was of his own doing—and with her consent, I might add. It seems that neither of us knows our daughters as well as we thought we did." He shifts his gaze back to me again. "And where exactly was Thalia when these bullets were making a mess of Sanders? Safely locked in her ivory tower, I hope?"

"She's gone."

Those dark eyes gleam in amusement. "Six days of marriage, and you've lost her already, Carrera? How careless."

I take a step toward the table and slam my palms down to mimic his stance. "They came for her."

He pauses. "What the fuck are you talking about?"

"They hit them in the parking lot. First, they took Thalia, then they came for my sister. Sanders was caught in the crossfire."

"They have my daughter?" He spits it out like he's chewing glass.

"Yes." I hold his gaze, refusing to look away.

In a flash of movement, I'm staring down the barrel of his gun.

"I should decorate the walls of this warehouse with your blood for allowing my daughter to be kidnapped."

"And then I'll paint a fucking Picasso with yours." Pulling his own gun, my father aims it at Santiago's head, and then at the line of cocked guns behind us. "And so on and so on. No one in this room would walk out alive. So, go ahead…take your revenge on the one Carrera who'll walk through hell to find your daughter."

What the fuck is he doing?

"I repeat, it was *your* bastard son who let my daughter fall into enemy hands," Santiago clips, barely containing his rage.

But my father hasn't garnered his reputation by backing down to anyone. *Especially not Dante Santiago.* Taking three calculated steps, now it's his turn to mock his adversary's stance, his low growl engulfing the room like rolling thunder. "Just like your bastard godson did with mine. If Sanders had stayed away from Lola, she wouldn't have been in New Jersey."

"This is going exactly how I imagined it would," I hear RJ mutter.

As The Reaper and The Devil square off against one another, a sense of anarchy builds in the warehouse like the final notes of an off-key concerto. Grayson and I exchange looks. He's still wearing that arrogant pretense, but there's no mistaking the flash of warning in his eyes.

It mirrors the one I know is reflected in mine.

We're proud men—princes who have the world at our feet. But even proud men can count the seconds of a ticking time bomb. There's too much bad blood between my father and Santiago for them to lead this charge. Thalia and Lola may be their daughters, but twenty years of animosity is going to get them killed.

There needs to be a mediator.

Someone with a vested interest in both women.

Someone who'd lay down his life for either one.

"Enough!" I roar, the passion in my voice causing both men to turn their heads. "Put your fucking guns down." When they continue glaring at each other, I raise my voice again. "I said, 'guns down'! In case you two have forgotten where you are, let me remind you... This is a warehouse in Brooklyn, New York—Santiago-owned territory governed by Edier Grayson's hand." I look to where the younger Colombian is watching me like a hawk. "And everyone within these state lines answers to him. Am I right?"

"Santi—"

"In turn, everyone within New Jersey's borders answers to me," I say, ignoring my father. "That makes *us* in charge here. Not you."

There's a long pause as my words hit home.

Taking a deep breath, I continue. "Last night, before everything went to hell, New York and New Jersey bridged a temporary alliance. It means that whatever bullshit happened before Sanders and Thalia walked out the doors of my casino and into enemy hands is irrelevant. It ends *now*... The sins of the fathers just got a fucking absolution by the next generation. Do you hear me?"

"He's right," Grayson says, earning himself one of Santiago's death glares. "We're not saying there aren't debts that need to be repaid." He flicks his dark eyes back to me. "And, trust me, the interest for those is still rising... But fighting amongst ourselves is hurting the women we're fighting over. Furthermore, I'd like to bring Sanders home before Carrera's bargain basement stitchwork finishes the job these bastards started."

I slide him a "fuck you" glare for that. I could've just as easily let him bleed to death.

"I'll allow it," Santiago affirms, through gritted teeth. "For now... For Thalia..."

"*No estaba pidiendo tu aprobación, cabrón,*" my father mutters.

The Colombian pins him with a sharp gaze. "I don't give a fuck if he was asking for my approval, or not. When it comes to the Carreras, I have the final word."

My father's lips twitch. "Actually, I believe that was your daughter, when she said, 'I do' to my son."

Another line of dominoes takes aim.

"I suggest we all take a seat and calm down," Grayson says evenly. "Did your security cameras catch anything?"

"Nothing." With a grimace, I pull out the nearest chair.

Santiago says nothing as he sinks back down into his own chair and drags the bottle of bourbon toward him. Moving swiftly, Grayson intercepts. He pours out five glasses and pushes each one in our direction.

My father stares at his glass as if he's just been handed a liquid heart attack. "I'm amenable, not stupid," he intones, pushing it away with the back of his hand.

I agree. However, I've also had enough stress and bullshit thrown at me in the last twelve hours to risk it. Slamming my bourbon, I slide his glass toward me for a second hit. "Problem solved."

Santiago watches the exchange in silence as he knocks his own drink back. His grip on the glass is a white-knuckle ride. Hell is about to be unleashed, but right now he's still picking at the locks.

"After two failed alliances, what makes you think this one will be any different?"

Picking up my father's glass, I toss it back in one. "Third time's the charm. I take it the bourbon is an apology for taking a shot at me last week?"

He frowns. "She didn't tell you."

"Tell me what?"

"Not my order, Carrera."

"How the fuck would Thalia know…?" I trail off with a curse. "You had an insider."

Santiago's smile never reaches his eyes. "You think I'd leave my daughter swimming with sharks without a weapon of mass destruction? She was being watched the moment she stepped foot in your penthouse. If you'd raised a hand to her, they would have shot it clean off."

"I'd never raise a hand to her," I say mildly. "Not in that sense, anyway…"

The cold smile disappears.

"I'll give you marks for creativity." I gesture to the bottle and refill my glass.

"Bribing my illegal alien housekeeper with a fake green card was inventive." Boom.

I already knew the score there, asshole.

"It seems the Russian needs a lesson in holding her tongue." Santiago pours himself another drink, barely flickering. "I may have underestimated you."

"More than you know." At his raised eyebrow, I add, "Tell me, Santiago, how's that new pilot of yours working out?"

I expected hellfire and brimstone. What I get is something far more unexpected. There's a faint flicker of respect in his black eyes, before it's suffocated by indifference.

I watch him exchange looks with Grayson. "Not well," he answers eventually. "Benito just had himself a tragic accident."

"How unfortunate. Almost as unfortunate as Svetlana's will be."

How unfortunate indeed. However, I need to veer this meeting back on track.

"This alliance won't fail because it goes beyond business. This is about blood. About family..."

Grayson scrapes a hand across his jaw. "Did you manage to get anything out of Sanders?"

"I did..." comes a low, controlled voice. Heads turn to where my father sits, deep in thought. "*I vecchi peccati hanno le ombre lunghe.*"

"Old sins have long shadows," Santiago translates, his expression darkening. "He heard them say this?"

My father nods. "There are some things you never forget. The moment he said it, I knew what we were up against." His gaze locks across the table. "I knew we couldn't do this alone."

"Anyone care to enlighten the rest of us?" I say, losing my temper.

My father grits his teeth. "Your *Abuelo* Alejandro, was a sick son a bitch who trafficked women. He enjoyed the hunt more than the kill. As such, it wasn't long before *La Societá Villefort* came calling."

"Like fucking poison." Santiago's grip tightens around his glass again.

"Their organization was mostly funded by trafficking. They controlled most of the networks, except the ones in and out of Mexico. In exchange for a huge cut, they offered him something money can't buy."

"Does that mean…?"

"No," my father snaps at my insinuation. "After that bastard died, *Villefort* came to me offering membership. They left with three less men. Still, they didn't take the rejection lightly, and I've kept a vigilant eye on my borders ever since." Letting out a curse, he finally reaches for the bourbon. "My knowledge of their inner workings is limited at best. However, *he* can tell us all we need to know."

I follow his line of sight to where Santiago sits.

"Actually, this is Knight's area of expertise," I hear Grayson say.

"And who the fuck is Knight?" I say sharply, bringing my fist down hard on the table. "I'm done with the coded bullshit. We need to lay everything out, right now. There are two women out there who are counting on it."

They're counting on us.

The older Colombian narrows his eyes, either to shield his contempt, or his respect. For the second time tonight, I'm suspecting the latter.

"Aiden Knight," he clarifies, leaning back in his chair. "He's a business associate of mine, going back twenty years. He launders money for me through his casinos on the French Riviera. He was knee-deep in *Villefort* until he cut himself free. In doing so, he brought the whole organization down. We believed it was dead and buried..."

There are emotions moving below his surface. Emotions he can't contain. My stomach lurches. *He's thinking about Thalia.* He knows she's in big trouble.

"Who's it affiliated with?" I demand, bringing my fist down on the table again. "Mafia? The Russians?"

"It's more complex than that. Back in the day, it offered an exclusive protection unit for billionaires, heads of state, royalty… They cleaned up their mess for a hefty price, and an even heftier sacrifice. They infiltrated governments. They were behind every decision on the world stage—"

"Illuminati bastard childs?"

"Something like that. They had stakes in every organized crime cell. Except mine and your father's, and a couple of others…" He shifts his gaze to the man sitting next to me. "We have no interest in politics, other than when it suits us. We play in a very different league… As do you," he adds, gifting me another concession. "Our reputations alone get us where we want to go."

Damn right they do.

"We find the ax, we find the key."

"I told you no more cryptic bullshit."

"*Villefort* has a crimson key insignia," Grayson interrupts. "They used to vomit that shit over everything. It's their calling card. Was there anything like that left behind in the parking lot?"

"I'll get my men to take another look." I pull out my phone to call Rocco. At the same time, Grayson turns to one of his black-clad ninjas.

"Get down to Canal Street with fifty others. Round up every Italian mafia cunt you come across. Anyone with an ax tattoo gets brought back here. You have two hours... Go."

"We're not dealing with chancers and petty criminals here," Santiago warns, a muscle working in his jaw. "Every major political assassination... Every conflict... Tommaso Zaccaria had a hand in it all."

"He's their leader?"

"Was. He and his five sons are long dead, save one. He has an Italian grandson..." He glances at Grayson, who's already tapping out a message on his phone.

Damn, this asshole's efficient.

"What else can you tell us?" With every passing second, I'm growing more impatient. I need Thalia back in my arms. I need her to understand why I did what I did... I just fucking *need* her.

"Not much, other than death was a kindness if you fell foul of their company. They were a bunch of depraved lunatics with a God complex. Their organization thrived on degradation and exploitation."

Fuck.

"And vengeance," Santiago finishes darkly. "Twenty years ago, we gave Interpol the keys to their house of cards and pissed all over their play time. Now, it seems, they're back to piss all over ours."

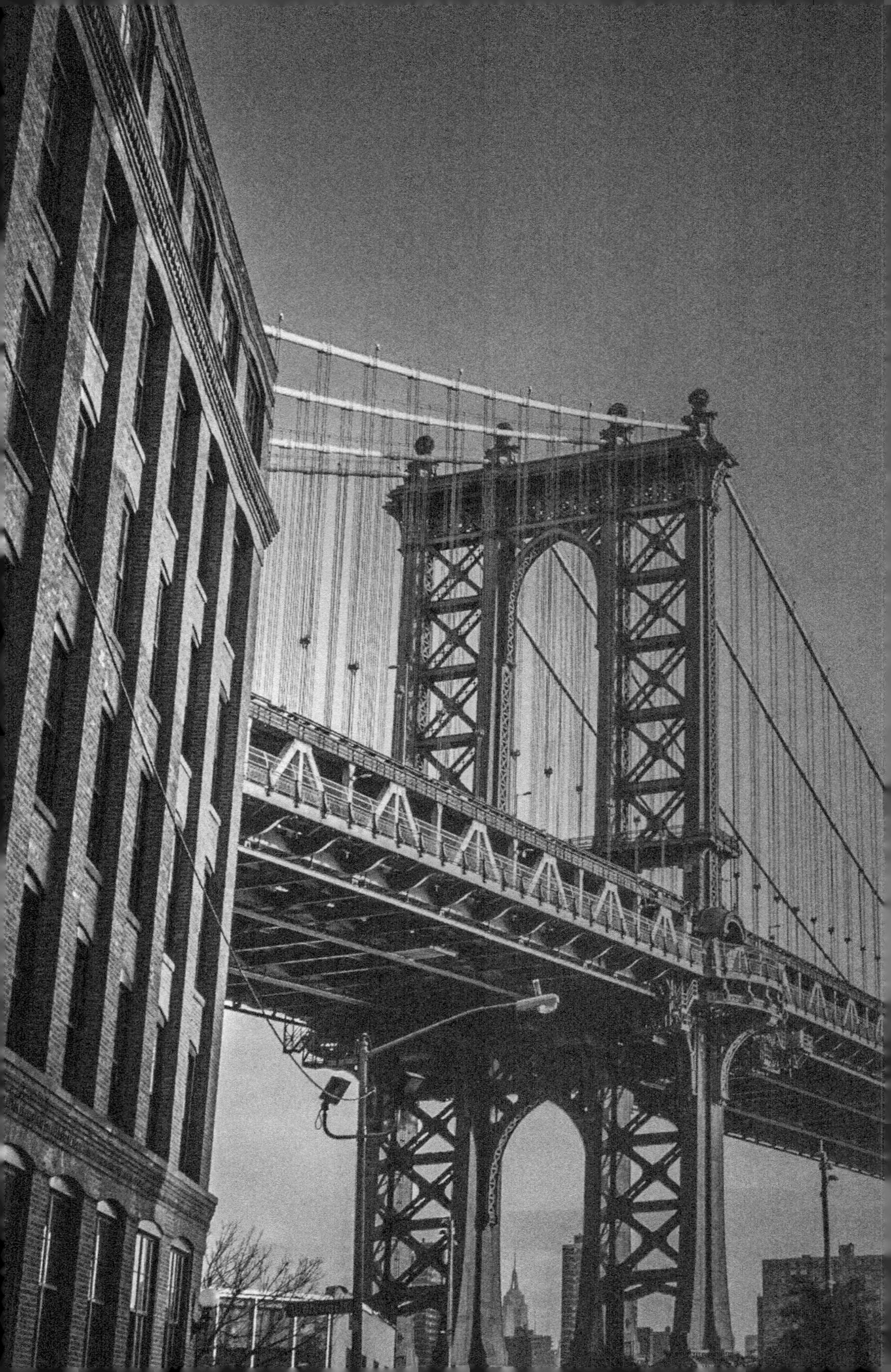

CHAPTER *Eight*

SANTI

Santiago's last words hang in the air like a rusty hook, one that's worn with time, and stained with sacrifice. The five of us sit in silence for a moment, absorbing the bleak portrait he just painted. Hearing the grim details of *La Societá Villefort* depravity, and realizing that whatever time we thought we had…

We don't.

I hear their screams in my head. I fucking hear them. *My sister… My wife…*

Somehow, I force their faces from my memory. If I let them take over, I'll lose focus. Their lives hinge on my ability to compartmentalize. To be analytical and strategic… My pulse slows to a steady hum as I slide back into the familiar skin of the cartel boss.

A man is most dangerous when he's calm.

"What were their last known whereabouts?" my father asks.

"South of France." Grayson reaches out to top off everyone's glass again. "There was a headquarters somewhere around Cannes. I'll get Knight to check it out. See if there's any movement at the estate."

A beginning… But if that's not enough. I'll raze every town and village in Europe, if I have to. I won't stop until I find them.

An incoming text from Rocco diverts my attention. I glance down at my phone, and his response has me reaching for the bourbon.

Nothing.

"Enjoying my hospitality, Carrera?"

I look up to find Santiago eyeing the near-empty bottle, as if I've stolen his favorite toy. Just for that, I pour myself another double.

"My head of security," I say, tapping the screen on my phone. "He swept the parking lot again—no crimson keys found."

"Interesting."

"Or telling..." I counter. "Why are you so convinced Ricci's ax and *Villefort's* key are in bed together? The man who freed Marco Bardi didn't wear a crimson key. He wore Ricci's insignia...an ax tattoo."

"Because they're operating as one unit," Grayson says, staring at his phone. All conversation ceases as four pairs of eyes follow his hand as he turns the screen around. "A preview of our incoming Canal Street delivery. My men work fast."

It's a close up of a man's bloody neck. Just like the one in the surveillance video, it bears an ax tattoo. *Unlike* the one in the video, a crimson key pin has been lodged deep in the center of it.

It's true. It's all fucking true. Ricci and *Villefort* have been a unified shadow darkening both our cities. All planned... All calculated...

"What about the timeline correlation?"

Every eye swings to where RJ has been sitting mute the whole meeting, taking everything in and watching it unfold. It doesn't surprise me. His silence is by design. While everyone around him wages war, he strategizes the counterattack.

"Who the fuck are you again?" Santiago drawls.

RJ returns his stony stare across the table. "A long-term casualty of *La Boda Roja*."

The Colombian regards him with mild curiosity, as if he's an irritating fly buzzing in and out of the conversation. But I know better. Behind RJ's arctic stare lies two decades of hatred. Twenty years of scars. Twenty years of silence.

After all, the man sitting across the table made him an orphan at three years old.

That's when the heart of his question hits me.

"Holy shit," I breathe. "*La Boda Roja.*"

Santiago growls. "Not this shit again."

"*La Boda Roja,*" I repeat again, this time through clenched teeth. "It happened around the same time as—"

"The fall of *Villefort*," my father says thoughtfully, his jaw tightening.

"Despite what you both claim, there *was* a third party involved at the wedding from hell." I swing my gaze from him to the Colombian. "They were Ricci's men, were they not?"

No one answers. Not that I expected them to. Besides, it was a rhetorical question. I'm playing Connect the Dots, not Truth or Dare.

Black

Crimson

Ax

Key

All four lines intersect, forming a perfect square.

"It was a power play," I deduce. "*Villefort* was sinking. Tommaso Zaccaria was behind bars. Don Ricci was at the bottom of the Hudson. What better way to carve inroads through American, Mexican, and Colombian borders?"

"Pit the two greatest cartels against one another and watch them destroy themselves for twenty years, extracting the ultimate revenge," my father adds flatly, as years of bloodshed and torment unravel on his face.

"*Corazones sangrantes*," I stiffen, my words soaked in blasphemy.

"*Sí*, bleeding hearts," he confirms, commanding everyone's attention. "Steal their beloved daughters and make them suffer a fate worse than death."

"We could've been a step ahead of this if *you* hadn't kept Bardi tied up in your basement," Santiago roars, turning on me.

"You think Bardi was part of *Villefort*?" I scoff. "Come on, even sociopaths have standards."

"The fact remains that if you hadn't chained her to your side of the river with lies, she would have been under our protection. Instead, you were so busy trying to climb to the top of the Carrera mountain, you didn't bother to look behind you."

I grip the edge of the table, ready to flip it in his face, when my father's words come back to me.

"Santiago has built an empire on his ability to mindfuck the soulless. Don't let him feed you a spark and let it draw you into an inferno."

He's trying to provoke me, so instead of giving him the reaction he wants, I give him the one he deserves.

"This all started in a New York nightclub, not New Jersey," I say, delivering the accusation with a sharper edge. "They would have taken Thalia regardless. Maybe you should be more worried about your own goddamn *mountain*."

RJ leans back in his chair. He's still turning pieces of information around in his head, trying to make them all fit. A deep line sinks in between his eyebrows as he runs his hands across his mouth. "Where did the shipping containers originate?"

"No idea," I snap, the harsh memory of the dead women lingering. "Why?"

He motions between Grayson and me. "You both had one land on your doorstep. Same white dresses. Same execution style… If you trace the origin of both shipping containers, we'll have a starting point, if not a location."

Before he's finished, Grayson and I are messaging the dockhands on our payroll at our respective port terminals. For fifteen minutes, no one speaks. No one touches another glass of bourbon. Each passing moment fades into the next as we wait for the confirmation, all of us primed and ready to paint the streets red.

Mine is the first phone to ring.

All eyes are on me as I answer, "Carrera."

"Bad time?" my contact asks, reading my tone.

"Just get on with it."

"I had to do some digging. 'Special shipments' like that one aren't exactly scanned and recorded, ya know."

"Then why are you wasting my time?"

He has the nerve to sound offended. "I wasn't able to track where those contents came from, but I can tell you the location of that particular container's last official log, six days prior."

Six days.

My mind wanders back to a night of tantalizing banter and stark honesty.

A night of submission and spaghetti…

"Carrera… You still there?"

I blink away the memory. "What's the location?"

"New Haven."

I freeze. "Are you sure?"

"Of course, I'm sure. Jesus, you think I'd call Santi Carrera with some half-cocked—?"

The line goes dead as I end the call and slide my phone back into my pocket. I'm about ten seconds away from losing my shit, when I look up and find myself in the twin firing line of both Valentin Carrera and Dante Santiago.

"Well?" Santiago demands.

Meanwhile, Grayson is staring down at his phone with the same grim look on his face.

"Santi," my father says sharply.

"The containers came from New Haven."

His static expression shifts. "Connecticut?"

The word is barely out of his mouth when Grayson slams his phone onto the table, his cool composure shot to shit. "Ours too. Port of New Haven. That's not even a cartel owned."

"It's Irish," I grit out. "Green, white and orange have had a lock on the Port of New Haven for over thirty years."

But why there? Why the diversion?

A criminal's actions are never without purpose. They're planned. Calculated. Timed...

Then I remember RJ's words about the timeline correlation.

Twenty years ago, two cartel kings met at a wedding in Mexico City. It ended in gunfire and bloodshed. Ten years ago, they met again at an old church on a suburban street in Hasbrouck Heights. Again, it ended in gunfire and bloodshed. Seven days ago, a Mexican heir and a Colombian *princesa* met in a casino in Atlantic City. This time, I'm going to make damn sure it's only the beginning.

"You two aren't the only ones who can hold a grudge," I say flatly. "Mahoney doesn't have daughters. He had four sons." I turn to my father. "Until ten years ago, when we killed them all in New Jersey."

"Sacred Heart," he mutters, and I watch the years peeling back in his mind. I also see the moment they come to a screeching halt. "*¡Hijo de su puta madre!* He didn't give the order to attack the church. He was following one."

Whoever controlled Ricci's crew twenty years ago, controlled him ten years ago.

Just like they control him and the Irish now.

"The minute I knew Thalia was gone, I had every main road in New Jersey on lockdown, and all private flights grounded. They would have sailed to New Haven and boarded a jet there."

The rage I feel in that moment isn't just vicious. It's primal. It surpasses the need to kill.

I'll make them all suffer.

I'll make them beg for mercy, as my wife and my sister did.

Santiago rises to his feet. "We need to find our daughters, Carrera," he says, addressing his adversary directly.

Something unspoken passes between them. This is bigger than decades of warfare. It's about choosing lifelines over bloodlines. It's about putting aside our differences for two women who have managed to navigate the wasteland between our two cartels, without the need to fire bullets.

For Thalia and Lola, we stand as one.

Starting now.

"If we do this, we do it properly," I say, jabbing my finger into the lacquered mahogany. "No surprises. No backhands. We fight together, until there's no longer a reason to do so..."

Until we either rescue Thalia and Lola or we bury them.

"Agreed." All eyes turn toward my father as he rises from his chair to join us. "My daughter was born the night of *La Boda Roja*. My *cielito* came into this world cursed by a cloud of vengeance. And now, that's who holds her life in his hands. Lola is the only thing from twenty years ago that matters now. Anything else is insignificant." The gold flecks in his eyes blaze with intent as he extends a steady hand across the table. "Our children have suffered enough."

Reaching across the table, Santiago takes his outstretched hand in a fierce hold. "I do this for my own."

It's as if the sun and moon have flipped inside out and upside down. Even if I lived a hundred lifetimes, I never thought I'd see Valentin Carrera and Dante Santiago make peace.

When kings pass judgment, there's no room for misinterpretation.

Fall in line.

A beat later, Grayson and I are cementing our own truce with a similar handshake.

New lines are drawn.

Torches are passed.

The East Coast alliance is sealed.

Slicing through the tension, Grayson gives a curt nod at the phone in my other hand. "Now that's settled, I want Sanders back in New York immediately. I'd prefer it if he isn't DOA when he gets here."

That makes one of us.

I dip my chin in acknowledgement and tap out a short text to Rocco.

Deal is sealed. Let Grayson's men inside.

The last thing I want to do is to keep that son of a bitch alive for a second longer, but releasing Sanders isn't the only concession I'll make in the fight to find my family. The Carreras and Santiagos will never be allies. Still, the only way to end a war isn't to fight my enemy… It's to fight beside him.

Grayson nods at the wall of armed men behind us, sending them scattering into formation. "This meeting is adjourned. We'll cover more ground by following up on separate leads. I'll head down to Canal Street and pay our Italian friends a visit."

"We'll keep tracking the containers," I affirm, but even as I say it, I know it's not enough. My soul craves blood. "Better still, a trip to New Haven is in order. Since Mahoney is so fond of showing up uninvited to places, I'll be happy to return the favor."

"We keep each other informed, and then meet back here in six hours."

"Make it five." At his raised eyebrow, I add, "There's no time to play games with this Irish fuck. He talks, or he doesn't. Either way he gets a bullet between his eyes."

The first of many to come.

The same beast of a *sicario* who met us at the door reappears. "This way, *Señor* Carrera. Time to escort you to your vehicles."

"That won't be necessary."

"I'm afraid *Señor* Grayson insists."

I glance over to find a hint of amusement on the Colombian's face.

Bastard.

I'm preparing to get the fuck out of this shithole when every phone in the vicinity goes off.

RJ answers immediately, while Grayson scowls down at his device. Rolling my neck, I check my caller ID before answering.

"What's wrong, Rocco? Sanders demanding an exit parade?"

"Elizabeth Terminal just went up in smoke."

All the noise in my head goes quiet. It's the kind of silence that spreads serenity like a balm before advancing with a knife. At the same time, I hear Grayson lose his cool on the other side of the warehouse.

Swinging around, we catch each other's eye.

"Our Newark port is in flames," I accuse.

"So is Red Hook Terminal," he snarls.

A dark thought enters my head. It's all I can do not to voice it without ramming my fist through the wall.

"What part of the terminal was hit?" I ask Rocco.

"The south office. The one housing our contact."

"*¡Hijo de su puta madre!*"

Losing all self-control, my fist collides with a nearby concrete support, sending shards of pain all the way up my shoulder—appearing to rattle the rafters. It's not until a second blast takes out the wall behind Santiago, pitching us in all directions like bowling pins, that the truth hits me as hard as losing Thalia did.

This meeting isn't ending with bullets.

It's ending with bombs.

CHAPTER
Nine

THALIA

"Leave her alone, *pinche cabrones! Fucking assholes!*"

"Lola, stop!" I grab her flailing arms and tug her away from the four guards who have come to escort me to *Il Labirinto*.

"Fight them, Thalia!" she says angrily, turning her frustrations onto me. "Why the fuck aren't you fighting them? What's wrong with you? You're not a pussy, you're a goddamn tiger."

"It's going to be okay… *I'm* going to be okay." I catch her face between my hands and force her to look at me. Attempting to convey a thousand comforts with my calm. Pleading with her to trust me.

She doesn't need to know that I'm selling her paper-thin assurances.

Not yet.

Truth is, I'm a nineteen-year-old woman who's scared to death—displaced, confused and drowning. But I'm also a daughter born into violence, and a wife married to sin.

I was a fool to think I could hold off those influences forever.

Tonight, I need to run headfirst at them. Embrace them. Turn them into a weapon of my own. Whatever shadows are lurking inside me need to come out to play. Whatever tainted blood fills my veins needs to bleed its truth. It's the only way I'm going to be able to survive this hell.

I was right. The whole auction was a farce, and there's been a change to protocol. Monroe Spader has me for the next five days to torture to his rotting heart's content. The only screams coming from that maze this week will be mine.

He won't be kind to me. Liars inflict pain to Band-aid their black souls. He plans to hit, beat, brand, rape...

"Get a move on, *puttana*," snaps one of the guards.

"My brother will destroy you for this." Lola rips her face away from my hands. "If you *hijos de sus putas madres* think your Black King is scary, you have no idea what Santi Carrera is capable—"

Her threats are cut off by disbelieving laughter.

"You live and die in this place, *señorita*. You're ghosts now. *Fantasmi*. No one will ever find you here."

"I *will* come back to this room, Lola," I say, grabbing her arm, forcing her attention back to me. "I won't leave you alone. I promise."

"I know." She flings her arms around my neck. She knows I have no choice. "You're a Carrera now," she whispers. "Strength and sacrifice bonds a family tighter than blood. Loyalty runs through your veins, Thalia. Just like it does ours."

Her words echo around my head as I'm dragged into the hallway.

I'm a Carrera and *a Santiago, Lola. Tonight, I'm part El Muerte, part scorpion.*

There's no one coming to rescue me. Lola's locked away. My father's influence can't reach me here. Even my prince of darkness won't be able to storm this castle in time.

I think of Edier's mother as I count the thirty-one winding steps to the ground floor. I think about what she overcame after being trafficked by the worst kind of sadist in her twenties. How even after everything she went through, she still managed to put all of her pieces back together again.

That's what fearless firebirds do. They shed their burning feathers and rise from the ashes. They're reborn from their tragedy...

I'll find my true strength in the flames. I'll fight. I'll claw. I'll sting. For every hurt Monroe Spader gives me, I'll be returning it, two-fold.

Tonight, I am my father's daughter.

Tonight, I am my husband's wife.

He's waiting for me at the gaping green entrance to the maze. Up close, the yaupon holly hedgerows are at least ten feet tall—a perfectly manicured screen for whatever he has planned for me. The sweet scent of summer heat is in the air, intermingled with red anticipation. Alice is about to tumble down a rabbit hole that's spiked with broken glass.

He's not wearing his cheap blue suit anymore. He's swapped it for some nerdy-looking khaki military fatigues.

All the better to hunt me with.

With his short stature, he looks like a short fat kid playing dress-up. But my derision is short-lived when I glance at the lacquered antique table next to him. It's strewn with cruel-looking implements and devices—some sexual, some medieval... *Some still bloody.*

"Mrs. Carrera," he greets expansively, his beady gaze oozing over my body like the toxic gunk at the bottom of a trash can.

"Spader, you lying piece of shit." My next words are lost to the stillness as my left cheek explodes in pain.

"*Silenzio!*" the guard growls. "You keep your mouth for screaming and sucking, *puttana*. Anything else is a disrespectful waste."

"Thank you for the lesson, Franco," Spader murmurs. "Manners maketh the cartel whore."

I press my palm against my skin to ease the sting. There's metal in my mouth. My vision is shooting stars and flashing lights. "How long have you been planning to kidnap Ella and me?"

How long have you been wanting to hurt us?

He reaches out to smooth a strand of dark hair away from my face. His touch seems to linger on and on. When I try to move away, I get shoved back to him by Franco.

"The moment your sweet sister stepped into a bar in Manhattan and allowed my associate to violate her."

"Bardi," I gasp out. "He works for you?"

His thin lips quirk. "They all do, Mrs. Carrera. The Irish, Don Ricci, Bardi... I, in turn, work for an organization who provides these... *services*. Amongst other things. You'd be surprised how much men will pay to taste the fear of a mafia or cartel princess, particularly if they've been wronged by their family. And there are so many who have been wronged by Dante Santiago, dear child." His voice drops to an obscene-like purr. "Not to mention, by your hot-headed new husband, who is making quite the name for himself these days."

I watch in horror as he raises his hand to his mouth to lick the fingers that just violated my skin. Still, I force myself to keep eye contact, even when my stomach starts roiling.

"How many pieces of silver did you cross the devil's palm for me?" I whisper.

"More than you think." He laughs and picks up a small hunting knife from the table. "You were my incentive, Thalia," he says, tilting his head with that toxic trash can expression again. "Well, initially I wanted your sister after seeing the tape Bardi made for us," he admits. "But from the moment I saw you, it was only a matter of time before we entered *Il Labirinto* together."

"You're sick!"

"Franco."

This time it's my right cheek that receives a savage reprimand. I stagger backward, gasping frantically, trying to fill my body with anything other than pain.

"Temper, temper, Thalia," he tuts. "You don't mind if I call you by your first name, do you? I think it's best we strip away the formalities, considering I'll be finding out just how loud you cry before dawn."

"This is bullshit," I rasp. "You were working for Santi long before Ella even met Bardi. You've been in his pocket for over a year. What else are you hiding?"

The guard advances on me again with a raised hand, but Spader waves him away.

"I have other skills, more intricate than procuring whores for Mr. Zaccaria's cash venture. I was tasked with escalating the destabilization on the East Coast, between your father's cartel and your husband's... And then you walked into Legado like a sacrificial lamb in shimmering red and caught everyone's attention." I freeze as he runs the tip of his blade along the curve of my shoulder, hovering over the strap of my dress. "I never dreamed Carrera would marry you. I never dreamed he'd fall so hard... A fool in love is a fool ripe for exploitation."

"My husband is no fool, Spader."

With a flick of his wrist, he slices through the delicate strap of my white slip dress, and I grab at the material to stop it from fluttering to the ground.

"Only a fool allows himself to be distracted. And *you* distracted him," he accuses, now focusing on the rise and fall of my chest. "It made you and Lola such easy targets. Once we found out about your sister's condition, she was no good to us. But you…you were a much more inviting proposition."

"You killed Sam," I whisper, the sickening twin blasts of the double gunshots ringing out in my head.

"On Legado's property, no less." He laughs again, before shifting the knife to my opposite shoulder, letting his threat rest on my skin next to my one remaining dress strap. "Now, who do you think Edier Grayson is going to blame for that?"

He takes off his glasses with his other hand and places them neatly in his front pocket. Moments later, there's the sound of angry barking behind me.

"We're not just here to line Zaccaria's pockets, are we?" I say in a rush. "There's something else he wants from this."

He hums in agreement but doesn't elaborate.

"The crimson keys," I blurt out, clutching at straws. "What do they represent?"

"When your father joins you in hell, be sure to ask him about it."

"Not if you're going there first." I flinch as his blade nicks my shoulder in punishment for my disrespect. "I want answers before you and your hellhounds chase me through this maze, Spader."

"Enough!" His expression turns feral as he leans forward, poisoning every inch of my eyeline, beads of sweat coating his top lip, his whole body reeking sour with nerves and excitement. "No more talking. Tonight we fight and fuck. Without your consent."

"You're a monster," I whisper.

"No, I'm a wolf, and now it's time for you to run, little lamb." With this, he slices through my last dress strap, tearing the ruined dress away from my hands. With a vicious shove he propels me, naked and faltering, toward the entrance to the maze. "Run, run, as fast as you can… It's time to begin your slaughter."

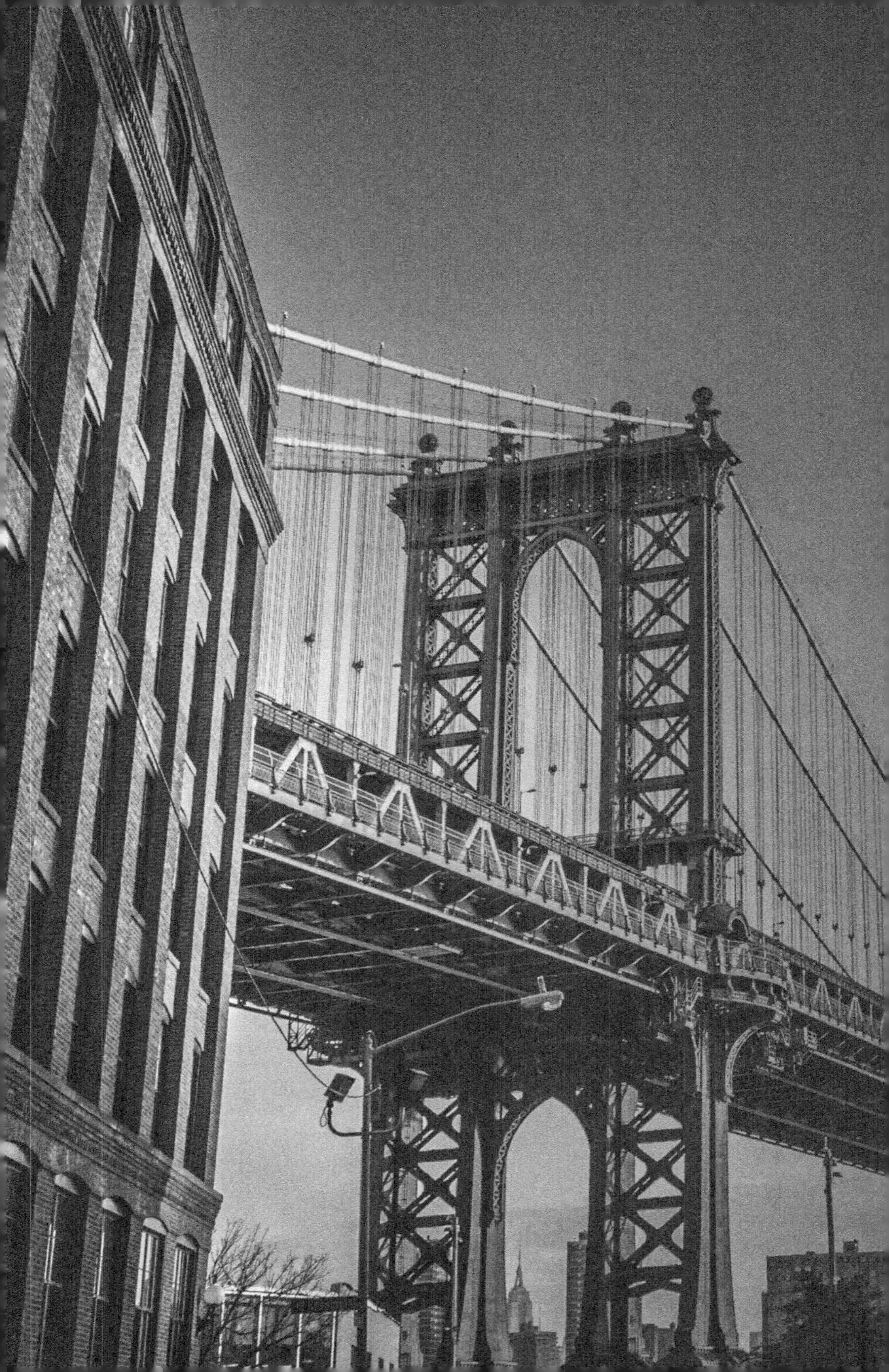

CHAPTER
Ten

SANTI

My visit to New Jersey ten years ago wasn't my first trip to America. Until that day, my version of America stopped at the Texas state line. Houston, to be exact. Base camp for all US cartel operations, and home to the other half of the Carrera bloodline:

The Harcourts.

I remember RJ's dad having a whole room at his house just for watching movies. It was all state of the art, with ninety-two decibels of surround sound that you could feel more than hear. A scream during a horror flick would burst an eardrum as fast as an explosion from an action movie would rattle your teeth.

That's why the explosion and flames don't feel real at first. For a split second, it's like I'm sitting on the outside, watching everything happen to someone else—like a movie.

But it's not.

Pressing my palms against the concrete floor, I lift my head to anarchy. *Fire. Smoke. Destruction.* It's the escalation of a fucking nightmare.

Slowly, I drag myself to my knees, and survey the damage. What used to be the south wall of the warehouse is now engulfed in a ball of multicolored flames. Dark smoke snakes around the jagged edges, inviting itself inside to consume what's left—a skeleton of twisted metal and crumbled brick.

What the hell just happened?

There's a muffled groan behind me. I turn to find RJ kneeling on one leg, his elbow braced against the other. He's holding his upper arm, a rare, rabid expression on his face.

"Shit!" I'm on my feet in half a second and by his side in even less. "Are you hurt?"

Gritting his teeth, he slides a narrowed gaze up at me. "No, I'm thinking *real* hard. Hell, yes, I'm hurt." He moves his hand, and blood pours from a wide gash in his bicep. "Piece of glass took out a chunk of my arm."

I catch another glimpse of the raging fire that's consuming one side of the warehouse. *We need to get the hell out of here.*

"Can you move?" A pointless question since I'm already dragging him to his feet.

Once vertical, he jerks his arm away. "Someone just tried to take us out, Santi... I can do more than move. I can kill the motherfucker with my bare hands, if I have to."

"*Muy bien*. Let's find the others and put that to the test."

We turn in opposite directions, and it doesn't take me long to find my father. Despite the gash slicing open his forehead, he's already on his feet with his gun drawn.

"Santi," he says, a mumbled *gracias a Dios* framing the edges of my name. "*¿Estás bien?*"

"*Sí*," I tell him. "I'm fine. RJ's fine. Where are Grayson and Santiago?"

At the mention of their names, his brief repose snaps like a brittle bone. "Already outside," he says, gesturing to his right. "Observing a mass cremation."

I turn to find six of Santiago's men lying motionless on the floor. Some are missing limbs, while others... Well, there's not much left to check for a pulse.

Santiago is waiting for us on the remains of the sidewalk outside. His dark skin is a criss-cross of bloody streaks and gore.

"Bombs, Carrera?" he roars when he sees us. "That's a coward's move."

My father lets out a hollow laugh. "You think we did this? If we came here to blow you to hell, do you think we'd stick around to hitch a ride? We're reckless, not suicidal."

We're neither. We're strategic executioners who do nothing without purpose. *Just like the fuckers who are lighting up the East Coast like the Fourth of July.*

I step in between them to diffuse the rising tension. "Let's think about this for one goddamn minute. Two cartel ports just went up in flames. The building hit on our side happened to be the terminal's south office, which is now a pile of fire and ash, along with the dockhand who tracked the container." I glance at Grayson, who's joined us, his face looking all kinds of fucked up. "You?"

"My insider went up in flames too."

"I don't believe in coincidences."

"Jesus Christ," RJ mutters. "We were being watched the whole time."

The chime of a text message diverts my attention. It's not mine. I have no idea where my phone ended up, after being blown to fuck and back. Everyone turns to where my father's head is bowed at the lit screen in his hand.

"*Dios mio*. What now?"

"The New Haven fire department was just called to Celtic Stone."

"That's Mahoney's place."

"Not anymore." Lifting his chin, he catches my eye. "Mahoney was inside."

I'm beginning to understand the power *Villefort* wields. Its dirty reach extends into all four corners of the world. There's no place to hide from them. Nothing our two cartels have done has ever gone unnoticed. Thalia and Lola were always living on borrowed time.

"They knew we were coming for Mahoney. They made sure he didn't talk."

Sirens and horns wail in the distance, drawing Grayson's attention toward the street where a crowd of onlookers are starting to gather, their eyes fixed to the orange flames licking the skyline.

"We need to get out of here," he says, motioning to the vehicles. "Fire department is three minutes out."

We're right back where we started, at square one with nothing but a handful of assumptions and theories. I'm not going anywhere until we realign our strategy.

"Mahoney is a pile of ash. How the hell do we get answers now?"

The corners of Grayson's mouth twitch. If I didn't know him any better, I'd swear he was smiling. "We offer a little cartel incentive. I'll deal with the fire department and meet you on Canal Street in an hour. There, we'll 'persuade' our *Villefort* friends to talk together."

Taking his lead, RJ nods to where our *sicarios* are reconvening. *That sure as hell isn't going to go unnoticed.* "We'll head back to base, and I'll fill Rocco in."

"Good. Go."

Meanwhile my father hasn't taken his eyes off his phone. I clasp his shoulder, understanding, now more than ever. "Go to *máma*. There's no guarantee Legado won't be next."

An hour later, I'm being greeted by the scent of copper and rotting meat. It doesn't take me long to find the source. Two steps into the Canal Street warehouse, and I'm ramming the toe of my shoe into a dead Italian's face.

He's not the only one. They're everywhere—dumped like discarded toys on the floor of a killer's playground. Twenty…maybe thirty. I stop counting the moment I encounter a line of Santiago guns, all aiming at my head.

"This is getting a little old," I say mildly.

"Lower your guns, men." Grayson follows me inside, unfazed by the carnage. "Carreras aren't the enemy here. Do I make myself clear? Now, fill us in on the pre-show."

One *sicario*, more muscle than man, steps forward and gestures around the room. "Most are Ricci's men. They were all wearing keys or tattoos. Those amenable to it, were questioned. Those who fired their weapons at us, died."

"Have they told you anything?"

"Him," the *sicario* clarifies. He nods behind us at the last remaining Italian. From the shades of his bloody suntan, he's already been beaten half-to-death. The chair he's tied to is more red than wood. "This one doesn't have the same pain threshold as the rest."

I don't ask permission, mainly because I don't give a fuck. Walking straight up to him, I inspect a familiar sight on his neck—a key pin jabbed in the center of the black ax tattoo.

"That looks unpleasant," I note, with a grim smile. "Has he started singing yet?"

"He said he'll only talk to a boss," the *sicario* mutters.

Well then, let the games begin.

Joining me, Grayson, rips the Italian's mouth gag down to his chin. "Name?"

"Vincenzo," he answers pitifully, his voice hoarse from screaming.

"Well, Vincenzo, it's your lucky day. You get two cartel bosses for the price of one. Guests first, Carrera..."

I can't tell if he's being serious or a dick. It doesn't matter either way.

"Knife," I order, holding out my hand. Within seconds, an impressive pocketknife is placed in my palm. "Let me tell you how this is going to work, Vincenzo..." Popping the blade, I watch his eyes widen as I circle him. "Nothing comes for free in this world. We're going to ask questions, and you're going to answer them. If your answer is to our liking, you pay for being a *hijo de tu puta madre* in blood." I tap the blade against his cheek. "That's son of a bitch, for the linguistically impaired." Straightening up, I continue to circle. "If you lie, or piss us off, we'll just slit your throat and call it a day. Got it?"

Not much of a choice, but he nods anyway.

"*Muy bien*. Question number one. Do you know who kidnapped my wife and sister?"

Think carefully, motherfucker.

He swallows hard. "No, no, I don't know his name."

I frown. "That's a shame." The moment I turn my hand sideways and aim for his throat, Vincenzo starts crying like a little bitch. "No, *per favore*! Please! I may not know his name, but I can describe him!"

Interesting.

"You have thirty seconds."

Red spit bubbles form at the corners of his mouth as frantic words tumble out of it. "American. *Corto*...uh, how do you say this in English? Short? *Sí*, short. With small eyes, like *ratto*...eh, rat. And he wore black glasses. Always eating *arachidi*."

Fucking peanuts.

There's only one man that fits that description. One man who managed to infiltrate both my inner circle and Grayson's... The same man who was at my fucking wedding.

That's the moment the cage unlocks and twenty-four hours of tension spills out in a rush of wrath and fury. "Spader," I growl between clenched teeth. I glance at Grayson who stands motionless, his jaw clenched.

I've always known betrayal wears many faces. What I never saw coming was the one orchestrated by a man dedicated to my climb to glory.

"You...you like?" the Italian stutters.

And the demons dance.

"Yes, Vincenzo, I like your answer. Unfortunately, I don't like looking at your fucking tattoo anymore, so I'm getting rid of it." He barely has a chance to register what I'm saying before I plunge the tip of my knife into the side of his neck. As three *sicarios* move in to hold him still, I flay a layer of his skin. By the end, he's both screaming prayers and cursing me to hell in Italian.

They're both unneeded. It's a superficial wound, and I was cursed to hell long before I was born.

When I'm done, I turn to Grayson. "All yours."

He doesn't waste any time. "Who's behind *La Societá Villefort* these days?"

The Italian hesitates a beat too long, and Grayson breaks his nose in one vicious punch.

Garbled words mix with his pleas for mercy. "He'll kill me if I tell—"

"We'll kill you if you don't," I mutter.

He passes a look back and forth between Grayson and me before letting out a ragged breath of resignation. "*Il Re Nero*. He calls himself The Black King."

"We need a name, Vincenzo, not an ego trip."

"Lorenzo Zaccaria."

"Fuuuck," Grayson hisses. "Tommaso's grandson. He's been moving in the shadows this whole time."

The Italian shakes in his chair. "Please, no more."

He considers him coldly. "Carrera stated how this was going to go upfront. We don't change the rules in the middle of a game." His gaze flits to the knife in my hand. "Can I borrow that?"

"Be my guest," I say, handing it over.

"Since you like tattoos so much, Vincenzo, let me give you some more." Driving forward, he works quickly, carving an S onto one cheek and a C onto the other. By the time he tosses the knife back, his eyes are dilated with fury. "Make this one count, Carrera. Not sure how much longer he's going to last."

I don't need *long*.

I need one word.

I prowl around him like a lion, the dying man tracking my every move. On the third rotation, I brace my hands on the arms of the chair, my face inches from his. When I speak, my tone is dangerously low—each word enunciated with all the hate that's boiling up inside me.

"Where did they take them?"

He hangs his head in despair. "Even if I tell you, they're probably already dead—or begging for death. What they do to women…"

Don't go there.

Don't think about it.

Grabbing a fistful of his hair, I jerk his head back. "Then I'll make everyone who touches them *beg* for it as well…starting with you."

He's been tortured, but he hasn't suffered. By the bleak look glazing his eyes, he finally understands the difference.

"Italy," he says weakly.

Italy… A surge of urgency paints my vision black. *So much distance to cover with so little time.*

"There's a town in the hills of northern Tuscany. It's where they take them and break them. I don't know the name of it, but locals call it '*Città Fantasma,*' after all the ghosts that haunt it. Rich men pay to do whatever they want with them there."

I release his hair, letting his head flop down like a broken doll's. Taking a step back, I stand shoulder to shoulder with Grayson, as Vincenzo's words sink into us.

We know exactly where we're headed next.

We're bringing them home together.

Closing the knife, I tuck it into my pocket. "I'm done here. You?"

"More than done."

At this, we both reach for our guns, take aim, and fire.

Two bullets.

One less *Villefort* disciple.

Zero margin for error.

I'm coming for you, Thalia.

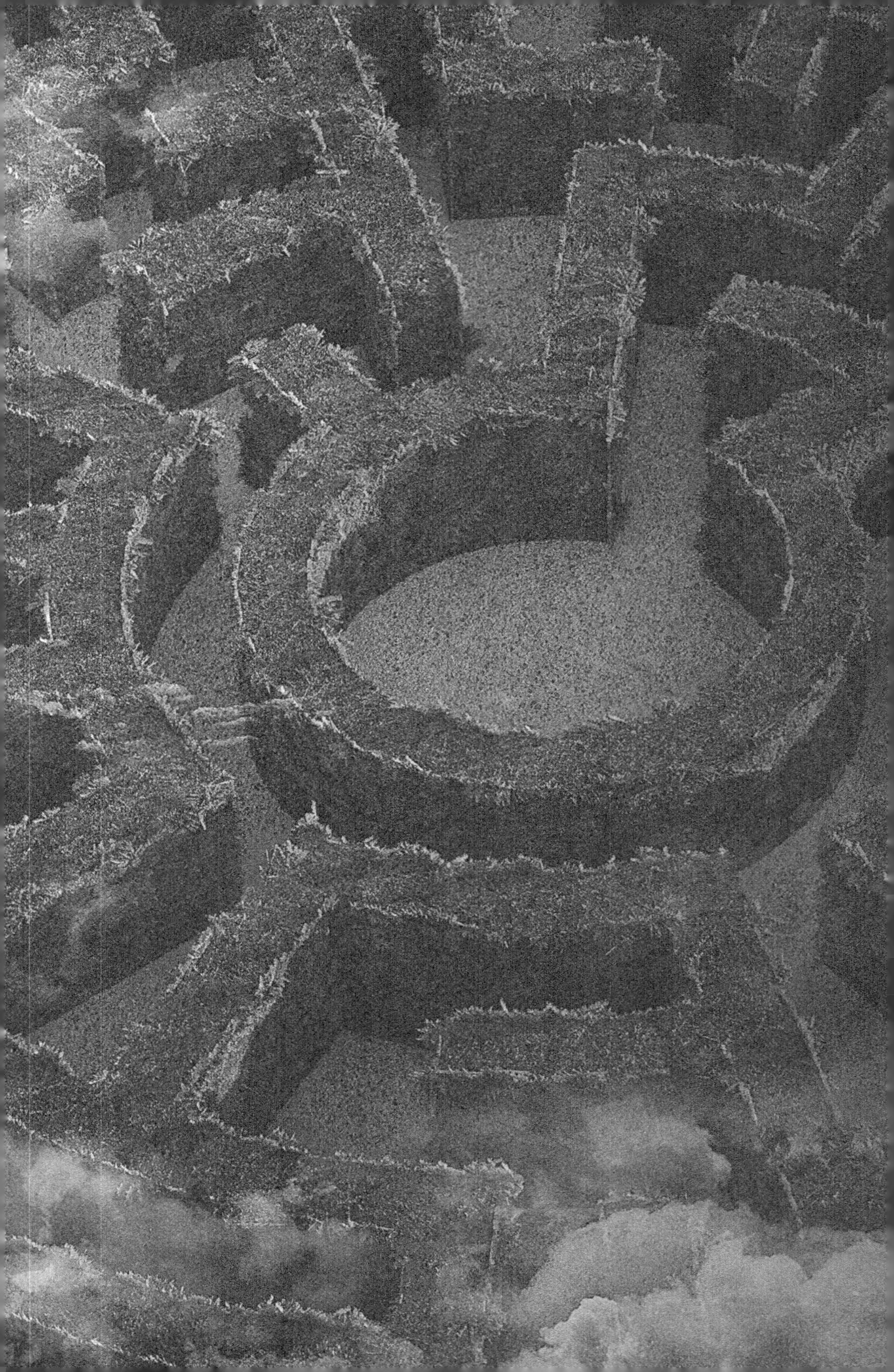

CHAPTER Eleven

THALIA

"*Run, Thalia! Don't let him catch you!*"

Everything hurts. I'm pushing my body to the limits, but Ella's war cry spurs me on more. My bare toes dig crescents into the soft sand as I force my legs to run faster… To chase the wind… To cross the finishing line in first place for once, instead of in second.

"You know your ponytail looks cute when you're trying hard to win like this."

Sam's mocking laughter is right there in my slipstream again. Despite my best efforts, I can't shake him loose. He's tucked himself in behind me and he's cruising. He's saving his final sprint to the end so he can be a dirty, fat show-off in front of everyone.

My lungs are on fire. Unfairness burns harder. I'm eleven, and he's fifteen, which means the race was rigged from the start. But pápa's watching alongside Ella today, and this makes me want to drown those stupid odds in the ocean.

We're only twenty feet out. My eyes are blurry. My fingertips are itching to reach out and claim what's mine. Ella's screams of encouragement are getting louder. In my head, I can picture my father's stern expression catching light to a rare smile.

Fifteen feet out, and Sam makes his move.

"So long, sucker," he hisses, breezing past me in a blur of black and blue.

"Go back to playing ponies and dolls like the little kid you are."

What a shithead!

Before I know it, I'm shoulder checking him. Knocking him off balance.

It doesn't matter that I'm half a foot shorter. The move is so unexpected he doesn't have time to check himself before he goes down in a crumpled heap of hurt boy pride and outrage.

"What the f—?"

I falter for the next couple of steps, caught off balance myself—my legs finding nothing but air before I'm hitting my stride again.

I can't hear Ella screaming anymore. My only focus is a line in the sand that's more precious to me than the one I just crossed with Sam.

In five strides, I'm there.

I won.

I freaking won.

Punching the air in delight, I collect my applause from the sand dunes, my heart thundering with happy beats. Even my father is clapping—though rules never mean much to him anyway.

"Cheat," Sam yells, picking himself up from the shoreline and brushing the beach out of his hair. His handsome face is stretched into a grin, and there's a glint of respect in his eyes that wasn't there ten minutes ago.

"You're just sore you didn't think of it first." I lift my eyebrows in a taunt. "Gotta be smart when you're playing to win."

"You were born to win, Thalia Santiago," he says with another laugh. "That's the kind of shit you'll never be able to trip up or outrun."

Does that go for fate too, Sam? I think wildly, remembering our race on the beach eight years ago in hazy snatches as I hit another dead end.

Cursing, I throw myself at the wall of yaupon holly hedge in despair—finding comfort in the way the needle-like branches bite and scratch at my skin.

I'm still alive... I'm still alive...

Just.

Tonight, my lungs are burning more than they ever did that day. Fear has added a new fuel to the cage. It's like all my oxygen is being held hostage.

Dusk fell hard when I wasn't paying attention. The long shadows have turned *Il Labirinto* into a warren of dark hallways. I've been running for my life for hours. Spader's dogs are still straining at their leashes.

"Run, Thalia! Don't let him catch you!"

I try a different path, cursing again in frustration when I have to double-back once more. That's when I hear rabid barking from the path running directly parallel to mine.

Too close.

He's too close.

"Come out, little lamb," he growls, turning my blood to ice. Meanwhile, his dogs are going nuts, sniffing and pawing at the thick hedgerow between us. "Fun fact time. The oldest maze in the world was built as a refuge for rich courtiers in eighteenth century England... Are you still seeking refuge, Thalia, or are you close to defeat?"

Never.

I sprint in the opposite direction, spilling out into the dead heart of this emerald-green mausoleum. It's huge, the size of a basketball court, with ten new paths leading off it in every direction. A near-empty space, with nothing to hide behind, other than an old stone table in the center.

I spin around in circles, unsure which path to choose next. Everything looks the same. There are no clubs or hearts to count my way to freedom. The whole maze is a blank deck of cards.

I can hear the snarling dogs close by again.

Panic rises up in my chest like dark magic, tricking me into fear and hopelessness. I glance at the stone table and see splashes of dark crimson staining the dirty gray.

Beat the monster.

Beat this fate.

But how?

The shadows are lengthening again. I can feel them creeping across my soul as I spin harder and faster, a sob tearing from my lips. Indecision has no place in this maze. I need to choose a path, and I need to choose it fast.

Darting forward, I nearly reach one when a dull agony is shredding my left calf—dragging my first scream of the night into the open.

"Shit!"

I tumble to the ground, but the movement only produces more pain. Glancing over my shoulder, terrified of what I might find, I stifle another scream when I see a wooden arrow protruding from my lower leg.

Shit, shit, shit.

I whimper as the pain ricochets like a pinball around my body. I try to stand up, and only end up lurching back to my knees.

"Fun fact number two, Thalia…" Turning in horror, I see Spader emerging from the opposite path with a silver crossbow in his hands and another arrow drawn and ready. His guard, Franco, follows closely behind, holding the leashes of two Rottweilers with drool stringing from their open mouths. "Another amusement for bored courtiers and royals was hunting deer."

I freeze as he raises his crossbow to shoulder height, deliberately aiming for my right thigh, his finger resting on the trigger.

"I thought you said I was a lamb?" I croak, miserably aware of my nakedness. Blocking out my humiliation, as I feel around the throbbing wound with my fingertips, coating them in sticky warmth. *The arrow tip doesn't seem to be in that deep.*

I grit my teeth and prepare to do the unthinkable.

I have to get up.

I have to keep running.

I can't do either with a fucking arrow sticking out of me.

Spader shrugs at my question. "Deer…lamb… You're all fair game to me."

Doing my best to ignore him, I take a firm grip at the base of the arrow shaft as he moves closer.

"But where are your tears, Thalia?" he demands, sounding disappointed. "I thought they'd be making a mess of you by now."

"They heard your fun fact medieval crap and decided not to stick around," I mutter, counting down the seconds in my head.

Three.

I see Santi's face. Clear as day.

Two.

I hear his nickname for me, over and over. As loud as Ella's war cry.

One.

I let the shadows inside me finally take over.

Wrenching the arrow free from my calf, I throw myself to the ground, muffling my screams in the scorched earth. At the same time, I feel a soft breeze grace my shoulder blades as Spader's arrow passes right over me, landing a couple of feet from my head.

"*Run, Thalia! Don't let him catch you!*"

I find myself back on my feet again and limping out a fast getaway. Behind me, I can hear Spader cursing my name and issuing angry instructions to Franco.

"Take the dogs back to the castle. I'll track this bitch myself all night if I have to."

I don't wait to hear more as I plunge deeper and deeper into the maze, ignoring the red-hot heat engulfing my leg—cannoning off yaupon holly hedge after yaupon holly hedge as I try to put some distance between me and my hunter.

I run and run, like Ella instructs me to, still clutching the bloody arrow I pulled from my own body—taking wrong turn after wrong turn, and weeping tears of sheer exhaustion because of it. *You can't have these tears though, Spader. This pain is all mine.*

Finding myself at another dead end, I stop for a moment to catch my breath—sucking in great lungfuls of air that make me dizzy and light-headed.

I can't stay here.

I have to keep moving.

But when I turn to retrace my steps, my access is blocked in the worst possible way.

"Trapped," Spader says, cocking his head indulgently at me, like I'm the last child to be found in a really messed-up game of hide and seek.

I stagger backward, pressing myself into the hedgerow—feeling the needle-like branches scratch and bite at my skin again.

Trapped.

He's swapped the crossbow for an old dagger, but the way the blade glints in the fading light is little comfort to me.

Trapped.

Before I can stop myself, I'm slithering to the ground like a wounded animal. Making myself as small as I can. Finding my last modicum of safety in the dark corners of this maze.

Above me, the North Star is low on the horizon. The moon is a weak promise. My calf is dripping red. My heart, even more so.

Help me, Ella. I can't see the line in the sand anymore.

"You've done well, little lamb," he praises, moving closer. "Most girls are being dragged unconscious back to the castle by now, but you…" He points the tip of his dagger in my direction. "You just gave me a whole evening's entertainment before the main event."

"Why me?" I croak, tightening my fingers around the bloody arrow.

"Ten years ago, your father and his associates destroyed a very profitable trafficking ring of mine in Honduras," he says, crouching down to my level, tapping the blade against his chin. "I've been waiting patiently for my vengeance ever since."

Without his glasses on, he looks even more rat-like and devious...

He looks vulnerable.

"What are you going to do to my body?" I whisper, holding his gaze as I slip the arrow behind my back.

"More English-devised torture, I expect," he admits with a shrug. "Let's just say I have a penchant for bestowing pain from all eras."

Somewhere, there's another countdown starting in my head.

Three.

He lunges forward and hauls me to my feet.

Two.

He hurls me up against the hedgerow and holds me prisoner by my throat. "Spread your legs for me, little lamb. I want to hear you bleat for me." When I refuse to do it, he squeezes and squeezes, until another shadow starts stealing my vision.

One.

"I'm going to make every fucking part of you bleed. Starting *here*." I feel the blunt handle of his dagger pushing between my legs.

Not in this lifetime.

With every ounce of strength I have left, I reach down between us and squeeze his cock as hard as I can, twisting it counter-clockwise to an ugly angle.

"You fucking bitch!" he squeals, stumbling away from me, clutching his crotch, his face the blotchy red color of rage and disbelief.

"I know my English history too, Mr. Spader," I rasp, advancing on him, naked and bloody like some fucking warrior queen. Canceling out his threats and curses with a descent so fast into my own darkness I can't feel the burn anymore. "I always liked the one about the asshole king who died with an arrow in his eye."

With that, I swing my arm and drive the sharp tip deep into his left socket.

CHAPTER
Twelve

THALIA

*O*nly in the darkness can you see the stars.

My mother keeps a framed copy of these words on her nightstand, next to photographs of me, Ella and *papá*, our half-sister, Isabella, as well as her childhood friend, Anna. When I was a child, I used to wriggle into her arms at dawn and watch them grow bolder and brighter with the rising sun.

I wanted so desperately to figure out what they meant.

I knew they must be important, just from their pride of place next to all the people she loved most in the world. But at eight years old, you tend not to dig too deep into subtexts. You stay safe on the surface to avoid being bitten by them.

One day, when I was older, I plucked up the courage to ask her, and her answer was as cryptic as the secret smile she reserves for our father. She said that they were like a footpath—like the one that led to our private beach—only this one led her all the way back to the missing pieces of her heart.

I've never forgotten her response.

In time, I learned the true meaning of Martin Luther King's words, but I never found a way to equate it with what she told me that day.

It's only now, as I'm chained to the wall in a pitch-black cellar, choking on agony and neglect, that I finally understand... She was once as desperate as I am, but somehow, in her own darkness, she found a way back to love.

Like I'll find my way back to him.

Because in the darkness, even hate has a softer shell.

The infection in my leg is burning me up with fever. I have no idea how long it's been since Zaccaria's men found me kneeling over Monroe Spader's dead body with his medieval dagger in my hand. The moment I finally beat the monster and crossed the line in first place again.

I crossed a ton of other ones too, but I'm past caring about lost morals. It's all about survival now, and if I have to kill again, I will. If I have to murder everyone in this godforsaken town to taste freedom again, *to taste love*, so be it.

This is the internal rhetoric—the drug—that drives my father. It's strange how I see it so clearly now, in a place where I can't actually see anything at all. I'd always assumed he was motivated by hate, but really, it's love—firstly, for our mother, and then for his children… For the first time, I'm seeing how all his pieces slot together to make him the uncompromising, complex, brutal man that he is.

If I ever get out of here alive, I'm going to tell him about my shadow, and he'll tell me about his darkness.

Please, God, let me get out of here.

Underneath the warm blanket of fever, everything hurts. Everything is polluted and stained. They dragged me here by my hair, and my scalp is sore. My leg is on fire. There's dried blood all over my hands and face, but it's not mine. I stabbed Spader twenty-three times until he died with my name on his lips, and I'm not sorry.

I'm not sorry.

This cellar is my punishment for fighting back, but I'll take it all, just as long as they spare Lola and Rosalia the worst.

Tick.

Tock.

Is that the sound of my time running out?

There's no lark down here. There's not even a window… There's just this never-ending night.

Tick.

Tock.

Pressing my spine into the stone wall, I tug listlessly at the restraints that bind my hands above me. My mind is a TV screen, flickering in and out of reality. Half here, half reliving that stupid race with Sam. He doesn't call me a cheat anymore, though. He calls me a murderer, and I smile in agreement.

Tick.

Tock.

I run my tongue along my lips. They're cracked and bleeding. I've had no food or water since I've been down here. If I don't get any soon, dehydration will be beating out infection for death's dark crown.

Tick.

Tock.

I swear I hear footsteps in the distance, but I'm starting to doubt my own thoughts. Next, the locks are turning. Heavy bolts are drawn back. A beat later, bright light is flooding into the cellar, and I'm flinching away like it's corrosive.

"Look at me, *puttana*."

I keep my face turned until rough fingers are digging into my chin and forcing the issue. Reluctantly, I blink away the blackness to find the face of evil himself standing right in front of me.

Lorenzo Zaccaria.

Coldly handsome.

Chillingly cruel.

"You don't play by my rules, *Señora* Carrera," he chides—his deep drawling indolence churning my stomach into bile. "A lamb isn't supposed to attack the wolf."

"Good girls aren't supposed to have shadows, either," I croak, wincing as he fists my hair and wrenches my head back to an agonizing angle.

"My dogs were hungry and restless," he murmurs, his dead eyes flickering over my face. "I sent them a Mexican meal…"

Lola.

"Please—"

"*Now* you beg for my mercy?" He sounds amused. "Don't worry, we'll keep her scarred, but alive… Same as you. You're much too valuable to waste so wantonly. The next time you face *Il Labirinto* though, you'll be doing it in chains."

"W-what is this place?" I whisper, forcing myself back from the beach. Forcing myself back to this cellar. *Never stop counting. Never stop seeking a way out.* "Men like you crave power, not money."

Tick.

Tock.

"Payback." He lets go of my hair, and my head flops forward. I'm too weak to hold it steady anymore. Too weak for pride. I don't even care that I'm naked. "Monroe Spader wasn't the only one wronged by your father, *señora*. My father and grandfather both suffered miserably in cages because of him."

Hysterical laughter bubbles up inside me. "Is that supposed to be ironic?"

This time, I feel his hand wrapping around my throat. A beat later, I'm being slammed up against the stone wall.

"Manners maketh the whore, *Señora* Carrera," he snarls. "Punishment is always bestowed on those who stray from that particular path of righteousness."

"Funny… That's the same thing Spader said, right before I turned your green maze into a bloodbath, *Lorenzo Zaccaria*."

He chuckles darkly. "So, you know who I am. You have an admirable spirit for a dying woman."

"I thought you said I was too valuable to waste?"

The grip on my throat tightens. "I might be willing to take a loss, this time around… After all, you just killed one of my best men."

Spots start dancing in my line of vision. "What do you want from me, an apology?"

There's a long pause.

"You Santiagos are all the same," he tuts eventually. "Your mouths are your weakest bullets."

"My father will be flattered by your efforts," I gasp out.

"Why's that?"

"Only a desperate man creates his own hilltop empire of deluded zombies to get even with his enemy."

"*Resurrecting, señora*," he corrects silkily, adjusting his grip—driving me so hard into the wall it feels like my skull is splitting. "This town is one of many we control across the world. You have no idea how formidable we really are."

"I can't breathe," I rasp, choking out a cough. Panic has my chest in a vise.

"Valentin Carrera is equally to blame for my family's misfortune," he continues, ignoring my plea. "His father, Alejandro, was once a loyal member of our organization—bleeding his influence across Mexico on our behalf. Then the cartel passed to his son, who inflicted immeasurable harm to our South American infrastructure. The same way immeasurable harm has just been unleashed on the

East Coast of America."

With this, he leans in close and hisses out a sinister word.

"Boom."

Bombs. He means bombs. The dirtiest of weapons—sly, secretive and devastating.

His dark secret curls a clenched fist around my heart. Everyone's life is in danger now—Santi, Edier, my father...

I'm close to unconsciousness when he finally loosens his grip. Air comes rushing back into my lungs, and I collapse against the wall. As I stand there, gasping and spluttering, he produces a bottle of water and holds it out to me like a beautiful, poisoned chalice.

To drink is to surrender.

To drink is survival.

Before I can make a choice, he's throwing the whole thing in my face.

After the initial shock settles, my tongue frantically laps at the droplets clinging to my cheeks and mouth. I tug at the chains, whimpering in frustration when I've licked myself dry.

"You're no better than my dogs," he says in disgust.

"More," I rasp.

"No."

"Please—"

"Beg for it, and you'll be denied. Earn it, and you'll be rewarded."

I'm too feverish to decipher his riddles. In my mind, I'm already back on the beach again. I'm ten feet out and winning. I see Ella... I see Sam...

Zaccaria turns to leave, my whole life dripping through his hands like the water that never reached my throat.

When the door slams shut, my last remaining stars extinguish.

My mother never told me there was a whole other level below darkness, and I just slammed, headfirst, into it.

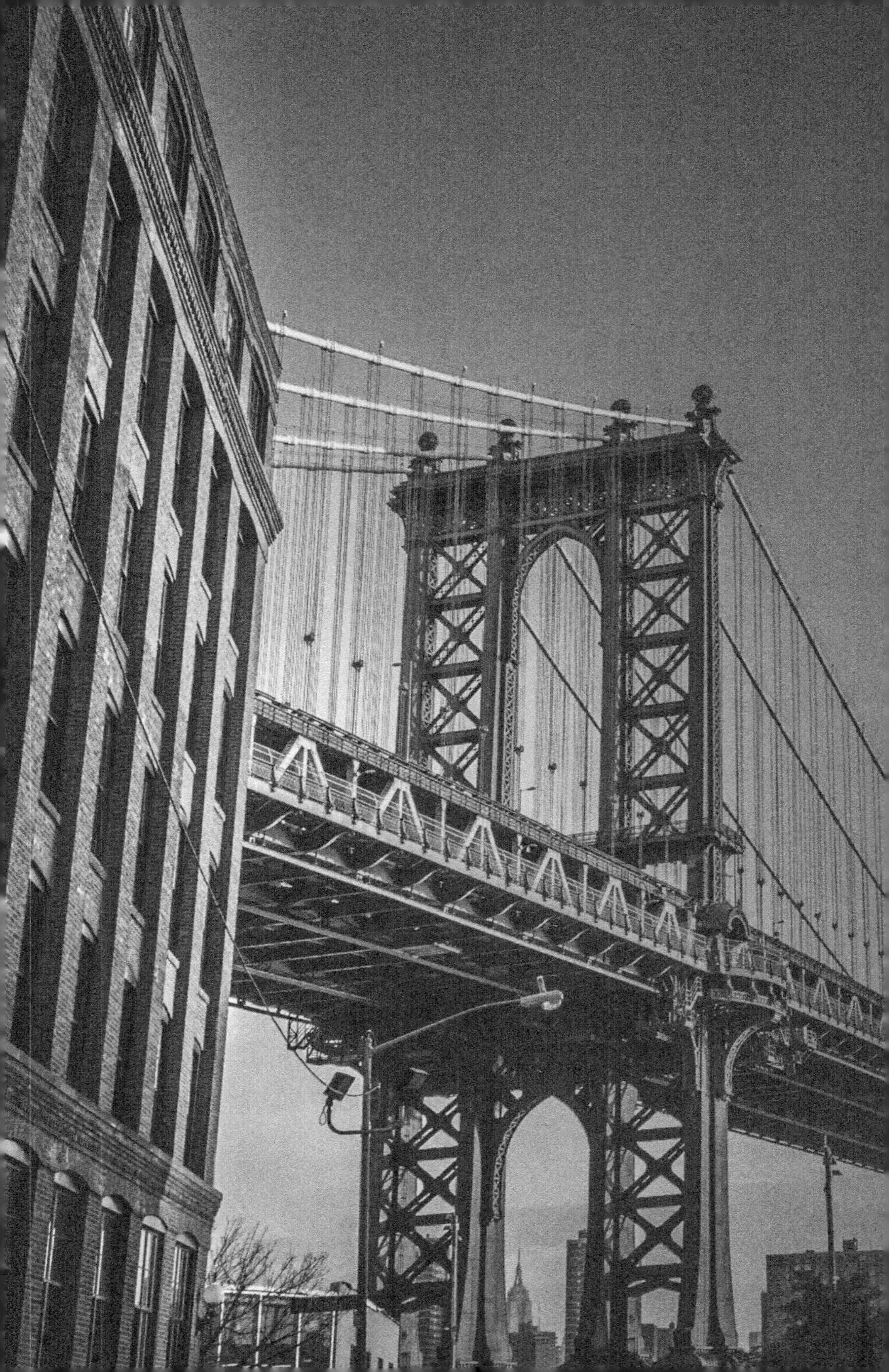

CHAPTER
Thirteen

SANTI

Grayson's fleet of private jets reach Florence shortly before nightfall. RJ and I are ready and waiting. We watch as the Colombian and two dozen of his best *sicarios* exit, their black military fatigues blending into the night—complimenting the thirty men behind us, along with the eight black SUVs.

He descends the airstairs with a phone attached to the side of his head and a scowl on his face. The moment his feet hit the tarmac, he's striding over to us. "*This* is your idea of being covert?" he says, gesturing to the army lining the runway. "Will the Special Ops forces be joining us as well?"

I jerk my head at his fleet of jets and disembarking men. "Just leveling the playing field. This is a joint effort, not a scorpion raid."

He pauses, taking in my black shirt and cargo pants with that now-familiar condescending look in his eyes. "Nice to know you don't always dress like a stockbroker."

"Says the man who walks around looking like he just fucked up a jewel heist."

Muttering a curse, RJ steps between us. "If you two are finished trading fashion tips, can we get on with it?" Ignoring my hardened stare, he turns toward Grayson. "Any word from the US?"

"If you're referring to the two cartel kingpins keeping our cities from burning to the ground, then no, they haven't killed each other yet. But 'ally' is a word Santiago and Carrera aren't familiar with, Harcourt. The sooner we end Zaccaria and return, the better."

"I couldn't agree more." Stepping around RJ, I glance at the phone in his hand. "Do we have a location?"

"I spoke to Knight just before we landed. Zaccaria bought himself a hilltop town in northern Tuscany ten years ago... His very own fortress of stone."

"What is it? A fucking castle?"

"From what he described, yes—and by design. Zaccaria's taken every precaution to ensure no one's getting in...*or out*."

"Not every precaution. What's our ETA?"

Grayson jerks his head at the waiting caravan. "Depending on how skilled your men are at handling Italian roads, we'll either arrive in an hour, or disappear over the side of a fucking motorway bridge."

Even that wouldn't stop me. If I have to crawl on my hands and knees to the gates of that fortress, so be it. I promised myself I'd find Thalia and bring her home.

I lied to her once.

I'd rather die before I do it twice.

We're walking toward the SUVs when Grayson pulls me to one side. "Remember, we're fighting as one tonight, Carrera."

"What the hell is that supposed to mean?"

"It means, our bullets fire *for* each other, not *at* each other. If this shit goes sideways, you'll have to put your life in the hands of a Santiago."

"I already have."

The weight of the words center me as I repeat my silent promise.

There's not a star in the sky as I lead our caravan of SUVs up the narrow, winding roads toward *Città Fantasma*. It contradicts everything I've heard about this part of the world, but it suits the plan. We're bringing a raging tempest with us. All light needs to be extinguished to disguise our impending slaughter.

We're about half a mile out, making up time on deserted country lanes, when the trees part and we catch our first glimpse of the town's imposing gray stone outer walls.

"Jesus Christ," RJ mutters, sliding forward from the backseat to take a better look. "Did we take a wrong turn into the twelfth century?"

I stare at the miles and miles of unbreachable parapets, hearing Vincenzo's words in my head.

"*Città Fantasma.*"

"Ghost town," Grayson echoes. "Sounds like a fucking invitation to create more inhabitants to me."

The approaching road climbs steeply. We kill the headlights for the last quarter of a mile and travel in total darkness. RJ's grip tightens around the back of Grayson's seat as I take another sharp turn.

"How the hell does someone buy up an entire town, no questions asked?"

"That's the power of *Villefort. Città Fantasma* doesn't need anyone's permission to exist, and those entrusted to protect its secrets are usually up to their eyes in dirty money."

My grip tightens on the wheel. We aren't good men, but we've never professed to be anything more than that. Those who wear the face of salvation while hiding their sins deserve to die a slow, painful death.

Speaking of inhuman bastards...

"Show me that image of Zaccaria again. I want to know which man to aim for first."

Grayson hands me his phone.

"Cold-looking fucker," I murmur, committing his face to memory. "He'll look even better with my bullets decorating his face."

"And Spader?"

"No one touches him, either." My fingers are choking the steering wheel now. "No man has ever suffered like that *maricon* will for his betrayal."

In response to my threat, the moon bows her head again, and more darkness descends.

We pull over five hundred feet before the arched entrance, just shy of the first line of security cameras. I watch as a couple of *sicarios* position themselves close by, ready to cut the feed on Grayson's signal.

There are no other cars around. No voices. No people.

Città Fantasma.

Moving swiftly, we exit the SUV and walk around to the rear. I pop the lift gate and start distributing the extra guns and ammo my contact in Florence arranged for us. Behind us, our men follow our lead.

Grayson glances down at the stash. "A grenade? Am I supposed to be impressed?"

Dropping a bullet into the magazine, I shoot him a side-eyed glare as I slam my palm against the base and shove it into the handgrip. "I'll be more impressed if you manage to throw it without blowing your own dick off."

I'm about to close the liftgate when I see RJ shove a small bottle into his rucksack. He's quick, but I'm quicker, and it's in my hands before he can snatch it back.

"Vodka?"

He points to his newly stitched bicep. "Pain relief."

Bullshit.

I go to tuck it away in my own rucksack when my head starts swimming, the lack of sleep finally getting to me. Now that we're here, right on the cusp of rescue, I'm aching. I'm agitated...

I'm crashing.

After forty-eight hours of continual motion, this lull feels like a detox—like someone just swung an anvil at my suit of armor. Fortunately, the vibration of my phone is the shot of adrenaline I need.

"What do you see?"

"Twenty scaling the perimeter walls on the north side right now," my lieutenant reports. "This place is locked down, and there are guards stationed all along, but there *are* weak spots." There's a weighted pause. "They definitely have the numbers."

"Maybe, but we have something they don't."

"What's that?"

"The element of surprise... Zaccaria sent a C4 calling card to anyone who knew of *Villefort's* resurrection. Until we make our move, we have the advantage."

"Give the orders, *jefe.*" There's a new respect in his voice.

He called me jefe.

I've led men into battle, but never into war. These are my father's men.

Mexican-trained *sicarios*. *Jefe* is what they call my father. It's a sign of respect and honor. To hear him call me that flips a switch inside me.

I'm *jefe*.

I'm *El Muerte*.

I'm bringing my family home.

"Time to switch to radio. Send another twenty over. On my signal, have the *sicarios* take out as many guards as they can. Use silencers. No fanfare. In the meantime, we'll keep the ones at the gate,"—I train my binoculars on the front archway where there are four men standing guard—"distracted."

"*Sí, jefe*. When it's clear, I'll send a message."

"I assume you have a plan for this 'distraction'?" Grayson asks, taking the binoculars from me to scope out the situation for himself. "Ten minutes and we can have snipers in place to take them out."

"We don't have ten minutes. Tell your men to cut the outside security feed and follow my lead." I shoot him a look. "I know that's going to make your head explode, Grayson, but try and keep up."

"Cocky bastard," I hear him mutter as we start to climb the rest of the road on foot.

I *am* a cocky bastard. If I was anything else, doubt would be creeping in by now. I can't allow thoughts of what awaits us on the other side of those walls to dilute my focus.

A hundred feet out, I unscrew RJ's vodka bottle. Taking a couple of deep swigs, I tip the rest down the front of my shirt as Grayson grabs my arm.

"What the hell are you doing?"

"Thinking outside the box."

It's risky. It's reckless. But other than going in, guns blazing, it's all I've got.

His grip tightens as I go to push past. "I run slick operations, Carrera—"

"Hang back in the shadows. When I start firing, don't *fucking* miss." Wrenching my arm away, I raise the radio, and give my lieutenant the order to start shooting guards from the rear.

Sliding my gun into the waistband of my pants, I make my way up to the guards, holding out my hands in mock surrender, staggering like I'm a drunk on *Día de los Muertos*. As predicted, I'm greeted the *Villefort* way—with their M27s aimed at my head, and a fuck load of angry Italian.

"I'm looking for the bar," I slur, throwing out my demand like I'm not two seconds away from being more bullet than bone.

The tallest one glares at me with contempt. *"Chi è questo imbecille?"*

"Did you...?" I pretend to sway again. "Did you just call me an idiot?"

Meanwhile, there's a faint commotion coming from the other side of the wall. I glance up to find half the parapet guards on this side have already disappeared.

"This is not a tourist stop," the guard hisses in broken English. "You are trespassing on private property. I will enjoy—"

He's cut off by an eruption of gunfire on the back side of the wall. Realization lights up his face as our *sicarios* spill out behind them, a spray of bullets announcing the arrival of the tempest. Before he can take aim, I have my finger on the trigger. With one shot, the back of his head is staining the road.

"You won't be enjoying anything anymore, you piece of shit," I tell the corpse, as the atmosphere thickens with the steady pulse of urgency.

The other three guards are down, courtesy of Grayson and RJ. But that was just the prelude. The real show begins as more guards come charging at us from every corner.

Grayson quickly reloads his gun, slamming the magazine in place. "Christ, they're multiplying."

Taking aim, I fire—sending another man to an early grave. "Go!" I shout, waving my gun toward the front entrance.

They take the lead and I follow behind, covering their asses as a bullet whizzes past, clipping my shoulder. I don't stop to inspect the damage. I can't allow anything to slow me down.

Through the archway, we find a network of narrow, cobblestone streets, with the silhouette of a castle looming large in front of us.

As we're sucked further into this ghost town, with its shuttered windows and boarded-up shops, the sound of fire power starts to dwindle.

"Where the fuck did all the guards go?" RJ says, voicing what we're all thinking. "It can't be this easy."

It's not.

The first explosion feels like the ground is crumbling beneath us. The walls of nearby buildings shake, setting off a chain reaction. Bomb after bomb detonates, destroying street after street, until the air is thick with smoke and flame.

"Zaccaria's gone," Grayson shouts, sprinting toward the castle. "We're too late."

Bleeding and frustrated, we sprint after him.

"What the hell is this?" RJ yells.

"It's a self-destruction plan. Destroy the evidence and everyone inside. We have to reach that castle, before it goes up in smoke too."

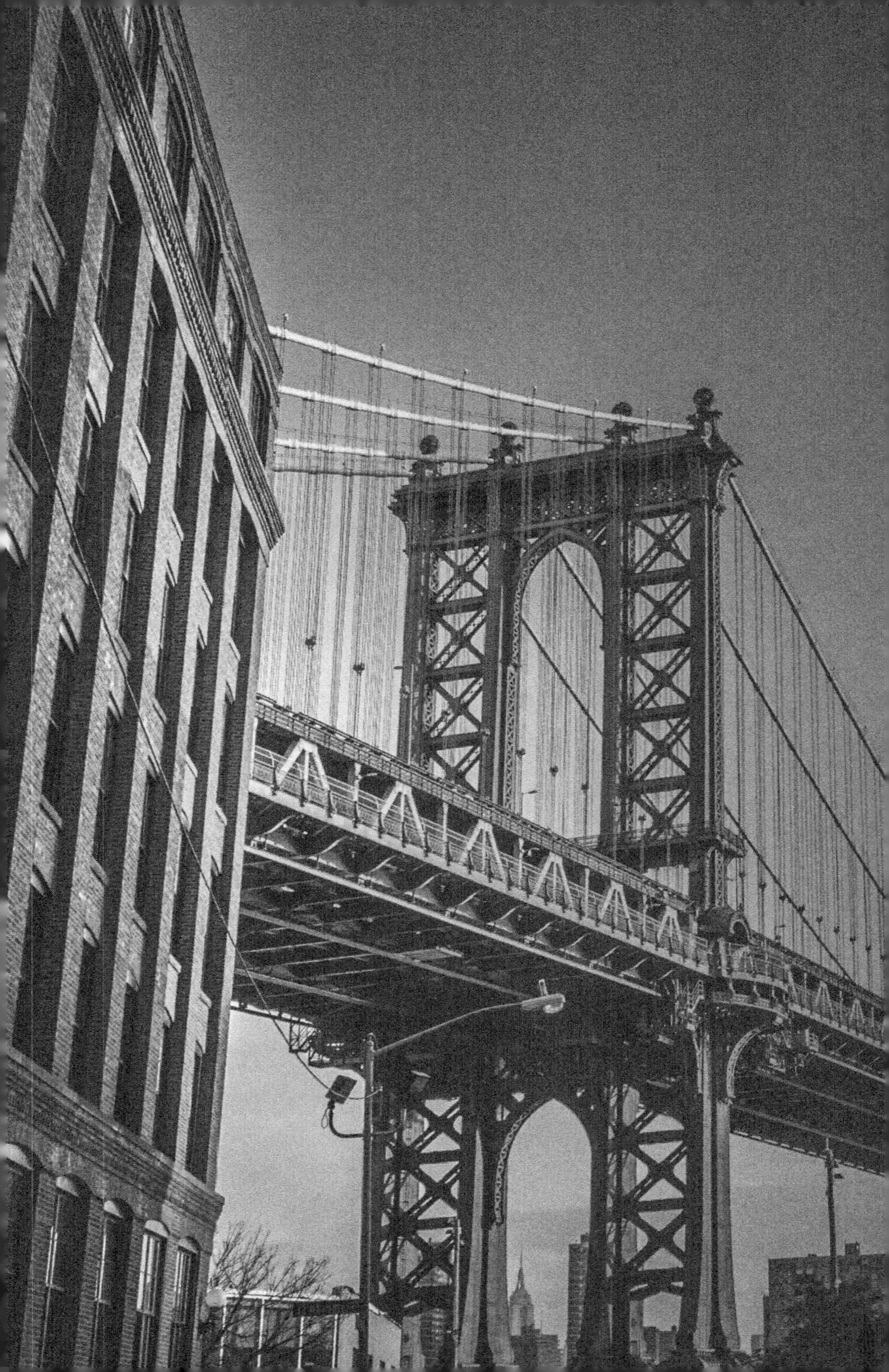

CHAPTER
Fourteen

SANTI

I thought we had the element of surprise on our side. Then another explosion goes off, sending stone scattering across the floor of the castle's front portico. That's when I realize stealth never mattered. Three generations have tried to destroy *Villefort*. Whether we coordinated a blitzkrieg or sent Zaccaria a RSVP to his own funeral, the outcome wouldn't have changed.

There was always a protocol for an invasion like ours.

Through the portico, we find ourselves in a courtyard. Grayson stops to reload his gun again. "Time's running out," he stresses, as if I don't feel the same weight pressing down on me.

The doors leading off this courtyard are mocking us. There are at least ten, all heading in ten different directions. *Ten opportunities for success or failure*.

"This place is like a goddamn labyrinth," I hear RJ say. "How the hell are we supposed to find *shit* before the whole thing blows?"

"We split up."

This catches everyone's attention.

Grayson nods. "He's right. Half our *sicarios* are gone and the rest are raining down bullets on any remaining *Villefort* guards. Which doors, Carrera?"

"Zaccaria trades in shadows, but he's a sadistic bastard who lives for the hunt. He wouldn't lead us away from destruction. He'd drive us straight into the heart of it and watch us burn…" I glance around the courtyard again. "We take the main entrance and the two doors closest. Hit me up on the radio the minute you find them, then you two get the fuck out of here."

"Don't you mean the three of us?" RJ says.

I reload my magazine in silence. I need him focused on the mission, not distracted by my choice. If I can't find Thalia and Lola, I won't be coming back to New Jersey. *If they burn, I burn.*

I take the center door, Grayson to my left, RJ to my right.

The first room I enter is a wide open space with a long glassless window, overlooking a field of black. I step closer to investigate, and then a strong arm is wrapping around my neck from behind and crushing my windpipe.

Fuck.

"You're here for *her*, aren't you?" leers a voice, as he tightens his grip around my throat.

I don't think, I react. Pulling my arm forward, I sink a hard elbow in his ribs—a move that barely causes him to stumble.

"Carrera," he seethes, spitting out my name like it's a curse. "She called for you, you know. She begged for you."

I sink another elbow into his ribs.

"There's a maze down there, Carrera." As he says it, he twists me toward the window. "I watched her run it. Right where you're standing. Spader outbid some very wealthy men for the privilege of degrading your whore wife first. He stripped her naked and chased her. We all watched her bleed."

I'm fighting to reach my pocket. All I can smell is smoke and rancid breath as the son of a bitch laughs.

"Would you like to hear the best part? I stood right here and jerked my dick raw to her screams, especially when his arrow hit its target."

His taunts sink behind my iron walls, slipping beneath my skin.

"I thought seeing her chained to the wall like a dog was the highlight of the night…" He trails off, another low laugh rumbling in his throat. "But that honor went to the *real* dogs, when they ripped your sister apart."

A wave of red crashes over my eyes. I'm a fusion of working parts—a machine hell bent on maximum destruction.

My wife is dead.

My sister is dead.

And this motherfucker is dead.

This time, my fingers make contact with my pocket, and I pull out my switchblade. Popping the button, I swing my arm backward and make contact with whatever the hell is there.

The man lets out a tortured hiss, and the pressure around my neck releases. I spin around to find him holding his own neck, attempting to pull my blade out. I'd love nothing more than to mutilate and dismember this *pendejo,* piece by piece, but I'm done with the small talk. With that in mind, I aim my gun at his forehead and pull the trigger.

Leaving him to rot, I continue my search down a cold stone hallway of closed doors. Behind every one is a woman. Some are Thalia's age, some are younger. They're all dead—their lifeless bodies strewn across their bed like broken dolls.

"Thalia?" I roar. "Where the fuck are you, *muñequita?*"

By the fifth room, I'm numb to the carnage. Numb to the waste. When I reach the sixth, a massive explosion rocks the castle, the impact slamming me into a wall so hard I see stars.

Images from that *pinche cabrón's* taunts seep into my mind as I search for my gun in a haze of dust and debris. I think of her running for her life, hunted like an animal...

Like a dog.

Bile rises up in my throat at the thought of my little sister being thrown to a pack of them.

At the end of the hallway is a winding stone staircase that leads down. I'm starting my descent when a voice comes through on my radio.

"Santi, I've got Lola. She's fucked up, but she's breathing."

His words are like a punch to the chest. "*Gracias a Dios.*"

Forgive me, Lola.

Drawing air back into my lungs, I refocus and resume my journey.

"What about Grayson?"

"He found some American girl still alive. *Sicarios* have cleared a path, and they're taking them to the SUVs. What's your location?"

I hesitate, then decide there's no point in lying. "I'm headed down into the cellar."

"You're going *where?*" His shock is clear enough to be heard on every channel. "Santi, this place is about to blow. Grayson's already on his way out."

He heaves out a jagged breath. "Committing suicide isn't going to save her."

Dying won't save her. But living without her won't save me.

"Take care of my sister, RJ."

I switch my radio off after that.

The steps are endless, taking me further and further down into the darkness. There's a dank smell down here that's permeating every sense. The clouds of dust are blinding, but when I hit the bottom, they seem to clear.

That's when I see her.

I always believed I didn't have a heart until Thalia stormed into my life and changed everything. For days, it's been beating to her rhythm. But now, *seeing her in a fucking cellar like this,* it's close to stopping.

She's chained to the far wall, her slim arms reaching high above her bowed head, her toes barely dusting the floor. Her naked body is a dirty canvas of gashes and bruises.

She's just hanging there.

Waiting for death.

I'm carving up the distance to reach her before her name leaves my mouth. *I need to touch her. I need to see her.* Cupping her jaw in both hands, I pull her head upright, and take a wrecking ball to the chest when I see the devil's handiwork all over her face.

But she's warm.

Her skin is fucking warm.

Keeping her head lifted with one hand, I check her pulse. It's faint, but it's there.

She's alive.

"Thalia, open your eyes. *Mi, amada...*"

Nothing. Meanwhile, in the distance, there's another massive explosion, and more clouds of dust come billowing down into the cellar.

Still cradling her head, I reach up to jerk the chains binding her wrists, but they're made of steel and concreted into the wall.

Fuck.

I can't shoot the chains while she's unconscious. She could move at any moment and catch the bullet instead.

I'm debating my next move when there's a dull crack and a section of the cellar's ceiling comes crashing down around us.

They say your life flashes before your eyes right before you die. I've taunted death more times than I can count, but at this moment, all I see is her...*us*... A tragically poetic story unfolding in a flurry of snapshots.

Thalia and I met in a snowstorm, and we're going to die in a fucking firestorm.

Orange and red start creeping into the far corners of the cellar. In a few moments, the heat and smoke will be punishing. I press my forehead to hers, cursing this world for ripping us apart. I deserve death. She doesn't. I'm destined for a place that no angel fears to tread.

"Fly high, *muñequita*..."

At the sound of my voice, her eyelids flutter, and then she's coughing violently.

"Come back to me, Thalia," I hiss, trying again to rouse her again. "Time to wake up."

"I'm so tired," she whispers.

"I need you to be strong one last time so I can shoot your chains. I need you to brace your fall. Can you do that?"

This time, when her eyelids flutter, I find myself staring into an ocean of pain.

"Thalia?"

"I'm ready," she croaks.

I step back, steadying my hand as I take aim and shoot—once, then twice. As her chains disintegrate, she flings her arms in front of her. Diving forward, I catch her seconds before she hits the ground—her warmth and fragility sinking into my chest.

I tighten a fierce hold around her.

I'm never letting her fall again.

Ripping off my shirt, I throw it around her naked body. There's so much I want to say. So much I want to atone for, but all that has to wait. Lifting her into my arms, I fight through the smoke and falling debris to find the staircase again. By the time we reach the hallway, we're both gasping for clean air.

"Santi," she wheezes, curling her arms around my neck. "I can't breathe."

"Stay with me, *muñequita*. Don't you fucking leave me now. Just a few more minutes. Keep your mouth covered."

I feel her press her face into my chest and nod.

Twist. Turn.

Right. Left.

I take each corner like I'm on fucking rails, but I didn't come this far to lose her now.

We spill out into the courtyard, moments before a final, deafening explosion sends the turrets of the castle caving inward. After that, I don't stop until I reach the front archway.

Through the haze, I see an outline of black fatigues approaching. I feel their footsteps vibrating up from the ground.

"Carrera!" Grayson reaches me first. "Jesus Christ." His face is a rare mask of fury when he sees the state of Thalia. "Give her to me."

"Fuck you."

I know I should hand her over, but something inside me won't let her go. *Can't let her go.*

"What are you going to do?" he snaps. "Crawl back to America?"

"If need be."

I've walked through fire for Thalia. I can walk a few more steps.

"Get in the back." He guides us toward the nearest SUV. "We've given half of Italy a firework display tonight. I've delayed the emergency departments for as long as I can."

Before I can swing inside the vehicle, RJ comes storming up to me. "Jesus fuck! You crazy bastard. Don't ever pull that shit again!"

"I don't plan to," I say bleakly. "Where's Lola?"

He nods to the SUV behind us.

"I need to see her."

Thalia's out cold as I lay her down gently on the backseat. Grayson leans over and fixes a portable oxygen mask over her face. "This will have to do until we reach a hospital. Go check on your sister. Do it fast. We need to move."

Following RJ over to the next SUV, I wait until he opens the rear driver's side door, and then for the second time tonight, my heart comes close to stopping. My baby sister is unrecognizable. Her petite body is riddled with bite marks, open wounds, and bruises.

"*Chaparrita?*" I murmur, leaning over her to cup her cheek. "I've come to take you home."

Lola barely opens her eyes. She's mumbling out incoherent words, wheezing as she thrashes her head back and forth. "Rosalia," she rasps, one word breaking through. "Where's Rosalia?"

Beside me, I feel RJ stiffen.

"Rosalia, who?" he asks cautiously.

"Leave her alone, RJ. She doesn't know what she's—"

But he's already pulling me out of the way, his huge arms braced on the doorframe to block me out. "Rosalia *who*, Lola?"

At his sharp tone, Lola's eyes flutter open. She doesn't answer, but something passes between them.

White knuckling the doorframe, he turns to an approaching Grayson. "The American girl. What does she look like?"

"Long hair. Dark. Hard to tell much—"

"Which SUV?"

"Last one."

Grayson slides me a look as RJ sprints off down the line of vehicles. "What the hell was that all about?"

"Smoke's fucked up his head." *I'll deal with his insubordination later.*

My gaze shifts back toward Lola. Once again, my loyalty is being tested. I'm not letting Thalia out of my arms—she's my wife. But Lola is my sister.

As if reading my thoughts, Grayson slides in next to Lola, making the decision for me. "Go take care of Thalia."

"She's my *familia*."

He nods at the SUV in front of us. "And she's mine. That makes us even."

After a twenty-four-hour detour via a private hospital in Florence for an emergency operation on Thalia's leg, and a night on oxygen for all of us, we're finally headed back to the US.

It only took a couple of million-dollar payouts to persuade two doctors to fly back with us. None of us escaped injury, but it's mostly superficial, with the effects of smoke inhalation and a couple of bullet holes thrown in for good measure.

Thalia's injuries were the worst. The infection in her leg was bordering on sepsis. Her other wounds weren't as serious, but just as brutal. She's yet to regain consciousness.

Autodefensa.

I lost count of how many stitches Lola needed to close all the dog bites on her arms.

And the third girl?

It took some digging, but a missing American mob princess doesn't go unnoticed in our circles. Especially one who's been stolen from our own backyard.

RJ is sitting in the seat beside me, carving craters into the cockpit door.

Lifting my glass, I take a long, slow drink. "How long?"

"Don't start," he says tightly.

"How long have you been involved with Gianni Marchesi's daughter?" His silence ticks my anger up a notch. "How long have you been fucking the New Jersey Don's—?"

"Since Lola crossed the border."

That's not the answer I expected. "A year and a half?"

His gaze takes a swing in my direction, scorching me with accusation. "Are you really going to lecture me about crossing battle lines, Santi?"

"Yes. Because shit like *this* happens," I motion to the back bedroom where Thalia is resting. "People get hurt when enemies don't play nice."

"The Marchesis and Carreras aren't enemies."

I glare at him over the rim of my glass. "It's a tepid alliance at best. Don't paint a bullet red and call it a rose."

"Do you regret *your* red bullet?"

I clench my teeth, his question taking me off guard.

"That's what I thought," he mutters. "You worry about your choices, and I'll worry about mine." Rising to his feet, he strides toward the front of the jet and disappears into the cockpit.

The seat is empty for all of thirty seconds, and then Edier Grayson is inviting himself into it. "What's his story?"

"Denial. And it's none of your fucking business."

"Your diplomacy skills leave a lot to be desired, Carrera," he says coldly.

"So my wife keeps telling me." I catch him eyeing up the bottle sitting between us. "*Gran Patron Añejo Burdeos* tequila. Carrera special."

I don't wait for him to ask. Pouring him a glass, I push it across the small table separating our seats.

"An improvement," he remarks. "Though I hate tequila."

"Stop being such a pussy."

Gritting his jaw, he slides the glass off the table and tips it back, draining it in one. "We need to talk about Lorenzo—"

"Save it. I've heard enough about *Villefort* these last two days. Our cartels fought a twenty-year war. This one will still be here tomorrow."

Rising from my seat, I make my way toward the back of the plane and into the small bedroom. The Italian doctor looks up from adjusting the IV stand. He nods a respectful greeting before swiftly making his exit.

Thalia is curled up on her side. She's bruised and weak, but she's clean and dressed in a red silk nightgown I found for her in Florence. Red reminds me of her. It's the color that's shaded every major event in our short marriage.

The color of blood.

Hate.

Passion.

Love?

I sit down on the edge of the bed, dusting my finger along the length of her cheek, before reaching into my pocket to retrieve the hope I've been holding on to these past few days.

Lifting her left hand, I slip her wedding rings back onto her third finger.

Where they belong.

"*Muñequita*," I murmur, pressing my lips to her forehead. "I've waited ten years to tell you a story. It's about how a thirteen-year-old boy sacrificed his loyalty for your innocence. Wake up, Thalia. I want to hear the one about how a queen sacrificed her innocence for loyalty."

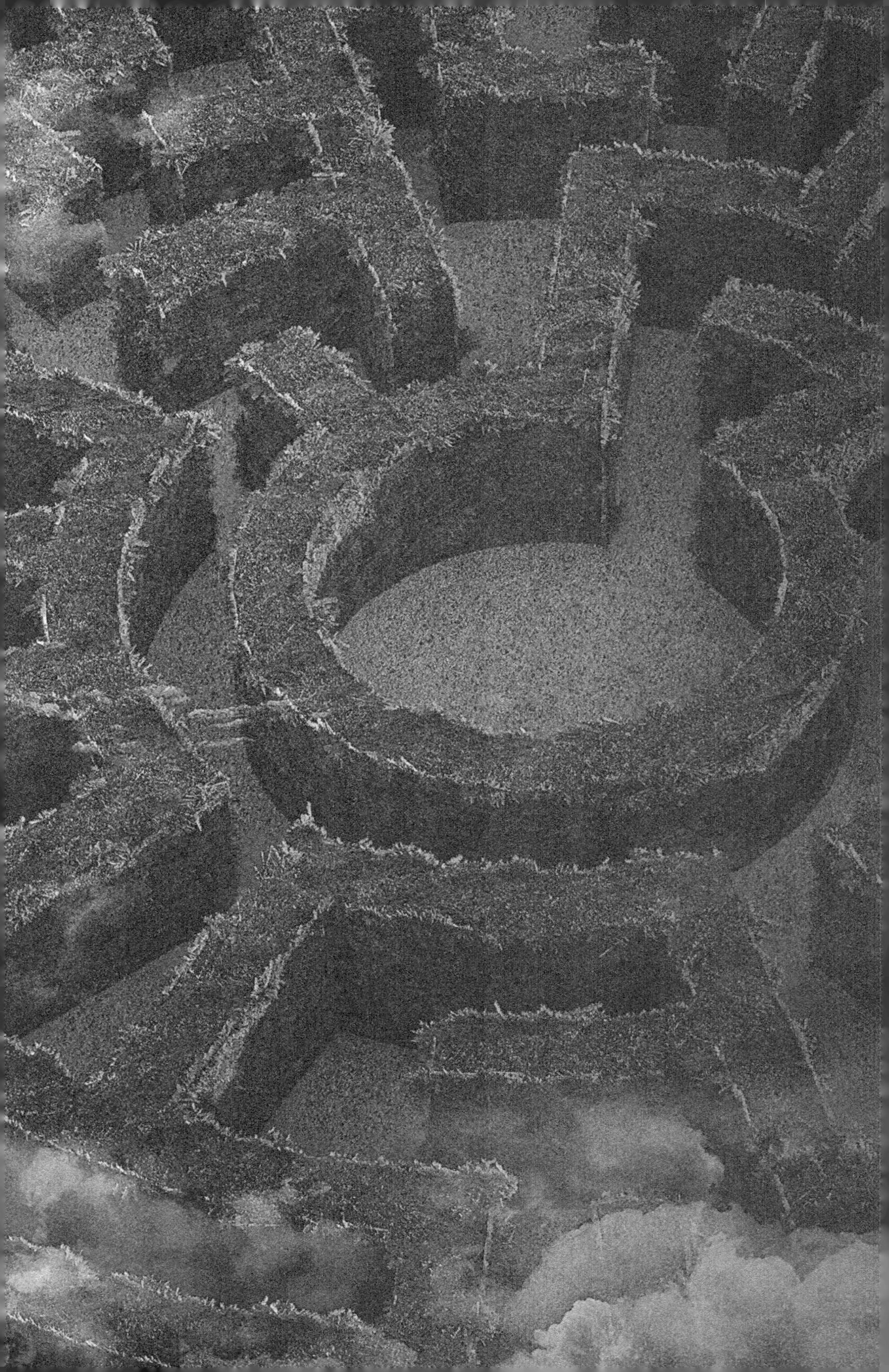

CHAPTER Fifteen

THALIA
Nine Days Later

Hope swims.
      Loss sinks.
But survival?

She's like the stagnant water of the two—a weightless woman who can't move forward with the current, but one who's too afraid to face the stormy oceans of her past.

Right now, she's cocooned in a fortress of white sheets with no desire to go anywhere. With no desire for much of anything anymore.

I don't want to feel.

I don't want to see.

I just want to *be*—floating in this bed that smells of lies and forgotten promises.

It's been nine days since Lola and I were rescued. Since a small hilltop town in northern Italy was decimated by cartel fire and fury. Since the life-saving operation in Florence to save my leg, and then the long, long flight back to America…

Or so I've been told.

I don't remember any of it, of course. I was unconscious the whole time. I learned the details from Ella who lies with me most days and nights, stroking my hair, whispering her warmth and reassurance so tenderly I'd cry from the beauty of it if I had any tears left to shed.

I never acknowledge her. I never react. I keep my eyes shut tight to reject a life I have no interest in living at the moment. I know where I am, though. I can sense it. I'm back in his room. In his bed. The floor-to-ceiling windows tempting me with a view of the New Jersey skyline.

It's not home.

It's not hell.

It's just…*stagnant.*

On the tenth day, the waters ripple. It begins with cigarette smoke wrapping its acrid scent around my senses. It continues with a presence so achingly familiar my eyelids flutter open of their own accord.

It's nighttime. There's the outline of a man standing by the window, a dark slur against the backdrop of neon. I listen to his vicious inhale, followed by a long, slow exhale—watching as the amber light of his cigarette rises and flares like a supernova, before falling back to his side. He repeats the motion several times, balancing his silence with weighted stares and history, before he finally speaks.

"Don't go back there, *muñequita,*" he says roughly. "Not yet. Stay with me for a while."

Muñequita?

Where have I heard that name before?

"Where's Ella?" I rasp. "I want Ella."

He pauses. "Your sister is in New York, as far as I'm aware."

"College," I whisper. "Did she—?"

"No idea. Call her up. Shoot the shit. I hear she's desperate to speak to you, but do it on your own time. I'm only interested in one of Santiago's daughters."

I'm not in the mood to be mocked. I turn my back on him, only to find the mattress dipping right beside me.

"Talk to me, Thalia."

"I don't talk to liars."

"How about the man who's been living in hell since you were taken."

His admission makes me blink. Here, in the dark, I swear I can feel his pain like it's my own. But Santi Carrera doesn't feel pain. He only knows how to give it.

Only in the darkness, can you see the stars.

"Did you burn it," I croak, sitting up slowly with the help of a brace of pillows behind me. Wincing from muscle stiffness and a throbbing ache in my leg. "Did you burn it back to hell?"

"Yes, *muñequita*," he says, moving closer until his face is a nodding silhouette, barely a foot in front of me. "The men who hurt you paid for it with their own deaths."

This time, I can feel his anger. It's a living breathing thing that fits the shape of my shadow perfectly.

"Even Lorenzo Zaccaria?"

There's another pause. "Soon."

It feels like a hammer blow to the chest. "He escaped," I say dully.

"He *will* die, Thalia. As *Santa Muerte* is my fucking witness."

It's not good enough. *Can't he see?* There is no future for us while that man is still alive. *I can't move forward. I'm too afraid to look back.*

Stagnant.

"Give me your gun. Tomorrow, I'll find him myself."

"And shoot your own foot off in the process?"

The trace of amusement in his voice makes me reach out and fist the front of his shirt in the dark. "You have no idea what I'm capable of anymore, Santi Carrera," I growl softly. "You have no idea what I had to do to survive…" My breath catches, and I release my hold.

"My firebird demands blood," he states, moving closer, a lingering scent of smoke and whiskey fanning across my face—churning up long-forgotten feelings deep inside me.

"Bardi," I grit out, causing him to retreat again with a curse.

Truth is, I have no idea what I am anymore. The girl I was before is gone. I lost half of her in a maze, and the other half in a cellar.

Somehow, I need to rise up from the ashes of this.

The mattress ripples as he stands. "My doctors are happy with your progress, but you need to rest. We'll talk more when you're stronger."

"Ella told me what happened," I say, falteringly. "With the raid, my leg… I heard her talking when she thought I was asleep."

There's a pause. "Your sister hasn't set foot in this apartment, Thalia."

"You're wrong. I heard her…" I trail off in confusion.

"I'm already straying close enough to your father's bullets by insisting you stay here. There's no way he'd allow your sister to cross state lines too."

"Then who—?"

"I have business to attend to." Soft light floods into the room as he opens the door. I catch a glimpse of his tall frame as he exits, before he's plunging me back into darkness again.

I slide under the bedsheets, his words spinning cartwheels in my head. If it wasn't Ella, then who held me? Comforted me? Bathed me? Made me feel their love when all I felt was numb?

The answer is as simple as it is bewildering.

My husband did.

CHAPTER *Sixteen*

THALIA

When I wake the next day, the neon skyline has dulled to a uniformed gray. Black clouds hang like dirty white lies over all the high-rises, and Santi's floor-to-ceiling windows are dotted with rain.

I lie there, debating whether to accept this new day or to crawl back inside my mind. Eventually, tolerance wins out, and I'm so thankful when I find a familiar figure perched on the edge of my bed, watching me.

"It's a shitty 'welcome home,' am I right?" She gestures to the window with a sigh. "You can always count on New Jersey weather to make a bad situation worse."

"Lola," I whisper, caught between sleep and disbelief. "Oh my God. I never thought I'd see you again!"

"I keep waiting for the stupid lark to show up," she blurts out, her face crumbling like an avalanche. "But he never does."

To anyone else, her words would sound crazy. To me, they're the sanest thing I've ever heard. Lola can't move on, either. She's stuck in her own motionless waters.

"Fuck, I'm sorry," she says, swiping at her tears with the back of her hand. "Ever since I've been home, I've been a mess."

"Don't be. You never, ever have to apologize for anything with me."

We stare at each other, taking in each other's scars, both the obvious ones and the hidden mutilations on the inside. She's wearing a simple black dress with a high neckline, but I can still see the fading red welts slashed into the side of her neck. There are yellowing bruises on both cheekbones, and a couple of wicked-looking gashes on her arms.

She looks haunted and beautiful, but very much *alive*.

"How's your leg?" she sniffs.

She doesn't ask what happened to it. She doesn't want to know, and I don't blame her. She already has enough nightmare material from that place to last a lifetime.

"Better."

"Thank God."

"The baby?" I hesitate, expecting the worst.

"Is fine."

"*Are you serious?*" There's a distant thud of joy in my chest as she rises from the bed to shut the door before scooting back to me.

"Sorry, I only have, like, ten minutes before my mother returns to my apartment. I can't breathe right now without her sticking a monitor on my finger and checking the oxygen levels. Santi's even worse. If it were up to him, he'd lock me up in a hospital and swallow the key."

"Are you sure?" I prompt again, greedy for lightness in a world that feels far too heavy right now.

"I'm sure," she confirms, smiling through her tears.

"Does Santi know?"

"Not yet. Fortunately, my doctor is open to every form of bribery." She holds up a slim hand to show me her lack of jewelry. "Hey, it's worth it. Once Sam is out of the hospital—"

"Sam?" I pounce on the name in disbelief. "Are you telling me Sam *survived?*"

This time, Lola's smile isn't a wilting flower. It's a sunflower turned toward the blazing sky. *Maybe someday I'll be able to smile like that again.*

"Santi heard the gunshots and found him in the parking lot. He and RJ saved him. He won't stop bitching about it, though..." Her face falls again. "Sam was shot in the stomach. He nearly bled out. He nearly died."

"Have you seen him? Does he know about the baby?" I'm tripping over my words like a drunk person now. Lola's news has me reeling.

She shakes her head. "Soon. For now, I'm biding my time... Picking my moment. Did Santi tell you about the truce between our families?"

"We haven't really spoken much about anything yet." I sink back down into my pillows again. *Whispers in the night aren't signed confessions.*

There's so much guilt and recrimination waiting for us.

We stare at each other again, and I know she's thinking the same thing. We're remembering two women chained to the gates of hell, fighting to keep them shut for as long as possible as the devil rattled the bars.

"I heard you screaming," she says, reaching out to take my hand. "That night in the maze? When you didn't come back to the room, I thought... I thought..." She leads her deduction into a sad, terrified silence.

"I can't do this," I whisper, moving my hand away. "Not yet."

"Don't punish yourself, Thalia," she pleads, her keen eyes flickering over my face. "For *anything*. Be kind to yourself. It's going to take a long time to come to terms with everything that happened."

Or what that night turned me into.

Reluctantly, she goes to stand. "I better get back. I'll come again soon, or maybe you can come find me? I'm in the apartment right below this one..." She pauses. "You know, *pápa* told me Santi didn't eat or sleep when he was trying to find us. He wouldn't rest until we were safe. The only reason he kept Sam alive was to extract information about our location. You know how much he wanted to kill him after what went down between us at Rutgers. The only reason he went to see Edier Grayson and your father—"

"He went to see my *father*?" I'm stunned. "Are they both still alive?"

"For now..." She shoots me a look before heading for the door. "If Santi doesn't allow him into Legado soon, he'll be mounting his severed head on the wall in the bar." She starts fiddling with the lock on the handle. "Look, I know he lied to you, Thalia... I know about the tape and the real reason he forced you to marry him. I know what he put you through is inexcusable, but sometimes the craziest decisions come from places that aren't overgrown with thorns."

"Like you and Sam," I say, feeling her words settle like soft snow on hard ground. Like a boy and a girl ten years ago, trying to make sense of a raging storm.

Muñequita.

"Did he tell you about Z-zaccaria?" I say, stumbling over the name.

As soon as I say it, black images invade my mind...

Begging for water.

Begging for my life.

"You mean that he escaped?" Her expression tightens. "Let's just say my brother has swapped one obsession for another. He'll find him, Thalia. He *will* make him pay."

She hovers in the doorway again, as if staked in place by a burning question. "I'll never forget the day they came to take you away to *Il Labirinto*. The look on your face... I don't think I'd ever have been that strong."

You are already, Lola. You just don't know it yet.

CHAPTER
Seventeen

THALIA

The hot water feels like sin.

The way it trickles down my body is like a long-held confession that's finally being spoken out loud.

I stay in the shower for hours, scrubbing every inch of my skin; attempting to wash the last of a green maze and a black cellar away.

If only it were that easy.

At least my leg has healed. After Lola left earlier, a blonde woman showed a doctor into my room to remove the bandages and stitches. When I asked where Svetlana was, she gave me a look as if to say that name was as dirty around here as my father's used to be.

The rest of me is still a fretwork of discolored bruises and welts, but the only real ache I have is in my heart. Everything feels like an off beat, and I don't know how to get myself back in rhythm.

Opening up the closet door, I discover a rail of old clothes from an old life. I choose out a couple of items, but nothing looks right.

I move to the next closet, stepping into Santi's extravagant haven of thousand-dollar dress suits and shirts. Shrugging into a black Brioni, I wander back over to the window, curling up the cuffs to my forearms. It's sundown, and there's still no sign of him.

In the end, I get sick of waiting and take the showdown to him.

My legs feel like cotton candy as I navigate the hallway toward the kitchen. After ten days in bed, each footstep feels like a mile. His black apartment is a scary place to be when you're all alone and haunted, too. I keep seeing yaupon holly hedges instead of walls. I tell myself beautiful lies to keep me calm.

You're safe now, Thalia. He can't find you here.

But I know that's bullshit.

The Black King can find me anywhere. His ghost town was just one of his many estates… He told me so himself.

The kitchen is empty, so I try the spare bedrooms. He's not in his office either, but our history invites me in anyway. I can smell spice and sandalwood, and the restrained violence in his embrace.

I run my finger along the desk surface where the first glass layer of my innocence was shattered. I curl my fingers around a crystal decanter, knowing exactly what it contains, because that's the flavor of his lust.

Everything in here looks and feels exactly like it did before. Except for me. And the opposite wall, which is now covered in photographs of people and places and old newspaper cuttings, with red string connecting them like a spider web of unsolved mysteries.

As I step closer, I start to recognize things, like the discarded shipping container that was our first cage, and Franco—the guard in Italy who beat me—now lying dead on the ground with his throat slit. I see a hilltop medieval town in flames. I see a fancy estate ablaze in the South of France. I see Aiden Knight, my father's business associate in Monaco and the owner of the Black Skies Casino, the place where I first discovered I could count cards at seventeen. Underneath is a picture of the man I stabbed in the eye and then in the chest twenty-three times without a shred of mercy.

All the red string seems to lead to one black and white photograph in the center. It's a blurry image of a tall man disembarking from a private jet, but I know who it is right away.

My stomach lurches.

Il Re Nero.

I reach out to touch it, to prove to myself he's not real—that here, in this room, he's just a 2D image with as much bite as a papercut. One finger turns into two, and before I know it, I'm pointing them at his dark head like I'm aiming the barrel of a gun.

"When his end comes, *muñequita*, he'll face more than imaginary bullets."

I spin around to find Santi standing in the doorway.

I've never seen him dressed in anything other than a suit before, but tonight, he's wearing black jeans slung low at his hips and a white T-shirt that defines every hard muscle in his chest and abdomen. There's a guarded expression on his handsome face, and more…*so much more.* But they're codes I can't crack and locks I don't have the key to. I used to think my father was the most unreadable man on Earth, but now I'm not so sure.

We stare at each other, the air fizzing with electricity. I don't know much of anything anymore, but I know I still want him.

Despite the lies.

Despite the trauma.

Still, I feel like I'm back in another maze, one with Santi in the center and me skirting the periphery paths.

Please let me find a way back to him.

He steps into the room, kicking the door shut, and then moves to stand beside me.

"You did all this?" I ask, swinging back to the wall collage, feeling his body heat warming up my skin, even though we're not touching.

"Zaccaria made it personal. I'm not resting until he's dead."

Santi's changed. There's a dangerous energy about him—a savageness doused in fury. I need him to hold me like he did when I was unconscious. Instead, he takes a step back and sits on the edge of his desk, reaching around for his decanter and pouring out two shots of *Añejo* tequila.

With the moment in pieces, I turn back to the wall again—my fingers straying to Monroe Spader's photograph.

"I killed him," I blurt out, unable to contain my dirty secret any longer.

"Good. You saved me a job." But there's an edge to his drawl that's all guilt.

"I never wanted to be like you or my father. But this world…this *fucking* world…" I suck in a harsh breath. "It was only a matter of time before it turned me into a murderer, too."

"It's never murder when it's self-defense. Or so my lawyers keep telling me."

"You don't understand," I say, blinking back my tears. "You will *never* understand because killing is a way of life for you. When I kill, I don't just take away their life. I destroy a part of mine as well."

His dark gaze is burning a hole in the back of my head.

"Talk to me, Thalia. I'm not one for heart-to-hearts, but occasionally they're warranted. This marriage is fucked without one."

"What did Lola tell you?"

"She said it was your story to share, but only when you felt ready to. Told me if I rushed you, she'd slam my balls in a vise."

"Did you see the m-maze?" The words get tangled up in my throat.

There's a pause. "I watched it burn."

"Thank you."

Thank you for rescuing me, for finding me in the darkness, for being so much more than I ever thought you were...

Heading over to the window, I press my palms and forehead to the glass, as if I'm trying to force some sense into my madness. It's late. A city of neon is reemerging. The cars down below are carving straight paths with yellow headlights.

It's time to jump into nothing.

To see if he catches me.

To see if we're strong enough to catch each other...

"I know why you didn't tell me about Bardi and the tape."

There's another pause at this, followed by clinking glass and pouring liquid.

"I think I knew the last time we were in this office together," I add, bracing myself when I hear his footsteps approaching.

"Enlighten me," he murmurs, slamming his large hands over mine—his wedding band gleaming bright in the declining light. A beat, later, he's pressing his hard body against me and sparking that flame between us, all over again. "What do you think you know, *muñequita*?"

"It's the same reason why you burned this world to the ground to find me." Feeling his lips feathering my neck, I tilt my head, daring him to sink his lust into me. "The same reason you saved Sam's life. The same reason you walked into a room with my father and Edier, knowing they had a bullet carved with your name on it... The same reason you've spent nine days holding me, bringing me back to life. The same reason why you saved me ten years ago in the snow, when you had every opportunity to kill me."

His hands clench briefly.

"Tell me the reason yourself, Santi," I whisper, enticing a truth from him that he doesn't want to admit to. "Tell me the word that binds us now. Tell me what you feel for me. Tell me what you're capable of."

Refusing to answer, he drops a hand to my shirt. I stand, stock still, as he wrestles with my buttons and his feelings. Pushing the shirt from my shoulders, he buries his face into my neck again.

"I thought I'd lost you."

"You did, and then you found me."

"No, Thalia," he says bitterly. "Not yet… But I will."

His elbows brush against my back as he rips his T-shirt off. His jeans follow, and then we're skin on skin again, fighting for purchase in a hailstorm of emotions.

"You need to let me go, Santi," I whisper. "You need to let me fly away like you did that night. I can't give you a heart that's already broken."

"You want me to admit what we are, only for you to smash it up in the hope we can fix it when your nightmares go away?" He scoffs. "You ask too much."

"Please, Santi…"

He kicks my feet apart with a growl and pulls my hips back. A beat later, the smooth head of his cock is pushing up against my pussy. "You belong to me, Thalia Carrera. You belong by my side. Somewhere along the way, our deception turned into truth. It's time you accepted it."

At this, he drives his cock inside me, stretching my walls around his thick girth, and stealing the breath from my lungs.

"Did they touch you like this, *muñequita*?" he growls, palming the base of my throat. "Did they touch what's mine?"

"I killed him before he could," I whisper.

"He deserves to die a thousand deaths for even thinking about it." He sinks in deeper. "*Dios mío…* You're fucking perfect."

I'm nowhere near wet enough, but there's never been a sweeter pain.

He needs this as much as I do: a beautiful farewell to a future that was never ours to lose.

Withdrawing, he spins me around to wrap my legs around his waist, and then he's crashing us backward into the glass. "If I told you that word, firebird," he says fiercely, seeking out my mouth. "Would you stay?"

I wrap my arms around his neck and kiss him back with a desperation that pushes tenderness into anarchy. At the same time, he lowers me back down onto his cock, and I groan into his mouth as he thrusts in so deep I'm splitting in two.

Santi doesn't fuck gently, and tonight is no exception. That violence inside him is tainting his touch.

I've changed since Italy, too. I crave that violence now. I don't want a reprieve, so I'm tugging his hair at the roots, sinking my teeth into his lips to taste that metal, begging for harder, faster, *more,* as his cock pistons in and out of me until sweat is dripping down both our shoulder blades.

He's taking me so hard, the whole window frame is shaking, but all I can concentrate on is the surge of pleasure building up inside me.

"Jesus…*fuck*," he curses, as he shifts his hips, slamming the back of my head against the glass.

"God, don't stop!" I'm reaching the tipping point, and I can feel his body straining to compete.

"I love how you come around my cock, Thalia Carrera," he snarls into my hair. "Your cunt worships me like I'm a fucking god."

My back arches, and my nails drag red across his skin. For a second, there's only light and pleasure, as molten heat detonates in my core. Somewhere in the distance, I hear him roaring out my name, and then he's coating the insides of my pussy—coming so hard, and for so long, I can feel it spilling out of me and dripping down our thighs.

Time stops.

Dimensions shift.

When I open my eyes, he's carrying me across the room and laying me down across his desk. Spreading my legs wide, we watch as more of his cum drips out of my pussy and onto the lacquered surface.

"What a fucking waste," he murmurs, gathering it up with a finger and pushing it back inside. "Every part of me belongs to you. The same as every part of you belongs to me." Wrapping his hand around the back of my neck, he pulls my head up to meet his mouth. "Love is a careless bastard who takes without permission, but he's *our* bastard, Thalia," he says huskily, sealing his words with a brief and brutal kiss. "You ripped my heart out ten years ago, and you never gave it back."

"You love me," I whisper.

"I love you," he confirms, dark eyes blazing. "And I'd rather die than see you walk out of that door tomorrow."

"If you love something—"

"Lock it up and throw away the key," he says, lining his cock up with my pussy again, but, this time, *for the first time,* his words are an empty threat.

When he starts fucking me for the second time, his desperation is just as raw as mine.

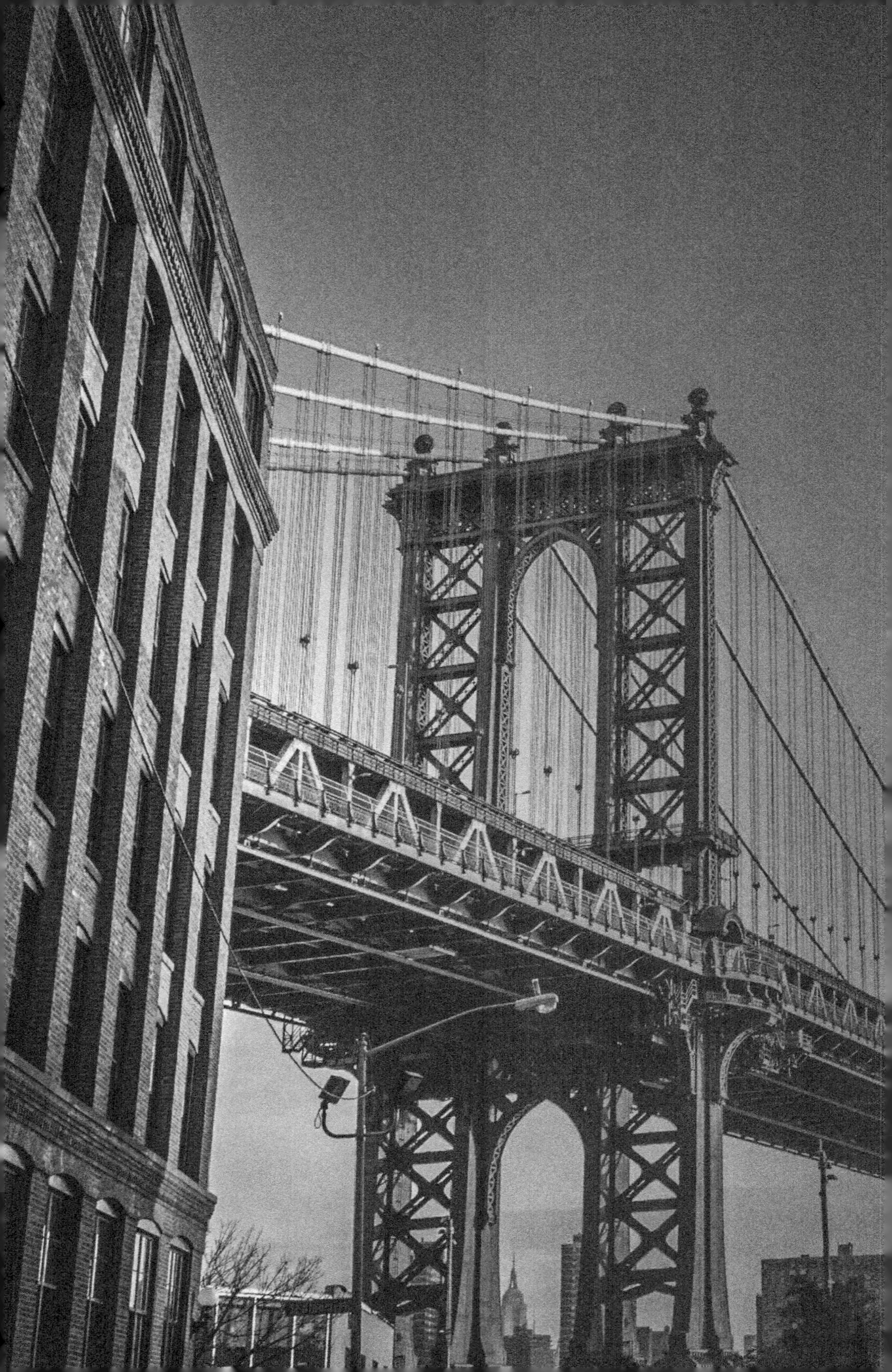

CHAPTER
Eighteen

SANTI

Sunrise spreads her colors across the Atlantic City skyline, and Thalia's decision is still a hollow echo in my mind. There's no more night to hold on to. No more watching the minutes tick away on the clock.

It's a new day, and our end.

And there's not a fucking thing I can do about it.

Turning away from the window, I watch her sleeping, her dark hair fanned out across the pillowcase. I brush a stray lock of it away from her face, telling myself that the memory of last night is enough, but it's an empty vow.

I trace my finger across her delicate jawline, skating the edges of her bruises. Every instinct I have is demanding I lock all the doors until I can prove to her that I'm the only one who can heal her.

I can't force her to stay, though. *Not this time.* Not after what she's been through. If I take away her freedom again, not only will I lose her forever, but I'll be no better than Zaccaria. I'd rather put a gun to my head than become another monster in her nightmares.

Still, as much as she's changed me, I'm still a selfish man.

I still want, and I still demand.

I still *need...*

Trailing my hand down the length of her neck, I take hold of the white bedsheet and yank it to her waist, exposing her small breasts. Brushing my fingers lightly over one dusky-pink nipple, my cock twitches as she moans and tosses her head from side to side,

Thinking dark thoughts, I tug the rest of the sheet away until she's fully bared to me. This time, I'm not filled with rage at seeing the red and purple marks on her skin. She doesn't know it yet, but there's a beauty in her scars. Each one is a test of survival. Each one a badge of strength.

She's still sleeping, Santi...

The man who saved her from that cellar knows what I'm doing right now is wrong, but the man who feeds off our violent connection doesn't give a shit about the rules. He's the one in control now. Before Thalia walks out that door, I'll be taking my fill of her anyway I can.

There's an edge of warning in the air, but I don't listen as I part her thighs.

Even in her sleep, she's wet for me, her lips glistening like a promise of glory. It's a heavy hit straight to my dick, seeing her gorgeous cunt splayed out like this. It's all I can do not to drive in so deep she'll never be free of us.

But this isn't just about my wants and needs. It's about showing her that a bastard like me can still give as well as take.

I lower my head and groan, the scent of her arousal, hypnotic.

The moment the first taste hits my senses, I'm lost—so fucking lost. My wife is like the sweetest sin.

I swirl my tongue in circles, savoring her, teasing her, memorizing her, as Thalia lets out another soft and tortured moan. My cock jerks at the sound. When I glance up, her eyes are still closed, but she's no longer asleep. She's walking a threadbare line between a dream state and reality, and it's one I intend to blur with more fucking pleasure than her body can handle.

I wrap my lips around her clit and suck hard. When she pants my name, I slide two fingers inside her slick heat, pumping in and out—creating a perfect rhythm—as her juices leak out, soaking my skin and the bedsheets beneath her.

Her pants turn to helpless whimpers, as she draws her knees up, toes curling, her fingers seeking out my hair. *Nothing will ever dull this flame.*

"Santi..."

This time when she says my name, there's no hushed lull. It's clear and present. *My firebird is awake.*

I could stop... I should stop.... But I don't. Instead, we hold each other's gazes, as I keep up the fierce tempo, continuing to fuck her with my tongue and fingers as she tips her head back and clenches the white pillowcase.

"What are you doing?" she rasps out, lust flushing her cheeks like burning embers.

"Enjoying my breakfast."

"We shouldn't..." She bites her lip, her head rolling back again. "Last night was—"

"Not enough." I punctuate my words with a graze of my teeth to her clit, forcing a cry from her throat. "Come for me." My order is rough and unforgiving. "I want my fucking name on your lips, *muñequita*. I want it to shatter these walls, and brand every single one of your thoughts."

"I have to leave," she whimpers.

"Then if I can't have your time, I'll take your pussy, right here, right now." My voice pitches low and savage. "When I let you go, it's going to be with the taste of you in my mouth."

In response, she arches her back and widens her legs for me, her fingers threading a tighter grip through my hair.

"I need you."

"Goddamn right, you do." Her confession does something raw and primal to me. Two fingers become three as I make a stunning mess of her pussy.

"Shit!"

Her cries are like a sinner's prayer to my ears. I welcome the pain as she fists my hair and twists, grinding herself against my face, until she's chasing the sunrise that's beating down on my back.

I watch her climax cresting, and then mercilessly drive her into it.

"Santi!" she screams, coming so hard around my fingers, I can feel her spasming. When her juices gush, I lap up every drop.

She's still gasping for air when I climb to my knees, my cock heavy and leaking pre-cum. Those hooded eyes watch as I fist the root, giving it a few savage strokes.

"*Dios mío*, Thalia, do you see what you do to me? Every fucking time." My groan is almost feral. This craving is too strong. I hold her stare as I work my cock harder...faster... Desperate for relief. Desperate to mark her. "This is all you, *muñequita*. Your scent, your voice, your touch..." The pressure at the base of my spine erupts as my balls tighten. "Fuck!"

A rush of blood blazes beneath my skin. Every vein in my body pulses her name. Thalia catalogues every move, not saying a word, spreading her pussy lips for me and arching upward to tease me right back.

It's too much. I groan out my release through clenched teeth, pumping thick ropes of cum all over her inner thighs and swollen cunt.

When my vision clears, I find her dragging her finger through my cum and smearing it into the scars on her body.

"In that maze, Spader had a knife."

I pause. She's opening a door for me. I'm afraid a single breath will slam it shut again.

"He cut the straps to my dress," she continues, her gaze lifting, watching warily for my reaction. "He sliced my skin, and then that arrow…"

Her next words catch in a sob, making my chest ache.

I can feel her pain.

Help me, Santi.

I can smell her blood.

Save me, Santi.

"Monroe is dead, *muñequita*." Caging her with my body, I take her jaw between my fingers to drag her above the surface of those dark waters. "He can't hurt you anymore."

She pulls away sharply. "That's the thing. He can. *He still is.* Every scar I have is because of him. Of both of them."

"Tell me what you need." I say, hearing her plea. "Say the word, and I'll give it to you. If I don't have it, then I'll steal it." *I'll kill and raze the world for you.* "Just tell me."

Her gaze is steady and fierce. "Every scar I have was created from hate. I need one created from something…*more.*"

Understanding immediately, I take my knife from the nightstand. Flipping her onto her back, I slide my hand up through the valley of her breasts to her throat. I tighten my hold, her pupils dilating with her escalating pulse rate. I watch her expression carefully for regret or fear, but there's only certainty and lust as I touch the blade to the soft swell of her stomach.

"Like this?"

Something flickers behind her gaze, and my cock is rock-hard again. There's a shadow there, moving…craving…

"Yes."

"Do you want me to hurt you, Thalia? Do you want me to make you bleed so you can hate me more? So you can hold onto it at night, tucking it away under your pillow when the doubts creep in? Your fucking father would love that."

"I don't want it, Santi. I *crave* it. What he did—what he made me do—it's all over me. I need to see something else when I look at my reflection."

It's a fucked-up request. I hate it, but the thought of marking her is so fucking tempting. I can already see the blood pooling against her pale skin.

Mine.

Maybe we both need to bleed...

Choosing my canvas carefully, I press my knife in harder. She hisses at the blade's sharp bite, but she never screams.

I work quickly after that, her blood beading with every flick of my wrist, rushing to chase each letter. When I'm done, I sit back, staring with reverence at my promise, as Thalia lowers her gaze to the word I carved into the soft skin above her pubic bone. She traces each letter, swirling her finger through the red rivulets, never flinching.

"*Siempre.*"

"Always," I confirm, our heated gazes colliding. "It's how long I'll wait for you, Thalia Carrera." Tossing the knife on the floor, I slip my hand under her neck, and pull her upright, our lips barely a breath apart. "Always. *Forever.* Whether it takes a month, a year, or ten years, I don't fucking care. I'll wait for you to come back to me." With that, I'm pushing her back to the mattress, my cock straining as I press against her opening, my lust heightened by the blood that's staining both our skin.

"*Siempre,*" I repeat huskily, driving into her and taking all she has left to give.

She chants my name with each brutal thrust as I fuck my own pain into her, leaving it so deep inside she'll never forget it. Her arms coil around my neck, her breath coming out in sharp, brittle pants as I fuck her like an animal. I was already on the edge. Now I'm a man possessed.

Obsessed.

The harder we fuck, the stronger the craving.

"More," she pants, with nothing between us but slick skin, blood, and lust.

"This pussy," I rasp, catching her mouth in a vicious kiss, forcing her to taste herself, "will only ever come for your husband. You're mine, Thalia

Carrera... *mine*."

I can't take her hard enough.

I can't get deep enough.

Mine. Mine. Mine.

I can feel her squeezing my cock. I slam my mouth against hers again as my last frantic thrusts send me careening over a cliff.

"*Eres mía por siempre!*" Throwing my head back, I roar as I come harder than I've ever come in my goddamn life.

Jesus Christ.

When the haze clears, and I can finally think straight, I realize Thalia is lying motionless beneath me.

That's when I know it's time.

Slowly, I pull out of her, *hating the break in connection*, and swing my legs out of bed. Thalia is quiet for a moment, drowning me in silence, before she's moving up behind me and snaking her arms around my chest.

Her touch only seems to hurt.

"Go."

"Santi..."

"*Go.*"

Tugging on a pair of jeans, I stalk into my office next door and slam the door behind me. Sinking into my desk chair, I pour myself a large glass of *Añejo*. Maybe a better man would've stayed and watched her leave, but as I told her when she first walked into my office...

I'm not a good man, and I never will be.

CHAPTER
Nineteen

SANTI

Time doesn't exist at the bottom of a bottle. Minutes turn into hours, and hours turn into days. Solitude doesn't count the tick of a clock as much as the pour of a drink.

Slumped behind my desk, I abandon my glass long enough to remove my wedding band. Gripping it between my thumb and my forefinger, I balance it on my desk and give it a spin. I watch, unblinking, as it swirls in dizzying circles, only to lose intensity with each revolution.

Tipping my half-empty glass back, I drink while observing its fight against gravity. I hate every off-beat *ping* as it hovers above the black lacquer, until it finally relents to the inevitable and clatters to a stop.

Frowning, I decide to roll the dice and go two-for-two, when my office door creaks open, followed by a familiar voice calling my name.

"Santi?"

I don't bother looking up. "You know what centripetal force is, Lola?"

She chuckles. "I believe we established at our ill-fated family dinner that science isn't my forté."

The corners of my mouth twitch. It feels foreign—uncomfortable—as if it's more an involuntary reaction than emotion.

Clamping my hand over my ring, I drag it toward the edge of the desk and hold it up. "It's what keeps this spinning in circles, but, like everything else, how long that lasts depends on the force. The tighter the grip, the longer it spins—but at some point, you can't hold on anymore. You have to let it go and watch it fall."

"Impressive. I guess you just destroyed the brawn versus brains debate."

I lift my chin to find my sister standing with her palm propped against the doorframe, hip cocked. She's wearing a loose-fitting yellow dress, which I grimly note matches her fading bruises.

"Meaning?" I ask, returning my attention to the gold band.

"Meaning stereotypes are almost always based on ignorance. The tough, bad guy with the IQ of a bar of soap... The four-eyed nerd with the mind of a diabolical genius... They're all sweeping generalizations."

My body stiffens, the color red hazing my already blurred vision. "Maybe more stock should be placed on those sweeping generalizations. Then signs aren't missed. People don't get hurt."

Muttering a curse under her breath, Lola invites herself into my office, standing over my desk like my own personal guilt warden. "Santi, there's no way you could've known about Monroe Spader. None of us did. Hell, the bastard did business right under Edier Grayson's nose, too, and he didn't smell a rat."

I glance up at her. "Not helping."

"Okay, so maybe that wasn't the best analogy, but you know what I mean. The only one who blames you for not seeing through Spader's act is *you*."

Then maybe everyone should take a few lessons in cause and effect.

I grit my teeth. "I'm the boss. I'm the husband. I'm the brother—"

"*¡Ay Dios mío!*" she groans. "You're also human, Santi—despite what you'd like to believe."

That's debatable.

Plenty would claim I'm just as much of an inhumane bastard as Spader and Zaccaria.

I lift my glass again, keeping my gaze fixed on my ring. It's a subtle hint for her to exit the same way she came in, but of course, this is Lola. Subtlety isn't a word in her vocabulary. Apparently, neither is distance, because she doesn't ask before offering herself a seat across from me.

Her expression tightens. "You look like hell."

"*Gracias.*"

It's meant to be sarcastic, but there's an off-key note of pride in there somewhere. *Good. Now the outside matches the inside.* I haven't bothered to shave in days, and my slacks and half-buttoned shirt have seen more than a few bottles of *Añejo*.

"How long have you been holed up in this office?"

Good question. One I can't be fucked with trying to figure out.

Swirling the amber liquid in my glass, I shrug. "A few hours? A day? Fuck, I don't know."

"Try two," she says sharply. "I've been trying to reach you for two days, Santi."

Forty-eight hours of spinning rings and silence. *And a shit ton of tequila...*

My last coherent memory is of my blood vow to Thalia. After hearing the penthouse door close, all I remember is grabbing the first bottle I could find and drowning in it.

"Nothing personal," I mutter, indulging myself with a slow sip.

"Nothing *personal*?" Leaning forward, she snaps her fingers in my face. "You had me bitch blocked. Your new gatekeeper almost got a foot up her ass for refusing to let me see you."

My new "gatekeeper" was just following orders. Which apparently Lola took as well as being fired as my secretary. A couple of days after returning to New Jersey, my stubborn sister tried to resume her duties. I didn't terminate her internship to be a dick. She needed to stop taking care of everyone else and get some fucking rest for once.

For all the good *that's* done.

"I haven't been in the mood for company."

"Even family?"

"*Especially* family."

My father to be exact. I scarcely remember him storming into my penthouse to find me passed out on the couch. With some concerted effort, I probably could've strung a few coherent words together before he and *máma* left for Mexico, but I had no interest in his pity.

Didn't care to twist that knife.

It didn't stop him from imparting a few last words of paternal wisdom, though.

"Love is not weakness, Santi. It takes a stronger man to let it go than to imprison it. A veces, el final es solo el comienzo."

"The end is only the beginning," I murmur, repeating his words.

She snorts. "You're starting to sound as cryptic as *pápa*."

I look away, ignoring that jab. "Speaking of cryptic, how long have you known about RJ screwing Rosalia Marchesi?"

Her face blanches. I've caught her off-guard, which was fully intended. I saw that look my sister and cousin shared in Italy. It was private.

Secret.

Exclusive.

Clearing her throat, she hesitates while examining her nails. "Since you had him tailing me at Rutgers."

I chuckle darkly, betrayal simmering beneath my splintered smirk. "Seems I was unaware of quite a few conspiracies around here."

She palms the back of her neck, uncomfortable, but cornered. "There was no *conspiracy*. I followed him to a restaurant in North Caldwell one night, and he swore me to secrecy. Seeing as how he knew I was chasing Sam, neither of us was in a place to—"

"He fucking *what*?"

"Santi, no one was trying to undermine your authority or stage a mutiny! You may own New Jersey, but you don't own *people*. You can't control who they care about. You, of all people, should know that," she huffs.

Letting out a hollow laugh, I raise my near-empty glass in a somber toast. "That's unfortunate. The objects of Carrera men's affections don't seem to have the longest life span."

Sighing, Lola reaches across the desk and grabs it out of my hand. "Drinking yourself into an early grave isn't helping Thalia."

"Did she tell you that?"

Now it's my sister's turn to avert her gaze.

"Didn't think so," I mutter. "Maybe a grave wouldn't be such a bad alternative."

She slams the glass down. "That shit isn't funny."

"Wasn't meant to be."

Her gaze lingers on me for a moment. "You love her."

The twitch from earlier is back, this time tipping the corners of my mouth. "Love is a never-ending riddle, don't you think?" Opening a side drawer, I pull out a new glass.

As I pour myself a new drink, Lola narrows those icy blue eyes.

"How so?"

I lean back in my chair, fresh *Añejo* poised at my lips. "At first, nothing makes sense, but you keep trying, getting all the wrong answers along the way, but getting closer each time." I motion the glass toward her. "Then, just when you think you've got shit figured out... When you lay everything on the line... You realize there are parts you skimmed over. Parts you didn't think mattered, when, in fact, they were the key to solving everything."

Picking up a discarded pen, she twirls it between her fingers. "Centripetal force and now metaphorical riddles? That's some deep shit, Santi. When did you get so philosophical?"

I nod to the crystal decanter on the edge of my desk. "About half a bottle ago." At her labored exhale, I frown, unable to ignore how her body is still riddled with bruises and endless stitches. "You're still hurt."

And water is wet... Way to point out the obvious, asshole.

Shrugging, she drops the pen. "They're healing."

"Are *you*? I hear your screams at night, *chaparrita*."

"I know," she says, knotting her fingers.

"When I think about what those sons of bitches did..." I can't say the words out loud. Not when *Añejo* is fueling my anger.

"Santi, don't," she pleads wearily. "I can't move on if I dwell in the past."

I drown the irony of her words at the bottom of my glass. "Thalia said the same thing."

My head understands, but my bastard of a heart, once again, refuses to see reason. It craves nothing more than to close out the world and dwell in a time when the sun rose and set with Thalia still in my bed.

"Is she okay?" I ask, and at Lola's reluctant expression, I add, "Grayson and I had a meeting earlier, in between bottles. Thalia wasn't exactly a welcome topic of conversation."

"It's not personal."

I huff out a sardonic laugh. "It absolutely *is* personal—and well-deserved. If the tables were turned, I wouldn't tell Sanders shit about you."

She hesitates, her fingers weaving a tangled web.

"Say what's on your mind, *chaparrita*." Tipping back what's left in my glass, I savor the burn. "I probably won't remember it, anyway."

Lifting her clasped hands to her mouth, she rests both thumbnails against her lower lip. "Thank you for saving his life."

Not like I had a choice.

"Don't make me your hero. If it wasn't for you and Thalia, I would've left him for dead."

She flinches. "Still, I'm grateful."

For once, I don't refill my glass. Instead, I stare at her, trying to decode her odd behavior. Lola was born with a crown of confidence. All this nervous stalling isn't like her.

"I'm grateful," she repeats, exhaling a harsh breath, "because thanks to you, our baby will have a father."

"I told you I didn't—" Every drop of alcohol evaporates from my system as her words sink in. "What did you just say?"

She lowers her hands. "I'm pregnant, Santi."

My fingers tighten around my empty glass. Slowly, I set it on the table, tempering my clipped tone. "How long have you known?"

"A few weeks... I found out after the Legado shooting. They ran bloodwork, and—"

My feet hit the marble. "You were pregnant when I brought you home from the hospital?" Shoving both hands in my hair, I pace out my frustration. "*Dios mío*, Lola, I fucking drugged you!"

Rising to her feet, she rounds the table and blocks my path. "Santi, calm down. You didn't know. I didn't get the chance to tell anyone because we were…"

Taken. Kidnapped. Stolen.

All three are accurate, but like Thalia, she doesn't talk about it. Instead, she wraps it up in something pretty, ignoring the crimson key print ribbon.

"I almost told Thalia that night, but I chickened out. I kept pouring my drinks away when she wasn't looking."

"I'm so sorry. I'm so fucking sorry…"

The apology that spills out shocks me almost as much as it does Lola, judging by the look on her face. Right or wrong, I've always stood by my actions, never offering justification or caring for forgiveness.

Absolution meant weakness.

Wrong.

So fucking wrong.

When you come close to losing the two most important people in your life, it changes your views.

Weakness isn't about sacrificing pride.

Weakness sacrifices love to uphold it.

She tugs at my wrists. "Santi! Would you listen to me? I don't blame you! You did what you thought was right. We're Carreras—we don't exactly subscribe to normal ideals and morality. Besides, I've been checked out, and we're both fine."

Both.

As in my sister and Sanders's baby.

A permanent link uniting them for life.

Slowly, I sink back into my chair. "You never stopped seeing him."

It's not a question, but she answers anyway. "Only for the six months *pápa* shipped me back to Mexico. Once I sweet talked my way back to Rhode Island…" She shakes her head, leaving the rest unspoken. "Yeah, ever since."

"Do you love him, Lola?"

The tension in her face melts into a serene smile. "More than anything."

"Does he love you?"

Sighing, she perches on the end of my desk. "I know you don't want to believe it, but yes, he does. There's a side to him no one sees, but me."

Too much fucking information.

"Let's keep it that way," I grumble. "When's the wedding?"

"What wedding?"

"That *pinche cab*—" At her biting look, I scrub a hand across my unshaven face. "I mean that *Santiago* knocked up my baby sister. You're telling me he's not even going to marry you?"

She rolls her eyes. "Welcome to the twenty-first century, Santi. Having a baby doesn't require a shotgun wedding."

If Sanders thinks he's going to turn my sister into a single mother, that *shotgun* will be aimed at his dick. "I thought you said you loved him."

"I do, but when we marry, it will be because we want to, not because we're forced to."

I wince. Although unintentional, she just shot a direct hit at a very thin nerve. Judging by how quickly her smile fades, she knows it, too.

Biting her lip, she squints her way through a half-assed apology. "Look, I didn't mean that the way it sounded…"

As fucked up as everything is, I can't help but chuckle. Carrera blood may dominate our gene pool, but *this* is pure Lachey. *Máma* has always had a penchant for unfiltered bluntness.

Speak first, think second, apologize when necessary.

Which, right now, is forcing me to take a good, hard look in the mirror.

Hooking my discarded wedding band around my thumb, I bring it to my face. For days, I've seen it as a promise. *A circle of hope.* Now, I see it for what Thalia saw when I slid hers onto her finger on our wedding day.

A fucking shackle.

"Yeah, you did," I say flatly. "But I deserve to hear it because you're right. No one should be forced into a marriage they don't want. It never ends well."

Silence fills my office as she absorbs my admission. "Give her time, Santi. You don't know what we went through. Nobody will ever know. Our bodies are healing, but what we saw, what we survived…" She shudders, a dark expression clouding her face. "It lingers. The memories are like poisonous seeds." Pinning me with a knowing stare, she adds, "Some things can't be uprooted with soothing words or with twenty bodyguards staking out her apartment."

Shit.

She knows I have eyes on New York.

"Those seeds are embedded in our minds. Given the right environment, they'll take hold. They'll fester black roses with thorns, and eventually that's all that will be left. We'll be their greatest victory." Glancing down, she dusts her fingers over her flat stomach. "Their living victims."

The sadness in her voice is like another dagger to the heart.

"Lola…"

Sliding off the edge of the desk, she rounds the corner to where I'm still reeling from her confession. "That's why she left," she says, laying a gentle hand on my shoulder. "It isn't because she doesn't love you, Santi. It's because she hasn't learned to love who she's become. They stole pieces of us and changed others. Until Thalia can come to terms with that, she doesn't have enough pieces left to give you."

I don't speak. I can't. The image she created has me by the throat.

As much as I fucking hate it, I've accepted Thalia's need for space. But until now, I've never understood it. Every demand of mine shattered the fragile pieces she was trying to rebuild.

As for my sister? I'm starting to understand her, too. She doesn't need my protection anymore. *She's a Carrera.*

Tipping her chin up, I tap her nose just like I did when we were kids. "You're going to make a good mom."

"Does that mean you're going to stop trying to kill the father?" she asks tentatively, hope flickering in her arctic blue eyes.

These motherfucking truces are going to be the death of me.

Sliding my desk drawer open, I pull out the silver bangle I've kept safe for her.

"My bracelet!" she says with a gasp.

"My only love sprung from my only hate," I recite, staring down at the inscription. I've analyzed those words to death these past few days. Twisting and turning them in my mind, only to come up with the same conclusion. "Do you ever get the feeling all of this was predestined?" I ask her, placing the bracelet in her waiting hand.

"How so?"

"They say love and hate are just different sides of the same coin. Reflections of each other, separated by a fraction of a degree. All this hate between our two families for all these years… Do you ever consider that it was only a matter of time before the coin flipped?" Bending my index finger, I run it across the ring still anchored to my thumb. "That our only love was always meant to spring from our only hate?"

Tilting her head, Lola slips Sanders's silver promise back on her arm as she contemplates more of my philosophical bullshit. "I don't think war fates love, Santi," she says finally. "I think love is what ends it." Giving me a shrewd smile, she turns toward the door.

"*Chaparrita.*"

Pausing, she glances over her shoulder. "Yeah?"

I grind my teeth, the unfamiliar taste of humility a bitter pill. I've always considered it to be a flaw, a pointless trait I've never bothered to learn. But for her—for Thalia—I'm willing to try.

"*Felicidades.*"

At my concession of congratulations, my sister's face lights up. Opening the door, she leaves me with one more thought. "Let her pick up her own pieces, Santi. Wait for her."

As the door quietly closes behind her, I slide my ring off the tip of my thumb, returning it to its rightful place on the third finger on my left hand.

"*Siempre.*"

CHAPTER Twenty

THALIA

"Dinner's on me tonight. Gluten free special. Any takers?" I drag my eyes away from a moody New York City skyline to find Ella standing in the living room doorway, brandishing a couple of takeout menus at me.

"*Gio's* has a crap selection of toppings, but *Little Italy* does a pretty average margarita," she adds, frowning at them. "Come to think of it, they're both crap. Next summer, you and I are taking a two-week trip to Rome. We're going to find a cafe near somewhere cool like the Pantheon and eat the real deal all day long…" She trails off in horror when she realizes what she's said. "Oh Gosh, Thalia, I didn't think... Italy is the last place you'd ever want to see again."

"Stop, please." Throwing off my silver quilt, I rise from the window seat where I've spent most of the last forty-eight hours, and gently fold my arms around her. "Can't blame a whole country for one man's evil."

"Except for Mussolini… Hey, are we back to that whole dictatorship thing again?"

Her joke falls flat. Just like my mouth that never seems to curve in either direction anymore. It's taking me back to the night I first met Santi, when I'd rushed out to meet Bardi, leaving her wrestling with deadlines while I wrestled with my conscience.

"Talk to me, Thalia," she mutters into my hair. "You're slowly dying on the inside. I can see the shades of blue in your eyes. You said you were lost in New Jersey, but I think you're more lost here…"

Without him.

I catch sight of the wedding rings on my finger, and my heart lurches. "It's not about Santi, Ella. This is about me."

She nods, pretending to understand. Hell, I don't even understand it myself. *I don't know how to rise from the ashes.*

To compensate, she hugs me tighter, and I commit it all to memory—her softness, her strength… I've always taken my lessons on courage from her. My sister has lived a living hell for eleven years, ever since her diagnosis with Lupus. I've been living mine for exactly fifteen days and counting.

It feels like forever, though.

"I wish they'd taken me instead," she mumbles.

"I'd have died a *thousand* times if they had," I say fiercely.

She pulls back and smooths a strand of hair away from my eyes. "I'll always blame myself, Thalia. I knew Bardi was a piece of work, but I accepted his stupid drink and attention anyway. If I hadn't been so low about Edier and that—"

"If it wasn't that night, it would have been on some other occasion," I interrupt swiftly. "Our cards were marked from before we were born." Somehow, I force a smile, and a change of subject. "When do you go back to college again?"

"Next week for the summer session. Have you considered, maybe, starting back with me?" she says hopefully.

No chance.

I can just imagine Santi's reaction if he found out I'd be hanging with a load of frat boys for the foreseeable. We may be separated right now, but the black SUV that's permanently parked outside my apartment tells me I'm gone, not forgotten. His presence is still tightly wrapped around me, all the way from New Jersey.

"I'm not sure college is for me, Ella. Not *after*…" I trail off with a hapless shrug.

Isn't it strange how you divide your life into subsections? Major events have the capacity to carve up your soul into the past and present.

"Will you at least think about it?"

"Sure," I lie.

She gives me a look. She knows a blasé concession when she hears it.

"So, pizza's out. How about gluten free Chinese?" She holds up the takeout brochures again.

"Sounds good," I say, heading for the door. "I'm going to lie down. Give me a shout when dinner arrives."

"But you haven't told me what you want yet!"

"Chow mein. Anything. Not fussy."

My bedroom is an even worse place to wallow in. Wherever I look, I see his face. Four blank walls seem to offer up the space for extra detail, too... Like the way he rakes his hand through his hair when he's pissed at me. How the light reflects off his face first thing in the morning. How he looked when he told me he loved me, as if it was a revelation to him that a bad man could feel anything other than bad things.

Sometime later, I hear my door open.

"I'll be there in a minute," I mumble.

"Wouldn't bother, food looks terrible," comes a deep drawl. "I brought you something else instead."

"*Pápa?*" I turn so violently all my bedsheets get tangled up in my legs.

Flicking on a side light, he leans against the far wall and crosses his arms, crowding out the space with his massive frame, his thick black hair framed with shadow, his dark eyes fully focused on me.

This time around, our silence is a dance of compassion—spinning words left unsaid into steps that I finally understand. I won't find comfort in his arms, like I do in Ella's. Instead, it's here in his presence. Just like it was there in a warehouse, a couple of weeks ago, when he formed a truce with his enemy in order to rescue me.

"W-what are you doing here?" I stutter, sitting up.

"I heard you were home."

Home.

But this isn't my home, either.

"How are you feeling, *mija*?" he asks.

Broken.

"Better."

He grimaces. "Christ. You're an even worse liar than your mother."

There's a second pause—an empty space just begging to be filled with another confession.

"I killed a man."

As I say it, I hold my breath, expecting the same reaction that I got from Santi. Instead, his head drops, as if the weight of my admission is a heavy crown to bear.

"You seem angry with me," I whisper.

"Not angry..." His dark gaze seeks out mine again as I draw my knees up to my chest for comfort. "There are two types of killers in this world, *mija*... Those who take without mercy, and those who carry the blood they spill inside their hearts until the only thing left for it to beat to is guilt."

My breath catches. It's as if he's reached inside my chest and seen the damage of my own pain.

"You need to let the guilt go before it consumes you. You need to finally accept who you are, and your place in this world."

"What if I can't?" I whisper.

"Then your worst fears about my business infecting you have already been realized."

"Want to know what the craziest thing about it is, *pápa*?"

"Crazier than you walking into Carrera's casino to scam fifty thousand out of the man when I have fifty billion in untraceable bank accounts?" he mocks, his black eyes glinting dangerously.

Turning my head, I press my cheek to my knee. "Without your blood in my veins, I would have died in that hellhole. I needed fire to survive, and you gave me an inferno."

There's a pause. "How did it feel to take a life?"

"Like a shadow was overwhelming me."

"Mine feels like a monster consuming me." Striding over to the bed, he slots his fingers under my chin and lifts my head toward him. "You are so like your mother in many ways, Thalia," he murmurs, his expression softening a fraction. "When she killed a man for the first time, she had this same conflict inside her."

I'm shocked. My mother is the model of restraint and fragility. I can't imagine her holding a gun, let alone firing one.

"She killed for love, not hate," he adds tersely. "The same as you. A long time ago, I told her to never doubt her decisions, to never apologize, and to never shed a fucking tear for anyone. Now, *again,* I say the same to you." His expression changes. "Don't fear the shadows, *mija.* They make you stronger, not weaker."

"That's good to know when Zaccaria finds me again."

"That's *never* going to happen." He drops my chin with a scowl. "For all your new husband's faults... For as much as I'd like to line him up against a wall in his fucking casino and let my bullets thank him for all he's done, I have no doubt he'll find Zaccaria and kill him. In the meantime, Edier has a hundred men protecting this apartment." His lips quirk. "Not forgetting the twenty or so unsanctioned Carrera men patrolling this block."

"You saw the black SUV outside?"

"I saw all five. Why buy flowers when protection is just as sweet?" He stops to weigh up his next words carefully. "He wouldn't rest until he'd found you, Thalia. He tripped and fell on the sword of his own deception, and now he's bleeding out for you."

"You sound way too calm about a Carrera falling in love with me, *pápa.*"

"Calm on the outside, *mija,*" he says dryly. "Best not to look too closely on the inside."

"I don't know how to find my way back to him," I blurt out, as he turns to leave.

"Then buy a fucking map," he says, sounding exasperated. "Matters of the heart are your mother's speciality, not mine."

"Bullshit," I argue, swinging my legs out of bed. "There are three types of killers, *pápa,* not two. The third killed for hate until his soul turned black. *Now,* he kills for love."

His deep, mocking laughter follows him out into the hallway. "I've been tortured, shot, and stabbed more times than I can count, Thalia Santiago, but do you know what the true definition of pain is? Having a daughter as smart as you are."

"Care to guess what the true definition of a father is?" I counter softly, making him stop and turn. "He's a man who does whatever it takes to make and keep his daughter's happiness."

"*Whatever* it takes," he agrees, brushing his fist against the doorframe, the corners of his mouth twitching. "Even if it means accepting a fucking Carrera as a son-in-law."

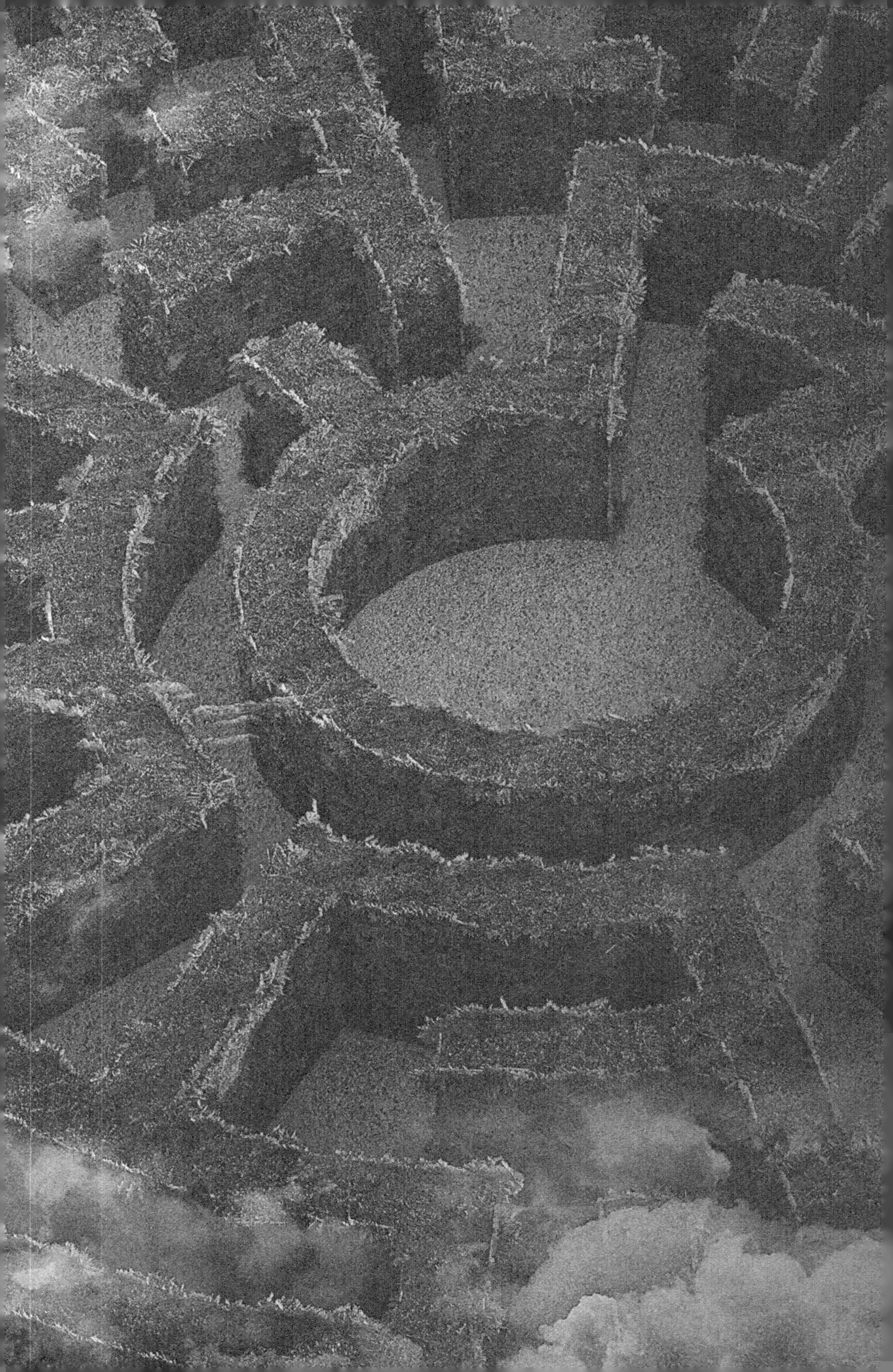

CHAPTER
Twenty-One

THALIA

That night, I toss and turn for hours, my nightmares making another tangled mess of my bedsheets.

I see mazes and cellars, spliced with a soundtrack of my father's words. I replay the moment I swing my arrow into Monroe Spader's eye, but it's a dark shadow, not blood, that comes pouring out of the wound. Next, I'm back on the beach with Sam. It's not a line in the sand I'm racing toward, however. It's my husband pointing a loaded gun at my head.

I wake to dusty beams of sunshine on my face. I'm damp with sweat and confusion. Still, I wake with the certainty that I'm done with staying motionless now. I don't want the past to catch and consume me before I've had a chance to touch the future.

I shower and wash my hair, running my fingers lightly over the raw skin where Santi carved his promise into me. Inhaling the sting, and relishing it...

Drawing strength from it.

It feels good to finally want to fix *me* for a change. For years, I've been the one trying to fix my father from his badness, and my sister from her illness... I don't know how the hell I'm going to achieve it, but I have a pretty good idea of where to start.

Dressing in black jeans, red Chucks, and a vintage music T-shirt, I leave my wet hair loose, with a brush of mascara and blush as my only make-up. Grabbing my purse from the living room, I head for the door.

"Where are you going?" Ella cries, appearing in the kitchen doorway, looking adorably confused by the fact that I look like a normal human being today instead of a sloth. "I just made pancakes. I even have the syrup."

"I'm off to buy a map," I say cryptically, barreling out of the door and straight into a wall of hard muscle.

"Jesus, Thalia, where's the fire?"

I look up to find my favorite bodyguard bruising up the hallway again.

"Reece!" Dropping my purse, I fling my arms around his huge waist, filling our reunion with apologies. "I'm sorry I ran off to New Jersey. I'm sorry I told you so many lies. I wanted to tell you the truth so many times." I pull back to look at him, convinced he's a mirage. "I thought my father was going to kill you after everything I did."

"It wasn't pretty, sweetheart, but I'm still alive. We both are," he finishes roughly, chucking my chin like he used to do when I was a kid. "How are you feeling?"

"I'm okay."

He goes to say something else, then changes his mind at the last second. "So, where are we headed?"

"Out."

"Care to be more specific?" he says, arching an eyebrow at me. "You know you can't leave this apartment without your security detail. So, what's the deal? Are you climbing out of a fifty-story window this time, or are you giving me an address so I can arrange men and vehicles?"

"Men and vehicles, please," I say, giving him a sheepish smile. "I need to see Edier Grayson right away."

Edier's office is situated on an ultra-stylish street on the Upper West Side, lined with sycamores, Corinthian columns, and gray stone porches. It's ruthlessly lavish, and brutally understated, and nothing about it surprises me in the slightest.

It's just so... *Edier.*

Art and design have a way of splashing color onto everything, including death and destruction. Somehow, my childhood friend will always find a way to combine the two.

Reece opens my car door for me, and I'm escorted through a line of armed guards and into an elegant white lobby with check marble floor tiles. From there, we take an elevator up to the top floor where I'm shown into a huge white room with black furniture.

Edier is sitting with his boots up on his desk, drumming his fingers lightly against the surface as he confers with a couple of his men. He looks up as we enter, his usual deadpan expression lifting in surprise when he sees me.

"Leave us," he snaps, indicating to Reece too.

As soon as the door shuts, his boots are slipping from the desk. "Thalia," he says, prowling up to me, looking just as much of a handsome, ruthless cartel king as Santi does. "Thank fuck you're okay."

"Thanks to you," I say, reaching out to touch his arm. "I mean it, Edier. I'll never forget it."

He frowns down at my hand that's now become the focus of the conversation. Edier has a habit of making you feel like the center of the universe, but he'll never let you reciprocate it. Since taking over New York, he keeps everyone at arm's length. Just ask my sister… She knows all about his hot and cold syndrome. Her fingers are covered in scars from trying to get close to his barbed wire fences.

"I'll take half the praise, but credit where it's due," he says, moving away, leaving my hand suspended in thin air. "As much as it pains me to admit it, your husband earned the rest."

At this, I drop my hand like a stone.

"How's Sam?"

"Still breathing. Stick around if you want confirmation. He's due here any minute."

"Three cheers for the epic survival rate among us," I say wearily. "I know what Santi did for me, Edier. I know what he risked."

He studies me for a moment before saying, "Fair enough."

"Is this place meant to be modeled on a monochrome war zone?" I glance around his office for a change of subject.

"Would you prefer it if I hung a picture of *Santa Muerte* on the wall, so you'd feel more at home?"

"You've been to Legado," I say quietly.

"I figured I may as well benefit financially from this truce while it's still holding. We've opened up our respective ports for a mutually beneficial trade deal. But something tells me you're not here to discuss the importation of Mexican and Colombian cocaine," he adds, catching sight of my face.

"When did you see him?"

"Yesterday."

"How is he?"

"His usual arrogant self," he says dryly. "The asshole had the nerve to demand a sixty-forty profit split."

The corners of my mouth can't help lifting as I settle into a spare chair. Edier swings into the opposite one, lifting his boots onto the desk again. He was always the older, cooler one when we were kids. Now, he's an ice man.

"What can I do for you, *Señorita* Santiago?" he says.

"*Señora* Carrera," I correct.

"Not for much longer, by the sounds of it."

I drop my gaze first. "He was the boy in the snow, Edier… Ten years ago, outside the church when we stole your bodyguard's car."

"I know."

I jerk my head up in surprise. "You *know*? Then why the hell didn't you tell me?"

He shrugs. "What difference would it have made? Before this truce, I still would have shot to kill. And I will afterward when it comes to a crashing conclusion," he finishes, flashing his teeth at me.

"But he saved my life. Twice!"

"Bad blood sticks better than past glories."

Damn stubborn villain. *Think of the map, Thalia.*

"Can I ask you a question?"

His dark eyes narrow to fixed points. "Depends. Is it personal?"

"Not this time, though I'd still like to know why you broke my sister's heart, and why you threw a scholarship away to that art college in London. Oh, and what did my father really offer you to climb his ranks so fast?"

"Professional it is, then," he says coldly.

We both know I'm holding my status around his neck like a noose. If I was anyone else, I'd be bleeding out by now.

"It's about your mom in Colombia…"

"Ah. I see where this is headed."

That's the other thing about Edier. He has an uncanny ability of guessing your intentions before you've spelled them out for him.

"It's a good idea," he continues with a frown. "You should talk to her. She can help you come to terms with everything that's happened." He scribbles down a number and hands it out to me.

"Do you know how she managed to move on from her own experiences?" I ask, hesitating a fraction before taking it and folding it into my purse.

"She found a purpose, and a good man." He narrows his eyes at me again.

"That's kind of why I'm here," I say, ignoring the dig. "I'd like to know if Senator Sanders still has links with any NGOs in New York?"

"The ones with projects to help trafficking victims?"

There he goes again, being all smart.

"Yes."

"I see." He steeples his hands as he considers my request. "Why did you come to me about this, and not Sam? The Senator is *his* stepfather."

"I figured Sam was still in the hospital. I wanted to test the waters before I brought it up with my father, too. He's requesting I go back to the island for a while, but I want something—"

"More?" Edier drops his feet from the desk. "I'm seeing the Senator tonight, as it so happens. You looking for a company, or a job?"

"Just a job," I say with another laugh. "I'm not looking for handouts, just a foot in the door. I've decided that counting cards isn't a fulfilling profession."

"Not that lucrative either, if you keep getting caught... Okay, leave it with me." He rises to his feet to show me out, but I stay sitting right where I am.

"Why are you such a monster to my sister?"

"Fuck off," he snarls, clearly taken aback by my question. "Besides, I *am* a monster."

"Any news on Zaccaria?" I glance at the photographs scattered all over his desk, as dark clouds start to form over my brief glimpse of recovery. Most are identical to the ones in Santi's office.

"Not yet, but we will," he reassures me, seeing the look on my face. "We've already had a sighting in South Africa. Carrera's had two in Morocco. The minute he hits US soil, we'll have our guns so far up his ass he'll be spitting out his last words with lead. After that, you can do the honors."

My stomach lurches. "My father told you I killed a man, didn't he?"

"I'm not here to be your conscience, bug."

"Bug?" I let out a burst of surprised laughter. "I can't remember the last time you called me that."

"Probably when he still thought fucking his right hand was a beautiful love affair," comes a wicked drawl from behind us.

"Sam!" I jump to my feet and rush over to him.

"One foot distance, sweetheart," he says, flinging his crutch at me like a barrier. "Let this body return to its former glory at its own pace."

His handsome face is drawn, but his expression is still a smirk away from a kiss and a punch.

"You look like you've been to hell and back," he remarks, looking me over too.

"Takes one to know one."

His dark eyes gleam. "Did you cry when you thought I was dead?"

"Did you cry at the thought of never having sleep again for the next eighteen years?" I say with a smile.

He freezes. "She told you?"

"I'll call you tomorrow morning, Thalia," Edier interrupts. "I'll let you know what the Senator says... Sam, see her out."

The elevator doors spring open on the ground floor. There's a crowd of sharp suits waiting, no doubt here for some meeting with Edier. It only takes me a second to register the sharpest one of all.

Santi.

The second our eyes meet, he's reaching out and slamming his hand across the doors to stop them closing.

"Get out," he hisses at Sam and Reece who are standing either side of me. "Take the next one. I'd like to speak with my wife in private."

"You're still a piece of shit, Carrera," Sam snarls, taking a threatening step forward. "No matter how many times you saved her life."

"You can thank me for saving your own life anytime you like," he snaps back, standing aside to let him exit. "You and I need words, too, but I'll deal with you in a moment."

"Please, Reece," I say quietly, turning to my bodyguard. "I'll come straight back down."

The Irishman complies with a scowl, shoulder checking Santi on his way out. Santi barely flinches. He's still devouring me with his dark gaze.

Stepping into the space they left, he lets the doors close behind him. As the carriage starts to rise, he slams his fist against the alarm and the whole thing staggers to a stop. He crowds me against the nearest wall and wraps his fingers around the base of my neck.

"I miss you, *muñequita*."

"I miss you too," I whisper, his nearness sending my senses into a tailspin. The pulse between my thighs is a throbbing live wire.

"I told you I love you. I'll make it enough for us."

"I need something for myself first, Santi. I need to feel more than just a victim."

He slams his other fist into the space above my head. "You're making me hate you."

"No, Santi," I argue. "That's just love gripping her claws even deeper into you."

"Tell me you feel the same way," he demands, brushing his lips against my cheek. "Tell me I'm your salvation. Give me a lie to hold on to, because right now, I'm finding too much comfort at the bottom of a bottle of *Añejo*."

"I feel the same way," I say, tipping my head back as he moves lower with his mouth, toward my collarbone. "That's not a lie. I loved you in the darkness, Santi Carrera, and I'll love you in the light."

"*Siempre*."

With a strangled groan, he steps back, and rams his fist against the alarm button.

The carriage continues to rise.

When the doors open, Edier's already there waiting. He slides a questioning look between us as Santi steps out, without so much as a backward glance at me.

When I make the return journey, it's with tears of confusion in my eyes.

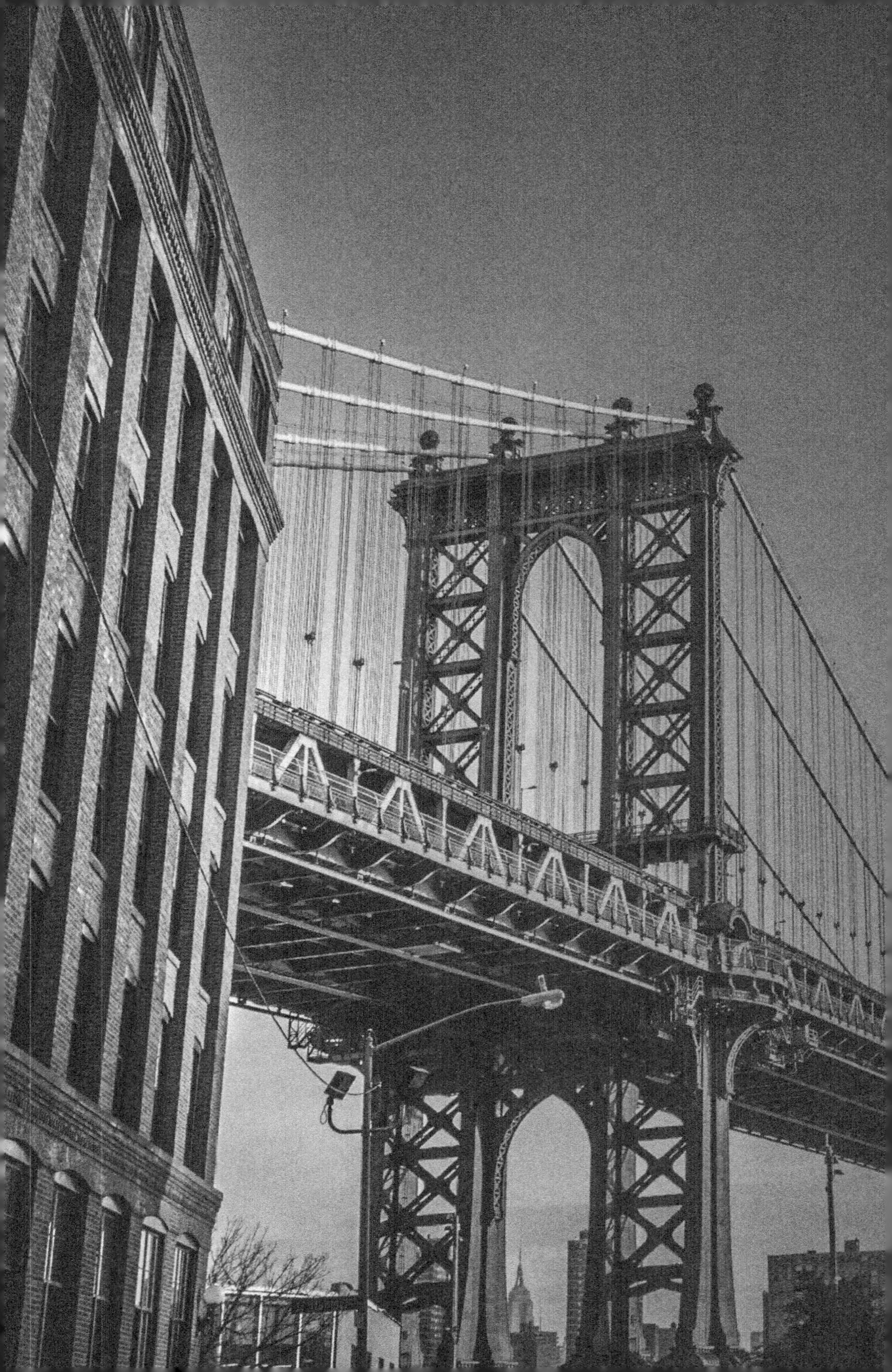

CHAPTER
Twenty-Two

SANTI

I'm in a New York state of mind...

Drunk, agitated, and lonely.

Yet again, RJ and I are parked across the street from Thalia's old apartment, watching a whole lot of nothing, and drinking a whole lot of tequila.

I find perpetual inebriation eases the sting of rejection.

Some people drink to dull their pain. Others drink to wallow in it. Me? I drink to keep the bullets inside my gun and my temper in check. It's why my inner circle doesn't bother with an intervention. The drunker I am, the easier their jobs, and less blood stains Legado's pristine floors.

Which is a good thing considering I'm one lawsuit away from setting fire to the damn thing myself.

Ignoring the side-eye from the driver's seat, I stare up at Thalia's apartment, drinking from the half-empty bottle of tequila until my lungs burn. I have no idea what day it is, or how many bottles I've had... I lost track somewhere around day five and bottle four. Taking onboard Lola's advice, I'd agreed to give her time—to let the seeds scatter, or whatever the analogy my sister used—and I was upholding it... Until I saw her in that elevator again, and all my good intentions went to hell.

Now, I'm back at square one, and drinking more than ever. Not that it's slowing me down. Day after day, I wake up with a hangover and a mission, only to pass out with a dozen false leads and double vision. It's two steps forward, four steps back, because this motherfucker Zaccaria is like a goddamn chameleon.

The moment we track him somewhere, he blends in and disappears.

Between my obsession with my enemy and my concern for my wife, my blood type has gone from AB to *Añejo*.

"New York has open container laws, you know," RJ mutters, flipping through radio stations.

I pause, the tip of the bottle inches from my lips. "You shot a dealer's kneecaps off yesterday for missing a coke drop. You're seriously worried about a class one misdemeanor?"

Since the sober are easily flustered by drunken logic, he just chokes the steering wheel with his hands. "If I knew 'pervert' was going to be part of the job description, I would've stayed in Houston."

"The job description is what I say it is," I correct, swinging the bottle toward him. "Besides, I don't think you're in any position to question shit."

As usual, any mention of his indiscretion ends arguments before they start. We've been treading in shallow waters since returning from Italy, moving in opposite circles and dancing around the whole Rosalia Marchesi situation. I haven't demanded any further explanation, and he sure as hell hasn't volunteered one.

I'm not too concerned. Just like everything else, the truth will come out eventually.

No one knows that better than me.

Releasing his death grip on the wheel, he exhales a frustrated breath and checks his phone again. "I'm not questioning. I'm advising. It's bad enough you have half our *sicarios* parked outside her apartment, twenty-four-seven, like dirty cops. If she finds out you're out here stalking her like some fucked up *Dateline* special, she's gonna have Grayson blow your nuts off."

"Don't be stupid," I scowl, tipping back another drink. "Grayson would go for the kill shot."

"You mean your ego?" he mutters. "It *is* the biggest target."

"I'm going to give you a pass on that one. Judging by the way you keep staring at your phone every five seconds, your attitude is coming from the fact your balls are in a jar at the vet."

The only rise I get out of him comes from his middle finger.

A flicker of light in Thalia's window draws my attention beyond the windshield. Seeing no movement, my focus returns to RJ and his incessant scrolling. Porn I could ignore... But this motherfucker is tapping "Rachel Marlow's" contact page like he's sending out Morse Code.

"Trouble in paradise?"

"Fuck off."

"You're my cousin, RJ—a damn good lieutenant. But don't think I won't break this bottle over your fucking skull for talking shit to me."

The rhythmic tic in his jaw is his only response. "No trouble, or paradise. Just silence."

Instead of being moody about it, the *cabrón* should accept it as a gift and move on. He's lucky we've been too busy driving back and forth across the Hudson for me to call attention to his ever-growing sins of omission. My second-in-command's actions in Tuscany will eventually be answered for, as well as Lola's confession concerning their dangerous liaison pact of secrecy.

The latter, I've decided to keep in my back pocket for now.

It's always good to have a trump card.

"Gianni Marchesi has her under lock and key, and for good reason. *Dios mío*, RJ, you stupid motherfucker. You know she's taken. Marchesi promised her hand at birth."

"Not Gianni," he bites out between clenched teeth. "Her grandfather. That bastard was as sick and sadistic as yours."

I shrug. *Not a hill I care to die on.* He's right. Alejandro Carrera and Marcello Marchesi were a pair of antichrists. Even death can't stop that kind of evil. They've probably overthrown hell by now and set up an underworld trafficking ring on the river Styx. Still, Italian arranged marriages tend to be more solid than a block of ice.

"Not sure Gianni has much of a choice. He can't break the contract without starting a war."

"Everyone has a choice."

"What's that supposed to mean?"

"Never mind." Shaking his head, he glances up at Thalia's window then levels his condescending gaze at me. "How long do you plan on playing the shitfaced stalker role tonight? I have things to do."

Lifting the bottle again, I smirk. "Oh? Like what?"

Cursing, he clasps his hands around the steering wheel again. "I really hate you sometimes."

"Get in line."

And it's a long fucking line, so he'd better bring a chair and some snacks. I've managed to alienate three-fourths of my friends and family. At this point, the entire Santi Carrera fan club could fit into the back of the SUV.

Dios mío, I need air.

I'm out of the passenger's seat before the interior light flashes, slamming the door on RJ's string of English and Spanish hybrid curses. With the bottle of *Añejo* still tucked in my hand, I cross the street, my eyes trained on her window.

Where is she?

We've been here for three hours. I know because I watched her and her bodyguard walk inside after following them from coffee house to restaurant to, surprisingly, a shooting range. That one, I didn't mind so much. The idea of my *muñequita* with her hands wrapped around the grip of a gun, aiming with intent…

Groaning, I turn the bottle up again, hoping like hell it'll dull my senses and my cock. I'm reaching down to adjust myself and relieve some of the pressure when a shadow flickers across the glass.

It's her.

Thalia is standing by the window, the sheer curtains doing nothing to hide her body as she pulls her T-shirt over her hand and then reaches behind her to unhook her bra.

Jesus Christ.

I've been tortured in many creative ways—cut, burned, shot, one Russian even tried to electrocute me. None of them comes close to the brutal agony of watching Thalia's unintentional striptease, knowing I can't do a goddamn thing about it.

So I watch her like the stalker RJ accuses me of being, until she runs her hands down her breasts, stopping to thumb her nipples…

That's when I lose it.

I fucking lose it.

I'm halfway to her apartment when my phone vibrates in my pocket. Too wrapped up in my own lust, I answer without checking the caller ID, assuming I'm getting an invitation to a private show. Instead, I get an irate Mexican with an American accent.

"Santi, as your second, your cousin, and most of all, your only source of common sense these days, I highly advise against what you're about to do."

"Noted," I say, ending the call.

As expected, when I reach her door, I'm greeted by the Irish pussy patrol.

"She doesn't want to see you, Carrera," her bodyguard growls.

"Did she tell you that?"

He scans a stern gaze down to where the bottle swings from my fingers. "You're drunk."

"Accurate, but it still doesn't answer my question."

It's obvious he's not used to being challenged. Clenching his fists, he takes a determined step forward. "Get the fuck out of here!"

"Not until I talk to Thalia." I meet his stride, because I don't fucking back down from anyone. I don't care that we'd take a bullet for the same woman. Right now, he's in my way.

Just as he goes for his gun, the door swings open.

"Geez, Reece! What's going on out here? It sounds like—" Her voice trails off as she notices me standing there. A beat later, an eerily familiar smile is turning downward in my direction.

Not exactly how I planned for this to go, but here we are.

"You must be Ella," I say, extending my hand. "I'm—"

"I know who you are," she clips. Folding her arms across her chest, she stares at my outstretched fingers as if they're about to wring her neck.

I know a roadblock when I see one. Lowering my hand, I jump tracks and try again.

"I see my wife has told you all about me."

"My *sister* has explained how you blackmailed her into marriage, yes."

I can see how these two are related. Beyond the striking physical resemblance, Ella Santiago shares her sister's same fierce protective streak. However, something tells me Thalia's big sister is more bark than bite.

My wife, on the other hand...

Reece steps in between us, his arms spread wide like a Santiago soccer goalie. "Go back inside, Ella. Señor Carrera was just leaving."

I palm the back of my neck, deciding whether or not to shoot this *pinche cabrón* in the head or the stomach for maximum suffering. "Look, if I can just—"

"Hey, Ells, who's at the...?" Thalia's steps falter when she sees me, and her eyes widen. "Santi." The breathy sound of my name on her lips turns my hard dick to granite. "What the hell are you doing here?"

Fuck, she looks beautiful. Fresh faced with no makeup, with her long dark hair tousled around her shoulders as she clutches at a short red robe that barely skims her thighs.

Perfection.

"I missed you again," I tell her honestly.

Reece spins around, the aforementioned gun, now pointing in my face. "Carrera. Out. Now!"

I don't flinch. If he thinks I'm intimidated by looking down the barrel of a gun, he doesn't know a damn thing about me. "Five minutes, Thalia," I say over his shoulder. "Please."

It's the "please" that gets to her. I knew it would. Thalia knows I'm not a man who grovels. I don't say "please" to anyone, except her...

Plus, I'm not above playing dirty.

She sighs. "Five minutes and then you're leaving. You promised, Santi."

There's that word again—promise. I'm starting to hate it, as much as I do space and time. But I'll take what I can get, so I nod, ignoring her bodyguard's disapproval as I follow her down a hallway and into a bedroom that screams her name. There's no fanfare or lace—just shades of color, with pictures of her family littering the walls and furniture.

It's simple and understated and perfect.

Just like her.

"Nice room," I say.

She shrugs. "It's no swanky black penthouse, but I'm free to come and go as I please." The moment she realizes what she's said, she sinks her teeth into her top lip and draws out a sigh. "Sorry, knee jerk reaction."

"Don't apologize." Lifting the bottle, I give her a wolfish smile. "It's true."

Eyeing the bottle with disdain, she grabs it out of my hand. "Santi, you need to lay off the *Añejo*."

"Why? Are you worried about my liver again, *muñequita*?" As the word rolls off my tongue, her eyes flash, causing me to step closer. "Besides, it's not my liver that's the problem."

"Look, if this is about what happened in the elevator earlier..."

"I'm not here about that."

Magnets can't help but be drawn to one another. Positives and negatives—they clash in the most violent of ways. *That's us.* And that's why Thalia's gaze lowers to the straining bulge in my pants, whether she wants it to or not.

That little gasp she lets out only fans the flame. Her steps are uneven as she backs into the dresser, the bottle clanging as she slides it across the polished wood.

"I thought you wanted to talk?"

"I did."

Step.

"And we have."

Step.

"Now I want to do other things."

I'm so fucking close to her I can smell the arousal gathering at the tops of her thighs. All I can think about is chasing it back inside her with my tongue.

"Santi, we can't."

"Thalia, it's been three days, and I'm going out of my mind." Cupping her face, I pin her against the dresser. "Do you know how often I dream of you? Your scent? Your taste? The way your pussy clenches around my cock when I'm fucking you?"

She shudders. "Don't—"

"Do you know how often I have to jerk off just to think straight? You've fucked up my head, Thalia. My head, my cock, my heart. All of it."

"Santi, you need to leave. I was just…" Absorbing my taunts, she gives me a soft groan. "I was just about to take a shower."

"Why get clean when getting dirty is so much more fun?" Taking her hand, I place it over my cock. "I'm not asking for anything, but some goddamn relief for the both of us. And then I'm gone."

She's weakening. I can feel it. The scales are about to tip in my favor.

"No strings, Thalia. Just sex. Hard. Rough. Fucking. Then I'll leave." Just as I'm reaching for the sash on her robe, she turns away.

"Go home, Santi. You're drunk."

Grabbing her neck, I spin her around into my chest. "And you're *mine!*"

Lifting her up by her hips, I set her down on the dresser. I don't ask for permission before pulling that fucking sash so hard it rips in two. "Hold your robe open and spread your legs," I say with a growl. "Offer it up to me, Thalia Carrera, and I'll take it all."

Her fingers are shaking as she peels back the red silk, her knees drifting open. At any other time, I'd be pausing to admire her body, but I'm too desperate tonight.

Too overdrawn.

Too denied.

There's no tenderness in my touch as I drag her to the edge of the dresser and thrust two fingers inside her pussy, pumping viciously.

"Santi!"

Her cries bounce off the walls in tune with the slick sounds of her own desire as I tear at my pants with my other hand. Within seconds, I have them pushed down my hips.

Thalia is still holding her robe open for me, her head tipped back in ecstasy. I pry her fingers away from the silk and wrap them tightly around my swollen cock. With my hand over hers, I guide her in rough, savage strokes. When she finds the rhythm I want, I release her.

"Look at me."

She opens her eyes, never breaking contact as I continue my brutal pace to destroy her cunt. Her touch is better than any high, and it's not long before I'm thrusting into her hand, and her inner muscles are clenching around my fingers.

"Shit! I'm coming!"

The words are barely out of her mouth before she's convulsing, a shattered cry tearing from the heart of her, as a trickle of pussy juice rolls down the inside of my arm.

She's still shaking as I rip my fingers away and push her legs wider, lining my dick up to fuck this madness out of my soul...

Until her palm comes crashing down against my chest.

Jerking my head up, I find her face flushed and her eyes conflicted.

"No, Santi."

"*No?*"

Son of a bitch.

I'm nearly out of my mind with lust. The need to come is greater than the need to breathe. The old Santi would have driven his cock in anyway and taken what's rightfully his. But this new Santi, this husband with a conscience, can't fucking do it.

Sober *or* drunk.

Growling out my frustration, I grab the back of her head, my fingers twisting in her hair. "You're going to be the death of me, *wife*," I repeat, the words starting to become my own personal creed.

I'm about to pull away and suffer in silence again, when she stops me with a hand on my arm. "Wait."

The entire room goes up in flames of anticipation as she sinks to her knees.

"Thalia, you don't have to—"

"Maybe I want to."

I've lusted over having those lips around my cock since the moment she fell into my office. But I also know I've been her first *everything*—and as wound up as I am, I'm incapable of being gentle.

"*Muñequita*—"

"I'm not asking, Santi. Give me the power for once."

"I don't give power, *mi amada*. But for you, I'll share it." I give her a dangerous smile. "Open your mouth."

She takes me in slow and deep, curling her fingers around the base of my cock. In response, I let out a slow hiss, my fingers fisting even tighter around her hair. She's inexperienced, but I don't care. Her mouth is wet and warm and feels like heaven.

I guide her movements, my vision blurring. Every time I hit the back of her throat, the craving gets stronger. After that, my restraint evaporates into thin air. I lead her in a brutal rhythm as I piston into her mouth. She takes it all, anchoring her nails into my ass, until my muscles ache...my balls ache...*everything aches for her.*

My palm slams against the top of the dresser, the tequila bottle rattling again as I come hard, spilling days of pent-up lust into her mouth. When the dark edges of my vision fade, I open my eyes to find her running a hand under her bottom lip, a victorious smile on her face.

Fuck, I love this woman.

Tugging her up to her feet, my fingers grip her chin with a touch of warning. "If I find out you've sucked any other man's cock, I'll slit his throat." Then I pull her against me and crush our mouths together again.

When we part, I brush my thumb over her lips, watching her smile falter.

"This doesn't change anything," she says. "I still meant what I said before I left."

"I know you did. I just needed a fix, and you're the most beautiful of highs."

Our next kiss is a lingering goodbye. I'll give her all the space she needs now, but maybe there's another way of keeping her close while she figures out all the shit she needs to figure out.

"Good luck with the job hunting, *muñequita*."

"Wait, how did you...?" She sighs in resignation. "Have you been stalking me?"

Smirking, I reach around her and retrieve my bottle before pausing at the door.

"*Siempre...*"

CHAPTER
Twenty-Three

THALIA
Three Weeks Later

"Thalia? Come quick! Your hot stalker's back again."

I glance up from my desk to find my colleague, Bonnie, leaning out of the fourth-floor window to catch a glimpse of the black Aston Martin, or more specifically the hot man standing next to it.

"It's my new shawl," I say, in mock exasperation, reaching for the swathe of crimson cashmere that's draped across the back of my chair, as I shut down my laptop and rise to my feet. "He can't get enough of it."

"Is that a kink? Did the generational gap just get wider?" My project manager shoots me a look—forty-five years of doubt, tinged with wonder that she might be missing out on something exciting.

"Only for him," I say with a laugh, leaning over to catch a glimpse, myself.

I only started at IFDF a couple of weeks ago, but it's a small company and routines tend to get noticed around here.

Santi sticks to his like clockwork.

At seven p.m. every night he's downstairs, come rain or shine. Black suit. Stormy vibes. Always leaning against the side panel, smoking one of his cigarettes, the silver trails rising up from his fingers like a prayer that only New York can answer. Readying himself for another half hour of polite small talk as he drives me home—something that's way *way* out of Santi Carrera's comfort zone, but one he's trying out just for me.

"Does dark and moody have a name?" Bonnie says, leaning out for another peek.

"Why waste time with introductions?" I say casually, watching her eyes widen to saucers at my wicked implication. "Bye, Bonnie, I'll see you tomorrow at nine a.m. for the project review meeting!"

With that, I grab my purse, and head for the elevator, pausing by the vending machine, and then dropping a chocolate bar on the counter for the receptionist as I pass. Lisa is usually the first in and last out of the office, so she deserves all the calories for that.

Slapping a caller on hold, she mouths me a "thank you", and blows me a kiss.

Santi looks up as I exit the building. Right away, his gaze drops to my shawl. For weeks, I've been wearing nothing but muted tones of gray and black, but when I was out shopping with Ella yesterday, I saw this in the front window of Saks, and I couldn't resist.

"Good day?" he asks, chucking away his cigarette, and opening up my door for me.

These are the rules to this agreement. We keep it brief. We keep it light. He's finally giving me the room to breathe, and in return, I'm giving him this precious hour where my safety falls under his protection—on the proviso he stops drinking eighteen bottles of *Añejo* a day.

"It was good, thanks." I slide my hands into my pockets, trying to ignore the scent of musk and sandalwood. It seems stronger tonight, like a temptation that's becoming harder and harder to resist. "We finally submitted the proposal for the rehabilitation project in Honduras."

He nods. "Want to know how mine went?"

"Did you torture anyone?"

"Not that I can recall."

"Kill anyone?"

The corners of his mouth start to curl. "Surprisingly, no. Although I may have sent Sanders an inappropriate impending fatherhood gift, which may result in him attempting to kill *me*."

"Oh dear," I say lightly. "Being a widow at nineteen wasn't part of my life goals, Santi. And to think I was just starting to wear bright colors again."

"You ready?" he says, gesturing to the empty passenger's seat.

"Thanks."

"Look at you fly," I hear him mutter.

I stop and turn. "What—?"

But he's already walking around to his side of the car and gesturing at the two black SUVs parked across the street.

I pause, finding I don't want an hour of stilted conversation tonight.

I want to make it tilt.

"There's a diner around the corner," I say in a rush. "Do you, maybe, want to go grab a coffee or something first…?" I trail off as his unblinking stare finds mine across the roof of the Aston Martin.

"Sounds good," he says, making his way back around to me. "Considering tomorrow may be my last day on this earth, a cup of bad filter coffee sounds like the perfect way to celebrate."

The first fifty feet are a tutorial in "awkward." Even small talk seems embarrassed to be in our company.

"How's Lola?" I mumble, as we reach the corner of the block.

"In a permanent state of nausea." His phone beeps, and he glances at the message. "Her new best friend is the toilet bowl, closely followed by root ginger and chamomile tea."

I can't help smiling at this. "My mom said she was the same when she was pregnant with me. She swears it's hereditary, so I'm totally screwed."

He falls silent again. I'm straying into a field that's loaded with land mines, and he's bracing himself for shrapnel.

"Do you want kids, Santi?" I ask quietly

"Figured they'd always be a part of my future at some point," he says, staring straight ahead. "Like erectile dysfunction, bad digestion and retirement homes."

I burst out laughing.

"You?" he asks.

"Definitely," I say, surprising myself.

Truth is, I'd never really thought about it before now, but there's something about this evening's clear warm night. Even the lights of New York can't keep the stars from shining, and it's making me want to break all the rules and talk secrets.

The diner is small and busy, but we find a blue leather booth at the end of the row.

I watch him slide in and stretch his arm out along the back of his seat, dominating the space and my attention at the same time.

Our waitress hands us two sticky menus and disappears.

Santi slaps his onto the table and glances about the diner, constantly checking and assessing until RJ and Rocco enter. They take up position at the counter, beneath a TV showing classic baseball game reruns. When I swing my gaze back to Santi, he's staring right at me.

I blush and drop my eyes to the menu, recognizing a glitch in the whole conversation-in-a-relationship thing. We're not at "small talk" anymore, but, at my instigation, we're nowhere near "dirty talk" either. We're stuck in the middle at a place called familiarity, which has giant black potholes in its roads.

"Are you hungry?"

"Not really."

"Two shit coffees it is, then."

I watch him raise his hand to our waitress. We're sitting right under a spotlight, and I see the dark shadows under his eyes when he turns to give her our order.

"How's Legado?" I ask, as soon as she disappears.

"Going down like a ship in a shitstorm." He rakes his hand through his hair and grimaces. "Anyone who tells you there's no such thing as bad publicity is a fucking liar. They've clearly never had two mass shootings and an abduction on their premises, either… But enough about my business, I want to hear about yours. Tell me about IFDF. I looked up the acronym on the internet and ended up on a porn site."

I can't help laughing again. "It stands for the International Freedom & Dignity Federation. It's a privately owned NGO with projects all over the world. Their head office is here in New York."

"How do they operate?"

"Do you really want to know, or are you just making polite conversation?"

"I'm a cartel boss, Thalia," he says, arching one eyebrow at me. "To me, conversations aren't polite; they're a necessary evil. But with my wife, they're essential, and occasionally enjoyable. Please continue."

"They receive funding from donors like USAID, UN Agencies and other high-net private foundations."

"What kind of stuff do you handle? Who do you help?"

"Mainly victims of anti-sex trafficking and sexual exploitation, human trafficking and modern slavery. The project we just submitted today focuses on the rescue and rehabilitation of children and young girls in West Africa…" I stop when I realize he's staring at me again. "Shit, am I boring you?"

"Not in the slightest. I love hearing about what you do. I love hearing you speak about anything other than the fucking weather, if I'm honest. Is this one of the Senator's legitimate side businesses? If so, nice of him to help his boss's daughter out."

"Senator Sanders is one of the founding members, yes, but I only requested a foot in the door," I grit out, hurt at his insinuation. "I still had to go through the whole interview process, and I'm starting as a project coordinator…"

That's when I realize he's smirking at me.

Bastard.

"Stop winding me up, Carrera!" I yell.

"But it's so easy to do, *Carrera*," he drawls back.

I go to punch his arm, but somehow our fingers get tangled up and crash back down to the table together as one. At the same time, our waitress arrives with our coffees. She bangs them down next to our hands and gives me a ghost of a wink.

"I'm not going to say, 'I miss you,' because that's against the rules," he says, dragging his coffee cup toward him and spilling half the contents onto the saucer.

"I miss you, too," I say softly, doing it anyway, because I'm being led astray by the warmth of his skin seeping into mine.

He lifts his coffee to his mouth and takes a sip, making me wait on tenterhooks.

"Bad girl," he says eventually, his dark eyes gleaming. "See how I've corrupted you?"

"Corrupted by a corrupt god," I muse thoughtfully. "Is there any hope left for me, do you think?"

"All the hope in the world, *muñequita*."

Soulful. That's how his voice sounds. Like his soul is full of me and my new ambitions, as well as his own, and it's making it fit to burst.

His phone beeps again, lighting up the table. I watch him glance at it, and then at RJ, who climbs down from his bar stool and heads for the exit.

"Is everything okay?"

"It's fine," he soothes.

"Don't lie to me, Santi. Is it Zaccaria?"

Saying his name out loud causes my stomach to churn. I'm healing well during my daylight hours, but my nights are still *Il Re Nero's* to terrorize. It doesn't matter how much Vicodin I take... The Black King still manages to take a sledgehammer to my medicated walls.

Santi's fingers tighten around mine. "We uncovered a *Villefort* trafficking network in Eastern Europe that led us all the way to the US. Your father and his team shut it down."

"But that's good, right?"

"Yes."

My heart sinks. "From the look on your face, that was just the bad entrée."

He blows out a heavy breath. "Zaccaria lost a significant money spinner when we destroyed his fortress in Italy. Grayson's convinced he's using another of his European estates to resurrect it."

I stare at him in horror. "Oh my God. Santi, we have to stop him."

"And we will. Unfortunately, the cunt's been buying up property all over the world for the past ten years using different pseudonyms and offshore accounts. Locating it is going to take some time... Hey..." Sliding a finger under my chin, he tips my head up to meet his fierce reassurance. "He's not coming within a thousand feet of you or Lola, *muñequita*... Not as long as there's still breath in my body. Do you hear me?"

"I hear you," I whisper. "So, what's the shitty dessert in all of this?"

"Are you sure you're not full on information yet?"

I shake my head.

"He's pissed about the truce," he says, dropping my chin. "Pissed with the Italians, or what's left of them. A man like that can't stew silently. He's putting on a show by having The Odessa flood our streets with heroin."

"The Odessa?" I say, frowning.

"Ukrainian mafia. They've always had a presence in New York and New Jersey, mostly in Brooklyn, but thanks to *Villefort's* extensive political connections, they've suddenly become the new players on a huge stage. They're bypassing the ports and flying the heroin in direct to both states. No checks.

Zaccaria even has sway over the DEA. It's the Bad Shit, too. Cut with Fentanyl. Highly addictive. With the hits on our dockside warehouses still hurting us, our profits just took a nosedive."

No wonder he looks so exhausted.

"Is there anything you can do?"

"Grayson's acting like a fucking diplomat, advising we set up a meet with Artem Lisko, the Don of Odessa here in New York. He wants to try and turn the tide in our favor before we declare an all-out turf war."

"Santi…"

I'm scared suddenly, even though I learned a long time ago that it's a redundant emotion to feel for men like him and my father. They live for the kill. They live for the danger. It's like trying to love a speeding bullet that's always pointed at someone, all the while praying that the one meant for him goes astray.

He releases my hand to drain the last of his coffee. "Fuck it, what does it matter... I'm dead tomorrow anyway, remember?" He shoots me another look over the rim of his white cup.

"What the *hell* did you buy Sam?" I say, temporarily distracted from my fears.

His lips start curving again. "A consultation with one of the best surgeons in the US."

I frown. "What for? His scars?"

"No, a vasectomy."

"A *vasectomy*?" I repeat, struggling to keep a straight face. "You're right. You really are a dead man walking."

"Will you come to my funeral?" he says idly, leaning forward, pressing his elbows into the table, bringing his face in so close to mine it's a fight not to lean in and press my lips against his.

"So long as I can wear red."

"It's our fucking color. I'd be pissed if you wore anything else."

I watch his gaze flicker to my mouth.

"You know, this is the first date we've ever had."

"And I didn't have to force you into it, either…" He leans back, breaking the spell.

Leaving me wanting more.

An easy calm blankets us as he reaches for his wallet and tosses a fifty on to the table.

"That's a good tip," I observe.

"Turns out, it was a great coffee."

Now, it's my turn to smile. "Are you flirting with me?" I say coyly, as he slides his wallet back into the inside pocket of his jacket.

"Nope. That's against the rules."

"When has that ever stopped you?"

He stands up, motioning for me to do the same. "Time to go. I have twenty minutes to get you across town, otherwise your Irish mountain of a bodyguard is going to accuse me of reneging on the deal and kick me all the way to Dublin."

We reach my apartment with a minute to spare, thanks to Santi driving like a maniac as usual, weaving in and out of traffic jams like he owns this city instead of the one across the Hudson.

He goes to open up the driver's door, when I grab his arm to stop him.

"Wait. I need to ask you something."

"Oh?"

"It's my birthday tomorrow, and I'm thinking of hitting up a casino to scratch a very bad itch I have for one last time..." I flick him a wicked grin. "You don't know of any casino owners who'd be okay being scammed out of fifty thousand dollars, do you?"

He doesn't answer at first. Instead, he leans over the console and runs a slow, leisurely finger down my cheek that makes my thighs clench and my heartbeat quicken.

"*Muñequita*," he says, his voice rough and low. "That's going to be the sweetest fucking money I've ever been cheated out of in my life. I'll even throw in dinner to make myself feel better about it."

"Then it's a date," I whisper.

"Our second in two days... Careful, *Señora* Carrera," he adds huskily. "That's more than most marriages have in a year."

CHAPTER
Twenty-Four

THALIA

It takes me over an hour, but I finally find it, crumpled and creased at the bottom of my overnight bag.

"Damn it."

"What's wrong?" Ella looks up from her laptop with a frown on her face. She's sitting cross-legged on the couch, with course notes and open textbooks scattered all around her like educational confetti. I can tell she's wrestling with an important assignment. It's only seven a.m., and she's been awake for longer than I have.

I hold up the claret-red designer dress to show her the state of it. "I wanted to wear this tonight, but it looks like a herd of elephants slept on it."

"Leave it on the chair behind you," she mutters, dropping her eyes back to her screen. "I'll swing by the dry cleaners on my way to class and beg Mia for a four-hour special."

"Why don't I make myself useful and drop it by myself," comes a soft voice from the doorway.

"*Máma*!" We cry in unison, our shock reverberating around the room like a high-pitched cannonball.

A split second later, we're throwing our arms around her, making a Santiago family reunion a mess of tears and joy in the middle of the living room, with our mother's elegant composure cracking just as hard as ours.

"What are you doing here?" Ella gasps.

"Your father has business here and I *insisted* on accompanying him."

My sister and I share a smile. We talk to our mother every day, but our father rarely allows her to leave his island compound. Most of the time, she's content to follow *pápa's* orders. Occasionally, like now, she'll drive her stiletto heel through his boot and insist on her freedom.

"Thalia, my beautiful girl," she says, turning to me to cup my cheek with her hand. "I wasn't going to miss your twentieth birthday for anything."

"And I've missed *you*," I mumble, diving into her slim shoulder again, feeling the weight of everything I've been through pushing against the thin barrier of my self-control. I've talked to her more on Skype these past few weeks than ever before, but there's nothing like being wrapped up in her warmth and reassurance.

"What time do you have to be at work, sweetheart?"

"In an hour," I sob, crumbling already.

"Ella," I hear her say. "It's been a long flight, and I'd love a coffee. Would you mind making me an extra strong espresso and bringing it to Thalia's room?"

"Sure. Where's *pápa*?"

"He's with Edier and Sam."

All having a crash course on Ukrainian curse words, no doubt.

"Come," she says, lifting my head from her damp shoulder and wiping away my tears. "I want to talk with you alone."

She leads me into my bedroom and sits me down on the edge of my quilt, still clasping my hand to her chest.

"*Máma*—"

"Shush. I want to say something to you first." She lifts my hand to her lips and kisses it gently. "I used to think that I was brave, Thalia Santiago, but you, my daughter, have the heart of a lioness and a tiger's soul."

"I lost your necklace," I mutter, staring at the floor. "They stole it from me in Italy."

"Objects aren't important," she chides. "It's the memories that live inside the moments that matter."

"But *pápa*—"

"Will buy me another," she reassures. "Sweetheart, I'm not even going to pretend to understand what you're going through, or what you're overcoming.

I'm not going to sit here and patronize and sympathize. But I want you to know that I'll always be here. Whatever you need. Whatever darkness you find yourself in…"

"*Only in darkness can we see the stars*," I whisper.

She lifts her brows in surprise. "You remembered the picture on my nightstand."

"I always think about that, and what you said to me. About how you found your way back to love when all hope was lost."

"And so will you," she muses. "I don't know much about your new husband, Thalia, but he burned bright when you needed him to, and *that* tells me everything."

"He thinks he's a bad man with no hope of redemption."

"What do *you* think?"

"That he's a bad man who feels more than he thinks he ought to."

She laughs. "In my experience, there are varying degrees of badness. Morality is a moving target in our world, but things like love? Family? Those are the true constants… From what I can tell, he's done what you've asked of him, because you *are* those two things to him, sweetheart. He's given you your space. He set you free. He's let you breathe and heal, and in doing so, we've all been rewarded in watching you soar again." She nudges me gently, the pride in her voice making my eyes sting. "For stubborn men like Santi Carrera and your father, bowing down to such a request is even harder than taking a bullet."

There's a knock at the door, and Ella enters with two steaming espresso cups.

"I brought one for you too, Thals."

"Time to get dressed," declares my mother, rising to her feet to take them from her and setting one down on my nightstand. "You don't want to be late for work. Oh, and I take it from the dress disaster, you're planning on going out later?"

I nod, giving her the trace of a smile. She returns it with a flick of a wink. "I see. Then we better get it cleaned up."

"Thanks, *máma*," I say quietly.

"You're welcome." She pauses in the doorway, an elegant vision in a white pant suit with her long, still-dark hair clouding up her shoulders. "Remember, Thalia, even during the day, the stars never really disappear. They're just waiting to shine for us again when we need them the most."

The rest of the day passes in a whirlwind of progress report reviews and updating budgets for our trafficking project in Nigeria.

Threading its way through every meeting and long-distance phone call is a ribbon of anticipation about tonight. In seeing Santi again, and returning to the scene of the crime as his wife, not as his enemy.

I'm not the same naïve nineteen-year-old girl who sneaked into his casino a couple of months ago. I've been broken and bruised since then.

I'm surer of who I am now. Of us. Of our place in this strange life of sin and sacrifice.

Most of all, I'm not afraid of loving him anymore. We're the only two people who can right each other's wrongs.

Bonnie's not in the main office as I grab my things together and power down my laptop. It means I'm not treated to her end-of-the-day hanging out of the window ritual to ogle my husband. When I spill out of the building, however, it's not Santi waiting for me, it's Reece.

"He was called away on business," he says tersely, watching my face fall. "He said he'll meet you at Legado later."

My skin starts prickling with uneasiness as he rushes me into the backseat. My heart sinks like a stone when I see at least ten of my father's men on the sidewalk behind me and five black SUVs parked nearby.

"What's going on, Reece?" I ask him. "This isn't extra security, it's an army."

"Nothing for you to worry about, Thalia," he croons, sliding into the passenger seat and nodding at the driver.

"Is my husband meeting with Edier?"

"I believe so."

"Is this about The Odessa and Lorenzo Zaccaria?"

He doesn't answer. Not that I expected him too. He's under strict instructions to keep me calm, oblivious, and out of harm's way. At the top of that list are orders not to divulge every facet of cartel warfare to me.

My apartment is dark and empty when I arrive home. Ella must still be in class. Flicking on a couple of side lights, I kick off my heels and the rest of my clothes and melt under a long hot shower.

Stepping out of a whirlpool of steam and into my bedroom, I'm distracted from my worries by the sight of the newly cleaned and pressed claret-red dress hanging on the back of my closet door.

Máma, you life saver.

I run my hand over the intricate beaded detail, remembering how much I hated it the first time I wore it. Back then, I chose it as the ultimate distraction. Tonight, I want all of his attention on me.

Lying on the center of my bed is a brand new pair of shiny red Louboutins, and a small black jewelry box. I can't help but smile when I open it up to find a beautiful star pendant studded with diamonds on a delicate silver chain. I love my mother more in that moment than I ever thought possible.

I take my time getting ready, straightening my long hair into a shiny dark waterfall, and making my eyes so smoky and sultry that Reece chokes on air when he sees me.

"Well?" I say, giving him a twirl.

"I thought you told Carrera to ditch the tequila," he accuses, fighting a grin. "The arrogant bastard's going to drink his own bar dry when he sees that dress."

No chance.

This evening, the only thing my husband is getting drunk on is me.

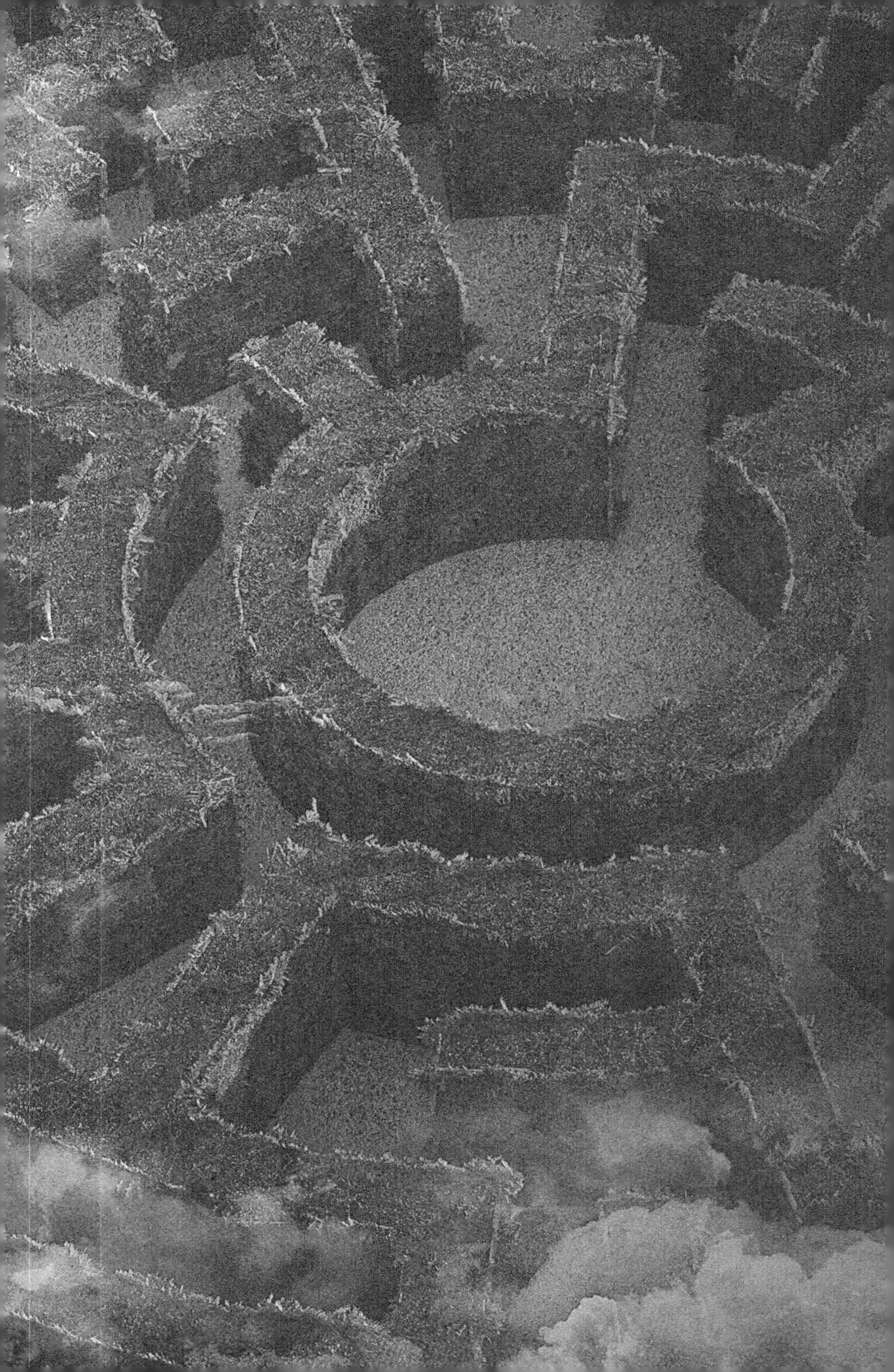

CHAPTER
Twenty-Five

THALIA

Despite Santi's talk about Legado's dwindling popularity yesterday, the *porte-cochére* is packed with expensive cars as Reece parks up next to a curtain of ivy.

The rose-gold tower of sin is beckoning. I slip out of the vehicle before my bodyguard can stop me, hurrying up the black marble steps and into the glass-fronted lobby.

I weave through the crowds of expensive colognes and perfumes toward the main elevator, under the assumption that Santi will be waiting for me in his office. But as I go to press the call button for a carriage, the large shadow of his second-in-command, RJ, materializes next to me.

"Nice déjà vu," he says, his mouth quirking up when he recognizes my dress. "Should I alert security that there's a card counter on the floor tonight?"

"I have it on good authority that the owner's going to let this one slide," I tell him, fighting a grin.

"Is that right?" He swallows a laugh. "Good to see you back, *Señora* Carrera. And of your own free will… He's waiting for you in one of the private blackjack rooms. Follow me."

Santi has his back turned to us as we enter. One wrist is resting on the bar counter in front of him, next to a cut glass tumbler, while the other is glued to his phone. His suit jacket has been thrown carelessly over the gold velvet bar stool nearby, and when he goes to rake his hand through his hair, the guns in his holster glint menacingly in the soft amber lights.

"I want updates throughout the evening," I hear him say, while I'm taking in the black velvet couches below the gilt-framed mirrors and the black gaming table in the center of the room. "We'll speak again before ten."

Hanging up, he chucks the phone across the bar counter in frustration, raking his hand through his hair again, as a vicious Spanish curse spills from his mouth.

"Santi," RJ murmurs.

"What is it?" he snaps.

"Your wife has arrived."

He turns, with his glass in his hand. When he sees me, he goes very still. A beat later, there's a click behind me as RJ excuses himself from our staring contest.

It lingers on and on, until I feel a giggle rising up inside me.

"Are you practicing your poker face, Santi?" I say slyly. "I thought we were playing a different game tonight."

That snaps him out of his trance.

"When you look like that, *muñequita*, I'll play any fucking game you want," he says huskily, reaching for his jacket.

"Don't," I tell him, and something in my voice makes him pause. "There's no need to hide your weapons from me. I'm done pretending that violence isn't a part of us. I'm done running from it."

I'm done running from you.

"If you say so." He tosses his jacket back down on the barstool and prowls up to where I'm standing. He circles me slowly like a hunter stalking his prey, his eyes so dark and penetrating I feel like he's inside me already.

The atmosphere is an electric storm on the horizon. He leaves my side for a second, and then the lock on the door turns.

"Ready to play?" he says, dropping a chaste kiss on my shoulder that makes the beat between my thighs dance to his tune.

"Who's dealing?" I say in a raspy voice.

"Birthday girls first." He gestures toward the gaming table.

I move to stand in the dealer's position by the loaded shoe, while he diverts to collect a chilled bottle of Dom Perignon and two flutes from the silver bucket on the bar counter.

"What are we playing for?" I ask, watching him pop the cork with ease and distribute the liquid gold between the glasses, his movements so self-assured that the beat between my thighs becomes relentless.

Handing me a glass, he slides his hand into his pocket and tosses a handful of familiar-looking gold and black chips onto the felt. "What do you say to fifty grand a piece?"

I feel that crazy swell of laughter rising up inside me again. "Sounds like a good place to start."

Taking a sip of my champagne, savoring the wicked fizz of bubbles on my tongue, I deal the first round as he pulls out the black chair opposite.

My heart races as he places ten thousand onto his betting box without even looking at his hand. In turn, I do the same, matching him chip for unknown playing card—throwing everything to chance.

"Why Legado?" he asks, studying my face as I deal us both a second card. "Why that dress? Why now?"

"I felt like going back to the beginning."

Glancing at his cards, he flips over a total of twenty. A second later, I'm flipping over a total of nineteen.

"Are you hustling me again, *muñequita*?" He shoots me a loaded look as he sweeps my losing chips toward his own stash.

"Never cheat the system in the same place twice," I say with a smile.

Another round. Another loss. I'm twenty thousand down already.

"It's a good job you're married to a rich man," he says dryly, winning again.

"I make my own money these days, Santi. Just in case you forgot."

I'm down to my last chip now.

My last bet.

I'm disappointed.

I never knew a game of blackjack could be so erotic. It's all in the slide of hand, the stolen glances, the charged pauses... My panties are so wet it's embarrassing.

"You need a better incentive to win," he declares, reaching into his pocket again and laying out the most beautiful diamond engagement ring I've ever seen on my betting box.

"What's that?" I gasp.

"Your birthday present," he says idly. "I figured it was time to replace a ring I bought for a woman I hated with one for the woman I love."

My breath catches.

"If you want it, that is," he adds, leaving his next words hanging.

If you want me...

With trembling fingers, I deal us both aces, and then I "draw" my way to a cool twenty-one without hesitation.

He tips his head back and laughs, chucking his seventeen across the table. "I fucking *knew* you were bluffing. *Dios mío*, you're good!"

"First rule of counting cards," I tell him, fighting another smile. "When someone accuses you of being a hustler, always distract them with innocence."

"Give me your hand."

I do as he asks, my stomach fluttering as he slips off my old ring and replaces it with a diamond that's so much more than *Hope*.

"Do you like it?" he inquires.

"Very much... What shall we play for next?"

He flicks me a wicked smirk. "Your panties."

"*What?*" I sputter.

I watch his mocking gaze trail a line of heat all the way down to my pussy. "The way you keep fidgeting, *muñequita*, tells me what's happening underneath your dress is pretty fucking similar to what's been happening in my pants since you walked into this room. I want to see if I'm right."

We're interrupted by a beep from his phone, still lying discarded on the bar counter.

"Well?" he asks, not even glancing at it. "Do we have a deal, or not?"

"Fine," I say through gritted teeth, ignoring the fire in my cheeks as I reach for the first card from the shoe. He can toy with me all he likes, but there's no way I'm taking my panties off and handing them over, just like that. His ego is way too big already.

"Are you flying back to me, firebird?" he murmurs suddenly, putting his hand on mine.

I shoot him a look from underneath my lashes. "Can I still keep my job? If I come back, I don't want any of this macho, cartel, barefoot and pregnant in the kitchen bullshit—"

"Of course, you can still keep your job," he says, sounding mildly offended that I'd even question it. "I know how important it is to you."

"And I still want to see Edier and Sam anytime I like without you throwing a shit fit."

"Is this a fair exchange, or a fucking landslide?" he mutters.

"And I'm redecorating your apartment because it's not a goddamn lair. Your soul is not as black as you think it is, Santi Carrera."

His dark eyes gleam. "What color is it, then?"

"Haven't decided. I'll let you know in the morning."

"That implies you're staying over tonight?"

"Are you going to let me play this card or not?" I say, losing my cool.

"Be my guest," he says, smirking as he finally releases his hold on my hand.

As predicted, I draw the Ten of Clubs.

As predicted, his second card is the King of Spades. Making his total a good twenty again.

I bite my lip, preparing to revel in his disappointment when I trump him with the Ace of Hearts, as I toss the final card of the game onto the table. But the smile is instantly wiped off my face when I look down to see the Six of Spades.

Sixteen.

"What…? How…?" I sputter again, as the deep rich sound of his laughter echoes around the private gaming room.

"First rule of being a criminal, Thalia," he says, his expression burning up with amusement. "Always fix the odds in your favor."

"How the hell did you do that?" I cry, launching myself at him across the table. "Tell me right now!"

But I never get my answer because my mouth is suddenly full of him, and then he's pulling me astride his lap and driving his tongue deep into the heart of my outrage.

Hot. Wet. Passionate and wild… I'm fisting his hair and moaning into our crazy kiss as he rises with me in his arms and sets me down on the edge of the gaming table. Tearing his mouth away, he slides a rough hand up my thigh to hook his finger into the gusset of my panties.

"You owe me a debt, *muñequita*," he says huskily, slamming a hand down next to my left hip. "And I'm here to collect."

Just then, there's a loud thumping on the door.

"Fuck off!" he roars, ripping my panties down my legs.

"Open up, boss," comes a loud voice. "Edier Grayson's on the line."

"Take a fucking message!"

"He says it's urgent."

Sliding a warm hand behind my neck he drags us together for one final, lingering, hotter-than-hell kiss. "Don't move from this room," he orders. "When I come back, I want your legs spread and waiting. Do you hear?"

I nod, dizzy with longing.

"And if I find out you've touched yourself in my absence, I'll be denying you orgasms for a week."

There's more thumping at the door.

"I'm coming!"

"Not yet, you're not," I whisper, curling my arms around his neck. "But you will later." My smile fades. "Please be careful."

"*Siempre*." He swipes the pad of his thumb across my lips. "Same goes for you. There are fifty of my men outside, and twenty of Grayson's, plus Reece who's still itching to dance an Irish *cèilidh* all over my ass… I'll be back in an hour."

CHAPTER
Twenty-Six

SANTI

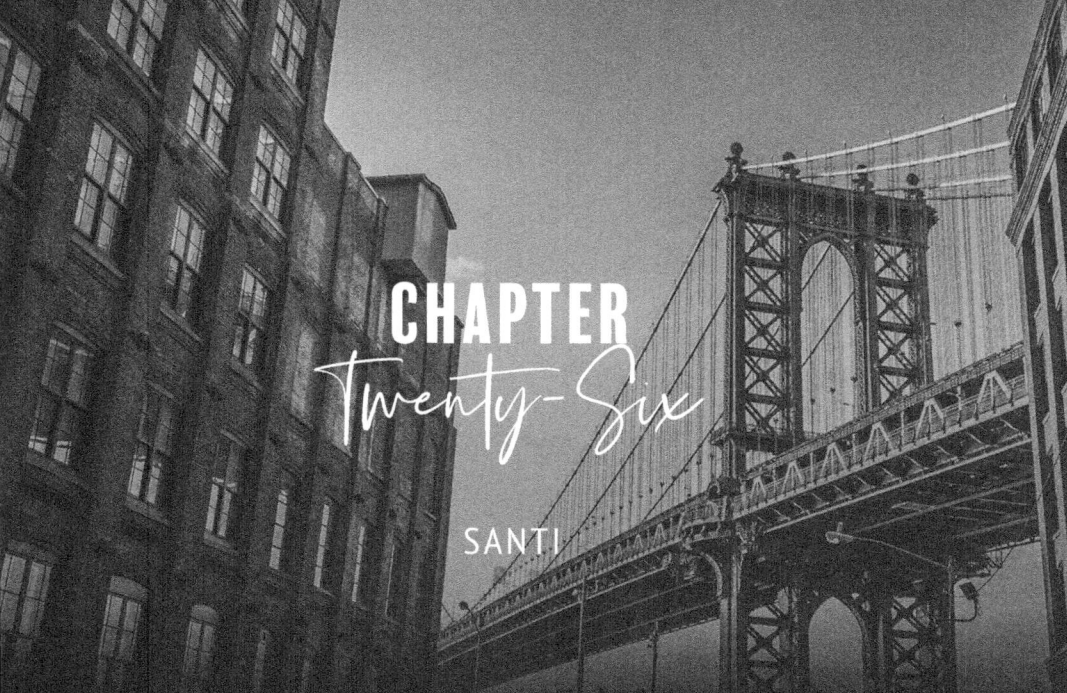

If death is the great equalizer, then life is the biased bitch paving its way—and tonight she's tipping the scales against me.

If it wasn't for the name connecting the two anchors of this meeting, I would never have left Thalia. But Grayson cockblocked me with the promise of blood, and after weeks of chasing Zaccaria all over the goddamn globe, even my wife's pussy couldn't keep me away.

That fucking Colombian better deliver, though. I'm suffering the worst case of blue balls in history because of him.

Killing the ignition, I stare at the run-down building across the street. Chipped white paint reveals a wooden frame in dire need of repair, and the faded blue awning boasting the name "Kyiv Kitchen" in dirty white block letters is anything but enticing.

From the outside it looks unassuming and forgettable…

Of course, evil never presents itself as a monster. It infiltrates with a shy smile, bowed head, and melodic laugh. It's only when your guard is down that the mask drops.

That's why men like me will always exist. We play the Jekyll and Hyde role to perfection. We flash our handsome faces, wear confidence like a cloak, and keep attention above our surfaces. By the time our own masks drop, it's too late.

That's also why Artem Lisko's Ukrainian restaurant looks like a subsidized shithole. I'd expect nothing less from a man tucked away in Lorenzo Zaccaria's back pocket.

I need to force all thoughts of Thalia out of my mind. Back in that blackjack room, I was a devoted husband. Parked outside the blue awning of Kyiv Kitchen, I'm a cartel boss.

Loading my gun, I slide it back into my holster, and make my way down the street to where Grayson is leaning against the passenger's side of an SUV. It's a deceptive stance. From an outsider's point of view, he's casually observing the scarce activity on a quiet Brighton Beach side street, situated on Brooklyn's coastline.

I know better these days. Behind that icy facade lies a mind in perpetual motion.

Stopping a couple of feet in front of him, I prop my hip against the front panel. "I hope you know what the hell you're doing. Walking into this sit-down without backup is like fucking a whore without a condom."

He cocks a dark eyebrow.

"Fuck you," I grumble, flipping my middle finger. "It's an expression. I meant by leaving Sanders and RJ in the trenches instead of inside with us. It's an open invitation to these *idiotas*."

"It's a concession, not an oversight." He glances over his shoulder at the restaurant, his murky gaze unreadable. "There were stipulations attached to this meeting. Lisko does his homework, Carrera. He knows who the key players are in every territory. Let him think what he wants."

It's an obvious divide and conquer. Grayson and I can hold our own, but with our seconds behind us as backup, we're an unbeatable force. Denying them access was a strategic move.

"Which means he knows what went down in Italy," I murmur to myself. *And if that's the case, Sanders and RJ are better off where they are.*

"I have a small army with their fingers on the trigger just waiting for my signal," he says. "Only an ignorant man would meet The Odessa without shields. You're a lot of things, Carrera, but ignorant isn't one of them." He nods to where ten of my best *sicarios* lie in wait before he strides toward the edge of the road.

Which is exactly why I brought them.

Grayson is methodical, not reckless. I knew he'd have backup. While I don't anticipate having any of those bullets aimed at me, I don't leave things to chance.

Pushing away from the SUV, I step forward until we're standing shoulder to shoulder. "Careful, Grayson... I think you're starting to like me."

His narrowed gaze slides to the side. "I tolerate you for the sake of Thalia and this truce."

"Fair enough."

Falling into silence, we move as one cohesive unit, crossing the street with intent. Just before we reach the ugly blue awning, he stops abruptly, his arm swinging across my chest.

I glance down. "You better have a damn good reason for doing that."

"I need you to keep that temper of yours in check," he warns. "I know how badly you want Zaccaria's head on a plate, but I guarantee he won't be in there. We're here to entice Lisko with a more lucrative import deal. He agreed to meet with us but..." He shakes his head.

"You don't trust him," I say flatly.

"I don't trust *anyone*, especially a man who does business with any faction of *Villefort*. Lisko isn't gullible, Carrera. His favorite color may be green, but it's closely followed by red. Do you get what I'm saying?"

And he calls me an arrogant bastard...

I'm starting to resent his tone. He may have facilitated this meeting, but I'm not part of his armed fan brigade. I have access to just as much intel as he does.

"Yes, I get you. Money opens doors, bullets close them. We're either entering into negotiations or a trap."

Either way, no one is keeping me from walking through those glass doors. I've spent too many sleepless nights and bottles of tequila chasing this phantom. It's grown into an obsession I have to see through or run the risk of Thalia and I spinning in circles for decades.

Neither of us say a word as the chime above the door announces our presence to the empty restaurant. We walk toward the back, and just as we approach the twin steel doors leading to the kitchen, a pungent aroma seeps through the cracks.

I arch an eyebrow. "Borscht?"

"Lisko has a thing about cooking during meetings." When I arch the other eyebrow, he shakes his head. "Don't ask."

With each of us taking a door, we swing them open to find Artem Lisko sitting behind a folding table, elbows propped and fingers steepled like he's the fucking *Godfather*.

"I was wondering how long you girls were going to dance outside my restaurant."

His joke obviously amuses him, his chins jiggling in unison as that Slavic accent rolls off his tongue like curdled milk. However, it's his smirk that catches my attention the most—a wide Cheshire Cat-like grin that spans the length of his fleshy face and bald head.

"You like to watch, Lisko?" I taunt, earning myself a sharp look from my left.

However, the Ukrainian Don doesn't seem as offended by the insult as he is entertained. "I like to 'see,' *Señor* Carrera," he says, drumming his fingers together. "Observation is the key to success."

"Actually, that's perseverance, but, hey, your house, your rules. Mind if we take a seat?" I don't wait for a response before pulling out one of the two folding metal chairs set across from him.

I can feel Grayson's agitation rising as he jerks out a chair, too.

Chuckling again, Lisko wags a stumpy finger across the table. "I like you, Carrera. You have balls. Few men would be so bold." That irritating smile widens, and he tilts his head at Grayson. "You should lighten up, yes? Take notes from your friend. All business, no fun shuts doors…*and ports*."

"Is that a threat?" he asks coldly.

"*Observation*," the Don repeats, his gaze sliding back to me as if the damn word is now our own private joke.

I'm about to tell him to get the fuck on with it, when a kitchen timer goes off.

Pushing away from the table, he rises to his feet. "Dinner is served." Waddling toward the stove, he dips a ladle into a steel pot and fills three bowls. "Have borscht…" he instructs, setting a bowl in front of both of us before taking his seat.

"Not hungry," Grayson snarls, biting down on each syllable instead.

Shrugging, Lisko tucks his napkin into his collar before taking a loud slurp.

Out of habit, I scan the room for signs of movement, finding nothing but silence. Lisko may be an irritating son of a bitch, but he didn't claim The Odessa's throne by being careless.

That's when Thalia's confession from earlier floats into my head. *"First *rule of counting cards... When someone accuses you of being a hustler, always distract them with innocence."*

I note his non-answers. His redirects. His hospitality. His cool demeanor.

Something isn't right.

"Likso, our offer—"

"Artem," he tuts, cutting Grayson off with a wave of his hand. "And I never talk business before borscht—is bad luck." Refilling his spoon, he lifts it with a lethal smile. "You should try. Is my mother's recipe. Family tradition passed down from generation to generation..." Just as the spoon touches his lips, he glances up at me. "Much like *Villefort*."

He might as well have tossed a grenade in my lap.

I'm halfway out of my chair, ready to shove that fucking spoon down his throat, when a strong hand clamps down on my shoulder.

"Lisko..." Grayson starts, when a throat clears across the table. Gritting his teeth, he tries again. "Artem, let's not be coy here. You know our distaste for your business partner. As a man seeped in *family values*, you can understand how *Villefort* isn't a favored topic."

The pressure on my shoulder intensifies, and I glare at him while lowering myself back into my chair. *If we were anywhere else, I would have broken his nose for that.*

Lisko drops his spoon, unfazed as it clatters against the table. "This business is not for fool-hearted men, Edier Grayson," he says, all earlier amusement evaporating into a scowl. "Flash your weaknesses, and they get noticed."

Anger coils around me like a serpent. It hisses. It rattles. It rises up, fangs bared, ready to strike. I see Thalia waiting for me in that room... I see Lola asleep in her apartment.

Both alone inside Legado.

I see a vicious circle.

My weaknesses.

"I have a good deal with Lorenzo," he continues, tugging the napkin away from his chin. "What can two warring cartels offer to make me change my mind?"

It's not a question.

It's a hook.

He's baiting us.

"Our ports are under reconstruction as we speak," Grayson answers tersely. "You'd have clear access at two points of entry, one in Santiago territory, one in Carrera. Surely, you can see the benefit of having multiple avenues of distribution rather than relying on one channel? If Zaccaria decides he's no longer interested in doing business, he won't cut ties, Lisko. He'll cut throats."

Instead of answering, Lisko picks up his spoon and returns to his bowl.

He's stalling.

The Odessa Don never had any intention of entertaining our offer.

Without taking my eyes off the fat fuck and his red-stained teeth, I slowly reach down, my fingers brushing my gun holster. As if hearing his own snake rattle, Grayson's gaze drops, then shifts back up, holding my stare as his hand slips under the table as well.

He knows, too

It's a trap.

There are no words, but the unspoken message we share is clear and distinct.

We go out fighting.

I pull my gun from its holster. At the faint click, Lisko glances up, thick red liquid dripping from his lips.

"Gun," he notes with disgust. "How unimaginative. You know why I conduct all business in Kyiv Kitchen, Carrera?"

It's a statement, not a question, so I don't offer an answer.

"It is good place to carve meat." An icy smile peels across his face, and there's an explosion of frenzied motion behind us.

Grayson and I pull our guns simultaneously, aiming them at his head. Seconds later, we're being slammed into from behind, sending them tumbling across the table as two butcher's knives are pressed against our throats.

"What are you waiting for, *pendejo*?" I roar, hatred boiling in my veins. "Do it!"

Sighing, the Ukrainian drops his spoon, that sadistic smile turning downward. "I hate cold borscht." He looks up, his expression tightening. "You no longer amuse me, *Señor* Carrera. Fortunately, more stimulating entertainment awaits me in New Jersey."

Another warning rattle.

Thalia.

The fangs sink deeper.

Lola.

Cold, hard rage simmers beside me. "You never had any intention of doing business."

"Not true, Grayson," Lisko tuts, wagging that goddamn finger again. "We do have business. It is just not with you. Lorenzo has missed his wayward lambs."

Fuck.

We both struggle, an effort which only earns us the sharp bite of a blade and a stream of warm red liquid trickling down our necks.

"Not a smart move to leave others to watch over your weaknesses," he muses.

I need that fucking gun.

"Did you know sheep are predictable?" He pauses as if I'm going to answer questions with a fucking butcher's knife to my jugular. "They have a strong instinct for danger. One that compels them to band together for protection. Is game of…" Glancing up at the ceiling, he snaps his fingers. "What do Americans call it…? Ah yes, Follow the Leader. One sheep moves, the other will follow. Is why so many are slaughtered. Hardwired instinct is stronger than learned intuition. Sad."

"You son of a bitch!" Grayson roars.

I try to speak, but there's no longer a separation of man and monster. The images of Thalia and Lola have caused the Jekyll and Hyde parts of me to run full force into one another.

We made them a flashing target. While we swung our dicks around, Zaccaria's been watching us. He's been waiting for his moment to strike. Once again, he's using Legado as a cage—trapping Thalia and Lola in a new nightmare.

"I'll kill you slowly, Lisko," I say darkly, holding his smug stare. There's so much adrenaline pumping through my veins, I barely feel a second swipe of the knife at my throat. "I'll cut you into pieces and serve you to your own mother."

The Ukrainian smiles, the sight of his beet-stained teeth fueling me. "Did you know sheep depend on sight to survive, Carrera? Is why they avoid shadows and darkness. What do you think happens to damaged little lambs when the lights go out?"

It's this image that tips the scale, sending the sliver of self-restraint I have left scattering across the floor. When I lunge, it's not to save my own life, but to avenge theirs.

Blinding hate sears my vision as I reach for the bowl of borscht in front of me, hurling it over my shoulder into the Ukrainian soldier's face. Caught off guard, he stumbles backward, giving me a wide enough breadth to hurl myself across the table. In seconds, my gun is in my hand, and I'm twisting around—the sound of Grayson's heated curses filling my ears as I fire two bullets.

One into the guard holding Grayson.

The other into the motherfucker trying to decapitate me.

As both guards hit the floor, Grayson grips his shoulder, biting out a muffled curse as blood pumps in between his fingers. Before I can survey the damage, Lisko mutters something in Ukrainian, then lumbers out of his chair, his hand going for his gun.

Not today, motherfucker.

Leaping over the flimsy card table, I collide into him, the force knocking both of us into the stove and my muzzle to his forehead. Familiar shouts and gunshots narrow into a vortex beyond the steel doors, as I stare into the eyes of the man who lured me away from my wife.

Suddenly, the monster inside me craves more than a bullet. It wants immoral justice.

"Since you like family recipes so much, let me share one of mine," I hiss. "It's a Carrera favorite."

Offering him a rare smile, I drive my knee into his stomach, the blow causing him to tilt forward just enough that I can grab the back of his neck, twist him around, and shove him face first into his fucking pot of borscht. His arms flail as he struggles, but I don't relent until he chokes on his *tradition* and drowns a painful death.

When I let go, his body collapses onto the floor, the pot tipping over on top of his lifeless body.

"Carrera."

Snapping out of my murderous rage, I turn to find Grayson, his shoulder soaked in blood, the same murderous glare in his eyes.

We sprint through the restaurant toward our waiting SUVs, our heavy steps sounding like the cadence of a drum pounding out our worst fears. Once we've crossed the street, we split in two different directions.

As I reach the driver's side door, Grayson calls out my name again. Looking up, I find an expression soaked in blood, honor, and determination. "No matter what happens, Zaccaria dies."

The bleak implication hits hard, driving the husband further into the shadows, while arming the monster with twenty years of redirected hate.

"He will," I promise. "If I have to claw my way up from hell and drag him down myself, he will."

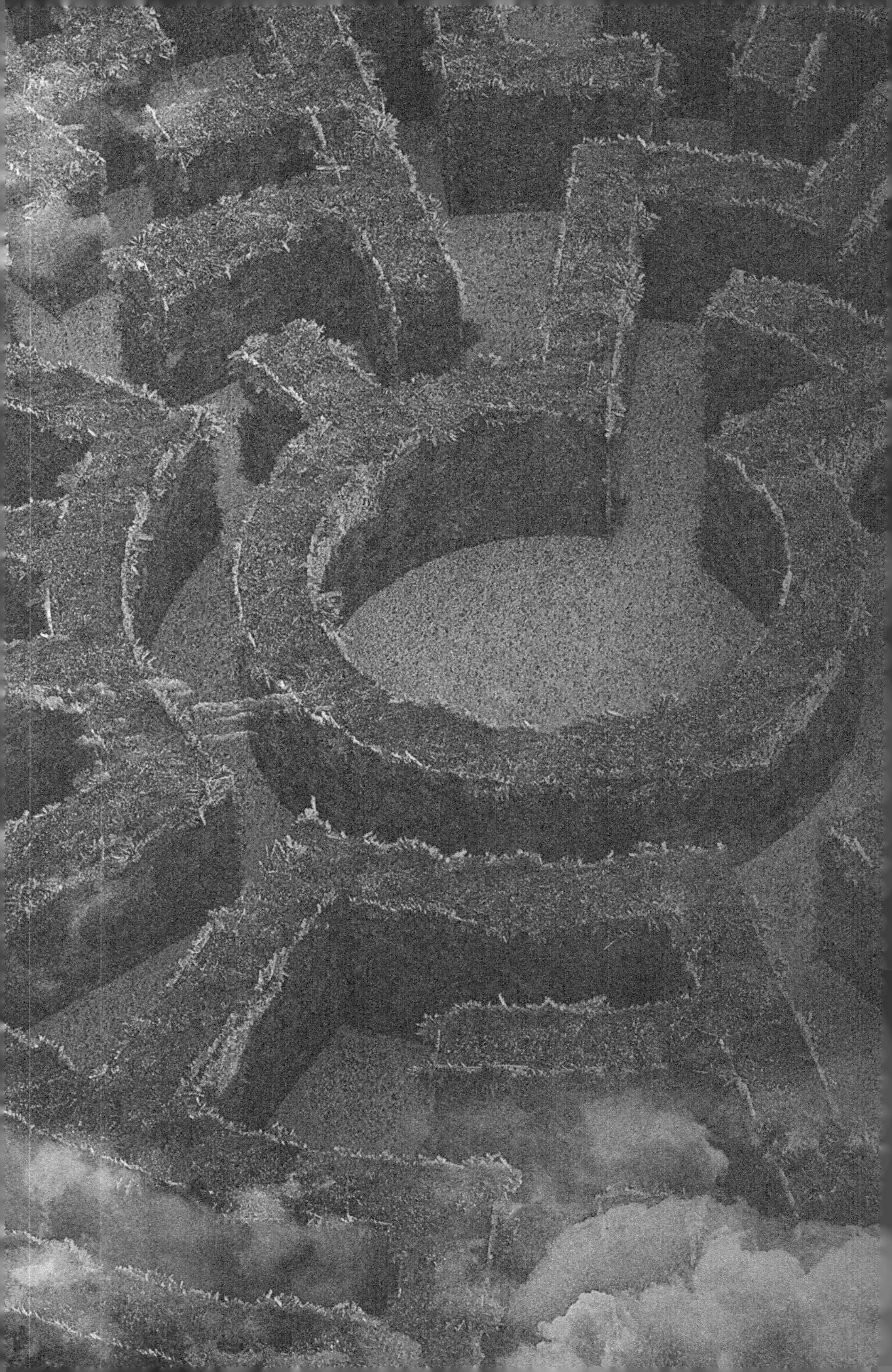

CHAPTER
Twenty-Seven

THALIA

Santi clearly doesn't trust me to save my orgasms for him. Fifteen minutes after he's gone, while I'm still cursing my husband for pocketing both my panties and my modesty on his way out, Reece steps into the room.

He stands like a sentry by the door as I perch on a gold barstool texting Lola to see if, by some miracle, she wants to drag herself away from her sick bed and come and join me down here. She's not answering any of them, though. She's not even reading them. In the end, I try calling, but it goes straight to voicemail.

I haven't touched a drop of champagne since Santi left. I don't much feel like celebrating anymore, because I know exactly where he's gone. Still, it's my birthday, so I need to be drinking *something* to take the edge off my sexual frustration and fears.

"Come and mix cocktails with me, Reece," I beg, sliding off the barstool and rounding the edge of the counter.

He shakes his head with a grimace. "No drinking on the job. You know your father's rules."

"Will you at least sit with me?"

With a sigh, he lumbers his giant six-foot-four frame over to the bar, running his hand back and forth over his bald head as if he's rubbing away his reluctance.

"Do you know any Tom Cruise tricks?" I joke, waving the cocktail shaker in his face.

When he doesn't answer, I bang the shaker down and start packing it with ice. I go to pour in a couple of shots of vodka when there's a loud thump outside the door, followed swiftly by another.

I glance at Reece to see if he's heard it too, but he just shrugs. "Gamblers getting rowdy. Carrera should be more selective with who he allows in."

"The crowd looked pretty elite and well-behaved tonight," I say doubtfully. "Do you think we should check?"

"Let Carrera's men deal with it," he says, waving it away.

He finds a discreet stereo behind the counter and switches on a chillingly haunting piece of classical music.

"What's this?" I ask, my arms prickling with goosebumps as he turns the volume up louder.

"Debussy."

"Doesn't seem like Santi's style. Something tells me he's more an anti-establishment kind of a guy."

My joke falls flat, so I finish making my Cosmopolitan in silence, convinced I can hear faint yelling above the music. The minor keys are sliding under my skin like rusty nails. I glance at the clock above the bar. Thirty minutes have passed since Santi left.

Reece's phone beeps.

"Who's that?"

"Your husband. He's been detained."

"Damn." I sit down on the stool next to him and take a sip of my cocktail.

With a grunt, he loosens the top button of his black shirt and places his gun down on the counter. It seems we're both settling in for a long night of staring at walls.

The music ends. Another track starts, and thirty minutes slowly trickles into an hour.

More messages come in for Reece, but nothing for me. I'm so bored, I find myself contemplating a game of Candy Crush.

"Do you know how long I've been working for your father?" Reece says suddenly, placing his phone next to his gun.

I shake my head. To me, Reece is a part of the fabric of my family. He's attended every birthday party. He's there in every photograph...

"Twenty-five years," he answers.

This shakes me from my web of inertia. "That's nearly as long as Edier's father."

"I was there in Miami when he met your mother."

Now, I'm really curious. "What was he like back then?"

There's a pause.

"Savage."

It's an ugly word that's not in keeping with the elegance of this room.

Uneasiness feathers my stomach as Reece swaps tracks to another piece of classical music, one where the staccato piano notes sound like stabbing knives.

"There's a kind of beauty in betrayal don't you think?" he says, making me choke on my drink. "She's like the perfect movie actress—a woman who you fantasize about for years—until one day you meet her in the street and she's even more fucking beautiful than you ever imagined."

"Reece—?"

"Did you know we share a birthday?"

I shake my head, staring back at a man who's as familiar to me as my own father, yet whose gaze has started flickering to my chest in a way that's anything but parental.

My uneasiness blooms into thorns.

"I bought myself a present. It's cost me nearly everything." Switching off the stereo, he reaches into the pocket of his black jeans and pulls out a small, crimson box. All of a sudden, the silence is more suffocating than the music. "Would you like to see?"

He places the box next to my cocktail. There's something about the color that chains me up in a cellar again and beats me until I'm begging for mercy.

"Open it."

"I really don't want—"

"I asked you to '*open it*'," he says through gritted teeth.

His pretense drops. The thorns multiply. My hand jerks back from the stem of my cocktail glass and Grey Goose vodka and Cointreau go slopping over the sides.

With trembling fingers, I open the box to find an ornate key resting on a black velvet cushion, with an inscription engraved into the stem.

La Società Villefort.

A beat later, I'm springing up from the barstool as every memory I've fought to repress over the last month rips my clothes off and shoves me toward the entrance of a maze again.

"What the hell, Reece?"

But disbelief is a feeble emotion when the truth is handed to me.

"I trusted you! We *all* trusted you!"

"Foolish girl," he sneers. "Never trust an obsession."

An obsession?

"Where's Santi?" I whisper.

He tilts his head at me in a way that's so reminiscent of Monroe Spader that I start trembling.

"Dead."

"I don't believe you!"

"Or he will be shortly…" He glances at the clock above the bar. "Allergic reaction to the Ukrainian national dish, I believe."

I stagger backward again, desperate to find purchase as my whole world disintegrates. All the while, Reece sits perched on his barstool, legs outstretched, watching my reaction with dispassion.

How did I never see the chips of ice in his eyes?

How did I never see the lie in his charm?

"Edier?" I rasp.

"Dead, too." He shrugs. "Borscht can be brutal on the digestion."

My legs give way, and I slither to the ground. "It was a trap. It's always been a trap… You let me slip my security all those times on purpose. You let me fall into Bardi's hands intentionally."

"That was the plan."

"But why?" I feel like I'm looking through a kaleidoscope of my life and all the patterns are changing.

"You."

"Me?" I can't seem to inhale enough air into my lungs, either.

"You," he repeats, rising to his feet. "Dear Thalia, the rage I felt when Spader was allowed to have you first…" He stops to suck in his regret through his teeth as I scramble to get further and further away from him. "I watched you as you ran, as you fell, *as you killed…* This time, you're going to run the maze for me."

Lunging forward, he grabs my wrist and drags me away from the door. Flinging it open, he hurls me out onto the main gaming floor.

It's empty. Disconcertingly so. Every single patron has disappeared, leaving cards and chips strewn across the tables and their chairs overturned. All that's left is a pile of dead *sicarios* in the center of the room.

The ghost town became a ghost casino.

This can't be happening to me.

"You might want to start running now," he advises, propping himself up against the doorframe, his gun hanging loosely by his side, a wicked caricature of the man I used to believe would die to protect me. "I don't have a pack of dogs, but I have silver bullets and dark, dark urges that are going to tear your body to shreds."

Nausea burns the back of my throat. His deception is a jammed screwdriver into the mechanism that makes all my muscles work.

I'm trembling with shock.

Shivering with revulsion.

"Run!" he roars, losing his patience. "Or Lola Carrera and the bastard baby growing inside her will pay for your disobedience!" At this, he hits a button on his iPhone, and Lola's screams and pleas explode like a dirty bomb into the casino. He clicks the recording off after a couple of seconds, but it's enough to have me staggering to my feet.

"Where do you want me to run to?" I rasp, a million thoughts colliding inside my head to form a single image of the loaded gun that Santi keeps in his nightstand.

"The whole casino is your maze, tonight, Thalia." A sinister smile stretches across his face. "Forty-two floors to chase you through all night long. There's no way in, and no way out. Every escape route is locked and bolted."

"W-what do you want from me?"

But I already know. *He's already intimated*, and the truth turns my stomach to bile.

"Zaccaria offered me the world, Thalia. Not money, not power, but *you*." His hungry gaze slips to my breasts again. "This obsession," he says, his voice thickening. "It drives a man to commit madness. The day you turned sixteen, I felt the roots burrow deep. For four years, I've waited for my chance, and now it's time. You have sixty seconds before the lights go out."

"W-what," I stutter, as he turns the tables so violently, I'm dizzy from the spin.

"You were stolen from the darkness. Now, it's time to return you to where you belong."

Backing away fast, my hip collides with a roulette table, and my high heels skid in a pool of crimson. When I encounter the sweeping marble steps leading up to the lobby, I hear another gun going off in my head.

Kicking off my shoes, I turn and run.

CHAPTER
Twenty-Eight

THALIA

He kills the lights just as the stairwell door is closing behind me, plunging everything into the kind of darkness where the demon under your childhood bed dwells.

Tonight, my demon is coming out to play, and I have forty-two flights of stairs to climb to have any chance of surviving him.

There's a low whine, and then a fierce buzzing sound as Legado's generators kick in, but the ethereal red glow overhead only lasts for a few seconds, before that's shut off as well.

I have no phone.

No flashlight.

Nothing.

Panic comes crashing over me like a wave, catching me in a riptide and dragging me under—scraping my mind against memories I've fought so hard to forget.

Santi's dead.

Edier's dead.

My grief hits me like a second wave, and this time there's no resurfacing from it.

I have to keep going, though. I have to believe it's a lie. I have to find that gun, kill Reece, and try to save Lola… *That's if she's still alive.*

Blinking back the tears, I swipe blindly for a handrail—my fingers connecting with the cool metal. Inching forward, I start to climb, following the rail as it coils around the corner and up to the next flight. Misjudging the distance in the dark, I stumble, my knees hitting the floor with an agony so sharp and unexpected I can't help crying out.

Blinking back more tears, I pick myself up and keep going, finding a kind of jerky rhythm in my shallow gasps of air. My eyes are beginning to adjust. There's a small skylight up ahead, and the emerging moon is trying hard to cast light into the darkest of places.

When I reach the thirty-first floor, I pause to catch my breath. That's when I hear the soft click of a door a couple of floors below. A beat later, Lola's screams are echoing up the stairwell.

Begging.

Pleading.

The recording shuts off again abruptly, and then I hear another door slam. I take the next couple of flights at a flat run, misjudging again. Falling *again*... In my head, I'm back in that maze, but this time it's made of concrete, not yaupon holly hedges, and I'm bouncing off hard walls instead of sharp twigs that bite and scratch at my skin.

Reaching the penthouse, I stumble through the door and into Santi's lobby, feeling a rush of smooth marble underfoot. Then, I'm tripping over something soft and solid lying on the floor.

Feeling around with my fingertips, I encounter loose hair, a nose, lips... I check for a pulse but there's an ominous chill to Santi's new housekeeper's skin.

Shit, shit, shit.

The apartment is a blanket of shadow. The moon has hidden herself in fear again. Following a blueprint in my head, I feel my way down the hallway, past the living room where, once upon a time, I waited for my fiancé on my wedding day.

A man who is now dead.

Breathing through another crashing wave of grief, I reach the doorway to his bedroom, and then another spine-chilling rendition of Lola's screams are chasing after me again.

Oh, God. No.

He's in Santi's apartment.

Wrenching the nightstand drawer open, I sift blindly through all the crap, until my fingers are closing around cold, unforgiving steel.

With no time to lose, I fling myself across the bed and tuck myself into the darkest corner of the room. With shaking hands, I train the muzzle at the doorway, and then I wait.

And wait.

I hear the tick tock of a distant clock again.

I hear the heavy tread of his boots.

His labored breathing...

Tick.

Tock.

His huge outline finally appears in the doorway.

You helped kill my husband, you bastard.

I aim the muzzle at what I imagine is his head.

"I know you're in here, Thalia... I can smell your perfume, angel. I can smell your fear."

No, Reece, that's the scent of anger and revenge.

That's the scent of my shadows.

"I switched up the rules... I need to see the object of my obsession as I devour what's left of her innocence, piece by luscious piece."

There's a loud click, and then the room is an ocean of blinding white light.

I act on instinct, firing five punishingly loud rounds in his direction with my eyes shut tight. The result is a cacophony of destruction—grunts, thuds, the sounds of wood splintering, glass shattering. I don't even realize I'm screaming until I'm all out of breath and rasping Santi's name.

When I finally open my eyes, Reece is lying in his own puddle of crimson, haloed by splintered wood and plaster, his face a mask of surprise and anger.

Blinking away the last sting of the light, I jump to my feet. "Where's Lola, you son of bitch?" I say, keeping my gun trained on him.

Reece just smiles that fucking smile again, and then he's lunging for his own gun. Before he can take aim, I'm firing three more rounds and obliterating what's left of his head.

And then there's silence.

But the clock is still ticking.

Lola.

I have to find Lola...

The lights are back on. Maybe the phones are working again?

Sliding past Reece's dead body, I sprint down the hallway toward Santi's office. Bursting into the room, filling my aching lungs with that heady smell of history again, I come to a crashing stop when I see a tall figure standing in front of the wall of unsolved *Villefort* mysteries. His back is turned to me. He's wearing a black suit, and with his hands in his pockets he looks so similar to...

"Santi!" I whisper.

"Not today," comes a flat drawl.

It's a voice that beat me. Tortured me. Denied me water. *Denied me air.*

"You."

Without thinking, I squeeze the trigger again, but Lorenzo Zaccaria doesn't even flinch as I fire round after useless round of an empty barrel at him.

"I've missed you, *puttana*," he says, leveling me with the same dead eyes that haunt my nightmares. "I've enjoyed leading your husband in loops and circles this past month."

"Stay the hell away from me!" I'm still pulling the redundant trigger, over and over, praying for a stuck bullet in the magazine to miraculously work itself free.

"Put the gun down," he says in a bored voice. "You'll need to conserve all your energy for where we're going. I take it from the Wild West show down the hallway that you've killed Reece?" He clucks in frustration. "And his obsession with you was making him so much easier to manipulate. You have a nasty habit of taking out my best men, *Señora* Carrera. You'll be punished for that."

"Where's Lola?" I cry, hurling the now useless gun at his head, but he sidesteps it at the last moment, and it goes crashing into the newspaper clippings and photographs, ripping the one of him from the wall.

All the red strings lead to The Black King.

He brushes imaginary dust from his lapel and grimaces. "She's not here. She slipped through our fingers, but her time will come."

"She's safe?" I find myself daring to believe him. "But the recordings...?"

"Were taken the night I set my dogs loose on her," he finishes tersely. "I suggested Reece use them to make you more amenable to what he wished to do to you. A confused mind makes for a far more pliable body to degrade. Would you care to guess how much money I made from my maze? Hunting mafia whores is far more lucrative than hunting big game."

"You bastard!"

I turn to run and find myself staring down the barrel of a gun as one of his men blocks my exit.

A beat later, Zaccaria is fisting my hair and hurling me backward over Santi's desk. The force is so violent, I go skidding across the surface, landing in a crumpled heap on the other side. Before I can catch my breath, I'm being dragged up by my hair again and punched twice in the face—fire exploding in my left cheek, and then above my left eye socket.

"Personal, just turned *extremely* personal," he says coldly, barely out of breath, as he drags me up by my hair for a third time. "And, by God, I'm going to make you suffer. Tell my pilot to start the engines," he snaps at his man in the doorway. "We're coming straight up."

I'm being dragged along the hallway, through the lobby, past the dead body of Santi's housekeeper, and back into the stairwell. I'm too numb to speak. I'm in too much pain to resist.

"Are you ready for your night flight, *puttana*? New Jersey is far more picturesque from the sky at midnight."

"My husband—"

"Is *dead, señora*... Edier Grayson is *dead*... Your father's private jet is rigged to blow in an hour, so soon your parents and sister will be *dead*..." Each of his vicious statements is elongated with a satisfied hiss. "I've made sure there'll be no one coming to rescue you this time."

The agony I feel in that moment is indescribable. I'm hauled through another door, and then the brutal cold night air is whipping all the breath from my lungs and pinning my red dress to my aching body. We're at the top of Legado, on the edge of a huge helipad I never even know existed. There's a black helicopter waiting for us a hundred feet away, with spinning blades and a crimson key stamped on the side door.

The noise is so deafening I don't hear the whine of bullets until the man next to Zaccaria drops to the ground. I don't hear the voice of the man I believed to be dead until he's yelling out words that slice the wind to ribbons.

"Stay the fuck where you are, Zaccaria! Let her go, and I'll make it a quick death."

I'm spun around with force. A merciless arm is crushing my chest, a Beretta

APX pressed to the side of my head, but all I see is my whole world pieced back together again.

Santi's standing twenty feet behind us, framed by a backdrop of a million shining stars. There's murder in his eyes, and a gun pointing in our direction. I watch his gaze dip to the state of my face, and his expression hardens.

"What happened to Lisko?" I hear Zaccaria ask.

"He couldn't handle his fucking food," Santi snarls. "Let my wife go, Zaccaria. Last warning."

He laughs, a loud and spiteful sound that rumbles unpleasantly against my back. "She's coming with me, Carrera. I'm having a new maze built especially for her. I'm going to make her run it every day until she's begging me to let her die."

"*¡Hijo de tu puta madre!*" he roars, adjusting his grip on the gun.

"Shoot him, Santi!" I twist against Zaccaria's arm, but in this position it's like trying to wrestle my way out of an anaconda's death grip. "Don't let him take me back to hell!"

"You're not going anywhere, *muñequita*."

The love and strength in his voice makes me want to fight even harder for him.

For us.

"Remember the snow?" I scream, as a crazy idea filters in through my fear. "Ten years ago, Santi. Do you remember what you did for me?"

"Shut the fuck up, *puttana*," Zaccaria hisses, dragging me backward toward the chopper, his gun still pressed against into the side of my head.

My eyes meet my husband's. Pleading. Trusting. "Do you remember?" I repeat at a whisper, my stomach lurching when I see the faint nod as he finally understands.

This time, there's a silent countdown going on in both of our heads.

Three

Two

One

When I hit the last number, I ram my elbow as hard as I can into Zaccaria's stomach. The moment I feel his grip loosen, I'm throwing myself to the side, and knocking him off balance. A beat later, Santi's bullet is ripping into Zaccaria's chest as the Italian's returning fire is slamming into him.

I scream again as I watch my husband go down.

Wrenching myself free, I half run, half crawl my way to where Santi is lying. There's a red stain spreading out across his white shirt. "Oh my God!" I whimper.

"Thalia," he hisses, sweeping aside my escalating panic as he slams his gun into the palm of my hand. "This is our one chance, *muñequita*. Don't let him get away."

Glancing over, I watch Zaccaria climbing across the back seat as the helicopter's landing skids start to lift from the helipad. In that moment, I see all the women he's hurt. *I see all the women he's going to hurt.*

Gripping the gun, I rise up from the ground.

I rise up from my ashes.

"Do it, *muñequita*."

I lift the gun and take aim, firing eight rounds at the tail rotor, and then watching as the helicopter veers violently off to one side, billowing gray smoke and flames. The moment it disappears from view, once gravity has taken her final savage shot, I'm flinging the gun away and turning back to Santi.

He's on his feet again and clutching at his shoulder.

"Don't tell Grayson, but your aim is better than his," he says through gritted teeth.

Five more steps and I'm back in his arms. I'm back in the only place I want to be.

"This birthday sucks," I mumble into his neck.

"Give me a week in a hospital, and I'll make it up to you."

"If I give you a lifetime, will you give me yours?"

He catches my mouth in a rough kiss that tastes of our future.

I kiss him back with one that tastes of shadows and stars.

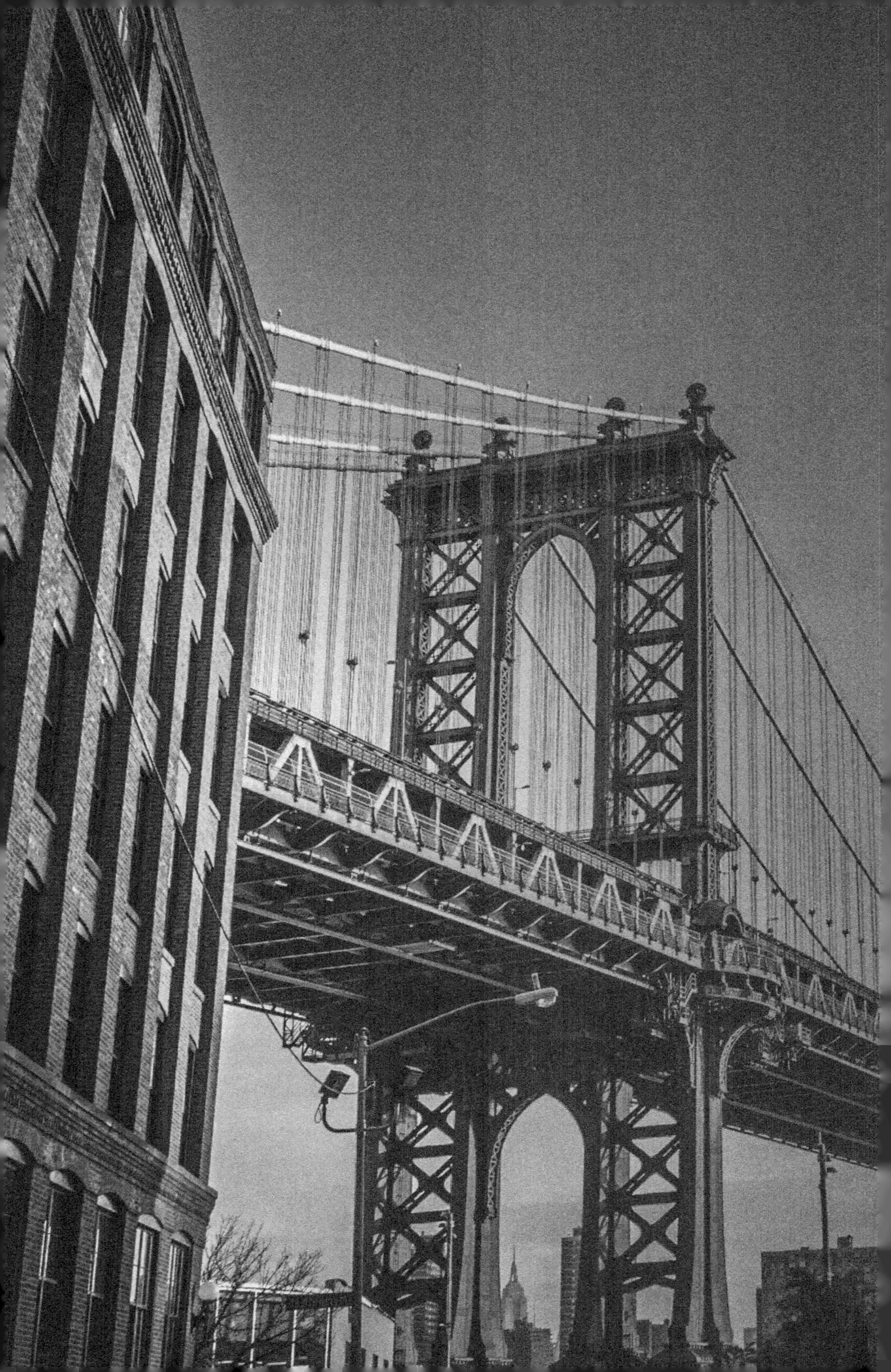

EPILOGUE

SANTI
One Year Later

They say when you find yourself standing at the end, return to the beginning. I remember thinking those exact words the night my world darkened, and my greatest sin became my ultimate salvation. With that in mind, it seems only fitting to bind our hearts in the same place that first breathed life into them.

A place where a snow angel showed me the meaning of courage.

The small vestibule at the back of Sacred Heart Church is draped in silence, and for the first time since Thalia entered my life, I chase it instead of running from it.

My request for solitude isn't a regression. It's a leap forward, stemming from a need to embrace the peace it offers rather than the loneliness.

Unbuttoning my tuxedo jacket, I lean back in my chair and slowly flip a quarter between my fingers, watching as fate is decided with the turn of a coin.

I'm so focused I barely register the door opening. Even then, I don't have to look up to know who's there. My father's presence can suffocate a room, just as quickly as command it.

"What are you doing?" he asks, coming to stand beside me.

"Thinking about something Lola said."

"Dangerous waters," he notes dryly, but I hear the amusement in his voice as he slides his hands in the pockets of his tuxedo pants.

I chuckle, my gaze still on the quarter. "It was last year, when Thalia asked for distance..." I explain, my brief smile fading. "But men like us aren't wired to back away as much as smother." Exhaling a rough breath, I close my fist around the coin. "Letting go tested my strength more than any bullet. Remembering the talk I had with Lola back then got me thinking about everything."

"Everything?" he repeats. "That's quite an extensive topic."

"*La Boda Roja*," I clarify. "The war with the Santiagos, my ambition, crossing paths with Thalia... I asked Lola if she'd ever considered if all of it was somehow predetermined. That it was only a matter of time before the two sides blurred and it stopped being heads or tails"—looking up, I meet his intrigued gaze—"and just became one coin."

He leans back against an antique desk to consider this, and once again, I note how similar we are. It's not just our matching tuxedos—simple, understated, and very un-Carrera-like. It's in the stubborn set of our jaws. The mirrored mannerisms. The slicked back dark hair, forced into submission to present an air of authority.

His choice not to sit down next to me isn't a power play, and for once in our relationship, I don't bristle at it. After forging a truce with our enemy, we forged our own. I'm no longer the heir fighting for his name. I'm the son who shares it with a willing king.

"What did she say?" he asks eventually.

"She said she didn't think war fated love. She believed love ended it.'"

Twenty years of hate and vengeance condensed in a piece of sage wisdom I've never forgotten. Priceless in its simplicity.

Frowning, I toss the quarter onto the desk beside him. "Which makes me wonder why it took decades of death and destruction to uncover such a simple truth. Why—"

"Why the sins of the fathers rested at the feet of the children to cleanse and rebuild," he finishes, without hesitation.

Today is meant for love and celebration, not for exorcising demons, so instead of expanding on all the "what-ifs" clouding my head, I nod.

"Something like that."

My father falls quiet again, the words hanging heavy between us. Removing his hands from his pockets, he clasps them at his chest and presses the pads of his thumbs together. "I've always taught you to never question what *is*, Santi—but to mold it into what you want. However, you and your sister aren't just Carreras.

You're Lacheys, and Lacheys question *everything*."

Now it's my turn to slide my hands in my pockets, the subtle humor in his tone when speaking about my mother curving my lips.

"Lacheys challenge what *is*, in order to create 'what can be.' Hate fights for dominance, but only love can share it." Rising to his feet, he claps a hand on my shoulder. "I didn't teach you that, Santi. You've taught me."

It's a concession I never expected to hear. Valentin Carrera doesn't accept defeat graciously, and he rarely admits fault.

My chest swells with honor. "*Gracias, pápa.*"

"They're about to start," he says, nodding toward the closed door. "Take a moment, reflect, and then get your ass to the altar. You have a bride to remarry."

Where this time around, he'll be standing beside me.

"You know, originally, a groom's best man was tasked with kidnapping the bride from her home." I laugh.

A devilish smile spreads across his face. "A mission you accomplished all on your own. You don't need my help doing anything, Santi. You've built your own legacy."

I smile to myself, counting his footsteps as they cross the room, only to stop at the door.

"Oh, and Santi?"

Glancing over my shoulder, I collide with that familiar, proud gaze.

"Thalia's heart may bear the Carrera name, but her soul will always be a Santiago." At the strain on my face, his perpetual stony expression softens. "A combination befitting a future queen. I look forward to getting to know both sides."

As he closes the door behind him, I pick up the coin and toss it in the air.

Heads.

Five minutes later, I'm still thinking about the impact of his words.

Thalia walked into my casino looking for a way to cheat darkness, only to find me—a man firmly entrenched in his own, framed by a hate I held so sacred. We've overcome obstacles that not many could survive. But the night she was ripped from my arms, forced vows became sworn ones.

Eleven years ago, I sacrificed my loyalty for her innocence.

A year ago, she sacrificed her innocence for my loyalty.

Today, we sacrifice the past for the promise of our future.

The sanctuary of Sacred Heart Church is nowhere near capacity. After everything that's happened in the last year, Thalia and I both wanted our second wedding to be intimate and more importantly, *contained*. Outside, the perimeter of the church is fortified by a double wall of armed Carrera and Santiago *sicarios*.

We're starting a new chapter, not trying to flip back to the prologue.

The interior has changed since the last time I was here. Today, it's bowing to a new era—pristine and unblemished by the violence inflicted on it by two warring families.

My father stands silent but proudly by my side at the altar, with RJ positioned on his left. As I wait for the back doors to open, I glance across to where Ella Santiago stands in her simple red silk maid of honor gown, with a soft smile and wise eyes. Just behind her stands my sister in a matching dress, but with a different kind of a smile. She's also fucking telepathic, judging by the way she's staring at me.

I don't know what possesses me, but I hold her gaze and mouth, *"Thank you."*

Lola's smile brightens as she mouths back, *"You're welcome."*

A wet gurgle from the front row causes a ripple of soft laughter, cutting the tension. Shifting my gaze, my own smile tugs my lips as I watch my niece reach up with both hands, grab her father's lower lip, and twist the fuck out of it. Unfazed, he pretends to bite down on her tiny fingers, earning himself another giggle.

Sam Sanders will never be my favorite person, but the bastard is one hell of a father. Beside him, Edier Grayson sits with one eye on the future, and his heart in the past, from what Thalia's intimated.

When the organ plays the first notes of the bridal march, everyone stands, eyes turned toward the back of the church.

I thought I was ready.

I was wrong.

When the double doors open, and Thalia takes her first step inside the sanctuary, it's like I'm seeing her for the first time, all over again. The same pressure squeezes my chest. The same punch hits my gut. When she walked into my office a year ago, she was a beautiful woman. Tonight, she's a goddess.

Her gown is white, but it's a concession I had no problem in making. Some traditions have their value, but it's the red roses woven into her veil that hold my attention the most.

Mi reina roja.

My red queen.

When her eyes meet mine, I see the same fire that captivated me the moment we first met. Taking her father's arm, they walk in perfect sync up the aisle, before coming to a stop three steps below the altar.

Santiago's face is unreadable as he turns to me. "Don't fuck it up, Carrera," he says dryly. "I still have a bullet with your name on it."

"*Pápa*," Thalia hisses.

Giving him a curt nod, I fight back a smirk. That's as close to an approval by Dante Santiago as it gets.

Turning to his daughter, he kisses her lightly on the cheek. "Beautiful, *mija*." Then, placing her hand in mine, he takes his seat in the front pew beside his wife, Eve.

"Been waiting for someone, Carrera?" Thalia teases me softly.

"Are you waiting for someone?"

They're the same words she spoke to me eleven years ago, standing knee-deep in snow outside these church walls. Back then, I thought she was innocent and brave—two qualities I still see in her—only now there's a third: *strength*.

"Only you, *muñequita*," I murmur. "I've only ever waited for you."

Receptions aren't for the bride and groom.

If it were up to Thalia and me, we'd already be locked inside our penthouse having our kind of fun on every redecorated surface. But to appease both our families, I had Legado's grand ballroom turned into a display of extravagance and excess.

I agreed to a simplistic wedding, not to a subdued celebration.

"We're magicians," Thalia says with a sigh, surveying the room.

"How do you figure that, *Señora* Carrera?" I ask, my fingers tracing the delicate dip between her shoulder blades.

I feel her shiver with longing as she motions with her champagne flute. "This is the first time in twenty years that all these people have been in the same room. It's either magic, or the power of alcohol."

I laugh, moving my fingers lower. "Maybe it's a little of both."

She's right. Family members from both cartels crowd around tables as if two vows just evaporated twenty years of bad blood. Grayson's parents sit at a table talking to Senator Sanders and his wife, Nina, while RJ's parents, my *Tío* Brody and *Tía* Adriana, hover by the bar with my father's second in command, Mateo, his wife Leighton, and my cousin, Stella.

As I down my fourth glass of champagne, my mother and father stride toward us, their pace hurried. Before I can brace myself, my mother throws herself into my arms, tears brimming her eyes.

"I'm so proud of you *mijo*," she whispers in my ear. "I always knew no matter what happened, no matter how deep the waters were where you fell, you'd always keep swimming."

They're the parting words she left me with when I left Mexico at eighteen to take over the world.

Ones I've never forgotten.

"*Gracias, máma.*"

Pulling away, she dabs at her eyes before turning to Thalia. "Welcome to the family, again, Thalia. We're proud to *officially* have you as a part of it." Holding her smile in place, she elbows my father, who darts an amused gaze at her before facing my wife.

"*Sí*," he echoes, a new respect in those hardened eyes. "*Tu eres familia*, Thalia."

You are family.

Three words weighted with meaning. The last time we were all together, he treated her as the enemy. In his way, it's an unspoken apology.

Thalia blushes, the impact of the moment hitting her just as heavily.

The sound of forks clanging in unison against dozens of glasses breaks the moment.

My mother gives me a knowing smile. "I believe it's time for your first dance, *Señor* and *Señora* Carrera."

And not a moment too soon.

Guiding my wife to the lowly lit dance floor, I take her in my arms, her nails lightly grazing my cheek in warning when I catch sight of Rosalia Marchesi out of the corner of my eye.

"What the fuck is *she* doing here?"

"I invited her."

"I thought you didn't want bloodshed?"

"Considering she's the reason, Lola and I didn't shed more than we did in Italy, I didn't think it'd be a problem." When I stiffen at the memory, she sighs. "Relax, Santi. Rosalia's here with her family." Arching an eyebrow, she directs my attention to a table of silent Marchesis. "As of right now, they're still our allies."

"The night is young, *mi amada*," I warn. "And RJ is still sober."

"This tension between you two needs to stop."

"It will, when he remembers the oath he made to this family, instead of making new ones..." I say, referring to Rosalia's own impending nuptials—an event that has sent my cousin into a spiral of strained silence and solitude. He's not talking to anyone these days, which in my line of work is a red flag. One that's about to get a bullet shot through it.

"Tread carefully, Santi…"

"If you insist." I spin her around, until all I see is her. "I just ended one fucking war. I don't feel like starting another one."

"That war is over. We're bound. Julieta ties us." Her serene smile directs to the edge of the dance floor where *máma* and Sanders's stepmother are cooing over my niece.

"I love Julieta, but she doesn't tie us, Thalia," I say, bending my head to brush my lips across her jaw. "She's a Sanders, not a Santiago. A permanent link needs Carrera and Santiago blood."

I feel her smile before I see it. "Then I guess we have some work to do."

The heat in her eyes causes mine to combust. "I'll have you pregnant tonight," I promise darkly, dipping her low. "I thought you wanted to wait?"

"Big words, Carrera… And maybe I'm open to persuasion these days."

"You should know by now, *muñequita*. I always get what I want."

Thalia throws her head back with a husky laugh, and I start counting down the minutes until I can make good on my promise and have her begging for mercy.

An hour later, only the dying embers of the reception remain. Most guests have departed, and I'm done waiting. I'm done with all the fucking goodbyes. Sweeping my wife off her feet, I carry her and her giggling protestations off toward the elevator. The moment the doors close, I'm taking her mouth in a violent kiss that shuts her up in the best possible way.

Stepping into our penthouse, I carry her across the lobby and into the living room where I finally lower her to the floor, just so I can trap her up against the window. Up here, looking out at the world with the woman I love in my arms, I feel like a god—one who stacked the odds, and beat his own destiny.

Some say that life is a game of chance where the deck is shuffled from birth and a single card is dealt that decides our fate. My father says that a man makes his own luck, though how far we push for that elusive "twenty-one" depends on how much is at stake, and how much we're willing to risk in order to win.

For Thalia, I risked it all, and in the end, love won.

Keep reading for more from Santi and Thalia...

BONUS
Chapters

AUTHOR NOTE

Dear Reader,

After releasing the Corrupt Gods duet, the most frequently asked question we received from readers was, *"but what happened after the truce?"*

At that time, the simple answer was…*to be continued…* However, in the middle of compiling this collection, Santi and Thalia decided they weren't quite finished with us yet.

We started writing this bonus material with the intention of giving our readers an exclusive second epilogue to Tainted Blood, but as usual, these characters had other plans.
Nearly ten thousand words later, we give you, "A Very Cartel Christmas…"

Feliz Navidad…

xoxo,

Cora and Catherine

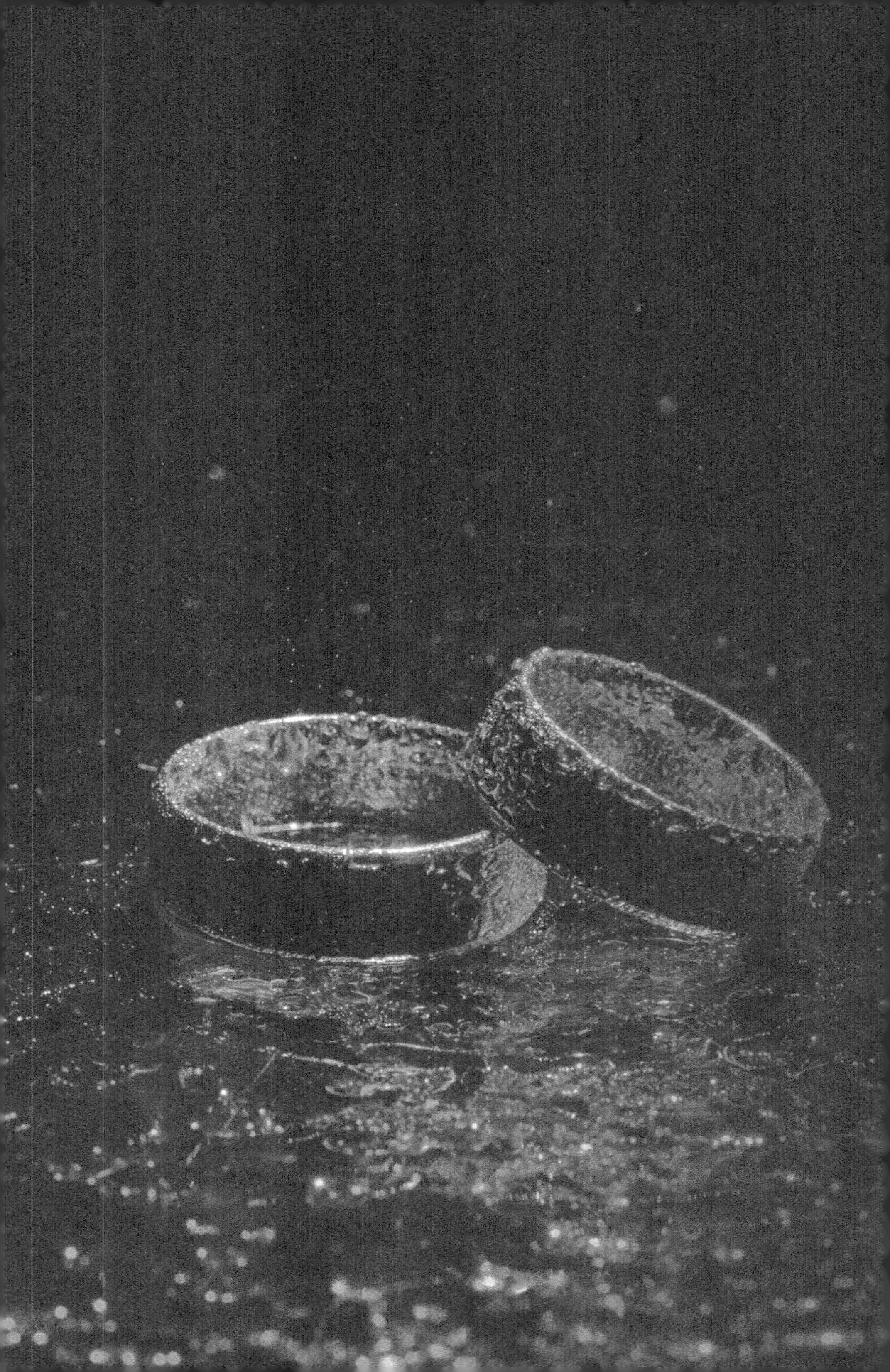

CHAPTER One

THALIA
Three Months Later

"Why does a family event always feel like I'm holding a fucking gun to my head?"

"Santi, it's Christmas," I plead, catching his eye in my dresser mirror as he stalks out of the walk-in closet, slamming the door behind him. "Can we, maybe, leave the gun talk alone for twenty-four hours?"

"Not when Santiago's in town." He stops behind me, his tall shadow falling over my dresser counter like a second threat.

"All that bad blood is in the past now," I remind him gently.

"Is it?"

Stifling a smile, I fix the first of the exquisitely cut diamond earrings he's just gifted me as an early Christmas present to my left earlobe. Marriage to him is like living with a holiday advent calendar, with each new day bringing me a new understanding of the man I love—which is how I can tell that beneath his usual "cool and caustic" he's edgy as hell.

Three guesses why...

"You ready?"

"Nearly." I switch to my other lobe, taking my sweet time about it because I'm having too much fun watching the steel bars of his composure crumble.

We haven't had many opportunities to see my parents since the wedding. Santi's empire expansion in Manhattan is taking up all his time, and my recent promotion to Project Leader at the NGO I work for has been keeping me super busy, as well.

"Christ, Thalia... Want any help with that?"

His irritation is like a coiled spring. Any minute now, he's going to explode.

"No, thank you." I place the empty jewelry box next to my perfume bottle and start lining it up neatly with my make-up brushes.

"You're doing this shit on purpose, *muñequita*."

"I don't know what you're talking about," I say, batting my lashes at him.

"Your call. But I'm warning you... One sarcastic comment from your father about how late we are, and I'll be holding my gun to his fucking head instead." He reels away from the dresser and stalks back over to the full-length mirror. To add emphasis to his threat, he slides his Glock into his holster and straightens the lapels of his black suit jacket.

"I know you didn't just mean that," I call out after him.

There's a pause. "Didn't I?"

"Play nice," I warn, "or you won't be receiving your gift from me later."

"So you're the one blackmailing *me* now?" He turns to sweep hungry, dark eyes over my elegant, red silk cocktail dress. "You look sensational, by the way. Fuck it. Let's blow everyone off, head straight to the airport, and spend our first Christmas together naked in the Caribbean."

Tempting... But I have a big secret to share, and I can't put it off for much longer. It has to be tonight. In New Jersey. With all our family present to minimize the bloodstains.

Or cover the walls...

"Not this time, Santi." I shake my head, my new earrings sparkling in the soft lights of our bedroom. "Everyone is downstairs waiting for us. If we bail, we'll regret it. My sister is already five drinks down because Edier has shown up with someone else's wife. Besides," I add, shooting him a look, "you've already risked bombs and bullets for me. Making polite small talk with my father will be a breeze after that."

"Not if we hit a verbal brick wall after ten seconds. There are only so many times you can ask how the fucking weather is in the middle of the Pacific."

"Maybe you should've thought about that before you forced me to marry you."

"*Maybe* you should have checked yourself before walking into the lion's den looking like my favorite meal." His scowl softens for a split-second, and I'm mesmerized. Santi's sharp edges will never be blunted, but these rare moments when he gives me a glimpse of just how much he loves me are *everything*.

"I love you, too," I say softly, reaching for my mascara wand.

His dark eyes glint. "I don't remember giving you a choice, but it brought me a whole lot of trouble in the process."

"Divorce me, then," I challenge, ignoring a vicious green wave of jealousy inside. "Make your life simple. Find some sweet, obedient girl who will serve you a healthy, home-cooked meal when you come home from a hard day of death, depravity, and torture."

"You sound like it's an option, *muñequita*." Cocking an eyebrow, he prowls back over to where I'm sitting in front of the dresser. Leaning down, he presses a palm to the base of my throat and brings his face level with mine. "*Never*," he adds with such savage finality it makes my heart flutter. He meets my eyes in the mirror again, the corners of his mouth lifting when he feels the nervous glide as I swallow. "Not even if you dropped to your knees, opened that pretty mouth wide, and begged me to."

My breath catches.

These dangerous games we play.

I live for them, for us, for everything we are and make together.

"Oh, Santi…" I sigh, reaching around to place my hand on his cock. "If I dropped to my knees, you wouldn't be able to deny me *anything*."

"Shall we put it to the test?" His eyes are gleaming with hot temptation now, making the pulse between my thighs throb.

"*After* this evening," I say firmly, and he pulls away from me with a curse. "It's only one night," I soothe, watching him drag his hand through his black hair in agitation. "Think of it as a game of ever-decreasing numbers. Fifty-six close friends and family to entertain, twenty-four varieties of canapé dishes, many, *many* expensive bottles of wine… You could always drink your way through it." Rising to my feet, I take two steps toward the closet to grab my purse and find myself swept up in his arms.

"*Señora Carrera*," he murmurs, dragging his stubble across my cheek, marking me, as he grinds his erection against my ass. "There isn't enough wine in my cellar to spin this evening into a good time. There's always this, though…" Catching the hem of my dress, he drags the silky material up my thigh and trails his fingers lightly over the heat of my pussy, making me gasp. "Give me your tongue," he orders, spinning me around.

"Don't be so demanding," I whisper, feeling his fingers slip inside my damp panties. Throwing my hands around his neck, I breathe in his rich, sinister scent of spice and cedarwood—the one that never fails to make my knees weak, anyway.

"Give me your fucking tongue, *muñequita*," he repeats, driving a brutal finger inside me without warning and forcing a helpless whimper from my lips. "Or I guarantee you won't be enjoying *all* the consequences for defying me."

"You're a bastard." Tipping my head back, I dig my fingernails into his shoulders. *Every day of our marriage is revelatory to him, too.* He knows I can't resist him when he's all bossy and dominant like this. "You never play fair, do you, Santi? Even now."

"Why the hell should I?" He pushes me backward onto our bed with a dark chuckle. "Did you forget what kind of man I am, *mi amada*?"

"I know exactly what kind of man you are, Santi Carrera," I say, my elbows digging into the white sheets as I open my legs wide for him, showing him just how much I want him. *How much I'll always want him.*

"Tell me." His eyes never leave my panties as he removes his jacket and gun holster before tugging at the perfectly tied black tie and tossing it on the floor.

"I know all about your scars and how they ache for me. I know how your black heart bleeds only red for me. You're the kind of man I call my husband."

With a hiss of approval, he follows me down, his huge frame forcing my legs even wider, his belt buckle brushing against my clit—eliciting another gasp from my lips.

Trapping my chin between his fingers, he slams his mouth onto mine, filling my senses with the burning heat and taste of him.

After a beat, he breaks away, his lips peeled back into a snarl. "If you ever mention the word 'divorce' to me again, I'll fuck you so hard, you'll forget everything but my name."

"Divorce," I gasp out as he reaches between us for his zipper. "Divorce, divorce, divorce…"

I'm still saying the word as he's ripping my panties down my thighs and then driving his cock inside me, making good on his threat.

"Fuck, Thalia," I hear him groan out as he hooks my knees over his shoulders and shoves in so deep there isn't a single part of me left untainted by him. I barely have time to catch my breath before he's driving me to the brink of my first orgasm with several brutal thrusts. "I will never stop wanting this. You…us."

"Us," I echo, thinking about my secret again as I pull him even closer.

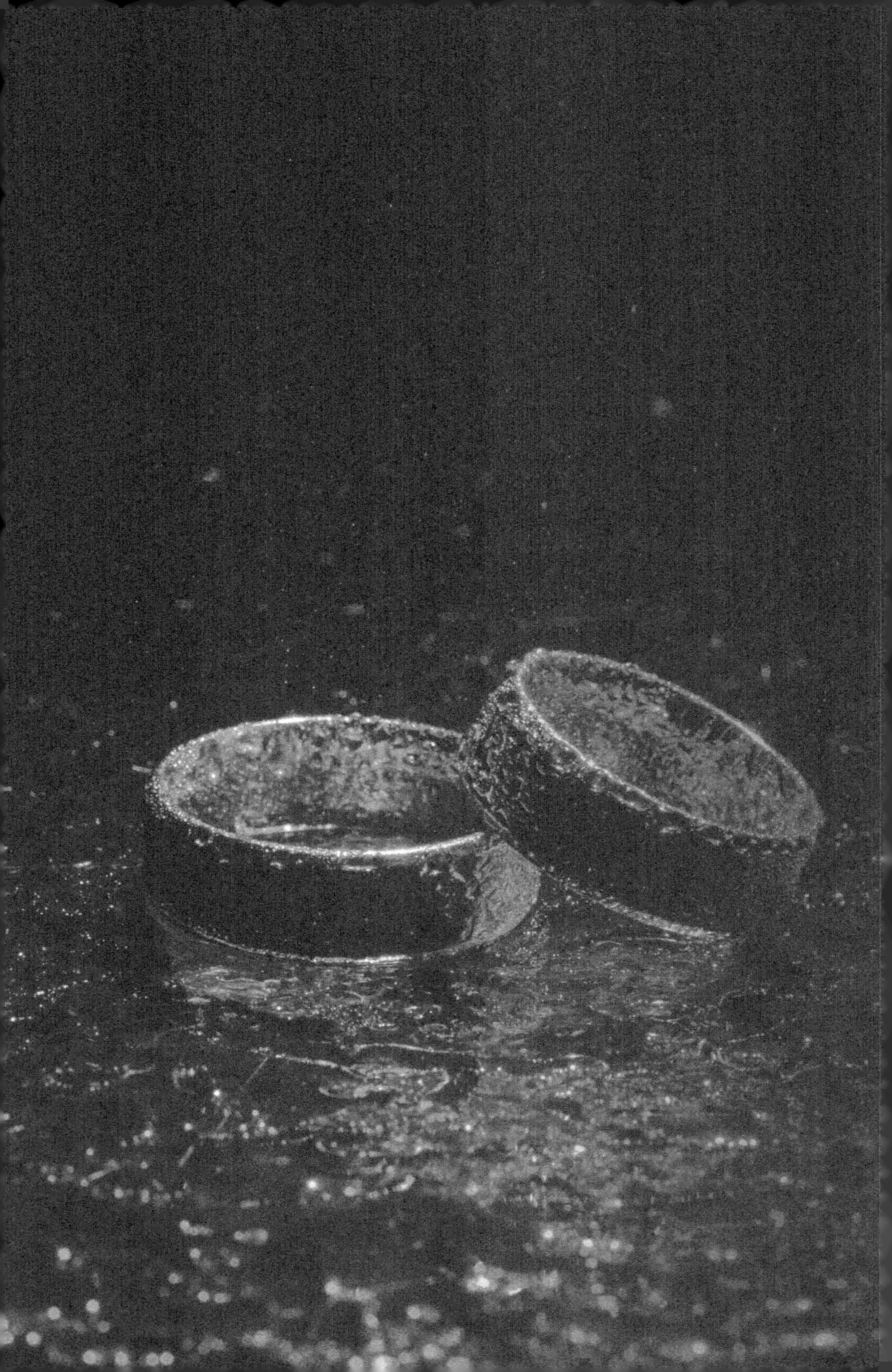

CHAPTER Two

THALIA

"I wish you'd let me change my outfit." I tug at the crumpled red silk as the elevator doors slide open. "I look like a hot mess."

"Bullshit." Santi exits the carriage first, before reaching back inside to grab my hand and drag me out after him. "You look perfect. Nothing says 'mine' like my wife wearing a dress stained with my cum."

I burst out laughing at this. "I think the whole world has gotten that memo already, Santi."

He smirks.

I melt.

"Doesn't hurt to repeat it." He drops my hand to trail his fingers down my spine.

"I can't decide if you're a neanderthal or a misogynist," I ponder, brushing his hand away.

"I'll be whatever you want me to be. Twenty minutes ago, you made me come so hard my balls are still aching."

I open my mouth for another smart retort and find myself full of him instead.

"Where's my Christmas gift?" he growls, breaking the kiss first.

"I told you to play nice," I whisper, pressing my palm to his jaw, amazed at how I could've hated him so much once, when all I see now is my future. "If you behave, you get lucky. Simple as that."

He blows out an impatient breath. "Let's get this fucking carnage over with then."

He strides toward the Platinum Bar, his hand pressed tight to the small of my back in another gesture of possession.

As we reach the doors, Lola comes sauntering out dressed to kill in an Alexander McQueen original, an off-the-shoulder, black lace corset gown that hugs her every curve.

She looks phenomenal, and I can't help but wonder…

Will I look that good after having a baby?

"*Feliz Navidad*, Carreras." She folds her brother into her arms. "Remember, you can't kill close relatives at this time of the year. It's against the rules."

He stiffens. "Fuck the rules. What the hell have you done?"

"Well…you know when you said you wanted the decorations to be low-key…"

"*Chaparrita*," he snarls. "If you've turned my casino bar into a goddamn winter wonderland—"

"It will be tasteful and festive, and Santi will be very grateful," I interrupt firmly.

Smiling, Lola flashes me a secret wink. "It's not so much 'baby brain' as 'motherhood mush' at this time of the year," she confides. "I'm on a crash course with Rudolph. Everything *has* to be perfect for Julieta's first Christmas."

"And it will be," I assure her, catching a flash of white and silver through the open doors.

Is that fake snow in there?

"Thank you, Thalia." She leans over to kiss my cheek. "At least *someone* in the family appreciates good taste."

"I appreciate her taste in men," Santi says sharply.

"Debatable when you see who she's married to," a voice drawls as Sam emerges from the bar, trailed by a stunningly beautiful girl who can't be more than seventeen or eighteen.

It's her eyes that captivate me the most.

They're old eyes.

Damaged eyes.

Angry at the universe eyes.

Her short black dress has three slashes across her cleavage, like a tiger's claw has swiped at it, but somehow it doesn't cheapen her. If anything, it's a warning.

"Side pieces aren't invited, Sanders." Santi gives her a brief once over, making that green wave of jealousy crash into my heart again. It's completely irrational. Santi would *never* touch another woman, but even so, I can't help myself.

"Don't be such a dick." Lola rolls her eyes at him before turning to the young girl. "Tatiana, meet my brother. Brother, meet Sam's half-sister."

I'm shocked. "Tatiana! Wow, I didn't recognize you!"

It's been four years since I last saw her. Back then, she was an awkward kid who spent more time in her bedroom than at the center of everyone's attention. As Senator Sanders's daughter, she was never going to be sweet and innocent forever, but there was an endearing lightness about her that I'd hoped was ingrained—a fragile sense of self beneath all the shy blushes.

What the hell happened?

"Thalia." She bridges the gap between us with over-confident strides and brushes her ice-cold lips against my cheek. "Nice to see you again."

"When did you grow up?" I muse, still reeling from the transformation.

Her smile stops right before it unfurls, freezing somewhere between a grimace and indifference.

"Turns out, I didn't have a choice."

I catch Sam's eye over her shoulder, but he doesn't seem to notice the complete one-eighty in his sister. *How can he not see the layers beneath her perfect tan skin that are ripped and bruised?*

"Sorry I missed your wedding," she says in a bored voice, turning to Santi.

"We survived," he says, with equal disinterest.

She looks him up and down like he's roadkill. "So I can see."

Shit.

"Have you, um, started college, Tatiana?" I ask, taking a hasty step between them. I've seen what my husband can do to those who don't respect him.

"Dropped out two weeks ago." She swings that weird, vacant gaze back to me. "I work full time at my mom's art gallery in Manhattan now."

"Sounds good."

"Are you going to give me a lecture about it, too?" she snaps, misreading my expression. "Because every other person in here seems to want to."

"Not everyone," Santi murmurs, moving past us toward the bar. "Some of us couldn't give a flying fuck. So nice to see your winning personality is a family trait, Sanders," he calls out to Sam over his shoulder.

Lola shoots Sam a warning look, and for once he keeps his mouth shut.

"Hey, I dropped out of college, too," I say, touching Tatiana's arm in a clumsy gesture of camaraderie.

She sees through it right away.

"Is that supposed to be a pep-talk?" She yanks her arm back. "You're such a great role model, *Thalia*," she adds, spitting my name at me. "If we all lived our lives according to you, we can look forward to marrying a criminal next."

For a brief moment her blue eyes flare with tears, and then she's storming back toward the bar herself.

CHAPTER
Three

SANTI

M y stride comes to a dead stop. Shooting my hand out, I clamp it firmly around Tatiana's wrist as she passes, causing her determined pace to falter. "Apologize."

Her chin snaps up. "Excuse me?"

"You heard me."

Behind us, Thalia takes a hesitant step forward. "Santi…"

I hold up my other hand to silence her. She may have taught me many things in our short time together, but tolerance isn't one of them. Not when it comes to someone questioning the integrity of my fucking queen.

"Thalia is my wife, *Tatiana*," I say, biting out the unpleasant taste of her name. "And no one disrespects her."

"Go to hell," she hisses, but she's not so brave underneath the prom bitch veneer. Her eyes are glistening, and she's trembling like a leaf.

"Eventually," I murmur. "However, the road leading there is paved with what's left of my enemies, Miss Sanders. If you prefer not to be one of them, I suggest you back the fuck up and take another path."

She glances over at her brother. "Aren't you going to do something?"

"Like what?" he says coldly. "Jump start the connection between your brain and your mouth?"

"Some brother you are." Her dark gaze glides across the four of us. Finding nothing but silence, she clenches her jaw and grits out a smile. "My apologies, *Señora* Carrera," she says tightly. "I hope you enjoy your party."

I lift an eyebrow as she spins around and disappears into the mingling crowd. "Is that girl a problem, Sanders?"

"Maybe, but she's not yours to handle." He presses a light kiss to Lola's temple. "I think I'll go make sure my stepfather hasn't corrupted Julieta already."

From the doorway, I watch, silently, as he makes his way to a far corner of the bar where Senator Sanders, a man who rules Capitol Hill like a legal underground, cradles my niece in his arms as if she's a delicate piece of fine china.

There are no battle lines when it comes to Julieta. While he wouldn't hesitate to put a bullet between my eyes, I have no doubt he'd take a whole gun's worth for that little girl.

It makes me wonder about the other branch of this twisted family tree.

Would Thalia's father look at our child the same way?

Could he see past his hangups with the guilty in order to love the innocent?

I shelve those thoughts as I take a sweeping glance around, finally registering the Christmas clusterfuck that used to be my casino bar. At the same time, there's another hushed *"uh-oh"* from my wife behind me.

I'm familiar with the phrase "when hell freezes over," but I've never witnessed it… *Until now.* The place is drenched in fake snow, gaudy silver tinsel, and enough LED lights to cause an entire Tri-State blackout.

"What do you think?" Lola asks proudly.

Gritting my teeth, I glare at my smiling sister out of the corner of my eye. "What happened to 'tasteful and festive'?"

Shrugging, she taps her finger against a blinking glitter snowflake. "Well, it's, *um*, festive…"

"It looks like someone took a hammer to a fucking disco ball."

"Santi…" Thalia warns softly.

Lola's bright smile fades. "You hate it."

I don't necessarily hate it as much as… *Okay, yeah, I fucking hate it.* This is mine and Thalia's first Christmas as husband and wife. I wanted her bathed in elegance and lavished by excess. Instead, my sister has turned my upscale holiday soirée into Frosty the Snowman's yuletide yeehaw.

It's on the tip of my tongue to tell her as much when I catch the eye of the most important woman in the world.

My wife's narrowed stare dares me to insult Lola's decorative disaster. The old Santi wouldn't have thought twice about speaking his mind. However, that man perished inside a dark cellar in Italy. The one who took his place was forced to learn patience and tolerance.

To know which battles to fight.

And which to let pass.

"It's perfectly...*shiny*," I say, baring my teeth. "Thank you, *chaparrita*."

Lola beams. "You were right," she says, tossing Thalia another conspiratorial wink. "He isn't as much of an asshole as he used to be."

My gaze snaps toward my wife. "Is that right?" I move closer, lowering my voice as I press my mouth against her ear. "Maybe a trip back upstairs will remind you just what kind of 'asshole' I can still be." Thalia shivers as I add, "The *only* one you get on your knees for."

"Santi," she groans, tipping her head to the side to give me full access to her neck. I'm about to take full advantage when her eyes flutter open, then widen. "Holy shit, is that a diamond?" Slipping from my grasp, Thalia grabs Lola's left hand and brings it to her face for inspection. "Oh my God, are you engaged?"

Lola catches sight of my expression, her cheeks paling.

Well, this night just gets better and better.

"*Chaparrita*..." I warn.

She scrunches up her nose. "Kind of..."

"How does one 'kind of' get engaged?"

Lola sighs. "Look, he asked me this morning, but there's no need for theatrics. We're doing this whole thing backward anyway, so tradition isn't exactly a priority. We have a baby, and we're already living together. A piece of paper making it legal isn't a big deal."

Thalia whistles. "Maybe not, but that rock sure as hell is."

She isn't kidding. I'm no expert, but it's at least six, maybe seven carats. Reflected off the right light, the damn thing could lead wayward ships to shore.

"Sam went a little overboard," Lola admits, rubbing her thumb across the massive diamond.

"Business must be good across the bridge."

"Don't act like you and Edier haven't played the good cop bad cop routine while razing the East Coast, Santi," she says pointedly. "That whole 'we hate each other' schtick won't hold weight after the—"

"Bruschetta!" Thalia exclaims, swiping two pieces of tomato covered crostini from a passing waiter's tray. Shoving one in Lola's mouth, she glares at her while quietly nibbling on the other.

"Champagne, *señor*?" the waiter asks.

I'd prefer a strong shot of *Añejo* tequila, but right now, I'd accept a glass of bourbon from the devil himself. Between insolent political progeny gate-crashing my party and my sister turning my casino into a decorative thrift store, alcohol really is the only thing that's going to get me through this night.

"*Gracias.*" Taking two flutes from the tray, I hand one to Lola, catching her curious gaze as I extend the other toward Thalia, who stares at it like it's liquid poison.

Mumbling a muffled "thank you," she grips the stem as I take my own glass.

Something isn't right.

"Thalia, what the hell is—?"

"My parents are here!" she exclaims, a curious blend of relief and anxiety swirling across her face. I follow her gaze to where my father-in-law is shadowing up the main bar, his lethal glare trained on me.

Because I'm a bastard who enjoys getting a rise out of him, I lift my champagne flute and dip my chin.

A benevolent gesture to anyone else.

A shot fired at the man in black.

I'm not surprised when his hand strays toward his inside pocket. I'd expect nothing less. His hot-headed reaction only cools when Eve touches his arm.

Thalia sighs. "I wish you wouldn't antagonize him like that."

"I was simply welcoming him to our party, *muñequita*."

"Maybe try saying 'hello' next time, instead of giving him the silent bullets. Eventually, you two are going to have to learn to be in the same room without the rest of us holding our breath. If not for me, then for…" Her voice trails off.

My gaze snaps to where Thalia worries her lip. "For what?"

There's a beat of silence, and then she turns, pressing a hand to my chest with a private smile. "Later."

I grab her wrist to stop her leaving. "I'm not a patient man, *muñequita*."

"Some things are worth the wait."

The gleam in her eyes sends fire up my spine. It's the taunt in her sultry tone, heavy with promise, that makes me bite back the instinct to force a confession out of her.

She's wrong, though. *Some* things aren't worth the wait.

Only one.

Her.

"Well, *I'm* going to go say 'hello.'" Thalia presses a soft, calming kiss to my cheek. "Try not to cause too much destruction while I'm gone."

"She's acting strange," I mutter to Lola, while watching her leave.

Lola waves her hand. "It's normal."

"What's normal?"

Her lashes flutter for a moment before she sputters, "Being the daughter of a kingpin and the wife of his former enemy." She narrows her eyes. "Why? What did *you* think I meant?"

Before I can answer, Sanders comes striding over, his daughter tucked in his arms, and a set of deep horizontal lines creasing his forehead.

Lola cocks her chin. "Everything okay?"

"She's teething," he grumbles, handing her over.

"And...?"

"And my father's solution was to dip her pacifier in whiskey."

Smothering a laugh, Lola cradles her daughter close to her chest, her gaze bouncing between me and her new fiancé. She's on guard, ready to be the voice of reason. I can't blame her. Sanders and I are a far worse combination than oil and water...

We're more like vinegar and milk.

"I hear you've made an honest woman of my sister, Sanders," I say, sliding my hands in my pockets. *Why beat around the bush when you can chop it down with an ax?*

The corners of his mouth tip. "If you're waiting for me to ask for your approval, you can fuck right off."

"Sam!" Lola hisses, which only makes his smirk widen.

A deep laugh rumbles in my throat. "I don't like you, Sanders, but I love my sister, and for some delusional reason, she doesn't think you're a piece of shit."

"Is that a 'welcome to the family'?" he mocks, stealing a glass of champagne from another passing waiter.

"That's a 'don't fucking hurt her or they'll never find your body.'"

He motions his glass toward the bar where Thalia is talking animatedly with her parents. "I could say the same to you."

"You have."

"It bears repeating a couple of hundred times."

Lola steps between us with a dramatic sigh. "Are you two done?"

"For now," I say, scowling at Sanders's arrogant expression.

"Good. Then Julieta would like to spend some quality time with her *Tío* Santi while her parents steal a few rare moments alone."

I groan inwardly. "Well, there went my appetite."

Her answer is to shove my niece into my arms and disappear with Sanders before I have time to form a rebuttal.

I have no fucking idea what to do with a baby, so I hold the squirming six-month-old out in front of me, her chubby legs spinning like the blades of a helicopter as she flashes me a shit-eating grin.

"You're enjoying this, aren't you?" I mutter.

"She's not a bomb, you know."

I glance over my shoulder to find RJ standing behind me, wearing a suit and a smirk, like a coat of armor.

I tuck my niece in my arms, trying to ignore the overpowering stench coming from her diaper. "Tell that to her ass."

He chuckles, his dark eyes scanning the perimeter of the room as usual. The man doesn't have an "off" switch, which is good for business, bad for the fuse tucked inside that fucked-up head of his.

I'm about to tell him to dial it down a few notches when his fingers tighten around a half-empty glass of what I know is Johnnie Walker Blue, his father's favorite scotch.

"Shit," he mutters.

I follow his heated glare to where a man with dark hair and even darker eyes is leaning against the bar, sipping a glass of something amber and potent.

Renzo Marchesi.

What the fuck is he doing here?

The surrounding air thickens with tension. I tilt my chin over my shoulder just in time to catch RJ take a step toward our uninvited guest.

Switching Julieta to my hip, I swing my arm out to block him. "Where the hell do you think you're going?"

"To get intel."

"Business or personal?"

He stiffens, straightening his suit jacket. "Does it matter?"

I've made my point, so I drop my arm and redirect my attention back toward the bar and the man gazing at us with cool indifference.

Watch yourself, culero.

RJ's nostrils flare as he exhales a staggered breath. I can tell he wants to tell me to 'fuck off', but he won't. While respected and powerful, he still knows his role in this cartel.

"I thought you cut ties with Rosalia?"

"I did," he says with a growl.

His words are full of conviction, and anyone else might buy that bullshit. But I can read him better than anyone. He's too emphatic. Too insistent. Too fucking curious.

This knee-jerk reaction just proves what I've suspected for months. This crazy *cabrón* is still caught up in whatever tangled web Rosalia Marchesi wrapped him up in two years ago.

The same woman promised to another man.

Dios mío… Feliz Navi-fucking-*dad.*

Rolling my eyes, I focus on more pressing problems. "Then what the hell is her brother doing here? This party is 'by invitation only,' and…*ouch, mother of fuck…*" Prying my knuckle out from between Julieta's baby fangs, I shake my hand as RJ tries to stifle a laugh. "And I'm positive New Jersey's Most Eligible Jackass didn't make the cut," I finish with a grimace.

"You invited his father, Gianni," he accuses, regaining his composure.

"Your point?"

"Gianni's handing over more of the day-to-day operations to Renzo these days. He's sent him here in his place."

How convenient.

Renzo was the quintessential product of excess and privilege until his brother died last year. Before then, he'd fucked and fought his way all over this state, leaving broken hearts and bodies in equal measure.

Unlike him, I embraced my name and my legacy from the day I was born, and held both with honor and pride, while Renzo spent thirty-three years pissing all over his heritage—a Sicilian-based, multiple venture monopoly with a stronghold on the Garden State for nearly four generations.

Classic middle child syndrome.

He wasn't Number One son, poised to be king and heir, nor was he the baby sister to be coddled and protected at all costs. So he rebelled, and over time, the sibling rivalry between Renzo and his older brother took on a darker 'Cain and Abel' quality.

Until *someone* gunned Rainero Marchesi down in a hotel room last fall.

"Word on the street is he's fucking obsessed with finding his brother's killer," RJ muses.

"Maybe he should take a look in the mirror."

He cocks an eyebrow, his gaze wandering back to Marchesi. "You think Renzo did it?"

Across the room, I catch Thalia's watchful eye. The corners of her mouth are turned down into a frown. *She's right.* I promised her no business this evening, so whatever Marchesi may or may not be up to by gatecrashing my party rests in RJ's capable hands.

Tonight is about family.

Mine.

Hers.

Ours.

Clapping my second-in-command on the shoulder, I tighten my hold on my niece, my eyes searching for, and finding, a pair of identical ones watching us from the other side of the room. "All I'm saying is a man doesn't spend his entire life on the wrong side of a tornado without learning when to lean into the spin."

CHAPTER Four

THALIA

"Is the bourbon not to your satisfaction, *papá*?" I say, gesturing to his untouched glass.

There's a crowd of curiosity surrounding us at the bar, but my father tends to have that effect on people. Aside from his reputation, he's taller than most men, and his favorite expression is a rock face in winter—both watchful and ruinous.

Only my mother, sister and I get to see the man behind the dark mask.

Mamá once told me that the contradiction in his heart is what holds hers captive.

I saw it for myself after he killed three men on the sidewalk outside a Miami restaurant on my sixth birthday.

I screamed.

He noticed.

Twenty minutes later, he was tucking me into my bed—fresh blood still staining his hands—with the lightest of kisses and rarest of smiles.

Bad one minute.

Good, the next.

Which version walked into Santi's party tonight?

"My drink is perfectly adequate, *mi hija*," he says smoothly, but his deep voice is kicking up chips of ice as he leans in to kiss my cheek. The restrained violence in his touch is enough to make me shiver.

Damn Santi for winding him up earlier. The truce between my family and my husband's is as fine as razor wire, and twice as deadly.

One wrong move, and everyone dies.

One secret unveiled and my world either crumbles or completes.

"Thalia, you look tired," my mother says, tugging me into her soft embrace. "Is it the new promotion? Are they working you too hard?"

"Is your new husband giving you shit?"

"You don't need to sound so hopeful, *papá*," I admonish. "Santi and I are fine. *I'm* fine," I add to my mother, giving her my best pacifying smile. "Doesn't the bar look great? Lola was in charge of the décor."

"Too much white," my father says dryly, never taking his eyes off me. "It could do with a splash of red."

"Is Ella around?" I blurt out, heading off the tension. "I haven't seen her yet."

"She's over by the window talking to Edier, so brace yourself for nuclear winter," comes a familiar mocking drawl as Sam's stepfather wanders over to join us. "Happy fucking ninety-proof-eggnog, princess. Great party." He yanks his tie loose and chucks my chin. "What time does your father get to hoist your husband up like a *piñata* and beat the living shit out of him?"

"If I didn't know you any better, Uncle Rick, I'd get you thrown out for that comment," I say, smothering a grin. His tongue is twice as sharp as Sam's and five times as wicked. More so when he's drunk...

I'm about to ask him if his daughter, Tatiana, is okay when he glances over my shoulder and lets out a raspish laugh. "Looks like Santiago will be swinging at a double *piñata* if Grayson's offspring doesn't find his festive cheer soon."

Reluctantly, I glance over to watch the inevitable fallout between Ella and Edier, something that happens with varying degrees of unhappiness whenever my sister and my father's cartel protégé are forced into close proximity.

As expected, my sister's features are tense and drawn. Edier's are harder than *papá*'s. Their voices never escalate, but I can feel the electricity from here.

It's charged.

Dangerous.

Denied.

Edier is the first to walk away. Whatever screwed up their friendship years ago clearly isn't going to be fixed tonight.

Turning toward the bar, the Colombian stops dead when he sees us all staring. His gaze dips to me and then slides to my father. A strange look passes between them, but before I have a chance to question it, Lola appears by my side.

"If you don't mind," she says, wafting us with floral Dior and easy smiles, while ignoring *papá's* own anti-Christmas scowl. "Thalia and I have something *very* important to discuss."

"How important?" I ask warily, allowing myself to be led to the far end of the bar.

"Look," she hisses, jerking her head in Santi's direction once we're safely out of earshot.

My stomach lurches.

He's holding Julieta.

He doesn't look remotely natural about it, though. If I'm honest, I've seen him handle live grenades with more ease. Still, it's enough for a heavy warmth to pool inside my heart.

"Okay, so he looks like he's inspecting a lab rat," she admits. "But it kind of suits him, don't you think?"

"He's not ready," I say, feeling panicked suddenly.

Neither am I.

Neither are our families.

I was a fool to think we were.

"When are men ever 'ready,' Thalia?" She laughs. "I take it you haven't told him yet?"

I go very still. "Told him what?"

"I see." She studies my face for a moment. *Guessing? Judging?*

"Lola—"

"No time like the present," she interrupts, taking off toward my husband, with a secret that she's cocked and loaded of her own accord...

But it's not hers to fire.

"Lola, wait!" I lunge for her arm, but she swings it out of reach.

By the time I go to follow, she's already halfway across the bar.

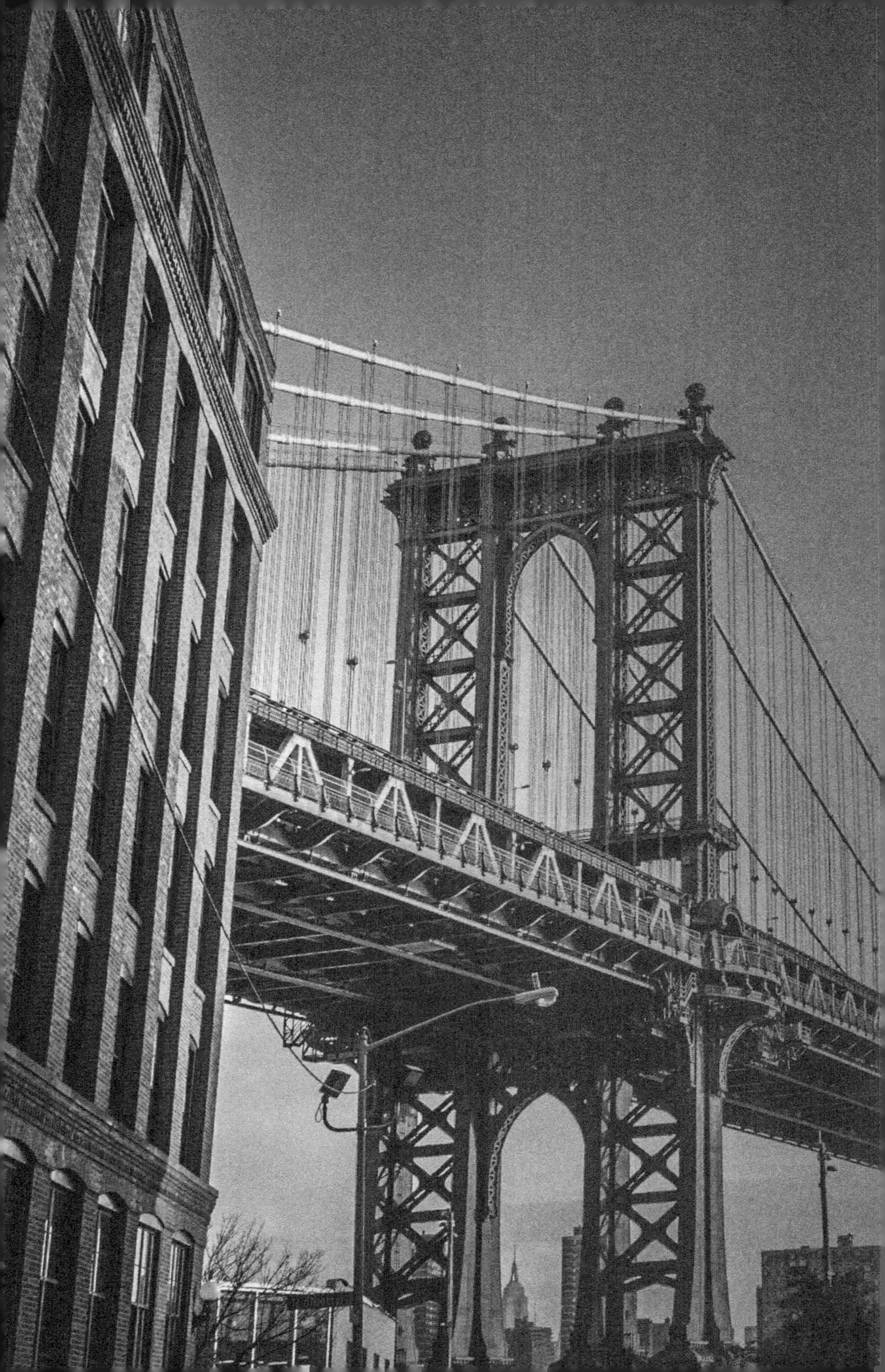

CHAPTER
Five

SANTI

It takes less than two seconds for my mother to steal Julieta from my arms. Shoving my hand in my pocket, I watch them together for a moment.

The natural affection flowing between them...

The love.

My mother has always been a fierce cartel queen, an outspoken wife, and a fair mother, but this is a side of her I've never seen. It's as if Julieta's birth has given her a new purpose and second chance. Maybe it's guilt stemming from missing out on so much of Lola's childhood, but the way she dotes on Sanders's daughter twists something ugly inside me.

I love my sister, and despite these conflicting feelings, the streets of New York and New Jersey would run red if anyone dared harm my niece, but jealousy isn't bound by familial ties.

I'm the first-born son.

I'm the heir to the throne.

I was supposed to give my parents their first grandchild, not my little sister.

My hand tightens around my champagne glass as I watch my father's hard expression soften. It's a whisper of emotion. One that's invisible to most people in this room. However, aside from my mother, I know Valentin Carrera better than anyone. His affection is exposed by the slight curve of his mouth and the downward tilt of his jaw as he settles an otherwise expressionless stare on Julieta.

It's a first I'll never give him.

But it's more than birth order rights. Something deep inside me can't help but wonder if he'll ever look at my child the way he looks at Lola's. Because while Carrera blood would run in its veins, so would Santiago's.

My mother catches my eye, her piercing blue gaze slicing through my defenses. "About time for this little girl to get a cousin, don't you think, *mijo*?"

I stiffen. It's not a blanket statement so much as a pointed arrow.

One that hits a little too close to home.

The moment Thalia and I said "I do" for the second time, I thought the time was right as well, but now, I'm not so sure.

My mind wanders back to my conversation with RJ about Renzo Marchesi and his murdered brother. Barely a year and a half separated those two. Italian Irish twins, people called them—Rainero the dominant prince, and Renzo the ice-cool loner with a trigger-happy finger who was more than happy to deliver Marchesi justice.

Fuck knows what went down between them, but if I've learned anything over the last few years, it's that history tends to repeat itself. Whether you're a Marchesi, a Grayson, a Harcourt, a Sanders, a Santiago, or a Carrera…rivalries will always exist.

The only way to carve a new path is to destroy the old one.

The Carreras are a strong family. My father has built an empire on loyalty and honor. However, twenty years of bad blood caused a chasm in its foundation.

Maybe Julieta should have her time to shine before adding another star.

"Thalia and I are more interested in taking over the world than populating it," I say firmly, shutting down any further inquisition.

I catch my mother's frown, right before Julieta grabs a handful of her long, red hair and squeals, drawing her attention back to her beloved granddaughter.

My father doesn't acknowledge my declaration. Instead, he gazes at my mother, running his palm over Julieta's dark hair before casually making his way to my side.

"The war is over, son," he says, sliding a hand in the pocket of his black slacks.

The move is eerily familiar, and I quickly remove my own as I give him a pointed look. "Is it?"

At first, he says nothing, his jaw ticking as the cords in his neck draw tightly. "Trust will never unite our families, Santi. For years we've had nothing in common but hate…"

"And now?"

"A crocodile and an anaconda will never peacefully coexist. Place them in the same habitat with the same prey, and you'll always get a power play."

"Is there a point to this, or have you been watching too much *Animal Planet*?" Pressing my tongue against my top teeth, I tip my head back and let out a rough breath, wondering where the hell he's going with this, but too on edge to care.

He flashes a tight smile. "Although they're natural enemies, there's one thing that will always unite them."

I cock an eyebrow.

"When one of their young is threatened, they'll both react with aggression."

"Toward each other," I remind him flatly. "Your science lesson would hold more relevance if there were a 'crococonda' involved."

His expression turns serious. "If there ever was one, it'd be the most protected creature in the world."

"Until it's used as a pawn."

The thin layer of peace bridging our two cartels is as genuine as Lola's fake snow. One wrong word, one misconstrued action, and it all could come crashing down. Then where would that "*protected creature*" be left?

I'll tell you…trapped in a tug-of-war between two corrupt gods.

"Santi, your child will command two armies and have the respect of three generations. If anyone dares challenge that, I can name two men who would fight to fire the first bullet."

I'm surprised. "You would stand beside Dante Santiago again to protect his bloodline?"

He shakes his head. "Not his bloodline, Santi. *Es un enlace común que cambia la historia.*"

"The common link that changes history," I translate, catching a blur of black and red out of the corner of my eye as Lola comes rushing toward us, drink in hand and laughing. Thalia is hot on her heels and not looking half as happy.

"What the hell is so funny?" I demand.

"*Shhh*," Lola chokes out, pressing her finger to her lips, nearly doubled over in laughter. "Just look shocked, okay? Act like I just told you Legado is on fire."

"What? Why?" I glance down at the half-empty glass in her hand. "How much champagne have you…? *Fuck!*" I hiss as the sharp point of her stiletto slams onto my foot. I glare at her, barely holding back the slew of curses resting behind my clenched teeth.

She grins. "*¡Perfecto!*"

Thalia skids to a stop behind my sister, her chest heaving. As she takes in my lethal expression, a resigned grimace twists her lips. "She told you, didn't she? I'm so sorry, I wanted it to be a surprise." She glares at a smug-faced Lola.

"*My* surprise."

I think back to the stolen moments together in our bedroom where she coyly denied me her mouth.

"What other egregious sins have you committed against me, *muñequita?*"

She recoils, a strange look on her face. "A *sin?* Is that really what you think of our baby, Santi?"

A hush falls across the room as I rear back in shock, her words hitting me like a wrecking ball. "What the hell did you just say to me?"

"Looks like Santa came way too early and fast this year," Sanders drawls, somewhere to my left, then chokes on his drink as Lola drives a sharp elbow into his ribcage.

Thalia glares at an unapologetic Lola, who leans back in Sanders's arms, a satisfied smile plastered across her face. "It's true. I'm pregnant," she repeats, this time her tone soft and unsure. "Just like Lola said."

"*Lola* didn't say shit," my sister announces proudly, "but it's about damn time *you* confessed."

A somber expression flits across Thalia's face, and her hands twist together, a motion that starts as a ripple and crashes into a torrent of well-wishes and congratulations.

While my eyes never leave hers, my mind spins in a dozen different directions. I don't know whether to pick her up and swing her around in my arms or carry her upstairs, strip her naked, and punish her for keeping something so life-changing from me. So, I say nothing, accepting the multiple toasts and claps on the back with a tight jaw and solemn nod.

Our sizzling connection is severed as my mother hands Julieta to Sam, then rushes between us, scooping Thalia in an exuberant hug. "I'm so thrilled for you! I know you…" She pulls back, her eyebrows drawing together in an awkward moment of uncertainty.

I'll be damned...

Talk about a one-two punch.

My mother is an unflappable woman who's rarely at a loss for words. This is an unprecedented moment, so I lean forward, invested in what's coming next.

Clearing her throat, my mother lifts her chin, then takes Thalia's hands in hers. "I know you have your mother, sister, and Lola here to help you, but it would mean the world to me to be a part of this, too."

Thalia's features soften. "I'd love that."

Smiling, my mother gives her one last squeeze, then glides back to my father and coils her arms around his neck. "Did you hear that, Val? We're going to be grandparents again. Our son is going to be a father!"

"*Sí, Cereza,*" he says, sliding his palm down her back, his gaze locked on me. "A common link that changes history."

Turning away from the incinerating heat of his stare, I glance down at my little sister. "You knew."

She shrugs. "I guessed. After watching you two tonight, I knew she was having a hard time telling you."

"That was a risky move, *chaparrita.*"

"Yeah, well, sometimes you two need a kick in the ass."

We're interrupted as my father clears his throat, a simple gesture that in normal settings wouldn't break a stride, but in the Platinum Bar of Legado Casino, it might as well have been a gunshot.

He holds up his glass of champagne, his dark eyes never leaving mine. "To my son, Santi, and his wife, Thalia. The birth of this child is the birth of a new era. Two families now bound by blood." He tips his drink across the bar to where Santiago stands, his expression unreadable. "To *our* grandchild."

After a few tense moments, the Colombian lifts his glass and nods.

Our fragile truce is holding... For now.

Amidst another round of applause and well-wishes, I catch Thalia's eye. Taking her hand, I draw her away from the celebration and down the hallway toward the elevator. As the carriage opens, we ride in silence toward the penthouse, the tension so thick it feels like a wool blanket.

Stepping out into the black marble lobby, I turn and cup her jaw between my fingers. "This was my gift?" I murmur.

She lets out a labored breath. "Yes. Although now I'm wondering if it's more of a burden."

Tightening my grip, I push her up against the nearest wall. "How long have you known?"

"A week," she admits, the bright tint of her cheeks fading as she glances away. "Santi, I've wanted to tell you for days, but I—"

"You didn't know how," I finish.

She nods, her troubled eyes seeking out mine again. "This baby will have my father's blood, too." She sucks in a sharp breath as my thumb glides up her throat and tips her chin.

"No, *muñequita*, it will have *yours*. You heard what my father said, 'bound by blood for life.'"

"Yes, but—"

"Do you remember that night we first met at Sacred Heart?"

I watch as the memory flickers in her eyes.

"Of course I do. You saved my life."

"I had no choice, *muñequita*. You stole a part of my heart, even as a thirteen-year-old boy. As children, we were bound by sacrifice. Ten years later, we were bound by circumstance, and now…"

"And now we're bound by blood," she says, repeating my father's words herself. "Does that mean you're happy about this baby?"

"You couldn't have given me a more perfect gift in the world, *mi amada*." To prove the weight of my words, I take her mouth in a reverent, but possessive kiss. As I press my palm against her still-taut stomach, I feel the lingering remnants of rivalry between our families evaporate only to be replaced with new promise. "*Mi hijo…*"

"Your son?" Thalia coils her arms around my waist and tips her chin. "You don't know that for sure. Not until fifteen weeks at least."

Only I do.

Out of death comes life and out of chaos comes strength.

"We've created a king, *muñequita*," I assure her, "and someday the world will bow at his feet."

"Will he be *El Muerte* or *El Diablo*?" she muses.

I consider her question before answering, "Neither. He'll be *El Príncipe Oscuro*."

She cocks an eyebrow. "The dark prince?"

I dance my tongue along the seam of her mouth as I lead her toward our bedroom. "Do you believe in destiny?"

"Why do you ask?"

Because I was always taught that a Carrera can never outrun destiny.

Because I grew up believing mine led to a collision course of darkness, not a blinding ray of light.

"When I was a boy in Mexico, legends were told about *La Boda Roja*," I tell her, taking her face between my hands again. "How two kings declared war, and only one dark prince could end it."

Thalia's steps falter. "But, *you* did."

"No, I calmed the storm. The only one who can truly end a war is a dark prince belonging to *both* kings."

"That's a lot of responsibility to place on a little boy, Santi."

"He'll rise to the challenge," I say confidently. "Carreras always do."

I go to push her backward again when she plants her heels. "And the Santiago in him?"

I smile. "Will keep the Carrera side in check." I lean in closer, breathing in her sweet scent. The one that always smells like home. Brushing her hair back, I trace patterns on her cheek with my thumb. "Just like his mother."

"I love you, Santi Carrera."

Her words hit hard. As many times as she's said them to me tonight, right now they feel different—as if a page has been turned revealing a crisp, blank chapter. One ready to be written with not only legacy, but strength and unity.

I once thought love was weak, a tool for a man's destruction.

Until Thalia.

My enemy's daughter taught me it possesses a strength hatred could never rival. It crosses oceans in sacrifice.

"Yo también te amo, Thalia Carrera," I tell her, repeating the words back to her in Spanish. I take her lips in another kiss, this one so fierce it flits on the edge of viciousness. *"Mi amada."* She moans out hotly as we tumble backward onto the bed. I pull her into a straddle position over my hips and kiss a fiery trail from her lips to her neck. *"Mi esposa."*

Her nails dig into my back. "Say the one that belongs to only me."

My hands run the length of her back, cupping her ass. Her heart races against mine as I shift my hips, pulling her flush against me. *"Mi muñequita."*

"Siempre." she whispers, and in that one word lies every promise made, every rule broken, and every fate fulfilled.

When I was a boy, I waded knee-deep in a snowstorm, reminding myself with every step that choices have consequences. That night, I chose her, and although I didn't realize it at the time, each choice I've made since has led me to this moment.

To my red queen.

To the love that saved me.

To the life we've created.

To the legacy that will entwine our stories forever.

Born SINNER

BOOK 0.5
CORRUPT GODS DUET

BORN SINNER

My sins will be her penance…

I came to this college for one reason—*her*.
A cartel princess.
Mexican royalty.
Sworn enemy of the Colombian ranks I'm destined to climb.

I'm meant to hate her.
Destroy her name and sacrifice her innocence.
But Lola Carrera isn't the delicate flower her family thinks she is.
And I just took a match to her ivory tower.

Obsession is a loaded gun…
And tonight, she's waging war with my patience.

"Every saint has a past and every sinner has a future."
—*Oscar Wilde*

PLAYLIST
In no particular order...

Bad Girl - Avril Lavigne, Marilyn Manson
Bad Boys Like Me - Hell Boulevard
I Get Off - Halestorm
Bite Your Kiss - DIAMANTE
Dirty Little Thing - Adelitas Way
Hit Me Like a Man - The Pretty Reckless
Headspin - Butcher Babies
Diamond In The Rough - The Nearly Deeds

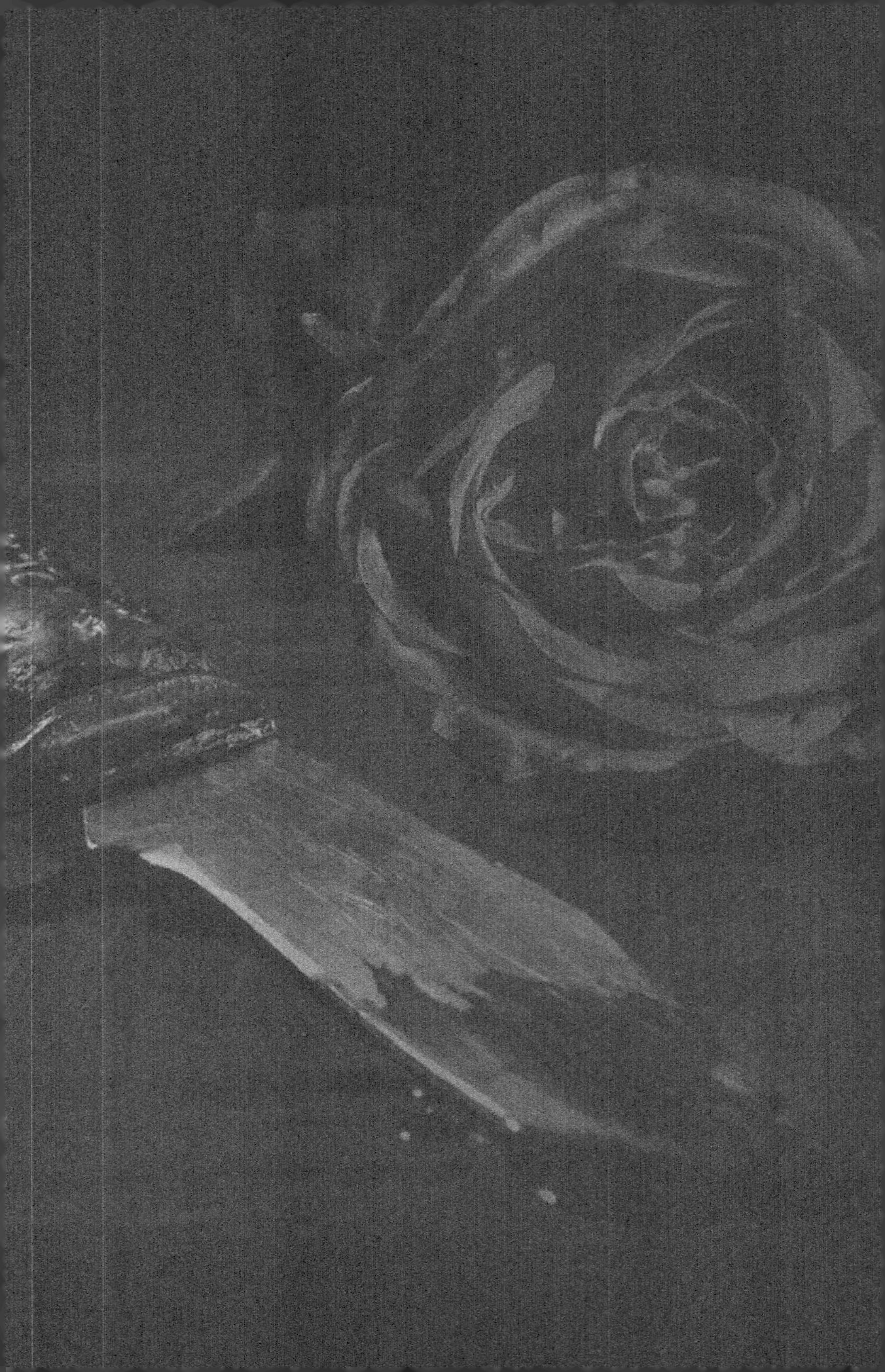

CHAPTER *One*

SAM

Obsession is a loaded gun.

The bullets started firing the moment she stepped into my party uninvited in a backless dress and heels, wearing confidence as a color and her smile as a taunt. Now, she's piling into my Arabescato marble kitchen with her girlfriends and tossing interested glances my way.

She wouldn't be this reckless if she knew who I was.

Danger has a scent, Lola Carrera, and I'm fucking wearing it.

She tries biting her lower lip and flashing those baby blues at me, like every other chick in this place. When I don't react, her smile slips, and she turns back to her friends.

Not me.

I never turn away.

For the next thirty minutes or so, I watch the rise and fall of her cigarette as shitty conversation and bad music sucks everything else around us into a whirlpool of mediocrity. I see it all—even from halfway across the crowded room of a five-thousand-square-foot apartment that a trust fund puked up for some over-privileged offspring.

Namely me.

When she sparks up her fifth Marlboro—*chain-smoking tonight, Lola?*—I track the silver trails to her mouth again, noting the shallow inhale and the subtle wrinkling of her nose. She doesn't like the taste, but she's playing a role at this college that demands an addiction. *Too bad it's not the one her daddy sells.*

I note every head tilt, every flick of her hair, every curve of those luscious ruby lips. I do it all with the same sick fascination I've been fighting since the day she arrived on New Jersey's Rutgers campus at the start of the semester. We've never spoken, we've never even touched, but you could say she fucks my mind on the regular.

I hate her.

I want her.

Taking another swig of beer, I focus on what she really is to throw cold water on my obsession. She's a two-faced innocent—a name I've been taught to hate all my life. A name I had every intention of exposing when she and her cunt brother, Santi Carrera, least expected it.

That was before I laid eyes on her.

"You want in on this, Sam?"

Lucas hands me a lit stub, and I accept it without thanks—declaring my dangerous mood to the world with a couple of savage tokes. Unlike Lola, I prefer to savor the burn of weed and nicotine instead of exhaling it fast like it's a bad word on a priest's tongue. I like the way it fills up every space in my lungs, because nothing else in my life will ever feel this whole.

"María! Hey, María!"

A loud voice rises above the music, making Dua Lipa marginally more bearable. We turn to find some prick named Troy Davis pushing through the party with a clear destination.

Her.

Yes, her. Because "Lola" isn't the name she trades under on American soil. "Lola" gets left behind the minute she crosses the border to disguise the fact that her daddy heads up one of the biggest drug cartels in Mexico. I'm betting her clique of virgin suicides would be kissing a new ass pretty damn fast if they knew she was a bona fide cartel princess.

But I know...

Let's just say I have connections, no matter how hard my senator stepfather tries to keep them from me.

"Aww, she's so *fuckable*." Lucas follows my gaze as my palm curls into a fist. "Word on the street is that her V-card is as good as her credit rating. You should totally hit it, bro. You've crushed more cherries on this campus than the juice bar."

"Are you still here?" I flick the dying stub at his chest, and he jumps back with a yelp, brushing imaginary ash from his designer shirt.

"What the *hell*?"

"Relax," I murmur lazily. "I'm sure Daddy will buy you a new one if you ask him nicely."

Lucas's stepfather is a big-shot politician in Washington too. We both have bank accounts that reflect the need for us to stay the fuck out of the headlines.

Troy's all up in Lola's face now. His arm keeps slipping around her waist.

I've never wanted to spill blood so badly.

"Who ordered the jock entrées?" I hear Lucas say in disgust. "Want me to call security?"

"Security" is a light word for the two heavies my stepfather insists on me keeping around. Senator Sanders's history of making enemies has created a claustrophobic existence for all his kids.

"Not yet." I crack open another bottle of Bud—my fourth. My head is starting to buzz, but it's doing *jack shit* for the thing I want it to dull the most.

"Suit yourself." He shrugs and starts chatting up some passing blonde. He knows there's no point in arguing with me. Besides, Rutgers's star quarterback is about to get his ass handed to him by yours truly, especially since I just watched him slip a tab of something extra special into Lola's Bacardi and Coke.

I catch the smirks on his teammates' mouths. I taste the acidity in Troy's intentions. Lola Carrera's precious V-card is about to be spanked and shredded all over my apartment, and she's not going to know a thing about it.

Unless...

The slow burn in my chest ignites, bursting into a dull red flame.

Obsession is a loaded gun, and tonight my patience is dead and bleeding.

No one, I repeat *no one*, gets to suck or fuck that body, other than me.

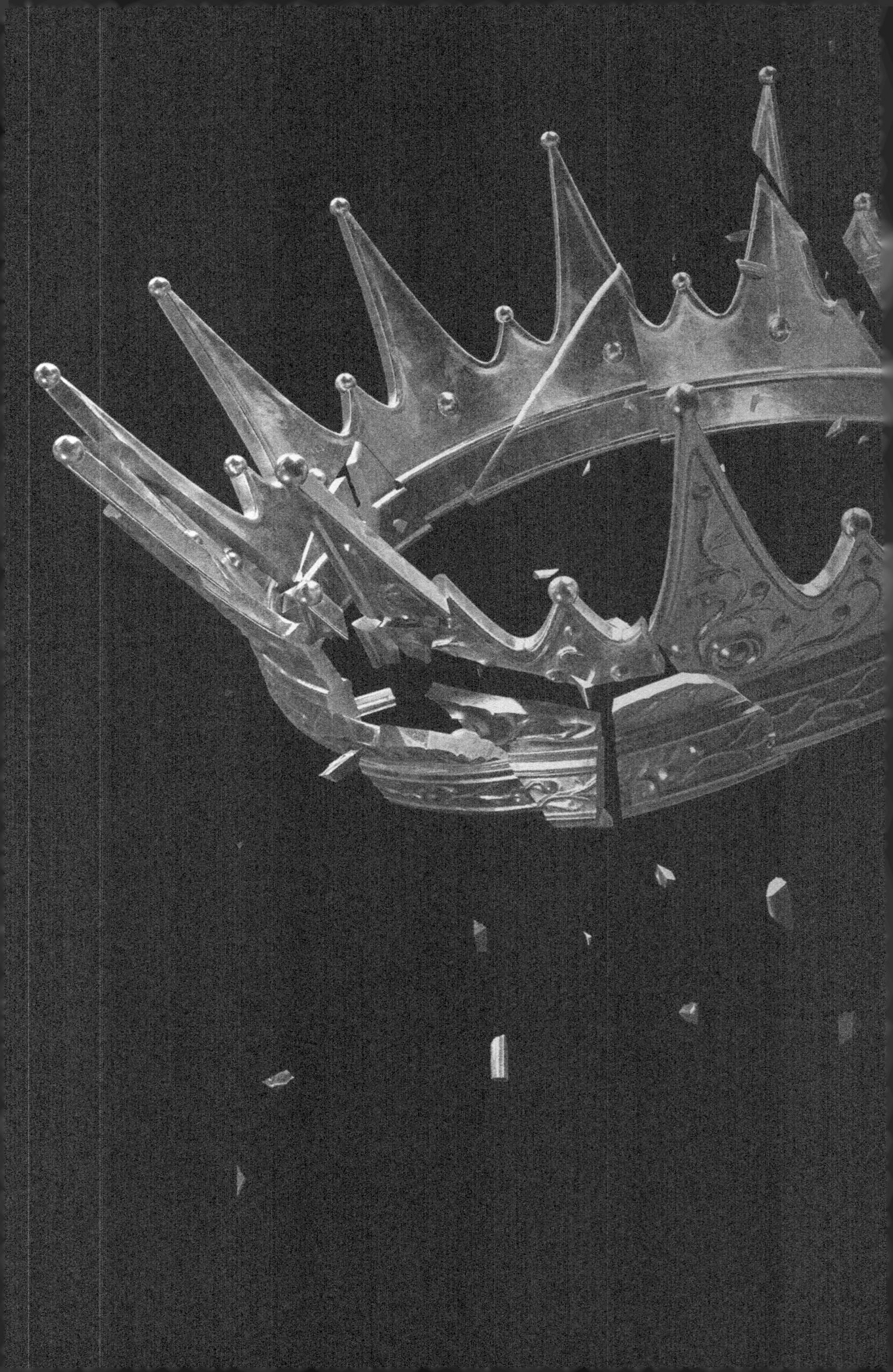

CHAPTER Two

LOLA

*T*rust no one. Suspect everyone.

The last words my father said to me before I left Mexico ring in one ear as Troy Davis's drunken shouts fill the other.

"María! Hey, María!"

Pinching the cigarette between my fingers, I lift it to my lips and inhale while pretending not to notice. The truth is, I'm still getting used to that name.

María.

I hate it, but it was a small price to pay in order to trade my sheltered existence for the American dream. *American freedom.*

My grip tightens, denting the filter. I don't feel so free right now. In fact, I feel more suffocated standing inside this lavish New Jersey apartment than I did locked inside my gilded border cage.

Blend in, Lola...

I've barely thought the words when a rush of heat ignites, licking along the skin on my bare shoulders. Glancing out of the corner of my eye, I track his movement.

Or lack thereof...

Sam Colton hasn't moved in fifteen minutes. I know; I've counted every one of them. He's still leaned against the far wall, his heel lazily braced against it as if daring it to crumble.

Daring it to deny his weight.

His hard, muscular, sinfully defined weight.

Exhaling a cloud of smoke, I glance down at my feet, ignoring the high-pitched chatter spreading like an infectious disease all around me. *This was a bad idea.*

I'm about to spout off a lame excuse and get the hell out of here when a figure appears behind me, and hot breath fans across my neck. "Damn, baby, look at you…"

Note to self: American men can't take a hint.

Sighing, I take another long drag off my cigarette. *Dios mío, these things are disgusting.*

Already planning my exit strategy, I glance over my shoulder to find Troy pressed way too close, his hooded gaze slowly sliding down my body.

Additional note to self: American men are also transparent as fuck.

Once he finally manages to look me in the eyes, he flashes a wide smile. I'll give him full marks for effort, but it's anything but sincere. Those perfect white teeth might as well end in two sharp points.

"That dress should come with a warning sign," he notes, trailing the back of his knuckles all the way down my arm to my wrist.

Lifting my chin, I blow a steady line of smoke right in his face. "It does: 'off-limits.'"

Those blond eyebrows raise toward a perfectly styled blond hairline. It's obvious he's confused as to why I'm not already on my knees sucking his dick—just like every other female at this party wants to.

The seething hatred coming from all four corners of the room is hot enough to spark a fire. There are at least half a dozen girls here willing to sell their souls to be me right now.

All because Troy Davis is a trophy dick.

Even with my short amount of time on campus, I know every facet of the *unwritten rule*: if given the opportunity to spread your legs for the star quarterback, you don't ask questions. You do it, then wear it as a badge of honor.

Maybe if I were any other girl.

I down half my rum and Coke, my gaze wandering over Troy's shoulder. Like a magnet, it settles back on that wall…and on *him.*

Sam Colton.

My brain spins a hundred different reasons as to why I should look away, but I don't. Instead, I memorize every strand of that messy dark hair and every inch of those tribal tattoos licking up his neck.

And if he were any other boy...

One I haven't been warned to stay away from with no explanation as to why...

I'm ripped away from Sam's cold stare as Troy winds his arm around my waist and pulls me against his chest. "Come on, don't be like that, María. I'm just being friendly."

Pinche sangrón. I clench my jaw, caging the insult behind my lips.

You're not royalty here, Lola.

You're a wide-eyed college student.

Just like the herd of half-drunk coeds standing in front of me. The ones winking at Troy's arm and giving me a wave of "thumbs up" signs.

Oblivious girls bleeding their naivety all over Sam Colton's apartment.

Sam...

Flicking a gaze over Troy's shoulder, I catch him passing a dangerous gaze at us before curling his lip. My hand trembles as I lift the red plastic cup again. I wish he'd stop staring at me like that.

Like I'm a stain on his precious marble flooring.

"Right," I mutter.

Chuckling, Troy brushes his lips against my ear. "Trust me," he whispers, tracing his index finger across the back of my hand.

Trust no one.

No one is your friend, cielito. They're only an enemy in waiting.

Suspect everyone.

Everyone is a snake. Some are just better at shedding their skin.

I swallow my father's warnings, liquid sloshing over the rim of my red cup as I jerk my hand away. *If I don't occupy my mouth, my true colors will fall out...* Troy's eyes follow every movement as I lift my drink, downing what's left. Just as the corners of his mouth tip up, I step forward.

Rules were meant to be broken—especially unwritten ones.

"Trust is earned, Troy." Flashing him a syrupy smile, I drop my half-smoked cigarette into his beer, accompanied by a chorus of horrified gasps.

My name is molded around multiple variations of "whore," but I'm already halfway across the room by the time they catch up to me.

Perfect, Lola. That was the exact opposite of "blending in…"

I'm supposed to swoon and bat my eyes. Instead, I placed a tiara on my head and unloaded a gun into the wall.

Safely immersed within the bowels of a makeshift dance floor, I sneak a look back at my friends. Their mouths are still gaping in shock. I let out a rough sigh while pretending to dance to the irritating base rattling the windows.

There will be a slew of questions waiting for me tomorrow. Apologies will have to be made. Bombs will need to be diffused. Diversions will have to be crafted...

But tonight, instinct is pumping too hard through my veins to ignore.

You don't grow up as the daughter of a kingpin without learning how to carve through bullshit to extract the truth. Troy Davis's truth is what makes him so dangerous. He's a viper hiding behind Polo shirts and boat shoes.

Luckily for me, I can read asshole frat boys.

As my gait slows, I glance to my right where a pair of midnight eyes are still watching me.

But not him.

I'd have better luck reading in the dark than reading Sam Colton.

I should be home.

I should be on the couch in my favorite pajamas watching Netflix, forgetting I ever agreed to come tonight.

But I'm not.

Twenty minutes after ditching everyone, I'm still leaning up against a wall at this party. At Sam's piece of shit—gritting my teeth, I look around at the marble and crystal *everything* and sigh—at his infuriatingly beautiful apartment.

"Why the hell am I still here?" I grumble out loud—except what falls from my mouth sounds nothing like what was in my head. Instead, it sounds like one long word dipped in caramel.

My stomach sloshes around at the thought.

"This is why Santi told you not to drink, Yola." I blink. "Loya." I blink again, the weight on my neck causing my chin to fall forward. "Yoya..."

What the hell kind of rum is Sam serving?

My head flops back, slamming against the wall with a hard thud. "Ow..." *That's going to hurt tomorrow.* I try to lift my hand to rub it, but the weight from my neck is now wrapped around my wrist. So I stand there, head back, knees bent, and arms heavy, swaying to a dancing orange light.

Up.

Down.

Left.

Right.

I blink again, the clouds in my eyes thinning enough for me to realize the light isn't dancing—it's moving.

And it's not just a light.

It's a fucking joint.

Squeezing my eyes shut, I count to five before opening them, only to collide with a familiar tattooed hand lifting the joint to a familiar mouth as familiar lips wrap around the end.

Sam.

As if I spoke his name out loud, he turns toward me. This time, he doesn't look right through me. He levels that icy glare like an earthquake, and I shiver under its weight. He's less than twenty feet away, but he might as well have me pressed against the wall with both hands wrapped around my neck.

My pulse races...

I can't breathe...

It's only when he pins me with that lethal stare again that I see it...

Darkness.

He's not just a rich bad boy with a chip on his shoulder—he's a jagged reef lying beneath a calm sea. And this place isn't just an apartment—it's a diamond-encrusted snake pit.

The realization is too much. The weight is too heavy. Both tangle in a knotted haze, dragging me down the wall. Just before I hit the floor, an arm hooks around my waist, pulling me to my feet. My brain barely stops spinning when a pair of lips press against my ear.

"What do you say we go someplace more private?"

I nod slowly, the words sounding thick and muddled in my head. Then I'm floating. Fingers dig into my arm, guiding me up, up, up…

So far up, I wonder if we'll ever reach the top.

I wonder what would happen if he let me go. I wonder how long it would take to hit the water. To sink beneath the surface and onto the reef… To stain clear blue water murky red…

My head lolls back. "Sam?"

A dark laugh rumbles beside me. "I'll be whoever you want me to be, baby."

"I don't feel so good, Sam."

"Don't worry…" he assures me. "Now that I've got that attitude dialed down, I'll make you feel better. *Trust me.*"

CHAPTER
Three

SAM

I sense the brunette while she's still circling, but I'm not quick enough to dodge the swoop.

"Hey," she chirps, crinkling her eyes at me. "Cool party, huh? Love the apartment. Your folks must be loaded."

Yeah, with piles of dirty money.

"Thanks," I say dryly, looking right through her. The roofie Troy slipped Lola must be out-of-this-world phenomenal. She's already swaying in her heels.

"Wanna give me a guided tour?"

Oh, Jesus... She's cute, but there's only one woman here who makes my dick hard.

"Maybe later," I lie.

Troy has Lola by the arm and he's guiding her toward the open glass staircase. By the time they reach the second floor, she's all over the place—her long, dark hair messing up her face as her head flops sideways onto his shoulder; her dress riding up to expose more tanned skin.

"Okay, well, make sure you come find me…" Brunette trails off as I push past her like the devil himself is hot on the heels of my Amiri check sneakers. Meanwhile, Lola's friends are waving her off with catcalls from below, looking as dickmatized by Troy Davis as she appears to be.

"Have fun, María!"

"Don't do anything I wouldn't do!"

Choke on those grins, you stupid bitches. She's a fucking Carrera. Don't they know she's smarter than that?

She shouldn't even be at my party. Her brother would never allow it, not if he knew my real last name was Sanders instead of Colton. I took my mother's maiden name the day I enrolled at Rutgers. Lola and I are both here under false pretenses to protect us from the war that's raging up and down the East Coast.

There's an invisible line drawn down this campus. It's the same one that divides New Jersey and New York, her family from mine, truth and lies... *Me from her.* We stay the fuck away from each other, or people die.

Santi Carrera is happy to enforce the rules for his baby sister, but he's not around right now and I get the feeling she had a little something to do with that. She's fighting for her freedom, just as much as I am, and that makes her fucking irresistible.

I move toward the stairs, fire and ice surging through my veins.

Protect her.

Reject her.

This contradiction is giving me a headache.

"Nice party, Colton."

Troy's crew try to block my access. All it takes is a single look from me and they're like sliding doors at the mall.

Pussies.

"It'd be even better without the dickhead parade showing up."

"Aw, you serious?" They clutch at their chests, all offended, like I just gang-banged their moms.

Fucking idiots.

"Get the hell out of my apartment," I say coldly.

"Or what?" says one cocky asshole.

"Or you won't be playing football for the rest of the season." I meet each of their shocked expressions in turn. "It's hard to find your own dick, let alone run ten steps, with two fractured ankles."

They wince.

"You're a sick man, Colton."

Tell me something I don't know.

I take the stairs three at a time and head straight for my bedroom. I know the mind games that provocative pricks like Troy Davis like to play. There's no love lost between us, and he'll come twice as hard knowing it's my bed he's defiling as well.

If he's touched her already...

Behind the door, it's a scene from every college chick's worst nightmare. Lola is passed out on the bed, her black minidress and heels already discarded on the floor. Troy's standing over her with his jeans around his ankles.

He looks up and smirks. "Come to join the party, Colton?"

"Consent's a tough word to purchase from the unconscious, frat boy." I glance at Lola's breasts in that black lingerie and feel my own traitorous dick stir. "You sure she's selling?"

"What's it to you? Pissed I'm buying first?"

"Wrong answer, asshole. Your libido lost its way, and the rest of you is about to pay." Reaching into my back pocket, I pull out the silver pocket knife the senator bought me for my eighth birthday. I learned to demand respect long before I learned to drive. I learned it on an island a long way away from a man who I have every intention of working for one day, no matter what my stepfather has to say about it. *You can't keep the bad away from the bad. We're like magnets around one another.*

Troy glances down at my hand, and the blood drains from his face. He yanks up his jeans and backs away from me like I'm the goddamn antichrist.

"What the *hell*, Colton? If you want the bitch so bad, you can have her."

"Did you touch her?" I tap the exposed blade against my lower lip as I saunter deeper into the room.

I find my answer in Troy's silence.

I press the blade into my lip until I can feel something hot and wet running down my chin. "Did you taste her?"

Troy looks like he's about to shit himself. "Just a kiss, man. I swear. I-I didn't know she was your girl."

Damn right, she is. "Didn't your mom ever teach you it's wrong to steal?"

"My mom's best friend is a vodka bottle. She didn't teach me *nothing*!"

"Poor little rich boys of the world unite." I swipe a hand across my jaw and it comes away red. "Get on your knees."

A tic jumps to life in his cheek. "Wh-what?"

My foot connects with his thigh, and a dark satisfaction fills my soul as he goes crashing to the floor. Crouching over him, I take his jaw between my fingers as he cringes away. "You fucked up, Troy Davis." With my other hand, I press the blade against the nervous glide of his throat. "You just violated my property, and that shit has consequences... Lift up your shirt."

He freezes. "No way."

"I said, lift up your *fucking* shirt."

A trembling hand shoots out and wrenches up his white Moncler Polo. "What the hell, Colton?" he says again weakly. "You a queer now?"

"No, Troy. I'm your end game." Changing my mind at the last second, I drop the knife from his throat and drive it down deep into the web of muscles above his kneecap, twisting as I go, severing a couple of tendons and all his hopes and dreams. Never mind a season on the bench; I've just gone and annihilated a promising football career at the age of twenty.

I feel nothing about it, though. No guilt. No regret.

Sweet. Fuck. All.

I told you I was ready for the big league, senator.

Troy screams, and I slam my hand across his mouth. "Inhale the pain," I order, bringing my face close to his. "Inhale it until you feel like your lungs are gonna explode, because that's only a fraction of what 'María' would have felt tomorrow morning if I hadn't shown up in time." Flashing him a grin, I pull the knife out, eliciting another muffled scream. "If I were you, Troy Davis, I'd get to a hospital in the next twenty minutes. You've had yourself a bad accident... Maybe you shouldn't drink so much next time. You feeling me?"

He nods, eyes glassy with pain. Compliant as a child.

Maybe he knows the truth about me. Maybe he's heard about the senator's reputation.

Removing my hand, I wipe his spit down the front of his polo shirt.

"Go... Get out of here."

"I-I can't move." He starts crying, snot trailing down his face like a well-fucked pussy.

Are they tears of relief or pain? Maybe it's the realization he'll never score a touchdown again. Either way, I doubt he'll be slipping a roofie into another chick's drink this side of never.

"Then you crawl, asshole. I'll count to ten, and then I'm introducing my knife to your other knee."

"Shit! Fuck! Okay!" He starts dragging his bleeding body toward the door, but my focus has already switched to her.

It's *all* about her.

I can't stop staring.

Turns out, I was missing the real masterpiece underneath her clothes.

I want her.

I fucking want her.

My gaze drops to the soft mound barely concealed beneath the black lace. *I bet she tastes like peaches and cream...*

She moans suddenly, her head falling to one side—hair strewn like dark seaweed across the flawless shores of her cheek.

Focus, Sam. Focus.

She's the daughter of the enemy. It's Mexico versus Colombia. It's the past versus our present. It's the fact that her daddy, Valentin Carrera, swore an oath years ago to bring death and destruction to the Santiago Cartel, an organization in which my stepfather is so entrenched, even his shit stinks of South America.

There's bad blood, and then there's this—a war so dangerous it kills people by seven degrees of separation.

She was meant to be my way into Santiago's organization. Mess her up a little. Fuck with her heart. Make everyone pay attention… Truth is, I'm done playing with wooden guns in safe, wooden houses, and being forced into a state of peace and tranquility when my black soul screams for anarchy. My stepfather argues that this war is the parents' fight. That their sins should absolve the next generation from bloodshed.

Screw that.

Not so long ago, he ruled the New York underground for Santiago. Now, I want a piece of his former action, and Santiago, *my godfather*, is the man to give it to me.

Running the edge of my knife across the unblemished plains of Lola's stomach, I follow the curve of her hipbone all the way to the black borderline of her panties. She moans again, and slurs out a word, but her eyes never open.

My lips twitch as an idea forms. The tip of the blade makes a shockingly white indentation before the first bud of crimson blooms.

I work quickly after that—a master of my wicked art—marking the flawless skin just left of her hipbone with a single letter that spans a couple of inches wide, and deep enough to scar.

S for my initial.

S for Santiago.

Rising from the bed, I admire my handiwork. What I've done to her is far worse than what Troy Davis could ever do. I've fucked with her body, and tomorrow that letter will be fucking with her mind.

I've finally announced my intention as a player in this war, but best of all? I've made Lola Carrera mine.

CHAPTER *Four*

LOLA

I wake in my apartment to the sound of my teeth chattering, each clap of enamel chipping away at my brain. Prying my eyes open, I wince at the sharp haze filtering through my lashes.

Fuck, it's bright.

I lift my arm to block out the sunlight, but the damn thing feels like a sack of bricks. Since gravity is waging war against me, I give up, letting it flop back down. *Big mistake.* The moment it lands across the bridge of my nose, I let out a hoarse cry as dozens of sharp knives plunge into my skull.

"What the hell?" My voice is barely audible. *Rough. Brittle.* Like my *Tío* Mateo sounded after taking a bullet to the chest a couple of years ago.

But I didn't get shot. This is New Jersey, not Mexico City.

Blowing out a queasy breath, I dig my elbow into the mattress and sit up, my body accompanying my chattering teeth in a symphony of tremors. When a sudden wave of nausea hits, I swallow hard, unsure if I'm going to black out or vomit all over my bed.

Breathe, Lola.

Dios mío, I must have had more to drink than I thought.

As my spinning head settles, I recall the single Bacardi and Coke I nursed all night. I was reckless, not stupid. I only allowed myself one drink, but I remember stumbling up a flight of stairs and then down a long hallway.

Someone was with me...

Beep! Beep! Beep!

"Argh, fuck!" Grabbing my head to stop the sound of my alarm from shattering my eardrums, I roll over, a sharp pain radiating across my abdomen as I search for my phone. "Shut up!" I growl. Dragging it off the nightstand, I hit all the buttons at once, praying one will stop the incessant noise.

Finally, silence.

Tossing it on the mattress, I flop back onto my pillow, when it hits me.

"Shit! Santi..." *I'm supposed to meet my brother for lunch.* Adrenaline spikes through my veins as I throw my comforter across the bed. It isn't until my feet hit the floor that I realize I'm naked.

Dread fills my chest as I force pieces of last night from behind the distorted opaque window clouding my mind. *How did I get home?*

Slowly, more jagged memories work their way out of the fog and into the light.

No. I couldn't have.

Troy Davis.

His hands.

A bed.

"Trust me, baby. I'm gonna treat this pussy good."

Trust me...

"No..." I breathe again, searching between my legs for signs of my worst fear. But there's no blood on my thighs, and I don't feel violated.

That's when a dark crimson stain catches my eye. The one smeared across the inside of my white comforter. It mocks me, daring me to come closer.

So, I do.

But as I twist toward the stained blanket, I draw in a sharp breath as another stinging pain shoots from my hip. Slowly, I glance down to see what could've caused such an ache.

What I see turns my blood to ice.

I'm bleeding all right, but not from a dick. Midway between my navel and left hip bone, someone carved a letter into my skin.

No, not someone. Troy Davis.

A fucking S.

I scream out in anger and frustration. I don't have to guess what that letter stands for. It speaks for itself.

Slut.

That bastard has no idea what he's done. One word—one *whisper* from me—and I can't count the number of ways he'd suffer, or the pieces of him that would end up scattered across all five boroughs.

And then I'd end up right back in Mexico behind the iron bars I just escaped.

This is why I'll be keeping Troy's assault and desecration to myself, as will every single one of my friends if they know what's good for them.

As far as they know, I'm María Diaz, the child of Cuban immigrants. They smile their plastic smiles, flip their blonde hair, and link arms with me, all while pretending they don't know exactly what I'm capable of.

They do. They just choose to lock it behind their gated suburban lies.

Fear is a deceptive spiritual guide.

Wrapping the sheet around myself, I shove everything away to deal with later. *Always later.* I can't afford to let the great Santi Carrera, my big brother, and the heir apparent of my father's empire, see weakness.

Because God forbid, I have a say in anything.

Santi left me alone in Mexico City two years ago to come to America and take control of our family's New Jersey cocaine distribution. No one asked me what I wanted.

Stay in Mexico and marry a nice boy, Lola.

Well, screw that.

Since my brother left, I've moved heaven and earth to follow him—which includes somehow convincing my overprotective parents to let me attend college in the heart of a warzone.

Making my way to the bathroom, I turn on the shower full blast. Before the water is even hot, I step inside, letting it wash away my sins. Even the ones I don't regret.

At least they were mine to make.

Control and freedom are two words I've craved but have been denied for years. Equal opportunity may be a right in the States, but things aren't so cut and dry where I'm from.

Not that women don't hold power in my world. I'm just not part of that exclusive club.

I'm Valentin Carrera's daughter. The king's innocent *cielito*—his little sky. I'm much too fragile to be tainted by the blood staining the hands of every member of my family. *Ay Dios mío*, I couldn't even cross the border and go to college without two huge bodyguards and my brother lurking behind every damn tree.

Maybe that's why I did it.

After stepping out of the shower, my mind spins like a Tilt-a-Whirl as I rush to throw on a pair of loose-fitting shorts and the least wrinkled shirt I can find.

I bite my lip while towel-drying my hair. My rebellion last night was stupid but exhilarating. I've kept a low profile since arriving on campus, so when my friend, Avery, suggested we blow off some steam, I was all in.

Party? *Hell yeah.* Booze? *Bring it.* Rich boys? *Even better.*

Then she said *his* name.

Sam Colton.

Slipping on a pair of sandals, I grab my phone and car keys and rush out the door, my hangover and stinging skin already forgotten. Instead, my head fills with a pair of watchful dark eyes.

Eyes so black I'm not sure there's a beginning or end. *Just infinite night.*

Taking the stairs two at a time, I keep a check on the time as I race across the parking lot toward my white BMW. I'm halfway there when a cool breeze licks down the back of my neck, causing my steps to falter.

My father's words ring like a church bell in my ears. *Always trust your instincts, cielito.*

"Is someone there?"

Of course, no one answers. The majority of the campus is still sleeping away their hangovers. Still, my feet refuse to move, cemented to the ground by a fatal curiosity.

I know all about the statistics of campus assault. I'm a prime target.

Young girl alone...

No one around to hear her cries for help...

It's a thought that should terrify me, but it doesn't. *It excites me.* There's something familiar in the air. Something forbidden and dangerous yet tantalizing and enticing.

Tightening my hold around the key fob, I hover my thumb over the panic button. "That's it," I mutter, shaking my head. "No more alcohol."

After settling behind the wheel, I lock the door and let out an unsettled breath. I can't shake the feeling I'm being watched.

Stalked.

Hunted.

As if my every move is a choreographed step in someone else's dance.

"You're losing it, Carrera." Starting the ignition, I turn to back out of the parking spot, when the wound on my stomach stings under the crude bandage I fashioned earlier. The corners of my mouth turn down, my momentary euphoria tanking at the bleak reminder.

I should've suggested we go to another party, but I didn't. Even though I knew better. Even though I've been cautioned.

"Stay away from Sam Colton, chaparrita. He's dangerous."

I rolled my eyes when my brother issued his warning. How could the hottest, most popular boy on campus be the most hazardous to my health? What the hell did he know about him that I didn't?

Temptation is a baited trap. Last night, I crept closer, knowing the second I touched the forbidden treat, a hair trigger would snap my neck.

But there's something about him… Something so mesmerizing it's worth the risk.

Danger is the most addictive drug and Sam has me hooked.

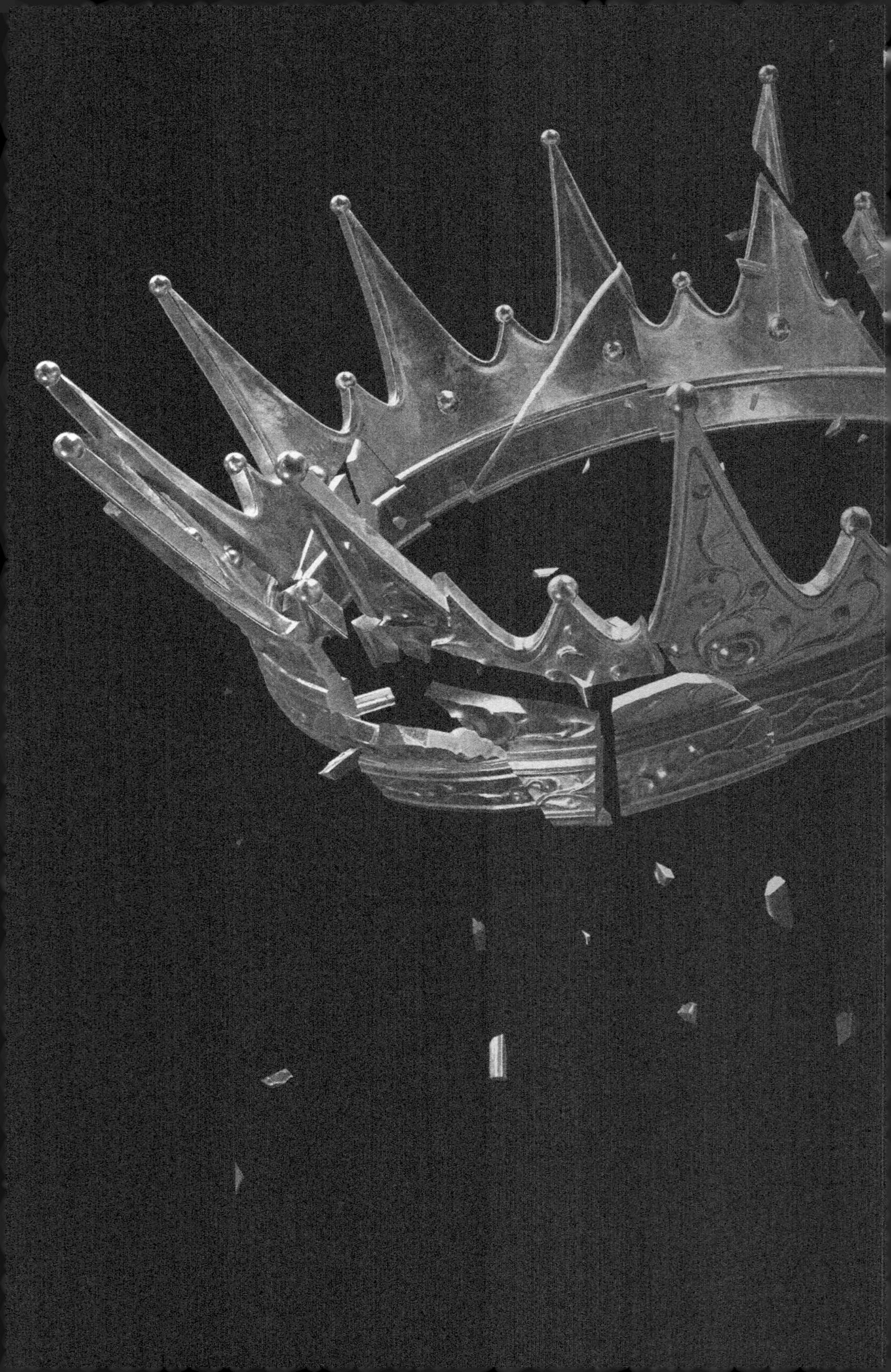

CHAPTER
Five

LOLA

"Not hungry?" My brother raises an eyebrow at me from across the small table.

I glance down at my untouched plate. "I don't like pizza."

Ugh, why did he have to pick an Italian restaurant? Thanks to our father, he has more money than all of New Jersey combined, yet here we sit in some godawful strip mall pizzeria.

"Bullshit. That ham and pineapple stuff is your favorite."

My stomach lurches. "Santi, please." I place my napkin on my plate, and *gracias a Dios*, it blocks the layer of grease from sight. "Will you lay off already?"

"No." He tosses me a lethal smirk.

I scrunch my nose in disgust. If we weren't in a public place, I'd punch it right off his face. Instead, I glare at him. "I'm sick, all right?" Crossing my arms, I slump into my chair. "I think I have the flu."

"You smell like last call." My big brother leans forward, the gold flecks in his eyes glinting with accusation. "The only thing you *have* is a hangover." I jump as he slams his palm onto the table. "What have I told you about the consequences of drinking around strangers?"

"That I could have fun?"

Santi's hand clenches, the vein in his temple pulsing with every grind of his teeth.

Christ, he's the spitting image of papá.

"You're testing me, *chaparrita*," he warns darkly.

I cringe at his childhood nickname for me. *Shorty.*

"You might get hurt," he continues, pausing on a slow inhale. "Where did you go last night? Felipé is getting his balls chopped off because of you."

My jaw drops. "What? Why?"

His eyes flash with an unforgiving truth no border walls can contain. "He's one of your personal guards, Lola. *Papá's* direct link to you besides me. What did you think would happen when you ditched him last night?"

Oh shit.

That's just it; I *didn't* think. Our father is merciless enough, but when it comes to me, he's inhuman. For some reason, I flip a switch in him that even *mamá* can't control.

Felipé is a pain in my ass, but he doesn't deserve *papá's* wrath.

"I'll call *papá*." I reach for my phone, my hands shaking so badly, I nearly knock over my water. "I'll tell him it was my"—I draw in a sharp breath as the tender flesh beside my hip burns—"my fault," I finish weakly. Keeping my gaze lowered, I try to pull up my father's coded contact in my phone.

Why won't my hand stop shaking?

I'm not afforded another attempt. Santi's bronzed one darts across the table and clamps on top of mine. "That's not how it works, and you know it. Actions have consequences. Unfortunately, Felipé will pay for yours."

I nod. It makes me sick to my stomach, but he's right. This is the way of our world, and no amount of pleading will change it.

As the pressure on my hand releases, I jerk my phone to my chest. *Bad move.* White, hot, pain tears through my body like a greased bobsled.

"Something's wrong."

It's not a question.

"Yeah." I wince, shifting in my chair. "Our father is about to castrate a man, and I'm about to throw up my spleen. Not a good day for vital organs."

Awesome, Lola. Crack a joke. That's always helpful.

He ignores my insolence. "Every time you move, you wince and clench your fists. You're hurt, so I'll ask again. Where were you last night?" He jabs a finger at me from across the table. "And don't lie to me."

"I sort of had a date." *Technically, it's not so much a lie as a bent truth.* "It didn't go so well."

"What does that mean?"

"He gave me a drink, and then it's all a big blur."

Santi's restrained anger explodes, his palms smacking the table again as his feet hit the floor. Glasses rattle and tip over, shattering into serrated pieces. "You deliberately put yourself in a vulnerable situation, opening the door for some asshole to roofie you? Of all the stupid—"

The entire restaurant falls silent as eyes shift toward us. This is the last thing either of us needs. "Santi," I plead in a low tone. "Please don't. Not here."

His gaze shifts to the left before he slowly sinks back into his seat. But I don't take my eyes off him. Just because the dragon isn't roaring, that doesn't mean he's not still breathing fire.

"Name," he says flatly.

"Santi…"

"Name, *chaparrita*. Don't make me seek it out myself." He issues the threat calmly, his nostrils flaring like a raging bull. "You won't like what happens."

I believe him.

"Troy Davis."

Santi pulls out his phone, and within seconds, he has someone on the line. "It's Carrera. Find a student named Troy Davis. Bring him to the docks and then wait for me there." Without another word, he disconnects the call and pockets his phone.

"What are you going to do?"

He holds my stare for one too many skipped heartbeats before speaking again, his tone dangerously calm. "You're a Carrera, Lola. You should know better than to let your guard down. Do you know how many men in this town would take a blade to you just to get to me? To get to *papá*?"

"No worries. Troy already took care of that," I mutter.

His eyes narrow into deadly slits. "Show me."

"*Here*? No!"

"I won't ask twice. You can show me, or I'll have RJ show me." He tilts his head to his left, where our cousin, Santi's second-in-command, sits watching our every move.

So that's who he was looking at.

"You wouldn't dare," I hiss, calling his bluff.

"Try me."

"You let him anywhere near me, and *papá* will shove a gun so far up your ass, you'll be burping bullets."

His full lips tip into a disturbing smile. "You think *papá* won't sanction my commands? Think again, *chaparrita*. I'm king in this state. You're just the kid who ditched her guard, went to a Santiago-affiliated party, and got herself roofied."

I glare at him, refusing his request, when his words blaze through my mind, leaving a scorched trail of deceit. "Wait, a *what* party?"

"Exactly," he scolds, folding his arms, his biceps straining beneath his white button-up shirt. "You have no idea the danger you've put yourself and this family in."

His accusation is like a punch to the chest. "I don't understand. How?"

Of course, he doesn't answer my question. He never does. This is Santi Carrera's world; we just live in it.

"Show me," he repeats, his jaw clenched.

Cursing under my breath, I tap the camera icon on my phone with more force than necessary.

"What are you doing?"

"Giving you what you asked for." As discreetly as possible, I lift the hem of my shirt and lower the elastic waistband on my shorts, quickly snapping a picture. Gritting my teeth, I shove my hand across the table. "They say a picture's worth a thousand words… Well, how about a letter?" I snort at my own joke as he takes my phone. "The bastard gave me a scarlet one. He carved an S for slut right next to my hip."

My heart stutters as fire sweeps up my brother's neck, igniting an all too familiar bloodlust in his eyes.

"It's not that bad," I whisper, shrinking into my seat. "Once it heals, I'll get a tattoo over it. It won't even show."

"The S is not for slut," he says in a clipped tone.

A few precious beats pass...

And then all hell breaks loose.

Santi stands, his expensive Santoni dress shoes hitting the tiles seconds before a roar rips from his chest. Flipping the table, he sends it flying across the restaurant and then storms out the door.

What the hell just happened?

I glance toward RJ, who simply shrugs and pulls a wad of bills from his pocket.

Oh, for fuck's sake...

It's not smart or rational, but I follow after my brother. It only takes a couple of steps to spot him leaning against the side of a building, a newly lit cigarette hanging from his lips.

By the time I reach him, I'm more than a little pissed off myself. "What the hell is wrong with you? And since when do you smoke?"

A little hypocritical, but whatever.

"Since about thirty seconds ago—right about the time I realized my sister started the next phase of this war."

"What's that supposed to mean?"

Leaving the burning embers tucked between his lips, he pulls his phone from his pocket and scrolls until he finds what he's looking for. Taking a long drag, he pulls the cigarette out of his mouth and holds up a picture. "Look familiar?"

My knees nearly buckle. *No. That can't be right.*

"Who's that?"

"Nora, my dock hand, who I compensated very well to clear all my shipments. She was on my payroll." He taps his middle finger against the rectangular thing lying beneath her. "Now she's on a metal slab at the medical examiner's office. A Carrera associate was about to perform her autopsy when he sent me this photo." He jabs the same finger toward the center of the screen, "And that, dear sister, is the same scarlet letter carved into her chest."

I can't breathe.

"S isn't for slut, Lola. It's for Santiago."

Breathe. Just breathe.

Dropping the barely-smoked cigarette onto the pavement, Santi stomps it out with the heel of his shoe while shoving his phone back into his pocket. "I told you to stay the fuck away from Colton."

"I have! What's he got to do with this anyway?"

"*Mamá.*"

The word is like another deep cut to my skin. Our father has sheltered me from most inner workings of the family business, save one. *Mamá's* role in the eighteen-year Carrera/Santiago feud is something that even the great Valentin Carrera could never hide.

Not when the ripple effect lasted well into our childhood.

A temporary alliance between Dante Santiago and my father turned into a third-party massacre at my *Tía* Adriana and *Tío* Brody's wedding. My mother, pregnant with me at the time, got caught in the line of fire, and it nearly killed both of us.

Papá laid the blame at Dante Santiago's feet, swearing vengeance against his cartel and its bloodline.

I shake my head. "But that has to do with the Santiago Cartel, and Sam—"

"Colton *is* the Santiago Cartel," he says coldly. "He's operating under a false name, *María*." I wince at his mocking drawl of my alias. "His real last name is Sanders, otherwise known as Senator Rick Sanders's stepson. You know, the former New York kingpin turned politician? Santiago *owns* New York," he stresses, shoving a hand through his thick, dark hair. "*Dios mío*, Lola!"

The way he spits out my name, it might as well be another curse word.

"How could *I* have known that?" I insist, my voice shaking as I defend myself. "You and *papá* don't tell me anything!"

"You weren't on a date last night," he accuses, taking two steps toward me. "You were with *him*. ¡No me mientas! Don't lie to me." His bitter expression turns deadly as he backs me against the building. "Right now, Troy Davis is being dragged from his hospital bed and will soon be chained to a metal beam. I'm already going to shred him into unrecognizable ribbons of flesh. It's your call whether his death will be quick or drawn out."

We stare at each other, my voice trapped in my throat.

"It'd be a shame if he endured unnecessary torture while paying for someone else's sins," he adds viciously.

My stomach lurches. "Fine! I was at Sam Colton's..." At Santi's dipped chin, I clench my teeth. "I mean Sam *Sanders's* party, but I swear Troy *did* put something in my drink. The last thing I remember is him taking me upstairs."

I force myself not to cringe as Troy's foreboding whispers from last night slithers through a hazy crack in my memory. *Trust me...*

My brother's eyes are crazed with hate as he draws his arm back and drives his fist into the wall. I cringe at the sickening sound.

"Sam didn't touch me, Santi!" I scream, looking up at him with pleading eyes. "We've never even spoken to each other." *Words as painful as they are accurate.*

I've never had to fight for a man's attention, but at that party, I'd locked gazes with him. I'd bitten my bottom lip, letting it slowly slide through my teeth.

Teasing him...

Enticing him...

And then nothing.

For a man who couldn't take his eyes off me, he sure as hell couldn't take a hint.

I never even wanted Troy Davis.

Guess the joke's on me.

"You think he didn't touch you?" A tight frown tugs at the corners of Santi's mouth. "Are you sure about that, *chaparrita*?" Cupping my chin, he leans close. "*This* is why *papá* didn't want you in America. You're too innocent. Too fucking trusting." His eyes flash with a hint of sadness as he pushes off the wall and walks away.

"Where are you going?" I call after him.

"To clean up your mess."

"Santi!"

He pauses but doesn't turn around. "You're my baby sister, Lola. *A Carrera.* By touching you, Sanders fired the first shot."

I wince at the ruthlessness in his voice. "What are you going to do?"

"Fire the last."

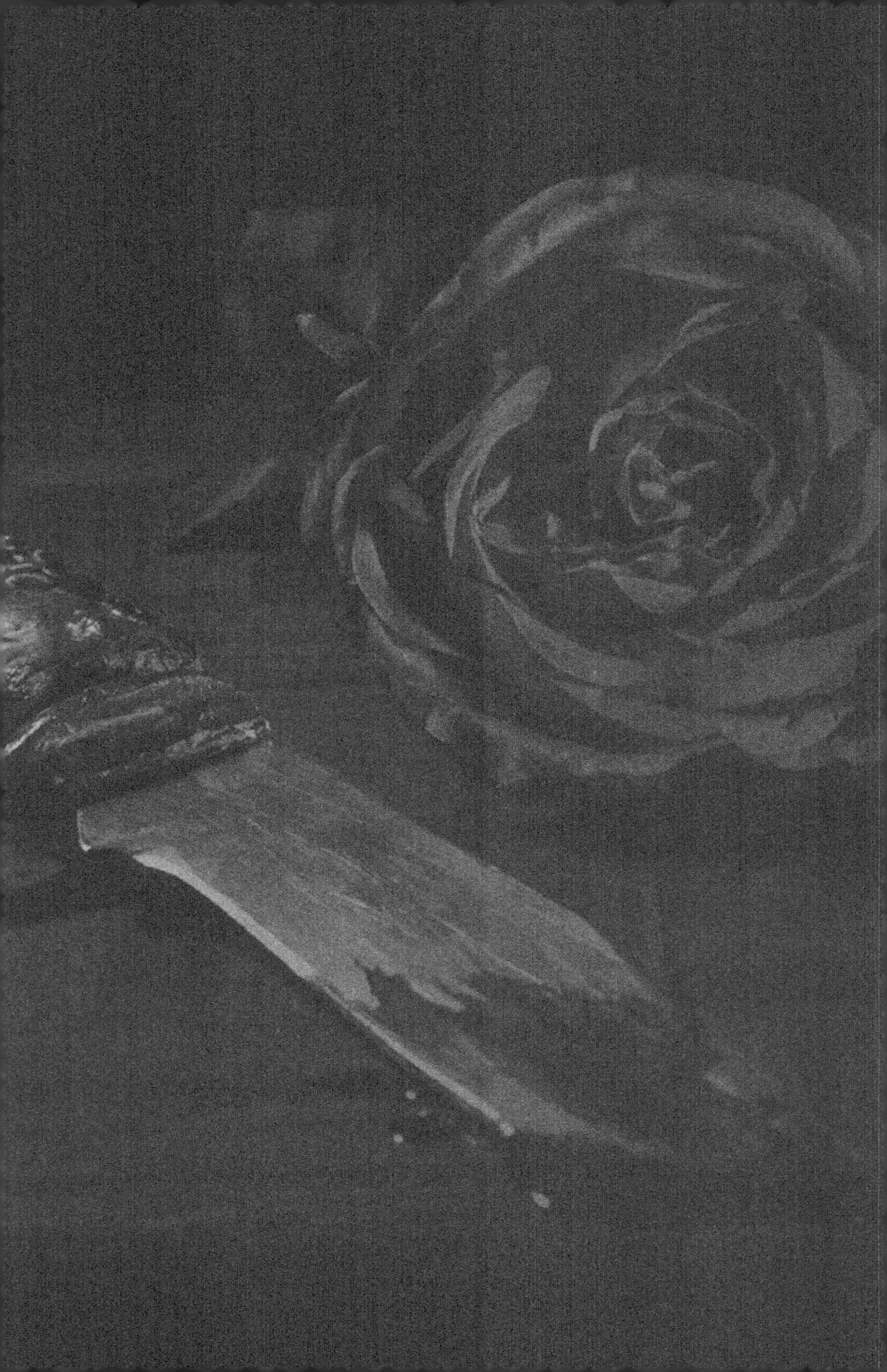

CHAPTER
Six

SAM

The table flips.

Pizza goes flying in all directions.

Blind rage heads for the front door, with sweet confusion trailing after him.

Flexing my grip, I loosen the gun's connection with the back of the guard's head as I glance at another security feed that shows Santi Carrera slamming his fist into the wall outside the restaurant.

"Expand on camera three," I order, and the terrified strip mall guard complies with shaking fingers. Within seconds, the main screen is a forty-six-inch display of satisfaction.

Some say it's an unparalleled feeling when your blade penetrates deep into the heart of your enemy. For me, their reaction is even better. The look on Carrera's face right now is more stunning than a sunset over the Grand Canyon.

It's a brief euphoria, though.

The dark clouds roll in the moment he takes Lola's chin. *The moment he touches what's mine.*

"P-please, don't hurt me."

I glance down to see that I've rammed the muzzle of my gun into the guard's head so hard his face is bowed over a keyboard.

"You've done well," I say, easing up on the contact again. "Don't ruin it. Tell anyone I was here, and you're a dead man." Tossing a couple of hundred-dollar bills onto the desk next to him, I drop my gun and exit the security booth.

By the time I reach my Bugatti, Lola is on the move. I placed a tracking device on her white BMW the night she switched my world to monotone. The moment she made it all about *her*.

Glancing at my cell, I watch her take a right. My lips curve into a smile.

So pretty.

So predictable.

I know exactly where she's headed—my apartment. She wants to raise hell about what I did last night, but I'll always be one step ahead. Once she reaches her destination, I have a fun surprise in store for her.

Lola, Lola, Lola.

She burns as bright as the sun, and I can never get enough.

Pulling out of the parking lot myself, I set a course for the opposite direction. If I can't have her body, I'll satisfy myself with the next best thing.

Twenty minutes later, I'm parking outside her apartment. I kill the block's security feed with a swipe of my finger. My phone starts beeping as I'm reaching the front door.

My office. Two hours.

I expected this. The senator has eyes and ears all over the East Coast. It was only a matter of time before I was dragged before his court of reckoning. *Well, guess what, stepdaddy dearest? I have a little reckoning of my own to toss around.*

Her apartment smells of her.

I cut a trail down the hallway, through her bedroom and into her bathroom. I run my finger over her bottles of perfumes and moisturizers, shampoos and conditioners. I find her birth control tablets stashed at the back of the vanity unit and force myself not to pop out every little yellow pill and crush them beneath the heel of my sneakers.

The idea of my child growing inside her turns my dick to stone.

My child.

No one else's...

Fuck.

Kids?

I'm driving myself insane with these thoughts. I'm only twenty years old. I can have any woman I want, but no one else can satisfy me like she can.

I want to use her.

Complete her.

Dirty up her tongue.

Stain her insides.

Spread her perfect ass cheeks and lavish attention on the most secret part of her.

Hissing out a curse, I fall against the vanity unit—gripping the white porcelain basin with one hand as I tear at my zipper with the other. Tipping my head back, I fill my lungs with her scent and her ghost as I work my cock like a man possessed.

Longing.

Needing.

Hard, for the diamond edges of this insatiable lust.

Fast, for how quick this descent into her madness has become.

My wrist aches.

My cock swells.

I groan in pain and elation as lightning zips down my spine and my balls draw tight to my body. I shoot my load so violently, thick ropes of it streak across the porcelain, blemishing the polished silver faucet and mirror.

With my head still swimming, I clean myself up and head for the door. I don't bother wiping away my sin. This won't be the last time I corrupt a part of Lola Carrera. As long as there's breath in *my* body, no other man will take their pleasure from hers.

My phone beeps again as I slip out of her apartment and make my way down the exit stairway to the parking lot.

You're in deep shit, Sam. Care to make it an abyss? I told you to stay away from her. My office. Time is ticking.

Despite my stepfather's fighting words, I'm in a conciliatory mood as I slide into the driver's seat. After checking Lola's car tracker and seeing she's headed home, I tap out a brief response.

On my way.

It's high time the senator had a lesson in generational deposition.

There's a new Sanders in town, and he better get used to it.

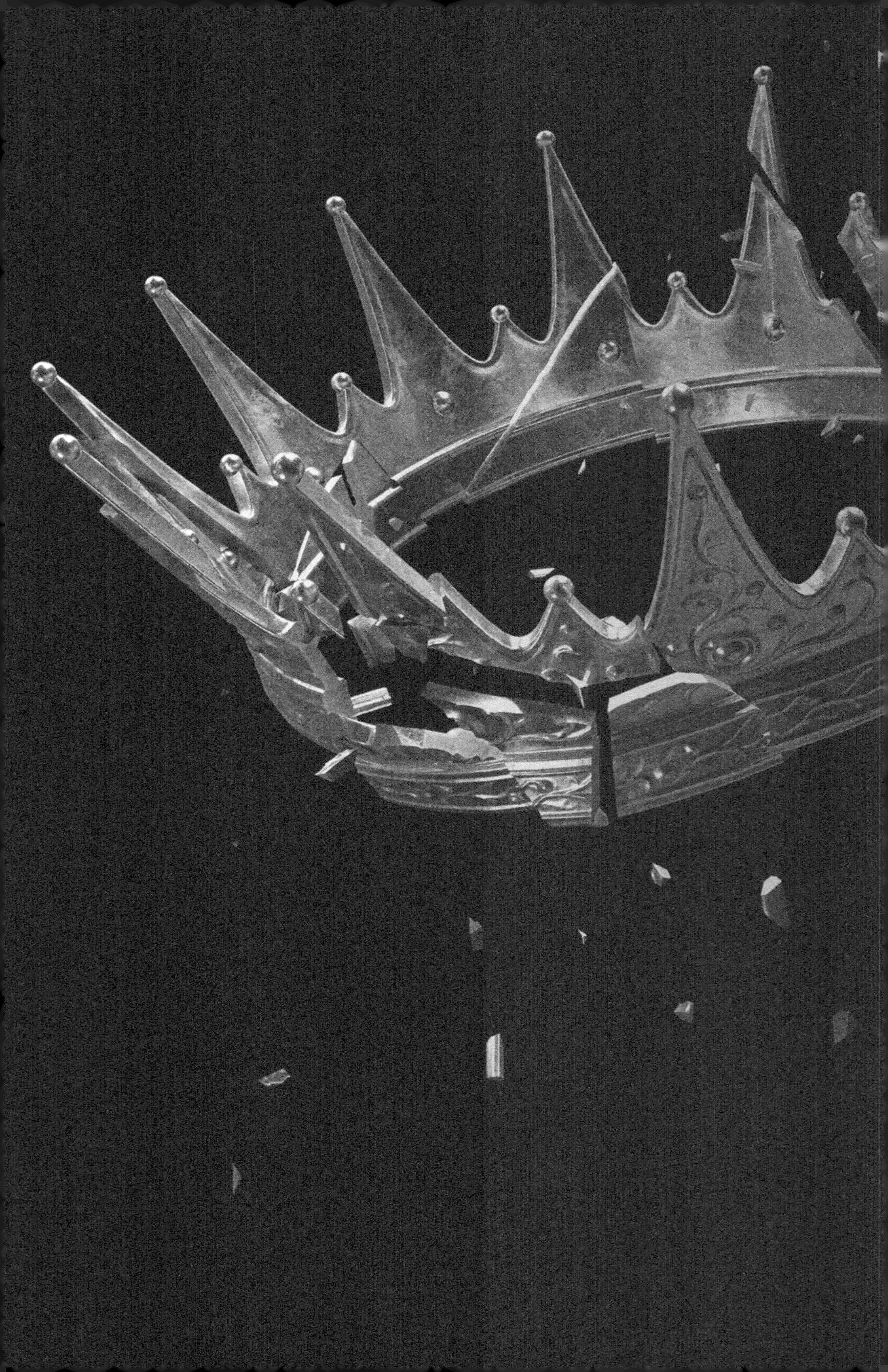

CHAPTER
Seven

LOLA

I shouldn't warn him.

I should go back to my apartment and let Santi dish out whatever punishment he sees fit. After all, Troy tried to rape me, and Sam…

Oh my God, did he brand me?

We've never said two words to each other before, but it seems he's happy to let his knife do the talking. I thought the new blood thrumming through the veins of the cartel underworld might dilute this feud between our families. Instead, it seems to have fortified it. Fueled it. Twisted it into something much darker…

Now, instead of standing on the outskirts of war, I've been forced across its borders and made into a casualty.

I shouldn't warn him.

The words repeat in my head as I pull my car into the parking lot outside his apartment. They burrow deep into my psyche as I climb the pretentious marble steps leading to his front door. They slice into my heart as I reach out a shaking finger and ring the doorbell.

Nothing.

I ring it again.

Nothing.

"Sam?" I press my face against the narrow window beside the door. There doesn't appear to be any movement, but I still call his name. "I know you're in there, Sam *Sanders*," I say, hissing the now-familiar last name. "You don't know who the hell you've messed with. Why don't you come out here and face me now that I'm conscious?"

Nothing.

Shit.

Exhaustion and nerves hit all at once, and I collapse forward, dropping my forehead against the glass. Heaving a sigh, I twist around until my back hits the brick wall next to it.

Nice. Real smooth, Lola.

I have no idea what I'm doing. I came here with no plan and no forethought. All I know is that I can't get Santi's words out of my head.

"Sam didn't touch me, Santi! We've never even spoken to each other."

"Are you sure about that, chaparrita?"

I thought I was. But now I can't seem to remember much of anything. And if Santi is right, and this S carved on me stands for Santiago, at some point late last night, I was alone with Colton.

Sanders...*whatever.*

Something dark and forbidden flares inside me. Something I can never speak of or acknowledge. The thought of him touching me should sicken me, but it doesn't.

Quite the opposite.

"It's just the drugs," I say with a groan, stepping away from the apartment. "Whatever Troy slipped in my drink messed up my head." Sighing, I turn to leave, when a piece of yellow paper stuck to the far side of the door catches my eye.

The closer I get, I realize it's a Post-it Note that someone has scribbled on. Ripping it off the door, I read it word for word and line for line. Then I read it twice more as a rush of heat crawls up my neck and stains my face.

When I read his words for the fourth time, I swear I can feel him watching me again.

My mouse doesn't want to be caught. Unless that's what she desires most... Better luck next time, dulzura.

CHAPTER
Eight

SAM

Senator Rick Sanders doesn't raise his voice. Even as a kid, growing up with my twin half-brother and sister, I can't recall a single time he yelled at us.

His methods of showing his displeasure are far more refined. When he's really pissed, like he is now, his gray eyes darken to cold steel and the sharp lines of his Armani suit take on all the comfort of razor blades.

It's his tone that chills the most. His easy drawl drops to a low and vicious rasp where every word, every vowel, *every inflection* returns to the tough Brooklyn streets where he grew up.

"What the fuck did you do last night, Sam?"

"You know exactly what I did, Daddio, and you know why I did it."

Leaning back in my chair, I gaze unseeingly at the white architrave in his five-million-dollar penthouse home office. My bodyguard-jailers work for him, not me, so I knew a call to the senator would have been made the moment Lola Carrera walked into my party.

Still, they have their uses. Tapping phones is another trick I learned before my eighth birthday. After that, I graduated fast. These days, there isn't a computer system I can't hack, which is how I know my worth to an organization like Santiago's.

Did she find the note yet?

"Nina is angry with you as well."

"Why?" I say, dropping my head. "She's not my mother. The first Mrs. Sanders is pushing up thorns in Calvary Cemetery, remember?"

So is my piece of shit, deadbeat dad if we're skipping down that happy trail. He was found with his throat slit the day Rick discovered I wasn't his. My stepfather doesn't like loose ends.

"Manners, Sam," he murmurs, his subtext clear. *Stop acting like a dick.*

I can't help it, even though I actually think my stepfather is pretty cool.

"You're just a kid playing in an adult world with very adult rules." The senator fixes me with a glare, and I return it with a grin.

"Are you jealous, Daddio? Before my stepmother came along, you'd screwed half of Manhattan's trophy wives, plus their mothers-in-law."

At this, there's a deep rumble of laughter behind me—a slow, dangerous, sleeper of a sound that hits me like a freight train.

Spinning around, I see the tall, inimitable, scary-as-hell figure of my godfather darkening up the doorway.

"The boy has your mouth, Sanders," he says, striding toward us. *Black jeans. Black shirt.* It's kind of fitting after all the death he's dealt in the last fifty years. "I believe the nature versus nurture debate just got resolved."

"Go fuck yourself, Dante," my stepfather drawls, seemingly unsurprised by the Colombian kingpin's appearance. He tosses a couple of photographs across the desk at him. "Turns out we share the same exquisite taste in women."

I catch a sideways glance, and my stomach drops. They're all of Lola from last night, approximately thirty minutes before Troy exited stage left at a bloody crawl.

The senator laughs when he notices the look on my face. "We expected you to screw her, not brand her, you stupid dickhead."

Wait, what?

"You're not pissed at what I did?" I say, frowning in confusion.

His eyes glint in amusement. "You've had your fun, Sam... Let's just say I wanted in on the action. Christ, you're even more belligerent than I am when backed into a corner."

What the hell is going on here?

"Does Santiago know who she is?"

"*Santiago* knew the moment she graced American soil," my godfather interrupts, cocking a dark eyebrow at me. "When my enemy's daughter happens to sweet-talk her way out of her heavily-armed Mexican compound and within touching distance of my territory, it would be remiss of me *not* to welcome her in with open arms."

Before I crush her with them.

I fill in that last part for myself.

"You played me, Daddio." Shades of red start misting up my vision. I hate being blindsided. *I hate that I don't have a plan in place to take the heat off their interest in her.*

But I will.

Because Lola is mine, not theirs.

"Reverse psychology, Sammio," he says, handing my own mockery back to me, fighting another grin. "Tell the cool kid to stay away from the hot new chick on campus, then watch the sparks fly."

"It was a test."

"A test," he confirms.

"You never had any issues about me working for Santiago."

"Sam," he says with a sigh. "I'd be the last fucking prick to lecture you about blurred lines and morality, but if you're planning to dance on the wrong side of the law, I'd prefer it if you partnered up with us. Edier Grayson is poised to take control of New York, and we want you as his second."

"You stepped in when it mattered most." I can feel Dante's dark eyes punching a hole in my face as he interjects. "I can't exact revenge on a body that's already damaged."

I know what he's talking about right away.

"Troy Davis." There's a pause. "Is he dead?"

"He will be soon, but not by my hand. Carrera got to him first. If it were one of my daughters he'd drugged and assaulted, there wouldn't be much of him left."

The look on his face sends a shiver through my body. *You don't fuck with this man and get to swap stories about it.*

He gestures at the bar in the corner. "Bourbon, Sanders."

"Get it yourself," comes the easy riposte.

"The knife in the quarterback's leg was a nice touch." I watch, heart hammering, as the Colombian helps himself to my stepfather's liquor. "Remind me to use it on the next Carrera we torture."

"But not Lola."

I say it too fast.

Too obvious.

"No, not Lola." He shoots me a look over the rim of his glass. "I have more creative designs on her than that. Even more creative than carving my initial into her skin."

I don't correct his assumption. Even though that letter, *that body*, belongs to me, not him.

I point to the photos on the desk. "Tell me what you're planning to do to her."

The temperature in the room drops sharply.

"That sounded dangerously close to an order," Dante says idly. "Can you spell the word respect, or would you like my fist to give you a lesson?"

"Let it go, Santiago," my stepfather warns. "There's no dick swinging in my office unless it's mine and my wife is doing the honors."

"Stay close to her." He finishes up his drink and pours himself another. "We arranged for her brother, Santi, to be out of town last night, but we won't be that lucky again for a while."

"Since when do you take such a keen interest in my sex life?" I say, losing my cool.

"Since the moment you flashed up on Lola Carrera's radar," Dante clips back. "She sees you, Sam... And when a cartel princess *sees*, she doesn't usually stop until she *gets*." He slams his glass down, that wicked smirk catching at the corners of his mouth again. "That's when you make things interesting. That's when there's no crueler torture than a bleeding heart."

CHAPTER
Nine

LOLA

My concentration is shot to hell.

After the fourth time scanning the same paragraph, I slam my social sciences book closed and toss it away. Groaning, I press my fingers against my closed eyelids as I sit cross-legged in the middle of my bed.

I have no clue what I just read.

Although, I shouldn't be shocked—there's no room left inside my head for useless information. I thought keeping busy the rest of the day would occupy all the space he's claimed, but that's an impossible feat.

Especially when it's just as marked with his name as my skin.

Even after eight hours of senseless shopping and a caffeine-infused coffeehouse crawl, I still can't get Sam, or his dark note, off my mind.

My elbows dig into the inside of my knees as I slump forward. Sinking my fingers into my hair, I tug at the strands as if somehow it will unroot memories from last night.

The ones of him.

The ones of him touching me.

Marking me.

Seeing me.

He witnessed me at my most vulnerable—naked and at his mercy. He could have added his enemy's innocence to his claims last night, but he didn't.

Why?

And why the hell am I even questioning it?

I should be counting my blessings that last night only cost me a physical scar. It could have been much worse. He could have left me with plenty more that would never heal.

Digging into the pocket of my shorts, I pull out a crumpled yellow piece of paper, my heart leaping into my throat as I smooth it out on my bare thigh.

My mouse doesn't want to be caught. Unless that's what she desires most... Better luck next time, dulzura.

Dulzura.

Sweetness? What the hell is that? I'm sure it wasn't meant as a term of endearment as much as a well-aimed dart. Just like all Santiagos, he managed to twist something innocent into something dark and perverted.

I should be furious. Instead, I want to twist back.

Which would be suicidal.

Sandwiching the Post-it Note between my palms, I press them against my lips almost as if in prayer. For what, I have no idea.

Forgiveness for my sins?

Strength not to commit more?

Wisdom to know the damn difference?

Sam Sanders... Just his name should be a cold slap of reality. If knowledge is power, then knowing who Sam Colton really is should drown this infatuation in a deep pool of vengeance.

So why don't I hate him?

Why do I still have his note?

Two more questions I don't have the answers to.

Unfolding my legs, I climb off my bed, wondering just how high this ledge is... The one I seem to have found myself cornered on with nowhere to run. No means of escape.

No way out but straight down.

Moving toward the window, I brush the curtain with the back of my hand. Unsurprisingly, my only view is a steel jaw and tense, folded arms. It's dark, but then again, so is RJ. I wouldn't be surprised if he bribes the sun just to exist in its light.

The streetlight casts a demonic glow across his expressionless face. He's not in a pleasant mood, and with good reason. I had him chasing me all over New Brunswick today like we were two rats in a bullet-ridden maze.

Courtesy of one overprotective future cartel king.

"Well played, Santi," I mutter.

My brother is nothing if not shrewd. My father has already punished one of my trusted bodyguards for my actions—RJ is his calculated replacement.

Slumping against the window frame, I let out a weary sigh. I never intentionally meant to cause Felipé harm. He was a good bodyguard. A good *sicario*. A good man. But in cartel life, good and bad are simply varying shades of the same intent—*loyalty.*

Felipé wasn't family.

But RJ is...

Santi knows damn well I'd never do anything impulsive and risk our cousin's life—*like ditch him to go to an enemy's party.*

The thought barely takes form in my head before he lifts his chin and meets my stare head-on. *Yep, he's pissed...* RJ doesn't smirk or sneer. He just continues to stare up at me, his arms pulled tightly across his white button-up as he leans up against the hood of his car.

He'd be a lot more pissed if he knew I saw him at that restaurant in North Caldwell a week ago. From what I witnessed, it seems I'm not the only one with my ass on the line.

Sighing, I pull my hand back and the curtain flutters back into place. *A caged princess with no prince in sight.* The Post-it Note feels like a tangle of thorns in my hand as I collapse against the wall.

Why the hell did I go to his place to try and warn him? That's a direct betrayal of not only my brother, but my entire family.

Because the thought of Sam getting hurt terrifies you, a voice in my head answers.

Which makes zero sense. The man has done nothing but play mind games with me, yet here I am...

Protecting him.

I push away from the window.

No. I'm stronger than this.

Balling the note, I toss it in the trash can next to my nightstand. "You're wrong, Sam," I promise under my breath. "This is one mouse you'll never catch."

Flopping back onto my bed, I reach for my textbook, when my phone rings. One glance at the caller ID, and I contemplate sending it straight to voicemail. I'm in no mood to play identity roulette right now. However, ever since arriving in America, I've learned there are two truths in life: I'll never escape my name, and Avery Thorpe will not be ignored.

Swiping the damn thing off the nightstand, I force pleasantries I don't feel. "Hi, Ave…"

"It's about damn time."

"Yeah, sorry about that." I glance toward the window where I know RJ still sits on the other side, brooding. "I had a lot of studying to do."

"It's Saturday." Before I can come up with a suitable rebuttal, she adds, "And that's bullshit. You haven't been home all day—we checked."

Shit.

"Look, I—"

"Spill, Diaz," she interrupts. "I want all the horny details."

My grip tightens around my phone. "What?"

"Troy…you lucky bitch. We all saw you go upstairs with him last night at the party. We looked for you later on, but someone said you'd left with him."

I wince. *I left…but not with Troy.*

"Someone saw wrong," I say flatly.

I might as well have said someone saw me sprout horns and a tail and then screw Satan on the hood of Sam's Bugatti.

"Own it, María. Hell, I'd tattoo that shit on my forehead if I were you."

I roll my eyes. "That'd make for an awkward job interview."

She laughs, a sound which slices through the thick tension that's been wrapped around me since meeting with Santi.

Rubbing my temple, I exhale a breath that's half-sigh and half-laugh. "Nothing happened, Avery. I turned him down, so he ditched me and hung around for a while."

Technically, it's not a lie. If Santi has had his way, Troy is probably doing a lot of hanging.

"I slept in my own bed last night…alone," I add, intercepting what I know to be a forthcoming assumption.

Again, technically not a lie.

"Whatever," she mutters. "We'll get it out of you tonight after a few drinks."

Wait, what?

"Tonight?"

"Don't tell me you forgot. Girls night?" When I don't say anything, she groans out her annoyance. "We planned it weeks ago."

Which is exactly why I forgot about it.

I've never had "girl" friends. I've never had many friends, period. Bearing the Carrera name doesn't lend itself to many sleepovers. This whole "sisterhood" thing is as foreign to me as America itself.

"I'll have to pass." I'm not in a partying mood after just getting roofied, plus Santi would lose his shit—and then pretty blonde girls become dead ones.

"Come on," she whines. "You owe it to us after ditching us last night."

What am I supposed to say to that? It's not like I can tell her the truth. So to avoid any more questions and another possible homicide, I relent.

"Fine." Drawing out the word with a groan, I crane my arm and snag a pen off my nightstand. "Where do I meet you?"

Damn it, I need something to write on. I scan my room, but besides my textbook, there's only one thing in sight.

One taunting piece of discarded yellow paper.

Swinging my legs off the side of the mattress, I clench my teeth as I hook my foot over the rim of the trashcan and then drag it toward me. Begrudgingly, I retrieve the crumpled Post-it Note, smoothing it out and then flipping it over, all while trying not to think about the lethal promise scrawled on the other side.

"The Foxhole, ten o'clock." she says as an engine revs in the background. "And María...?"

"Yeah?"

"Dress to kill."

I stiffen as the line goes dead. Slowly, I turn the Post-it Note back over, re-reading my enemy's words as a graphic warning flares inside my head.

"That's what I'm worried about," I whisper softly.

I stare at my reflection in the bathroom mirror, a horrified expression looking back at me. One sliced into a distorted, crude mosaic crafted by *him*.

His scent lingers somewhere deep in my subconscious. A vicious haven of leather and barbed wire.

One foot moves in front of the other until I'm pressed up against the counter. Reaching forward, I touch the glass, trailing my finger along the dried stains.

I may be a virgin, but I'm not totally innocent. I know what the hell is all over my mirror.

And basin.

And faucets.

Cum.

"You son of a bitch," I hiss, dropping my hand and clenching my fists by my side. Only the words lack conviction. There's no offense entwined with my insult, only fire.

The wrong kind.

I'm furious he invaded my apartment. I'm fearful of how he did it so easily.

But most of all, I'm turned on.

I don't know what game Sam's playing, but it has taken a dangerous turn. He's marked me, and now he's marked the one place I call my own. It's a message I should return with a lipstick-kissed bullet, but I can't ignore the coiling in my belly or the unbearable ache between my legs.

Thoughts of him consume me as carnal need takes over. I close my eyes, diluted justification swimming behind them as my hand slides inside the waistband of my shorts. *It will almost be like we came together...*

Sam...

However, the moment my finger slides in between my wet folds, my eyes fly open in horror. *This is what he wants...* Pissed, I jerk my hand out of my shorts, the elastic waistband snapping back into place with a pop.

No. I won't give him the satisfaction.

"Nice try, asshole." Bending down, I open a cabinet door under the counter, swinging it hard against the wooden base. Armed with a towel in one hand and Windex in the other, I go to erase every trace of him…and then I freeze.

Because some messed-up, masochistic part of me doesn't want to.

Common sense tells me I'm taking a dangerous risk by leaving it there, but logic isn't in control right now—lust is.

Sighing out a frustrated breath, I drop the towel and my clothes into a pile on the bathroom floor. I don't care about the consequences as I turn the shower on full blast and step under a waterfall of scalding hot punishment.

As I lather, images of Sam force their way into my head. His hand pumping his thick cock. His face twisted in Machiavellian pleasure while coming with my name on his lips.

My hand creeps lower.

No, Lola. Don't do it.

I grit my teeth, forcing my hand back up my body, wincing as my fingers graze my still tender hip. Blinking water from my eyes, I glance down at the letter he carved into my skin. I trace the jagged curve that starts at the top, following down its forbidden path.

"S isn't for slut, Lola. It's for Santiago."

The words are sharp shards of ice driven straight into my chest.

Did he do it out of hate, or was it something darker?

"Damn you, Sanders…" Quickly rinsing off, I slam my hand onto the faucet and turn the water off.

Why do I let him get to me like this?

Shoving my hand against the shower door, I drag the discarded towel off the floor and wrap it around my body, not bothering to dry off first.

And then I see it again…

His salacious calling card.

Ripping the towel off, I stomp toward the glass and scrub the mirror and basin until they're both spotless. Taking slow, ragged breaths to diffuse my anger, I hastily shake out the towel and wrap it back around my dripping skin.

It's only then that I realize what I've done.

So much for getting clean. I just coated myself in my stalker's cum.

Wandering back into my bedroom, I open my closet, revealing row after row of designer dresses. However, only one catches my eye.

Dress to kill…

Swallowing any lingering reservation, I reach for the one I know with every fiber of my being I shouldn't wear.

Short, shiny, and silver.

I hope Sam Sanders has the good sense to stay away tonight.

Otherwise, those words may be prophetic.

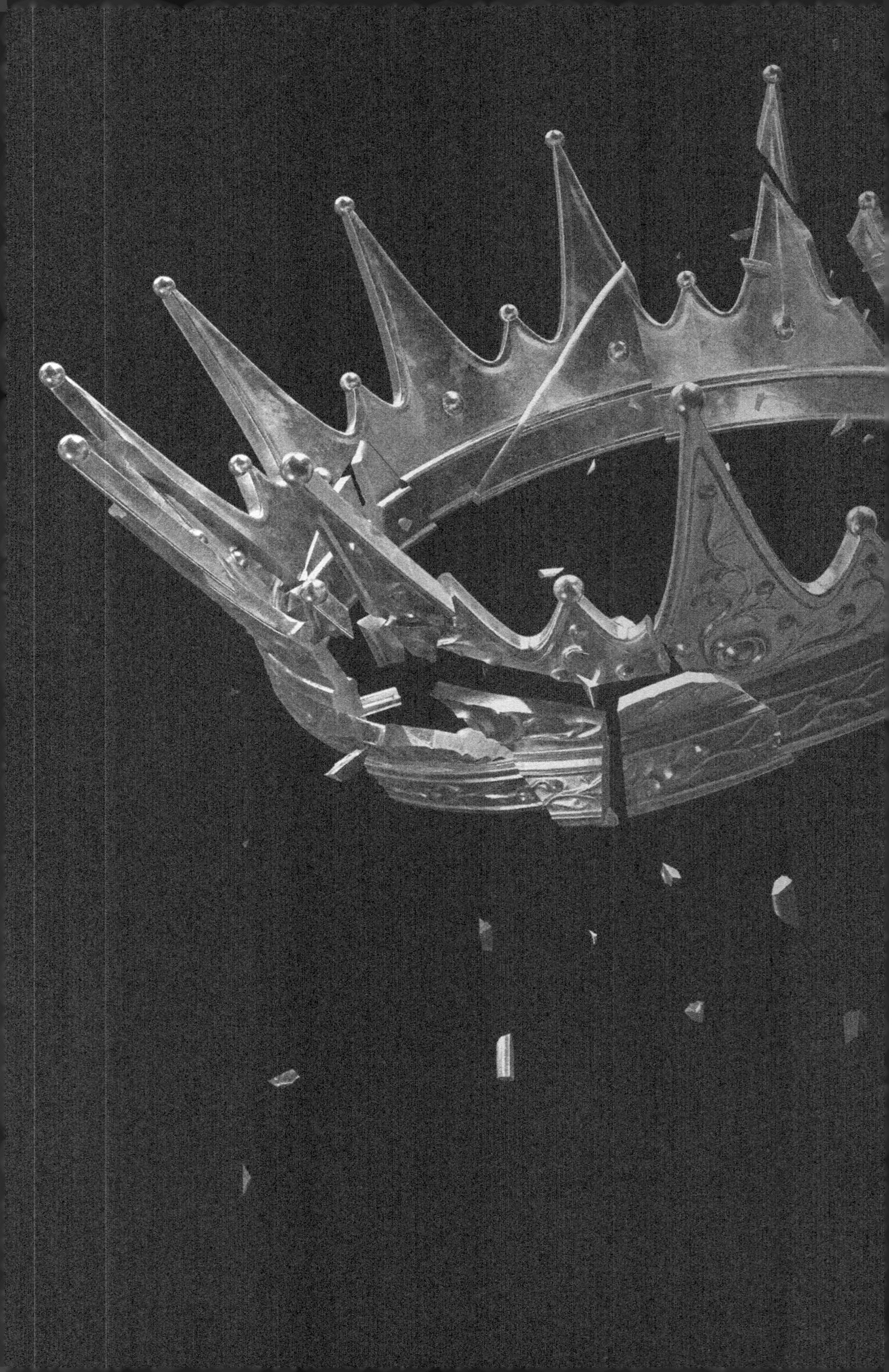

CHAPTER
Ten

LOLA

The line is already three drunks deep by the time I make my way to the bar. Alcohol is the last thing I should have right now, but my liver is the least of my worries. I need something eighty-proof to get me through the night.

After a few unproductive moments of waiting my turn, I take matters into my own hands. Paying little attention to the dirty looks being shot my way, I push through the crowd and squeeze into a small pocket toward the front.

A bartender, who looks like he just stepped off the pages of an underwear ad, pauses in front of me. "What can I get for you?"

I don't hesitate. "A shot of *Añejo* tequila."

If I'm going to play a king's game, I might as well drink like one.

He lifts an eyebrow. "You got an ID hidden in the dress somewhere?"

My smile is anything but sweet. Reaching into my bra, I pull out the fake ID Avery and I bought our first week on campus and hand it to him. I'd like to tell him where he can shove it, but I've already landed myself on Santi's radar enough as it is.

He barely even looks at it before tossing it back and turning to face the wall of liquor bottles behind him. While I wait, I scan the perimeter, looking for Avery and the rest of my friends in the sea of shadowed faces.

Nothing.

Damn it.

I have no idea why it was so imperative we come here tonight. The Foxhole isn't anything special. It's just your typical nightclub—thirty-five hundred square feet of chrome acting as reflectors for the magenta and purple stage lights.

And in case one inch of space missed the cotton candy colored memo, the disco ball hanging in the center of the dance floor is there to drive the point home.

Jesus, where'd that guy go to pour my drink—Mexico?

I'm leaning over the bar, trying to see where he could've gone, when I feel a hand grab my ass from behind.

"What the hell?" I spin around, nearly tumbling into another pretentious polo shirt stretched across a broad chest.

Ay Dios mío... Did Rutgers issue one to every damn idiot with an acceptance letter and a dick?

Grabbing hold of the bar, I steady myself while staring into a pair of bloodshot green eyes.

"Sorry, baby," he slurs. "If you're gonna flash the goods, don't be shocked when someone tries a sample."

I fight to rein in my temper. *If he only knew...* Instead of smirking, he should be counting his blessings that we're in New Jersey. Twenty-five hundred miles south and every one of those perfect white teeth would be scattered across the floor.

Along with that hand.

And other favored appendages.

Luckily, both our nights are saved when the bartender clears his throat behind me. "Francesca?"

I twist back around. "Huh?"

He flips my ID between his fingers and holds it up between us. "Francesca Romano..." Glancing down at it, he cocks an eyebrow. "From Louisville, Kentucky?"

I cringe. The guy who sold us the fake IDs promised efficacy, not accuracy.

I keep my mouth shut and pay for my drink, deciding to slip the guy an extra twenty just to be safe. By the time I turn back around, the idiot who grabbed my ass is nowhere to be found. Instinctively, I sling an accusing glare to my right, only to find RJ scrolling through his phone, still sitting at the same high-top table he's been brooding over since following me through the door.

I let out a relieved breath. Despite my thoughts to the contrary, I have no desire to be the cause of another man's death.

Glancing up, he catches my eye, his bored expression turning to granite. Although stuffed in a designer suit, his oversized frame looks out of place sitting in the middle of a trendy dance club. He doesn't look like he's here to have a good time. He looks like he's here to shoot up the place.

Which, to be fair, isn't out of the realm of possibility.

RJ's last name may be Harcourt, but he's a Carrera to his core—and just like Santi, he's deadliest when he's silent.

Don't poke the bear, Lola...

But I can't help myself. I'm hardwired to push boundaries.

Tossing him a salutatory wave, I arch an eyebrow at the phone clutched in his hand and free the snarky smile I've held back since leaving my apartment.

He scowls in response, dropping his phone on the table like it burned him. *That's what I thought. Busted, big guy.* My smile widens, which causes him to fold his arms tightly across his chest and stare at the shot in my hand like it's a glass of battery acid.

Sighing, I leave him and his euthanized sense of humor behind and meander my way through the crowded club. *I miss my cousin.* The one who used to play hide-and-go-seek with me all over the estate. The one who snuck me my first taste of tequila behind the counter of his father's Houston cantina.

The one who used to laugh.

RJ doesn't laugh much anymore. Not since he abandoned his Texas roots and followed Santi to New Jersey two years ago to become his second-in-command and first shield.

The brother and cousin I once knew are gone. They've molded themselves into replicas of their fathers.

Leaving those thoughts behind, I stop a few feet away from the dance floor, my gaze sliding up a private staircase leading to a roped off VIP area. For the second time tonight, the same thought floats through my head.

If they only knew...

If only I didn't have to hide. If only I could flash my last name like an all-access pass, *that's* where I'd be instead of fighting for a drink at a crowded bar.

"María! Over here!"

I glance over my shoulder to find Avery waving frantically from the edge of the dance floor. From the looks of it, she took her own wardrobe advice to heart. That fire-engine red number she's wearing is *almost* a dress.

If it covered her ass.

"All right, María Díaz," I mutter under my breath. "It's showtime."

I don't waste time sipping my shot—I inhale it. Warmth floods my veins, my eyes closing for a beat as thoughts of my stalker invade my head. *As the feel of him still sticks to my skin.*

Not only has he infected my mind, he's branded me...*twice.*

Once without my consent, and once in spite of it.

Opening my eyes again, I stare at the dance floor and at Avery and my friends' smiling faces. With each passing second, my anger escalates.

I envy their blissful ignorance. They're not mice. They're not trapped by a sadistic Santiago just waiting to strike.

That's it.

I slam my empty glass onto the crowded table beside me, ignoring a wave of irritated protests as I stalk toward the dance floor.

How dare Sam violate my apartment and then dismiss me. I'm the daughter of a drug lord. I don't get caught in someone else's head-on collision.

I cause my own.

The base is heavy, and the beat is loud—perfect for drowning out the thoughts poisoning my head. There's no talking. No bullshitting. It's too damn loud to do anything but let the tequila take over.

Before long, everything fades into the background. I just dance, pretending to be normal for a few unguarded moments, until I feel a hard chest press up against me from behind. I stiffen as two rough hands anchor onto my hips, pulling me against something even harder.

Shit. If RJ sees this, we're both screwed.

An automatic reaction has me scanning scan the club, searching for a pair of murderous eyes. Thankfully, the crowd is too thick, allowing me to wiggle out of the guy's hold before the Mexican *sicario* in my cousin erupts and incites a riot.

Twisting around, I extend my arm to put a safe amount of space between us. "No thanks," I yell over the music.

"Why?" he shouts back, those damn hands making a grab for my hips again. "You got a guy or something?"

It doesn't matter if I've "got" a guy, a girl, or a gorilla. If he touches me again, he'll be pulling back a bloody stump.

"No, I—" The minute I look up, the words die on my tongue. On the second level—right in the heart of the VIP area I was just pining over—stands the man I've been waiting for.

Sam is draped over the railing, wearing that irritatingly familiar blasé expression, as if daring it to fall.

A blurry memory breaks through the haze. I remember thinking the same thing last night as I watched him leaning against the wall. How even his stance seemed like a challenge…

"What the hell is he doing here?"

A pair of dry lips dust my ear. "Who?"

I don't bother answering. *Who* isn't the right question. It's *why*.

The longer I stare, the harder Sam stares. *Pinche cabrón.* Has he been here the whole time? Just watching me like the stalker he is?

He wants a show? For the first time, I offer him a loaded smile. *I'll give him one.*

"Nobody," I shout back. "Let's dance." Before he can grab me again, I shuffle around behind him, causing him to do a one-eighty.

However, my attention isn't on my dance partner. It's one floor up, locked in a battle of wills.

I want a front row seat too, you son of a bitch.

Oblivious, the guy follows my lead and turns to face the VIP area as well. Once again, he hooks an arm around my waist, this time pressing his chest so tightly against my back his shirt sticks to my bare skin. I play the game with cat-like finesse, purring up against him while holding Sam's volatile glare.

The blank expression is gone. His arms are no longer leisurely draped over the railing. Now, he's choking the life out of it.

Instead of deterring me, it spurs me on.

I don't know if it's because I'm taunting him, or if it's because he's jealous—*but screw it.* I'm turning up the heat and pushing the needle to find out once and for all.

Lifting one arm, I coil it around the guy's neck and drop down low, my shiny silver dress riding up my thighs. Slowly and methodically, I rise to the sound of a strained groan behind me.

I know I'm playing another dangerous game, but I've already poured gasoline on a lit flame. All that's left is to watch it burn.

Unfortunately, my attention is forced away from my fiery creation, when a wandering hand slides up the inside of my thigh.

"Hey!" Spinning around, I shove my fist into his chest. "If you value your testicles, you won't do that again."

The asshole has the nerve to look shocked, muttering, "Tease..." before stalking off the dance floor toward the bar.

"Well, that backfired." I palm the back of my neck just as Avery gives me two thumbs up from a few feet away—like she did last night with Troy.

I'm seriously starting to question the people I've chosen to surround myself with. Their judge of character leaves a lot to be desired.

I grind my teeth together. I'm not exactly a shining beacon of sensibility, myself. I have no idea what this thing is between Sam and me. *And that savage look in his eyes?* I don't know if it's because he wants to hate me or hates that he wants me.

I tell myself not to—but it's useless. My gaze draws back up to the VIP area, only to find the railing empty. He's nowhere to be found.

My heart sinks.

It's neither. He just hates me.

Dejected, I wave my hand to get RJ's attention. Other than pointing toward the ladies' room, then motioning for him to stay put, I don't bother to tell anyone where I'm going as I walk toward the back of the club.

Maybe a few moments of solitude behind a bathroom stall will unfuck my head.

Just as I take my place at the end of a long line, the back door opens, and two girls reenter the club clutching packs of cigarettes and lighters in their hands.

Outside.

That's where I need to go.

Hurrying, I abandon my spot and chase them down a few steps away from the door. "Hi," I say, toning down my accent while pointing at their hands. "Can I bum one of those?"

I have no intention of smoking it. I just need an excuse to be on the other side of that door.

The taller one shrugs and flips the cardboard top open. "Knock yourself out."

Smiling in gratitude, I slide one cigarette from the pack. Before I can even take a step, the same girl lays a heavy hand on my shoulder.

"You plan to light that on someone's tailpipe, honey?" Chuckling, she flicks her thumb on her lighter, presenting me with a dancing flame.

Guess, I'm smoking it now...

I force another smile. "Oh, right. Thank you." Tucking it between my lips, I lean down and suck on the filter, inhaling the disgusting thing until the end burns a bright orange.

Dios mío, I need air.

Throwing all my weight against the door, I tumble out into a dark alleyway and nearly gag. *Air yes—fresh air, not so much.* All I can smell is rancid garbage and this stupid cigarette.

But at least I can finally breathe.

Mostly.

Leaning against the bricks, I take a long drag and sigh. "What the hell is happening to me?"

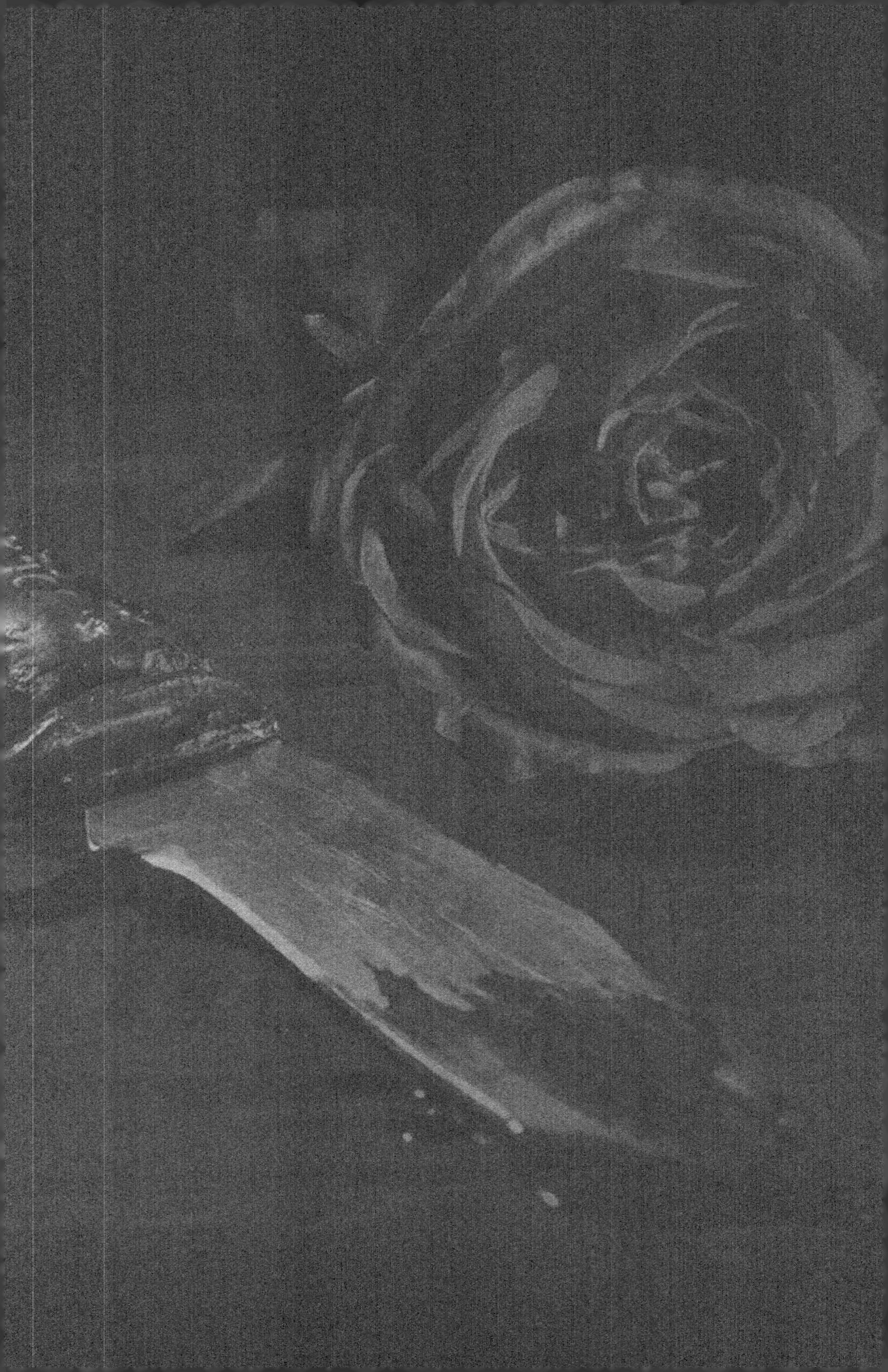

CHAPTER
Eleven

SAM

I can't take my eyes off her dress. It's fucking hypnotic. The way the silver material skims her breasts and hips makes it even more precious than gold to me.

It comes with a warning—a precursor to violence.

So far, there are two victims in this club who didn't read the fine print… The man who pinched her ass as she stood at the bar? *He's on his way to the ER with two broken wrists.* The man who dared to dance with her just now? *He'll soon be lying unconscious in a bathroom stall.*

No hesitation.

No regrets.

After Santiago requested I stay close to Lola, we've been moving in ever-decreasing circles around one another.

Never speaking.

Always watching.

Switching venues from the college campus to this club, my Mexican *dulzura* shining brighter than the sun, as I keep in the shadows.

Tonight, she's the one who's picking up the pace. She's meeting my eyes, returning my hunger, flirting with other men on purpose to tempt me into the spotlight…

All we're doing here is building anticipation for the final scene.

Our crash is inevitable.

"Want another drink, buddy?"

"Bourbon," I tell the bartender, tossing a twenty onto the counter. *I'm in league with the devil these days. I may as well start drinking like him.*

Taking a swig, I watch as Lola leaves the dance floor, her silver dress catching in the club's disco balls—reflecting the kind of sin I want to drown in.

She's moving toward the bathroom stalls, ditching her idiot friends on the dance floor, and murmuring a "stay, boy," at her discreet bodyguard.

Finishing up my drink, I follow ten steps behind, smiling to myself as she ducks out of the line by the ladies' room and heads toward the fire exit at the end of the hallway.

She disappears into the night.

I go to follow when my phone starts chiming. Yanking the device out of my back pocket, I check the ID and accept the call immediately.

"Troublemaking again, Sanders?" comes a familiar clipped drawl.

I bark out a rough laugh. There are few men I'd take orders from, never mind ridicule, but I respect the hell out of Edier Grayson. I'd even go so far as to call him a friend.

He's five years older than me, but he's not the kind of man who judges age over the ability to fire a gun.

His father is Dante Santiago's second. As such, we grew up together. Stole cars and smoked weed together. *Dared to share our dreams of another life together.*

I stopped running from destiny long before he did.

At eighteen, he was all set to study fine arts at Goldsmiths in London. Then he switched from a kid to a killer overnight. Trading pencils for bullets, he's spent the last couple of years in South America slaughtering the last of Santiago's enemies and shoring up the distribution channels from Cartagena until a recent move to the East Coast brought his talents to the US.

He's cool as fuck...

With a sting like a scorpion.

And if the tone of his voice is anything to go by? *He's pissed as hell.*

"Where are you?"

"New Brunswick."

He blows out a breath. "I want you back in NYC within the hour. I need a closure and then a clean-up. You good for that?"

It's another test. One that requires a gun, two fists, and an absence of morality.

Check, check, and double check. The more I integrate myself in the organization, the more sway I'll have over Lola Carrera's fate.

"I'll be there in fifty," I tell him as silver swims with crimson. "Message me the address."

Hanging up, I slip into the alley. She's standing a couple of feet away in the moonlight with her back turned. *Braced.* A perfect silhouette that's mine for the taking.

As I watch, she tips her head back and exhales, her long dark hair tumbling to her waist as tendrils of smoke coil around her like a dirty halo. She's smoking to justify why she's out here, but the time for pretense is over.

We both know what she's waiting for.

Me.

This.

When she hears the soft click of the door closing behind me, her shoulders stiffen. The lit cigarette drops from her fingers, flaring orange as it hits the asphalt by her heels.

I move fast. Before she has a chance to speak, my hand is clamped across her mouth, and I'm spinning her face-first into the wall.

"Have you come here to play, little mouse?" I murmur as the sweet scent from her apartment is amplified a thousand times.

It's all around me.

Consuming me.

Eliciting the filthiest thoughts.

I think of my cum smearing her mirror and basin.

I think of my cum dripping from her lips.

She moans her response into my hand. She tries to fight me off, bucking her hips and twisting. *Not that I'd expect anything less...*

I press her body even harder into the wall, crushing my own knuckles in the process and drawing blood. Her flighty breaths are music to my ears. I need to return to New York, but first, I'll leave my Mexican *dulzura* with a dirty narrative to replay in my absence.

Keeping one hand on her mouth, I trail my fingers up the damp heat of her inner thighs. She shudders and stops fighting the minute I reach her panties.

Wet.

Soaking.

I couldn't stay away from her if I tried.

"Is this for me, Lola?" I say huskily, resisting the urge to slide her panties to the side and sink my middle finger inside her. "Such a gift from my angel in black, *and silver*. Because that's what you are...*the fucking death of me*."

She moans again, squirming helplessly against my touch.

"I hate you, too," I say with a low chuckle. "You know, I'd fuck you right here in this alley if I thought it would loosen these chains between us." I lean in closer. Citrus... *My heaven and my hell*. "Turns out, they're unbreakable, but I think you know that already."

Glancing down, I bite out a groan when I see how flawlessly we fit together.

Her ass.

My dick.

Her pussy.

My fingers.

I won't be satisfied until every part of her is submitting to me. *Demanding me.*

Maybe it's time to leave a different kind of memory on her body—a reminder of just how brutal and beautiful our connection is.

Dropping my hand from her pussy, I reach for the gun tucked into the back waistband of my Levis and commence a new path up the inside of her thighs, swapping warm skin for cold steel.

Moans turn to muffled screams.

"You keep me in a prison cell for you, Lola," I accuse, kicking her legs apart. "With rusty bars on the windows and a broken lock. As punishment, I'm going to blur the lines between fear and lust. The first time you come for me will be from the sweetest act of violence."

Muffled screams turn to whimpers, as I drag the muzzle across her clit.

I do it again, and again, rubbing out a rhythm that has her whimpering, and me throbbing against the zipper of my jeans, leaking pre-cum.

My lips twitch as she slams her palms against the wall and widens her legs even more for me. It's a full-blown smile when she starts grinding up and down the barrel of my gun, seeking relief from something that's just as filthy as I am.

I press harder.

I rub faster.

My mind briefly wanders back a few hours ago in her bathroom, when I was just as unforgiving with myself.

I finger the trigger to flood the moment with even more danger. She shudders but doesn't stop. *She can't stop.* We're not just crossing lines anymore. We're fucking obliterating them. Normal doesn't exist for us. When you're born into the threat of violence, it warps everything.

Dropping my hand from her mouth, I force my fingers between her teeth, needing to feel the strength of her orgasm as strands of black silk whip across my face—nearly coming myself as she bites down hard with another scream, piercing the skin.

Afterward, we collapse forward, both breathing hard.

"Soon," I gasp, removing my gun from between her thighs. Despising it. Envying it. "Soon, every part of you will be mine, Lola."

"Soon," she whispers in concession, one cheek pressed tightly against the brickwork—as twisted up by this as I am.

Not that I'm giving her a choice, either way.

She stays motionless where she is as I slide back into the shadows, thinking how stunning she looks all destroyed like this.

She waits until she thinks I've gone, but I'll never leave her alone while she's vulnerable. Instead, I watch unseen as she peels herself away from the wall. Her steps are unsteady as she heads toward the door.

Mission accomplished.

She won't be thinking about anything else now until the next time we meet.

And there will always be a next time with her.

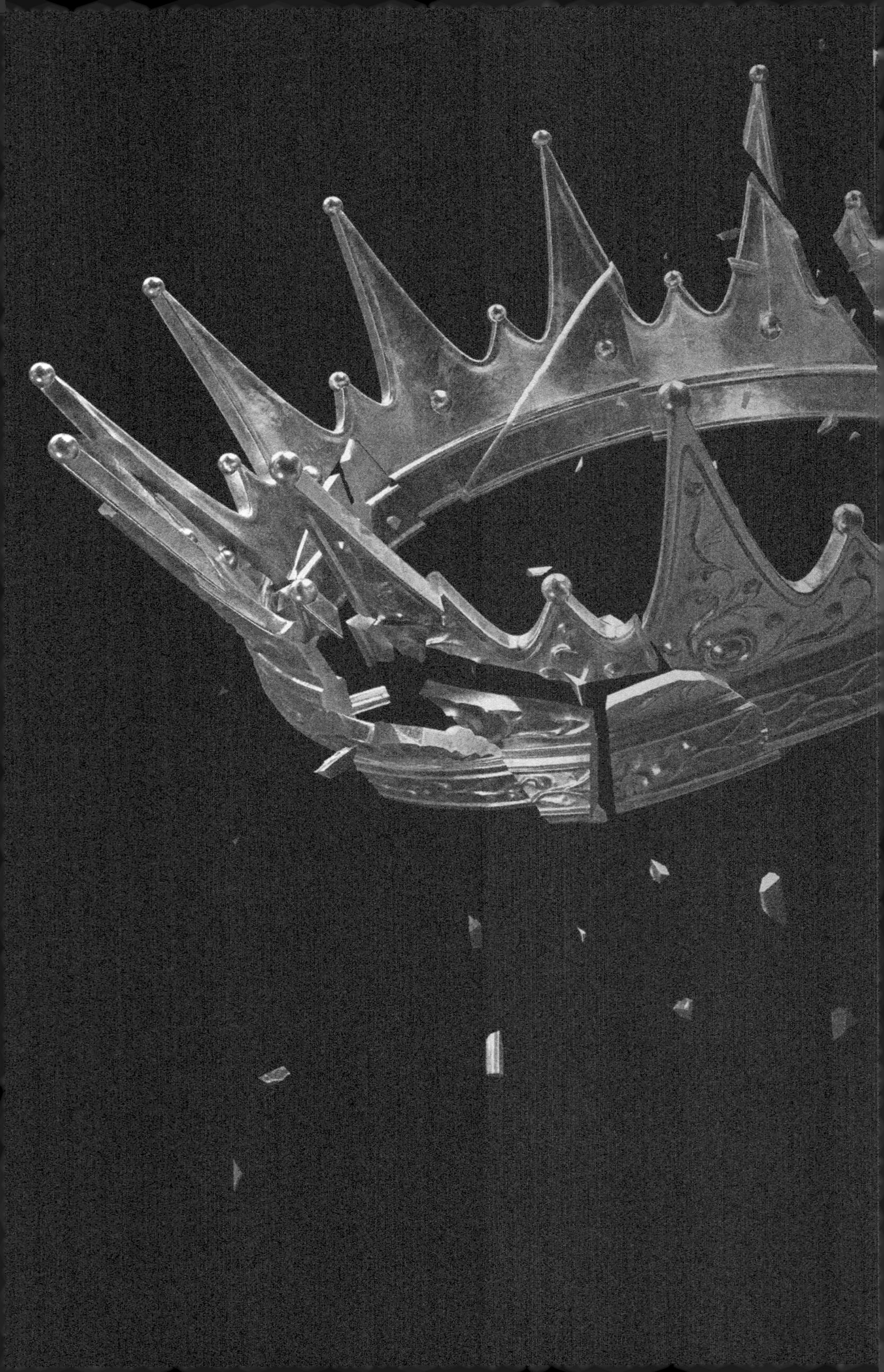

CHAPTER
Twelve

LOLA

My mother has a saying...

Chasing butterflies only leads you into repetitive circles. Pretend they don't exist, and they'll flutter back into the palm of your hand.

At ten years old, I took those words at face value. I spent hours sitting cross-legged on the bright green lawns of our estate, my arms spread wide and my palms up.

Waiting.

A butterfly never landed in my hand. They always darted around me, close enough to admire, but just out of reach.

I realize now—as most things with my family—it was a metaphorical warning. Butterflies are just like boys. Chase them, and they fly away. Leave them be, and they come to you.

A valuable lesson I wish I'd remembered days ago. *Four to be exact.*

A full ninety-six hours since I've seen or heard from Sam.

After our alleyway encounter, he just disappeared—as if successfully breaking me meant there was no more game left to play.

He'd won. I'd lost. End of story.

Only it wasn't—at least for me.

I always have the last word, but he left me speechless while he rode away like some kind of dark knight. So, instead of pretending he didn't exist, I chased a butterfly.

I've become the stalker.

For four days, I've driven by his apartment at all hours of the night just to catch a glimpse of him. I've casually inquired on his whereabouts around campus. Worst of all...? I've stood in the alleyway outside the Foxhole, shamelessly waiting for him to reappear.

I've spun in so many circles, I've made myself dizzy.

So after receiving nothing but silence, I decided it was time to put Eden Lachey Carrera's motherly advice to the test.

That's how I ended up here, at a dive college bar, sharing a plate of nachos with some frat boy I don't even like.

I suppose Alex-*what's-his-name* is nice enough—*cheap as hell*—but nice. However, I'm not interested. Not even those All-American dimples can divert my attention away from the man who owns my thoughts.

I used to crave normalcy—a clichéd, bland existence. Thanks to Sam and his filthy brand of debauchery, I now crave rebellion. I hunger to push boundaries and test my own limits. I wait for the sun to go down so I can dance in the darkness.

His darkness.

Sighing, I toss a half-eaten tortilla chip onto my plate and pull a fresh water bottle from my purse. Unscrewing the cap, I drink slowly so I don't have to engage in pointless small talk.

"You know they have water here, right?"

Resting the rim of the bottle against my bottom lip, I give him a half-hearted smile. "I have a rule against drinking things that aren't sealed these days." At his furrowed brow, I add, "A girl can never be too careful."

But she can definitely be too desperate—something I hope to rectify tonight.

There's an awkward silence as Alex spins his phone in lazy circles on the table. "So, what's your major?"

It's all I can do not to roll my eyes. This is what this sick obsession of mine has come to—engaging in useless chatter with a cardboard placeholder.

"Don't have one yet," I say, sliding out of the sticky booth. "I'm only a few weeks into my freshman year." Before he can offer up another mundane question, I hold up one finger while already walking away. "Be right back. Have to use the ladies' room."

Of course, I'm headed nowhere near the ladies' room... *Again.*

Weaving my way around scratched tables and barstools, I disappear down a secluded hallway toward what I hope is the back door.

One that leads to another darkened alley, maybe...?

Nostalgia is a ruthless bitch.

But before I can take another step, a firm hand is wrapping around my arm and dragging me into an alcove.

"Where the hell do you think you're going?"

Gritting my teeth, I tug my arm out of RJ's claw-like grip and spin around ready to spit fire. "Outside."

"Don't think so."

If I have to deal with one more male ego...

"Don't you have something better to do than babysit me?"

Wrong thing to say, Lola.

Even bathed in shadow, I see the hard clench of his jaw and the warning in those onyx eyes. "Yeah, I do—like run this goddamn East Coast operation for your brother. Unfortunately, little *chaparrita* decided to swim with the sharks and got herself bit."

I recoil at the sharp accusation. RJ Harcourt is as efficient as they come. He doesn't believe in wasting time or resources doing mundane tasks or...

Chasing butterflies.

I cross my arms over my chest. "That's not fair."

"Life isn't fair, Lola. If it was..." His voice trails off, leaving the rest unspoken.

Left to ambiguous interpretation.

Only, he forgets how well I know him. How I see through that iron façade of his, right down to his hidden truth.

If it was, Santi would be here with you while I called the shots, I think, silently finishing his bold presumption for myself.

I know he's loyal to my brother, but there has always been an unspoken, underlying rivalry between them. RJ is a year older, and after a childhood filled with death and loss, he's much more streetwise. Whereas Santi boasts birthright and stealth, RJ operates on survival and brawn.

They're a dormant volcano just waiting for the right storm. Carrera men crave power, not servitude. I worry what will happen when they inevitably clash.

Speaking of volcanoes…

"Shouldn't you be on a date of your own?" I ask with a conspiratorial smile.

"What the fuck is that supposed to mean?"

Heaving out an exasperated sigh, I slump against the wall. "Don't try and play innocent with me, RJ. I'm better at it than you." I should probably drop and refrain from waving any more red flags, but I don't. "You know exactly what, or should I say *who* I'm talking about. Long, curly, brown hair? Legs like a ballerina? Two boulders on her chest the size of—"

He clamps his hand over my mouth. "That's enough."

I smile against his palm, remembering his obsession with his phone the other night and knowing who was most likely on the other line. *The same woman I've seen him tucked in dark corners with for weeks now.*

"Who is she?" I mumble into his palm.

"Nobody."

I cock an eyebrow, my words still muffled as I counter, "Didn't look like *nobody* to me."

He presses harder, flattening my lips. "You know nothing, Lola. You got me?"

In response, I stare down at the hand still smooshing my face and wait. Letting out a rough growl, he draws back and shoves it in his pocket.

"Yeah," I tell him, elated not to be the only one in this family with secrets. "I got you. What Santi doesn't know won't hurt him. *You got me?*"

RJ grunts out a reluctant affirmation.

"Good." I nod. "Now that that's settled, how about you head back to Newark?"

"And do what?"

"Tell my brother I left my date early, and I'm now safe and sound and *alone* in my apartment."

It's his turn to cock an eyebrow. "And you think he's gonna buy that bullshit?"

"If you're the one shoveling it? Yes."

I can all but hear the scales tipping back and forth in his head. It's a gamble—one that requires a lot of trust and faith. Two unfamiliar words when it comes to Carrera men.

Finally, RJ exhales on a harsh breath. "You'll go straight home after this?"

Right. Despite what he wants me to think he's agreeing to, we both know he'll be following me home anyway. The man is secretive, not suicidal.

However, just like a few nights ago at the club, I give him a mock salute. "Scout's honor."

He shakes his head. "You're trouble, Carrera."

"Takes one to know one, Harcourt."

Raking one hand over the top of his closely-cropped dark hair, he ruffles mine with the other. "One of these days, you're gonna go looking for it in the wrong place, and instead of causing trouble, you're gonna fall neck deep in the middle of it."

"Duly noted," I say, giving him a small smile. I have no interest in pressing my luck, so with a quick pat to his chest, I speed walk back to the table.

Alex glances up, his forehead wrinkling as I slide back into the booth. "Everything okay?"

"Fine," I counter, waving a dismissive hand, as if I haven't been missing for over fifteen minutes. "Long line. You know how it is."

By the look on his face, he doesn't, but then again, neither do I. I'm just trying to keep him from asking questions he doesn't want the answers to.

"So, María, what do you say we—?"

"I'm really tired," I blurt out, padding the statement with an exaggerated yawn. "Do you mind taking me home?"

"We've been here less than half an hour."

I offer a lukewarm smile. *Yeah, and my chances of catching a butterfly is slim to none at this point.* It seems my mother's sage advice doesn't apply to a certain rebel without a conscience.

I'd be wasting both of our time if I pretended otherwise.

"I'm sorry. I have a really bad headache all of a sudden." I tilt my head, trying to appear apologetic. "Raincheck?"

He's not happy as he snatches a twenty-dollar bill from his wallet and then slams it face down onto the table.

That makes two of us.

Something aches all right, but it's definitely not my head.

This was a huge mistake.

I'm barely present as Alex pulls his blue Prius into the parking lot outside my apartment building. I should've never agreed to this date.

I should've learned my lesson about stepping outside the lines a week ago.

"Thanks. I really appreciate—" My words are cut off by a pair of demanding lips.

My palms shoot forward against his chest, but just before I push him away, a taunting voice whispers inside my head...*Don't chase butterflies—provoke them.*

So, dancing on a very thin tightrope, I do the unthinkable.

I let it happen.

Alex-*what's-his-name's* kiss is wet and uninspiring, a pathetic substitute for the forbidden one I can't stop craving. The cruel touch of a man and his gun—both of which I dreamed about last night in such vivid detail, I woke up blushing from the sheer depravity of it.

Nothing like the fumbling, hurried hand attempting to unbutton my dress.

No. This is all wrong.

"Stop!" Shoving him away, I tumble into the passenger's seat, wiping the remnants of his sloppy kiss away with the back of my hand.

"Come on, baby," he urges, diving his hand into my hair and twisting the strands around his fingers. "Don't play hard to get."

Damn, that hurts.

"I'm not trying to." Wincing, I pull away, only to get yanked back across the console. "But I also don't put out on the first date."

Or at all...

"That's not what I heard."

I glare up at him, his smug accusation as cold as my brother's soul. "What the hell did you hear?"

My date leans in, his breath hot on my cheek. "Everybody's saying you fucked Troy Davis at Sam Colton's party."

Emotion clouds my judgment, and I don't think; I swing, a damn impressive right hook catching him across the chin.

"Son of a bitch!" he yells, releasing my hair to cover his face. "What the fuck?"

Holy shit, I have no idea what the hell just happened. It's as if the brand on my hip has infected my blood with venom. I'm drunk with power and feeding off the poison coursing through my veins.

Maybe I'm not as innocent as everyone thinks.

"I'm getting out now." I smile sweetly, the glassy confusion in his eyes fueling my sadistic enjoyment. "And if I hear a word around campus that anything happened between you and me other than a kiss goodnight, your football career will be over faster than Troy's." *And if Troy's unfortunate warehouse destination is any indication, his life as well.* "Are we clear?"

Alex's face blanches. "Get out of my car, you crazy bitch."

Opening the passenger's side door, I blow him a kiss and make my way toward my apartment, a strange smile on my face.

Maybe I didn't catch a butterfly tonight, but I caught the scent of something way more potent.

My own darkness.

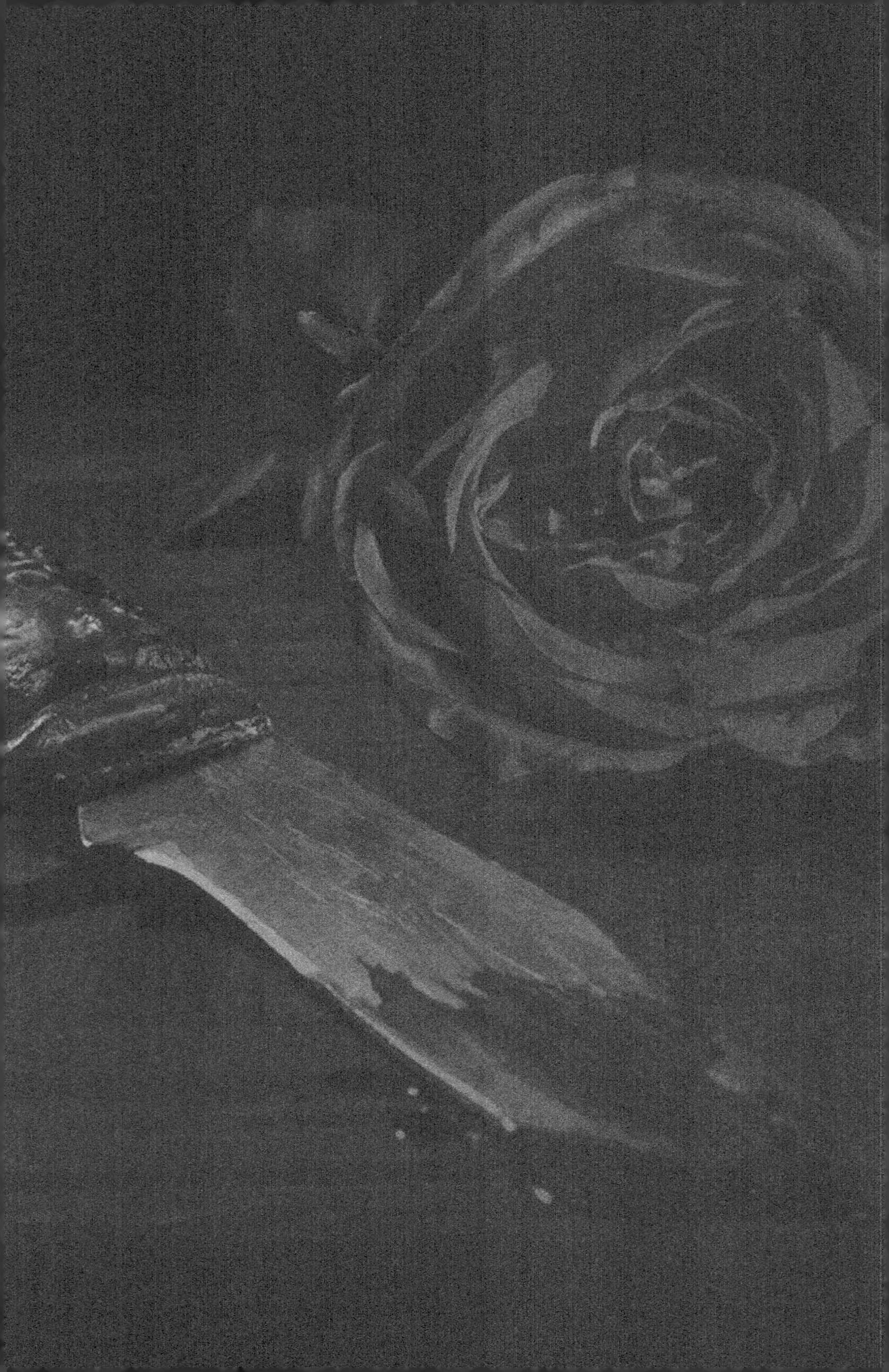

"Finish him," he orders, turning away from the bruised and bloodied man hanging by his wrists from the meat hook—suspended between life and death.

I take out my gun and pull the trigger, making the Russian my fourth kill in as many days. Murdering the last of my boyhood along with Savio the snitch.

People try to take advantage during a power change. It's like they think the incoming king has cracks of stupidity in his crown. The moment Edier stepped foot in New York, the Russians started flexing their muscles. A couple of trusted Santiago dealers ended up with their throats slit, so retribution was demanded.

After this week, no one will be questioning Edier's authority in this town again.

Twenty-six dead.

A Bratva cell in flames.

Even the Italians down on Canal Street have stopped strutting their shit like peacocks on a day outing.

It scares me how easily I've slipped into this new life. It's like a designer suit with bloodstains that's been tailored just for me.

I find Edier waiting outside the meat warehouse.

"Tell Reece to get rid of the bodies." His face is still as fuck, no flickers of emotion, but you know what they say about those kinds of waters... "You did well."

"Do I get a glitter sticker and a lollipop?"

Edier stares at me for a beat before his lips start twitching. "There he is.... Sam the sarcastic pain-in-the-ass. I was beginning to think you'd undergone a personality transplant at that fancy college of yours."

"Ex-college," I correct, as he folds a piece of gum into his mouth and pockets the wrapper. He chews slowly. Methodically. A twenty-five-year-old cartel prince with the habits of a high school chick.

"You're playing with fire."

"Nice day to get burned."

His eyebrows lift at my tone. "Seems the joker grew teeth."

"I'm not handing her over to Santiago," I warn.

"Who says you have a choice?"

Cursing under my breath, I start walking toward my Bugatti. I've been gone for too long. I have a tracking device on her car. I've hacked the college and her apartment security cameras. I know the moment she wakes up and the hour she falls asleep, but it's still not enough.

I can feel the weight of my gun pressing against my heart. *The same gun that made such a pretty mess of that composure.*

I start the engine as Edier taps on the window.

"Screw her out of your system, and then I want you back in New York by Friday," he says tersely. "She's a Carrera, Sam... I don't need to spell out all the bullshit that comes with that name."

I jerk out a nod, tearing at my lower lip in frustration. *And obsessions don't just "leave your system," Edier. They dig deep with spikes until nothing shakes them lose. They puncture your lungs so you need their fucking air to survive.*

Something flashes in his dark eyes. Something close to sympathy.

"Listen, Ella Santiago arrives here next week for a late transfer into NYU, and I want you supervising her protection. If anything happens to the devil's daughter on my watch, I'll end up on a meat hook next to Savio. You hear me?"

I jerk out another nod.

"Go." Taking a step back from the car, he slides his hands into his pockets. "And don't come back until you're breathing Santiago fumes again, not Carrera's."

I boomerang straight back to New Brunswick, braking with a screech outside her apartment—parking at an angle and blocking off two spaces.

I checked the trackers on the way here, my mood souring somewhere along the Garden State Freeway. Her place is in darkness, but I know exactly where she is, and she knows she'll be getting punished for it.

Taking the fire exit stairs, I do what I need to do, and then I'm swinging back into my Bugatti to move it to a more discreet location around the side of the building.

Just as well.

A minute later, Santi Carrera pulls up and stalks inside, leaving three of his men by the door.

Soon after, a blue Ford Prius is parking nearby.

I watch the scene play out in grim silence, knowing I can't make a goddamn move with her brother and his *sicarios* in the vicinity. Instead, I satisfy myself with the fact I'll be adding a fifth kill to my lack of conscience by the end of the night.

I'm starting to forget who I was before Lola. Did I crack jokes like Edier said I did? *Act more carefree?*

As soon as she exits the car, I'm ramming a fresh magazine into my Glock. Ten minutes later, I'm rear-ending a blue Ford Prius off the road and watching some college prick piss himself with fear.

When I return to her apartment, I'm still buzzing with unrestrained violence, bloody knuckles, and a Lola-shaped hole in my heart that only she can fill.

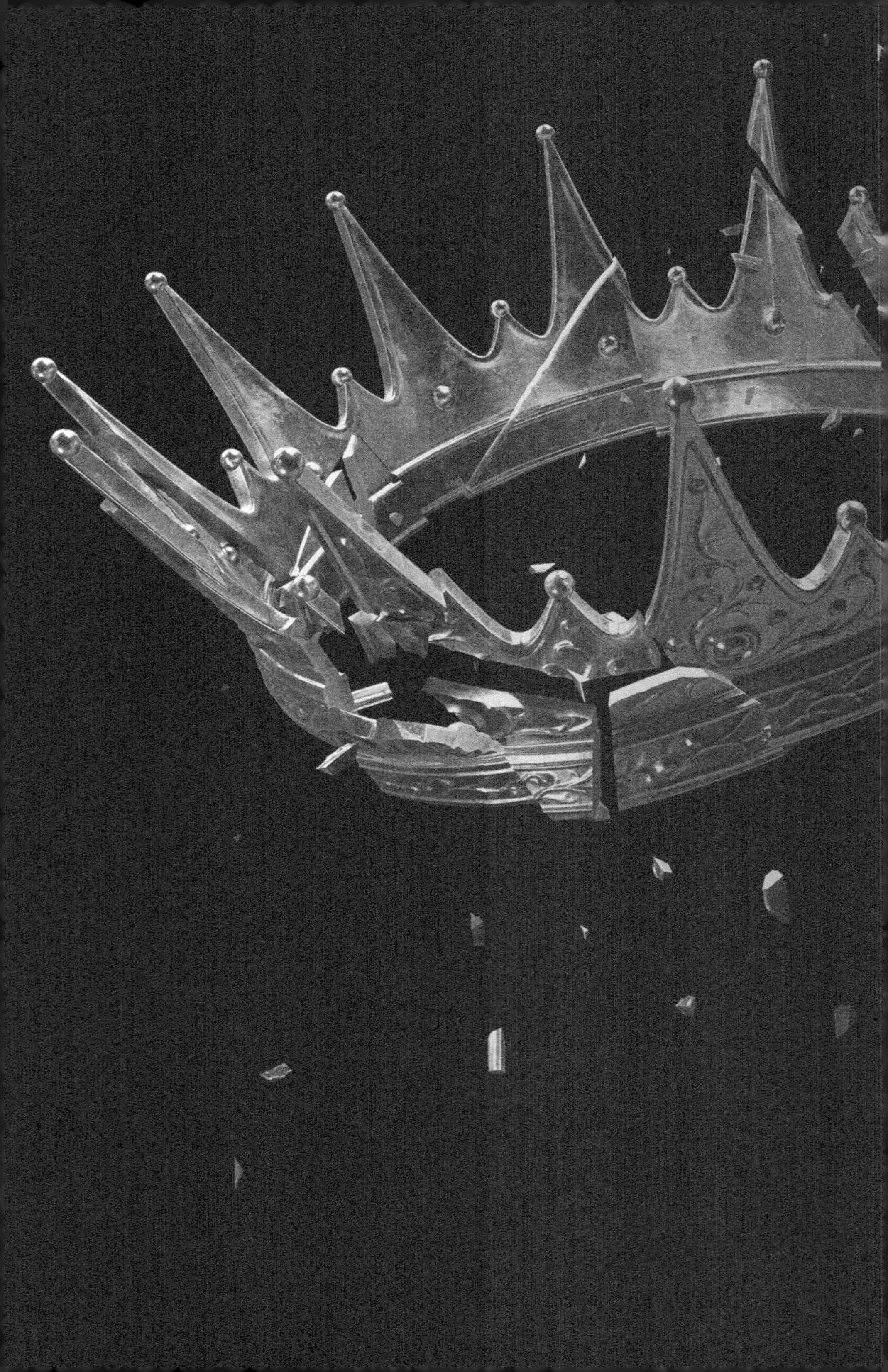

Apparently, we both like playing with fire.

Now, not only do I have my designated babysitter back on duty, it seems the powers-that-be have called in reinforcements.

Three to be exact.

A fortified wall of emotionless *sicarios* who don't give a damn what I want or think.

Super.

Although I can't see anything, my confidence is in control and leading the charge, while common sense lounges somewhere three or four rungs down the ladder.

Another of my father's warnings filters through my head as I cross the threshold into the living room. *Arrogance can be your strongest asset or your weakest flaw.*

Arrogance is why I don't bother turning on the lights.

Or maybe the mouse just wants to be caught.

"You're late."

I stumble into the wall, letting out something between a gasp and a shriek, when the lamp beside the couch clicks on. Harsh yellow light spills across the room, illuminating the man sitting on my couch. His favored slicked-back dark hair is wild and chaotic, casting a stark contrast against the pristine white leather and giving him a sinister glow. Three buttons on his shirt are open at the collar, highlighting the strained muscles in his neck that lead to one hell of a pissed-off scowl.

Adrenaline deflates from my chest, and I sigh in both relief and irritation. "¡*Ay Dios mío*, Santi! What the hell?"

"Pack your shit," he deadpans, his expression tight.

"Excuse me?"

"Did I stutter?" Rising to his feet, my brother crosses the room, all six foot four inches of him looming over me like a warden. "You're leaving for Mexico tonight."

I stare up at him, blinking rapidly as if the movement will force clarity into those five words. "What?"

"You heard what I said."

"I have a life here!" I shout, my panic escalating as I move in front of him, blocking his path. "My *own* life with my *own* friends. I don't want to leave it."

"I didn't ask what you wanted, *chaparrita*. You're leaving, and that's final."

Final. He growls the word like *papá*. As if his command is the damn gospel. As if I'm not an adult with a brain and free will. *Granted, an adult who disobeyed him and got herself roofied and branded, but that's beside the point...*

I fling my arms around like a broken windmill. "Do I not get a say in this?"

"No."

I want him to yell. Instead, he remains rigid and stoic.

"Santi!"

"This is not up for discussion." He steps forward, and I automatically step back. "I warned you to stay away from Sanders, and you wouldn't listen. Now they know."

"Know *what*?" I demand. "And who's *they*?" He's talking in circles, and I'm tired of standing on the outside of them while trying to decipher Carrera cryptic talk.

"Dante Santiago," he bites out between clenched teeth. "My contacts in New York saw him pay Senator Sanders a visit a few days ago. Care to guess the main topic of conversation?"

My stomach plummets to my feet. "Me?"

He doesn't confirm nor deny. Instead, he paces in front of me, another trait he inherited from our father. The more he paces, the faster he talks. "Your cover is blown, *chaparrita*. They know María Diaz is an alias. They know who you are, and now they're going to use you to get to me and *papá*. We can't take that chance, so you're going back to Mexico where the cartel can protect you."

I can't stop staring at the dark circles flashing under his eyes every time he passes me. Jesus, it looks like he hasn't slept in days…maybe weeks. I noticed it at the pizzeria, but it's gotten worse. His obsession with this feud between our family and the Santiagos is consuming him.

"There's nothing I can do to change your mind?"

"No." When he faces me, I recoil, the brother I grew up with disappearing behind the hardened mask of a criminal. "You're in over your head, Lola. You're drowning, and you don't even know it."

A surge of fury courses through me, prompting me to hurl my purse against the wall. "Damn it, Santi! I'm eighteen, not eight! You can't force me to leave the country. I'm just as much of a Carrera as you are. For Christ's sake, I just punched a guy in the face for trying to get into my pants."

Which was absolutely the wrong thing to say.

Santi's dark eyebrows shoot up to his messy hairline. "You *what?*"

"Focus, please," I huff, redirecting the conversation. "The point is that you can't keep ordering me around like this. You're my brother, not my father."

He gets deathly quiet. The strained kind of quiet where you know you've fucked up. The kind that fills the air with so much static it crackles. "You're right," he says calmly. "I'm not." His jaw tics as he reaches into his pocket and pulls out his phone. Without a word, he presses a single button.

"What are you doing?" I whisper.

His narrowed eyes snap to mine. "Proving a point."

Within seconds, he's speaking into the phone in rapid Spanish. It's my native language, so, of course, I understand every word, yet somehow it all gets muddled in my brain, hovering in that space between willful ignorance and denied truth.

Before the fog in my head can clear, he presses another button and holds the phone between us.

"*Cielito*," a deep, heavily accented voice rumbles.

Oh fuck.

"*Papá?*" I have no idea why his name exits my mouth as a question. There's no mistaking Valentin Carrera's voice. I've witnessed grown men piss themselves at the mere sound of it.

"We had a deal, *cielito*."

"I know, *papá*, but—"

"No buts," he clips, cutting off my protest. "Your *mamá* and I allowed you to attend school under the direct supervision and discretion of your brother. Santi has informed me that your alias and safety have been compromised."

I glare at my brother. *Snitch.* "But, *papá…*"

"*¡Silencio!*"

I jump at the harsh command in his tone. My father has never raised his hand to me, but that doesn't mean he isn't terrifying. I may be *papá's* little girl, but even *I* know when to shut the hell up.

"I almost lost you once at the hands of Dante Santiago," he continues. "I will not risk my daughter's life again. Your brother and I have many enemies, *cielito*. Enemies who would love nothing more than to see you suffer for our sins. So, you *will* pack your shit, and you *will* board my jet with RJ and return to Mexico City immediately."

Oh great, a traveling companion.

I don't know what possesses me to ask, "And if I don't?"

Dumb, Lola. Dumb, dumb, dumb.

Even Santi lifts an eyebrow.

"Lola…" It's a grave warning. My father only uses my given name when I'm about to fall out of his good graces. It's a dark place no one wants to find themselves, whether family, friend, or foe.

I swallow hard. "*Sí, papá.*"

"Santi," he growls. "Take me off speaker phone."

Obeying, my brother disappears into the kitchen to discuss cartel business with our father in an unnecessarily hushed tone. He could act out their entire battle strategy in an interpretive dance for all I care. I'm not interested in anything they have to say. I'm too devastated at the blow I've just been dealt.

My taste of freedom.

My chance at a normal life.

All gone because of a stupid obsession.

I wander around my apartment, soaking in the last moments of normalcy I have left. Sighing, I trail my hand over the white leather couch Santi cursed to hell for over an hour as he carried it up two flights of stairs. I dust my finger along the top of the flat screen TV, still hanging crooked on the wall after RJ refused to use a leveler.

All snapshots of independence soon to be a distant memory.

Stopping next to the window, I move the curtain to gaze out at the empty parking lot, when a flash of color catches my eye, causing my stomach to somersault.

A yellow Post-it Note is stuck to the glass. With a shaking hand, I tear it away and read the familiar slanted handwriting.

When the mouse strays, she gets punished. Slowly, painfully, until she begs for mercy. This time, it won't be steel that draws it from her. The hunt is on, dulzura.

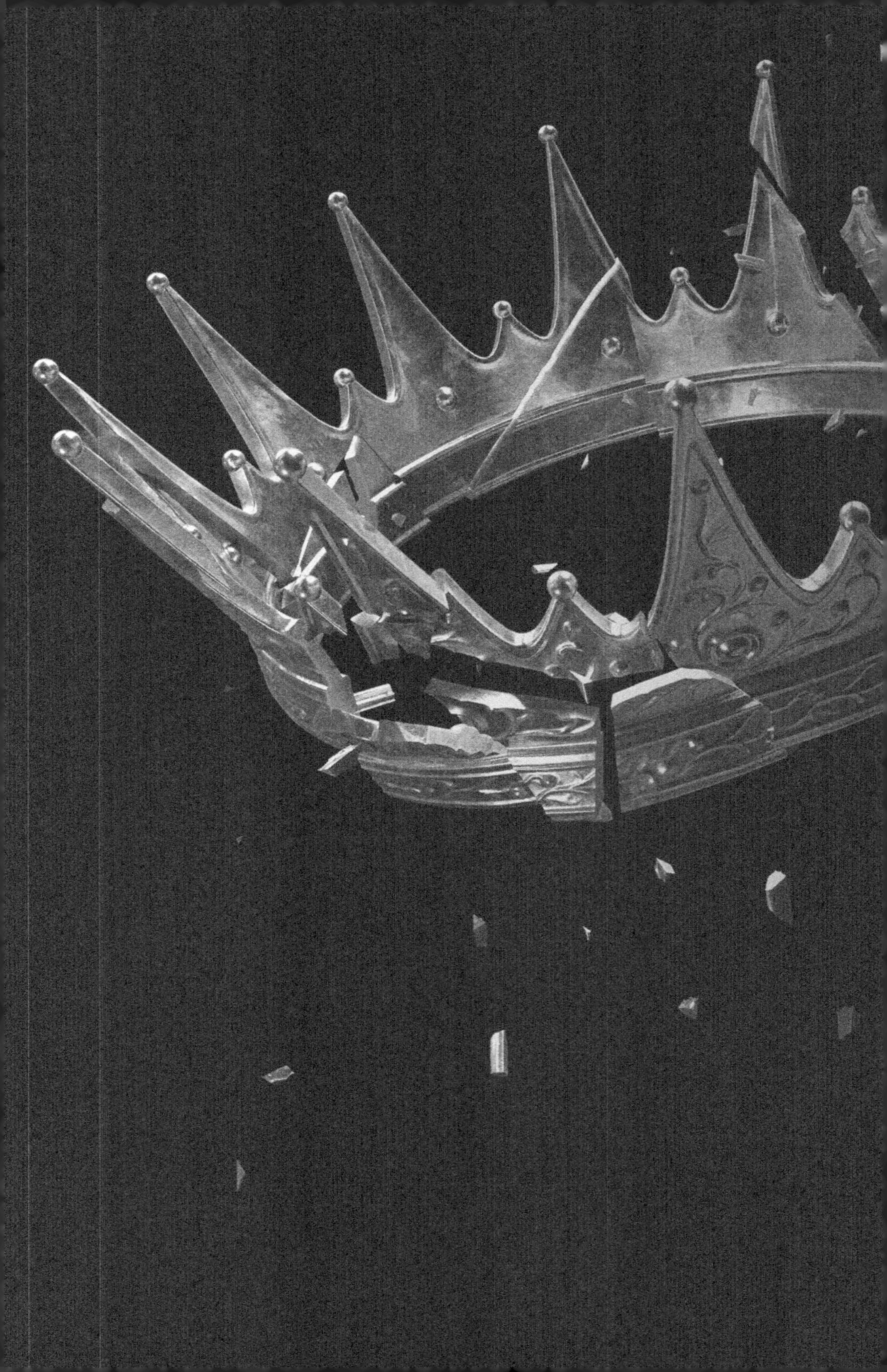

CHAPTER
Fifteen

LOLA

The pulse in my neck beats a furious rhythm. *It's him.*

He was here, inside my apartment again.

But how? When?

When the mouse strays, she gets punished.

Lifting my head off the glass, I stare out the window. One that gives a perfect view of the parking lot. *Right where Alex's car was parked.*

I fist my hands, the note crumpling in my damp palm as I stumble backward.

He saw us.

Common sense tells me to feel violated again. Instead, my cheeks heat with desire.

It's exactly what you wanted…

Thoughts swirl in my head of Sam standing where I am now, watching Alex kiss me. Watching him try to undress me. Watching as I fought back, the Carrera in me surfacing like an uncaged animal.

Did it infuriate him?

Did his dick harden as he watched?

Images spin through my mind faster than I can control them. It's sick and twisted, but I can't stop. The more I think about him—his jaw tight, his need strong, and his hate for me, a barrel of gasoline with my taunting a lit match—the wetter I get.

I can't breathe.

"Lola?"

I jump as my brother's voice rumbles behind me.

"Shit!" Quickly shoving the note into my bra, I turn around, trying to mask arousal as annoyance. "Stop sneaking up on me like that!" As soon as my heart starts beating again, I shift a nervous glance back at the window. "How long had you been here before I walked in?"

"A few minutes. Why?"

No reason. Just wondering if you crossed paths with my stalker. "Never mind."

With as much dignity as possible, I walk past him toward the bedroom, when he grabs my arm.

"What the hell, Santi? Do you or do you not want me to pack?"

He holds out his hand. "Give me your keys."

"You're kidding me, right?"

"Do I look like I'm kidding?"

No, he looks like he's about to throw me over his shoulder and carry me back to Mexico.

There's no hope in changing his mind. I've been a part of this family long enough to know a losing battle when I see one.

Sighing, I gesture toward the far wall where the contents of my purse lay scattered across the floor. "Help yourself."

Rolling his eyes, he crosses the room and bends down to sift through the strewn contents. After pocketing my keys, he runs a hand through his unruly hair. "I have to make arrangements with RJ. I'll be back in half an hour. Be ready."

Once again, I heave out a heavy sigh.

Santi tips my chin with his forefinger, the hard lines in his face softening. "*Chaparrita*, I'm not doing this to punish you."

"It doesn't feel like it."

"You're my baby sister, Lola. My responsibility. I couldn't live with myself if anything happened to you." His hold tightens. "You have to understand that family is everything to me. I'll kill for you. I'll die for you. And any man who hurts you will suffer until his last breath."

Damn it. His fierce loyalty is making it hard to hate him right now. "I know."

And therein lies the problem. *I do know.* His words aren't just idle threats.

He won't rest until Sam pays. Not only for crossing territory lines, but for drawing Carrera blood.

For daring to taint the innocence of Valentin Carrera's daughter.

The gold flecks in Santi's brown eyes glitter with affection. "I love you, kid."

"I love you too," I mumble. *It'd be so much easier if I didn't.*

With a brotherly kiss to my forehead, he leaves me alone with my wayward thoughts and a ticking time clock. Closing the door behind him, I turn and slump against it.

Half an hour.

Half an hour and then it's goodbye freedom, hello shackles and chains. I love my family with all my heart, but they're slowly suffocating me.

"You're in over your head, Lola. You're drowning, and you don't even know it."

How the hell am I supposed to learn to swim if I'm never allowed to sink?

But you did sink, a voice in my head whispers. *You sank hard, just like the enemy's blade did into your skin. You moaned for him. You chased the ruthless path of a loaded gun as he dragged it against you. He did more than slice your skin—he sliced through your last shred of restraint.*

Biting my lip, I reach into my bra and pull out the Post-it Note. Smoothing out the wrinkles, I read the words again, memorizing each slanted line as I wander back across the living room.

When the mouse strays, she gets punished. Slowly, painfully, until she begs for mercy. This time, it won't be steel that draws it from her. The hunt is on, dulzura.

The hunt is on.

What does that even mean? Is he watching me right now?

Before I can stop myself, I wander back to the window. Scraping my teeth over my bottom lip, I lean against the wooden frame and scour the parking lot.

He's a Santiago associate—my family's sworn enemy. I'm meant to hate him and everything he stands for. According to Santi and *papá*, he wants nothing more than to hurt me.

To kill me.

So, why simply mark me? Why use his gun in that alley instead of his cock? He's had every chance to taint Valentin Carrera's daughter. To take my virginity and leave me bleeding until I gasped my last breath.

So why didn't he?

I stared across the room into those intense, dark eyes the night of his party, and then again in the nightclub. They weren't drenched in hate. If anything, they radiated lust.

And something else...

Something more unsettling.

Obsession.

I know because it courses through my own veins, too.

I think of his cool demeanor and that midnight black hair, wild and a little long—as reckless and chaotic as the man himself.

He's a silent predator, stalking with beauty and grace and then devouring with the appetite of an entire pack. *Just like he did in the alley when he blurred the line between desire and death.*

He saved me that night from Troy Davis. I can't remember it or prove it, but I know in my soul he did.

As if pulled by a magnetic force, my fingers trail down my dress, between my breasts, down my stomach, and hover just inside of my hip. I touch the still tender S with the tip of my finger. Over and over, I trace the brand he gave me, each pass hardening my nipples to stiff peaks.

I wonder if he's outside this window watching me right now?

"What game are you playing, Sam?" I muse, imagining him standing in the parking lot and looking up at me through the window.

When the mouse strays, she gets punished.

Maybe in another lifetime, yes, but in half an hour, I'll be on a plane to Mexico. Our cat and mouse game is over. There will be no punishment. No begging. No hunt.

No more butterflies to catch.

I'll never see him again, and he'll never see me again.

Unless I let him see me now.

I don't know what possesses me to unbutton the first button at the top of my dress, but the moment I do, a rush of heat pools between my legs so unbearably strong, I can't control myself. I unbutton another...then another... then another...until the entire thing is barely hanging onto my shoulders. I can't see anything outside the window. It's too dark, but I feel him. He's out there watching…*waiting.*

What I'm doing is dangerous. RJ could have left with Santi, or he could be standing guard right outside cataloging my every move. I don't see him lurking about, but that's hardly comforting. Cousin or not, as my brother's right-hand man, he wouldn't hesitate to throw me under the bus.

Electricity sizzles down my spine at the contradiction. Two dark knights—one here to protect my purity, the other here to destroy it.

This is what being a Carrera means. Daring to walk into fire. Balancing on the thin wires tracing my name. Risking the fall just to satiate an innate need to shatter society's perfect ideals.

If I'm going to be convicted, I might as well commit the crime.

My fingers travel up my arm and curl around the strap resting on my shoulder. I'm lightheaded as it slides down my skin, ashamed of my own wantonness, but too far gone to stop. Trailing my hand across my chest, I reach for the strap clinging to my other shoulder, when a faint ringing sound catches my attention.

Turning, I stare across the room at the cell phone lying face down on the floor by my purse, and my stomach clenches.

I don't have to look to know it's RJ. There's no doubt in my mind he's caught an unintentional glimpse of Sam's private show, and he's calling to warn me of my brother's impending wrath.

My heavy footsteps carry me across the room where I pick up my phone, my indiscretion searing the metal into my palm. The screen is blank, save two words.

Unknown Caller.

Of course. My family uses burner phones. Always helpful when avoiding the DEA. Sighing, I hit the accept button. "RJ, come on… I thought we had a deal. I'm already in enough trouble. Can we just keep this between—?"

A rough breath hisses through the line, licking my ear with its forbidden tongue.

"RJ?"

He doesn't answer, but the breathing grows heavier…lethal…more insistent. There's an underlying growl hidden in the silence that ignites my skin.

It's him.

I don't know how I know; I just do.

Closing my eyes, I imagine his gaze following my every move as that wicked tongue licks his full lips.

"Can you see me, Sam?" I whisper. "Do you want to see your creation?"

Wandering back to the window, I stare into the pitch-black night. Once I verify my cousin is nowhere to be found, my restraint snaps. Emboldened by lust, I push the remaining strap of my dress off my shoulder, not flinching as the material slips past my waist and pools at my feet.

I'm standing in front of my second-floor window in a lacy black bra and thong, breathing as heavily as if he were standing behind me, his lips brushing my neck.

Slowly, I run my fingers along the S puckering the skin on my hip, a strange pride filling my chest. "What does this mean?" I ask, placing a hand against the glass. "Am I marked for death? Or am I marked for *you*?"

As if in response, a bright orange glow ignites in the hazy dark, and then just as quickly, disappears. Startled, I take a few steps back, logic trying to force its way through whatever spell I'm under.

However, instead of getting dressed as any sane person would do, I lick my lips. "Sam...?" I call out, testing him by slowly dragging a bra strap down my shoulder. "Do you like what you see? Is this what you thought about when you got yourself off in my bathroom? Do you want me, or do you just like to watch?"

The image in my head returns, bringing with it an insatiable ache between my thighs. As if commanded, I slide my other strap down, teasing a nipple through the thin lace of my bra. "Did you see me with Alex tonight? What would you have done if I'd let him touch me?" I'm growing delirious with lust, my pussy throbbing at the thought of my father's enemy watching me... Hearing me... "Would you have stopped me? Would you have killed him for it? Do you want to punish me, Sam?"

Fuck, I can't take it anymore. I slip my hand into my panties, gasping as my finger finds my clit.

"What if I'd let him fuck me?" I groan, rubbing furious circles. The pleasure is so intense it lifts me onto my toes, forcing me to bow my head. "What would you have done?"

In my mind, it's no longer my finger torturing my clit. *It's his.* Stars burst behind my closed eyes as the fantasy pushes me closer to the edge.

"I'm a virgin, you know. Does that get you off?" *Shit*! The glass fogs as I sink my finger inside my wet heat, pumping just like I know he would do. "I'm leaving, Sam." My body is shaking with need, words tumbling out of my mouth with reckless abandon. "Your mouse is being taken away. You could've been my first. Now another will take what's yours. Does that piss you off?"

Letting out a tortured cry, I return to my clit, chasing an orgasm carved in his image.

Pretending my hand is his mouth...his tongue...

"Would you take me hard? Over and over until I bled your name? Until there wasn't a part of me that didn't belong to you?" *That's it.* The thought of him claiming and dominating me is too much. "Sam!" Collapsing against the window, I come violently, his name a hoarse cry on my lips.

When the euphoria of my orgasm finally fades, I slump against the window, my forehead and breasts pressed against the glass, and my hand still tucked inside my panties.

What's even more pathetic?

The fantasy will never be enough.

Quickly ending the call, I block the unknown number in a panic and push away from the window, staring blankly at my reflection—at my half-naked body and the crude S carved into the inside of my hip.

"You're in over your head, Lola. You're drowning, and you don't even know it."

My brother is right. I'm drowning. I'm getting myself off in front of a window to the thought of my family's sworn enemy, for Christ's sake. The man who desecrated my body in the name of war, not desire.

"That is a metal slab at the medical examiner's office... And that, dear sister, is the same scarlet letter carved into her chest." Santi's warning blares like a siren in my head.

"*Dios mío*, what the hell's wrong with me?"

Shame burns my cheeks as I draw the curtains, gathering my dress from the floor and quickly buttoning it. Backing away, I disappear into my bedroom and pull my suitcase from the back of my closet, my mind a cyclone of self-loathing and sadness.

My family is right. I'm just a pawn.

A stupid mouse who took the bait.

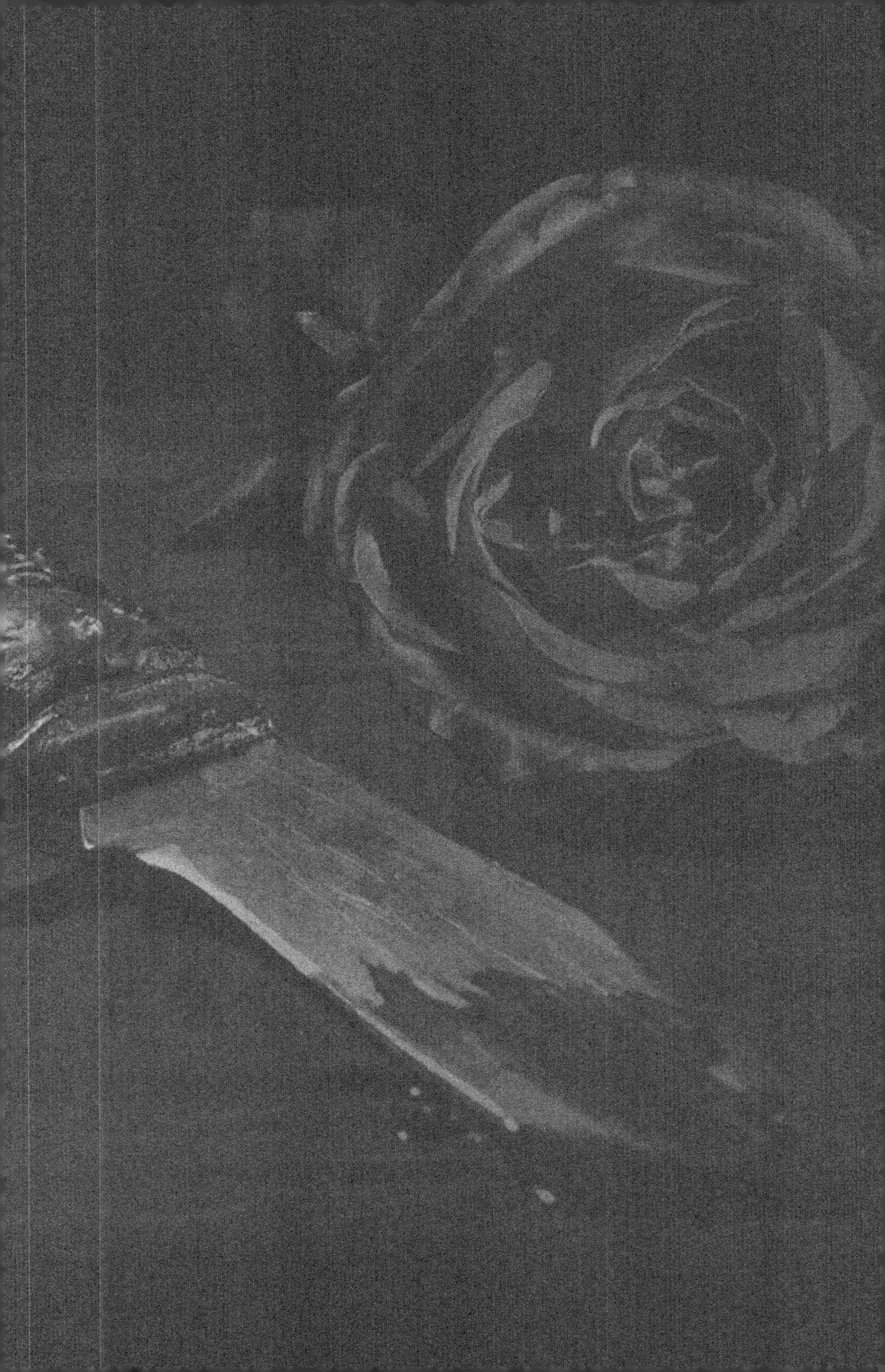

CHAPTER
Sixteen

SAM

It takes me less than sixty seconds to hack into her apartment's maintenance system and cut the lights dead. It takes me another five to pistol-whip her bodyguard so hard he'll be seeing double for a week. He doesn't look like the kind of fucker who'd waiver a shot at revenge, but I'll deal with that fall out later.

Lust and jealousy are dangerous weapons, and after watching Lola Carrera come so hard against a window the fucking glass fogged up, there's no army in the world that could stop me from sinking my cock into her pussy tonight.

"I'm leaving, Sam."

Never.

Her whispered admission sliced through the last strands of my sense and reason. Her breathless taunts made a bonfire out of my self-control. Lola is only going one way tonight, and that's with me. Predators don't barter with their prey. There are no pretty deals, sneaky underhands, or backstreet bargains. They stalk and they pounce, they steal and they break.

Her front door is open, and it smells like an invitation.

I don't make a sound as I slip inside, the heavy stillness crushing me like a velvet fist. I move slowly, cat-like, along the hallway, even though I know every inch of this apartment by heart. I head straight for the bedroom because that's where she's leading me. The sweet scent of her arousal is unmistakable beneath the generic florals and citrus.

I pause in the doorway, my anticipation turning my cock to stone. We're breaking the rules again. We're crashing through more unseen barriers. *Do bad things with me, Lola... Sharing our pleasure will be double the fun.*

I push the door open, the smallest creak shattering the silence. I hear her breathing in the darkness. *Rapid, shallow rasps.* Sounds that are so easy to make screams out of.

The curtains are closed. The moon is in hiding. I'm a thief in the night as I cross the room to reach the bed, stealing hearts and virtue with a fucking smile on my face. That's when she makes her move, darting for the hallway in a flurry of frantic footsteps. Her soft cry shatters the silence again as she runs straight into me.

I grab her arm and throw her up against a nearby wall, pressing a hand over her delicate mouth as my hips hold her body prisoner. "Strike a pose, *Lola Carrera*," I say huskily, drunk off her fury and her fragility. "The show's not over until I say it is."

Her muffled cries grow louder against my palm, and her sharp teeth snag on my skin.

Frustrated, I spin her around and crush my throbbing erection into her ass. *Holy fuck.* The feeling of her heat pressed up against me again is blowing all my late-night fantasies out of the water. It's enough to make my hand slip from her mouth.

"Get the hell off me!" She leverages her foot against the wall to try and tip me backward.

"Is that really what you want?"

"*Want?*" She toys with the word like it's an unwanted gift. "You don't *want* me, Sam Colton... Sanders... Whatever the hell your name is. You can drop the façade right now. I know where your allegiance lies. You saw Troy Davis roofie me, so you took your opportunity. You branded me for *him*... You branded me for *Dante Santiago*."

"I branded you for *me*." I drop my mouth to her shoulder as she hisses out a single rebuke.

"What about the other night? In the alleyway?" I catch the hitch in her breath.

"Don't deny you wanted it."

"Bullshit I did! It was sick. You're sick!"

"Then we'll be sick together." Incensed, I suck on her skin as hard as I can, creating another mark that won't be so easy to cover up. She yelps and shudders, but, again, she's not so easily conquered.

"My brother will be back any minute, and when he sees you—"

"He'll what?" I wrench her dress up around her hips, grinning to myself when she doesn't yank it back down again. "Tell me something, Lola… Is he coming here to drag you back to Mexico? Will you be a willing passenger, or will you be screaming inside the whole time because Daddy is taking all your dreams and wishes and drowning them in a river named Carrera?"

Her body sags. I've just deconstructed her truth into something real and ugly.

Like a bastard, I take advantage of the situation and ram my knee between her legs, spreading them wider.

"How long have you known?" she rasps. She's almost compliant as I brush my thumbs against the underside of her breasts.

"The day you started at Rutgers." I slide a hand between her thighs, trailing upwards; smirking as she pushes back on me, biting out a moan.

"That was over a month ago… Santiago could have come for me anytime—"

"But he didn't." I reach the damp apex of her thighs and slide a finger inside her panties. I'm so close to losing my shit over this woman it's unreal. One more breathy moan and I'll be destroying her virginity for the rest of the night.

"Am I supposed to offer my *gratitude*?" Hissing out the word, she tries to push me away again. "Do you know what he did to my mother eighteen years ago? *To me?*"

"Toss a story in the air and the facts will fall differently every time, Lola. Your father sent him and my stepfather an invitation to their own fucking murders. They got lucky. Your dad got pissed. Cue two decades of East Coast anarchy."

"You're a liar!"

"And you're a fucking lunatic," I snarl, losing my temper. "Flashing your pussy in that nightclub… Sucking that asshole's face earlier."

She stills. "Did you hurt him?"

"Damn right I did." I pinch her swollen clit in delicious punishment, inhaling her pained groans like they're oxygen.

"*¡Ay Dios mío!*" she gasps, and shudders, cursing me in Spanish. "*¡Hijo de su puta madre!*"

She's right. I am a son of a bitch. In more ways than one. At this, I drive my middle finger so deep inside her she loses her balance, slamming her palms against the wall as I circle and stretch her, prepping her for an even bigger surprise.

"You're crazy!" she cries, angling her hips for more.

"Crazy for you. Do you like it, Lola? Does it pique your interest? Are you going to climb down from your ivory tower to take a closer look? Maybe we should climb back *up* together?" With this, I give her exactly what she needs, ramming a second finger inside her. I pump mercilessly in and out of her body as she curses again.

"God, I hate you!"

"Feeling's mutual."

"You're a creep," she groans, squeezing my fingers as her pussy starts quivering.

"You're a tease."

"You're a filthy Santiago *pendejo!*"

"And you're *mine!*"

Ripping my fingers away, I spin her back around, smashing our mouths together to drown out her next insult. I taste peaches and cream, relief and desperation, before shouts and heavy footsteps in the parking lot outside send us spiraling back to earth.

Shit.

Tearing my mouth from hers, I slam my hand down in its place. "Don't make a fucking sound. I mean it, Lola. There's a fine line between the two factions of this war, and we're slow-dancing on the edge of it."

I think fast. I have exactly sixty seconds before Santi Carrera sees what I did to his second-in-command and starts redecorating her apartment in my blood.

There's a stairwell at the end of her hallway. It leads to the side of the building where my car is parked. I hear Lola's silent question in my head, and my mind is made up.

Wherever I'm going, she's coming too.

CHAPTER
Seventeen

SAM

If looks could kill, Lola would have sent me to hell and back a couple of times over by now.

She's in the passenger's seat of my Bugatti, her hands tied to the Jesus handle above her head. I can't tell if she's madder at me for kidnapping her or at herself for coming all over my fingers as her brother was storming the stairs. We made it out with seconds to spare, and now we're speeding down the freeway and into the eye of the storm.

Not knowing Santiago's intentions toward Lola pushed my obsession into a wasteland of uncertainty. *And then she hit me with that sexy-as-fuck floor show.*

In that moment, ambition, lust, *Santiago*…all that other stuff ceased to exist. There's only her to drown in now, and what a great death it promises to be.

We drive for five hours straight, kissing the coastline all the way up to New England. At two a.m., I see a derelict road sign for some roach motel a couple of miles shy of Newport, Rhode Island.

Pulling into the parking lot, I kill the engine.

"Are you going to play nice, Lola?" Turning to her, I trail a finger down one flawless cheek, feeling a surge of hope when she doesn't unleash a string of Spanish insults at me.

"You have no idea what you've done," she whispers, looking vulnerable and so fucking beautiful, I want to kiss all her doubt and hesitation away.

She's wrong. I know exactly what I've done. By taking her, I haven't just declared a new war on the Carreras, I've declared war on my own side too. We're on the run from the two biggest criminal organizations in the world, and I couldn't be happier about it.

I think I need a drink to process it, though.

"Let me go," she urges, her blue eyes wide and wary. "I'll tell Santi it was a mistake—"

"Didn't we cover this already?" Leaning over, I press my mouth against hers. *Will she bite me or accept me?* "There are no rules when it comes to you and me anymore, Lola. Only the ones we make together."

She rears back, her dark eyebrows drawing together. "Is it me you really want, Sam? Or is it my submission? When the sun comes up, will my heart just be another casualty of this war?"

I know what she's doing. She wants me to hurt her with a lie. She needs to convince herself that she's not a traitor to the family she loves. That way, she can absolve herself of the guilt she tastes when we kiss.

But absolution is for those without sin, and Lola Carrera and I have bathed in those bloody waters all our lives.

Sinking a hand into her hair, I twist the thick strands around my fingers and hold her so close we're sharing the same breath. "If all I wanted from you was a fucking conquest, *dulzura*, I would've spread your legs that night in my bedroom."

"But—"

"I want *everything*," I growl against her lips. "Every piece of you… Even the confused and broken ones you try to hide."

Those wicked blue eyes flash. "Then kiss me again," she says breathlessly, "and maybe I'll consider it."

Grabbing the back of her head, I crash our mouths together, swallowing every moan like it's a Michelin star meal. When she strains to reach more of me, I feel like I've won the moon and stars on a game of chance.

"How can you be so sure about us?" She breaks away again, panting.

"Because I *know you*, Lola Carrera." I hold her face prisoner between my hands, forcing her to look at me. "I know the pain you feel from this conflict. I know how much you hate smoking cigarettes, even when you pretend otherwise. I know your tiger spirit would have happily carved up Troy Davis's knee yourself if I hadn't beaten you to it... I love that when you look to the horizon it's the world you see, and not the borders of Mexico." I go to kiss her again. I can't help myself. "Stay awhile, little mouse. You might find you don't hate me as much as you think you do."

"That's a lot of hate to make right."

"Give me this night, Lola. I'll wrap it around us so fucking tight, you'll never want to break free."

"I'll give you more than that," she says, curling her arms around my neck as soon as I loosen her restraints. "But only if you swear it in blood."

The motel room is sparse, but functional. The whole interior is bathed in grays and browns, but her colors are blinding.

Kicking the door shut, I grab her by the wrist and spin her back into my arms for another violent kiss.

After that, clothes become skin, and heated promises take center stage.

Throwing her backward onto the bed, I pull her legs apart, impatient to taste every part of her. This time, there are no guns. No violence. Her body is a roadmap to her universe, and her hair is a messy dark web across the white pillowcase.

She tastes of *everything*.

"If this is what dawn feels like, I never want the day to end." With a groan, I drag myself away from her pussy, my chin glistening with the residue of her third orgasm as I settle between her legs. Holding her heavy-lidded gaze, I line my dick up for the ultimate prize. "Mine."

"Yours," she rasps, sinking her head back into the pillow, her small hands resting on my shoulders to brace herself.

With that one word, I drive in so deep her nails leave crimson welts across my skin, her slick warmth gripping me so tight I'm close to shooting my load right away.

"Harder," she whispers as I shudder to a stop. "Faster."

"Not if you want twenty-eight chapters and an epilogue," I gasp out.

She laughs softly and pulls my mouth down to hers. "I didn't know you made jokes."

"Not recently. With you, I'm relearning."

At that, she smiles.

"How much do you hate me now?" I say a couple of minutes later.

"Make me come again, and I'll tell you." Lifting her hips, she makes herself so full of me I can't tell where she ends and I begin.

We come together, and it's off-the-wall spectacular—a fucking fusion of lust, obsession, and everything that's perfectly imperfect about us.

Her back arches.

My mind is drunk.

Turns out, she doesn't hate me that much, after all.

She hates me even less when, lying tangled up in sheets and exhaustion, I give her my knife and instruct her to carve an L into my chest.

My oath in blood, just like I promised.

Two letters.

Two lives.

Two hearts that refuse to beat for a war that tries so hard to define them.

CHAPTER
Eighteen

LOLA

While my beautiful captor slept, I dressed in darkness and spilled our truth onto a dirty piece of motel stationary.

Now, standing by the bed and clutching the note in my hand, I'm as stained as the white sheet covering Sam's newly-branded chest. Unshed tears burn the back of my eyes as I reach down and trace a feather-light touch across the dark red L bleeding through the cheap linen.

"Mine," I whisper, echoing his earlier claim.

He doesn't respond. Those intense eyes remain closed as I trail my hand from his chest to his face. He's too lost in the depths of a dream to know what's about to happen. To understand why I have to go through with what I'm about to do.

It's not in spite of him. It's *for* him.

He asked me to give him the night, and I did. I gave him that and more. I gave him me—body and soul.

Heart.

And whether or not he believes it when he wakes, I've already given him all of my tomorrows. Every single one. But defiance always comes with a price, and ours is one I must pay alone.

For me.

For him.

For peace.

And for a chance at happiness for either of us.

I wish I could tell him goodbye, but I know he'd just try to stop me. He'd argue we could simply keep driving. Away from New Jersey. Away from Mexico. Away from the loyalties and responsibilities tying us to both.

But it would never be far enough.

Deep down, we both know it's impossible to outrun Valentin Carrera or Dante Santiago. Eventually, we'd be found, and depending on who got there first, one of us would answer with our life.

That's no way to live.

However, I'm leaving here more confident than I arrived. Thanks to Sam, I'm no longer afraid of who I am. By weakening me, he strengthened me.

Because of him, I found my voice.

Besides, if I've learned anything while being in America, it's that when something blocks your path, you don't try to run through it...

You find a way around it.

Fighting back the emotion threatening to bubble to the surface, I glance down at the paper in my hand, silently reading the words one last time.

The ones I stole from him and twisted into a fate I must endure alone.

When the mouse strays, she gets punished. Slowly and painfully until she wins her freedom. When that time comes, the hunt is on. Catch me, and I'm yours forever.

With a soft kiss goodbye, I place the tear-stained note on the nightstand and close the door behind me, returning to the chains he shattered.

"What the hell do you mean you don't know where he is?"

I force myself not to flinch under the lead weight of my father's murderous stare. He's pacing the entire length of my apartment with Santi balancing out the act by marching his heavy-footed gait in the opposite direction.

They look like two pinballs bouncing off an electric fence. *If pinballs could raze an entire city with one glance.*

Valentin Carrera is one of the two most feared men in the world. Looking him in the eye with a lie on my lips is terrifying. My father loves me, but he also has the power to lock me away from civilization.

And from Sam.

"Just what I said," I say calmly while twisting my fingers into a pretzel. "I don't know where Sam went after I escaped, *papá*. He could be anywhere in the world by now."

Hopefully, I'm right, and he stays there until this storm blows over.

At that, my brother pauses, his gaze narrowing as he turns those accusing eyes my way. "And he just let you escape? Just like that?"

"Yep," I say, popping the "p" at the end.

"You want us to believe that Sam *fucking* Sanders went through all the trouble to carve up your skin, then kidnap you, only to decide you weren't worth the gas to chase down?"

I glare back at him. "You make it sound like he had a choice."

He lifts a dark, slanted eyebrow. "Didn't he?"

"No! I'm not some idiot college girl who can't fight her way out of a paper bag, Santi! I keep trying to tell you that" Folding my arms across my chest, I sink deeper into the leather cushions of my couch, adding under my breath, "You just refuse to listen."

"*Cielito*, you have to understand, you are priceless to us. If anything had happened to you..." My father's voice trails off, unable to simultaneously give voice to his fear *and* keep his rage in check.

The deep love in his eyes wars with the budding one locked away in my heart. The one I can never speak of for risk losing it forever.

I hate lying to them. The two men shoving their hands through their dark hair, carelessly dislodging both their favored slicked back styles while wearing out my hardwood floor, have always been my heroes. *My dark knights.*

But now there's another.

And his safety trumps my loyalty.

"I know, *papá*," I say softly. "And I'm sorry for the trouble I've caused Santi, and I'm sorry for worrying you so much that you had to fly here, and—"

"You didn't do anything, *cielito*. Once again, the Santiagos have dared to tread on sacred ground. No man hurts my daughter and lives."

And that is exactly why I told them the story I did. Why, after skipping town, *hell, the state*, with Sam, and then showing back up nearly eighteen hours later to a *sicario* and testosterone infused apartment, I knew I had to do some fancy tap dancing to cover both our asses.

So, I lied.

I couldn't hide what we'd done. Not only did we leave a trail of destruction in our wake, but a neighbor saw us leave, giving the police a description of Sam's Bugatti and his license plate. By the time we made it to Rhode Island, the sharp jaws of truth were already snapping at our necks.

So I drew first blood.

I told my father and brother the story they wanted to hear. The story of how after Sam kidnapped me, I'd waited until he stopped for gas near New Haven, Connecticut, and then I'd run for my life.

The reality of what happened was substantially less dramatic.

The part where I hitchhiked my way across three states is true, however, I'd waited to call Santi until I was safely tucked inside the borders of New Jersey to give Sam plenty of lead time, not because I didn't have access to a phone.

I spoke nothing of Newport or the run-down motel where Sam's cock left a delicious scar inside me, matching the one carved on my skin.

When I finished, war raged across my father's weathered face.

A bloodthirsty look settled in my brother's eyes.

And me? I kept my silent promise to my darkest and dirtiest knight.

I did what I had to do.

I played the role of the virginal victim while painting him all the colors of a diabolical villain. If I knew it would've protected him, I would've happily shouldered all the blame. But my father and brother are so deeply entrenched in this Carrera/Santiago war, they wouldn't have believed me anyway.

A familiar lie is always more palatable than an uncomfortable truth.

That doesn't mean I don't have my own penance to pay.

My time in America is over. I'd already been ordered back to Mexico before Sam and I took off... After my return, I knew I'd never see the bright lights of the New York skyline again.

"Please, *papá*," I beg, fighting to knit the fragile fibers of peace back together as they unravel before my eyes. "Don't fan the flames of a war Santi and I will have to extinguish."

"Speak for yourself," my brother says, violence flickering in his dark glare. "I've been ready to fight this battle for years. All I needed was an excuse." One corner of his mouth tips up in a wicked smile. "So, I suppose I owe Sanders a thank you before I put a bullet between his eyes."

He might as well have fired it into my own chest.

"*Papá!*" I beg, turning toward the formidable man now looming over me. "Do something!"

"I am." Glancing toward the front door, he nods to where an expressionless RJ stands guard. "Tell the pilot to get the jet ready. My daughter will be arriving at Teterboro in half an hour." He snaps his challenge-filled gaze my way. "She's going home."

"*Sí.*" It's the first and last word RJ utters before pressing a button on his phone, a silent warning in his eyes. *Remember our deal...*

Three against one aren't good odds for anyone. But when you're the king's daughter returning from battle wearing the insignia of his sworn enemy, they're damn near impossible.

Closing my eyes, I soak in one final moment of freedom before wordlessly making my way toward my bedroom to pack up my new life…

And reluctantly return to the one I left behind.

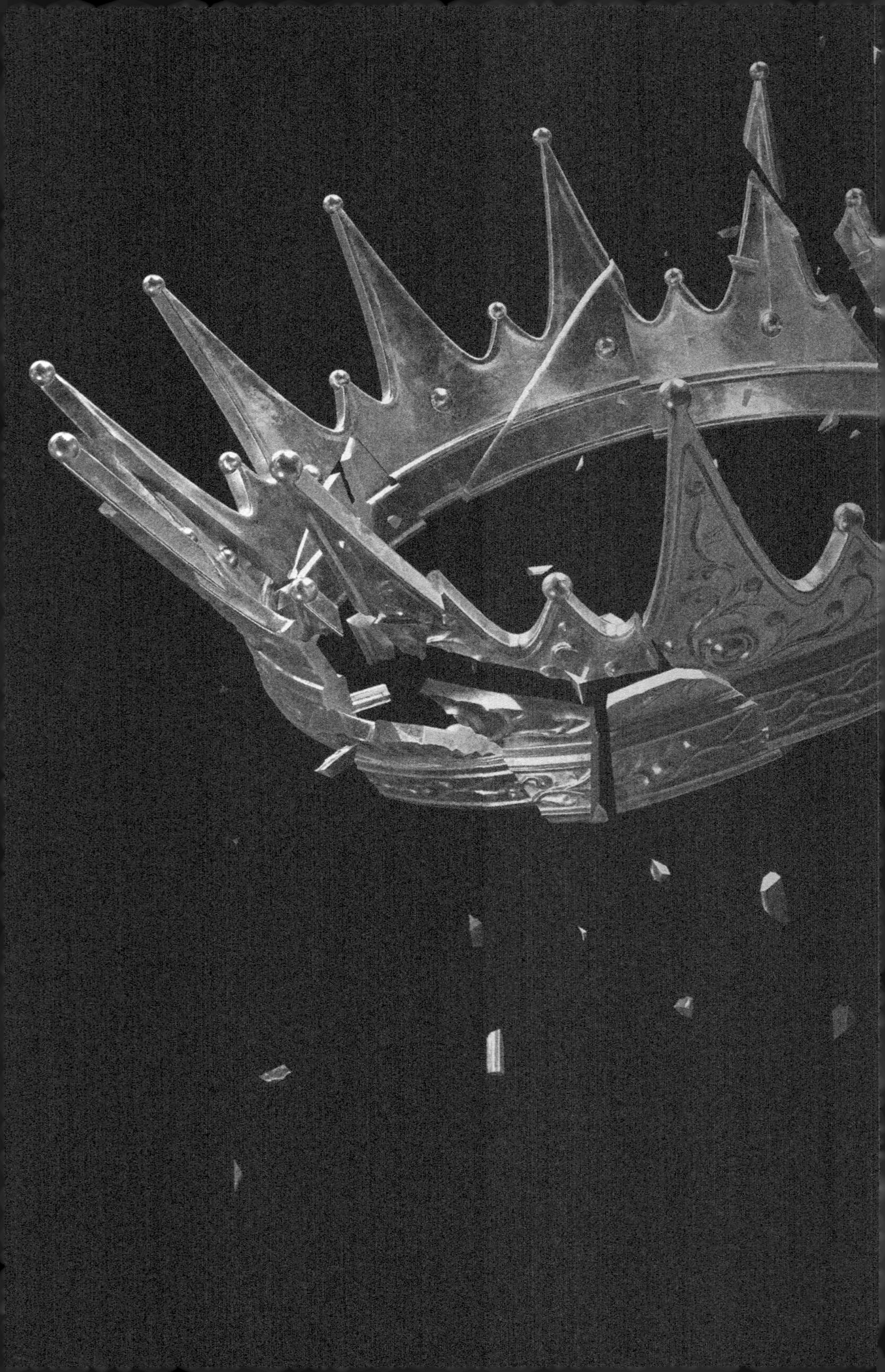

EPILOGUE

LOLA
Seven Months Later

"Hey, Daniela! Wait up!"

Adjusting the heavy backpack slipping down my arm, I smile at the bubbly blonde waving at me from across the quad. *Vanessa, I think is her name.* She's a nice girl, a little too talkative at times, but harmless.

I should know. My father and brother personally vetted every student on Northgate's campus. This place is nothing like Rutgers. With only two thousand students, it's almost impossible to blend in, so my family keeps their finger on its pulse, allowing no margin for error.

No dark corners for Santiago masks to hide.

Or so they think.

"Everything okay?" I ask, forcing as much of my native accent from the words as possible. No need to raise suspicion and make pretty blonde girls dead.

I laugh to myself. *Who knew that phrase could be used twice in one lifetime?*

She nods, her pale cheeks stained red from the biting wind. "A few of us are going out tonight. You should come. We can celebrate your birthday."

"I'm not allowed to go to bars."

"This is college, not high school!" She laughs. "You're free to have fun, Daniela. Our parents have no control over us here."

Maybe for her. Her white-picket-fenced suburban life doesn't know a damn thing about control. About the dangers of bearing a name the world condemns as evil.

I grit my teeth as a looming shadow darts behind a lecture hall building.

Free is a four-letter word where I come from, nothing more. Especially now that I have twice the security. Luckily, RJ is family, otherwise Santi would've wasted no time in slitting his throat for failing to protect me from what he perceived as Dante Santiago's wrath.

Now *Miguel the Destroyer* has become my three-hundred-pound shadow, stepping where I step, breathing where I breathe. At any given time, he and at least three other men hover about, boxing me inside an invisible shield. One wrong move or misguided touch and the snow blanketing this campus will run red.

I shrug. "Maybe some other time."

There won't be a next time, and she knows it. Thankfully, she doesn't voice the questions pooling in her bright green eyes. "You're a mysterious girl, Daniela Torres," she mutters, walking away.

Daniela Torres.

It's the name my father assigned me before allowing me to return to the States with my entourage in tow. It took twenty-four long weeks of solitude and repentance to earn my way back into his favor. Mercifully, after six months of atoning for my sins in Mexico, *mamá* became my champion—the calm voice of reason in a chaotic war.

"Give her a second chance," she crooned into *papá's* ear. *"She's a free spirit, Val. A hummingbird thrives on perpetual motion. Clip its wings, and it dies."*

Mamá always had a way of bending *papá's* iron-will.

Begrudgingly, he conceded, enrolling Daniela Torres at a Newport, Rhode Island school where the biggest danger came from crossing the street.

I allow a secret smile to tug at my lips. I care nothing about this school. However, its location calls to my soul.

Because it's ours.

Making my way back to my heavily guarded apartment, I slip my key in the door as four shadows close in behind me. "*Buenas noches,*" I say in a sing-songy voice, bidding Miguel and his men goodnight with a private smirk.

Once I close the door, the air inside the darkened room changes. Turning the lock, I let my backpack slide off my arm while slowly drowning in the charged electricity of his presence.

"Did you miss me?" I whisper.

My answer is a firm grip around the back of my neck as I'm slammed against the wall, my pulse thumping a furious beat under his rough fingers. Sam doesn't greet me with a kiss or a soft caress. His greedy hands tear at my leggings until they're nothing but ribbons of confetti littering the floor.

"Catch me, and I'm yours forever," he growls, reciting the words from my note through clenched teeth. "Well, I've caught you, *dulzura*. There's no escape from me now."

The heat of his warning skates down my neck.

"What if I run?" I ask, biting my lip.

"I'll catch you again."

"What if I scream?"

His hand slides up my throat, gripping my chin and twisting it until it brushes his unshaven cheek. "I'll steal it from your lips."

"And if I fight?"

"I'll come twice as hard."

He seals his promise with a graze of his teeth against my jaw while thrusting a finger deep inside me. I moan at his rough possession. *This is the game we play.* Intruder and victim. The same act that started our torrid affair now feeds our addiction.

The dark can't mask what has only grown stronger with time. I feel him everywhere: in the air, on my skin, in my soul...

I spin around, and like two magnets, our mouths crash together, drinking the life from each other to soothe the thirst our separation caused. His bare chest rubs against my breasts, the scarred L carved into his flesh fanning the flames of my desire.

L for Lola.

L for lust.

L for love.

"Happy birthday, Lola." He hums out a dark, satisfied groan as his tongue laps my arousal off his fingers. He lowers his hand, and I shake in anticipation at the sound of his jeans unzipping. "What's your wish?"

"Freedom," I whisper, gasping as he pins my back against the wall. "Blood and salvation."

As I voice my demands, Sam grabs the back of my thighs and lifts me off the ground. Instinctively, I wrap my legs around his waist, crying out as he thrusts inside me, the searing pain easing the ache in my heart.

"Blood I can give you, *dulzura*. You have to earn the rest for yourself."

He's right. It's a battle fought with patience, not force. I'll embrace my role as a pawn in this cartel chess game. I'll move strategically across the board, hiding in plain sight from both deadly kings.

For now, we're forced to play by their rules.

But one day, I'll graduate. One day, I'll return to him, and we'll break these chains binding him to Colombia and me to Mexico. One day, we'll cross this thorn-riddled line drawn between our two families.

"For now…" I groan, his possessive thrusts driving me toward the edge of ecstasy.

For now, we'll meet in darkness.

Fuck in secret.

Love in silence.

Sam pauses, our bodies joined and aching for release. "And then what?"

I smile, soaking in the strained moments of peace before he shatters me once again.

"Checkmate."

ACKNOWLEDGMENTS

Cora's Acknowledgments

Catherine, what a wild, caffeine-infused, no-sleep having, when-did-I-last-shower, oh-I-forgot-to-eat, how-is-that-only-five-hundred-words, what-time-zone-are-we-in ride it's been. I'm pretty sure we've both aged five years in the last four months, but *we f'ing did it*. Thanks for taking this journey with me.

Ronda, thank you for keeping my head above water. Thank you for telling me to stop listening to my head and listen to my heart. Just…thank *you*.

Crystal, thanks for your unwavering support and for giving me a much-needed dose of reality when deadlines got close and I checked out.

Murphy, thank you for always listening when I needed an ear. You are one of the most genuine people I've ever had the pleasure of knowing.

Ginger, my translation goddess, thanks for correcting all my Spanish *oopsies* and for making sure my Carrera men and women always sound authentic. Maybe in five more books, I won't ask you fifty times to differentiate between the expression and the insult when I'm bilingual-cursing. Sorry about the 101 screenshots at one a.m. #doeskarateinspanish

Gillian Leonard: I have no idea how you managed to edit two back-to-back books so quickly, but I love you to the moon and back for it. #teamkumquat.

Thanks to Stephanie Rush for your last-minute proofreading of our bonus material!

Carrera's Guerreras: You are one hell of a beta team. I don't tell you enough how amazing you are, so I'm doing it now. Love you all!

Lots of love to my reader group, Cora's Twisted Alpha Addicts for being my fam and to my AMAZING street team, Cora's Twisted Capos for your unyielding support.

Huge thanks to my publicist, Danielle Sanchez, and the amazing team at Wildfire Marketing Solutions. You are, simply put, the best.

Thank you to the bloggers, bookstagrammers, and especially readers for your constant support and love, and for supporting this crazy Carrera world I've created. It means more than you'll ever know.

A special thank you to my family for bringing me food when I forgot to eat, for not acknowledging when I'd been in the same pajamas for a week, and for not commenting on the family of ferrets living in my unwashed hair. Thanks for giving me space and silence and for understanding that being an author isn't glamorous. I love you more than words can say.

Lastly, thanks to every single reader for your support of our "hey, you know what would be cool…" project and for loving these second-generation cartel families.

Now, I'm going to finally shower…

And maybe lay off the coffee for a while.

Eh, probably not.

Catherine's Acknowledgments

To my husband: a man who advocates female rights as naturally as breathing, and who works so hard to implement projects that help human trafficking victims, amongst many others… Thank you for your insights into International Development, and for holding our family together through every storm. You give us roots and wings. Plus, you walk the dog twice a day.

To my two beautiful girls. I'm running out of adjectives again. Let's just say that I love how you bring me cups of tea and hugs when I'm writing. I love that I've inspired you to write yourselves.

Cora, my author guru! The pain was worth it! I love these characters that we created with all my heart—they're almost as crazy as we are. Thank you from the bottom of my green tea for your love, support and 4 a.m. messages.

Sammy, Anne, Sally, Joanne, and Julia. Thank you for cheering me on from the sidelines. You've been there from the beginning and you're more priceless than gold. A special thank you to Greta for answering all my Italian translation requests, no matter what time of the day!

To my wonderful PAs, Siobhan, and Joanne. Thank you for keeping my life in order. And to my amazing Street Team! I would be hopelessly lost without you—special high-fives to Joy, Jayne, Ashley, Piia, Chelle, Janie, Isidora, Sarah, Tracey, Sandra, Sophie, Kay, Lucy, Anna, and Laura.

To Maria at Steamy Designs. Thank you for taking on all my demands, not disowning me, and for weaving your magic.

And finally, to the readers. You make every invasive scan, test and operation worth it. I'll be writing these stories for you until they pry my laptop away from my lifeless fingers. Thank you for making all my dreams come true.

xx

#fuckcancer

ABOUT
Cora Kenborn

Cora Kenborn is a *USA Today* Bestselling author of over twenty-five multi-genre novels, including the Carrera Cartel Trilogy.

While best known for her dark and gritty romances, Cora infuses sharp banter and a shocking blindside in every story she writes. She loves a brooding antihero who falls hard for a feisty heroine who stands beside him, not behind him.

Although she's a native North Carolinian, Cora claims the domestic Southern Belle gene skipped a generation, so she spends any free time convincing her family that microwaved mac and cheese counts as fine dining.

Oh, and autocorrect thinks she's obsessed with ducks.

Sign up for her newsletter and get exclusive updates at www.corakenborn.com

ABOUT Catherine Wiltcher

Catherine Wiltcher is an international bestselling author of fifteen dark romance novels, including the Santiago Trilogy. A stage 4 cancer thriver and a self-confessed alpha addict, she writes flawed characters who always fall hard and deep for one another.

She lives in the UK with her husband and two young daughters. If she ever found herself stranded on a desert island, she'd like a large pink gin to keep her company... Cillian Murphy wouldn't be a bad shout, either.

Sign up to her newsletter for book updates and exclusives!
www.catherinewiltcher.com/newsletter

ALSO BY
Cora Kenborn

CARRERA CARTEL TRILOGY
(Dark Mafia Romance)

Carrera Cartel: The Collection (*w/bonus novel*)

Blurred Red Lines

Faded Gray Lines

Drawn Blue Lines

CORRUPT GODS WORLD
Spinoff of Carrera Cartel
(Dark Mafia Romance)

Corrupt Gods Collection (*w/bonus chapters*)

Born Sinner

Bad Blood

Tainted Blood

Bullets and Thorns

UNDERWORLD KINGS
(Dark Mafia Romance)

City of Thieves

LES CAVALIERS DE L'OMBRE DUET
(Dark Mafia Romance)

Darkest Deeds

MIAMI BRATVA DUET
Spinoff of Les Cavaliers de l'ombre
(Dark Mafia Romance)

Illicit Acts

Wicked Ways

LORDS OF LYRE SERIES
(Rockstar Suspense Romance)

Fame and Obsession

Fame and Secrets

Fame and Lies

STANDALONES
(Dark/Romantic Suspense)

Sixth Sin

Cast Stones

STANDALONES
(Contemporary/Sports Romance)

Shallow

Playboy Pitcher

Adrenaline

STANDALONES
(Romantic Comedy)

Unsupervised

Swamp Happens: The Complete Collection

STANDALONES
(Paranormal/Dark Urban Fantasy Romance)

Cursed In Love

ALSO BY
Catherine Wittcher

THE SANTIAGO TRILOGY
(Dark Mafia)

The Santiago Trilogy
Hearts of Darkness
Hearts Divine
Hearts On Fire

THE GRAYSON DUET
(Dark Mafia)

Shadow Man
Reckless Woman

CORRUPT GODS
(Dark Mafia)

Corrupt Gods Collection *(w/bonus chapters)*
Born Sinner
Bad Blood
Tainted Blood
Rush & Ruin

UNDERWORLD KINGS
(Dark Mafia)

City of Thieves

STANDALONES

Devils & Dust
Black Skies Riviera
Unwrapping the Billionaire
Hot Nights In Morocco
Cast Stones

Printed in Great Britain
by Amazon